Agatha Christie is known throughout the world as the Queen of Crime. Her books have sold over a billion copies in English with another billion in 100 foreign languages. She is the most widely published author of all time and in any language, outsold only by the Bible and Shakespeare. She is the author of 80 crime novels and short story collections, 19 plays, and six novels written under the name of Mary Westmacott.

Agatha Christie's first novel, *The Mysterious Affair at Styles*, was written towards the end of the First World War, in which she served as a VAD. In it she created Hercule Poirot, the little Belgian detective who was destined to become the most popular detective in crime fiction since Sherlock Holmes. It was eventually published by The Bodley Head in 1920.

In 1926, after averaging a book a year, Agatha Christie wrote her masterpiece. *The Murder of Roger Ackroyd* was the first of her books to be published by Collins and marked the beginning of an author-publisher relationship which lasted for 50 years and well over 70 books. *The Murder of Roger Ackroyd* was also the first of Agatha Christie's books to be dramatised – under the name *Alibi* – and to have a successful run in London's West End. *The Mousetrap*, her most famous play of all, opened in 1952 and is the longest-running play in history.

Agatha Christie was made a Dame in 1971. She died in 1976, since when a number of books have been published posthumously: the bestselling novel *Sleeping Murder* appeared later that year, followed by her autobiography and the short story collections *Miss Marple's Final Cases*, *Problem at Pollensa Bay* and *While the Light Lasts*. In 1998 *Black Coffee* was the first of her plays to be novelised by another author, Charles Osborne.

THE AGATHA CHRISTIE COLLECTION

The Man in the Brown Suit
The Secret of Chimneys
The Seven Dials Mystery
The Mysterious Mr Quin
The Sittaford Mystery
The Hound of Death
The Listerdale Mystery
Why Didn't They Ask Evans?
Parker Pyne Investigates
Murder is Easy
And Then There Were None
Death Comes as the End
Sparkling Cyanide
Crooked House
They Came to Baghdad
Destination Unknown
Spider's Web*
The Unexpected Guest*
Ordeal by Innocence
The Pale Horse
Endless Night
Passenger to Frankfurt

Poirot

The Mysterious Affair at Styles
Murder on the Links
Poirot Investigates
The Murder of Roger Ackroyd
The Big Four
The Mystery of the Blue Train
Black Coffee*
Peril at End House
Lord Edgware Dies
Murder on the Orient Express
Three Act Tragedy
Death in the Clouds
The ABC Murders
Murder in Mesopotamia
Cards on the Table
Murder in the Mews
Dumb Witness
Death on the Nile
Appointment with Death
Hercule Poirot's Christmas
Sad Cypress
One, Two, Buckle My Shoe
Evil Under the Sun
Five Little Pigs
The Hollow
The Labours of Hercules
Taken at the Flood

Mrs McGinty's Dead
After the Funeral
Hickory Dickory Dock
Dead Man's Folly
Cat Among the Pigeons
The Adventure of the Christmas Pudding
The Clocks
Third Girl
Hallowe'en Party
Elephants Can Remember
Poirot's Early Cases
Curtain: Poirot's Last Case

Marple

The Murder at the Vicarage
The Thirteen Problems
The Body in the Library
The Moving Finger
A Murder is Announced
They Do It With Mirrors
A Pocket Full of Rye
4.50 from Paddington
The Mirror Crack'd from Side to Side
A Caribbean Mystery
At Bertram's Hotel
Nemesis
Sleeping Murder
Miss Marple's Final Cases

Tommy & Tuppence

The Secret Adversary
Partners in Crime
N or M?
By the Pricking of My Thumbs
Postern of Fate

Published as Mary Westmacott

Giant's Bread
Unfinished Portrait
Absent in the Spring
The Rose and the Yew Tree
A Daughter's a Daughter
The Burden

Memoirs

An Autobiography
Come, Tell Me How You Live

Play Collections

The Mousetrap and Selected Plays
Witness for the Prosecution and Selected Plays

* novelised by Charles Osborne

Agatha Christie

POIROT
IN THE ORIENT

·

MURDER IN MESOPOTAMIA

·

DEATH ON THE NILE

·

APPOINTMENT WITH DEATH

·

HarperCollinsPublishers

HarperCollins*Publishers*
77–85 Fulham Palace Road,
Hammersmith, London W6 8JB
www.**fire**and**water**.com

This edition first published 2001
1 3 5 7 9 8 6 4 2

This collection copyright © Agatha Christie Limited 2001

Murder in Mesopotamia copyright Agatha Christie Mallowan 1936
Death on the Nile copyright Agatha Christie Mallowan 1937
Appointment With Death copyright Agatha Christie Mallowan 1938

ISBN 0 00 712072 9

Typeset by Palimpsest Book Production Limited,
Polmont, Stirlingshire
Printed and bound in Great Britain by
Omnia Books Limited, Glasgow

CONTENTS

MURDER IN MESOPOTAMIA

AGATHA CHRISTIE

A NEW POIROT STORY

R.H. MACARTNEY

Dedicated to
My many archaeological friends
in Iraq and Syria

CONTENTS

BY GILES REILLY, MD

The events chronicled in this narrative took place some four years ago. Circumstances have rendered it necessary, in my opinion, that a straightforward account of them should be given to the public. There have been the wildest and most ridiculous rumours suggesting that important evidence was suppressed and other nonsense of that kind. Those misconstructions have appeared more especially in the American Press.

For obvious reasons it was desirable that the account should not come from the pen of one of the expedition staff, who might reasonably be supposed to be prejudiced.

I therefore suggested to Miss Amy Leatheran that she should undertake the task. She is obviously the person to do it. She had a professional character of the highest, she is not biased by having any previous connection with the University of Pittstown Expedition to Iraq and she was an observant and intellectual eye-witness.

It was not very easy to persuade Miss Leatheran to undertake this task – in fact, persuading her was one of the hardest jobs of my professional career – and even after it was completed she displayed a curious reluctance to let me see the manuscript. I discovered that this was partly due to some critical remarks she had made concerning my daughter Sheila. I soon disposed of that, assuring her that as children criticize their parents freely in print nowadays, parents are only too delighted when their offspring come in for their share of abuse! Her other objection was extreme modesty about her literary style. She hoped I would 'put the grammar right and all that.' I have, on the contrary, refused to alter so much as a single word. Miss Leatheran's style in my opinion is vigorous, individual and entirely apposite. If she calls Hercule Poirot 'Poirot' in one paragraph and 'Mr Poirot' in the next, such a variation is both interesting and suggestive. At one moment she is, so to speak, 'remembering her manners' (and hospital nurses are great sticklers for etiquette) and at the next her interest in what she is telling is that of a pure human being – cap and cuffs forgotten!

The only thing I have done is to take the liberty of writing a first chapter – aided by a letter kindly supplied by one of Miss Leatheran's friends. It is intended to be in the nature of a frontispiece – that is, it gives a rough sketch of the narrator.

CHAPTER I
FRONTISPIECE

In the hall of the Tigris Palace Hotel in Baghdad a hospital nurse was finishing a letter. Her fountain-pen drove briskly over the paper.

> . . . Well, dear, I think that's really all my news. I must say it's been nice to see a bit of the world – though England for me every time, thank you. The *dirt* and the *mess* in Baghdad you wouldn't believe – and not romantic at all like you'd think from the *Arabian Nights*! Of course, it's pretty just on the river, but the town itself is just awful – and no proper shops at all. Major Kelsey took me through the bazaars, and of course there's no denying they're *quaint* – but just a lot of rubbish and hammering away at copper pans till they make your head ache – and not what I'd like to use myself unless I was sure about the cleaning. You've got to be so careful of verdigris with copper pans.
>
> I'll write and let you know if anything comes of the job that Dr Reilly spoke about. He said this American gentleman was in Baghdad now and might come and see me this afternoon. It's for his wife – she has 'fancies', so Dr Reilly said. He didn't say any more than that, and of course, dear, one knows what that *usually means* (but I hope not actually D.T.s!). Of course, Dr Reilly didn't *say* anything – but he had a look – if you know what I mean. This Dr Leidner is an archaeologist and is digging up a mound out in the desert somewhere for some American museum.
>
> Well, dear, I will close now. I thought what you told me about little Stubbins was simply *killing*! Whatever did Matron say?
>
> No more now.
> Yours ever,
> Amy Leatheran

Enclosing the letter in an envelope, she addressed it to Sister Curshaw, St Christopher's Hospital, London.

As she put the cap on her fountain-pen, one of the native boys approached her.

'A gentleman come to see you. Dr Leidner.'

Nurse Leatheran turned. She saw a man of middle height with slightly stooping shoulders, a brown beard and gentle, tired eyes.

Dr Leidner saw a woman of thirty-five, of erect, confident bearing. He saw a good-humoured face with slightly prominent blue eyes and glossy brown hair. She looked, he thought, just what a hospital nurse for a nervous case ought to look. Cheerful, robust, shrewd and matter-of-fact.

Nurse Leatheran, he thought, would do.

CHAPTER 2

INTRODUCING AMY LEATHERAN

I don't pretend to be an author or to know anything about writing. I'm doing this simply because Dr Reilly asked me to, and somehow when Dr Reilly asks you to do a thing you don't like to refuse.

'Oh, but, doctor,' I said, 'I'm not literary – not literary at all.'

'Nonsense!' he said. 'Treat it as case notes, if you like.'

Well, of course, you *can* look at it that way.

Dr Reilly went on. He said that an unvarnished plain account of the Tell Yarimjah business was badly needed.

'If one of the interested parties writes it, it won't carry conviction. They'll say it's biased one way or another.'

And of course that was true, too. I was in it all and yet an outsider, so to speak.

'Why don't you write it yourself, doctor?' I asked.

'I wasn't on the spot – you were. Besides,' he added with a sigh, 'my daughter won't let me.'

The way he knuckles under to that chit of a girl of his is downright disgraceful. I had half a mind to say so, when I saw that his eyes were twinkling. That was the worst of Dr Reilly. You never knew whether he was joking or not. He always said things in the same slow melancholy way – but half the time there was a twinkle underneath it.

'Well,' I said doubtfully, 'I suppose I *could*.'

'Of course you could.'

'Only I don't quite know how to set about it.'

'There's a good precedent for that. Begin at the beginning, go on to the end and then leave off.'

'I don't even know quite where and what the beginning was,' I said doubtfully.

'Believe me, nurse, the difficulty of beginning will be nothing to the difficulty of knowing how to stop. At least that's the way it is with me when I have to make a speech. Someone's got to catch hold of my coat-tails and pull me down by main force.'

'Oh, you're joking, doctor.'

'It's profoundly serious I am. Now what about it?'

Another thing was worrying me. After hesitating a moment or two I said: 'You know, doctor, I'm afraid I might tend to be – well, a little *personal* sometimes.'

'God bless my soul, woman, the more personal you are the better! This is a story of human beings – not dummies! Be personal – be prejudiced – be catty – be anything you please! Write the thing your own way. We can always prune out the bits that are libellous afterwards! You go ahead. You're a sensible woman, and you'll give a sensible common-sense account of the business.'

So that was that, and I promised to do my best.

And here I am beginning, but as I said to the doctor, it's difficult to know just where to start.

I suppose I ought to say a word or two about myself. I'm thirty-two and my name is Amy Leatheran. I took my training at St Christopher's and after that did two years maternity. I did a certain amount of private work and I was for four years at Miss Bendix's Nursing Home in Devonshire Place. I came out to Iraq with a Mrs Kelsey. I'd attended her when her baby was born. She was coming out to Baghdad with her husband and had already got a children's nurse booked who had been for some years with friends of hers out there. Their children were coming home and going to school, and the nurse had agreed to go to Mrs Kelsey when they left. Mrs Kelsey was delicate and nervous about the journey out with so young a child, so Major Kelsey arranged that

I should come out with her and look after her and the baby. They would pay my passage home unless we found someone needing a nurse for the return journey.

Well, there is no need to describe the Kelseys – the baby was a little love and Mrs Kelsey quite nice, though rather the fretting kind. I enjoyed the voyage very much. I'd never been a long trip on the sea before.

Dr Reilly was on board the boat. He was a black-haired, long-faced man who said all sorts of funny things in a low, sad voice. I think he enjoyed pulling my leg and used to make the most extraordinary statements to see if I would swallow them. He was the civil surgeon at a place called Hassanieh – a day and a half's journey from Baghdad.

I had been about a week in Baghdad when I ran across him and he asked when I was leaving the Kelseys. I said that it was funny his asking that because as a matter of fact the Wrights (the other people I mentioned) were going home earlier than they had meant to and their nurse was free to come straightaway.

He said that he had heard about the Wrights and that that was why he had asked me.

'As a matter of fact, nurse, I've got a possible job for you.'

'A case?'

He screwed his face up as though considering.

'You could hardly call it a case. It's just a lady who has – shall we say – fancies?'

'Oh!' I said.

(One usually knows what *that* means – drink or drugs!)

Dr Reilly didn't explain further. He was very discreet. 'Yes,' he said. 'A Mrs Leidner. Husband's an American – an American Swede to be exact. He's the head of a large American dig.'

And he explained how this expedition was excavating the site of a big Assyrian city something like Nineveh. The expedition house was not actually very far from Hassanieh, but it was a lonely spot and Dr Leidner had been worried for some time about his wife's health.

'He's not been very explicit about it, but it seems she has these fits of recurring nervous terrors.'

'Is she left alone all day amongst natives?' I asked.

'Oh, no, there's quite a crowd – seven or eight. I don't fancy she's ever been alone in the house. But there seems to be no doubt that she's worked herself up into a queer state. Leidner has any amount of work on his shoulders, but he's crazy about his wife and it worries him to know she's in this state. He felt he'd be happier if he knew that some responsible person with expert knowledge was keeping an eye on her.'

'And what does Mrs Leidner herself think about it?'

Dr Reilly answered gravely:

'Mrs Leidner is a very lovely lady. She's seldom of the same mind about anything two days on end. But on the whole she favours the idea.' He added, 'She's an odd woman. A mass of affection and, I should fancy, a champion liar – but Leidner seems honestly to believe that she is scared out of her life by something or other.'

'What did she herself say to you, doctor?'

'Oh, she hasn't consulted me! She doesn't like me anyway – for several reasons. It was Leidner who came to me and propounded this plan. Well, nurse, what do you think of the idea? You'd see something of the country before you go home – they'll be digging for another two months. And excavation is quite interesting work.'

After a moment's hesitation while I turned the matter over in my mind: 'Well,' I said, 'I really think I might try it.'

'Splendid,' said Dr Reilly, rising. 'Leidner's in Baghdad now. I'll tell him to come round and see if he can fix things up with you.'

Dr Leidner came to the hotel that afternoon. He was a middle-aged man with a rather nervous, hesitating manner. There was something gentle and kindly and rather helpless about him.

He sounded very devoted to his wife, but he was very vague about what was the matter with her.

'You see,' he said, tugging at his beard in a rather perplexed manner that I later came to know to be characteristic of him, 'my wife is really in a very nervous state. I – I'm quite worried about her.'

'She is in good physical health?' I asked.

'Yes – oh, yes, I think so. No, I should not think there was anything the matter with her physically. But she – well – imagines things, you know.'

'What kind of things?' I asked.

But he shied off from the point, merely murmuring perplexedly:

11

'She works herself up over nothing at all . . . I really can see no foundations for these fears.'

'Fears of what, Dr Leidner?'

He said vaguely, 'Oh, just – nervous terrors, you know.'

Ten to one, I thought to myself, it's drugs. And he doesn't realize it! Lots of men don't. Just wonder why their wives are so jumpy and have such extraordinary changes of mood.

I asked whether Mrs Leidner herself approved of the idea of my coming.

His face lighted up.

'Yes. I was surprised. Most pleasurably surprised. She said it was a very good idea. She said she would feel very much safer.'

The word struck me oddly. *Safer*. A very queer word to use. I began to surmise that Mrs Leidner might be a mental case.

He went on with a kind of boyish eagerness.

'I'm sure you'll get on very well with her. She's really a very charming woman.' He smiled disarmingly. 'She feels you'll be the greatest comfort to her. I felt the same as soon as I saw you. You look, if you will allow me to say so, so splendidly healthy and full of common sense. I'm sure you're just the person for Louise.'

'Well, we can but try, Dr Leidner,' I said cheerfully. 'I'm sure I hope I can be of use to your wife. Perhaps she's nervous of natives and coloured people?'

'Oh, dear me no.' He shook his head, amused at the idea. 'My wife likes Arabs very much – she appreciates their simplicity and their sense of humour. This is only her second season – we have been married less than two years – but she already speaks quite a fair amount of Arabic.'

I was silent for a moment or two, then I had one more try.

'Can't you tell me at all what it is your wife is afraid of, Dr Leidner?' I asked.

He hesitated. Then he said slowly, 'I hope – I believe – that she will tell you that herself.'

And that's all I could get out of him.

CHAPTER 3
GOSSIP

It was arranged that I should go to Tell Yarimjah the following week.

Mrs Kelsey was settling into her house at Alwiyah, and I was glad to be able to take a few things off her shoulders.

During that time I heard one or two allusions to the Leidner expedition. A friend of Mrs Kelsey's, a young squadron-leader, pursed his lips in surprise as he exclaimed: 'Lovely Louise. So that's her latest!' He turned to me. 'That's our nickname for her, nurse. She's always known as Lovely Louise.'

'Is she so very handsome then?' I asked.

'It's taking her at her own valuation. *She* thinks she is!'

'Now don't be spiteful, John,' said Mrs Kelsey. 'You know it's not only she who thinks so! Lots of people have been very smitten by her.'

'Perhaps you're right. She's a bit long in the tooth, but she has a certain attraction.'

'You were completely bowled over yourself,' said Mrs Kelsey, laughing.

The squadron-leader blushed and admitted rather shame-facedly: 'Well, she has a way with her. As for Leidner himself, he worships the ground she walks on – and all the rest of the expedition has to worship too! It's expected of them!'

'How many are there altogether?' I asked.

'All sorts and nationalities, nurse,' said the squadron-leader cheerfully. 'An English architect, a French Father from Carthage – he does the inscriptions – tablets and things, you know. And then there's Miss Johnson. She's English too – sort of general bottle-washer. And a little plump man who does the photography – he's an American. And the Mercados. Heaven knows what nationality they are – Dagos of some kind! She's quite young – a snaky-looking creature – and oh! doesn't she hate Lovely Louise! And there are a couple of youngsters and that's the lot. A few odd fish, but nice on the whole – don't you agree, Pennyman?'

He was appealing to an elderly man who was sitting thoughtfully twirling a pair of pince-nez.

The latter started and looked up.

'Yes – yes – very nice indeed. Taken individually, that is. Of course, Mercado is rather a queer fish –'

'He has such a very *odd* beard,' put in Mrs Kelsey. 'A queer limp kind.'

Major Pennyman went on without noticing her interruption.

'The young 'uns are both nice. The American's rather silent, and the English boy talks a bit too much. Funny, it's usually the other way round. Leidner himself is a delightful fellow – so modest and unassuming. Yes, individually they are all pleasant people. But somehow or other, I may have been fanciful, but the last time I went to see them I got a queer impression of something being wrong. I don't know what it was exactly . . . Nobody seemed quite natural. There was a queer atmosphere of tension. I can explain best what I mean by saying that they all passed the butter to each other too politely.'

Blushing a little, because I don't like airing my own opinions too much, I said: 'If people are too much cooped up together it's got a way of getting on their nerves. I know that myself from experience in hospital.'

'That's true,' said Major Kelsey, 'but it's early in the season, hardly time for that particular irritation to have set in.'

'An expedition is probably like our life here in miniature,' said Major Pennyman. 'It has its cliques and rivalries and jealousies.'

'It sounds as though they'd got a good many newcomers this year,' said Major Kelsey.

'Let me see.' The squadron-leader counted them off on his fingers. 'Young Coleman is new, so is Reiter. Emmott was out last year and so were the Mercados. Father Lavigny is a newcomer. He's come in place of Dr Byrd, who was ill this year and couldn't come out. Carey, of course, is an old hand. He's been out ever since the beginning, five years ago. Miss Johnson's been out nearly as many years as Carey.'

'I always thought they got on so well together at Tell Yarimjah,' remarked Major Kelsey. 'They seemed like a happy family – which is really surprising when one considers what human nature is! I'm sure Nurse Leatheran agrees with me.'

'Well,' I said, 'I don't know that you're not right! The rows I've known in hospital and starting often from nothing more than a dispute about a pot of tea.'

'Yes, one tends to get petty in close communities,' said Major Pennyman. 'All the same I feel there must be something more to it in this case. Leidner is such a gentle, unassuming man, with really a remarkable amount of tact. He's always managed to keep his expedition happy and on good terms with each other. And yet I *did* notice that feeling of tension the other day.'

Mrs Kelsey laughed.

'And you don't see the explanation? Why, it leaps to the eye!'

'What do you mean?'

'*Mrs* Leidner, of course.'

'Oh come, Mary,' said her husband, 'she's a charming woman – not at all the quarrelsome kind.'

'I didn't say she was quarrelsome. She *causes* quarrels!'

'In what way? And why should she?'

'Why? Why? Because she's bored. She's not an archaeologist, only the wife of one. She's bored shut away from any excitements and so she provides her own drama. She amuses herself by setting other people by the ears.'

'Mary, you don't know in the least. You're merely imagining.'

'Of course I'm imagining! But you'll find I'm right. Lovely Louise doesn't look like the Mona Lisa for nothing! She mayn't mean any harm, but she likes to see what will happen.'

'She's devoted to Leidner.'

'Oh! I dare say, I'm not suggesting vulgar intrigues. But she's an *allumeuse*, that woman.'

'Women are so sweet to each other,' said Major Kelsey.

'I know. Cat, cat, cat, that's what you men say. But we're usually right about our own sex.'

'All the same,' said Major Pennyman thoughtfully, 'assuming all Mrs Kelsey's uncharitable surmises to be true, I don't think it would quite account for that curious sense of tension – rather like the feeling there is before a thunderstorm. I had the impression very strongly that the storm might break any minute.'

'Now don't frighten nurse,' said Mrs Kelsey. 'She's going there in three days' time and you'll put her right off.'

'Oh, you won't frighten me,' I said, laughing.

All the same I thought a good deal about what had been said. Dr Leidner's curious use of the word 'safer' recurred to me. Was it his wife's secret fear, unacknowledged or expressed perhaps, that was reacting on the rest of the party? Or was it the actual tension (or perhaps the unknown cause of it) that was reacting on *her* nerves?

I looked up the word *allumeuse* that Mrs Kelsey had used in a dictionary, but couldn't get any sense out of it.

'Well,' I thought to myself, 'I must wait and see.'

CHAPTER 4

I ARRIVE IN HASSANIEH

Three days later I left Baghdad.

I was sorry to leave Mrs Kelsey and the baby, who was a little love and was thriving splendidly, gaining her proper number of ounces every week. Major Kelsey took me to the station and saw me off. I should arrive at Kirkuk the following morning, and there someone was to meet me.

I slept badly, I never sleep very well in a train and I was troubled by dreams. The next morning, however, when I looked out of the window it was a lovely day and I felt interested and curious about the people I was going to see.

As I stood on the platform hesitating and looking about me I saw a young man coming towards me. He had a round pink face, and really, in all my life, I have never seen anyone who seemed so exactly like a young man out of one of Mr P. G. Wodehouse's books.

'Hallo, 'allo, 'allo,' he said. 'Are you Nurse Leatheran? Well, I mean you must be – I can see that. Ha ha! My name's Coleman. Dr Leidner sent me along. How are you feeling? Beastly journey and all that? Don't I know these trains! Well, here we are – had any breakfast? This your kit? I say, awfully modest, aren't you? Mrs Leidner has four suitcases and a trunk – to say nothing of a hat-box and a patent pillow, and this, that and the other. Am I talking too much? Come along to the old bus.'

There was what I heard called later a station wagon waiting outside. It was a little like a wagonette, a little like a lorry and a little like a car. Mr Coleman helped me in, explaining that I had better sit next to the driver so as to get less jolting.

Jolting! I wonder the whole contraption didn't fall to pieces! And nothing like a road – just a sort of track all ruts and holes.

Glorious East indeed! When I thought of our splendid arterial roads in England it made me quite homesick.

Mr Coleman leaned forward from his seat behind me and yelled in my ear a good deal.

'Track's in pretty good condition,' he shouted just after we had been thrown up in our seats till we nearly touched the roof.

And apparently he was speaking quite seriously.

'Very good for you – jogs the liver,' he said. 'You ought to know that, nurse.'

'A stimulated liver won't be much good to me if my head's split open,' I observed tartly.

'You should come along here after it's rained! The skids are glorious. Most of the time one's going sideways.'

To this I did not respond.

Presently we had to cross the river, which we did on the craziest ferry-boat you can imagine. It was a mercy we ever got across, but everyone seemed to think it was quite usual.

It took us about four hours to get to Hassanieh, which, to my surprise, was quite a big place. Very pretty it looked, too, before we got there from the other side of the river – standing up quite white and fairy-like with minarets. It was a bit different, though, when one had crossed the bridge and come right into it. Such a smell and everything ramshackle and tumble-down, and mud and mess everywhere.

Mr Coleman took me to Dr Reilly's house, where, he said, the doctor was expecting me to lunch.

Dr Reilly was just as nice as ever, and his house was nice too, with a bathroom and everything spick and span. I had a nice bath, and by the time I got back into my uniform and came down I was feeling fine.

Lunch was just ready and we went in, the doctor apologizing for his daughter, who he said was always late. We'd just had a very good dish of eggs in sauce when she came in and Dr Reilly said, 'Nurse, this is my daughter Sheila.'

She shook hands, hoped I'd had a good journey, tossed off her hat, gave a cool nod to Mr Coleman and sat down.

'Well, Bill,' she said. 'How's everything?'

He began to talk to her about some party or other that was to come off at the club, and I took stock of her.

I can't say I took to her much. A thought too cool for my liking.

An off-hand sort of girl, though good-looking. Black hair and blue eyes – a pale sort of face and the usual lipsticked mouth. She'd a cool, sarcastic way of talking that rather annoyed me. I had a probationer like her under me once – a girl who worked well, I'll admit, but whose manner always riled me.

It looked to me rather as though Mr Coleman was gone on her. He stammered a bit, and his conversation became slightly more idiotic than it was before, if that was possible! He reminded me of a large stupid dog wagging its tail and trying to please.

After lunch Dr Reilly went off to the hospital, and Mr Coleman had some things to get in the town, and Miss Reilly asked me whether I'd like to see round the town a bit or whether I'd rather stop in the house. Mr Coleman, she said, would be back to fetch me in about an hour.

'Is there anything to see?' I asked.

'There are some picturesque corners,' said Miss Reilly. 'But I don't know that you'd care for them. They're extremely dirty.'

The way she said it rather nettled me. I've never been able to see that picturesqueness excuses dirt.

In the end she took me to the club, which was pleasant enough, overlooking the river, and there were English papers and magazines there.

When we got back to the house Mr Coleman wasn't there yet, so we sat down and talked a bit. It wasn't easy somehow.

She asked me if I'd met Mrs Leidner yet.

'No,' I said. 'Only her husband.'

'Oh,' she said. 'I wonder what you'll think of her?'

I didn't say anything to that. And she went on: 'I like Dr Leidner very much. Everybody likes him.'

That's as good as saying, I thought, that you don't like his wife.

I still didn't say anything and presently she asked abruptly: 'What's the matter with her? Did Dr Leidner tell you?'

I wasn't going to start gossiping about a patient before I got there even, so I said evasively: 'I understand she's a bit rundown and wants looking after.'

She laughed – a nasty sort of laugh – hard and abrupt.

'Good God,' she said. 'Aren't nine people looking after her already enough?'

'I suppose they've all got their work to do,' I said.

'Work to do? Of course they've got work to do. But Louise comes first – she sees to that all right.'

'No,' I said to myself. 'You *don't* like her.'

'All the same,' went on Miss Reilly, 'I don't see what she wants with a professional hospital nurse. I should have thought amateur assistance was more in her line; not someone who'll jam a thermometer in her mouth, and count her pulse and bring everything down to hard facts.'

Well, I must admit it, I was curious.

'You think there's nothing the matter with her?' I asked.

'Of course there's nothing the matter with her! The woman's as strong as an ox. "Dear Louise hasn't slept." "She's got black circles under her eyes." Yes – put there with a blue pencil! Anything to get attention, to have everybody hovering round her, making a fuss of her!'

There was something in that, of course. I had (what nurse hasn't?) come across many cases of hypochondriacs whose delight it is to keep a whole household dancing attendance. And if a doctor or a nurse were to say to them: 'There's nothing on earth the matter with you!' Well, to begin with they wouldn't believe it, and their indignation would be as genuine as indignation can be.

Of course it was quite possible that Mrs Leidner might be a case of this kind. The husband, naturally, would be the first to be deceived. Husbands, I've found, are a credulous lot where illness is concerned. But all the same, it didn't quite square with what I'd heard. It didn't, for instance, fit in with that word 'safer'.

Funny how that word had got kind of stuck in my mind.

Reflecting on it, I asked: 'Is Mrs Leidner a nervous woman? Is she nervous, for instance, of living out far from anywhere?'

'What is there to be nervous of? Good heavens, there are ten of them! And they've got guards too – because of the antiquities. Oh, no, she's not nervous – at least –'

She seemed struck by some thought and stopped – going on slowly after a minute or two.

'It's odd your saying that.'

'Why?'

'Flight-Lieutenant Jervis and I rode over the other day. It was in the morning. Most of them were up on the dig. She was sitting writing a letter and I suppose she didn't hear us coming. The boy

19

who brings you in wasn't about for once, and we came straight up on to the verandah. Apparently she saw Flight-Lieutenant Jervis's shadow thrown on the wall – and she fairly screamed! Apologized, of course. Said she thought it was a strange man. A bit odd, that. I mean, even if it was a strange man, why get the wind up?'

I nodded thoughtfully.

Miss Reilly was silent, then burst out suddenly:

'I don't know what's the matter with them this year. They've all got the jumps. Johnson goes about so glum she can't open her mouth. David never speaks if he can help it. Bill, of course, never stops, and somehow his chatter seems to make the others worse. Carey goes about looking as though something would snap any minute. And they all watch each other as though – as though – Oh, I don't know, but it's *queer*.'

It was odd, I thought, that two such dissimilar people as Miss Reilly and Major Pennyman should have been struck in the same manner.

Just then Mr Coleman came bustling in. Bustling was just the word for it. If his tongue had hung out and he had suddenly produced a tail to wag you wouldn't have been surprised.

'Hallo-allo,' he said. 'Absolutely the world's best shopper – that's me. Have you shown nurse all the beauties of the town?'

'She wasn't impressed,' said Miss Reilly dryly.

'I don't blame her,' said Mr Coleman heartily. 'Of all the one-horse tumble-down places!'

'Not a lover of the picturesque or the antique, are you, Bill? I can't think why you are an archaeologist.'

'Don't blame me for that. Blame my guardian. He's a learned bird – fellow of his college – browses among books in bedroom slippers – that kind of man. Bit of a shock for him to have a ward like me.'

'I think it's frightfully stupid of you to be forced into a profession you don't care for,' said the girl sharply.

'Not forced, Sheila, old girl, not forced. The old man asked if I had any special profession in mind, and I said I hadn't, and so he wangled a season out here for me.'

'But haven't you any idea really what you'd *like* to do? You *must* have!'

'Of course I have. My idea would be to give work a miss

altogether. What I'd like to do is to have plenty of money and go in for motor-racing.'

'You're absurd!' said Miss Reilly.

She sounded quite angry.

'Oh, I realize that it's quite out of the question,' said Mr Coleman cheerfully. 'So, if I've got to do something, I don't much care what it is so long as it isn't mugging in an office all day long. I was quite agreeable to seeing a bit of the world. Here goes, I said, and along I came.'

'And a fat lot of use you must be, I expect!'

'There you're wrong. I can stand up on the dig and shout "*Y'Allah*" with anybody! And as a matter of fact I'm not so dusty at drawing. Imitating handwriting used to be my speciality at school. I'd have made a first-class forger. Oh, well, I may come to that yet. If my Rolls-Royce splashes you with mud as you're waiting for a bus, you'll know that I've taken to crime.'

Miss Reilly said coldly: 'Don't you think it's about time you started instead of talking so much?'

'Hospitable, aren't we, nurse?'

'I'm sure Nurse Leatheran is anxious to get settled in.'

'You're always sure of everything,' retorted Mr Coleman with a grin.

That was true enough, I thought. Cocksure little minx.

I said dryly: 'Perhaps we'd better start, Mr Coleman.'

'Right you are, nurse.'

I shook hands with Miss Reilly and thanked her, and we set off.

'Damned attractive girl, Sheila,' said Mr Coleman. 'But always ticking a fellow off.'

We drove out of the town and presently took a kind of track between green crops. It was very bumpy and full of ruts.

After about half an hour Mr Coleman pointed to a big mound by the river bank ahead of us and said: 'Tell Yarimjah.'

I could see little black figures moving about it like ants.

As I was looking they suddenly began to run all together down the side of the mound.

'Fidos,' said Mr Coleman. 'Knocking-off time. We knock off an hour before sunset.'

The expedition house lay a little way back from the river.

The driver rounded a corner, bumped through an extremely narrow arch and there we were.

The house was built round a courtyard. Originally it had occupied only the south side of the courtyard with a few unimportant out-buildings on the east. The expedition had continued the building on the other two sides. As the plan of the house was to prove of special interest later, I append a rough sketch of it here.

All the rooms opened on to the courtyard, and most of the windows – the exception being in the original south building where there were windows giving on the outside country as well. These windows, however, were barred on the outside. In the south-west corner a staircase ran up to a long flat roof with a parapet running the length of the south side of the building which was higher than the other three sides.

Mr Coleman led me along the east side of the courtyard and round to where a big open verandah occupied the centre of the south side. He pushed open a door at one side of it and we entered a room where several people were sitting round a tea-table.

'Toodle-oodle-oo!' said Mr Coleman. 'Here's Sairey Gamp.'

The lady who was sitting at the head of the table rose and came to greet me.

I had my first glimpse of Louise Leidner.

CHAPTER 5

TELL YARIMJAH

I don't mind admitting that my first impression on seeing Mrs Leidner was one of downright surprise. One gets into the way of imagining a person when one hears them talked about. I'd got it firmly into my head that Mrs Leidner was a dark, discontented kind of woman. The nervy kind, all on edge. And then, too, I'd expected her to be – well, to put it frankly – a bit vulgar.

She wasn't a bit like what I'd imagined her! To begin with, she was very fair. She wasn't a Swede, like her husband, but she might have been as far as looks went. She had that blonde Scandinavian fairness that you don't very often see. She wasn't a young woman. Midway between thirty and forty, I should say. Her face was rather haggard, and there was some grey hair mingled with the

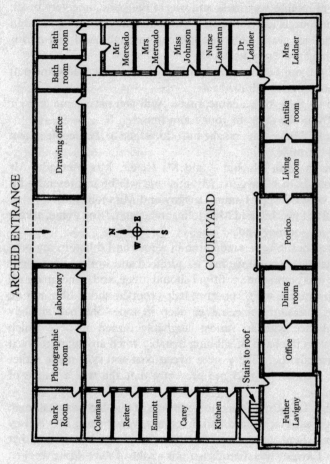

ARCHED ENTRANCE

| Bath room | Bath room | | Mr Mercado | Mrs Mercado | Miss Johnson | Nurse Leatheran | Dr Leidner | |
| Drawing office | | | | | | | | Mrs Leidner |

COURTYARD

Laboratory								Antika room
Photographic room								Living room
Dark Room	Coleman	Reiter	Emmott	Carey	Kitchen		Portico.
					Stairs to roof	Dining room	
						Office	
						Father Lavigny	

Plan of the expedition house at Tell Yarimjah

fairness. Her eyes, though, were lovely. They were the only eyes
I've ever come across that you might truly describe as violet. They
were very large, and there were faint shadows underneath them.
She was very thin and fragile-looking, and if I say that she had
an air of intense weariness and was at the same time very much
alive, it sounds like nonsense – but that's the feeling I got. I felt,
too, that she was a lady through and through. And that means
something – even nowadays.

She put out her hand and smiled. Her voice was low and soft
with an American drawl in it.

'I'm so glad you've come, nurse. Will you have some tea? Or
would you like to go to your room first?'

I said I'd have tea, and she introduced me to the people sitting
round the table.

'This is Miss Johnson – and Mr Reiter. Mrs Mercado. Mr
Emmott. Father Lavigny. My husband will be in presently. Sit
down here between Father Lavigny and Miss Johnson.'

I did as I was bid and Miss Johnson began talking to me, asking
about my journey and so on.

I liked her. She reminded me of a matron I'd had in my probationer days whom we had all admired and worked hard for.

She was getting on for fifty, I should judge, and rather mannish
in appearance, with iron-grey hair cropped short. She had an
abrupt, pleasant voice, rather deep in tone. She had an ugly
rugged face with an almost laughably turned-up nose which
she was in the habit of rubbing irritably when anything troubled
or perplexed her. She wore a tweed coat and skirt made rather
like a man's. She told me presently that she was a native of
Yorkshire.

Father Lavigny I found just a bit alarming. He was a tall man
with a great black beard and pince-nez. I had heard Mrs Kelsey
say that there was a French monk there, and I now saw that
Father Lavigny was wearing a monk's robe of some white woollen
material. It surprised me rather, because I always understood that
monks went into monasteries and didn't come out again.

Mrs Leidner talked to him mostly in French, but he spoke to
me in quite fair English. I noticed that he had shrewd, observant
eyes which darted about from face to face.

Opposite me were the other three. Mr Reiter was a stout, fair
young man with glasses. His hair was rather long and curly, and

he had very round blue eyes. I should think he must have been a lovely baby, but he wasn't much to look at now! In fact he was just a little like a pig. The other young man had very short hair cropped close to his head. He had a long, rather humorous face and very good teeth, and he looked very attractive when he smiled. He said very little, though, just nodded if spoken to or answered in monosyllables. He, like Mr Reiter, was an American. The last person was Mrs Mercado, and I couldn't have a good look at her because whenever I glanced in her direction I always found her staring at me with a kind of hungry stare that was a bit disconcerting to say the least of it. You might have thought a hospital nurse was a strange animal the way she was looking at me. No manners at all!

She was quite young – not more than about twenty-five – and sort of dark and slinky-looking, if you know what I mean. Quite nice-looking in a kind of way, but rather as though she might have what my mother used to call 'a touch of the tar-brush'. She had on a very vivid pullover and her nails matched it in colour. She had a thin bird-like eager face with big eyes and rather a tight, suspicious mouth.

The tea was very good – a nice strong blend – not like the weak China stuff that Mrs Kelsey always had and that had been a sore trial to me.

There was toast and jam and a plate of rock buns and a cutting cake. Mr Emmott was very polite passing me things. Quiet as he was he always seemed to notice when my plate was empty.

Presently Mr Coleman bustled in and took the place beyond Miss Johnson. There didn't seem to be anything the matter with *his* nerves. He talked away nineteen to the dozen.

Mrs Leidner sighed once and cast a wearied look in his direction but it didn't have any effect. Nor did the fact that Mrs Mercado, to whom he was addressing most of his conversation, was far too busy watching me to do more than make perfunctory replies.

Just as we were finishing, Dr Leidner and Mr Mercado came in from the dig.

Dr Leidner greeted me in his nice kind manner. I saw his eyes go quickly and anxiously to his wife's face and he seemed to be relieved by what he saw there. Then he sat down at the other end of the table, and Mr Mercado sat down in the vacant place by Mrs Leidner. He was a tall, thin, melancholy man, a good deal older than his wife, with a sallow complexion and a queer, soft, shapeless-looking beard. I was glad when he came in, for his wife stopped staring at me and transferred her attention to him, watching him with a kind of anxious impatience that I found rather odd. He himself stirred his tea dreamily and said nothing at all. A piece of cake lay untasted on his plate.

There was still one vacant place, and presently the door opened and a man came in.

The moment I saw Richard Carey I felt he was one of the handsomest men I'd seen for a long time – and yet I doubt if that were really so. To say a man is handsome and at the same time to say he looks like a death's head sounds a rank contradiction, and yet it was true. His head gave the effect of having the skin stretched unusually tight over the bones – but they were beautiful bones. The lean line of jaw and temple and forehead was so sharply outlined that he reminded me of a bronze statue. Out of this lean brown face looked two of the brightest and most intensely blue eyes I have ever seen. He stood about six foot and was, I should imagine, a little under forty years of age.

Dr Leidner said: 'This is Mr Carey, our architect, nurse.'

He murmured something in a pleasant, inaudible English voice and sat down by Mrs Mercado.

Mrs Leidner said: 'I'm afraid the tea is a little cold, Mr Carey.'

He said: 'Oh, that's quite all right, Mrs Leidner. My fault for being late. I wanted to finish plotting those walls.'

Mrs Mercado said, 'Jam, Mr Carey?'

Mr Reiter pushed forward the toast.

And I remembered Major Pennyman saying: '*I can explain best what I mean by saying that they all passed the butter to each other a shade too politely.*'

Yes, there was something a little odd about it . . .

A shade formal . . .

You'd have said it was a party of strangers – not people who had known each other – some of them – for quite a number of years.

CHAPTER 6

FIRST EVENING

After tea Mrs Leidner took me to show me my room.

Perhaps here I had better give a short description of the arrangement of the rooms. This was very simple and can easily be understood by a reference to the plan.

On either side of the big open porch were doors leading into the two principal rooms. That on the right led into the dining-room, where we had tea. The one on the other side led into an exactly similar room (I have called it the living-room) which was used as a sitting-room and kind of informal workroom – that is, a certain amount of drawing (other than the strictly architectural) was done there, and the more delicate pieces of pottery were brought there to be pieced together. Through the living-room one passed into the antiquities-room where all the finds from the dig were brought in and stored on shelves and in pigeon-holes, and also laid out on big benches and tables. From the antika-room there was no exit save through the living-room.

Beyond the antika-room, but reached through a door which gave on the courtyard, was Mrs Leidner's bedroom. This, like the other rooms on that side of the house, had a couple of barred windows looking out over the ploughed countryside. Round the corner next to Mrs Leidner's room, but with no actual communicating door, was Dr Leidner's room. This was the first of the rooms on the east side of the building. Next to it was the room that was to be mine. Next to me was Miss Johnson's, with Mr and Mrs Mercado's beyond. After that came two so-called bathrooms.

(When I once used that last term in the hearing of Dr Reilly he laughed at me and said a bathroom was either a bathroom or not a bathroom! All the same, when you've got used to taps and proper plumbing, it seems strange to call a couple of mud-rooms with a tin hip-bath in each of them, and muddy water brought in kerosene tins, *bathrooms*!)

All this side of the building had been added by Dr Leidner to the original Arab house. The bedrooms were all the same, each with a window and a door giving on to the courtyard. Along the north side were the drawing-office, the laboratory and the photographic rooms.

To return to the verandah, the arrangement of rooms was much the same on the other side. There was the dining-room leading into the office where the files were kept and the cataloguing and typing was done. Corresponding to Mrs Leidner's room was that of Father Lavigny, who was given the largest bedroom; he used it also for the decoding – or whatever you call it – of tablets.

In the south-west corner was the staircase running up to the roof. On the west side were first the kitchen quarters and then four small bedrooms used by the young men – Carey, Emmott, Reiter and Coleman.

At the north-west corner was the photographic-room with the dark-room leading out of it. Next to that the laboratory. Then came the only entrance – the big arched doorway through which we had entered. Outside were sleeping quarters for the native servants, the guard-house for the soldiers, and stables, etc., for the water horses. The drawing-office was to the right of the archway occupying the rest of the north side.

I have gone into the arrangements of the house rather fully here because I don't want to have to go over them again later.

As I say, Mrs Leidner herself took me round the building and finally established me in my bedroom, hoping that I should be comfortable and have everything I wanted.

The room was nicely though plainly furnished – a bed, a chest of drawers, a wash-stand and a chair.

'The boys will bring you hot water before lunch and dinner – and in the morning, of course. If you want it any other time, go outside and clap your hands, and when the boy comes say, *jib mai' har.* Do you think you can remember that?'

I said I thought so and repeated it a little haltingly.

'That's right. And be sure and shout it. Arabs don't understand anything said in an ordinary "English" voice.'

'Languages are funny things,' I said. 'It seems odd there should be such a lot of different ones.'

Mrs Leidner smiled.

'There is a church in Palestine in which the Lord's Prayer is written up in – ninety, I think it is – different languages.'

'Well!' I said. 'I must write and tell my old aunt that. She *will* be interested.'

Mrs Leidner fingered the jug and basin absently and shifted the soap-dish an inch or two.'

'I do hope you'll be happy here,' she said, 'and not get too bored.'

'I'm not often bored,' I assured her. 'Life's not long enough for that.'

She did not answer. She continued to toy with the washstand as though abstractedly.

Suddenly she fixed her dark violet eyes on my face.

'What exactly did my husband tell you, nurse?'

Well, one usually says the same thing to a question of that kind.

'I gathered you were a bit run-down and all that, Mrs Leidner,' I said glibly. 'And that you just wanted someone to look after you and take any worries off your hands.'

She bent her head slowly and thoughtfully.

'Yes,' she said. 'Yes – that will do very well.'

That was just a little bit enigmatic, but I wasn't going to question it. Instead I said: 'I hope you'll let me help you with anything there is to do in the house. You mustn't let me be idle.'

She smiled a little.

'Thank you, nurse.'

Then she sat down on the bed and, rather to my surprise, began to cross-question me rather closely. I say rather to my surprise because, from the moment I set eyes on her, I felt sure that Mrs Leidner was a lady. And a lady, in my experience, very seldom displays curiosity about one's private affairs.

But Mrs Leidner seemed anxious to know everything there was to know about me. Where I'd trained and how long ago. What had brought me out to the East. How it had come about that Dr Reilly had recommended me. She even asked me if I had ever been in America or had any relations in America. One or two other questions she asked me that seemed quite purposeless at the time, but of which I saw the significance later.

Then, suddenly, her manner changed. She smiled – a warm sunny smile – and she said, very sweetly, that she was very glad I had come and that she was sure I was going to be a comfort to her.

She got up from the bed and said: 'Would you like to come

up to the roof and see the sunset? It's usually very lovely about this time.'

I agreed willingly.

As we went out of the room she asked: 'Were there many other people on the train from Baghdad? Any men?'

I said that I hadn't noticed anybody in particular. There had been two Frenchmen in the restaurant-car the night before. And a party of three men whom I gathered from their conversation had to do with the Pipe line.

She nodded and a faint sound escaped her. It sounded like a small sigh of relief.

We went up to the roof together.

Mrs Mercado was there, sitting on the parapet, and Dr Leidner was bending over looking at a lot of stones and broken pottery that were laid in rows. There were big things he called querns, and pestles and celts and stone axes, and more broken bits of pottery with queer patterns on them than I've ever seen all at once.

'Come over here,' called out Mrs Mercado. 'Isn't it *too* too beautiful?'

It certainly was a beautiful sunset. Hassanieh in the distance looked quite fairy-like with the setting sun behind it, and the River Tigris flowing between its wide banks looked like a dream river rather than a real one.

'Isn't it lovely, Eric?' said Mrs Leidner.

The doctor looked up with abstracted eyes, murmured, 'Lovely, lovely,' perfunctorily and went on sorting potsherds.

Mrs Leidner smiled and said: 'Archaeologists only look at what lies beneath their feet. The sky and the heavens don't exist for them.'

Mrs Mercado giggled.

'Oh, they're very queer people – you'll soon find *that* out, nurse,' she said.

She paused and then added: 'We are all *so* glad you've come. We've been so very worried about dear Mrs Leidner, haven't we, Louise?'

'Have you?'

Her voice was not encouraging.

'Oh, yes. She really has been *very* bad, nurse. All sorts of alarms and excursions. You know when anybody says to me of someone, "It's just nerves," I always say: but what could be *worse*? Nerves are the core and centre of one's being, aren't they?'

'Puss, puss,' I thought to myself.

Mrs Leidner said dryly: 'Well, you needn't be worried about me any more, Marie. Nurse is going to look after me.'

'Certainly I am,' I said cheerfully.

'I'm sure that will make all the difference,' said Mrs Mercado. 'We've all felt that she ought to see a doctor or do *something*. Her nerves have really been all to pieces, haven't they, Louise dear?'

'So much so that I seem to have got on *your* nerves with them,' said Mrs Leidner. 'Shall we talk about something more interesting than my wretched ailments?'

I understood then that Mrs Leidner was the sort of woman who could easily make enemies. There was a cool rudeness in her tone (not that I blamed her for it) which brought a flush to Mrs Mercado's rather sallow cheeks. She stammered out something, but Mrs Leidner had risen and had joined her husband at the other end of the roof. I doubt if he heard her coming till she laid her hand on his shoulder, then he looked up quickly. There was affection and a kind of eager questioning in his face.

Mrs Leidner nodded her head gently. Presently, her arm through his, they wandered to the far parapet and finally down the steps together.

'He's devoted to her, isn't he?' said Mrs Mercado.

'Yes,' I said. 'It's very nice to see.'

She was looking at me with a queer, rather eager sidelong glance.

'What do you think is really the matter with her, nurse?' she asked, lowering her voice a little.

'Oh, I don't suppose it's much,' I said cheerfully. 'Just a bit run-down, I expect.'

Her eyes still bored into me as they had done at tea. She said abruptly: 'Are you a mental nurse?'

'Oh, dear, no!' I said. 'What made you think that?'

She was silent for a moment, then she said: 'Do you know how queer she's been? Did Dr Leidner tell you?'

I don't hold with gossiping about my cases. On the other hand, it's my experience that it's often very hard to get the truth out of relatives, and until you know the truth you're often working in the dark and doing no good. Of course, when there's a doctor in charge, it's different. He tells you what it's necessary for you to know. But in this case there wasn't a doctor in charge. Dr Reilly had never been called in professionally. And in my own mind I wasn't at all sure that Dr Leidner had told me all he could have done. It's often the husband's instinct to be reticent – and more honour to him, I must say. But all the same, the more I knew the better I could tell which line to take. Mrs Mercado (whom I put down in my own mind as a thoroughly spiteful little cat) was clearly dying to talk. And frankly, on the human side as well as the professional, I wanted to hear what she had to say. You can put it that I was just everyday curious if you like.

I said, 'I gather Mrs Leidner's not been quite her normal self lately?'

Mrs Mercado laughed disagreeably.

'Normal? I should say not. Frightening us to death. One night it was fingers tapping on her window. And then it was a hand without an arm attached. But when it came to a yellow face pressed against the window – and when she rushed to the window there was nothing there – well, I ask you, it *is* a bit creepy for all of us.'

'Perhaps somebody was playing a trick on her,' I suggested.

'Oh, no, she fancied it all. And only three days ago at dinner they were firing shots in the village – nearly a mile away – and she jumped up and screamed out – it scared us all to death. As for Dr Leidner, he rushed to her and behaved in the most ridiculous way. "It's nothing, darling, it's nothing at all," he kept saying. I think, you know, nurse, men sometimes *encourage* women in these hysterical fancies. It's a pity because it's a bad thing. Delusions shouldn't be encouraged.'

'Not if they *are* delusions,' I said dryly.

'What else could they be?'

I didn't answer because I didn't know what to say. It was a funny business. The shots and the screaming were natural enough – for anyone in a nervous condition, that is. But this queer story of a spectral face and hand was different. It looked to me like one of two things – either Mrs Leidner had made the story up (exactly as a child shows off by telling lies about something that never happened in order to make herself the centre of attraction) or else it was, as I had suggested, a deliberate practical joke. It was the sort of thing, I reflected, that an unimaginative hearty sort of young fellow like Mr Coleman might think very funny. I decided to keep a close watch on him. Nervous patients can be scared nearly out of their minds by a silly joke.

Mrs Mercado said with a sideways glance at me:

'She's very romantic-looking, nurse, don't you think so? The sort of woman things *happen* to.'

'Have many things happened to her?' I asked.

'Well, her first husband was killed in the war when she was only twenty. I think that's very pathetic and romantic, don't you?'

'It's one way of calling a goose a swan,' I said dryly.

'Oh, nurse! What an extraordinary remark!'

It was really a very true one. The amount of women you hear say, 'If Donald – or Arthur – or whatever his name was – had *only* lived.' And I sometimes think but if he had, he'd have been a stout, unromantic, short-tempered, middle-aged husband as likely as not.

It was getting dark and I suggested that we should go down. Mrs Mercado agreed and asked if I would like to see the laboratory. 'My husband will be there – working.'

I said I would like to very much and we made our way there. The place was lighted by a lamp, but it was empty. Mrs Mercado showed me some of the apparatus and some copper ornaments that were being treated, and also some bones coated with wax.

'Where can Joseph be?' said Mrs Mercado.

She looked into the drawing-office, where Carey was at work. He hardly looked up as we entered, and I was struck by the extraordinary look of strain on his face. It came to me suddenly: 'This man is at the end of his tether. Very soon, something will snap.' And I remembered somebody else had noticed that same tenseness about him.

As we went out again I turned my head for one last look at him. He was bent over his paper, his lips pressed very closely together, and that 'death's head' suggestion of his bones very strongly marked. Perhaps it was fanciful, but I thought that he looked like a knight of old who was going into battle and knew he was going to be killed.

And again I felt what an extraordinary and quite unconscious power of attraction he had.

We found Mr Mercado in the living-room. He was explaining the idea of some new process to Mrs Leidner. She was sitting on a straight wooden chair, embroidering flowers in fine silks, and I was struck anew by her strange, fragile, unearthly appearance. She looked a fairy creature more than flesh and blood.

Mrs Mercado said, her voice high and shrill: 'Oh, *there* you are, Joseph. We thought we'd find you in the lab.'

He jumped up looking startled and confused, as though her entrance had broken a spell. He said stammeringly: 'I – I must go now. I'm in the middle of – the middle of –'

He didn't complete the sentence but turned towards the door.

Mrs Leidner said in her soft, drawling voice: 'You must finish telling me some other time. It was very interesting.'

She looked up at us, smiled rather sweetly but in a far-away manner, and bent over her embroidery again.

In a minute or two she said: 'There are some books over there, nurse. We've got quite a good selection. Choose one and sit down.'

I went over to the bookshelf. Mrs Mercado stayed for a minute or two, then, turning abruptly, she went out. As she passed me I saw her face and I didn't like the look of it. She looked wild with fury.

In spite of myself I remembered some of the things Mrs Kelsey had said and hinted about Mrs Leidner. I didn't like to think they were true because I liked Mrs Leidner, but I wondered, nevertheless, if there mightn't perhaps be a grain of truth behind them.

I didn't think it was all her fault, but the fact remained that dear ugly Miss Johnson, and that common little spitfire Mrs Mercado, couldn't hold a candle to her in looks or in attraction. And after all, men are men all over the world. You soon see a lot of that in my profession.

Mercado was a poor fish, and I don't suppose Mrs Leidner really cared two hoots for his admiration – but his wife cared. If I wasn't mistaken, she minded badly and would be quite willing to do Mrs Leidner a bad turn if she could.

I looked at Mrs Leidner sitting there and sewing at her pretty flowers, so remote and far away and aloof. I felt somehow I ought to warn her. I felt that perhaps she didn't know how stupid and unreasoning and violent jealousy and hate can be – and how little it takes to set them smouldering.

And then I said to myself, 'Amy Leatheran, you're a fool. Mrs

Leidner's no chicken. She's close on forty if she's a day, and she must know all about life there is to know.'

But I felt that all the same perhaps she didn't.

She had such a queer untouched look.

I began to wonder what her life had been. I knew she'd only married Dr Leidner two years ago. And according to Mrs Mercado her first husband had died about fifteen years ago.

I came and sat down near her with a book, and presently I went and washed my hands for supper. It was a good meal – some really excellent curry. They all went to bed early and I was glad, for I was tired.

Dr Leidner came with me to my room to see I had all I wanted.

He gave me a warm handclasp and said eagerly:

'She likes you, nurse. She's taken to you at once. I'm so glad. I feel everything's going to be all right now.'

His eagerness was almost boyish.

I felt, too, that Mrs Leidner had taken a liking to me, and I was pleased it should be so.

But I didn't quite share his confidence. I felt, somehow, that there was more to it all than he himself might know.

There was *something* – something I couldn't get at. But I felt it in the air.

My bed was comfortable, but I didn't sleep well for all that. I dreamt too much.

The words of a poem by Keats, that I'd had to learn as a child, kept running through my head. I kept getting them wrong and it worried me. It was a poem I'd always hated – I suppose because I'd had to learn it whether I wanted to or not. But somehow when I woke up in the dark I saw a sort of beauty in it for the first time.

'*Oh say what ails thee, knight at arms, alone – and* (what was it?) – *palely loitering . . .* ? I saw the knight's face in my mind for the first time – it was Mr Carey's face – a grim, tense, bronzed face like some of those poor young men I remembered as a girl during the war . . . and I felt sorry for him – and then I fell off to sleep again and I saw that the Belle Dame sans Merci was Mrs Leidner and she was leaning sideways on a horse with an embroidery of flowers in her hands – and then the horse stumbled and everywhere there were bones coated in wax, and I woke up all goose-flesh and shivering, and told myself that curry never *had* agreed with me at night.

CHAPTER 7

THE MAN AT THE WINDOW

I think I'd better make it clear right away that there isn't going to be any local colour in this story. I don't know anything about archaeology and I don't know that I very much want to. Messing about with people and places that are buried and done with doesn't make sense to me. Mr Carey used to tell me that I hadn't got the archaeological temperament and I've no doubt he was quite right.

The very first morning after my arrival Mr Carey asked if I'd like to come and see the palace he was – *planning* I think he called it. Though how you can plan for a thing that's happened long ago I'm sure I don't know! Well, I said I'd like to, and to tell the truth, I was a bit excited about it. Nearly three thousand years old that palace was, it appeared. I wondered what sort of palaces they had in those days, and if it would be like the pictures I'd seen of Tutankhamen's tomb furniture. But would you believe it, there was nothing to see but *mud*! Dirty mud walls about two feet high – and that's all there was to it. Mr Carey took me here and there telling me things – how this was the great court, and there were some chambers here and an upper storey and various other rooms that opened off the central court. And all I thought was, 'But how does he *know*?' though, of course, I was too polite to say so. I can tell you it *was* a disappointment! The whole excavation looked like nothing but mud to me – no marble or gold or anything handsome – my aunt's house in Cricklewood would have made a much more imposing ruin! And those old Assyrians, or whatever they were, called themselves *kings*. When Mr Carey had shown me his old 'palaces', he handed me over to Father Lavigny, who showed me the rest of the mound. I was a little afraid of Father Lavigny, being a monk and a foreigner and having such a deep voice and all that, but he was very kind – though rather vague. Sometimes I felt it wasn't much more real to him than it was to me.

Mrs Leidner explained that later. She said that Father Lavigny was only interested in 'written documents' – as she called them. They wrote everything on clay, these people, queer, heathenish-looking marks too, but quite sensible. There were even school tablets – the teacher's lesson on one side and the pupil's effort on the back of it. I confess that that did interest me rather – it seemed so human, if you know what I mean.

Father Lavigny walked round the work with me and showed me what were temples or palaces and what were private houses, and also a place which he said was an early Akkadian cemetery. He spoke in a funny jerky way, just throwing in a scrap of information and then reverting to other subjects.

He said: 'It is strange that you have come here. Is Mrs Leidner really ill, then?'

'Not exactly ill,' I said cautiously.

He said: 'She is an odd woman. A dangerous woman, I think.'

'Now what do you mean by that?' I said. 'Dangerous? How dangerous?'

He shook his head thoughtfully.

'I think she is ruthless,' he said. 'Yes, I think she could be absolutely ruthless.'

'If you'll excuse me,' I said, 'I think you're talking non-sense.'

He shook his head.

'You do not know women as I do,' he said.

And that was a funny thing, I thought, for a monk to say. But of course I suppose he might have heard a lot of things in confession. But that rather puzzled me, because I wasn't sure if monks heard confessions or if it was only priests. I supposed he *was* a monk with that long woollen robe – all sweeping up the dirt – and the rosary and all!

'Yes, she could be ruthless,' he said musingly. 'I am quite sure of that. And yet – though she is so hard – like stone, like marble – yet she is afraid. What is she afraid of?'

That, I thought, is what we should all like to know!

At least it was possible that her husband did know, but I didn't think anyone else did.

He fixed me with a sudden bright, dark eye.

'It is odd here? You find it odd? Or quite natural?'

'Not quite natural,' I said, considering. 'It's comfortable enough as far as the arrangements go – but there isn't quite a comfortable feeling.'

'It makes *me* uncomfortable. I have the idea' – he became suddenly a little more foreign – 'that something prepares itself. Dr Leidner, too, he is not quite himself. Something is worrying him also.'

'His wife's health?'

'That perhaps. But there is more. There is – how shall I say it – an uneasiness.'

And that was just it, there was an uneasiness.

We didn't say any more just then, for Dr Leidner came towards us. He showed me a child's grave that had just been uncovered. Rather pathetic it was – the little bones – and a pot or two and some little specks that Dr Leidner told me were a bead necklace.

It was the workmen that made me laugh. You never saw such a lot of scarecrows – all in long petticoats and rags, and their heads tied up as though they had toothache. And every now and then, as they went to and fro carrying away baskets of earth, they began to sing – at least I suppose it was meant to be singing – a queer sort of monotonous chant that went on and on over and over again. I noticed that most of their eyes were terrible – all covered with discharge, and one or two looked half blind. I was just thinking what a miserable lot they were when Dr Leidner said, 'Rather a fine-looking lot of men, aren't they?' and I thought what a queer world it was and how two different people could see the same thing each of them the other way round. I haven't put that very well, but you can guess what I mean.

After a bit Dr Leidner said he was going back to the house for a mid-morning cup of tea. So he and I walked back together and he told me things. When *he* explained, it was all quite different. I sort of *saw* it all – how it used to be – the streets and the houses, and he showed me ovens where they baked bread and said the Arabs used much the same kind of ovens nowadays.

We got back to the house and found Mrs Leidner had got up. She was looking better today, not so thin and worn. Tea came in almost at once and Dr Leidner told her what had turned up during the morning on the dig. Then he went back to work and Mrs Leidner asked me if I would like to see some of the finds they had made up to date. Of course I said 'Yes,' so she took me through into the antika-room. There was a lot of stuff lying about – mostly broken pots it seemed to me – or else ones that were all mended and stuck together. The whole lot might have been thrown away, I thought.

'Dear, dear,' I said, 'it's a pity they're all so broken, isn't it? Are they really worth keeping?'

Mrs Leidner smiled a little and she said: 'You mustn't let Eric hear you. Pots interest him more than anything else, and some of these are the oldest things we have – perhaps as much as seven thousand years old.' And she explained how some of them came from a very deep cut on the mound down towards the bottom, and how, thousands of years ago, they had been broken and mended with bitumen, showing people prized their things just as much then as they do nowadays.

'And now,' she said, 'we'll show you something more exciting.'

And she took down a box from the shelf and showed me a beautiful gold dagger with dark-blue stones in the handle.

I exclaimed with pleasure.

Mrs Leidner laughed.

'Yes, everybody likes gold! Except my husband.'

'Why doesn't Dr Leidner like it?'

'Well, for one thing it comes expensive. You have to pay the workmen who find it the weight of the object in gold.'

'Good gracious!' I exclaimed. 'But why?'

'Oh, it's a custom. For one thing it prevents them from stealing. You see, if they *did* steal, it wouldn't be for the archaeological value but for the intrinsic value. They could melt it down. So we make it easy for them to be honest.'

She took down another tray and showed me a really beautiful gold drinking-cup with a design of rams' heads on it.

Again I exclaimed.

'Yes, it is beautiful, isn't it? These came from a prince's grave. We found other royal graves but most of them had been plundered. This cup is our best find. It is one of the most lovely ever found anywhere. Early Akkadian. Unique.'

Suddenly, with a frown, Mrs Leidner brought the cup up close to her eyes and scratched at it delicately with her nail.

'How extraordinary! There's actually wax on it. Someone must have been in here with a candle.' She detached the little flake and replaced the cup in its place.

After that she showed me some queer little terracotta figurines – but most of them were just rude. Nasty minds those old people had, I say.

When we went back to the porch Mrs Mercado was sitting polishing her nails. She was holding them out in front of her admiring the effect. I thought myself that anything more hideous than that orange red could hardly have been imagined.

Mrs Leidner had brought with her from the antika-room a very delicate little saucer broken in several pieces, and this she now proceeded to join together. I watched her for a minute or two and then asked if I could help.

'Oh, yes, there are plenty more.' She fetched quite a supply of broken pottery and we set to work. I soon got into the hang of it and she praised my ability. I suppose most nurses are handy with their fingers.

'How busy everybody is!' said Mrs Mercado. 'It makes me feel dreadfully idle. Of course I *am* idle.'

'Why shouldn't you be if you like?' said Mrs Leidner.

Her voice was quite uninterested.

At twelve we had lunch. Afterwards Dr Leidner and Mr Mercado cleaned some pottery, pouring a solution of hydrochloric acid over it. One pot went a lovely plum colour and a pattern of bulls' horns came out on another one. It was really quite magical. All the dried mud that no washing would remove sort of foamed and boiled away.

Mr Carey and Mr Coleman went out on the dig and Mr Reiter went off to the photographic-room.

'What will you do, Louise?' Dr Leidner asked his wife. 'I suppose you'll rest for a bit?'

I gathered that Mrs Leidner usually lay down every afternoon.

'I'll rest for about an hour. Then perhaps I'll go out for a short stroll.'

'Good. Nurse will go with you, won't you?'

'Of course,' I said.

'No, no,' said Mrs Leidner, 'I like going alone. Nurse isn't to feel so much on duty that I'm not allowed out of her sight.'

'Oh, but I'd like to come,' I said.

'No, really, I'd rather you didn't.' She was quite firm – almost peremptory. 'I must be by myself every now and then. It's necessary to me.'

I didn't insist, of course. But as I went off for a short sleep myself it struck me as odd that Mrs Leidner, with her nervous terrors, should be quite content to walk by herself without any kind of protection.

When I came out of my room at half-past three the courtyard was deserted save for a little boy with a large copper bath who was washing pottery, and Mr Emmott, who was sorting and arranging it. As I went towards them Mrs Leidner came in through the archway. She looked more alive than I had seen her yet. Her eyes shone and she looked uplifted and almost gay.

Dr Leidner came out from the laboratory and joined her. He was showing her a big dish with bulls' horns on it.

'The prehistoric levels are being extraordinarily productive,' he said. 'It's been a good season so far. Finding that tomb right at the beginning was a real piece of luck. The only person who might complain is Father Lavigny. We've had hardly any tablets so far.'

'He doesn't seem to have done very much with the few we have had,' said Mrs Leidner dryly. 'He may be a very fine epigraphist but he's a remarkably lazy one. He spends all his afternoons sleeping.'

'We miss Byrd,' said Dr Leidner. 'This man strikes me as slightly unorthodox – though, of course, I'm not competent to judge. But one or two of his translations have been surprising, to say the least of it. I can hardly believe, for instance, that he's right about that inscribed brick, and yet he must know.'

After tea Mrs Leidner asked me if I would like to stroll down to the river. I thought that perhaps she feared that her refusal to let me accompany her earlier in the afternoon might have hurt my feelings.

I wanted her to know that I wasn't the touchy kind, so I accepted at once.

It was a lovely evening. A path led between barley fields and then through some flowering fruit trees. Finally we came to the edge of the Tigris. Immediately on our left was the Tell with the workmen singing in their queer monotonous chant. A little to our right was a big water-wheel which made a queer groaning noise. It used to set my teeth on edge at first. But in the end I got fond of it and it had a queer soothing effect on me. Beyond the water-wheel was the village from which most of the workmen came.

'It's rather beautiful, isn't it?' said Mrs Leidner.

'It's very peaceful,' I said. 'It seems funny to me to be so far away from everywhere.'

'Far from everywhere,' repeated Mrs Leidner. 'Yes. Here at least one might expect to be safe.'

I glanced at her sharply, but I think she was speaking more to herself than to me, and I don't think she realized that her words had been revealing.

We began to walk back to the house.

Suddenly Mrs Leidner clutched my arm so violently that I nearly cried out.

'Who's that, nurse? What's he doing?'

Some distance ahead of us, just where the path ran near the expedition house, a man was standing. He wore European clothes and he seemed to be standing on tiptoe and trying to look in at one of the windows.

As we watched he glanced round, caught sight of us, and immediately continued on the path towards us. I felt Mrs Leidner's clutch tighten.

'Nurse,' she whispered. 'Nurse . . .'

'It's all right, my dear, it's all right,' I said reassuringly.

The man came along and passed us. He was an Iraqi, and as soon as she saw him near to, Mrs Leidner relaxed with a sigh.

'He's only an Iraqi after all,' she said.

We went on our way. I glanced up at the windows as I passed. Not only were they barred, but they were too high from the ground to permit of anyone seeing in, for the level of the ground was lower here than on the inside of the courtyard.

'It must have been just curiosity,' I said.

Mrs Leidner nodded.

'That's all. But just for a minute I thought –'

She broke off.

I thought to myself. 'You thought *what*? That's what I'd like to know. *What* did you think?'

But I knew one thing now – that Mrs Leidner was afraid of a definite flesh-and-blood person.

....
NIGHT ALARM

It's a little difficult to know exactly what to note in the week that followed my arrival at Tell Yarimjah.

Looking back as I do from my present standpoint of knowledge I can see a good many little signs and indications that I was quite blind to at the time.

To tell the story properly, however, I think I ought to try to recapture the point of view that I actually held – puzzled, uneasy and increasingly conscious of *something* wrong.

For one thing *was* certain, that curious sense of strain and constraint was *not* imagined. It was genuine. Even Bill Coleman the insensitive commented upon it.

'This place gets under my skin,' I heard him say. 'Are they always such a glum lot?'

It was David Emmott to whom he spoke, the other assistant. I had taken rather a fancy to Mr Emmott, his taciturnity was not, I felt sure, unfriendly. There was something about him that seemed very steadfast and reassuring in an atmosphere where one was uncertain what anyone was feeling or thinking.

'No,' he said in answer to Mr Coleman. 'It wasn't like this last year.'

But he didn't enlarge on the theme, or say any more.

'What I can't make out is what it's all about,' said Mr Coleman in an aggrieved voice.

Emmott shrugged his shoulders but didn't answer.

I had a rather enlightening conversation with Miss Johnson. I liked her very much. She was capable, practical and intelligent. She had, it was quite obvious, a distinct hero worship for Dr Leidner.

On this occasion she told me the story of his life since his young days. She knew every site he had dug, and the results of the dig. I would almost dare swear she could quote from every lecture he had ever delivered. She considered him, she told me, quite the finest field archaeologist living.

'And he's so simple. So completely unworldly. He doesn't know the meaning of the word conceit. Only a really great man could be so simple.'

'That's true enough,' I said. 'Big people don't need to throw their weight about.'

'And he's so light-hearted too, I can't tell you what fun we used to have – he and Richard Carey and I – the first years we were out here. We were such a happy party. Richard Carey worked with him in Palestine, of course. Theirs is a friendship of ten years or so. Oh, well, I've known him for seven.'

'What a handsome man Mr Carey is,' I said.

'Yes – I suppose he is.'

She said it rather curtly.

'But he's just a little bit quiet, don't you think?'

'He usedn't to be like that,' said Miss Johnson quickly. 'It's only since –'

She stopped abruptly.

'Only since –?' I prompted.

'Oh, well.' Miss Johnson gave a characteristic motion of her shoulders. 'A good many things are changed nowadays.'

I didn't answer. I hoped she would go on – and she did – prefacing her remarks with a little laugh as though to detract from their importance.

'I'm afraid I'm rather a conservative old fogey. I sometimes think that if an archaeologist's wife isn't really interested, it would be wiser for her not to accompany the expedition. It often leads to friction.'

'Mrs Mercado –' I suggested.

'Oh, her!' Miss Johnson brushed the suggestion aside. 'I was really thinking of Mrs Leidner. She's a very charming woman – and one can quite understand why Dr Leidner "fell for her" – to use a slang term. But I can't help feeling she's out of place here. She – it unsettles things.'

So Miss Johnson agreed with Mrs Kelsey that it was Mrs Leidner who was responsible for the strained atmosphere. But then where did Mrs Leidner's own nervous fears come in?

'It unsettles *him*,' said Miss Johnson earnestly. 'Of course I'm – well, I'm like a faithful but jealous old dog. I don't like to see him so worn out and worried. His whole mind ought to be on the work – not taken up with his wife and her silly fears! If she's nervous of coming to out-of-the-way places, she ought to have stayed in America. I've no patience with people who come to a place and then do nothing but grouse about it!'

And then, a little fearful of having said more than she meant to say, she went on: 'Of course I admire her very much. She's a lovely woman and she's got great charm of manner when she chooses.'

And there the subject dropped.

I thought to myself that it was always the same way – wherever women are cooped up together, there's bound to be jealousy. Miss Johnson clearly didn't like her chief's wife (that was perhaps natural) and unless I was much mistaken Mrs Mercado fairly hated her.

Another person who didn't like Mrs Leidner was Sheila Reilly. She came out once or twice to the dig, once in a car and twice with some young man on a horse – on two horses I mean, of course. It was at the back of my mind that she had a weakness for the silent young American, Emmott. When he was on duty at the dig she used to stay talking to him, and I thought, too, that *he* admired *her*.

One day, rather injudiciously, I thought, Mrs Leidner commented upon it at lunch.

'The Reilly girl is still hunting David down,' she said with a little laugh. 'Poor David, she chases you up on the dig even! How foolish girls are!'

Mr Emmott didn't answer, but under his tan his face got rather red. He raised his eyes and looked right into hers with a very curious expression – a straight, steady glance with something of a challenge in it.

She smiled very faintly and looked away.

I heard Father Lavigny murmur something, but when I said 'Pardon?' he merely shook his head and did not repeat his remark.

That afternoon Mr Coleman said to me: 'Matter of fact I didn't like Mrs L. any too much at first. She used to jump down my throat every time I opened my mouth. But I've begun to understand her better now. She's one of the kindest women I've ever met. You find yourself telling her all the foolish scrapes you ever got into before you know where you are. She's got her knife into Sheila Reilly, I know, but then Sheila's been damned rude to her once or twice. That's the worst of Sheila – she's got no manners. And a temper like the devil!'

That I could well believe. Dr Reilly spoilt her.

'Of course she's bound to get a bit full of herself, being the only young woman in the place. But that doesn't excuse her talking to Mrs Leidner as though Mrs Leidner were her great-aunt. Mrs L.'s not exactly a chicken, but she's a damned good-looking woman. Rather like those fairy women who come out of marshes with lights and lure you away.' He added bitterly, 'You wouldn't find Sheila luring anyone. All she does is to tick a fellow off.'

I only remember two other incidents of any kind of significance.

One was when I went to the laboratory to fetch some acetone to get the stickiness off my fingers from mending the pottery. Mr Mercado was sitting in a corner, his head was laid down on his arms and I fancied he was asleep. I took the bottle I wanted and went off with it.

That evening, to my great surprise, Mrs Mercado tackled me.

'Did you take a bottle of acetone from the lab?'

'Yes,' I said. 'I did.'

'You know perfectly well that there's a small bottle always kept in the antika-room.'

She spoke quite angrily.

'Is there? I didn't know.'

'I think you did! You just wanted to come spying round. I know what hospital nurses are.'

I stared at her.

'I don't know what you're talking about, Mrs Mercado,' I said with dignity. 'I'm sure I don't want to spy on anyone.'

'Oh, no! Of course not. Do you think I don't know what you're here for?'

Really, for a minute or two I thought she must have been drinking. I went away without saying any more. But I thought it was very odd.

The other thing was nothing very much. I was trying to entice a pi dog pup with a piece of bread. It was very timid, however, like all Arab dogs – and was convinced I meant no good. It slunk away and I followed it – out through the archway and round the corner of the house. I came round so sharply that before I knew I had cannoned into Father Lavigny and another man who were standing together – and in a minute I realized that the second man was the same one Mrs Leidner and I had noticed that day trying to peer through the window.

I apologized and Father Lavigny smiled, and with a word of farewell greeting to the other man he returned to the house with me.

'You know,' he said. 'I am very ashamed. I am a student of Oriental languages and none of the men on the work can understand me! It is humiliating, do you not think? I was trying my Arabic on that man, who is a townsman, to see if I got on better – but it still wasn't very successful. Leidner says my Arabic is too pure.'

That was all. But it just passed through my head that it was odd the same man should still be hanging round the house.

That night we had a scare.

It must have been about two in the morning. I'm a light sleeper, as most nurses have to be. I was awake and sitting up in bed by the time that my door opened.

'Nurse, nurse!'

It was Mrs Leidner's voice, low and urgent.

I struck a match and lighted the candle.

She was standing by the door in a long blue dressing-gown. She was looking petrified with terror.

'There's someone – someone – in the room next to mine . . . I heard him – scratching on the wall.'

I jumped out of bed and came to her.

'It's all right,' I said. 'I'm here. Don't be afraid, my dear.'

She whispered: 'Get Eric.'

I nodded and ran out and knocked on his door. In a minute he was with us. Mrs Leidner was sitting on my bed, her breath coming in great gasps.

'I heard him,' she said. 'I heard him – scratching on the wall.'

'Someone in the antika-room?' cried Dr Leidner.

He ran out quickly – and it just flashed across my mind how differently these two had reacted. Mrs Leidner's fear was entirely personal, but Dr Leidner's mind leaped at once to his precious treasures.

'The antika-room!' breathed Mrs Leidner. 'Of course! How stupid of me!'

And rising and pulling her gown round her, she bade me

47

come with her. All traces of her panic-stricken fear had vanished.

We arrived in the antika-room to find Dr Leidner and Father Lavigny. The latter had also heard a noise, had risen to investigate, and had fancied he saw a light in the antika-room. He had delayed to put on slippers and snatch up a torch and had found no one by the time he got there. The door, moreover, was duly locked, as it was supposed to be at night.

Whilst he was assuring himself that nothing had been taken, Dr Leidner had joined him.

Nothing more was to be learned. The outside archway door was locked. The guard swore nobody could have got in from outside, but as they had probably been fast asleep this was not conclusive. There were no marks or traces of an intruder and nothing had been taken.

It was possible that what had alarmed Mrs Leidner was the noise made by Father Lavigny taking down boxes from the shelves to assure himself that all was in order.

On the other hand, Father Lavigny himself was positive that he had (a) heard footsteps passing his window and (b) seen the flicker of a light, possibly a torch, in the antika-room.

Nobody else had heard or seen anything.

The incident is of value in my narrative because it led to Mrs Leidner's unburdening herself to me on the following day.

CHAPTER 9
MRS LEIDNER'S STORY

We had just finished lunch. Mrs Leidner went to her room to rest as usual. I settled her on her bed with plenty of pillows and her book, and was leaving the room when she called me back.

'Don't go, nurse, there's something I want to say to you.'

I came back into the room.

'Shut the door.'

I obeyed.

She got up from the bed and began to walk up and down the room. I could see that she was making up her mind to something and I didn't like to interrupt her. She was clearly in great indecision of mind.

At last she seemed to have nerved herself to the required point. She turned to me and said abruptly: 'Sit down.'

I sat down by the table very quietly. She began nervously: 'You must have wondered what all this is about?'

I just nodded without saying anything.

'I've made up my mind to tell you – everything! I must tell someone or I shall go mad.'

'Well,' I said, 'I think really it would be just as well. It's not easy to know the best thing to do when one's kept in the dark.'

She stopped in her uneasy walk and faced me.

'Do you know what I'm frightened of?'

'Some man,' I said.

'Yes – but I didn't say whom – I said what.'

I waited.

She said: '*I'm afraid of being killed!*'

Well, it was out now. I wasn't going to show any particular concern. She was near enough to hysterics as it was.

'Dear me,' I said. 'So that's it, is it?'

Then she began to laugh. She laughed and she laughed – and the tears ran down her face.

'The way you said that!' she gasped. 'The way you said it . . .'

'Now, now,' I said. 'This won't do.' I spoke sharply. I pushed her into a chair, went over to the washstand and got a cold sponge and bathed her forehead and wrists.

'No more nonsense,' I said. 'Tell me calmly and sensibly all about it.'

That stopped her. She sat up and spoke in her natural voice.

'You're a treasure, nurse,' she said. 'You make me feel as though I'm six. I'm going to tell you.'

'That's right,' I said. 'Take your time and don't hurry.'

She began to speak, slowly and deliberately.

'When I was a girl of twenty I married. A young man in one of our State departments. It was in 1918.'

'I know,' I said. 'Mrs Mercado told me. He was killed in the war.'

But Mrs Leidner shook her head.

'That's what she thinks. That's what everybody thinks. The truth is something different. I was a queer patriotic, enthusiastic girl, nurse, full of idealism. When I'd been married a few months I discovered – by a quite unforeseeable accident – that my husband was a spy in German pay. I learned that the information supplied by him had led directly to the sinking of an American transport and the loss of hundreds of lives. I don't know what most people would have done . . . But I'll tell you what I did. I went straight to my father, who was in the War Department, and told him the truth. Frederick *was* killed in the war – but he was killed in America – shot as a spy.'

'Oh dear, dear!' I ejaculated. 'How terrible!'

'Yes,' she said. 'It was terrible. He was so kind, too – so gentle . . . And all the time . . . But I never hesitated. Perhaps I was wrong.'

'It's difficult to say,' I said. 'I'm sure I don't know what one would do.'

'What I'm telling you was never generally known outside the State department. Ostensibly my husband had gone to the Front and had been killed. I had a lot of sympathy and kindness shown me as a war widow.'

Her voice was bitter and I nodded comprehendingly.

'Lots of people wanted to marry me, but I always refused. I'd had too bad a shock. I didn't feel I could ever *trust* anyone again.'

'Yes, I can imagine feeling like that.'

'And then I became very fond of a certain young man. I wavered. An amazing thing happened! I got an anonymous letter – from Frederick – saying that if I ever married another man, he'd kill me!'

'From Frederick? From your dead husband?'

'Yes. Of course, I thought at first I was mad or dreaming . . . At last I went to my father. He told me the truth. My husband hadn't been shot after all. He'd escaped – but his escape did him no good. He was involved in a train wreck a few weeks later and his dead body was found amongst others. My father had kept the fact of his escape from me, and since the man had died anyway he had seen no reason to tell me anything until now.

'But the letter I received opened up entirely new possibilities. Was it perhaps a fact that my husband was still alive?

'My father went into the matter as carefully as possible. And he declared that as far as one could humanly be sure the body that was buried as Frederick's *was* Frederick's. There had been a certain amount of disfiguration, so that he could not speak with absolute cast-iron certainty, but he reiterated his solemn belief that Frederick was dead and that this letter was a cruel and malicious hoax.

'The same thing happened more than once. If I seemed to be on intimate terms with any man, I would receive a threatening letter.'

'In your husband's handwriting?'

She said slowly: 'That is difficult to say. I had no letters of his. I had only my memory to go by.'

'There was no allusion or special form of words used that could make you sure?'

'No. There *were* certain terms – nicknames, for instance – private between us – if one of those had been used or quoted, then I should have been quite sure.'

'Yes,' I said thoughtfully. 'That is odd. It looks as though it *wasn't* your husband. But is there anyone else it could be?'

'There is a possibility. Frederick had a younger brother – a boy of ten or twelve at the time of our marriage. He worshipped Frederick and Frederick was devoted to him. What happened to this boy, William his name was, I don't know. It seems to me possible that, adoring his brother as fanatically as he did, he may have grown up regarding me as directly responsible for his death. He had always been jealous of me and may have invented this scheme by way of punishment.'

'It's possible,' I said. 'It's amazing the way children do remember if they've had a shock.'

'I know. This boy may have dedicated his life to revenge.'

'Please go on.'

'There isn't much more to tell. I met Eric three years ago. I meant never to marry. Eric made me change my mind. Right up to our wedding day I waited for another threatening letter. None came. I decided that whoever the writer might be, he was either dead, or tired of his cruel sport. *Two days after our marriage I got this.*'

Drawing a small attaché-case which was on the table towards her, she unlocked it, took out a letter and handed it to me.

The ink was slightly faded. It was written in a rather womanish hand with a forward slant.

You have disobeyed. Now you cannot escape. You must be Frederick Bosner's wife only! You have got to die.

'I was frightened – but not so much as I might have been to begin with. Being with Eric made me feel safe. Then, a month later, I got a second letter.'

I have not forgotten. I am making my plans. You have got to die. Why did you disobey?

'Does your husband know about this?'

Mrs Leidner answered slowly.

'He knows that I am threatened. I showed him both letters when the second one came. He was inclined to think the whole thing a hoax. He thought also that it might be someone who wanted to blackmail me by pretending my first husband was alive.'

She paused and then went on.

'A few days after I received the second letter we had a narrow escape from death by gas poisoning. Somebody entered our apartment after we were asleep and turned on the gas. Luckily I woke and smelled the gas in time. Then I lost my nerve. I told Eric how I had been persecuted for years, and I told him that I was sure this madman, whoever he might be, did really mean to kill me. I think that for the first time I really did think it *was* Frederick. There was always something a little ruthless behind his gentleness.

'Eric was still, I think, less alarmed than I was. He wanted to go to the police. Naturally I wouldn't hear of that. In the end we agreed that I should accompany him here, and that it might be wise if I didn't return to America in the summer but stayed in London and Paris.

'We carried out our plan and all went well. I felt sure that now everything would be all right. After all, we had put half the globe between ourselves and my enemy.

'And then – a little over three weeks ago – I received a letter – with an Iraq stamp on it.'

She handed me a third letter.

You thought you could escape. You were wrong. You shall not be false to me and live. I have always told you so. Death is coming very soon.

'And a week ago – *this*! Just lying on the table here. It had not even gone through the post.'

I took the sheet of paper from her. There was just one phrase scrawled across it.

I have arrived.

She stared at me.

'You see? You understand? He's going to kill me. It may be Frederick – it may be little William – *but he's going to kill me.*'

Her voice rose shudderingly. I caught her wrist.

'Now – now,' I said warningly. 'Don't give way. We'll look after you. Have you got any sal volatile?'

She nodded towards the washstand and I gave her a good dose.

'That's better,' I said, as the colour returned to her cheeks.

'Yes, I'm better now. But oh, nurse, do you see why I'm in this state? When I saw that man looking in through my window, I thought: *he's come* . . . Even when *you* arrived I was suspicious. I thought you might be a man in disguise –'

'The idea!'

'Oh, I know it sounds absurd. But you might have been in league with him perhaps – not a hospital nurse at all.'

'But that's nonsense!'

'Yes, perhaps. But I've got beyond sense.'

Struck by a sudden idea, I said: 'You'd *recognize* your husband, I suppose?'

She answered slowly.

'I don't even know that. It's over fifteen years ago. I mightn't recognize his face.'

Then she shivered.

'I saw it one night – but it was a *dead* face. There was a tap, tap, tap on the window. And then I saw a face, a dead face, ghastly and grinning against the pane. I screamed and screamed . . . And they said there wasn't anything there!'

I remembered Mrs Mercado's story.

'You don't think,' I said hesitatingly, 'that you *dreamt* that?'

'I'm sure I didn't!'

I wasn't so sure. It was the kind of nightmare that was quite likely under the circumstances and that easily might be taken for a waking occurrence. However, I never contradict a patient. I soothed Mrs Leidner as best I could and pointed out that if any stranger arrived in the neighbourhood it was pretty sure to be known.

I left her, I think, a little comforted, and I went in search of Dr Leidner and told him of our conversation.

'I'm glad she told you,' he said simply. 'It has worried me dreadfully. I feel sure that all those faces and tappings on the window-pane have been sheer imagination on her part. I haven't known what to do for the best. What do you think of the whole thing?'

I didn't quite understand the tone in his voice, but I answered promptly enough.

'It's possible,' I said, 'that these letters may be just a cruel and malicious hoax.'

'Yes, that is quite likely. But what are we to *do*? They are driving her mad. I don't know what to think.'

I didn't either. It had occurred to me that possibly a woman might be concerned. Those letters had a feminine note about them. Mrs Mercado was at the back of my mind.

Supposing that by some chance she had learnt the facts of Mrs Leidner's first marriage? She might be indulging her spite by terrorizing the other woman.

I didn't quite like to suggest such a thing to Dr Leidner. It's so difficult to know how people are going to take things.

'Oh, well,' I said cheerfully, 'we must hope for the best. I think Mrs Leidner seems happier already from just talking about it. That's always a help, you know. It's bottling things up that makes them get on your nerves.'

'I'm very glad she has told you,' he repeated. 'It's a good sign. It shows she likes and trusts you. I've been at my wits' end to know what to do for the best.'

It was on the tip of my tongue to ask him whether he'd thought of giving a discreet hint to the local police, but afterwards I was glad I hadn't done so.

What happened was this. On the following day Mr Coleman was going in to Hassanieh to get the workmen's pay. He was also taking in all our letters to catch the air mail.

The letters, as written, were dropped into a wooden box on the dining-room window-sill. Last thing that night Mr Coleman took them out and was sorting them out into bundles and putting rubber bands round them.

Suddenly he gave a shout.

'What is it?' I asked.

He held out a letter with a grin.

'It's our Lovely Louise – she really *is* going balmy. She's addressed a letter to someone at 42nd Street, Paris, France. I don't think that can be right, do you? Do you mind taking it to her and asking what she *does* mean? She's just gone off to bed.'

I took it from him and ran off to Mrs Leidner with it and she amended the address.

It was the first time I had seen Mrs Leidner's handwriting, and I wondered idly where I had seen it before, for it was certainly quite familiar to me.

It wasn't till the middle of the night that it suddenly came to me.

Except that it was bigger and rather more straggling, *it was extraordinarily like the writing on the anonymous letters.*

New ideas flashed through my head.

Had Mrs Leidner conceivably written those letters *herself*?

And did Dr Leidner half-suspect the fact?

CHAPTER 10

SATURDAY AFTERNOON

Mrs Leidner told me her story on a Friday.

On the Saturday morning there was a feeling of slight anti-climax in the air.

Mrs Leidner, in particular, was inclined to be very offhand with me and rather pointedly avoided any possibility of a *tête-à-tête*. Well, *that* didn't surprise me! I've had the same thing happen to me again and again. Ladies tell their nurses things in a sudden burst of confidence, and then, afterwards, they feel uncomfortable about it and wish they hadn't! It's only human nature.

I was very careful not to hint or remind her in any way of what she had told me. I purposely kept my conversation as matter-of-fact as possible.

Mr Coleman had started in to Hassanieh in the morning, driving himself in the lorry with the letters in a knapsack. He also had one or two commissions to do for the members of the expedition. It was pay-day for the men, and he would have to go to the bank and bring out the money in coins of small denominations. All this was a long business and he did not expect to be back until the afternoon. I rather suspected he might be lunching with Sheila Reilly.

Work on the dig was usually not very busy on the afternoon of pay-day as at three-thirty the paying-out began.

The little boy, Abdullah, whose business it was to wash pots, was established as usual in the centre of the courtyard, and again, as usual, kept up his queer nasal chant. Dr Leidner and Mr Emmott were going to put in some work on the pottery until Mr Coleman returned, and Mr Carey went up to the dig.

Mrs Leidner went to her room to rest. I settled her as usual and then went to my own room, taking a book with me as I did not feel sleepy. It was then about a quarter to one, and a couple of hours passed quite pleasantly. I was reading *Death in a Nursing Home* – really a most exciting story – though I don't think the author knew much about the way nursing homes are run! At any rate I've never known a nursing home like that! I really felt inclined to write to the author and put him right about a few points.

When I put the book down at last (it was the red-haired parlourmaid and I'd never suspected her once!) and looked at my watch I was quite surprised to find it was twenty minutes to three!

I got up, straightened my uniform, and came out into the courtyard.

Abdullah was still scrubbing and still singing his depressing chant, and David Emmott was standing by him sorting the scrubbed pots, and putting the ones that were broken into boxes to await mending. I strolled over towards them just as Dr Leidner came down the staircase from the roof.

'Not a bad afternoon,' he said cheerfully. 'I've made a bit of a clearance up there. Louise will be pleased. She's complained lately that there's not room to walk about. I'll go and tell her the good news.'

He went over to his wife's door, tapped on it and went in.

It must, I suppose, have been about a minute and a half later that he came out again. I happened to be looking at the door when he did so. It was like a nightmare. He had gone in a brisk, cheerful man. He came out like a drunken one – reeling a little on his feet, and with a queer dazed expression on his face.

'Nurse –' he called in a queer, hoarse voice. 'Nurse –'

I saw at once something was wrong and I ran across to him.

He looked awful – his face was all grey and twitching, and I saw he might collapse any minute.

'My wife . . .' he said. 'My wife . . . Oh, my God . . .'

I pushed past him into the room. Then I caught my breath.

Mrs Leidner was lying in a dreadful huddled heap by the bed.

I bent over her. She was quite dead – must have been dead an hour at least. The cause of death was perfectly plain – a terrific blow on the front of the head just over the right temple. She must have got up from the bed and been struck down where she stood.

I didn't handle her more than I could help.

I glanced round the room to see if there was anything that might give a clue, but nothing seemed out of place or disturbed. The windows were closed and fastened, and there was no place where the murderer could have hidden. Obviously he had been and gone long ago.

I went out, closing the door behind me.

Dr Leidner had collapsed completely now. David Emmott was with him and turned a white, inquiring face to me.

In a few low words I told him what had happened.

As I had always suspected, he was a first-class person to rely on in trouble. He was perfectly calm and self-possessed. Those blue eyes of his opened very wide, but otherwise he gave no sign at all.

He considered for a moment and then said: 'I suppose we must notify the police as soon as possible. Bill ought to be back any minute. What shall we do with Leidner?'

'Help me to get him into his room.'

He nodded.

'Better lock this door first, I suppose,' he said.

He turned the key in the lock of Mrs Leidner's door, then drew it out and handed it to me.

'I guess you'd better keep this, nurse. Now then.'

Together we lifted Dr Leidner and carried him into his own room and laid him on his bed. Mr Emmott went off in search of brandy. He returned, accompanied by Miss Johnson.

Her face was drawn and anxious, but she was calm and capable, and I felt satisfied to leave Dr Leidner in her charge.

I hurried out into the courtyard. The station wagon was just coming in through the archway. I think it gave us all a shock to see Bill's pink, cheerful face as he jumped out with his familiar 'Hallo, 'allo, 'allo! Here's the oof!' He went on gaily, 'No highway robberies –'

He came to a halt suddenly. 'I say, is anything up? What's the matter with you all? You look as though the cat had killed your canary.'

Mr Emmott said shortly: 'Mrs Leidner's dead – killed.'

'*What?*' Bill's jolly face changed ludicrously. He stared, his eyes goggling. 'Mother Leidner dead! You're pulling my leg.'

'Dead?' It was a sharp cry. I turned to see Mrs Mercado behind me. 'Did you say Mrs Leidner had been *killed*?'

'Yes,' I said. 'Murdered.'

'No!' she gasped. 'Oh, no! I won't believe it. Perhaps she's committed suicide.'

'Suicides don't hit themselves on the head,' I said dryly. 'It's murder all right, Mrs Mercado.'

She sat down suddenly on an upturned packing-case.

She said, 'Oh, but this is horrible – *horrible* . . .'

Naturally it was horrible. We didn't need *her* to tell us so! I wondered if perhaps she was feeling a bit remorseful for the harsh feelings she had harboured against the dead woman, and all the spiteful things she had said.

After a minute or two she asked rather breathlessly: 'What are you going to do?'

Mr Emmott took charge in his quiet way.

'Bill, you'd better get in again to Hassanieh as quick as you can. I don't know much about the proper procedure. Better get hold of Captain Maitland, he's in charge of the police here, I think. Get Dr Reilly first. He'll know what to do.'

Mr Coleman nodded. All the facetiousness was knocked out of him. He just looked young and frightened. Without a word he jumped into the station wagon and drove off.

Mr Emmott said rather uncertainly, 'I suppose we ought to have a hunt round.' He raised his voice and called: 'Ibrahim!'

'*Na'am.*'

The house-boy came running. Mr Emmott spoke to him in Arabic. A vigorous colloquy passed between them. The boy seemed to be emphatically denying something.

At last Mr Emmott said in a perplexed voice, 'He says there's not been a soul here this afternoon. No stranger of any kind. I suppose the fellow must have slipped in without their seeing him.'

'Of course he did,' said Mrs Mercado. 'He slunk in when the boys weren't looking.'

'Yes,' said Mr Emmott.

The slight uncertainty in his voice made me look at him inquiringly.

He turned and spoke to the little pot-boy, Abdullah, asking him a question.

The boy replied vehemently at length.

The puzzled frown on Mr Emmott's brow increased.

'I don't understand it,' he murmured under his breath. 'I don't understand it at all.'

But he didn't tell me what he didn't understand.

CHAPTER 11
....
AN ODD BUSINESS

I'm adhering as far as possible to telling only my personal part in the business. I pass over the events of the next two hours, the arrival of Captain Maitland and the police and Dr Reilly. There was a good deal of general confusion, questioning, all the routine business, I suppose.

In my opinion we began to get down to brass tacks about five o'clock when Dr Reilly asked me to come with him into the office. He shut the door, sat down in Dr Leidner's chair, motioned me to sit down opposite him, and said briskly: 'Now, then, nurse, let's get down to it. There's something damned odd here.'

I settled my cuffs and looked at him inquiringly.

He drew out a notebook.

'This is for my own satisfaction. Now, what time was it exactly when Dr Leidner found his wife's body?'

'I should say it was almost exactly a quarter to three,' I said.

'And how do you know that?'

'Well, I looked at my watch when I got up. It was twenty to three then.'

'Let's have a look at this watch of yours.'

I slipped it off my wrist and held it out to him.

'Right to the minute. Excellent woman. Good, that's *that*

59

fixed. Now, did you form any opinion as to how long she'd been dead?'

'Oh, really, doctor,' I said, 'I shouldn't like to say.'

'Don't be so professional. I want to see if your estimate agrees with mine.'

'Well, I should say she'd been dead at least an hour.'

'Quite so. I examined the body at half-past four and I'm inclined to put the time of death between 1.15 and 1.45. We'll say half-past one at a guess. That's near enough.'

He stopped and drummed thoughtfully with his fingers on the table.

'Damned odd, this business,' he said. 'Can you tell me about it – you were resting, you say? Did you hear anything?'

'At half-past one? No, doctor. I didn't hear anything at half-past one or at any other time. I lay on my bed from a quarter to one until twenty to three and I didn't hear anything except that droning noise the Arab boy makes, and occasionally Mr Emmott shouting up to Dr Leidner on the roof.'

'The Arab boy – yes.'

He frowned.

At that moment the door opened and Dr Leidner and Captain Maitland came in. Captain Maitland was a fussy little man with a pair of shrewd grey eyes.

Dr Reilly rose and pushed Dr Leidner into his chair.

'Sit down, man. I'm glad you've come. We shall want you. There's something very queer about this business.'

Dr Leidner bowed his head.

'I know.' He looked at me. 'My wife confided the truth to Nurse Leatheran. We mustn't keep anything back at this juncture, nurse, so please tell Captain Maitland and Dr Reilly just what passed between you and my wife yesterday.'

As nearly as possible I gave our conversation verbatim.

Captain Maitland uttered an occasional ejaculation. When I had finished he turned to Dr Leidner.

'And this is all true, Leidner – eh?'

'Every word Nurse Leatheran has told you is correct.'

'What an extraordinary story!' said Dr Reilly. 'You can produce these letters?'

'I have no doubt they will be found amongst my wife's belongings.'

'She took them out of the attaché-case on her table,' I said.

'Then they are probably still there.'

He turned to Captain Maitland and his usually gentle face grew hard and stern.

'There must be no question of hushing this story up, Captain Maitland. The one thing necessary is for this man to be caught and punished.'

'You believe it actually is Mrs Leidner's former husband?' I asked.

'Don't you think so, nurse?' asked Captain Maitland.

'Well, I think it is open to doubt,' I said hesitatingly.

'In any case,' said Dr Leidner, 'the man is a murderer – and I should say a dangerous lunatic also. He *must* be found, Captain Maitland. He must. It should not be difficult.'

Dr Reilly said slowly: 'It may be more difficult than you think . . . eh, Maitland?'

Captain Maitland tugged at his moustache without replying.

Suddenly I gave a start.

'Excuse me,' I said, 'but there's something perhaps I ought to mention.'

I told my story of the Iraqi we had seen trying to peer through the window, and of how I had seen him hanging about the place two days ago trying to pump Father Lavigny.

'Good,' said Captain Maitland, 'we'll make a note of that. It will be something for the police to go on. The man may have some connection with the case.'

'Probably paid to act as a spy,' I suggested. 'To find out when the coast was clear.'

Dr Reilly rubbed his nose with a harassed gesture.

'That's the devil of it,' he said. 'Supposing the coast wasn't clear – eh?'

I stared at him in a puzzled fashion.

Captain Maitland turned to Dr Leidner.

'I want you to listen to me very carefully, Leidner. This is a review of the evidence we've got up to date. After lunch, which was served at twelve o'clock and was over by five and twenty to one, your wife went to her room accompanied by Nurse Leatheran, who settled her comfortably. You yourself went up to the roof, where you spent the next two hours, is that right?'

'Yes.'

'Did you come down from the roof at all during that time?'

'No.'

'Did anyone come up to you?'

'Yes, Emmott did pretty frequently. He went to and fro between me and the boy, who was washing pottery down below.'

'Did you yourself look over into the courtyard at all?'

'Once or twice – usually to call to Emmott about something.'

'On each occasion the boy was sitting in the middle of the courtyard washing pots?'

'Yes.'

'What was the longest period of time when Emmott was with you and absent from the courtyard?'

Dr Leidner considered.

'It's difficult to say – perhaps ten minutes. Personally I should say two or three minutes, but I know by experience that my sense of time is not very good when I am absorbed and interested in what I am doing.'

Captain Maitland looked at Dr Reilly. The latter nodded. 'We'd better get down to it,' he said.

Captain Maitland took out a small notebook and opened it.

'Look here, Leidner, I'm going to read to you exactly what every member of your expedition was doing between one and two this afternoon.'

'But surely –'

'Wait. You'll see what I'm driving at in a minute. First Mr and Mrs Mercado. Mr Mercado says he was working in his laboratory. Mrs Mercado says she was in her bedroom shampooing her hair. Miss Johnson says she was in the living-room taking impressions of cylinder seals. Mr Reiter says he was in the dark-room developing plates. Father Lavigny says he was working in his bedroom. As to the two remaining members of the expedition, Carey and Coleman, the former was up on the dig and Coleman was in Hassanieh. So much for the members of the expedition. Now for the servants. The cook – your Indian chap – was sitting immediately outside the archway chatting to the guard and plucking a couple of fowls. Ibrahim and Mansur, the house-boys, joined him there at about 1.15. They both remained there laughing and talking until 2.30 – *by which time your wife was already dead.*'

Dr Leidner leaned forward.

'I don't understand – you puzzle me. What are you hinting at?'

'Is there any means of access to your wife's room except by the door into the courtyard?'

'No. There are two windows, but they are heavily barred – and besides, I think they were shut.'

He looked at me questioningly.

'They were closed and latched on the inside,' I said promptly.

'In any case,' said Captain Maitland, 'even if they had been open, no one could have entered or left the room that way. My fellows and I have assured ourselves of that. It is the same with all the other windows giving on the open country. They all have iron bars and all the bars are in good condition. To have got into your wife's room, a stranger *must* have come through the arched doorway into the courtyard. But we have the united assurance of the guard, the cook and the house-boy that *nobody did so.*'

Dr Leidner sprang up.

'What do you mean? What do you mean?'

'Pull yourself together, man,' said Dr Reilly quietly. 'I know it's a shock, but it's got to be faced. The *murderer didn't come from outside* – so he must have come from *inside*. It looks as though Mrs Leidner must have been murdered *by a member of your own expedition.*'

CHAPTER 12

'I DIDN'T BELIEVE . . .'

'No. No!'

Dr Leidner sprang up and walked up and down in an agitated manner.

'It's impossible what you say, Reilly. Absolutely impossible. One of *us*? Why, every single member of the expedition was devoted to Louise!'

A queer little expression pulled down the corners of Dr Reilly's mouth. Under the circumstances it was difficult for him to say anything, but if ever a man's silence was eloquent his was at that minute.

'Quite impossible,' reiterated Dr Leidner. 'They were all

devoted to her, Louise had such wonderful charm. Everyone felt it.'

Dr Reilly coughed.

'Excuse me, Leidner, but after all that's only your opinion. If any member of the expedition had disliked your wife they would naturally not advertise the fact to you.'

Dr Leidner looked distressed.

'True – quite true. But all the same, Reilly, I think you are wrong. I'm sure everyone was fond of Louise.'

He was silent for a moment or two and then burst out:

'This idea of yours is infamous. It's – it's frankly incredible.'

'You can't get away from – er – the facts,' said Captain Maitland.

'Facts? Facts? Lies told by an Indian cook and a couple of Arab house-boys. You know these fellows as well as I do, Reilly, so do you, Maitland. Truth as truth means nothing to them. They say what you want them to say as a mere matter of politeness.'

'In this case,' said Dr Reilly dryly, 'they are saying what we *don't* want them to say. Besides, I know the habits of your household fairly well. Just outside the gate is a kind of social club. Whenever I've been over here in the afternoon I've always found most of your staff there. It's the natural place for them to be.'

'All the same I think you are assuming too much. Why shouldn't this man – this devil – have got in earlier and concealed himself somewhere?'

'I agree that that is not actually impossible,' said Dr Reilly coolly. 'Let us assume that a stranger *did* somehow gain admission unseen. He would have to remain concealed until the right moment (and he certainly couldn't have done so in Mrs Leidner's room, there is no cover there) and take the risk of being seen entering the room and leaving it – with Emmott and the boy in the courtyard most of the time.'

'The boy. I'd forgotten the boy,' said Dr Leidner. 'A sharp little chap. But surely, Maitland, the boy *must* have seen the murderer go into my wife's room?'

'We've elucidated that. The boy was washing pots the whole afternoon with one exception. Somehow around half-past one – Emmott can't put it closer than that – he went up to the roof and was with you for ten minutes – that's right, isn't it?'

'Yes. I couldn't have told you the exact time but it must have been about that.'

'Very good. Well, during that ten minutes, the boy, seizing his chance to be idle, strolled out and joined the others outside the gate for a chat. When Emmott came down he found the boy absent and called him angrily, asking him what he meant leaving his work. As far as I can see, *your wife must have been murdered during that ten minutes.*'

With a groan Dr Leidner sat down and hid his face in his hands.

Dr Reilly took up the tale, his voice quiet and matter-of-fact.

'The time fits in with my evidence,' he said. 'She'd been dead about three hours when I examined her. The only question is – who did it?'

There was a silence. Dr Leidner sat up in his chair and passed a hand over his forehead.

'I admit the force of your reasoning, Reilly,' he said quietly. 'It certainly *seems* as though it were what people call "an inside job". But I feel convinced that somewhere or other there is a mistake. It's plausible but there must be a flaw in it. To begin with, you are assuming that an amazing coincidence has occurred.'

'Odd that you should use that word,' said Dr Reilly.

Without paying any attention Dr Leidner went on: 'My wife receives threatening letters. She has reason to fear a certain person. Then she is – killed. And you ask me to believe that she is killed – not by that person – but by someone entirely different! I say that that is ridiculous.'

'It seems so – yes,' said Reilly meditatively.

He looked at Captain Maitland. 'Coincidence – eh? What do you say, Maitland? Are you in favour of the idea? Shall we put it up to Leidner?'

Captain Maitland gave a nod.

'Go ahead,' he said shortly.

'Have you ever heard of a man called Hercule Poirot, Leidner?'

Dr Leidner stared at him, puzzled.

'I think I have heard the name, yes,' he said vaguely. 'I once heard a Mr Van Aldin speak of him in very high terms. He is a private detective, is he not?'

'That's the man.'

'But surely he lives in London, so how will that help us?'

'He lives in London, true,' said Dr Reilly, 'but this is where the coincidence comes in. He is now, not in London, but in Syria, and *he will actually pass through Hassanieh on his way to Baghdad tomorrow*!'

'Who told you this?'

'Jean Berat, the French consul. He dined with us last night and was talking about him. It seems he has been disentangling some military scandal in Syria. He's coming through here to visit Baghdad, and afterwards returning through Syria to London. How's that for a coincidence?'

Dr Leidner hesitated a moment and looked apologetically at Captain Maitland.

'What do you think, Captain Maitland?'

'Should welcome co-operation,' said Captain Maitland promptly. 'My fellows are good scouts at scouring the countryside and investigating Arab blood feuds, but frankly, Leidner, this business of your wife's seems to me rather out of my class. The whole thing looks confoundedly fishy. I'm more than willing to have the fellow take a look at the case.'

'You suggest that I should appeal to this man Poirot to help us?' said Dr Leidner. 'And suppose he refuses?'

'He won't refuse,' said Dr Reilly.

'How do you know?'

'Because I'm a professional man myself. If a really intricate case of, say, cerebro-spinal meningitis comes my way and I'm invited to take a hand, I shouldn't be able to refuse. This isn't an ordinary crime, Leidner.'

'No,' said Dr Leidner. His lips twitched with sudden pain. 'Will you then, Reilly, approach this Hercule Poirot on my behalf?'

'I will.'

Dr Leidner made a gesture of thanks.

'Even now,' he said slowly, 'I can't realize it – that Louise is really dead.'

I could bear it no longer.

'Oh! Doctor Leidner,' I burst out, 'I – I can't tell you how badly I feel about this. I've failed so badly in my duty. It was my job to watch over Mrs Leidner – to keep her from harm.'

Dr Leidner shook his head gravely.

'No, no, nurse, you've nothing to reproach yourself with,' he said slowly. 'It's *I*, God forgive me, who am to blame . . . *I didn't believe* – all along I didn't believe . . . I didn't dream for one moment that there was any *real* danger . . .'

He got up. His face twitched.

'*I let her go to her death* . . . Yes, I let her go to her death – *not believing* –'

He staggered out of the room.

Dr Reilly looked at me.

'I feel pretty culpable too,' he said. 'I thought the good lady was playing on his nerves.'

'I didn't take it really seriously either,' I confessed.

'We were all three wrong,' said Dr Reilly gravely.

'So it seems,' said Captain Maitland.

CHAPTER 13

HERCULE POIROT ARRIVES

I don't think I shall ever forget my first sight of Hercule Poirot. Of course, I got used to him later on, but to begin with it was a shock, and I think everyone else must have felt the same!

I don't know what I'd imagined – something rather like Sherlock Holmes – long and lean with a keen, clever face. Of course, I knew he was a foreigner, but I hadn't expected him to be *quite* as foreign as he was, if you know what I mean.

When you saw him you just wanted to laugh! He was like something on the stage or at the pictures. To begin with, he wasn't above five-foot five, I should think – an odd, plump little man, quite old, with an enormous moustache, and a head like an egg. He looked like a hairdresser in a comic play!

And this was the man who was going to find out who killed Mrs Leidner!

I suppose something of my disgust must have shown in my face, for almost straightaway he said to me with a queer kind of twinkle:

'You disapprove of me, *ma soeur*? Remember, the pudding proves itself only when you eat it.'

The proof of the pudding's in the eating, I *suppose* he meant.

Well, that's a true enough saying, but I couldn't say I felt much confidence myself!

Dr Reilly brought him out in his car soon after lunch on

Sunday, and his first procedure was to ask us all to assemble together.

We did so in the dining-room, all sitting round the table. Mr Poirot sat at the head of it with Dr Leidner one side and Dr Reilly the other.

When we were all assembled, Dr Leidner cleared his throat and spoke in his gentle, hesitating voice.

'I dare say you have all heard of M. Hercule Poirot. He was passing through Hassanieh today, and has very kindly agreed to break his journey to help us. The Iraqi police and Captain Maitland are, I am sure, doing their very best, but – but there are circumstances in the case' – he floundered and shot an appealing glance at Dr Reilly – 'there may, it seems, be difficulties . . .'

'It is not all the square and overboard – no?' said the little man at the top of the table. Why, he couldn't even speak English properly!

'Oho, he *must* be caught!' cried Mrs Mercado. 'It would be unbearable if he got away!'

I noticed the little foreigner's eyes rest on her appraisingly.

'He? Who is *he*, madame?' he asked.

'Why, the murderer, of course.'

'Ah! the murderer,' said Hercule Poirot.

He spoke as though the murderer was of no consequence at all! We all stared at him. He looked from one face to another.

'It is likely, I think,' he said, 'that you have none of you been brought in contact with a case of murder before?'

There was a general murmur of assent.

Hercule Poirot smiled.

'It is clear, therefore, that you do not understand the A B C of the position. There are unpleasantnesses! Yes, there are a lot of unpleasantnesses. To begin with, there is *suspicion*.'

'Suspicion?'

It was Miss Johnson who spoke. Mr Poirot looked at her thoughtfully. I had an idea that he regarded her with approval. He looked as though he were thinking: 'Here is a sensible, intelligent person!'

'Yes, mademoiselle,' he said. 'Suspicion! Let us not make the bones about it. *You are all under suspicion here in this house.* The cook, the house-boy, the scullion, the pot-boy – yes, and all the members of the expedition too.'

Mrs Mercado started up, her face working.

'How *dare* you? How dare you say such a thing? This is odious – unbearable! Dr Leidner – you can't sit here and let this man – let this man –'

Dr Leidner said wearily: 'Please try and be calm, Marie.'

Mr Mercado stood up too. His hands were shaking and his eyes were bloodshot.

'I agree. It is an outrage – an insult –'

'No, no,' said Mr Poirot. 'I do not insult you. I merely ask you all to face facts. *In a house where murder has been committed, every inmate comes in for a certain share of suspicion.* I ask you what evidence is there that the murderer came from outside at all?'

Mrs Mercado cried: 'But of course he did! It stands to reason! Why –' She stopped and said more slowly, 'Anything else would be incredible!'

'You are doubtless correct, madame,' said Poirot with a bow. 'I explain to you only how the matter must be approached. First I assure myself of the fact that everyone in this room is innocent. After that I seek the murderer elsewhere.'

'Is it not possible that that may be a little late in the day?' asked Father Lavigny suavely.

'The tortoise, *mon père*, overtook the hare.'

Father Lavigny shrugged his shoulders.

'We are in your hands,' he said resignedly. 'Convince yourself as soon as may be of our innocence in this terrible business.'

'As rapidly as possible. It was my duty to make the position clear to you, so that you may not resent the impertinence of any questions I may have to ask. Perhaps, *mon père*, the Church will set an example?'

'Ask any questions you please of me,' said Father Lavigny gravely.

'This is your first season out here?'

'Yes.'

'And you arrived – when?'

'Three weeks ago almost to a day. That is, on the 27th of February.'

'Coming from?'

'The Order of the Pères Blancs at Carthage.'

'Thank you, *mon père*. Were you at any time acquainted with Mrs Leidner before coming here?'

69

'No, I had never seen the lady until I met her here.'

'Will you tell me what you were doing at the time of the tragedy?'

'I was working on some cuneiform tablets in my own room.'

I noticed that Poirot had at his elbow a rough plan of the building.

'That is the room at the south-west corner corresponding to that of Mrs Leidner on the opposite side?'

'Yes.'

'At what time did you go to your room?'

'Immediately after lunch. I should say at about twenty minutes to one.'

'And you remained there until – when?'

'Just before three o'clock. I had heard the station wagon come back – and then I heard it drive off again. I wondered why, and came out to see.'

'During the time that you were there did you leave the room at all?'

'No, not once.'

'And you heard or saw nothing that might have any bearing on the tragedy?'

'No.'

'You have no window giving on the courtyard in your room?'

'No, both the windows give on the countryside.'

'Could you hear at all what was happening in the courtyard?'

'Not very much. I heard Mr Emmott passing my room and going up to the roof. He did so once or twice.'

'Can you remember at what time?'

'No, I'm afraid I can't. I was engrossed in my work, you see.'

There was a pause and then Poirot said:

'Can you say or suggest anything at all that might throw light on this business? Did you, for instance, notice anything in the days preceding the murder?'

Father Lavigny looked slightly uncomfortable.

He shot a half-questioning look at Dr Leidner.

'That is rather a difficult question, monsieur,' he said gravely. 'If you ask me I must reply frankly that in my opinion Mrs Leidner was clearly in dread of someone or something. She was definitely nervous about strangers. I imagine she had a reason for this nervousness of hers – but I *know* nothing. She did not confide in me.'

Poirot cleared his throat and consulted some notes that he held in his hand. 'Two nights ago I understand there was a scare of burglary.'

Father Lavigny replied in the affirmative and retailed his story of the light seen in the antika-room and the subsequent futile search.

'You believe, do you not, that some unauthorized person was on the premises at that time?'

'I don't know what to think,' said Father Lavigny frankly. 'Nothing was taken or disturbed in any way. It might have been one of the house-boys –'

'Or a member of the expedition?'

'Or a member of the expedition. But in that case there would be no reason for the person not admitting the fact.'

'But it *might* equally have been a stranger from outside?'

'I suppose so.'

'Supposing a stranger *had* been on the premises, could he have concealed himself successfully during the following day and until the afternoon of the day following that?'

He asked the question half of Father Lavigny and half of Dr Leidner. Both men considered the question carefully.

'I hardly think it would be possible,' said Dr Leidner at last with some reluctance. 'I don't see where he could possibly conceal himself, do you, Father Lavigny?'

'No – no – I don't.'

Both men seemed reluctant to put the suggestion aside.

Poirot turned to Miss Johnson.

'And you, mademoiselle? Do you consider such a hypothesis feasible?'

After a moment's thought Miss Johnson shook her head.

'No,' she said. 'I don't. Where could anyone hide? The bed-rooms are all in use and, in any case, are sparsely furnished. The dark-room, the drawing-office and the laboratory were all in use the next day – so were all these rooms. There are no cupboards or corners. Perhaps, if the servants were in collusion –'

'That is possible, but unlikely,' said Poirot.

He turned once more to Father Lavigny.

'There is another point. The other day Nurse Leatheran here

71

noticed you talking to a man outside. She had previously noticed that same man trying to peer in at one of the windows on the outside. It rather looks as though the man were hanging round the place deliberately.'

'That is possible, of course,' said Father Lavigny thoughtfully.

'Did you speak to this man first, or did he speak to you?'

Father Lavigny considered for a moment or two.

'I believe – yes, I am sure, that he spoke to me.'

'What did he say?'

Father Lavigny made an effort of memory.

'He said, I think, something to the effect was this the American expedition house? And then something else about the Americans employing a lot of men on the work. I did not really understand him very well, but I endeavoured to keep up a conversation so as to improve my Arabic. I thought, perhaps, that being a townee he would understand me better than the men on the dig do.'

'Did you converse about anything else?'

'As far as I remember, I said Hassanieh was a big town – and we then agreed that Baghdad was bigger – and I think he asked whether I was an Armenian or a Syrian Catholic – something of that kind.'

Poirot nodded.

'Can you describe him?'

Again Father Lavigny frowned in thought.

'He was rather a short man,' he said at last, 'and squarely built. He had a very noticeable squint and was of fair complexion.'

Mr Poirot turned to me.

'Does that agree with the way you would describe him?' he asked.

'Not exactly,' I said hesitatingly. 'I should have said he was tall rather than short, and very dark-complexioned. He seemed to me of a rather slender build. I didn't notice any squint.'

Mr Poirot gave a despairing shrug of the shoulders.

'It is always so! If you were of the police how well you would know it! The description of the same man by two different people – never does it agree. Every detail is contradicted.'

'I'm fairly sure about the squint,' said Father Lavigny. 'Nurse Leatheran may be right about the other points. By the way, when

I said *fair*, I only meant fair for an *Iraqi*. I expect nurse would call that dark.'

'Very dark,' I said obstinately. 'A dirty dark-yellow colour.'

I saw Dr Reilly bite his lips and smile.

Poirot threw up his hands.

'*Passons!*' he said. 'This stranger hanging about, he may be important – he may not. At any rate he must be found. Let us continue our inquiry.'

He hesitated for a minute, studying the faces turned towards him round the table, then, with a quick nod, he singled out Mr Reiter.

'Come, my friend,' he said. 'Let us have your account of yesterday afternoon.'

Mr Reiter's pink, plump face flushed scarlet.

'Me?' he said.

'Yes, you. To begin with, your name and your age?'

'Carl Reiter, twenty-eight.'

'American – yes?'

'Yes, I come from Chicago.'

'This is your first season?'

'Yes. I'm in charge of the photography.'

'Ah, yes. And yesterday afternoon, how did you employ yourself?'

'Well – I was in the dark-room most of the time.'

'*Most* of the time – eh?'

'Yes. I developed some plates first. Afterwards I was fixing up some objects to photograph.'

'Outside?'

'Oh no, in the photographic-room.'

'The dark-room opens out of the photographic-room?'

'Yes.'

'And so you never came outside the photographic-room?'

'No.'

'Did you notice anything that went on in the courtyard?'

The young man shook his head.

'I wasn't noticing anything,' he explained. 'I was busy. I heard the car come back, and as soon as I could leave what I was doing I came out to see if there was any mail. It was then that I – heard.'

'And you began to work in the photographic-room – when?'

'At ten minutes to one.'

'Were you acquainted with Mrs Leidner before you joined this expedition?'

The young man shook his head.

'No, sir. I never saw her till I actually got here.'

'Can you think of *anything* – any incident – however small – that might help us?'

Carl Reiter shook his head.

He said helplessly: 'I guess I don't know anything at all, sir.'

'Mr Emmott?'

David Emmott spoke clearly and concisely in his pleasant soft American voice.

'I was working with the pottery from a quarter to one till a quarter to three – overseeing the boy Abdullah, sorting it, and occasionally going up to the roof to help Dr Leidner.'

'How often did you go up to the roof?'

'Four times, I think.'

'For how long?'

'Usually a couple of minutes – not more. But on one occasion after I'd been working a little over half an hour I stayed as long as ten minutes – discussing what to keep and what to fling away.'

'And I understand that when you came down you found the boy had left his place?'

'Yes. I called him angrily and he reappeared from outside the archway. He had gone out to gossip with the others.'

'That settles the only time he left his work?'

'Well, I sent him up once or twice to the roof with pottery.'

Poirot said gravely: 'It is hardly necessary to ask you, Mr Emmott, whether you saw anyone enter or leave Mrs Leidner's room during that time?'

Mr Emmott replied promptly.

'I saw no one at all. Nobody even came out into the courtyard during the two hours I was working.'

'And to the best of your belief it was half-past one when both you and the boy were absent and the courtyard was empty?'

'It couldn't have been far off that time. Of course, I can't say *exactly*.'

Poirot turned to Dr Reilly.

'That agrees with your estimate of the time of death, doctor?'

'It does,' said Dr Reilly.

Mr Poirot stroked his great curled moustaches.

'I think we can take it,' he said gravely, 'that Mrs Leidner met her death during that ten minutes.'

CHAPTER 14

ONE OF US?

There was a little pause – and in it a wave of horror seemed to float round the room.

I think it was at that moment that I first believed Dr Reilly's theory to be right.

I *felt* that the murderer was in the room. Sitting with us – listening. *One of us . . .*

Perhaps Mrs Mercado felt it too. For she suddenly gave a short sharp cry.

'I can't help it,' she sobbed. 'I – it's so *terrible!*'

'Courage, Marie,' said her husband.

He looked at us apologetically.

'She is so sensitive. She feels things so much.'

'I – I was so fond of Louise,' sobbed Mrs Mercado.

I don't know whether something of what I felt showed in my face, but I suddenly found that Mr Poirot was looking at me, and that a slight smile hovered on his lips.

I gave him a cold glance, and at once he resumed his inquiry.

'Tell me, madame,' he said, 'of the way you spent yesterday afternoon?'

'I was washing my hair,' sobbed Mrs Mercado. 'It seems awful not to have known anything about it. I was quite happy and busy.'

'You were in your room?'

'Yes.'

'And you did not leave it?'

'No. Not till I heard the car. Then I came out and I heard what had happened. Oh, it was *awful!*'

'Did it surprise you?'

Mrs Mercado stopped crying. Her eyes opened resentfully.

'What do you mean, M. Poirot? Are you suggesting –?'

'What should I mean, madame? You have just told us how

fond you were of Mrs Leidner. She might, perhaps, have confided in you.'

'Oh, I see . . . No – no, dear Louise never told me anything – anything *definite*, that is. Of course, I could see she was terribly worried and nervous. And there were those strange occurrences – hands tapping on the windows and all that.'

'Fancies, I remember you said,' I put in, unable to keep silent.

I was glad to see that she looked momentarily disconcerted.

Once again I was conscious of Mr Poirot's amused eye glancing in my direction.

He summed up in a businesslike way.

'It comes to this, madame, you were washing your hair – you heard nothing and you saw nothing. Is there anything at all you can think of that would be a help to us in any way?'

Mrs Mercado took no time to think.

'No, indeed there isn't. It's the deepest mystery! But I should say there is no doubt – no doubt *at all* that the murderer came from outside. Why, it stands to reason.'

Poirot turned to her husband.

'And you, monsieur, what have you to say?'

Mr Mercado started nervously. He pulled at his beard in an aimless fashion.

'Must have been. Must have been,' he said. 'Yet how could anyone wish to harm her? She was so gentle – so kind –' He shook his head. 'Whoever killed her must have been a fiend – yes, a fiend!'

'And you yourself, monsieur, how did you pass yesterday afternoon?'

'I?' he stared vaguely.

'You were in the laboratory, Joseph,' his wife prompted him.

'Ah, yes, so I was – so I was. My usual tasks.'

'At what time did you go there?'

Again he looked helplessly and inquiringly at Mrs Mercado.

'At ten minutes to one, Joseph.'

'Ah, yes, at ten minutes to one.'

'Did you come out in the courtyard at all?'

'No – I don't think so.' He considered. 'No, I am sure I didn't.'

'When did you hear of the tragedy?'

'My wife came and told me. It was terrible – shocking. I could hardly believe it. Even now, I can hardly believe it is true.'

Suddenly he began to tremble.

'It is horrible – horrible . . .'

Mrs Mercado came quickly to his side.

'Yes, yes, Joseph, we feel that. But we mustn't give way. It makes it so much more difficult for poor Dr Leidner.'

I saw a spasm of pain pass across Dr Leidner's face, and I guessed that this emotional atmosphere was not easy for him. He gave a half-glance at Poirot as though in appeal. Poirot responded quickly.

'Miss Johnson?' he said.

'I'm afraid I can tell you very little,' said Miss Johnson. Her cultured well-bred voice was soothing after Mrs Mercado's shrill treble. She went on: 'I was working in the living-room – taking impressions of some cylinder seals on plasticine.'

'And you saw or noticed nothing?'

'No.'

Poirot gave her a quick glance. His ear had caught what mine had – a faint note of indecision.

'Are you quite sure, mademoiselle? Is there something that comes back to you vaguely?'

'No – not really –'

'Something you saw, shall we say, out of the corner of your eye hardly knowing you saw it.'

'No, certainly not,' she replied positively.

'Something you *heard* then. Ah, yes, something you are not quite sure whether you heard or not?'

Miss Johnson gave a short, vexed laugh.

'You press me very closely, M. Poirot. I'm afraid you are encouraging me to tell you what I am, perhaps, only imagining.'

'Then there was something you – shall we say – imagined?'

Miss Johnson said slowly, weighing her words in a detached way: 'I have imagined – since – that at some time during the afternoon I heard a very faint cry . . . What I mean is that I daresay I *did* hear a cry. All the windows in the living-room were open and one hears all sorts of sounds from people working in the barley fields. But you see – since – I've got the idea into my head that it was – that it was Mrs Leidner I heard. And that's made me rather unhappy. Because if I'd jumped up and run along to her room – well, who knows? I might have been in time . . .'

Dr Reilly interposed authoritatively.

'Now, don't start getting that into your head,' he said. 'I've no doubt but that Mrs Leidner (forgive me, Leidner) was struck down almost as soon as the man entered the room, and it was that blow that killed her. No second blow was struck. Otherwise she would have had time to call for help and make a real outcry.'

'Still, I might have caught the murderer,' said Miss Johnson.

'What time was this, mademoiselle?' asked Poirot. 'In the neighbourhood of half-past one?'

'It must have been about that time – yes.' She reflected a minute.

'That would fit in,' said Poirot thoughtfully. 'You heard nothing else – the opening or shutting of a door, for instance?'

Miss Johnson shook her head.

'No, I do not remember anything of that kind.'

'You were sitting at a table, I presume. Which way were you facing? The courtyard? The antika-room? The verandah? Or the open countryside?'

'I was facing the courtyard.'

'Could you see the boy Abdullah washing pots from where you were?'

'Oh, yes, if I looked up, but of course I was very intent on what I was doing. All my attention was on that.'

'If anyone had passed the courtyard window, though, you would have noticed it?'

'Oh, yes, I am almost sure of that.'

'And nobody did so?'

'No.'

'But if anyone had walked, say, across the middle of the courtyard, would you have noticed that?'

'I think – probably not – unless, as I said before, I had happened to look up and out of the window.'

'You did not notice the boy Abdullah leave his work and go out to join the other servants?'

'No.'

'Ten minutes,' mused Poirot. 'That fatal ten minutes.'

There was a momentary silence.

Miss Johnson lifted her head suddenly and said: 'You know,

M. Poirot, I think I have unintentionally misled you. On thinking it over, I do not believe that I could possibly have heard any cry uttered in Mrs Leidner's room from where I was. The antika-room lay between me and her – and I understand her windows were found closed.'

'In any case, do not distress yourself, mademoiselle,' said Poirot kindly. 'It is not really of much importance.'

'No, of course not. I understand that. But you see, it *is* of importance to me, because I feel I might have done something.'

'Don't distress yourself, dear Anne,' said Dr Leidner with affection. 'You must be sensible. What you heard was probably one Arab bawling to another some distance away in the fields.'

Miss Johnson flushed a little at the kindliness of his tone. I even saw tears spring to her eyes. She turned her head away and spoke even more gruffly than usual.

'Probably was. Usual thing after a tragedy – start imagining things that aren't so at all.'

Poirot was once more consulting his notebook.

'I do not suppose there is much more to be said. Mr Carey?'

Richard Carey spoke slowly – in a wooden mechanical manner.

'I'm afraid I can add nothing helpful. I was on duty at the dig. The news was brought to me there.'

'And you know or can think of nothing helpful that occurred in the days immediately preceding the murder?'

'Nothing at all.'

'Mr Coleman?'

'I was right out of the whole thing,' said Mr Coleman with – was it just a shade of regret – in his tone. 'I went into Hassanieh yesterday morning to get the money for the men's wages. When I came back Emmott told me what had happened and I went back in the bus to get the police and Dr Reilly.'

'And beforehand?'

'Well, sir, things were a bit jumpy – but you know that already. There was the antika-room scare and one or two before that – hands and faces at the window – you remember, sir,' he appealed to Dr Leidner, who bent his head in assent. 'I think, you know, that you'll find some Johnny *did* get in from outside. Must have been an artful sort of beggar.'

Poirot considered him for a minute or two in silence.

'You are an Englishman, Mr Coleman?' he asked at last.

'That's right, sir. All British. See the trade-mark. Guaranteed genuine.'

'This is your first season?'

'Quite right.'

'And you are passionately keen on archaeology?'

This description of himself seemed to cause Mr Coleman some embarrassment. He got rather pink and shot the side look of a guilty schoolboy at Dr Leidner.

'Of course – it's all very interesting,' he stammered. 'I mean – I'm not exactly a brainy chap . . .'

He broke off rather lamely. Poirot did not insist.

He tapped thoughtfully on the table with the end of his pencil and carefully straightened an inkpot that stood in front of him.

'It seems then,' he said, 'that that is as near as we can get for the moment. If any one of you thinks of something that has for the time being slipped his or her memory, do not hesitate to come to me with it. It will be well now, I think, for me to have a few words alone with Dr Leidner and Dr Reilly.'

It was the signal for a breaking up of the party. We all rose and filed out of the door. When I was half-way out, however, a voice recalled me.

'Perhaps,' said M. Poirot, 'Nurse Leatheran will be so kind as to remain. I think her assistance will be valuable to us.'

I came back and resumed my seat at the table.

CHAPTER 15
....
POIROT MAKES A SUGGESTION

Dr Reilly had risen from his seat. When everyone had gone out he carefully closed the door. Then, with an inquiring glance at Poirot, he proceeded to shut the window giving on the courtyard. The others were already shut. Then he, too, resumed his seat at the table.

'*Bien!*' said Poirot. 'We are now private and undisturbed. We can speak freely. We have heard what the members of the expedition have to tell us and – But yes, *ma soeur*, what is it that you think?'

I got rather red. There was no denying that the queer little man had sharp eyes. He'd seen the thought passing through my mind – I suppose my face *had* shown a bit too clearly what I was thinking!

'Oh, it's nothing –' I said hesitating.

'Come on, nurse,' said Dr Reilly. 'Don't keep the specialist waiting.'

'It's nothing really,' I said hurriedly. 'It only just passed through my mind, so to speak, that perhaps even if anyone did know or suspect something it wouldn't be easy to bring it out in front of everybody else – or even, perhaps, in front of Dr Leidner.'

Rather to my astonishment, M. Poirot nodded his head in vigorous agreement.

'Precisely. Precisely. It is very just what you say there. But I will explain. That little reunion we have just had – it served a purpose. In England before the races you have a parade of the horses, do you not? They go in front of the grandstand so that everyone may have an opportunity of seeing and judging them. That is the purpose of my little assembly. In the sporting phrase, I run my eye over the possible starters.'

Dr Leidner cried out violently, 'I do not believe for one minute that *any* member of my expedition is implicated in this crime!'

Then, turning to me, he said authoritatively: 'Nurse, I should be much obliged if you would tell M. Poirot here and now exactly what passed between my wife and you two days ago.'

Thus urged, I plunged straightaway into my own story, trying as far as possible to recall the exact words and phrases Mrs Leidner had used.

When I had finished, M. Poirot said: 'Very good. Very good. You have the mind neat and orderly. You will be of great service to me here.'

He turned to Dr Leidner.

'You have these letters?'

'I have them here. I thought that you would want to see them first thing.'

Poirot took them from him, read them, and scrutinized them carefully as he did so. I was rather disappointed that he didn't dust powder over them or examine them with a microscope or anything like that – but I realized that he wasn't a very young man and that his methods were probably not very up to date. He just read them in the way that anyone might read a letter.

Having read them he put them down and cleared his throat.

'Now,' he said, 'let us proceed to get our facts clear and in order. The first of these letters was received by your wife shortly after her marriage to you in America. There had been others but these she destroyed. The first letter was followed by a second. A very short time after the second arrived you both had a near escape from coal-gas poisoning. You then came abroad and for nearly two years no further letters were received. They started again at the beginning of your season this year – that is to say within the last three weeks. That is correct?'

'Absolutely.'

'Your wife displayed every sign of panic and, after consulting Dr Reilly, you engaged Nurse Leatheran here to keep your wife company and allay her fears?'

'Yes.'

'Certain incidents occurred – hands tapping at the window – a spectral face – noises in the antika-room. You did not witness any of these phenomena yourself?'

'No.'

'In fact nobody did except Mrs Leidner?'

'Father Lavigny saw a light in the antika-room.'

'Yes, I have not forgotten that.'

He was silent for a minute or two, then he said: 'Had your wife made a will?'

'I do not think so.'

'Why was that?'

'It did not seem worth it from her point of view.'

'Is she not a wealthy woman?'

'Yes, during her lifetime. Her father left her a considerable sum of money in trust. She could not touch the principal. At her death it was to pass to any children she might have – and failing children to the Pittstown Museum.'

Poirot drummed thoughtfully on the table.

'Then we can, I think,' he said, 'eliminate one motive from the case. It is, you comprehend, what I look for first. *Who benefits by the deceased's death?* In this case it is a museum. Had it been otherwise, had Mrs Leidner died intestate but possessed of a considerable fortune, I should imagine that it would prove an interesting question as to who inherited the money – you – or a former husband. But there would have been this difficulty, the former husband would have had to resurrect himself in order to claim it, and I should imagine that he would then be in danger of arrest, though I hardly fancy that the death penalty would be exacted so long after the war. However, these speculations need not arise. As I say, I settle first the question of money. For the next step I proceed always to suspect the husband or wife of the deceased! In this case, in the first place, you are proved never to have gone near your wife's room yesterday afternoon, in the second place you lose instead of gain by your wife's death, and in the third place –'

He paused.

'Yes?' said Dr Leidner.

'In the third place,' said Poirot slowly, 'I can, I think, appreciate devotion when I see it. I believe, Dr Leidner, that your love for your wife was the ruling passion of your life. It is so, is it not?'

Dr Leidner answered quite simply: 'Yes.'

Poirot nodded.

'Therefore,' he said, 'we can proceed.'

'Hear, hear, let's get down to it,' said Dr Reilly with some impatience.

Poirot gave him a reproving glance.

'My friend, do not be impatient. In a case like this everything must be approached with order and method. In fact, that is my rule in every case. Having disposed of certain possibilities, we now approach a very important point. It is vital that, as you say – all the cards should be on the table – there must be nothing kept back.'

'Quite so,' said Dr Reilly.

'That is why I demand the whole truth,' went on Poirot.

Dr Leidner looked at him in surprise.

'I assure you, M. Poirot, that I have kept nothing back. I have told you everything that I know. There have been no reserves.'

'*Tout de même*, you have not told me *everything*.'

'Yes, indeed. I cannot think of any detail that has escaped me.'

He looked quite distressed.

Poirot shook his head gently.

'No,' he said. '*You have not told me, for instance, why you installed Nurse Leatheran in the house.*'

Dr Leidner looked completely bewildered.

'But I have explained that. It is obvious. My wife's nervousness – her fears . . .'

Poirot leaned forward. Slowly and emphatically he wagged a finger up and down.

'No, no, no. There is something there that is not clear. Your wife is in danger, yes – she is threatened with death, yes. You send – *not for the police* – not for a private detective even – but for a *nurse*! It does not make the sense, that!'

'I – I –' Dr Leidner stopped. The colour rose in his cheeks. 'I thought –' He came to a dead stop.

'Now we are coming to it,' Poirot encouraged him. 'You thought – what?'

Dr Leidner remained silent. He looked harassed and unwilling.

'See you,' Poirot's tone became winning and appealing, 'it all rings what you have told me, *except for that*. Why a *nurse*? There is an answer – yes. In fact, there can be only one answer. *You did not believe yourself in your wife's danger.*'

And then with a cry Dr Leidner broke down.

'God help me,' he groaned. 'I didn't. I didn't.'

Poirot watched him with the kind of attention a cat gives a mouse-hole – ready to pounce when the mouse shows itself.

'What *did* you think then?' he asked.

'I don't know. I don't know . . .'

'But you do know. You know perfectly. Perhaps I can help you – with a guess. *Did you, Dr Leidner, suspect that these letters were all written by your wife herself?*'

There wasn't any need for him to answer. The truth of Poirot's guess was only too apparent. The horrified hand he held up, as though begging for mercy, told its own tale.

I drew a deep breath. So I *had* been right in my half-formed guess! I recalled the curious tone in which Dr Leidner had asked me what I thought of it all. I nodded my head slowly and thoughtfully, and suddenly awoke to the fact that M. Poirot's eyes were on me.

'Did you think the same, nurse?'

'The idea did cross my mind,' I said truthfully.

'For what reason?'

I explained the similarity of the handwriting on the letter that Mr Coleman had shown me.

Poirot turned to Dr Leidner.

'Had you, too, noticed that similarity?'

Dr Leidner bowed his head.

'Yes, I did. The writing was small and cramped – not big and generous like Louise's, but several of the letters were formed the same way. I will show you.'

From an inner breast pocket he took out some letters and finally selected a sheet from one, which he handed to Poirot. It was part of a letter written to him by his wife. Poirot compared it carefully with the anonymous letters.

'Yes,' he murmured. 'Yes. There are several similarities – a curious way of forming the letter *s*, a distinctive *e*. I am not a handwriting expert – I cannot pronounce definitely (and for that matter, I have never found two handwriting experts who agree on any point whatsoever) – but one can at least say this – the similarity between the two handwritings is very marked. It seems highly probable that they were all written by the same person. But it is not *certain*. We must take all contingencies into mind.'

He leaned back in his chair and said thoughtfully: 'There are three possibilities. First, the similarity of the handwriting is pure coincidence. Second, that these threatening letters were written by Mrs Leidner herself for some obscure reason. Third, that they were written by someone *who deliberately copied her handwriting*. Why? There seems no sense in it. One of these three possibilities must be the correct one.'

He reflected for a minute or two and then, turning to Dr Leidner, he asked, with a resumal of his brisk manner: 'When the possibility that Mrs Leidner herself was the author of these letters first struck you, what theory did you form?'

Dr Leidner shook his head.

'I put the idea out of my head as quickly as possible. I felt it was monstrous.'

'Did you search for no explanation?'

'Well,' he hesitated. 'I wondered if worrying and brooding over the past had perhaps affected my wife's brain slightly. I thought she might possibly have written those letters to herself without being conscious of having done so. That is possible, isn't it?' he added, turning to Dr Reilly.

Dr Reilly pursed up his lips.

'The human brain is capable of almost anything,' he replied vaguely.

But he shot a lightning glance at Poirot, and as if in obedience to it, the latter abandoned the subject.

'The letters are an interesting point,' he said. 'But we must concentrate on the case as a whole. There are, as I see it, three possible solutions.'

'Three?'

'Yes. Solution one: the simplest. Your wife's first husband is still alive. He first threatens her and then proceeds to carry out his threats. If we accept this solution, our problem is to discover how he got in or out without being seen.

'Solution two: Mrs Leidner, for reasons of her own (reasons probably more easily understood by a medical man than a layman), writes herself threatening letters. The gas business is staged by her (remember, it was she who roused you by telling you she smelt gas). But, *if Mrs Leidner wrote herself the letters, she cannot be in danger from the supposed writer.* We must, therefore, look elsewhere for the murderer. We must look, in fact, amongst the members of your staff. Yes,' in answer to a murmur of protest from Dr Leidner, 'that is the only logical conclusion. To satisfy a private grudge one of them killed her. That person, I may say, was probably aware of the letters – or was at any rate aware that Mrs Leidner feared or was pretending to fear someone. That fact, in the murderer's opinion, rendered the murder quite safe for him. He felt sure it would be put down to a mysterious outsider – the writer of the threatening letters.

'A variant of this solution is that the murderer actually wrote the letters himself, being aware of Mrs Leidner's past history. But in that case it is not quite clear *why* the criminal should have copied Mrs Leidner's own handwriting since, as far as we can see, it would be more to his or her advantage that they should appear to be written by an outsider.

'The third solution is the most interesting to my mind. I suggest that the letters are genuine. They are written by Mrs Leidner's first husband (or his younger brother), *who is actually one of the expedition staff.*'

CHAPTER 16

THE SUSPECTS

Dr Leidner sprang to his feet.

'Impossible! Absolutely impossible! The idea is absurd!'

Mr Poirot looked at him quite calmly but said nothing.

'You mean to suggest that my wife's former husband is one of the expedition *and that she didn't recognize him*?'

'Exactly. Reflect a little on the facts. Some fifteen years ago your wife lived with this man for a few months. Would she know him if she came across him after that lapse of time? I think not. His face will have changed, his build will have changed – his voice may not have changed so much, but that is a detail he can attend to himself. And remember, *she is not looking for him amongst her own household*. She visualizes him as somewhere *outside* – a stranger. No, I do not think she would recognize him. And there is a second possibility. The young brother – the child of those days who was so passionately devoted to his elder brother. He is now a man. Will she recognize a child of ten or twelve years old in a man nearing thirty? Yes, there is young William Bosner to be reckoned with. Remember, his brother in his eyes may not loom as a traitor but as a patriot, a martyr for his own country – Germany. In his eyes *Mrs Leidner* is the traitor – the monster who sent his beloved brother to death! A susceptible child is capable of great hero worship, and a young mind can easily be obsessed by an idea which persists into adult life.'

'Quite true,' said Dr Reilly. 'The popular view that a child forgets easily is not an accurate one. Many people go right through life in the grip of an idea which has been impressed on them in very tender years.'

'*Bien*. You have these two possibilities. Frederick Bosner, a man by now of fifty odd, and William Bosner, whose age would be something short of thirty. Let us examine the members of your staff from these two points of view.'

'This is fantastic,' murmured Dr Leidner. '*My* staff! The members of my own expedition.'

'And consequently considered above suspicion,' said Poirot

dryly. 'A very useful point of view. *Commençons!* Who could emphatically *not* be Frederick or William?'

'The women.'

'Naturally. Miss Johnson and Mrs Mercado are crossed off. Who else?'

'Carey. He and I have worked together for years before I even met Louise –'

'And also he is the wrong age. He is, I should judge, thirty-eight or nine, too young for Frederick, too old for William. Now for the rest. There is Father Lavigny and Mr Mercado. Either of them might be Frederick Bosner.'

'But, my dear sir,' cried Dr Leidner in a voice of mingled irritation and amusement, 'Father Lavigny is known all over the world as an epigraphist and Mercado has worked for years in a well-known museum in New York. It is *impossible* that either of them should be the man you think!'

Poirot waved an airy hand.

'Impossible – impossible – I take no account of the word! The impossible, always I examine it very closely! But we will pass on for the moment. Who else have you? Carl Reiter, a young man with a German name, David Emmott –'

'He has been with me two seasons, remember.'

'He is a young man with the gift of patience. *If* he committed a crime, it would not be in a hurry. All would be very well prepared.'

Dr Leidner made a gesture of despair.

'And lastly, William Coleman,' continued Poirot.

'He is an Englishman.'

'*Pourquoi pas?* Did not Mrs Leidner say that the boy left America and could not be traced? He might easily have been brought up in England.'

'You have an answer to everything,' said Dr Leidner.

I was thinking hard. Right from the beginning I had thought Mr Coleman's manner rather more like a P. G. Wodehouse book than like a real live young man. Had he really been playing a part all the time?

Poirot was writing in a little book.

'Let us proceed with order and method,' he said. 'On the first count we have two names. Father Lavigny and Mr Mercado. On the second we have Coleman, Emmott and Reiter.

'Now let us pass to the opposite aspect of the matter – means and opportunity. *Who amongst the expedition had the means and the opportunity of committing the crime?* Carey was on the dig, Coleman was in Hassanieh, you yourself were on the roof. That leaves us Father Lavigny, Mr Mercado, Mrs Mercado, David Emmott, Carl Reiter, Miss Johnson and Nurse Leatheran.'

'Oh!' I exclaimed, and I bounded in my chair.

Mr Poirot looked at me with twinkling eyes.

'Yes, I'm afraid, *ma soeur*, that you have got to be included. It would have been quite easy for you to have gone along and killed Mrs Leidner while the courtyard was empty. You have plenty of muscle and strength, and she would have been quite unsuspicious until the moment the blow was struck.'

I was so upset that I couldn't get a word out. Dr Reilly, I noticed, was looking highly amused.

'Interesting case of a nurse who murdered her patients one by one,' he murmured.

Such a look as I gave him!

Dr Leidner's mind had been running on a different tack.

'Not Emmott, M. Poirot,' he objected. 'You can't include him. He was on the roof with me, remember, during that ten minutes.'

'Nevertheless we cannot exclude him. He could have come down, gone straight to Mrs Leidner's room, killed her, and *then* called the boy back. Or he might have killed her on one of the occasions when he had *sent the boy up to you*.'

Dr Leidner shook his head, murmuring: 'What a nightmare! It's all so – fantastic.'

To my surprise Poirot agreed.

'Yes, that's true. *This is a fantastic crime.* One does not often come across them. Usually murder is very sordid – very simple. But this is unusual murder . . . I suspect, Dr Leidner, that your wife was an unusual woman.'

He had hit the nail on the head with such accuracy that I jumped.

'Is that true, nurse?' he asked.

Dr Leidner said quietly: 'Tell him what Louise was like, nurse. You are unprejudiced.'

I spoke quite frankly.

'She was very lovely,' I said. 'You couldn't help admiring her and wanting to do things for her. I've never met anyone like her before.'

'Thank you,' said Dr Leidner and smiled at me.

'That is valuable testimony coming from an outsider,' said Poirot politely. 'Well, let us proceed. Under the heading of *means and opportunity* we have seven names. Nurse Leatheran, Miss Johnson, Mrs Mercado, Mr Mercado, Mr Reiter, Mr Emmott and Father Lavigny.'

Once more he cleared his throat. I've always noticed that foreigners can make the oddest noises.

'Let us for the moment assume that our third theory is correct. That is that the murderer is Frederick or William Bosner, and that Frederick or William Bosner is a member of the expedition staff. By comparing both lists we can narrow down our suspects on this count to four. Father Lavigny, Mr Mercado, Carl Reiter and David Emmott.'

'Father Lavigny is out of the question,' said Dr Leidner with decision. 'He is one of the Pères Blancs in Carthage.'

'And his beard's quite real,' I put in.

'*Ma soeur*,' said Poirot, 'a murderer of the first class *never* wears a false beard!'

'How do you know the murderer is of the first class?' I asked rebelliously.

'Because if he were not, the whole truth would be plain to me at this instant – and it is not.'

That's pure conceit, I thought to myself.

'Anyway,' I said, reverting to the beard, 'it must have taken quite a time to grow.'

'That is a practical observation,' said Poirot.

Dr Leidner said irritably: 'But it's ridiculous – quite ridiculous. Both he and Mercado are well-known men. They've been known for years.'

Poirot turned to him.

'You have not the true version. You do not appreciate an important point. *If Frederick Bosner is not dead – what has he been doing all these years?* He must have taken a different name. He must have built himself up a career.'

'As a Père Blanc?' asked Dr Reilly sceptically.

'It is a little fantastic that, yes,' confessed Poirot. 'But we cannot put it right out of court. Besides, these other possibilities.'

'The young 'uns?' said Reilly. 'If you want my opinion, on the face of it there's only one of your suspects that's even plausible.'

'And that is?'

'Young Carl Reiter. There's nothing actually against him, but come down to it and you've got to admit a few things – he's the right age, he's got a German name, he's new this year and he had the opportunity all right. He'd only got to pop out of his photographic place, cross the courtyard to do his dirty work and hare back again while the coast was clear. If anyone were to have dropped into the photographic-room while he was out of it, he can always say later that he was in the dark-room. I don't say he's your man but if you are going to suspect someone I say he's by far and away the most likely.'

M. Poirot didn't seem very receptive. He nodded gravely but doubtfully.

'Yes,' he said. 'He is the most plausible, but it may not be so simple as all that.'

Then he said: 'Let us say no more at present. I would like now, if I may, to examine the room where the crime took place.'

'Certainly.' Dr Leidner fumbled in his pockets, then looked at Dr Reilly.

'Captain Maitland took it,' he said.

'Maitland gave it to me,' said Reilly. 'He had to go off on that Kurdish business.'

He produced the key.

Dr Leidner said hesitatingly: 'Do you mind – if I don't – Perhaps, nurse –'

'Of course. Of course,' said Poirot. 'I quite understand. Never do I wish to cause you unnecessary pain. If you will be good enough to accompany me, *ma soeur*.'

'Certainly,' I said.

CHAPTER 17

THE STAIN BY THE WASHSTAND

Mrs Leidner's body had been taken to Hassanieh for the post-mortem, but otherwise her room had been left exactly as it was. There was so little in it that it had not taken the police long to go over it.

To the right of the door as you entered was the bed. Opposite the door were the two barred windows giving on the countryside. Between them was a plain oak table with two drawers that served Mrs Leidner as a dressing-table. On the east wall there was a line of hooks with dresses hung up protected by cotton bags and a deal chest of drawers. Immediately to the left of the door was the washstand. In the middle of the room was a good-sized plain oak table with a blotter and inkstand and a small attaché-case. It was in the latter that Mrs Leidner had kept the anonymous letters. The curtains were short strips of native material – white striped with orange. The floor was of stone with some goatskin rugs on it, three narrow ones of brown striped with white in front of the two windows and the washstand, and a larger better quality one of white with brown stripes lying between the bed and the writing-table.

There were no cupboards or alcoves or long curtains – nowhere, in fact, where anyone could have hidden. The bed was a plain iron one with a printed cotton quilt. The only trace of luxury in the room were three pillows all made of the best soft and billowy down. Nobody but Mrs Leidner had pillows like these.

In a few brief words Dr Reilly explained where Mrs Leidner's body had been found – in a heap on the rug beside the bed.

To illustrate his account, he beckoned me to come forward.

'If you don't mind, nurse?' he said.

I'm not squeamish. I got down on the floor and arranged myself as far as possible in the attitude in which Mrs Leidner's body had been found.

'Leidner lifted her head when he found her,' said the doctor. 'But I questioned him closely and it's obvious that he didn't actually change her position.'

'It seems quite straightforward,' said Poirot. 'She was lying on the bed, asleep or resting – someone opens the door, she looks up, rises to her feet –'

'And he struck her down,' finished the doctor. 'The blow would produce unconsciousness and death would follow very shortly. You see –'

He explained the injury in technical language.

'Not much blood, then?' said Poirot.

'No, the blood escaped internally into the brain.'

'*Eh bien,*' said Poirot, 'that seems straightforward enough – except for one thing. *If* the man who entered was a stranger, why did not Mrs Leidner cry out at once for help? If she had screamed she would have been heard. Nurse Leatheran here would have heard her, and Emmott and the boy.'

'That's easily answered,' said Dr Reilly dryly. '*Because it wasn't a stranger.*'

Poirot nodded.

'Yes,' he said meditatively. 'She may have been *surprised* to see the person – but she was not *afraid.* Then, as he struck, she *may* have uttered a half-cry – too late.'

'The cry Miss Johnson heard?'

'Yes, if she *did* hear it. But on the whole I doubt it. These mud walls are thick and the windows were closed.'

He stepped up to the bed.

'You left her actually lying down?' he asked me.

I explained exactly what I had done.

'Did she mean to sleep or was she going to read?'

'I gave her two books – a light one and a volume of memoirs. She usually read for a while and then sometimes dropped off for a short sleep.'

'And she was – what shall I say – quite as usual?'

I considered.

'Yes. She seemed quite normal and in good spirits,' I said. 'Just a shade off-hand, perhaps, but I put that down to her having confided in me the day before. It makes people a little uncomfortable sometimes.'

Poirot's eyes twinkled.

'Ah, yes, indeed, me, I know that well.'

He looked round the room.

'And when you came in here after the murder, was everything as you had seen it before?'

I looked round also.

'Yes, I think so. I don't remember anything being different.'

'There was no sign of the weapon with which she was struck?'

'No.'

Poirot looked at Dr Reilly.

'What was it in your opinion?'

The doctor replied promptly:

'Something pretty powerful, of a fair size and without any sharp corners or edges. The rounded base of a statue, say – something like that. Mind you, I'm not suggesting that that *was* it. But that type of thing. The blow was delivered with great force.'

'Struck by a strong arm? A man's arm?'

'Yes – unless –'

'Unless – what?'

Dr Reilly said slowly: 'It is just possible that Mrs Leidner might have been on her knees – in which case, the blow being delivered from above with a heavy implement, the force needed would not have been so great.'

'*On her knees*,' mused Poirot. 'It is an idea – that.'

'It's only an idea, mind,' the doctor hastened to point out. 'There's absolutely nothing to indicate it.'

'But it's possible.'

'Yes. And after all, in view of the circumstances, it's not fantastic. Her fear might have led her to kneel in supplication rather than to scream when her instinct would tell her it was too late – that nobody could get there in time.'

'Yes,' said Poirot thoughtfully. 'It is an idea . . .'

It was a very poor one, I thought. I couldn't for one moment imagine Mrs Leidner on her knees to anyone.

Poirot made his way slowly round the room. He opened the windows, tested the bars, passed his head through and satisfied himself that by no means could his shoulders be made to follow his head.

'The windows were shut when you found her,' he said. 'Were they also shut when you left her at a quarter to one?'

'Yes, they were always shut in the afternoon. There is no gauze over these windows as there is in the living-room and dining-room. They are kept shut to keep out the flies.'

'And in any case no one could get in that way,' mused Poirot. 'And the walls are of the most solid – mud-brick – and there are no trap-doors and no sky-lights. No, there is only one way into this room – *through the door*. And there is only one way to the door *through the courtyard*. And there is only one entrance to the courtyard – *through the archway*. And outside the archway there were five people and they all tell the same story, and I do not think, me, that they are lying . . . No, they are not lying. They are not bribed to silence. The murderer was *here* . . .'

I didn't say anything. Hadn't I felt the same thing just now when we were all cooped up round the table?

Slowly Poirot prowled round the room. He took up a photograph from the chest of drawers. It was of an elderly man with a white goatee beard. He looked inquiringly at me.

'Mrs Leidner's father,' I said. 'She told me so.'

He put it down again and glanced over the articles on the dressing-table – all of plain tortoiseshell – simple but good. He looked up at a row of books on a shelf, repeating the titles aloud.

'*Who were the Greeks? Introduction to Relativity. Life of Lady Hester Stanhope. Crewe Train. Back to Methuselah. Linda Condon.* Yes, they tell us something, perhaps. She was not a fool, your Mrs Leidner. She had a mind.'

'Oh! she was a *very* clever woman,' I said eagerly. 'Very well read and up in everything. She wasn't a bit ordinary.'

He smiled as he looked over at me.

'No,' he said. 'I've already realized that.'

He passed on. He stood for some moments at the washstand, where there was a big array of bottles and toilet creams.

Then, suddenly, he dropped on his knees and examined the rug.

Dr Reilly and I came quickly to join him. He was examining a small dark brown stain, almost invisible on the brown of the rug. In fact it was only just noticeable where it impinged on one of the white stripes.

'What do you say, doctor?' he said. 'Is that blood?'

Dr Reilly knelt down.

'Might be,' he said. 'I'll make sure if you like?'

'If you would be so amiable.'

Mr Poirot examined the jug and basin. The jug was standing on the side of the washstand. The basin was empty, but beside the washstand there was an empty kerosene tin containing slop water.

He turned to me.

'Do you remember, nurse? Was this jug *out* of the basin or *in* it when you left Mrs Leidner at a quarter to one?'

'I can't be sure,' I said after a minute or two. 'I rather think it was standing in the basin.'

'Ah?'

'But you see,' I said hastily, 'I only think so because it usually was. The boys leave it like that after lunch. I just feel that if it hadn't been in I should have noticed it.'

He nodded quite appreciatively.

'Yes. I understand that. It is your hospital training. If everything had not been just so in the room, you would quite unconsciously have set it to rights hardly noticing what you were doing. And after the murder? Was it like it is now?'

I shook my head.

'I didn't notice then,' I said. 'All I looked for was whether there was any place anyone could be hidden or if there was anything the murderer had left behind him.'

'It's blood all right,' said Dr Reilly, rising from his knees. 'Is it important?'

Poirot was frowning perplexedly. He flung out his hands with petulance.

'I cannot tell. How can I tell? It may mean nothing at all. I can say, if I like, that the murderer touched her – that there was blood on his hands – very little blood, but still blood – and so he came over here and washed them. Yes, it may have been like that. But I cannot jump to conclusions and say that it *was* so. That stain may be of no importance at all.'

'There would have been very little blood,' said Dr Reilly dubiously. 'None would have spurted out or anything like that. It would have just oozed a little from the wound. Of course, if he'd probed it at all . . .'

I gave a shiver. A nasty sort of picture came up in my mind. The vision of somebody – perhaps that nice pig-faced photographic boy, striking down that lovely woman and then bending over her probing the wound with his finger in an awful gloating fashion and his face, perhaps, quite different . . . all fierce and mad . . .

Dr Reilly noticed my shiver.

'What's the matter, nurse?' he said.

96

'Nothing – just goose-flesh,' I said. 'A goose walking over my grave.'

Mr Poirot turned round and looked at me.

'I know what you need,' he said. 'Presently when we have finished here and I go back with the doctor to Hassanieh we will take you with us. You will give Nurse Leatheran tea, will you not, doctor?'

'Delighted.'

'Oh, no doctor,' I protested. 'I couldn't think of such a thing.'

M. Poirot gave me a little friendly tap on the shoulder. Quite an English tap, not a foreign one.

'You, *ma soeur*, will do as you are told,' he said. 'Besides, it will be of advantage to me. There is a good deal more that I want to discuss, and I cannot do it here where one must preserve the decencies. The good Dr Leidner he worshipped his wife and he is sure – oh, so sure – that everybody else felt the same about her! But that, in my opinion, would not be human nature! No, we want to discuss Mrs Leidner with – how do you say? – the gloves removed. That is settled then. When we have finished here, we take you with us to Hassanieh.'

'I suppose,' I said doubtfully, 'that I ought to be leaving anyway. It's rather awkward.'

'Do nothing for a day or two,' said Dr Reilly. 'You can't very well go until after the funeral.'

'That's all very well,' I said. 'And supposing *I* get murdered too, doctor?'

I said it half jokingly and Dr Reilly took it in the same fashion and would, I think, have made some jocular response.

But M. Poirot, to my astonishment, stood stock-still in the middle of the floor and clasped his hands to his head.

'Ah! if that were possible,' he murmured. 'It is a danger – yes – a great danger – and what can one do? How can one guard against it?'

'Why, M. Poirot,' I said, 'I was only joking! Who'd want to murder me, I should like to know?'

'You – or another,' he said, and I didn't like the way he said it at all. Positively creepy.

'But why?' I persisted.

He looked at me very straight then.

'I joke, mademoiselle,' he said, 'and I laugh. *But there are some things that are no joke.* There are things that my profession has taught me. And one of these things, the most terrible thing, is this: *Murder is a habit . . .*'

CHAPTER 18

TEA AT DR REILLY'S

Before leaving, Poirot made a round of the expedition house and the outbuildings. He also asked a few questions of the servants at second hand – that is to say, Dr Reilly translated the questions and answers from English to Arabic and *vice versa*.

These questions dealt mainly with the appearance of the stranger Mrs Leidner and I had seen looking through the window and to whom Father Lavigny had been talking on the following day.

'Do you really think that fellow had anything to do with it?' asked Dr Reilly when we were bumping along in his car on our way to Hassanieh.

'I like all the information there is,' was Poirot's reply.

And really, that described his methods very well. I found later that there wasn't anything – no small scrap of insignificant gossip – in which he wasn't interested. Men aren't usually so gossipy.

I must confess I was glad of my cup of tea when we got to Dr Reilly's house. M. Poirot, I noticed, put five lumps of sugar in his.

Stirring it carefully with his teaspoon he said: 'And now we can talk, can we not? We can make up our minds who is likely to have committed the crime.'

'Lavigny, Mercado, Emmott or Reiter?' asked Dr Reilly.

'No, no – that was theory number three. I wish to concentrate now on theory number two – leaving aside all question of a mysterious husband or brother-in-law turning up from the past. Let us discuss now quite simply which member of the expedition had the means and opportunity to kill Mrs Leidner, and who is likely to have done so.'

'I thought you didn't think much of that theory.'

'Not at all. But I have some natural delicacy,' said Poirot reproachfully. 'Can I discuss in the presence of Dr Leidner the motives likely to lead to the murder of his wife by a member of the expedition? That would not have been delicate at all. I had to sustain the fiction that his wife was adorable and that everyone adored her!

'But naturally it was not like that at all. Now we can be brutal and impersonal and say what we think. We have no longer to consider people's feelings. And that is where Nurse Leatheran is going to help us. She is, I am sure, a very good observer.'

'Oh, I don't know about that,' I said.

Dr Reilly handed me a plate of hot scones – 'To fortify yourself,' he said. They were very good scones.

'Come now,' said M. Poirot in a friendly, chatty way. 'You shall tell me, *ma soeur*, exactly what each member of the expedition felt towards Mrs Leidner.'

'I was only there a week, M. Poirot,' I said.

'Quite long enough for one of your intelligence. A nurse sums up quickly. She makes her judgments and abides by them. Come, let us make a beginning. Father Lavigny, for instance?'

'Well, there now, I really couldn't say. He and Mrs Leidner seemed to like talking together. But they usually spoke French and I'm not very good at French myself though I learnt it as a girl at school. I've an idea they talked mainly about books.'

'They were, as you might say, companionable together – yes?'

'Well, yes, you might put it that way. But, all the same, I think Father Lavigny was puzzled by her and – well – almost annoyed by being puzzled, if you know what I mean.'

And I told him of the conversation I had had with him out on the dig that first day when he had called Mrs Leidner a 'dangerous woman'.

'Now that is very interesting,' M. Poirot said. 'And she – what do you think she thought of him?'

'That's rather difficult to say, too. It wasn't easy to know what Mrs Leidner thought of people. Sometimes, I fancy, *he* puzzled *her*. I remember her saying to Dr Leidner that he was unlike any priest she had ever known.'

'A length of hemp to be ordered for Father Lavigny,' said Dr Reilly facetiously.

'My dear friend,' said Poirot. 'Have you not, perhaps, some patients to attend? I would not for the world detain you from your professional duties.'

'I've got a whole hospital of them,' said Dr Reilly.

And he got up and said a wink was as good as a nod to a blind horse, and went out laughing.

'That is better,' said Poirot. 'We will have now an interesting conversation *tête-à-tête*. But you must not forget to eat your tea.'

He passed me a plate of sandwiches and suggested my having a second cup of tea. He really had very pleasant, attentive manners.

'And now,' he said, 'let us continue with your impressions. Who was there who in your opinion did *not* like Mrs Leidner?'

'Well,' I said, 'it's only my opinion and I don't want it repeated as coming from me.'

'Naturally not.'

'But in my opinion little Mrs Mercado fairly hated her!'

'Ah! And Mr Mercado?'

'He was a bit soft on her,' I said. 'I shouldn't think women, apart from his wife, had ever taken much notice of him. And Mrs Leidner had a nice kind way of being interested in people and the things they told her. It rather went to the poor man's head, I fancy.'

'And Mrs Mercado – she was not pleased?'

'She was just plain jealous – that's the truth of it. You've got to be very careful when there's a husband and wife about, and that's a fact. I could tell you some surprising things. You've no idea the extraordinary things women get into their heads when it's a question of their husbands.'

'I do not doubt the truth of what you say. So Mrs Mercado was jealous? And she hated Mrs Leidner?'

'I've seen her look at her as though she'd have liked to kill her – oh, gracious!' I pulled myself up. 'Indeed, M. Poirot, I didn't mean to say – I mean, that is, not for one moment –'

'No, no. I quite understand. The phrase slipped out. A very convenient one. And Mrs Leidner, was she worried by this animosity of Mrs Mercado's?'

'Well,' I said, reflecting, 'I don't really think she was worried at all. In fact, I don't even know whether she noticed it. I thought once of just giving her a hint – but I didn't like to. Least said soonest mended. That's what I say.'

'You are doubtless wise. Can you give me any instances of how Mrs Mercado showed her feelings?'

I told him about our conversation on the roof.

'So she mentioned Mrs Leidner's first marriage,' said Poirot thoughtfully. 'Can you remember – in mentioning it – did she look at you as though she wondered whether you had heard a different version?'

'You think she may have known the truth about it?'

'It is a possibility. She may have written those letters – and engineered a tapping hand and all the rest of it.'

'I wondered something of the same kind myself. It seemed the kind of petty revengeful thing she might do.'

'Yes. A cruel streak, I should say. But hardly the temperament for cold-blooded, brutal murder unless, of course –'

He paused and then said: 'It is odd, that curious thing she said to you. "*I know why you are here.*" What did she mean by it?'

'I can't imagine,' I said frankly.

'She thought you were there for some ulterior reason apart from the declared one. What reason? And why should she be so concerned in the matter. Odd, too, the way you tell me she stared at you all through tea the day you arrived.'

'Well, she's not a lady, M. Poirot,' I said primly.

'That, *ma soeur*, is an excuse but not an explanation.'

I wasn't quite sure for the minute what he meant. But he went on quickly.

'And the other members of the staff?'

I considered.

'I don't think Miss Johnson liked Mrs Leidner either very much. But she was quite open and above-board about it. She as good as admitted she was prejudiced. You see, she's very devoted to Dr Leidner and had worked with him for years. And of course, marriage does change things – there's no denying it.'

'Yes,' said Poirot. 'And from Miss Johnson's point of view it would be an unsuitable marriage. It would really have been much more suitable if Dr Leidner had married *her*.'

'It would really,' I agreed. 'But there, that's a man all over. Not one in a hundred considers suitability. And one can't really blame Dr Leidner. Miss Johnson, poor soul, isn't so much to look at. Now Mrs Leidner was really beautiful – not young, of course – but oh! I wish you'd known her. There was something about her . . . I remember Mr Coleman saying she was like a thingummyjig that came to lure people into marshes. That wasn't a very good way of putting it, but – oh, well – you'll laugh at me, but there *was* something about her that was – well – unearthly.'

'She could cast a spell – yes, I understand,' said Poirot.

'Then I don't think she and Mr Carey got on very well either,' I went on. 'I've an idea *he* was jealous just like Miss Johnson. He was always very stiff with her and so was she with him. You know – she passed him things and was very polite and called him Mr Carey rather formally. He was an old friend of her husband's of course, and some women can't stand their husband's old friends. They don't like to think that anyone knew them before they did – at least that's rather a muddled way of putting it –'

'I quite understand. And the three young men? Coleman, you say, was inclined to be poetic about her.'

I couldn't help laughing.

'It was funny, M. Poirot,' I said. 'He's such a matter-of-fact young man.'

'And the other two?'

'I don't really know about Mr Emmott. He's always so quiet and never says much. She was very nice to him always. You know – friendly – called him David and used to tease him about Miss Reilly and things like that.'

'Ah, really? And did he enjoy that?'

'I don't quite know,' I said doubtfully. 'He'd just look at her. Rather funnily. You couldn't tell what he was thinking.'

'And Mr Reiter?'

'She wasn't always very kind to him,' I said slowly. 'I think he got on her nerves. She used to say quite sarcastic things to him.'

'And did he mind?'

'He used to get very pink, poor boy. Of course, she didn't *mean* to be unkind.'

And then suddenly, from feeling a little sorry for the boy, it came over me that he was very likely a cold-blooded murderer and had been playing a part all the time.

'Oh, M. Poirot,' I exclaimed. 'What do you think *really* happened?'

He shook his head slowly and thoughtfully.

'Tell me,' he said. 'You are not afraid to go back there tonight?'

'Oh *no*,' I said. 'Of course, I remember what you said, but who would want to murder *me*?'

'I do not think that anyone could,' he said slowly. 'That is partly why I have been so anxious to hear all you could tell me. No, I think – I am sure – you are quite safe.'

'If anyone had told me in Baghdad –' I began and stopped.

'Did you hear any gossip about the Leidners and the expedition before you came here?' he asked.

I told him about Mrs Leidner's nickname and just a little of what Mrs Kelsey had said about her.

In the middle of it the door opened and Miss Reilly came in. She had been playing tennis and had her racquet in her hand.

I gathered Poirot had already met her when he arrived in Hassanieh.

She said how-do-you-do to me in her usual off-hand manner and picked up a sandwich.

'Well, M. Poirot,' she said. 'How are you getting on with our local mystery?'

'Not very fast, mademoiselle.'

'I see you've rescued nurse from the wreck.'

'Nurse Leatheran has been giving me valuable information about the various members of the expedition. Incidentally I have learnt a good deal – about the victim. And the victim, mademoiselle, is very often the clue to the mystery.'

Miss Reilly said: 'That's rather clever of you, M. Poirot. It's certainly true that if ever a woman deserved to be murdered Mrs Leidner was that woman!'

'Miss Reilly!' I cried, scandalized.

She laughed, a short, nasty laugh.

'Ah!' she said. 'I thought you hadn't been hearing quite the truth. Nurse Leatheran, I'm afraid, was quite taken in, like many other people. Do you know, M. Poirot, I rather hope that this case isn't going to be one of your successes. I'd quite like the murderer of Louise Leidner to get away with it. In fact, I wouldn't much have objected to putting her out of the way myself.'

I was simply disgusted with the girl. M. Poirot, I must say, didn't turn a hair. He just bowed and said quite pleasantly:

'I hope, then, that you have an alibi for yesterday afternoon?'

There was a moment's silence and Miss Reilly's racquet went clattering down on to the floor. She didn't bother to pick it up. Slack and untidy like all her sort! She said in a rather breathless voice: 'Oh, yes, I was playing tennis at the club. But, seriously,

M. Poirot, I wonder if you know anything at all about Mrs Leidner and the kind of woman she was?'

Again he made a funny little bow and said: 'You shall inform me, mademoiselle.'

She hesitated a minute and then spoke with a callousness and lack of decency that really sickened me.

'There's a convention that one doesn't speak ill of the dead. That's stupid, I think. The truth's always the truth. On the whole it's better to keep your mouth shut about living people. You might conceivably injure them. The dead are past that. But the harm they've done lives after them sometimes. Not quite a quotation from Shakespeare but very nearly! Has nurse told you of the queer atmosphere there was at Tell Yarimjah? Has she told you how jumpy they all were? And how they all used to glare at each other like enemies? That was Louise Leidner's doing. When I was a kid out here three years ago they were the happiest, jolliest lot imaginable. Even last year they were pretty well all right. But this year there was a blight over them – and it was *her* doing. She was the kind of woman who won't let anybody else be happy! There *are* women like that and she was one of them! She wanted to break up things always. Just for fun – or for the sense of power – or perhaps just because she was made that way. And she was the kind of woman who had to get hold of every male creature within reach!'

'Miss Reilly,' I cried, 'I don't think that's true. In fact I *know* it isn't.'

She went on without taking the least notice of me.

'It wasn't enough for her to have her husband adore her. She had to make a fool of that long-legged shambling idiot of a Mercado. Then she got hold of Bill. Bill's a sensible cove, but she was getting him all mazed and bewildered. Carl Reiter she just amused herself by tormenting. It was easy. He's a sensitive boy. And she had a jolly good go at David.

'David was better sport to her because he put up a fight. He felt her charm – but he wasn't having any. I think because he'd got sense enough to know that she didn't really care a damn. And that's why I hate her so. She's not sensual. She doesn't *want* affairs. It's just cold-blooded experiment on her part and the fun of stirring people up and setting them against each other. She dabbled in that too. She's the sort of woman who's never had a row with anyone in her life – but rows always happen where she is! She *makes* them happen. She's a kind of female Iago. She *must* have drama. But she doesn't want to be involved *herself*. She's always outside pulling strings – looking on – enjoying it. Oh, do you see *at all* what I mean?'

'I see, perhaps, more than you know, mademoiselle,' said Poirot.

I couldn't make his voice out. He didn't sound indignant. He sounded – oh, well, I can't explain it.

Sheila Reilly seemed to understand, for she flushed all over her face.

'You can think what you choose,' she said. 'But I'm right about her. She was a clever woman and she was bored and she experimented – with people – like other people experiment with chemicals. She enjoyed working on poor old Johnson's feelings and seeing her bite on the bullet and control herself like the old sport she is. She liked goading little Mercado into a white-hot frenzy. She liked flicking *me* on the raw – and she could do it too, every time! She liked finding out things about people and holding it over them. Oh, I don't mean crude blackmail – I mean just letting them know that she *knew* – and leaving them uncertain what she meant to do about it. My God, though, that woman was an artist! There was nothing crude about *her* methods!'

'And her husband?' asked Poirot.

'She never wanted to hurt him,' said Miss Reilly slowly. 'I've never known her anything but sweet to him. I suppose she was fond of him. He's a dear – wrapped up in his own world – his digging and his theories. And he worshipped her and thought her perfection. That might have annoyed some women. It didn't annoy her. In a sense he lived in a fool's paradise – and yet it wasn't a fool's paradise because to him she was what he thought her. Though it's hard to reconcile that with –'

She stopped.

'Go on, mademoiselle,' said Poirot.

She turned suddenly on me.

'What have you said about Richard Carey?'

'About Mr Carey?' I asked, astonished.

'About her and Carey?'

'Well,' I said, 'I've mentioned that they didn't hit it off very well –'

To my surprise she broke into a fit of laughter.

'Didn't hit it off very well! You fool! He's head over ears in love with her. And it's tearing him to pieces – because he worships Leidner too. He's been his friend for years. That would be enough for her, of course. She's made it her business to come between them. But all the same I've fancied –'

'*Eh bien?*'

She was frowning, absorbed in thought.

'I've fancied that she'd gone too far for once – that she was not only biter but bit! Carey's attractive. He's as attractive as hell . . . She was a cold devil – but I believe she could have lost her coldness with him . . .'

'I think it's just scandalous what you're saying,' I cried. 'Why, they hardly spoke to each other!'

'Oh, didn't they?' She turned on me. 'A hell of a lot you know about it. It was "Mr Carey" and "Mrs Leidner" in the house, but they used to meet outside. She'd walk down the path to the river. And he'd leave the dig for an hour at a time. They used to meet among the fruit trees.

'I saw him once just leaving her, striding back to the dig, and she was standing looking after him. I was a female cad, I suppose. I had some glasses with me and I took them out and had a good look at her face. If you ask me, I believe she cared like hell for Richard Carey . . .'

She broke off and looked at Poirot.

'Excuse my butting in on your case,' she said with a sudden rather twisted grin, 'but I thought you'd like to have the local colour correct.'

And she marched out of the room.

'M. Poirot,' I cried. 'I don't believe one word of it all!'

He looked at me and he smiled, and he said (very queerly I thought): 'You can't deny, nurse, that Miss Reilly has shed a certain – illumination on the case.'

CHAPTER 19

A NEW SUSPICION

We couldn't say any more just then because Dr Reilly came in, saying jokingly that he'd killed off the most tiresome of his patients.

He and M. Poirot settled down to a more or less medical discussion of the psychology and mental state of an anonymous letter-writer. The doctor cited cases that he had known professionally, and M. Poirot told various stories from his own experience.

'It is not so simple as it seems,' he ended. 'There is the desire for power and very often a strong inferiority complex.'

Dr Reilly nodded.

'That's why you often find that the author of anonymous letters is the last person in the place to be suspected. Some quiet inoffensive little soul who apparently can't say Bo to a goose – all sweetness and Christian meekness on the outside – and seething with all the fury of hell underneath!'

Poirot said thoughtfully: 'Should you say Mrs Leidner had any tendency to an inferiority complex?'

Dr Reilly scraped out his pipe with a chuckle.

'Last woman on earth I'd describe that way. No repressions about her. Life, life and more life – that's what she wanted – and got, too!'

'Do you consider it a possibility, psychologically speaking, that she wrote those letters?'

'Yes, I do. But if she did, the reason arose out of her instinct to dramatize herself. Mrs Leidner was a bit of a film star in private life! She *had* to be the centre of things – in the limelight. By the law of opposites she married Leidner, who's about the most retiring and modest man I know. He adored her – but adoration by the fireside wasn't enough for her. She had to be the persecuted heroine as well.'

'In fact,' said Poirot, smiling, 'you don't subscribe to his theory that she wrote them and retained no memory of her act?'

'No, I don't. I didn't turn down the idea in front of him. You can't very well say to a man who's just lost a dearly loved wife that that same wife was a shameless exhibitionist, and that she drove him nearly crazy with anxiety to satisfy her sense of the dramatic. As a matter of fact it wouldn't be safe to tell any man the truth about his wife! Funnily enough, I'd trust most women with the truth about their husbands. Women can accept the fact that a man is a rotter, a swindler, a drug-taker, a confirmed liar, and a general swine without batting an eyelash and without its impairing their affection for the brute in the least! Women are wonderful realists.'

'Frankly, Dr Reilly, what *was* your exact opinion of Mrs Leidner?'

Dr Reilly lay back in his chair and puffed slowly at his pipe.

'Frankly – it's hard to say! I didn't know her well enough. She'd got charm – any amount of it. Brains, sympathy . . . What else? She hadn't any of the ordinary unpleasant vices. She wasn't sensual or lazy or even particularly vain. She was, I've always thought (but I've no proofs of it), a most accomplished liar. What I don't know (and what I'd like to know) is whether she lied to herself or only to other people. I'm rather partial to liars myself. A woman who doesn't lie is a woman without imagination and without sympathy. I don't think she was really a man-hunter – she just liked the sport of bringing them down "with my bow and arrow". If you get my daughter on the subject –'

'We have had that pleasure,' said Poirot with a slight smile.

'H'm,' said Dr Reilly. 'She hasn't wasted much time! Shoved her knife into her pretty thoroughly, I should imagine! The younger generation has no sentiment towards the dead. It's a pity all young people are prigs! They condemn the "old morality" and then proceed to set up a much more hard-and-fast code of their own. If Mrs Leidner had had half a dozen affairs Sheila would probably have approved of her as "living her life fully" – or "obeying her blood instincts". What she doesn't see is that Mrs Leidner was acting true to type – *her* type. The cat *is* obeying its blood instinct when it plays with the mouse! It's made that way. Men aren't little boys to be shielded and protected. They've got to meet cat women – and faithful spaniel, yours-till-death adoring women, and hen-pecking nagging bird women – and all the rest of it! Life's a battlefield – not a picnic! I'd like to see Sheila honest enough to come off her high horse and admit that she hated Mrs Leidner for good old thorough-going personal reasons. Sheila's about the only young girl in this place and she naturally assumes that she ought to have it all her own way with the young things in trousers. Naturally it annoys her when a woman, who in her view is middle-aged and who has already two husbands to her credit, comes along and licks her on her own ground. Sheila's a nice child, healthy and reasonably good-looking and attractive to the other sex as she should be. But Mrs Leidner was something out of the ordinary in that line. She'd got just that sort of calamitous magic that plays the deuce with things – a kind of Belle Dame sans Merci.'

I jumped in my chair. What a coincidence his saying that!

'Your daughter – I am not indiscreet – she has perhaps a *tendresse* for one of the young men out there?'

'Oh, I don't suppose so. She's had Emmott and Coleman dancing attendance on her as a matter of course. I don't know that she cares for one more than the other. There are a couple of young Air Force chaps too. I fancy all's fish that comes to her net at present. No, I think it's age daring to defeat youth that annoys her so much! She doesn't know as much of the world as I do. It's when you get to my age that you really appreciate a schoolgirl complexion and a clear eye and a firmly knit young body. But a woman over thirty can listen with rapt attention and throw in a word here and there to show the talker what a fine fellow he is – and few young men can resist that! Sheila's a pretty girl – but Louise Leidner was beautiful. Glorious eyes and that amazing golden fairness. Yes, she was a beautiful woman.'

Yes, I thought to myself, he's right. Beauty's a wonderful thing. She *had* been beautiful. It wasn't the kind of looks you were jealous of – you just sat back and admired. I felt that first day I met her that I'd do *anything* for Mrs Leidner!

All the same, that night as I was being driven back to Tell Yarimjah (Dr Reilly made me stay for an early dinner) one or two things came back to my mind and made me rather uncomfortable. At the time I hadn't believed a word of all Sheila Reilly's outpouring. I'd taken it for sheer spite and malice.

But now I suddenly remembered the way Mrs Leidner had insisted on going for a stroll by herself that afternoon and wouldn't hear of me coming with her. I couldn't help wondering if perhaps, after all, she *had* been going to meet Mr Carey . . . And of course, it *was* a little odd, really, the way he and she spoke to each other so formally. Most of the others she called by their Christian names.

He never seemed to look at her, I remembered. That might be because he disliked her – or it might be just the opposite . . .

I gave myself a little shake. Here I was fancying and imagining all sorts of things – all because of a girl's spiteful outburst! It just showed how unkind and dangerous it was to go about saying that kind of thing.

Mrs Leidner *hadn't* been like that at all . . .

Of course, she *hadn't* liked Sheila Reilly. She'd really been – almost catty about her that day at lunch to Mr Emmott.

Funny, the way he'd looked at her. The sort of way that you couldn't possibly tell what he was thinking. You never could tell what Mr Emmott was thinking. He was so quiet. But very nice. A nice dependable person.

Now Mr Coleman was a foolish young man if there ever was one!

I'd got to that point in my meditations when we arrived. It was just on nine o'clock and the big door was closed and barred.

Ibrahim came running with his great key to let me in.

We all went to bed early at Tell Yarimjah. There weren't any lights showing in the living-room. There was a light in the drawing-office and one in Dr Leidner's office, but nearly all the other windows were dark. Everyone must have gone to bed even earlier than usual.

As I passed the drawing-office to go to my room I looked in. Mr Carey was in his shirt sleeves working over his big plan.

Terribly ill, he looked, I thought. So strained and worn. It gave me quite a pang. I don't know what there was about Mr Carey – it wasn't what he *said* because he hardly said anything – and that of the most ordinary nature, and it wasn't what he *did*, for that didn't amount to much either – and yet you just couldn't help noticing him, and everything about him seemed to matter more than it would about anyone else. He just *counted*, if you know what I mean.

He turned his head and saw me. He removed his pipe from his mouth and said: 'Well, nurse, back from Hassanieh?'

'Yes, Mr Carey. You're up working late. Everybody else seems to have gone to bed.'

'I thought I might as well get on with things,' he said.

'I was a bit behind-hand. And I shall be out on the dig all tomorrow. We're starting digging again.'

'Already?' I asked, shocked.

He looked at me rather queerly.

'It's the best thing, I think. I put it up to Leidner. He'll be in Hassanieh most of tomorrow seeing to things. But the rest of us will carry on here. You know it's not too easy all sitting round and looking at each other as things are.'

He was right there, of course. Especially in the nervy, jumpy state everyone was in.

'Well, of course you're right in a way,' I said. 'It takes one's mind off if one's got something to do.'

The funeral, I knew, was to be the day after tomorrow.

He had bent over his plan again. I don't know why, but my heart just ached for him. I felt certain that he wasn't going to get any sleep.

'If you'd like a sleeping draught, Mr Carey?' I said hesitatingly.

He shook his head with a smile.

'I'll carry on, nurse. Bad habit, sleeping draughts.'

'Well, good night, Mr Carey,' I said. 'If there's anything I can do –'

'Don't think so, thank you, nurse. Good night.'

'I'm terribly sorry,' I said, rather too impulsively I suppose.

'Sorry?' He looked surprised.

'For – for everybody. It's all so dreadful. But especially for you.'

'For me? Why for me?'

'Well, you're such an old friend of them both.'

'I'm an old friend of Leidner's. I wasn't a friend of hers particularly.'

He spoke as though he had actually disliked her. Really, I wished Miss Reilly could have heard him!

'Well, good night,' I said and hurried along to my room.

I fussed around a bit in my room before undressing. Washed out some handkerchiefs and a pair of wash-leather gloves and wrote up my diary. I just looked out of my door again before I really started to get ready for bed. The lights were still on in the drawing-office and in the south building.

I suppose Dr Leidner was still up and working in his office.

I wondered whether I ought to go and say goodnight to him. I hesitated about it – I didn't want to seem officious. He might be busy and not want to be disturbed. In the end, however, a sort of uneasiness drove me on. After all, it couldn't do any harm. I'd just say goodnight, ask if there was anything I could do and come away.

But Dr Leidner wasn't there. The office itself was lit up but there was no one in it except Miss Johnson. She had her head down on the table and was crying as though her heart would break.

It gave me quite a turn. She was such a quiet, self-controlled woman. It was pitiful to see her.

'Whatever is it, my dear?' I cried. I put my arm round her and patted her. 'Now, now, this won't do at all . . . You mustn't sit here crying all by yourself.'

She didn't answer and I felt the dreadful shuddering sobs that were racking her.

'Don't, my dear, don't,' I said. 'Take a hold on yourself. I'll go and make you a cup of nice hot tea.'

She raised her head and said: 'No, no, its all right, nurse. I'm being a fool.'

'What's upset you, my dear?' I asked.

She didn't answer at once, then she said: 'It's all too awful . . .'

'Now don't start thinking of it,' I told her. 'What's happened has happened and can't be mended. It's no use fretting.'

She sat up straight and began to pat her hair.

'I'm making rather a fool of myself,' she said in her gruff voice. 'I've been clearing up and tidying the office. Thought it was best to *do* something. And then – it all came over me suddenly –'

'Yes, yes,' I said hastily. 'I know. A nice strong cup of tea and a hot-water bottle in your bed is what you want,' I said.

And she had them too. I didn't listen to any protests.

'Thank you, nurse,' she said when I'd settled her in bed, and she was sipping her tea and the hot-water bottle was in. 'You're a nice kind sensible woman. It's not often I make such a fool of myself.'

'Oh, anybody's liable to do that at a time like this,' I said. 'What with one thing and another. The strain and the shock and the police here, there and everywhere. Why, I'm quite jumpy myself.'

She said slowly in rather a queer voice: 'What you said in there is true. What's happened has happened and can't be mended . . .'

She was silent for a minute or two and then said – rather oddly, I thought: 'She was never a nice woman!'

Well, I didn't argue the point. I'd always felt it was quite natural for Miss Johnson and Mrs Leidner not to hit it off.

I wondered if, perhaps, Miss Johnson had secretly had a feeling that she was pleased Mrs Leidner was dead, and had then been ashamed of herself for the thought.

I said: 'Now you go to sleep and don't worry about anything.'

I just picked up a few things and set the room to rights. Stockings over the back of the chair and coat and skirt on a hanger. There was a little ball of crumpled paper on the floor where it must have fallen out of a pocket.

I was just smoothing it out to see whether I could safely throw it away when she quite startled me.

'Give that to me!'

I did so – rather taken aback. She'd called out so peremptorily. She snatched it from me – fairly snatched it – and then held it in the candle flame till it was burnt to ashes.

As I say, I was startled – and I just stared at her.

I hadn't had time to see what the paper was – she'd snatched it so quick. But funnily enough, as it burned it curled over towards me and I just saw that there were words written in ink on the paper.

It wasn't till I was getting into bed that I realized why they'd looked sort of familiar to me.

It was the same handwriting as that of the anonymous letters.

Was *that* why Miss Johnson had given way to a fit of remorse? Had it been her all along who had written those anonymous letters?

CHAPTER 20
MISS JOHNSON, MRS MERCADO, MR REITER

I don't mind confessing that the idea came as a complete shock to me. I'd never thought of associating *Miss Johnson* with the letters. Mrs Mercado, perhaps. But Miss Johnson was a real lady, and so self-controlled and sensible.

But I reflected, remembering the conversation I had listened to that evening between M. Poirot and Dr Reilly, that that might be just *why*.

If it were Miss Johnson who had written the letters it explained a lot, mind you. I didn't think for a minute Miss Johnson had had anything to do with the murder. But I *did* see that her dislike of Mrs Leidner might have made her succumb to the temptation of, well – putting the wind up her – to put it vulgarly.

She might have hoped to frighten away Mrs Leidner from the dig.

But then Mrs Leidner had been murdered and Miss Johnson had felt terrible pangs of remorse – first for her cruel trick and also, perhaps, because she realized that those letters were acting as a very good shield to the actual murderer. No wonder she had broken down so utterly. She was, I was sure, a decent soul at heart. And it explained, too, why she had caught so eagerly at my consolation of 'what's happened's happened and can't be mended.'

And then her cryptic remark – her vindication of herself – 'she was never a nice woman!'

The question was, what was *I* to do about it?

I tossed and turned for a good while and in the end decided I'd let M. Poirot know about it at the first opportunity.

He came out next day, but I didn't get a chance of speaking to him what you might call privately.

We had just a minute alone together and before I could collect myself to know how to begin, he had come close to me and was whispering instructions in my ear.

'Me, I shall talk to Miss Johnson – and others, perhaps, in the living-room. You have the key of Mrs Leidner's room still?'

'Yes,' I said.

'*Très bien.* Go there, shut the door behind you and give a cry – not a scream – a cry. You understand what I mean – it is alarm – surprise that I want you to express – not mad terror. As for the excuse if you are heard – I leave that to you – the stepped toe or what you will.'

At that moment Miss Johnson came out into the courtyard and there was no time for more.

I understood well enough what M. Poirot was after. As soon as he and Miss Johnson had gone into the living-room I went across to Mrs Leidner's room and, unlocking the door, went in and pulled the door to behind me.

I can't say I didn't feel a bit of a fool standing up in an empty room and giving a yelp all for nothing at all. Besides, it wasn't so easy to know just how loud to do it. I gave a pretty loud 'Oh' and then tried it a bit higher and a bit lower.

Then I came out again and prepared my excuse of a stepped (stubbed I *suppose* he meant!) toe.

But it soon appeared that no excuse would be needed. Poirot and Miss Johnson were talking together earnestly and there had clearly been no interruption.

'Well,' I thought, 'that settles that. Either Miss Johnson imagined that cry she heard or else it was something quite different.'

I didn't like to go in and interrupt them. There was a deck-chair on the porch so I sat down there. Their voices floated out to me.

'The position is delicate, you understand,' Poirot was saying. 'Dr Leidner – obviously he adored his wife –'

'He worshipped her,' said Miss Johnson.

'He tells me, naturally, how fond all his staff was of her! As for them, what can they say? Naturally they say the same thing. It is politeness. It is decency. It *may* also be the truth! But also it may *not*! And I am convinced, mademoiselle, that the key to this enigma lies in a complete understanding of Mrs Leidner's character. If I could get the opinion – the honest opinion – of every member of the staff, I might, from the whole, build up a picture. Frankly, that is why I am here today. I knew Dr Leidner would be in Hassanieh. That makes it easy for me to have an interview with each of you here in turn, and beg your help.'

'That's all very well,' began Miss Johnson and stopped.

'Do not make me the British *clichés*,' Poirot begged. 'Do not say it is not the cricket or the football, that to speak anything but well of the dead is not done – that – *enfin* – there is loyalty! Loyalty it is a pestilential thing in crime. Again and again it obscures the truth.'

'I've no particular loyalty to Mrs Leidner,' said Miss Johnson dryly. There was indeed a sharp and acid tone in her voice. 'Dr Leidner's a different matter. And, after all, she was his wife.'

'Precisely – precisely. I understand that you would not wish to speak against your chief's wife. But this is not a question of a testimonial. It is a question of sudden and mysterious death. If I am to believe that it is a martyred angel who has been killed it does not add to the easiness of my task.'

'I certainly shouldn't call her an angel,' said Miss Johnson and the acid tone was even more in evidence.

'Tell me your opinion, frankly, of Mrs Leidner – as a woman.'

'H'm! To begin with, M. Poirot, I'll give you this warning. I'm prejudiced. I am – we all were – devoted to Dr Leidner. And, I suppose, when Mrs Leidner came along, we were jealous. We resented the demands she made on his time and attention. The devotion he showed her irritated us. I'm being truthful, M. Poirot, and it isn't very pleasant for me. I resented her presence here – yes, I did, though, of course, I tried never to show it. It made a difference to us, you see.'

'Us? You say us?'

'I mean Mr Carey and myself. We're the two old-timers, you see. And we didn't much care for the new order of things. I suppose that's natural, though perhaps it was rather petty of us. But it *did* make a difference.'

'What kind of a difference?'

'Oh! to everything. We used to have such a happy time. A good deal of fun, you know, and rather silly jokes, like people do who work together. Dr Leidner was quite light-hearted – just like a boy.'

'And when Mrs Leidner came she changed all that?'

'Well, I suppose it wasn't her *fault*. It wasn't so bad last year. And please believe, M. Poirot, that it wasn't anything she *did*. She's always been charming to me – quite charming. That's why I've felt ashamed sometimes. It wasn't her fault that little things she said and did seemed to rub me up the wrong way. Really, nobody could be nicer than she was.'

'But nevertheless things were changed this season? There was a different atmosphere.'

'Oh, entirely. Really. I don't know what it was. Everything seemed to go wrong – not with the work – I mean with us – our tempers and our nerves. All on edge. Almost the sort of feeling you get when there is a thunderstorm coming.'

'And you put that down to Mrs Leidner's influence?'

'Well, it was never like that before she came,' said Miss

Johnson dryly. 'Oh! I'm a cross-grained, complaining old dog. Conservative – liking things always the same. You really mustn't take any notice of me, M. Poirot.'

'How would you describe to me Mrs Leidner's character and temperament?'

Miss Johnson hesitated for a moment. Then she said slowly: 'Well, of course, she was temperamental. A lot of ups and downs. Nice to people one day and perhaps wouldn't speak to them the next. She was very kind, I think. And very thoughtful for others. All the same you could see she had been thoroughly spoilt all her life. She took Dr Leidner's waiting on her hand and foot as perfectly natural. And I don't think she ever really appreciated what a very remarkable – what a really great – man she had married. That used to annoy me sometimes. And of course she was terribly highly strung and nervous. The things she used to imagine and the states she used to get into! I was thankful when Dr Leidner brought Nurse Leatheran here. It was too much for him having to cope both with his work and with his wife's fears.'

'What is your own opinion of these anonymous letters she received?'

I had to do it. I leaned forward in my chair till I could just catch sight of Miss Johnson's profile turned to Poirot in answer to his question.

She was looking perfectly cool and collected.

'I think someone in America had a spite against her and was trying to frighten or annoy her.'

'*Pas plus sérieux que ça?*'

'That's my opinion. She was a very handsome woman, you know, and might easily have had enemies. I think, those letters were written by some spiteful woman. Mrs Leidner being of a nervous temperament took them seriously.'

'She certainly did that,' said Poirot. 'But remember – the last of them arrived by hand.'

'Well, I suppose that *could* have been managed if anyone had given their minds to it. Women will take a lot of trouble to gratify their spite, M. Poirot.'

They will indeed, I thought to myself!

'Perhaps you are right, mademoiselle. As you say, Mrs Leidner was handsome. By the way, you know Miss Reilly, the doctor's daughter?'

'Sheila Reilly? Yes, of course.'

Poirot adopted a very confidential, gossipy tone.

'I have heard a rumour (naturally I do not like to ask the doctor) that there was a *tendresse* between her and one of the members of Dr Leidner's staff. Is that so, do you know?'

Miss Johnson appeared rather amused.

'Oh, young Coleman and David Emmott were both inclined to dance attendance. I believe there was some rivalry as to who was to be her partner in some event at the club. Both the boys went in on Saturday evenings to the club as a general rule. But I don't know that there was anything in it on her side. She's the only young creature in the place, you know, and so she's by way of being the belle of it. She's got the Air Force dancing attendance on her as well.'

'So you think there is nothing in it?'

'Well – I don't know.' Miss Johnson became thoughtful. 'It is true that she comes out this way fairly often. Up to the dig and all that. In fact, Mrs Leidner was chaffing David Emmott about it the other day – saying the girl was running after him. Which was rather a catty thing to say, I thought, and I don't think he liked it . . . Yes, she was here a good deal. I saw her riding towards the dig on that awful afternoon.' She nodded her head towards the open window. 'But neither David Emmott nor Coleman were on duty that afternoon. Richard Carey was in charge. Yes, perhaps she *is* attracted to one of the boys – but she's such a modern unsentimental young woman that one doesn't know quite how seriously to take her. I'm sure I don't know which of them it is. Bill's a nice boy, and not nearly such a fool as he pretends to be. David Emmott is a dear – and there's a lot to him. He is the deep, quiet kind.'

Then she looked quizzically at Poirot and said: 'But has this any bearing on the crime, M. Poirot?'

M. Poirot threw up his hands in a very French fashion.

'You make me blush, mademoiselle,' he said. 'You expose me as a mere gossip. But what will you, I am interested always in the love affairs of young people.'

'Yes,' said Miss Johnson with a little sigh. 'It's nice when the course of true love runs smooth.'

Poirot gave an answering sigh. I wondered if Miss Johnson was thinking of some love affair of her own when she was a girl. And I

118

wondered if M. Poirot had a wife, and if he went on in the way you always hear foreigners do, with mistresses and things like that. He looked so comic I couldn't imagine it.

'Sheila Reilly has a lot of character,' said Miss Johnson. 'She's young and she's crude, but she's the right sort.'

'I take your word for it, mademoiselle,' said Poirot.

He got up and said, 'Are there any other members of the staff in the house?'

'Marie Mercado is somewhere about. All the men are up on the dig today. I think they wanted to get out of the house. I don't blame them. If you'd like to go up to the dig –'

She came out on the verandah and said, smiling to me: 'Nurse Leatheran won't mind taking you, I dare say.'

'Oh, certainly, Miss Johnson,' I said.

'And you'll come back to lunch, won't you, M. Poirot?'

'Enchanted, mademoiselle.'

Miss Johnson went back into the living-room where she was engaged in cataloguing.

'Mrs Mercado's on the roof,' I said. 'Do you want to see her first?'

'It would be as well, I think. Let us go up.'

As we went up the stairs I said: 'I did what you told me. Did you hear anything?'

'Not a sound.'

'That will be a weight off Miss Johnson's mind at any rate,' I said. 'She's been worrying that she might have done something about it.'

Mrs Mercado was sitting on the parapet, her head bent down, and she was so deep in thought that she never heard us till Poirot halted opposite her and bade her good morning.

Then she looked up with a start.

She looked ill this morning, I thought, her small face pinched and wizened and great dark circles under her eyes.

'*Encore moi*,' said Poirot. 'I come today with a special object.'

And he went on much in the same way as he had done to Miss Johnson, explaining how necessary it was that he should get a true picture of Mrs Leidner.

Mrs Mercado, however, wasn't as honest as Miss Johnson had been. She burst into fulsome praise which, I was pretty sure, was quite far removed from her real feelings.

119

'Dear, *dear* Louise! It's so hard to explain her to someone who didn't know her. She was such an *exotic* creature. Quite different from anyone else. You felt that, I'm sure, nurse? A martyr to nerves, of course, and full of fancies, but one put up with things in her one wouldn't from anyone else. And she was so *sweet* to us all, wasn't she, nurse? And so *humble* about herself – I mean she didn't know anything about archaeology, and she was so eager to learn. Always asking my husband about the chemical processes for treating the metal objects and helping Miss Johnson to mend pottery. Oh, we were all *devoted* to her.'

'Then it is not true, madame, what I have heard, that there was a certain tenseness – an uncomfortable atmosphere – here?'

Mrs Mercado opened her opaque black eyes very wide.

'Oh! who *can* have been telling you that? Nurse? Dr Leidner? I'm sure *he* would never notice anything, poor man.'

And she shot a thoroughly unfriendly glance at me.

Poirot smiled easily.

'I have my spies, madame,' he declared gaily. And just for a minute I saw her eyelids quiver and blink.

'Don't you think,' asked Mrs Mercado with an air of great sweetness, 'that after an event of this kind, everyone always pretends a lot of things that never were? You know – tension, atmosphere, a "feeling that something was going to happen"? I think people just *make up* these things afterwards.'

'There is a lot in what you say, madame,' said Poirot.

'And it really *wasn't* true! We were a thoroughly happy family here.'

'That woman is one of the most utter liars I've ever known,' I said indignantly, when M. Poirot and I were clear of the house and walking along the path to the dig. 'I'm sure she simply hated Mrs Leidner really!'

'She is hardly the type to whom one would go for the truth,' Poirot agreed.

'Waste of time talking to her,' I snapped.

'Hardly that – hardly that. If a person tells you lies with her lips she is sometimes telling you truth with her eyes. What is she afraid of, little Madame Mercado? I saw fear in her eyes. Yes – decidedly she is afraid of something. It is very interesting.'

'I've got something to tell you, M. Poirot,' I said.

Then I told him all about my return the night before and my

strong belief that Miss Johnson was the writer of the anonymous letters.

'So *she's* a liar too!' I said. 'The cool way she answered you this morning about these same letters!'

'Yes,' said Poirot. 'It was interesting, that. *For she let out the fact she knew all about those letters.* So far they have not been spoken of in the presence of the staff. Of course, it is quite possible that Dr Leidner told her about them yesterday. They are old friends, he and she. But if he did not – well – then it is curious and interesting, is it not?'

My respect for him went up. It was clever the way he had tricked her into mentioning the letters.

'Are you going to tackle her about them?' I asked.

M. Poirot seemed quite shocked by the idea.

'No, no, indeed. Always it is unwise to parade one's knowledge. Until the last minute I keep everything here,' he tapped his forehead. 'At the right moment – I make the spring – like the panther – and, *mon Dieu!* the consternation!'

I couldn't help laughing to myself at little M. Poirot in the role of a panther.

We had just reached the dig. The first person we saw was Mr Reiter, who was busy photographing some walling.

It's my opinion that the men who were digging just hacked out walls wherever they wanted them. That's what it looked like anyway. Mr Carey explained to me that you could feel the difference at once with a pick, and he tried to show me – but I never saw. When the man said '*Libn*' – mud-brick – it was just ordinary dirt and mud as far as I could see.

Mr Reiter finished his photographs and handed over the camera and the plate to his boy and told him to take them back to the house.

Poirot asked him one or two questions about exposures and film packs and so on which he answered very readily. He seemed pleased to be asked about his work.

He was just tendering his excuses for leaving us when Poirot plunged once more into his set speech. As a matter of fact it wasn't quite a set speech because he varied it a little each time to suit the person he was talking to. But I'm not going to write it all down every time. With sensible people like Miss Johnson he went straight to the point, and with some of the others he had to beat about the bush a bit more. But it came to the same in the end.

'Yes, yes, I see what you mean,' said Mr Reiter. 'But indeed, I do not see that I can be much help to you. I am new here this season and I did not speak much with Mrs Leidner. I regret, but indeed I can tell you nothing.'

There was something a little stiff and foreign in the way he spoke, though, of course, he hadn't got any accent – except an American one, I mean.

'You can at least tell me whether you liked or disliked her?' said Poirot with a smile.

Mr Reiter got quite red and stammered: 'She was a charming person – most charming. And intellectual. She had a very fine brain – yes.'

'*Bien!* You liked her. And she liked you?'

Mr Reiter got redder still.

'Oh, I – I don't know that she noticed me much. And I was unfortunate once or twice. I was always unlucky when I tried to do anything for her. I'm afraid I annoyed her by my clumsiness. It was quite unintentional . . . I would have done *any*thing –'

Poirot took pity on his flounderings.

'Perfectly – perfectly. Let us pass to another matter. Was it a happy atmosphere in the house?'

'Please?'

'Were you all happy together? Did you laugh and talk?'

'No – no, not exactly that. There was a little – stiffness.'

He paused, struggling with himself, and then said: 'You see, I am not very good in company. I am clumsy. I am shy. Dr Leidner always he has been most kind to me. But – it is stupid – I cannot overcome my shyness. I say always the wrong thing. I upset water jugs. I am unlucky.'

He really looked like a large awkward child.

'We all do these things when we are young,' said Poirot, smiling. 'The poise, the *savoir faire*, it comes later.'

Then with a word of farewell we walked on.

He said: 'That, *ma soeur*, is either an extremely simple young man or a very remarkable actor.'

I didn't answer. I was caught up once more by the fantastic notion that one of these people was a dangerous and cold-blooded murderer. Somehow, on this beautiful still sunny morning it seemed impossible.

CHAPTER 21

MR MERCADO, RICHARD CAREY

'They work in two separate places, I see,' said Poirot, halting.

Mr Reiter had been doing his photography on an outlying portion of the main excavation. A little distance away from us a second swarm of men were coming and going with baskets.

'That's what they call the deep cut,' I explained. 'They don't find much there, nothing but rubbishy broken pottery, but Dr Leidner always says it's very interesting, so I suppose it must be.'

'Let us go there.'

We walked together slowly, for the sun was hot.

Mr Mercado was in command. We saw him below us talking to the foreman, an old man like a tortoise who wore a tweed coat over his long striped cotton gown.

It was a little difficult to get down to them as there was only a narrow path or stair and basket-boys were going up and down it constantly, and they always seemed to be as blind as bats and never to think of getting out of the way.

As I followed Poirot down he said suddenly over his shoulder: 'Is Mr Mercado right-handed or left-handed?'

Now that was an extraordinary question if you like!

I thought a minute, then: 'Right-handed,' I said decisively.

Poirot didn't condescend to explain. He just went on and I followed him.

Mr Mercado seemed rather pleased to see us.

His long melancholy face lit up.

M. Poirot pretended to an interest in archaeology that I'm sure he couldn't have really felt, but Mr Mercado responded at once.

He explained that they had already cut down through twelve levels of house occupation.

'We are now definitely in the fourth millennium,' he said with enthusiasm.

I always thought a millennium was in the future – the time when everything comes right.

Mr Mercado pointed out belts of ashes (how his hand did shake! I wondered if he might possibly have malaria) and he explained how the pottery changed in character, and about burials – and how they had had one level almost entirely composed of infant burials – poor little things – and about flexed position and orientation, which seemed to mean the way the bones were lying.

And then suddenly, just as he was stooping down to pick up a kind of flint knife that was lying with some pots in a corner, he leapt into the air with a wild yell.

He spun round to find me and Poirot staring at him in astonishment.

He clapped his hand to his left arm.

'Something stung me – like a red-hot needle.'

Immediately Poirot was galvanized into energy.

'Quick, *mon cher*, let us see. Nurse Leatheran!'

I came forward.

He seized Mr Mercado's arm and deftly rolled back the sleeve of his khaki shirt to the shoulder.

'There,' said Mr Mercado pointing.

About three inches below the shoulder there was a minute prick from which the blood was oozing.

'Curious,' said Poirot. He peered into the rolled-up sleeve. 'I can see nothing. It was an ant, perhaps?'

'Better put on a little iodine,' I said.

I always carry an iodine pencil with me, and I whipped it out and applied it. But I was a little absent-minded as I did so, for my attention had been caught by something quite different. Mr Mercado's arm, all the way up the forearm to the elbow, was marked all over by tiny punctures. I knew well enough what *they were – the marks of a hypodermic needle.*

Mr Mercado rolled down his sleeve again and recommenced his explanations. Mr Poirot listened, but didn't try to bring the conversation round to the Leidners. In fact, he didn't ask Mr Mercado anything at all.

Presently we said goodbye to Mr Mercado and climbed up the path again.

'It was neat that, did you not think so?' my companion asked.

'Neat?' I asked.

M. Poirot took something from behind the lapel of his coat and surveyed it affectionately. To my surprise I saw that it was a long sharp darning needle with a blob of sealing wax making it into a pin.

'M. Poirot,' I cried, 'did you do that?'

'I was the stinging insect – yes. And very neatly I did it, too, do you not think so? You did not see me.'

That was true enough. *I* never saw him do it. And I'm sure Mr Mercado hadn't suspected. He must have been quick as lightning.

'But, M. Poirot, why?' I asked.

He answered me by another question.

'Did you notice anything, sister?' he asked.

I nodded my head slowly.

'Hypodermic marks,' I said.

'So now we know something about Mr Mercado,' said Poirot. 'I suspected – but I did not *know*. It is always necessary to *know*.'

'And you don't care how you set about it!' I thought, but didn't say.

Poirot suddenly clapped his hand to his pocket.

'Alas, I have dropped my handkerchief down there. I concealed the pin in it.'

'I'll get it for you,' I said and hurried back.

I'd got the feeling, you see, by this time, that M. Poirot and I were the doctor and nurse in charge of a case. At least, it was more like an operation and he was the surgeon. Perhaps I oughtn't to say so, but in a queer way I was beginning to enjoy myself.

I remember just after I'd finished my training, I went to a case in a private house and the need for an immediate operation arose, and the patient's husband was cranky about nursing homes. He just wouldn't hear of his wife being taken to one. Said it had to be done in the house.

Well, of course it was just splendid for me! Nobody else to have a look in! I was in charge of everything. Of course, I was terribly nervous – I thought of everything conceivable that doctor could want, but even then I was afraid I might have forgotten something. You never know with doctors. They ask for absolutely anything sometimes! But everything went splendidly! I had each thing ready as he asked for it, and he actually told me I'd done first-rate after it was over – and that's a thing most doctors wouldn't bother to do! The G.P. was very nice too. And I ran the whole thing myself!

The patient recovered, too, so everybody was happy.

Well, I felt rather the same now. In a way M. Poirot reminded me of that surgeon. *He* was a little man, too. Ugly little man with a face like a monkey, but a wonderful surgeon. He knew instinctively just where to go. I've seen a lot of surgeons and I know what a lot of difference there is.

Gradually I'd been growing a kind of confidence in M. Poirot. I felt that he, too, knew exactly what he was doing. And I was getting to feel that it was my job to help him – as you might say – to have the forceps and the swabs and all handy just when he wanted them. That's why it seemed just as natural for me to run off and look for his handkerchief as it would have been to pick up a towel that a doctor had thrown on the floor.

When I'd found it and got back I couldn't see him at first. But at last I caught sight of him. He was sitting a little way from the mound talking to Mr Carey. Mr Carey's boy was standing near with that great big rod thing with metres marked on it, but just at that moment he said something to the boy and the boy took it away. It seemed he had finished with it for the time being.

I'd like to get this next bit quite clear. You see, I wasn't quite sure what M. Poirot did or didn't want me to do. He might, I mean, have sent me back for that handkerchief *on purpose*. To get me out of the way.

It was just like an operation over again. You've got to be careful to hand the doctor just what he wants and not what he *doesn't* want. I mean, suppose you gave him the artery forceps at the wrong moment, and were late with them at the right moment! Thank goodness I know my work in the theatre well enough. I'm not likely to make mistakes there. But in this business I was really the rawest of raw little probationers. And so I had to be particularly careful not to make any silly mistakes.

Of course, I didn't for one moment imagine that M. Poirot didn't want me to hear what he and Mr Carey were saying. But he might have thought he'd get Mr Carey to talk better if I wasn't there.

Now I don't want anybody to get it into their heads that I'm the kind of woman who goes about eavesdropping on private conversations. I wouldn't do such a thing. Not for a moment. Not however much I wanted to.

And what I mean is if it *had* been a private conversation I wouldn't for a moment have done what, as a matter of fact, I actually did do.

As I looked at it I was in a privileged position. After all, you hear many a thing when a patient's coming round after an anaesthetic. The patient wouldn't want you to hear it – and usually has no idea you *have* heard it – but the fact remains you *do* hear it. I just took it that Mr Carey was the patient. He'd be none the worse for what he didn't know about. And if you think that I was just curious, well, I'll admit that I *was* curious. I didn't want to miss anything I could help.

All this is just leading up to the fact that I turned aside and went by a roundabout way up behind the big dump until I was a foot from where they were, but concealed from them by the corner of the dump. And if anyone says it was dishonourable I just beg to disagree. *Nothing* ought to be hidden from the nurse in charge of the case, though, of course, it's for the doctor to say what shall be *done*.

I don't know, of course, what M. Poirot's line of approach had been, but by the time I'd got there he was aiming straight for the bull's eye, so to speak.

'Nobody appreciates Dr Leidner's devotion to his wife more than I do,' he was saying. 'But it is often the case that one learns more about a person from their enemies than from their friends.'

'You suggest that their faults are more important than their virtues?' said Mr Carey. His tone was dry and ironic.

'Undoubtedly – when it comes to murder. It seems odd that as far as I know nobody has yet been murdered for having too perfect a character! And yet perfection is undoubtedly an irritating thing.'

'I'm afraid I'm hardly the right person to help you,' said Mr Carey. 'To be perfectly honest, Mrs Leidner and I didn't hit it off particularly well. I don't mean that we were in any sense of the word enemies, but we were not exactly friends. Mrs Leidner was, perhaps, a shade jealous of my old friendship with her husband. I, for my part, although I admired her very much and thought she was an extremely attractive woman, was just a shade resentful of her influence over Leidner. As a result we were quite polite to each other, but not intimate.'

'Admirably explained,' said Poirot.

I could just see their heads, and I saw Mr Carey's turn sharply as though something in M. Poirot's detached tone struck him disagreeably.

M. Poirot went on: 'Was not Dr Leidner distressed that you and his wife did not get on together better?'

Carey hesitated a minute before saying: 'Really – I'm not sure. He never said anything. I always hoped he didn't notice it. He was very wrapped up in his work, you know.'

'So the truth, according to you, is that you did not really like Mrs Leidner?'

Carey shrugged his shoulders.

'I should probably have liked her very much if she hadn't been Leidner's wife.'

He laughed as though amused by his own statement.

Poirot was arranging a little heap of broken potsherds. He said in a dreamy, far-away voice: 'I talked to Miss Johnson this morning. She admitted that she was prejudiced against Mrs Leidner and did not like her very much, although she hastened to add that Mrs Leidner had always been charming to her.'

'All quite true, I should say,' said Carey.

'So I believed. Then I had a conversation with Mrs Mercado. She told me at great length how devoted she had been to Mrs Leidner and how much she had admired her.'

Carey made no answer to this, and after waiting a minute or two Poirot went on: 'That – I did not believe! Then I come to you and that which you tell me – well, again – *I* do *not believe* . . .'

Carey stiffened. I could hear the anger – repressed anger – in his voice.

'I really cannot help your beliefs – or your disbeliefs, M. Poirot. You've heard the truth and you can take it or leave it as far as I am concerned.'

Poirot did not grow angry. Instead he sounded particularly meek and depressed.

'Is it my fault what I do – or do not believe? I have a sensitive ear, you know. And then – there are always plenty of stories going about – rumours floating in the air. One listens – and perhaps – one learns something! Yes, there *are* stories . . .'

Carey sprang to his feet. I could see clearly a little pulse that beat in his temple. He looked simply splendid! So lean and so brown – and that wonderful jaw, hard and square. I don't wonder women fell for that man.

'What stories?' he asked savagely.

Poirot looked sideways at him.

'Perhaps you can guess. The usual sort of story – about you and Mrs Leidner.'

'What foul minds people have!'

'*N'est-ce pas?* They are like dogs. However deep you bury an unpleasantness a dog will always root it up again.'

'And you believe these stories?'

'I am willing to be convinced – of the truth,' said Poirot gravely.

'I doubt if you'd know the truth if you heard it,' Carey laughed rudely.

'Try me and see,' said Poirot, watching him.

'I will then! You shall have the truth! I hated Louise Leidner – there's the truth for you! I hated her like hell!'

CHAPTER 22

DAVID EMMOTT, FATHER LAVIGNY AND A DISCOVERY

Turning abruptly away, Carey strode off with long, angry strides.

Poirot sat looking after him and presently he murmured: 'Yes – I see . . .'

Without turning his head he said in a slightly louder voice: 'Do not come round the corner for a minute, nurse. In case he turns his head. Now it is all right. You have my handkerchief? Many thanks. You are most amiable.'

He didn't say anything at all about my having been listening – and how he knew I *was* listening I can't think. He'd never once looked in that direction. I was rather relieved he didn't say anything. I mean, I felt all right with *myself* about it, but it might have been a little awkward explaining to him. So it was a good thing he didn't seem to want explanations.

'Do you think he did hate her, M. Poirot?' I asked.

Nodding his head slowly with a curious expression on his face, Poirot answered.

'Yes – I think he did.'

Then he got up briskly and began to walk to where the men

129

were working on the top of the mound. I followed him. We couldn't see anyone but Arabs at first, but we finally found Mr Emmott lying face downwards blowing dust off a skeleton that had just been uncovered.

He gave his pleasant, grave smile when he saw us.

'Have you come to see round?' he asked. 'I'll be free in a minute.'

He sat up, took his knife and began daintily cutting the earth away from round the bones, stopping every now and then to use either a bellows or his own breath. A very insanitary proceeding the latter, I thought.

'You'll get all sorts of nasty germs in your mouth, Mr Emmott,' I protested.

'Nasty germs are my daily diet, nurse,' he said gravely. 'Germs can't do anything to an archaeologist – they just get naturally discouraged trying.'

He scraped a little more away round the thigh bone. Then he spoke to the foreman at his side, directing him exactly what he wanted done.

'There,' he said, rising to his feet. 'That's ready for Reiter to photograph after lunch. Rather nice stuff she had in with her.'

He showed us a little verdigris copper bowl and some pins. And a lot of gold and blue things that had been her necklace of beads.

The bones and all the objects were brushed and cleaned with a knife and kept in position ready to be photographed.

'Who is she?' asked Poirot.

'First millennium. A lady of some consequence perhaps. Skull looks rather odd – I must get Mercado to look at it. It suggests death by foul play.'

'A Mrs Leidner of two thousand odd years ago?' said Poirot.

'Perhaps,' said Mr Emmott.

Bill Coleman was doing something with a pick to a wall face.

David Emmott called something to him which I didn't catch and then started showing M. Poirot round.

When the short explanatory tour was over, Emmott looked at his watch.

'We knock off in ten minutes,' he said. 'Shall we walk back to the house?'

'That will suit me excellently,' said Poirot.

We walked slowly along the well-worn path.

'I expect you are all glad to get back to work again,' said Poirot.

Emmott replied gravely: 'Yes, it's much the best thing. It's not been any too easy loafing about the house and making conversation.'

'Knowing all the time *that one of you was a murderer*.'

Emmott did not answer. He made no gesture of dissent. I knew now that he had had a suspicion of the truth from the very first when he had questioned the house-boys.

After a few minutes he asked quietly: 'Are you getting anywhere, M. Poirot?'

Poirot said gravely: 'Will you help me to get somewhere?'

'Why, naturally.'

Watching him closely, Poirot said: 'The hub of the case is Mrs Leidner. I want to know about Mrs Leidner.'

David Emmott said slowly: 'What do you mean by know about her?'

'I do not mean where she came from and what her maiden name was. I do not mean the shape of her face and the colour of her eyes. I mean her – herself.'

'You think that counts in the case?'

'I am quite sure of it.'

Emmott was silent for a moment or two, then he said: 'Maybe you're right.'

'And that is where you can help me. You can tell me what sort of a woman she was.'

'Can I? I've often wondered about it myself.'

'Didn't you make up your mind on the subject?'

'I think I did in the end.'

'*Eh bien?*'

But Mr Emmott was silent for some minutes, then he said: 'What did nurse think of her? Women are said to sum up other women quickly enough, and a nurse has a wide experience of types.'

Poirot didn't give me any chance of speaking even if I had wanted to. He said quickly: 'What I want to know is what a *man* thought of her?'

Emmott smiled a little.

'I expect they'd all be much the same.' He paused and said,

'She wasn't young, but I think she was about the most beautiful woman I've ever come across.'

'That's hardly an answer, Mr Emmott.'

'It's not so far off one, M. Poirot.'

He was silent a minute or two and then he went on: 'There used to be a fairy story I read when I was a kid. A Northern fairy tale about the Snow Queen and Little Kay. I guess Mrs Leidner was rather like that – always taking Little Kay for a ride.'

'Ah yes, a tale of Hans Andersen, is it not? And there was a girl in it. Little Gerda, was that her name?'

'Maybe. I don't remember much of it.'

'Can't you go a little further, Mr Emmott?'

David Emmott shook his head.

'I don't even know if I've summed her up correctly. She wasn't easy to read. She'd do a devilish thing one day, and a really fine one the next. But I think you're about right when you say that she's the hub of the case. That's what she always wanted to be – *at the centre of things*. And she liked to get *at* other people – I mean, she wasn't just satisfied with being passed the toast and the peanut butter, she wanted you to turn your mind and soul inside out for her to look at it.'

'And if one did not give her that satisfaction?' asked Poirot.

'Then she could turn ugly!'

I saw his lips close resolutely and his jaw set.

'I suppose, Mr Emmott, you would not care to express a plain unofficial opinion as to who murdered her?'

'I don't know,' said Emmott. 'I really haven't the slightest idea. I rather think that, if I'd been Carl – Carl Reiter, I mean – I would have had a shot at murdering her. She was a pretty fair devil to him. But, of course, he asks for it by being so darned sensitive. Just invites you to give him a kick in the pants.'

'And did Mrs Leidner give him – a kick in the pants?' inquired Poirot.

Emmott gave a sudden grin.

'No. Pretty little jabs with an embroidery needle – that was her method. He *was* irritating, of course. Just like some blubbering, poor-spirited kid. But a needle's a painful weapon.'

I stole a glance at Poirot and thought I detected a slight quiver of his lips.

'But you don't really believe that Carl Reiter killed her?' he asked.

'No. I don't believe you'd kill a woman because she persistently made you look a fool at every meal.'

Poirot shook his head thoughtfully.

Of course, Mr Emmott made Mrs Leidner sound quite inhuman. There was something to be said on the other side too.

There had been something terribly irritating about Mr Reiter's attitude. He jumped when she spoke to him, and did idiotic things like passing her the marmalade again and again when he knew she never ate it. I'd have felt inclined to snap at him a bit myself.

Men don't understand how their mannerisms can get on women's nerves so that you feel you just have to snap.

I thought I'd just mention that to Mr Poirot some time.

We had arrived back now and Mr Emmott offered Poirot a wash and took him into his room.

I hurried across the courtyard to mine.

I came out again about the same time they did and we were all making for the dining-room when Father Lavigny appeared in the doorway of his room and invited Poirot in.

Mr Emmott came on round and he and I went into the dining-room together. Miss Johnson and Mrs Mercado were there already, and after a few minutes Mr Mercado, Mr Reiter and Bill Coleman joined us.

We were just sitting down and Mercado had told the Arab boy to tell Father Lavigny lunch was ready when we were all startled by a faint, muffled cry.

I suppose our nerves weren't very good yet, for we all jumped, and Miss Johnson got quite pale and said: '*What was that?* What's happened?'

Mrs Mercado stared at her and said: 'My dear, what *is* the matter with you? It's some noise outside in the fields.'

But at that minute Poirot and Father Lavigny came in.

'We thought someone was hurt,' Miss Johnson said.

'A thousand pardons, mademoiselle,' cried Poirot. 'The fault is mine. Father Lavigny, he explains to me some tablets, and I take one to the window to see better – and, *ma foi*, not looking where I was going, I steb the toe, and the pain is sharp for the moment and I cry out.'

'We thought it was another murder,' said Mrs Mercado, laughing.

'Marie!' said her husband.

His tone was reproachful and she flushed and bit her lip.

Miss Johnson hastily turned the conversation to the dig and what objects of interest had turned up that morning. Conversation all through lunch was sternly archaeological.

I think we all felt it was the safest thing.

After we had had coffee we adjourned to the living-room. Then the men, with the exception of Father Lavigny, went off to the dig again.

Father Lavigny took Poirot through into the antika-room and I went with them. I was getting to know the things pretty well by now and I felt a thrill of pride – almost as though it were my own property – when Father Lavigny took down the gold cup and I heard Poirot's exclamation of admiration and pleasure.

'How beautiful! What a work of art!'

Father Lavigny agreed eagerly and began to point out its beauties with real enthusiasm and knowledge.

'No wax on it today,' I said.

'Wax?' Poirot stared at me.

'Wax?' So did Father Lavigny.

I explained my remark.

'Ah, *je comprends*,' said Father Lavigny. 'Yes, yes, candle grease.'

That led direct to the subject of the midnight visitor. Forgetting my presence they both dropped into French, and I left them together and went back into the living-room.

Mrs Mercado was darning her husband's socks and Miss Johnson was reading a book. Rather an unusual thing for her. She usually seemed to have something to work at.

After a while Father Lavigny and Poirot came out, and the former excused himself on the score of work. Poirot sat down with us.

'A most interesting man,' he said, and asked how much work there had been for Father Lavigny to do so far.

Miss Johnson explained that tablets had been scarce and that there had been very few inscribed bricks or cylinder seals. Father Lavigny, however, had done his share of work on the dig and was picking up colloquial Arabic very fast.

That led the talk to cylinder seals, and presently Miss Johnson fetched from a cupboard a sheet of impressions made by rolling them out on plasticine.

I realized as we bent over them, admiring the spirited designs, that these must be what she had been working at on that fatal afternoon.

As we talked I noticed that Poirot was rolling and kneading a little ball of plasticine between his fingers.

'You use a lot of plasticine, mademoiselle?' he asked.

'A fair amount. We seem to have got through a lot already this year – though I can't imagine how. But half our supply seems to have gone.'

'Where is it kept, mademoiselle?'

'Here – in this cupboard.'

As she replaced the sheet of impressions she showed him the shelf with rolls of plasticine, Durofix, photographic paste and other stationery supplies.

Poirot stooped down.

'And this – what is this, mademoiselle?'

He had slipped his hand right to the back and had brought out a curious crumpled object.

As he straightened it out we could see that it was a kind of mask, with eyes and mouth crudely painted on it in Indian ink and the whole thing roughly smeared with plasticine.

'How perfectly extraordinary!' cried Miss Johnson. 'I've never seen it before. How did it get there? And what is it?'

'As to how it got there, well, one hiding-place is as good as another, and I presume that this cupboard would not have been turned out till the end of the season. As to what it *is* – that, too, I think, is not difficult to say. *We have here the face that Mrs Leidner described.* The ghostly face seen in the semi-dusk outside her window – without body attached.'

Mrs Mercado gave a little shriek.

Miss Johnson was white to the lips. She murmured: 'Then it was *not* fancy. It was a trick – a wicked trick! But who played it?'

'Yes,' cried Mrs Mercado. 'Who could have done such a wicked, wicked thing?'

Poirot did not attempt a reply. His face was very grim as he went into the next room, returned with an empty cardboard box in his hand and put the crumpled mask into it.

'The police must see this,' he explained.

'It's horrible,' said Miss Johnson in a low voice. 'Horrible!'

'Do you think everything's hidden here somewhere?' cried Mrs Mercado shrilly. 'Do you think perhaps the weapon – the club she was killed with – all covered with blood still, perhaps . . . Oh! I'm frightened – I'm frightened . . .'

Miss Johnson gripped her by the shoulder.

'Be quiet,' she said fiercely. 'Here's Dr Leidner. We mustn't upset him.'

Indeed, at that very moment the car had driven into the courtyard. Dr Leidner got out of it and came straight across and in at the living-room door. His face was set in lines of fatigue and he looked twice the age he had three days ago.

He said in a quiet voice: 'The funeral will be at eleven o'clock tomorrow. Major Deane will read the service.'

Mrs Mercado faltered something, then slipped out of the room.

Dr Leidner said to Miss Johnson: 'You'll come, Anne?'

And she answered: 'Of course, my dear, we'll all come. Naturally.'

She didn't say anything else, but her face must have expressed what her tongue was powerless to do, for his face lightened up with affection and a momentary ease.

'Dear Anne,' he said. 'You are such a wonderful comfort and help to me. My dear old friend.'

He laid his hand on her arm and I saw the red colour creep up in her face as she muttered, gruff as ever: 'That's all right.'

But I just caught a glimpse of her expression and knew that, for one short moment, Anne Johnson was a perfectly happy woman.

And another idea flashed across my mind. Perhaps soon, in the natural course of things, turning to his old friend for sympathy, a new and happy state of things might come about.

Not that I'm really a matchmaker, and of course it was indecent to think of such a thing before the funeral even. But after all, it *would* be a happy solution. He was very fond of her, and there was no doubt she was absolutely devoted to him and would be perfectly happy devoting the rest of her life to him. That is, if she could bear to hear Louise's perfections sung all the time. But women can put up with a lot when they've got what they want.

Dr Leidner then greeted Poirot, asking him if he had made any progress.

Miss Johnson was standing behind Dr Leidner and she looked hard at the box in Poirot's hand and shook her head, and I realized that she was pleading with Poirot not to tell him about the mask. She felt, I was sure, that he had enough to bear for one day.

Poirot fell in with her wish.

'These things march slowly, monsieur,' he said.

Then, after a few desultory words, he took his leave.

I accompanied him out to his car.

There were half a dozen things I wanted to ask him, but somehow, when he turned and looked at me, I didn't ask anything after all. I'd as soon have asked a surgeon if he thought he'd made a good job of an operation. I just stood meekly waiting for instructions.

Rather to my surprise he said: 'Take care of yourself, my child.'

And then he added: 'I wonder if it is well for you to remain here?'

'I must speak to Dr Leidner about leaving,' I said. 'But I thought I'd wait until after the funeral.'

He nodded in approval.

'In the meantime,' he said, 'do not try to find out too much. You understand, I do not want you to be clever!' And he added with a smile, 'It is for you to hold the swabs and for me to do the operation.'

Wasn't it funny, his actually saying that?

Then he said quite irrelevantly: 'An interesting man, that Father Lavigny.'

'A monk being an archaeologist seems odd to me,' I said.

'Ah, yes, you are a Protestant. Me, I am a good Catholic. I know something of priests and monks.'

He frowned, seemed to hesitate, then said: 'Remember, he is quite clever enough to turn you inside out if he likes.'

If he was warning me against gossiping I felt that I didn't need any warning!

It annoyed me, and though I didn't like to ask him any of the things I really wanted to know, I didn't see why I shouldn't at any rate say one thing.

'You'll excuse me, M. Poirot,' I said. 'But it's "stubbed your toe", not *stepped* or *stebbed*.'

'Ah! Thank you, *ma soeur*.'

'Don't mention it. But it's just as well to get a phrase right.'

'I will remember,' he said – quite meekly for him.

And he got in the car and was driven away, and I went slowly back across the courtyard wondering about a lot of things.

About the hypodermic marks on Mr Mercado's arm, and what drug it was he took. And about that horrid yellow smeared mask. And how odd it was that Poirot and Miss Johnson hadn't heard my cry in the living-room that morning, whereas we had all heard Poirot perfectly well in the dining-room at lunch-time – and yet Father Lavigny's room and Mrs Leidner's were just the same distance from the living-room and the dining-room respectively.

And then I felt rather pleased that I'd taught *Doctor* Poirot one English phrase correctly!

Even if he *was* a great detective he'd realize he *didn't* know *everything*!

CHAPTER 23
I GO PSYCHIC

The funeral was, I thought, a very affecting affair. As well as ourselves, all the English people in Hassanieh attended it. Even Sheila Reilly was there, looking quiet and subdued in a dark coat and skirt. I hoped that she was feeling a little remorseful for all the unkind things she had said.

When we got back to the house I followed Dr Leidner into the office and broached the subject of my departure. He was very nice about it, thanked me for what I had done (Done! I had been worse than useless) and insisted on my accepting an extra week's salary.

I protested because really I felt I'd done nothing to earn it.

'Indeed, Dr Leidner, I'd rather not have any salary at all. If you'll just refund me my travelling expenses, that's all I want.'

But he wouldn't hear of that.

'You see,' I said, 'I don't feel I deserve it, Dr Leidner. I mean, I've – well, I've failed. She – my coming didn't save her.'

'Now don't get that idea into your head, nurse,' he said earnestly. 'After all, I didn't engage you as a female detective. I never dreamt my wife's life was in danger. I was convinced it was all nerves and that she'd worked herself up into a rather curious mental state. You did all anyone could do. She liked and trusted you. And I think in her last days she felt happier and safer because of your being here. There's nothing for you to reproach yourself with.'

His voice quivered a little and I knew what he was thinking. *He* was the one to blame for not having taken Mrs Leidner's fears seriously.

'Dr Leidner,' I said curiously. 'Have you ever come to any conclusion about those anonymous letters?'

He said with a sigh: 'I don't know what to believe. Has M. Poirot come to any definite conclusion?'

'He hadn't yesterday,' I said, steering rather neatly, I thought, between truth and fiction. After all, he hadn't until I told him about Miss Johnson.

It was on my mind that I'd like to give Dr Leidner a hint and see if he reacted. In the pleasure of seeing him and Miss Johnson together the day before, and his affection and reliance on her, I'd forgotten all about the letters. Even now I felt it was perhaps rather mean of me to bring it up. Even if she had written them, she had had a bad time after Mrs Leidner's death. Yet I did want to see whether that particular possibility had ever entered Dr Leidner's head.

'Anonymous letters are usually the work of a woman,' I said. I wanted to see how he'd take it.

'I suppose they are,' he said with a sigh. 'But you seem to forget, nurse, that these may be genuine. They may actually be written by Frederick Bosner.'

'No, I haven't forgotten,' I said. 'But I can't believe somehow that that's the real explanation.'

'I do,' he said. 'It's all nonsense, his being one of the expedition staff. That is just an ingenious theory of M. Poirot's. I believe that the truth is much simpler. The man is a madman, of course. He's been hanging round the place – perhaps in disguise of some kind. And somehow or other he got in on that fatal afternoon. The servants may be lying – they may have been bribed.'

'I suppose it's possible,' I said doubtfully.

Dr Leidner went on with a trace of irritability.

'It is all very well for M. Poirot to suspect the members of my expedition. I am perfectly certain *none* of them have anything to do with it! I have worked with them. I *know* them!'

He stopped suddenly, then he said: 'Is that your experience, nurse? That anonymous letters are usually written by women?'

'It isn't always the case,' I said. 'But there's a certain type of feminine spitefulness that finds relief that way.'

'I suppose you are thinking of Mrs Mercado?' he said.

Then he shook his head.

'Even if she were malicious enough to wish to hurt Louise she would hardly have the necessary knowledge,' he said.

I remembered the earlier letters in the attaché-case.

If Mrs Leidner had left that unlocked and Mrs Mercado had been alone in the house one day pottering about, she might easily have found them and read them. Men never seem to think of the simplest possibilities!

'And apart from her there is only Miss Johnson,' I said, watching him.

'That would be quite ridiculous!'

The little smile with which he said it was quite conclusive. The idea of Miss Johnson being the author of the letters had never entered his head! I hesitated just for a minute – but I didn't say anything. One doesn't like giving away a fellow woman, and besides, I had been a witness of Miss Johnson's genuine and moving remorse. What was done was done. Why expose Dr Leidner to a fresh disillusion on top of all his other troubles?

It was arranged that I should leave on the following day, and I had arranged through Dr Reilly to stay for a day or two with the matron of the hospital whilst I made arrangements for returning to England either via Baghdad or direct via Nissibin by car and train.

Dr Leidner was kind enough to say that he would like me to choose a memento from amongst his wife's things.

'Oh, no, really, Dr Leidner,' I said. 'I couldn't. It's much too kind of you.'

He insisted.

'But I should like you to have something. And Louise, I am sure, would have wished it.'

Then he went on to suggest that I should have her tortoiseshell toilet set!

'Oh, no, Dr Leidner! Why, that's a most *expensive* set. I couldn't, really.'

'She had no sisters, you know – no one who wants these things. There is no one else to have them.'

I could quite imagine that he wouldn't want them to fall into Mrs Mercado's greedy little hands. And I didn't think he'd want to offer them to Miss Johnson.

He went on kindly: 'You just think it over. By the way, here is the key of Louise's jewel case. Perhaps you will find something there you would rather have. And I should be very grateful if you would pack up – all her clothes. I daresay Reilly can find a use for them amongst some of the poor Christian families in Hassanieh.'

I was very glad to be able to do that for him, and I expressed my willingness.

I set about it at once.

Mrs Leidner had only had a very simple wardrobe with her and it was soon sorted and packed up into a couple of suitcases. All her papers had been in the small attaché-case. The jewel case contained a few simple trinkets – a pearl ring, a diamond brooch, a small string of pearls, and one or two plain gold bar brooches of the safety-pin type, and a string of large amber beads.

Naturally I wasn't going to take the pearls or the diamonds, but I hesitated a bit between the amber beads and the toilet set. In the end, however, I didn't see why I shouldn't take the latter. It was a kindly thought on Dr Leidner's part, and I was sure there wasn't any patronage about it. I'd take it in the spirit it had been offered, without any false pride. After all, I *had* been fond of her.

Well, that was all done and finished with. The suitcases packed, the jewel case locked up again and put separate to give to Dr Leidner with the photograph of Mrs Leidner's father and one or two other personal little odds and ends.

The room looked bare and forlorn emptied of all its accoutrements, when I'd finished. There was nothing more for me to do – and yet somehow or other I shrank from leaving the room. It seemed as though there was something still to do there – something I ought to *see* – or something I ought to have *known*.

I'm not superstitious, but the idea *did* pop into my head that perhaps Mrs Leidner's spirit was hanging about the room and trying to get in touch with me.

I remember once at the hospital some of us girls got a planchette and really it wrote some very remarkable things.

Perhaps, although I'd never thought of such a thing, I might be mediumistic.

As I say, one gets all worked up to imagine all sorts of foolishness sometimes.

I prowled round the room uneasily, touching this and that. But, of course, there wasn't anything in the room but bare furniture. There was nothing slipped behind drawers or tucked away. I couldn't hope for anything of that kind.

In the end (it sounds rather batty, but as I say, one gets worked up) I did rather a queer thing.

I went and lay down in the bed and closed my eyes.

I deliberately tried to forget who and what I was. I tried to think myself back to that fatal afternoon. I was Mrs Leidner lying here resting, peaceful and unsuspicious.

It's extraordinary how you *can* work yourself up.

I'm a perfectly normal matter-of-fact individual – not the least bit spooky, but I tell you that after I'd lain there about five minutes I began to *feel* spooky.

I didn't try to resist. I deliberately encouraged the feeling.

I said to myself: 'I'm Mrs Leidner. I'm Mrs Leidner. I'm lying here – half asleep. Presently – very soon now – the door's going to open.'

I kept on saying that – as though I were hypnotizing myself.

'It's just about half-past one . . . it's just about the time . . . The door is going to open . . . *the door is going to open* . . . I shall see who comes in . . .'

I kept my eyes glued on that door. Presently it was going to open. I should *see* it open. And I should see *the person who opened it.*

I must have been a little over-wrought that afternoon to imagine I could solve the mystery that way.

But I did believe it. A sort of chill passed down my back and settled in my legs. They felt numb – paralysed.

'You're going into a trance,' I said. 'And in that trance you'll see . . .'

And once again I repeated monotonously again and again:
'The door is going to open – the door is going to open . . .'
The cold numbed feeling grew more intense.

And then, slowly, *I saw the door just beginning to open.*

It was horrible.

I've never known anything so horrible before or since.

I was paralysed – chilled through and through. I couldn't move. For the life of me I couldn't have moved.

And I was terrified. Sick and blind and dumb with terror.

That slowly opening door.

So noiseless.

In a minute I should see . . .

Slowly – slowly – wider and wider.

Bill Coleman came quietly in.

He must have had the shock of his life!

I bounded off the bed with a scream of terror and hurled myself across the room.

He stood stock-still, his blunt pink face pinker and his mouth opened wide with surprise.

'Hallo-allo-allo,' he said. 'What's up, nurse?'

I came back to reality with a crash.

'Goodness, Mr Coleman,' I said. 'How you startled me!'

'Sorry,' he said with a momentary grin.

I saw then that he was holding a little bunch of scarlet ranunculus in his hand. They were pretty little flowers and they grew wild on the sides of the Tell. Mrs Leidner had been fond of them.

He blushed and got rather red as he said: 'One can't get any flowers or things in Hassanieh. Seemed rather rotten not to have any flowers for the grave. I thought I'd just nip in here and put a little posy in that little pot thing she always had flowers in on her table. Sort of show she wasn't forgotten – eh? A bit asinine, I know, but – well – I mean to say.'

I thought it was very nice of him. He was all pink with embarrassment like Englishmen are when they've done anything sentimental. I thought it was a very sweet thought.

'Why, I think that's a very nice idea, Mr Coleman,' I said.

And I picked up the little pot and went and got some water in it and we put the flowers in.

I really thought much more of Mr Coleman for this idea of his. It showed he had a heart and nice feelings about things.

He didn't ask me again what made me let out such a squeal and I'm thankful he didn't. I should have felt a fool explaining.

'Stick to common sense in future, woman,' I said to myself as I settled my cuffs and smoothed my apron. 'You're not cut out for this psychic stuff.'

I bustled about doing my own packing and kept myself busy for the rest of the day.

Father Lavigny was kind enough to express great distress at my leaving. He said my cheerfulness and common sense had been such a help to everybody. Common sense! I'm glad he didn't know about my idiotic behaviour in Mrs Leidner's room.

'We have not seen M. Poirot today,' he remarked.

I told him that Poirot had said he was going to be busy all day sending off telegrams.

Father Lavigny raised his eyebrows.

'Telegrams? To America?'

'I suppose so. He said, "All over the world!" but I think that was rather a foreign exaggeration.'

And then I got rather red, remembering that Father Lavigny was a foreigner himself.

He didn't seem offended though, just laughed quite pleasantly and asked me if there were any news of the man with the squint.

I said I didn't know but I hadn't heard of any.

Father Lavigny asked me again about the time Mrs Leidner and I had noticed the man and how he had seemed to be standing on tiptoe and peering through the window.

'It seems clear the man had some overwhelming interest in Mrs Leidner,' he said thoughtfully. 'I have wondered since whether the man could possibly have been a European got up to look like an Iraqi?'

That was a new idea to me and I considered it carefully. I had taken it for granted that the man was a native, but of course when I came to think of it, I was really going by the cut of his clothes and the yellowness of his skin.

Father Lavigny declared his intention of going round outside the house to the place where Mrs Leidner and I had seen the man standing.

'You never know, he might have dropped something. In the detective stories the criminal always does.'

'I expect in real life criminals are more careful,' I said.

I fetched some socks I had just finished darning and put them on the table in the living-room for the men to sort out when they came in, and then, as there was nothing much more to do, I went up on the roof.

Miss Johnson was standing there but she didn't hear me. I got right up to her before she noticed me.

But long before that I'd seen that there was something very wrong.

She was standing in the middle of the roof staring straight in front of her, and there was the most awful look on her face. As though she'd seen something she couldn't possibly believe.

It gave me quite a shock.

Mind you, I'd seen her upset the other evening, but this was quite different.

'My dear,' I said, hurrying to her, 'whatever's the matter?'

She turned her head at that and stood looking at me – almost as if she didn't see me.

'What is it?' I persisted.

She made a queer sort of grimace – as though she were trying to swallow but her throat were too dry. She said hoarsely: 'I've just seen something.'

'What have you seen? Tell me. Whatever can it be? You look all in.'

She gave an effort to pull herself together, but she still looked pretty dreadful.

She said, still in that same dreadful choked voice: '*I've seen how someone could come in from outside – and no one would ever guess.*'

I followed the direction of her eyes but I couldn't see anything.

Mr Reiter was standing in the door of the photographic-room and Father Lavigny was just crossing the courtyard – but there was nothing else.

I turned back puzzled and found her eyes fixed on mine with the strangest expression in them.

'Really,' I said, 'I don't see what you mean. Won't you explain?'

But she shook her head.

'Not now. Later. We *ought* to have seen. Oh, we ought to have seen!'

'If you'd only tell me –'

But she shook her head.

'I've got to think it out first.'

And pushing past me, she went stumbling down the stairs.

I didn't follow her as she obviously didn't want me with her. Instead I sat down on the parapet and tried to puzzle things out. But I didn't get anywhere. There was only the one way into the courtyard – through the big arch. Just outside it I could see the water-boy and his horse and the Indian cook talking to him. Nobody could have passed them and come in without their seeing him.

I shook my head in perplexity and went downstairs again.

CHAPTER 24

MURDER IS A HABIT

We all went to bed early that night. Miss Johnson had appeared at dinner and had behaved more or less as usual. She had, however, a sort of dazed look, and once or twice quite failed to take in what other people said to her.

It wasn't somehow a very comfortable sort of meal. You'd say, I suppose, that that was natural enough in a house where there'd been a funeral that day. But I know what I mean.

Lately our meals had been hushed and subdued, but for all that there had been a feeling of comradeship. There had been sympathy with Dr Leidner in his grief and a fellow feeling of being all in the same boat amongst the others.

But tonight I was reminded of my first meal there – when Mrs Mercado had watched me and there had been that curious feeling as though something might snap any minute.

I'd felt the same thing – only very much intensified – when we'd sat round the dining-room table with Poirot at the head of it.

Tonight it was particularly strong. Everyone was on edge – jumpy – on tenterhooks. If anyone had dropped something I'm sure somebody would have screamed.

As I say, we all separated early afterwards. I went to bed almost at once. The last thing I heard as I was dropping off to sleep was Mrs Mercado's voice saying goodnight to Miss Johnson just outside my door.

I dropped off to sleep at once – tired by my exertions and even more by my silly experience in Mrs Leidner's room. I slept heavily and dreamlessly for several hours.

I awoke when I did awake with a start and a feeling of impending catastrophe. Some sound had woken me, and as I sat up in bed listening I heard it again.

An awful sort of agonized choking groan.

I had lit my candle and was out of bed in a twinkling. I snatched up a torch, too, in case the candle should blow out. I came out of my door and stood listening. I knew the sound wasn't far away. It came again – from the room immediately next to mine – Miss Johnson's room.

I hurried in. Miss Johnson was lying in bed, her whole body contorted in agony. As I set down the candle and bent over her, her lips moved and she tried to speak – but only an awful hoarse whisper came. I saw that the corners of her mouth and the skin of her chin were burnt a kind of greyish white.

Her eyes went from me to a glass that lay on the floor evidently where it had dropped from her hand. The light rug was stained a bright red where it had fallen. I picked it up and ran a finger over the inside, drawing back my hand with a sharp exclamation. Then I examined the inside of the poor woman's mouth.

There wasn't the least doubt what was the matter. Somehow or other, intentionally or otherwise, she'd swallowed a quantity of corrosive acid – oxalic or hydrochloric, I suspected.

I ran out and called to Dr Leidner and he woke the others, and we worked over her for all we were worth, but all the time I had an awful feeling it was no good. We tried a strong solution of carbonate of soda – and followed it with olive oil. To ease the pain I gave her a hypodermic of morphine sulphate.

David Emmott had gone off to Hassanieh to fetch Dr Reilly, but before he came it was over.

I won't dwell on the details. Poisoning by a strong solution of hydrochloric acid (which is what it proved to be) is one of the most painful deaths possible.

It was when I was bending over her to give her the morphia that she made one ghastly effort to speak. It was only a horrible strangled whisper when it came.

'*The window . . .*' she said. '*Nurse . . . the window . . .*'

But that was all – she couldn't go on. She collapsed completely.

I shall never forget that night. The arrival of Dr Reilly. The arrival of Captain Maitland. And finally with the dawn, Hercule Poirot.

He it was who took me gently by the arm and steered me into the dining-room, where he made me sit down and have a cup of good strong tea.

'There, *mon enfant*,' he said, 'that is better. You are worn out.'

Upon that, I burst into tears.

'It's too awful,' I sobbed. 'It's been like a nightmare. Such awful suffering. And her eyes . . . Oh, M. Poirot – her eyes . . .'

He patted me on the shoulder. A woman couldn't have been kinder.

'Yes, yes – do not think of it. You did all you could.'

'It was one of the corrosive acids.'

'It was a strong solution of hydrochloric acid.'

'The stuff they use on the pots?'

'Yes. Miss Johnson probably drank it off before she was fully awake. That is – unless she took it on purpose.'

'Oh, M. Poirot, what an awful idea!'

'It is a possibility, after all. What do you think?'

I considered for a moment and then shook my head decisively.

'I don't believe it. No, I don't believe it for a moment.' I hesitated and then said, 'I think she found out something yesterday afternoon.'

'What is that you say? She found out something?'

I repeated to him the curious conversation we had had together.

Poirot gave a low soft whistle.

'*La pauvre femme!*' he said. 'She said she wanted to think it over – eh? That is what signed her death warrant. If she had only spoken out – then – at once.'

He said: 'Tell me again her exact words.'

I repeated them.

'She saw how someone could have come in from outside without any of you knowing? Come, *ma soeur*, let us go up to the roof and you shall show me just where she was standing.'

We went up to the roof together and I showed Poirot the exact spot where Miss Johnson had stood.

'Like this?' said Poirot. 'Now what do I see? I see half the

148

courtyard – and the archway – and the doors of the drawing-office and the photographic-room and the laboratory. Was there anyone in the courtyard?'

'Father Lavigny was just going towards the archway and Mr Reiter was standing in the door of the photographic-room.'

'And still I do not see in the least how anyone could come in from outside and none of you know about it . . . But *she* saw . . .'

He gave it up at last, shaking his head.

'*Sacré nom d'un chien – va!* What *did* she see?'

The sun was just rising. The whole eastern sky was a riot of rose and orange and pale, pearly grey.

'What a beautiful sunrise!' said Poirot gently.

The river wound away to our left and the Tell stood up outlined in gold colour. To the south were the blossoming trees and the peaceful cultivation. The water-wheel groaned in the distance – a faint unearthly sound. In the north were the slender minarets and the clustering fairy whiteness of Hassanieh.

It was incredibly beautiful.

And then, close at my elbow, I heard Poirot give a long deep sigh.

'Fool that I have been,' he murmured. 'When the truth is so clear – so clear.'

CHAPTER 25

SUICIDE OR MURDER?

I hadn't time to ask Poirot what he meant, for Captain Maitland was calling up to us and asking us to come down.

We hurried down the stairs.

'Look here, Poirot,' he said. 'Here's another complication. The monk fellow is missing.'

'Father Lavigny?'

'Yes. Nobody noticed it till just now. Then it dawned on somebody that he was the only one of the party not around, and we went to his room. His bed's not been slept in and there's no sign of him.'

The whole thing was like a bad dream. First Miss Johnson's death and then the disappearance of Father Lavigny.

The servants were called and questioned, but they couldn't

throw any light on the mystery. He had last been seen at about eight o'clock the night before. Then he had said he was going out for a stroll before going to bed.

Nobody had seen him come back from that stroll.

The big doors had been closed and barred at nine o'clock as usual. Nobody, however, remembered unbarring them in the morning. The two house-boys each thought the other one must have done the unfastening.

Had Father Lavigny ever returned the night before? Had he, in the course of his earlier walk, discovered anything of a suspicious nature, gone out to investigate it later, and perhaps fallen a third victim?

Captain Maitland swung round as Dr Reilly came up with Mr Mercado behind him.

'Hallo, Reilly. Got anything?'

'Yes. The stuff came from the laboratory here. I've just been checking up the quantities with Mercado. It's H.C.L. from the lab.'

'The laboratory – eh? Was it locked up?'

Mr Mercado shook his head. His hands were shaking and his face was twitching. He looked a wreck of a man.

'It's never been the custom,' he stammered. 'You see – just now – we're using it all the time. I – nobody ever dreamt –'

'Is the place locked up at night?'

'Yes – all the rooms are locked. The keys are hung up just inside the living-room.'

'So if anyone had a key to that they could get the lot.'

'Yes.'

'And it's a perfectly ordinary key, I suppose?'

'Oh, yes.'

'Nothing to show whether she took it herself from the laboratory?' asked Captain Maitland.

'She didn't,' I said loudly and positively.

I felt a warning touch on my arm. Poirot was standing close behind me.

And then something rather ghastly happened.

Not ghastly in itself – in fact it was just the incongruousness that made it seem worse than anything else.

A car drove into the courtyard and a little man jumped out. He was wearing a sun helmet and a short thick trench coat.

He came straight to Dr Leidner, who was standing by Dr Reilly, and shook him warmly by the hand.

'*Vous voilà, mon cher,*' he cried. 'Delighted to see you. I passed this way on Saturday afternoon – en route to the Italians at Fugima. I went to the dig but there wasn't a single European about and alas! I cannot speak Arabic. I had not time to come to the house. This morning I leave Fugima at five – two hours here with you – and then I catch the convoy on. *Eh bien*, and how is the season going?'

It was ghastly.

The cheery voice, the matter-of-fact manner, all the pleasant sanity of an everyday world now left far behind. He just bustled in, knowing nothing and noticing nothing – full of cheerful bonhomie.

No wonder Dr Leidner gave an inarticulate gasp and looked in mute appeal at Dr Reilly.

The doctor rose to the occasion.

He took the little man (he was a French archaeologist called Verrier who dug in the Greek islands, I heard later) aside and explained to him what had occurred.

Verrier was horrified. He himself had been staying at an Italian dig right away from civilization for the last few days and had heard nothing.

He was profuse in condolences and apologies, finally striding over to Dr Leidner and clasping him warmly by both hands.

'What a tragedy! My God, what a tragedy! I have no words. *Mon pauvre collègue.*'

And shaking his head in one last ineffectual effort to express his feelings, the little man climbed into his car and left us.

As I say, that momentary introduction of comic relief into tragedy seemed really more gruesome than anything else that had happened.

'The next thing,' said Dr Reilly firmly, 'is breakfast. Yes, I insist. Come, Leidner, you must eat.'

Poor Dr Leidner was almost a complete wreck. He came with us to the dining-room and there a funereal meal was served. I think the hot coffee and fried eggs did us all good, though no one actually felt they wanted to eat. Dr Leidner drank some coffee and sat twiddling his bread. His face was grey, drawn with pain and bewilderment.

After breakfast, Captain Maitland got down to things.

I explained how I had woken up, heard a queer sound and had gone into Miss Johnson's room.

'You say there was a glass on the floor?'

'Yes. She must have dropped it after drinking.'

'Was it broken?'

'No, it had fallen on the rug. (I'm afraid the acid's ruined the rug, by the way.) I picked the glass up and put it back on the table.'

'I'm glad you've told us that. There are only two sets of fingerprints on it, and one set is certainly Miss Johnson's own. The other must be yours.'

He was silent for a moment, then he said: 'Please go on.'

I described carefully what I'd done and the methods I had tried, looking rather anxiously at Dr Reilly for approval. He gave it with a nod.

'You tried everything that could possibly have done any good,' he said. And though I was pretty sure I had done so, it was a relief to have my belief confirmed.

'Did you know exactly what she had taken?' Captain Maitland asked.

'No – but I could see, of course, that it was a corrosive acid.'

Captain Maitland asked gravely: 'Is it your opinion, nurse, that Miss Johnson deliberately administered this stuff to herself?'

'Oh, no,' I exclaimed. 'I never thought of such a thing!'

I don't know why I was so sure. Partly, I think, because of M. Poirot's hints. His 'murder is a habit' had impressed itself on my mind. And then one doesn't readily believe that anyone's going to commit suicide in such a terribly painful way.

I said as much and Captain Maitland nodded thoughtfully. 'I agree that it isn't what one would choose,' he said. 'But if anyone were in great distress of mind and this stuff were easily obtainable it might be taken for that reason.'

'*Was* she in great distress of mind?' I asked doubtfully.

'Mrs Mercado says so. She says that Miss Johnson was quite unlike herself at dinner last night – that she hardly replied to anything that was said to her. Mrs Mercado is quite sure that Miss Johnson was in terrible distress over something and that the idea of making away with herself had already occurred to her.'

'Well, I don't believe it for a moment,' I said bluntly.

Mrs Mercado indeed! Nasty slinking little cat!

'Then what *do* you think?'

'I think she was murdered,' I said bluntly.

He rapped out his next question sharply. I felt rather that I was in the orderly room.

'Any reasons?'

'It seems to me by far and away the most possible solution.'

'That's just your private opinion. There was no reason why the lady should be murdered?'

'Excuse me,' I said, 'there was. She found out something.'

'Found out something? What did she find out?'

I repeated our conversation on the roof word for word.

'She refused to tell you what her discovery was?'

'Yes. She said she must have time to think it over.'

'But she was very excited by it?'

'Yes.'

'*A way of getting in from outside.*' Captain Maitland puzzled over it, his brows knit. 'Had you no idea at all of what she was driving at?'

'Not in the least. I puzzled and puzzled over it but I couldn't even get a glimmering.'

Captain Maitland said: 'What do you think, M. Poirot?'

Poirot said: 'I think you have there a possible motive.'

'For murder?'

'For murder.'

Captain Maitland frowned.

'She wasn't able to speak before she died?'

'Yes, she just managed to get out two words.'

'What were they?'

'*The window . . .*'

'The window?' repeated Captain Maitland. 'Did you understand to what she was referring?'

I shook my head.

'How many windows were there in her bedroom?'

'Just the one.'

'Giving on the courtyard?'

'Yes.'

'Was it open or shut? Open, I seem to remember. But perhaps one of you opened it?'

'No, it was open all the time. I wondered –'

I stopped.

'Go on, nurse.'

'I examined the window, of course, but I couldn't see anything unusual about it. I wondered whether, perhaps, somebody changed the glasses that way.'

'Changed the glasses?'

'Yes. You see, Miss Johnson always takes a glass of water to bed with her. I think that glass must have been tampered with and a glass of acid put in its place.'

'What do you say, Reilly?'

'If it's murder, that was probably the way it was done,' said Dr Reilly promptly. 'No ordinary moderately observant human being would drink a glass of acid in mistake for one of water – if they were in full possession of their waking faculties. But if anyone's accustomed to drinking off a glass of water in the middle of the night, that person might easily stretch out an arm, find the glass in the accustomed place, and still half asleep, toss off enough of the stuff to be fatal before realizing what had happened.'

Captain Maitland reflected a minute.

'I'll have to go back and look at that window. How far is it from the head of the bed?'

I thought.

'With a very long stretch you could just reach the little table that stands by the head of the bed.'

'The table on which the glass of water was?'

'Yes.'

'Was the door locked?'

'No.'

'So whoever it was could have come in that way and made the substitution?'

'Oh, yes.'

'There would be more risk that way,' said Dr Reilly. 'A person who is sleeping quite soundly will often wake up at the sound of a footfall. If the table could be reached from the window it would be the safer way.'

'I'm not only thinking of the glass,' said Captain Maitland absent-mindedly.

Rousing himself, he addressed me once again.

'It's your opinion that when the poor lady felt she was dying she was anxious to let you know that somebody had substituted acid for water through the open window? Surely the person's *name* would have been more to the point?'

'She mayn't have known the name,' I pointed out.

'Or it would have been more to the point if she'd managed to hint what it was that she had discovered the day before?'

Dr Reilly said: 'When you're dying, Maitland, you haven't always got a sense of proportion. One particular fact very likely obsesses your mind. That a murderous hand had come through the window may have been the principal fact obsessing her at the minute. It may have seemed to her important that she should let people know that. In my opinion she wasn't far wrong either. It *was* important! She probably jumped to the fact that you'd think it was suicide. If she could have used her tongue freely, she'd probably have said "It wasn't suicide. I didn't take it myself. Somebody else must have put it near my bed *through the window*."'

Captain Maitland drummed with his fingers for a minute or two without replying. Then he said:

'There are certainly two ways of looking at it. It's either suicide or murder. Which do you think, Dr Leidner?'

Dr Leidner was silent for a minute or two, then he said quietly and decisively: 'Murder. Anne Johnson wasn't the sort of woman to kill herself.'

'No,' allowed Captain Maitland. 'Not in the normal run of things. But there might be circumstances in which it would be quite a natural thing to do.'

'Such as?'

Captain Maitland stooped to a bundle which I had previously noticed him place by the side of his chair. He swung it on to the table with something of an effort.

'There's something here that none of you know about,' he said. 'We found it under her bed.'

He fumbled with the knot of the covering, then threw it back, revealing a heavy great quern or grinder.

That was nothing in itself – there were a dozen or so already found in the course of the excavations.

What riveted our attention on this particular specimen was a dull, dark stain and a fragment of something that looked like hair.

'That'll be your job, Reilly,' said Captain Maitland. 'But I

shouldn't say that there's much doubt about this being the
instrument with which Mrs Leidner was killed!'

NEXT IT WILL BE ME!

It was rather horrible. Dr Leidner looked as though he were going
to faint and I felt a bit sick myself.

Dr Reilly examined it with professional gusto.

'No fingerprints, I presume?' he threw out.

'No fingerprints.'

Dr Reilly took out a pair of forceps and investigated delicately.

'H'm – a fragment of human tissue – and hair – fair blonde
hair. That's the unofficial verdict. Of course, I'll have to make a
proper test, blood group, etc., but there's not much doubt. Found
under Miss Johnson's bed? Well, well – so *that's* the big idea. She
did the murder, and then, God rest her, remorse came to her and
she finished herself off. It's a theory – a pretty theory.'

Dr Leidner could only shake his head helplessly.

'Not Anne – not Anne,' he murmured.

'I don't know where she hid this to begin with,' said Captain
Maitland. 'Every room was searched after the first crime.'

Something jumped into my mind and I thought, 'In the stationery cupboard,' but I didn't say anything.

'Wherever it was, she became dissatisfied with its hiding-place
and took it into her own room, which had been searched with
all the rest. Or perhaps she did that after making up her mind
to commit suicide.'

'I don't believe it,' I said aloud.

And I couldn't somehow believe that kind nice Miss Johnson
had battered out Mrs Leidner's brains. I just couldn't *see* it
happening! And yet it *did* fit in with some things – her fit of
weeping that night, for instance. After all, I'd said 'remorse'
myself – only I'd never thought it was remorse for anything but
the smaller, more insignificant crime.

'I don't know what to believe,' said Captain Maitland. 'There's
the French Father's disappearance to be cleared up too. My men
are out hunting around in case he's been knocked on the head
and his body rolled into a convenient irrigation ditch.'

'Oh! I remember now –' I began.

Everyone looked towards me inquiringly.

'It was yesterday afternoon,' I said. 'He'd been cross-questioning me about the man with a squint who was looking in at the window that day. He asked me just where he'd stood on the path and then he said he was going out to have a look round. He said in detective stories the criminal always dropped a convenient clue.'

'Damned if any of my criminals ever do,' said Captain Maitland. 'So that's what he was after, was it? By Jove, I wonder if he *did* find anything. A bit of a coincidence if both he and Miss Johnson discovered a clue to the identity of the murderer at practically the same time.'

He added irritably, 'Man with a squint? Man with a squint? There's more in this tale of that fellow with a squint than meets the eye. I don't know why the devil my fellows can't lay hold of him!'

'Probably because he hasn't got a squint,' said Poirot quietly.

'Do you mean he faked it? Didn't know you could fake an actual squint.'

Poirot merely said: 'A squint can be a very useful thing.'

'The devil it can! I'd give a lot to know where that fellow is now, squint or no squint!'

'At a guess,' said Poirot, 'he has already passed the Syrian frontier.'

'We've warned Tell Kotchek and Abu Kemal – all the frontier posts, in fact.'

'I should imagine that he took the route through the hills. The route lorries sometimes take when running contraband.'

Captain Maitland grunted.

'Then we'd better telegraph Deir ez Zor?'

'I did so yesterday – warning them to look out for a car with two men in it whose passports will be in the most impeccable order.'

Captain Maitland favoured him with a stare.

'*You* did, did you? Two men – eh?'

Poirot nodded.

'There are two men in this.'

'It strikes me, M. Poirot, that you've been keeping quite a lot of things up your sleeve.'

Poirot shook his head.

'No,' he said. 'Not really. The truth came to me only this morning when I was watching the sunrise. A very beautiful sunrise.'

I don't think that any of us had noticed that Mrs Mercado was in the room. She must have crept in when we were all taken aback by the production of that horrible great bloodstained stone.

But now, without the least warning, she set up a noise like a pig having its throat cut.

'Oh, my God!' she cried. 'I see it all. I see it all now. *It was Father Lavigny.* He's mad – religious mania. He thinks women are sinful. *He's killing them all.* First Mrs Leidner – then Miss Johnson. And next it will be *me . . .*'

With a scream of frenzy she flung herself across the room and clutched Dr Reilly's coat.

'I won't stay here, I tell you! I won't stay here a day longer. There's danger. There's danger all round. He's hiding somewhere – waiting his time. He'll spring out on me!'

Her mouth opened and she began screaming again.

I hurried over to Dr Reilly, who had caught her by the wrists. I gave her a sharp slap on each cheek and with Dr Reilly's help I sat her down in a chair.

'Nobody's going to kill you,' I said. 'We'll see to that. Sit down and behave yourself.'

She didn't scream any more. Her mouth closed and she sat looking at me with startled, stupid eyes.

Then there was another interruption. The door opened and Sheila Reilly came in.

Her face was pale and serious. She came straight to Poirot.

'I was at the post office early, M. Poirot,' she said, 'and there was a telegram there for you – so I brought it along.'

'Thank you, mademoiselle.'

He took it from her and tore it open while she watched his face.

It did not change, that face. He read the telegram, smoothed it out, folded it up neatly and put it in his pocket.

Mrs Mercado was watching him. She said in a choked voice: 'Is that – from America?'

'No, madame,' he said. 'It is from Tunis.'

She stared at him for a moment as though she did not understand, then with a long sigh, she leant back in her seat.

'Father Lavigny,' she said. 'I *was* right. I've always thought there was something queer about him. He said things to me once – I suppose he's mad . . .' She paused and then said, 'I'll be quiet. But I *must* leave this place. Joseph and I can go in and sleep at the Rest House.'

'Patience, madame,' said Poirot. 'I will explain everything.'

Captain Maitland was looking at him curiously.

'Do you consider you've definitely got the hang of this business?' he demanded.

Poirot bowed.

It was a most theatrical bow. I think it rather annoyed Captain Maitland.

'Well,' he barked. 'Out with it, man.'

But that wasn't the way Hercule Poirot did things. I saw perfectly well that he meant to make a song and dance of it. I wondered if he really *did* know the truth, or if he was just showing off.

He turned to Dr Reilly.

'Will you be so good, Dr Reilly, as to summon the others?'

Dr Reilly jumped up and went off obligingly. In a minute or two the other members of the expedition began to file into the room. First Reiter and Emmott. Then Bill Coleman. Then Richard Carey and finally Mr Mercado.

Poor man, he really looked like death. I suppose he was mortally afraid that he'd get hauled over the coals for carelessness in leaving dangerous chemicals about.

Everyone seated themselves round the table very much as we had done on the day M. Poirot arrived. Both Bill Coleman and David Emmott hesitated before they sat down, glancing towards Sheila Reilly. She had her back to them and was standing looking out of the window.

'Chair, Sheila?' said Bill.

David Emmott said in his low pleasant drawl, 'Won't you sit down?'

She turned then and stood for a minute looking at them. Each was indicating a chair, pushing it forward. I wondered whose chair she would accept.

In the end she accepted neither.

'I'll sit here,' she said brusquely. And she sat down on the edge of a table quite close to the window.

'That is,' she added, 'if Captain Maitland doesn't mind my staying?'

I'm not quite sure what Captain Maitland would have said. Poirot forestalled him.

'Stay by all means, mademoiselle,' he said. 'It is, indeed, necessary that you should.'

She raised her eyebrows.

'Necessary?'

'That is the word I used, mademoiselle. There are some questions I shall have to ask you.'

Again her eyebrows went up but she said nothing further. She turned her face to the window as though determined to ignore what went on in the room behind her.

'And now,' said Captain Maitland, 'perhaps we shall get at the truth!'

He spoke rather impatiently. He was essentially a man of action. At this very moment I felt sure that he was fretting to be out and doing things – directing the search for Father Lavigny's body, or alternatively sending out parties for his capture and arrest.

He looked at Poirot with something akin to dislike.

'If the beggar's got anything to say, why doesn't he say it?'

I could see the words on the tip of his tongue.

Poirot gave a slow appraising glance at us all, then rose to his feet.

I don't know what I expected him to say – something dramatic certainly. He was that kind of person.

But I certainly didn't expect him to start off with a phrase in Arabic.

Yet that is what happened. He said the words slowly and solemnly – and really quite religiously, if you know what I mean.

'*Bismillahi ar rahman ar rahim.*'

And then he gave the translation in English.

'In the name of Allah, the Merciful, the Compassionate.'

CHAPTER 27

BEGINNING OF A JOURNEY

'*Bismillahi ar rahman ar rahim*. That is the Arab phrase used before starting out on a journey. *Eh bien*, we too start on a journey. A journey into the past. A journey into the strange places of the human soul.'

I don't think that up till that moment I'd ever felt any of the so-called 'glamour of the East'. Frankly, what had struck me was the *mess* everywhere. But suddenly, with M. Poirot's words, a queer sort of vision seemed to grow up before my eyes. I thought of words like Samarkand and Ispahan – and of merchants with long beards – and kneeling camels – and staggering porters carrying great bales on their backs held by a rope round the forehead – and women with henna-stained hair and tattooed faces kneeling by the Tigris and washing clothes, and I heard their queer wailing chants and the far-off groaning of the water-wheel.

They were mostly things I'd seen and heard and thought nothing much of. But now, somehow they seemed *different* – like a piece of fusty old stuff you take into the light and suddenly see the rich colours of an old embroidery . . .

Then I looked round the room we were sitting in and I got a queer feeling that what M. Poirot said was true – we *were* all starting on a journey. We were here together now, but we were all going our different ways.

And I looked at everyone as though, in a sort of way, I were seeing them for the first time – *and* for the last time – which sounds stupid, but it was what I felt all the same.

Mr Mercado was twisting his fingers nervously – his queer light eyes with their dilated pupils were staring at Poirot. Mrs Mercado was looking at her husband. She had a strange watchful look like a tigress waiting to spring. Dr Leidner seemed to have shrunk in some curious fashion. This last blow had just crumpled him up. You might almost say he wasn't in the room at all. He was somewhere far away in a place of his own. Mr Coleman was looking straight at Poirot. His mouth was slightly open and his eyes protruded. He looked almost idiotic. Mr Emmott was looking down at his feet and I couldn't see his face properly. Mr Reiter looked bewildered. His mouth was pushed out in a pout and that made him look more like a nice clean pig than ever. Miss Reilly was looking steadily out of the window. I don't know what she was thinking or feeling. Then I looked at Mr Carey, and somehow his face hurt me and I looked away. There we were, all of us. And somehow I felt that when M. Poirot had finished we'd all be somewhere quite different . . .

It was a queer feeling . . .

Poirot's voice went quietly on. It was like a river running evenly between its banks . . . running to the sea . . .

'From the very beginning I have felt that to understand this case one must seek not for external signs or clues, but for the truer clues of the clash of personalities and the secrets of the heart.

'And I may say that though I have now arrived at what I believe to be the true solution of the case, *I have no material proof of it*. I *know* it is so, because it *must* be so, because *in no other way* can every single fact fit into its ordered and recognized place.

'And that, to my mind, is the most satisfying solution there can be.'

He paused and then went on:

'I will start my journey at the moment when I myself was brought into the case – when I had it presented to me as an accomplished happening. Now, every case, in my opinion, has a definite *shape* and *form*. The pattern of this case, to my mind, all revolved round the personality of Mrs Leidner. Until I knew *exactly what kind of a woman Mrs Leidner was* I should not be able to know why she was murdered and who murdered her.

'That, then, was my starting point – the personality of Mrs Leidner.

'There was also one other psychological point of interest – the curious state of tension described as existing amongst the members of the expedition. This was attested to by several different witnesses – some of them outsiders – and I made a note that although hardly a starting point, it should nevertheless be borne in mind during my investigations.

'The accepted idea seemed to be that it was directly the result of Mrs Leidner's influence on the members of the expedition, but for reasons which I will outline to you later this did not seem to me entirely acceptable.

'To start with, as I say, I concentrated solely and entirely on the personality of Mrs Leidner. I had various means of assessing that personality. There were the reactions she produced in a number of people, all varying widely in character and temperament, and there was what I could glean by my own observation. The scope of the latter was naturally limited. But I *did* learn certain facts.

'Mrs Leidner's tastes were simple and even on the austere side. She was clearly not a luxurious woman. On the other hand, some embroidery she had been doing was of an extreme fineness and beauty. That indicated a woman of fastidious and artistic taste. From the observation of the books in her bedroom I formed a further estimate. She had brains, and I also fancied that she was, essentially, an egoist.

'It had been suggested to me that Mrs Leidner was a woman whose main preoccupation was to attract the opposite sex – that she was, in fact, a sensual woman. This I did not believe to be the case.

'In her bedroom I noticed the following books on a shelf: *Who were the Greeks?*, *Introduction to Relativity*, *Life of Lady Hester Stanhope*, *Back to Methuselah*, *Linda Condon*, *Crewe Train*.

'She had, to begin with, an interest in culture and in modern science – that is, a distinct intellectual side. Of the novels, *Linda Condon*, and in a lesser degree *Crewe Train*, seemed to show that Mrs Leidner had a sympathy and interest in the independent woman – unencumbered or entrapped by man. She was also obviously interested by the personality of Lady Hester Stanhope. *Linda Condon* is an exquisite study of the worship of her own beauty by a woman. *Crewe Train* is a study of a passionate individualist, *Back to Methuselah* is in sympathy with the intellectual rather than the emotional attitude to life. I felt that I was beginning to understand the dead woman.

'I next studied the reactions of those who had formed Mrs Leidner's immediate circle – and my picture of the dead woman grew more and more complete.

'It was quite clear to me from the accounts of Dr Reilly and others that Mrs Leidner was one of those women who are endowed by Nature not only with beauty but with the kind of calamitous magic which sometimes accompanies beauty and can, indeed, exist independently of it. Such women usually leave a trail of violent happenings behind them. They bring disaster –

sometimes on others – sometimes on themselves.

'I was convinced that Mrs Leidner was a woman who essentially worshipped *herself* and who enjoyed more than anything else the sense of *power*. Wherever she was, she *must* be the centre of the universe. And everyone round her, man or woman, had got to acknowledge her sway. With some people that was easy. Nurse Leatheran, for instance, a generous-natured woman with a romantic imagination, was captured instantly and gave in ungrudging manner full appreciation. But there was a second way in which Mrs Leidner exercised her sway – the way of fear. Where conquest was too easy she indulged a more cruel side to her nature – but I wish to reiterate emphatically that it was not what you might call *conscious* cruelty. It was as natural and unthinking as is the conduct of a cat with a mouse. Where consciousness came in, she was essentially kind and would often go out of her way to do kind and thoughtful actions for other people.

'Now of course the first and most important problem to solve was the problem of the anonymous letters. Who had written them and why? I asked myself: Had Mrs Leidner written them *herself*?

'To answer this problem it was necessary to go back a long way – to go back, in fact, to the date of Mrs Leidner's first marriage. It is here we start on our journey proper. The journey of Mrs Leidner's life.

'First of all we must realize that the Louise Leidner of all those years ago is essentially the same Louise Leidner of the present time.

'She was young then, of remarkable beauty – that same haunting beauty that affects a man's spirit and senses as no mere material beauty can – and she was already essentially an egoist.

'Such women naturally revolt from the idea of marriage. They may be attracted by men, but they prefer to belong to themselves. They are truly *La Belle Dame sans Merci* of the legend. Nevertheless Mrs Leidner *did* marry – and we can assume, I think, that her husband must have been a man of a certain force of character.

'Then the revelation of his traitorous activities occurs and Mrs Leidner acts in the way she told Nurse Leidner. She gave information to the Government.

'Now I submit that there was a psychological significance in her action. She told Nurse Leatheran that she was a very patriotic idealistic girl and that that feeling was the cause of her action. But it is a well-known fact that we all tend to deceive ourselves as to the motives for our own actions. Instinctively we select the best-sounding motive! Mrs Leidner may have believed herself that it was patriotism that inspired her action, but I believe myself that it was really the outcome of an unacknowledged desire to get rid of her husband! She disliked domination – she disliked the feeling of belonging to someone else – in fact she disliked playing second fiddle. She took a patriotic way of regaining her freedom.

'But underneath her consciousness was a gnawing sense of guilt which was to play its part in her future destiny.

'We now come directly to the question of the letters. Mrs Leidner was highly attractive to the male sex. On several occasions she was attracted by them – but in each case a threatening letter played its part and the affair came to nothing.

'Who wrote those letters? Frederick Bosner or his brother William or *Mrs Leidner herself*?

'There is a perfectly good case for either theory. It seems clear to me that Mrs Leidner was one of those women who do inspire devouring devotions in men, the type of devotion which can become an obsession. I find it quite possible to believe in a Frederick Bosner to whom Louise, his wife, mattered more than anything in the world! She had betrayed him once and he dared not approach her openly, but he was determined at least that she should be his or no one's. He preferred her death to her belonging to another man.

'On the other hand, if Mrs Leidner had, deep down, a dislike of entering into the marriage bond, it is possible that she took this way of extricating herself from difficult positions. She was a huntress who, the prey once attained, had no further use for it! Craving drama in her life, she invented a highly satisfactory drama – a resurrected husband forbidding the banns! It satisfied her deepest instincts. It made her a romantic figure, a tragic heroine, and it enabled her not to marry again.

'This state of affairs continued over a number of years. Every time there was any likelihood of marriage – a threatening letter arrived.

'*But now we come to a really interesting point.* Dr Leidner came upon the scene – and no forbidding letter arrived! Nothing stood in the way of her becoming Mrs Leidner. Not until *after* her marriage did a letter arrive.

'At once we ask ourselves – why?

'Let us take each theory in turn.

. . . '*If* Mrs Leidner wrote the letters herself the problem is easily explained. Mrs Leidner really *wanted* to marry Dr Leidner. And so she *did* marry him. But in that case, *why did she write herself a letter afterwards?* Was her craving for drama too strong to be suppressed? And why only those two letters? After that no other letter was received until a year and a half later.

'Now take the other theory, that the letters were written by her first husband, Frederick Bosner (or his brother). Why did the threatening letter arrive *after* the marriage? Presumably Frederick could not have *wanted* her to marry Leidner. Why, then, did he not stop the marriage? He had done so successfully on former occasions. And why, *having waited till the marriage had taken place*, did he then resume his threats?

'The answer, an unsatisfactory one, is that he was somehow or other unable to protest sooner. He may have been in prison or he may have been abroad.

'There is next the attempted gas poisoning to consider. It seems extremely unlikely that it was brought about by an outside agency. The likely persons to have staged it were Dr and Mrs Leidner themselves. There seems no conceivable reason why *Dr* Leidner should do such a thing, so we are brought to the conclusion that *Mrs* Leidner planned and carried it out herself.

'Why? More drama?

'After that Dr and Mrs Leidner go abroad and for eighteen months they lead a happy, peaceful life with no threats of death to disturb it. They put that down to having successfully covered their traces, but such an explanation is quite absurd. In these days going abroad is quite inadequate for that purpose. And especially was that so in the case of the Leidners. He was the director of a museum expedition. By inquiry at the museum, Frederick Bosner could at once have obtained his correct address. Even granting that he was in too reduced circumstances to pursue the couple himself there would be no bar to his continuing his threatening letters. And it seems to me that a man with his obsession would certainly have done so.

'Instead nothing is heard of him until nearly two years later when the letters are resumed.

'*Why* were the letters resumed?

'A very difficult question – most easily answered by saying that Mrs Leidner was bored and wanted more drama. But I was not quite satisfied with that. This particular form of drama seemed to me a shade too vulgar and too crude to accord well with her fastidious personality.

'The only thing to do was to keep an open mind on the question.

'There were three definite possibilities: (1) the letters were written by Mrs Leidner herself; (2) they were written by Frederick Bosner (or young William Bosner); (3) they might have been written *originally* by either Mrs Leidner or her first husband, but they were now *forgeries* – that is, they were being written by a *third* person who was aware of the earlier letters.

'I now come to direct consideration of Mrs Leidner's entourage.

'I examined first the actual opportunities that each member of the staff had had for committing the murder.

'Roughly, on the face of it, *anyone* might have committed it (as far as opportunity went), with the exception of three persons.

'Dr Leidner, by overwhelming testimony, had never left the roof. Mr Carey was on duty at the mound. Mr Coleman was in Hassanieh.

'But those alibis, my friends, were not *quite* as good as they looked. I except Dr Leidner's. There is absolutely no doubt that he was on the roof all the time and did not come down until quite an hour and a quarter after the murder had happened.

'But was it *quite* certain that Mr Carey was on the mound all the time?

'And had Mr Coleman *actually been in Hassanieh* at the time the murder took place?'

Bill Coleman reddened, opened his mouth, shut it and looked round uneasily.

Mr Carey's expression did not change.

Poirot went on smoothly.

'I also considered one other person who, I satisfied myself, would be perfectly capable of committing murder *if she felt strongly enough*. Miss Reilly has courage and brains and a certain quality of ruthlessness. When Miss Reilly was speaking to me on the subject of the dead woman, I said to her, jokingly, that I hoped she had an alibi. I think Miss Reilly was conscious then that she had had in her heart the desire, at least, to kill. At any rate she immediately uttered a very silly and purposeless lie. She said she had been playing tennis on that afternoon. The next day I learned from a casual conversation with Miss Johnson that far from playing tennis, Miss Reilly *had actually been near this house at the time of the murder*. It occurred to me that Miss Reilly, if not guilty of the crime, might be able to tell me something useful.'

He stopped and then said quietly: 'Will you tell us, Miss Reilly, what you did *see* that afternoon?'

The girl did not answer at once. She still looked out of the window without turning her head, and when she spoke it was in a detached and measured voice.

'I rode out to the dig after lunch. It must have been about a quarter to two when I got there.'

'Did you find any of your friends on the dig?'

'No, there seemed to be no one there but the Arab foreman.'

'You did not see Mr Carey?'

'No.'

'Curious,' said Poirot. 'No more did M. Verrier when he went there that same afternoon.'

He looked invitingly at Carey, but the latter neither moved nor spoke.

'Have you any explanation, Mr Carey?'

'I went for a walk. There was nothing of interest turning up.'

'In which direction did you go for a walk?'

'Down by the river.'

'Not back towards the house?'

'No.'

'I suppose,' said Miss Reilly, 'that you were waiting for some-one who didn't come.'

He looked at her but didn't answer.

Poirot did not press the point. He spoke once more to the girl.

'Did you see anything else, mademoiselle?'

'Yes. I was not far from the expedition house when I noticed the expedition lorry drawn up in a wadi. I thought it was rather queer. Then I saw Mr Coleman. He was walking along with his head down as though he were searching for something.'

'Look here,' burst out Mr Coleman, 'I –'

Poirot stopped him with an authoritative gesture.

'Wait. Did you speak to him, Miss Reilly?'

'No. I didn't.'

'Why?'

The girl said slowly: 'Because, from time to time, he started and looked round with an extraordinary furtive look. It – gave me an unpleasant feeling. I turned my horse's head and rode away. I don't think he saw me. I was not very near and he was absorbed in what he was doing.'

'Look here,' Mr Coleman was not to be hushed any longer. 'I've got a perfectly good explanation for what – I admit – looks a bit fishy. As a matter of fact, the day before I had slipped a jolly fine cylinder seal into my coat pocket instead of putting it in the antika-room – forgot all about it. And then I discovered I'd been and lost it out of my pocket – dropped it somewhere. I didn't want to get into a row about it so I decided I'd have a jolly good search on the quiet. I was pretty sure I'd dropped it on the way to or from the dig. I rushed over my business in Hassanieh. Sent a walad to do some of the shopping and got back early. I stuck the bus where it wouldn't show and had a jolly good hunt for over an hour. And didn't find the damned thing at that! Then I got into the bus and drove on to the house. Naturally, everyone thought I'd just got back.'

'And you did not undeceive them?' asked Poirot sweetly.

'Well, that was pretty natural under the circumstances, don't you think?'

'I hardly agree,' said Poirot.

'Oh, come now – don't go looking for trouble – that's *my* motto! But you can't fasten anything on me. I never went into the courtyard, and you can't find anyone who'll say I did.'

'That, of course, has been the difficulty,' said Poirot. 'The evidence of the servants that *no one entered the courtyard from outside*. But it occurred to me, upon reflection, that that was really *not* what they had said. They had sworn that *no stranger* had entered the premises. They had not been asked *if a member of the expedition* had done so.'

'Well, you ask them,' said Coleman. 'I'll eat my hat if they saw me or Carey either.'

'Ah! but that raises rather an interesting question. They would notice *a stranger* undoubtedly – but would they have even *noticed* a member of the expedition? The members of the staff are passing in and out all day. The servants would hardly notice their going and coming. It is possible, I think, that either Mr Carey or Mr Coleman *might* have entered and the servants' minds would have no remembrance of such an event.'

'Bunkum!' said Mr Coleman.

Poirot went on calmly: 'Of the two, I think Mr Carey was the least likely to be noticed going or coming. Mr Coleman had started to Hassanieh in the car that morning and he would be expected to return in it. His arrival on foot would therefore be noticeable.'

'Of course it would!' said Coleman.

Richard Carey raised his head. His deep-blue eyes looked straight at Poirot.

'Are you accusing me of murder, M. Poirot?' he asked.

His manner was quite quiet but his voice had a dangerous undertone.

Poirot bowed to him.

'As yet I am only taking you all on a journey – my journey towards the truth. I had now established one fact – that all the members of the expedition staff, and also Nurse Leatheran, could in actual *fact* have committed the murder. That there was very little likelihood of some of them having committed it was a secondary matter.

'I had examined *means* and *opportunity*. I next passed to *motive*. I discovered that *one and all of you could be credited with a motive!*'

'Oh! M. Poirot,' I cried. 'Not *me*! Why, I was a stranger. I'd only just come.'

'*Eh bien, ma soeur*, and was not that *just what Mrs Leidner had been fearing*? A stranger from *outside*?'

'But – but – Why, Dr Reilly knew all about me! He suggested my coming!'

'How much did he really know about you? *Mostly what you yourself had told him.* Imposters have passed themselves off as hospital nurses before now.'

'You can write to St. Christopher's,' I began.

'For the moment will you silence yourself. Impossible to proceed while you conduct this argument. I do not say I suspect you *now*. All I say is that, keeping the open mind, you might quite easily be someone other than you pretended to be. There are many successful female impersonators, you know. Young William Bosner might be something of that kind.'

I was about to give him a further piece of my mind. Female impersonator indeed! But he raised his voice and hurried on with such an air of determination that I thought better of it.

'I am going now to be frank – brutally so. It is necessary. I am going to lay bare the underlying structure of this place.

'I examined and considered every single soul here. To begin with Dr Leidner, I soon convinced myself that his love for his wife was the mainspring of his existence. He was a man torn and ravaged with grief. Nurse Leatheran I have already mentioned. If she were a female impersonator she was a most amazingly successful one, and I inclined to the belief that she was exactly what she said she was – a thoroughly competent hospital nurse.'

'Thank you for nothing,' I interposed.

'My attention was immediately attracted towards Mr and Mrs Mercado, who were both of them clearly in a state of great agitation and unrest. I considered first Mrs Mercado. Was she capable of murder, and if so for what reasons?

'Mrs Mercado's physique was frail. At first sight it did not seem possible that she could have had the physical strength to strike down a woman like Mrs Leidner with a heavy stone implement. If, however, Mrs Leidner had been on her knees at the time, the thing would at least be *physically possible*. There are ways in which one woman can induce another to go down on her knees. Oh! not emotional ways! For instance, a woman might be turning up the hem of a skirt and ask another woman to put in the pins for her. The second woman would kneel on the ground quite unsuspectingly.

'But the motive? Nurse Leatheran had told me of the angry glances she had seen Mrs Mercado direct at Mrs Leidner. Mr Mercado had evidently succumbed easily to Mrs Leidner's spell. But I did not think the solution was to be found in mere jealousy. I was sure Mrs Leidner was not in the least interested really in Mr

Mercado – and doubtless Mrs Mercado was aware of the fact. She might be furious with her for the moment, but for *murder* there would have to be greater provocation. But Mrs Mercado was essentially a fiercely maternal type. From the way she looked at her husband I realized, not only that she loved him, but that she would fight for him tooth and nail – and more than that – *that she envisaged the possibility of having to do so*. She was constantly on her guard and uneasy. The uneasiness was for him – not for herself. And when I studied Mr Mercado I could make a fairly easy guess at what the trouble was. I took means to assure myself of the truth of my guess. Mr Mercado was a drug addict – in an advanced stage of the craving.

'Now I need probably not tell you all that the taking of drugs over a long period has the result of considerably blunting the moral sense.

'Under the influence of drugs a man commits actions that he would not have dreamed of committing a few years earlier before he began the practice. In some cases a man has committed murder – and it has been difficult to say whether he was wholly responsible for his actions or not. The law of different countries varies slightly on that point. The chief characteristic of the drug-fiend criminal is overweening confidence in his own cleverness.

'I thought it possible that there was some discreditable incident, perhaps a criminal incident, in Mr Mercado's past which his wife had somehow or other succeeded in hushing up. Nevertheless his career hung on a thread. If anything of this past incident were bruited about, Mr Mercado would be ruined. His wife was always on the watch. But there was Mrs Leidner to be reckoned with. She had a sharp intelligence and a love of power. She might even induce the wretched man to confide in her. It would just have suited her peculiar temperament to feel she knew a secret which she could reveal at any minute with disastrous effects.

'Here, then, was a possible motive for murder on the part of the Mercados. To protect her mate, Mrs Mercado, I felt sure, would stick at nothing! Both she and her husband had had the opportunity – during that ten minutes when the courtyard was empty.'

Mrs Mercado cried out, 'It's not *true!*'

Poirot paid no attention.

'I next considered Miss Johnson. Was *she* capable of murder?

'I thought she was. She was a person of strong will and iron self-control. Such people are constantly repressing themselves – and one day the dam bursts! But if Miss Johnson had committed the crime it could only be for some reason connected with Dr Leidner. If in any way she felt convinced that Mrs Leidner was spoiling her husband's life, then the deep unacknowledged jealousy far down in her would leap at the chance of a plausible motive and give itself full rein.

'Yes, Miss Johnson was distinctly a possibility.

'Then there were the three young men.

'First Carl Reiter. If, by any chance, one of the expedition staff was William Bosner, then Reiter was by far the most likely person. But if he *was* William Bosner, then he was certainly a most accomplished actor! If he were merely *himself*, had he any reason for murder?

'Regarded from Mrs Leidner's point of view, Carl Reiter was far too easy a victim for good sport. He was prepared to fall on his face and worship immediately. Mrs Leidner despised undiscriminating adoration – and the door-mat attitude nearly always brings out the worst side of a woman. In her treatment of Carl Reiter Mrs Leidner displayed really deliberate cruelty. She inserted a gibe here – a prick there. She made the poor young man's life a hell to him.'

Poirot broke off suddenly and addressed the young man in a personal, highly confidential manner.

'*Mon ami*, let this be a lesson to you. You are a *man*. Behave, then, like a *man*! It is against Nature for a man to grovel. Women and Nature have almost exactly the same reactions! Remember it is better to take the largest plate within reach and fling it at a woman's head than it is to wriggle like a worm whenever she looks at you!'

He dropped his private manner and reverted to his lecture style.

'Could Carl Reiter have been goaded to such a pitch of torment that he turned on his tormentor and killed her? Suffering does queer things to a man. I could not be *sure* that it was *not* so!

'Next William Coleman. His behaviour, as reported by Miss Reilly, is certainly suspicious. If he was the criminal it could only be because his cheerful personality concealed the hidden one of William Bosner. I do not think William Coleman, as William

Coleman, has the temperament of a murderer. His faults might lie in another direction. Ah! perhaps Nurse Leatheran can guess what they would be?'

How *did* the man do it? I'm sure I didn't look as though I was thinking anything at all.

'It's nothing really,' I said, hesitating. 'Only if it's to be all truth, Mr Coleman *did* say once himself that he would have made a good forger.'

'A good point,' said Poirot. 'Therefore if he had come across some of the old threatening letters, he could have copied them without difficulty.'

'Oy, oy, oy!' called out Mr Coleman. 'This is what they call a frame-up.'

Poirot swept on.

'As to his being or not being William Bosner, such a matter is difficult of verification. But Mr Coleman has spoken of a *guardian* – not of a father – and there is nothing definitely to veto the idea.'

'Tommyrot,' said Mr Coleman. 'Why all of you listen to this chap beats me.'

'Of the three young men there remains Mr Emmott,' went on Poirot. 'He again might be a possible shield for the identity of William Bosner. Whatever *personal reasons* he might have for the removal of Mrs Leidner I soon realized that I should have no means of learning them from him. He could keep his own counsel remarkably well, and there was not the least chance of provoking him nor of tricking him into betraying himself on any point. Of all the expedition he seemed to be the best and most dispassionate judge of Mrs Leidner's personality. I think that he always knew her for exactly what she was – but what impression her personality made on him I was unable to discover. I fancy that Mrs Leidner herself must have been provoked and angered by his attitude.

'I may say that of all the expedition, *as far as character and capacity were concerned*, Mr Emmott seemed to me the most fitted to bring a clever and well-timed crime off satisfactorily.'

For the first time, Mr Emmott raised his eyes from the toes of his boots.

'Thank you,' he said.

There seemed to be just a trace of amusement in his voice.

'The last two people on my list were Richard Carey and Father Lavigny.

'According to the testimony of Nurse Leatheran and others, Mr Carey and Mrs Leidner disliked each other. They were both civil with an effort. Another person, Miss Reilly, propounded a totally different theory to account for their attitude of frigid politeness.

'I soon had very little doubt that Miss Reilly's explanation was the correct one. I acquired my certitude by the simple expedient of provoking Mr Carey into reckless and unguarded speech. It was not difficult. As I soon saw, he was in a state of high nervous tension. In fact he was – and is – very near a complete nervous breakdown. A man who is suffering up to the limit of his capacity can seldom put up much of a fight.

'Mr Carey's barriers came down almost immediately. He told me, with a sincerity that I did not for a moment doubt, that he hated Mrs Leidner.

'And he was undoubtedly speaking the truth. He *did* hate Mrs Leidner. But *why* did he hate her?

'I have spoken of women who have a calamitous magic. But men have that magic too. There are men who are able without the least effort to attract women. What they call in these days *le sex appeal*! Mr Carey had this quality very strongly. He was to begin with devoted to his friend and employer, and indifferent to his employer's wife. That did not suit Mrs Leidner. She *must* dominate – and she set herself out to capture Richard Carey. But here, I believe, something entirely unforeseen took place. She herself for perhaps the first time in her life, fell a victim to an overmastering passion. She fell in love – really in love – with Richard Carey.

'And he – was unable to resist her. Here is the truth of the terrible state of nervous tension that he has been enduring. He has been a man torn by two opposing passions. He loved Louise Leidner – yes, but he also hated her. He hated her for undermining his loyalty to his friend. There is no hatred so great as that of a man who has been made to love a woman against his will.

'I had here all the motive that I needed. I was convinced that *at certain moments* the most natural thing for Richard Carey to do would have been to strike with all the force of his arm at the beautiful face that had cast a spell over him.

'All along I had felt sure that the murder of Louise Leidner was a *crime passionnel*. In Mr Carey I had found an ideal murderer for that type of crime.

'There remains one other candidate for the title of murderer – Father Lavigny. My attention was attracted to the good Father straightaway by a certain discrepancy between his description of the strange man who had been seen peering in at the window and the one given by Nurse Leatheran. In all accounts given by different witnesses there is usually *some* discrepancy, but this was absolutely glaring. Moreover, Father Lavigny insisted on a certain characteristic – a squint – which ought to make identification much easier.

'But very soon it became apparent that *while Nurse Leatheran's description was substantially accurate,* Father Lavigny's was *nothing of the kind*. It looked almost as though Father Lavigny was deliberately misleading us – as though he did *not want the man caught*.

'But in that case *he must know something about this curious person*. He had been seen talking to the man but we had only his word for what they had been talking about.

'What had the Iraqi been doing when Nurse Leatheran and Mrs Leidner saw him? Trying to peer through the window – Mrs Leidner's window, so they thought, but I realized when I went and stood where they had been, that it might equally have been the *antika-room window*.

'The night after that an alarm was given. Someone was in the antika-room. Nothing proved to have been taken, however. The interesting point to me is that when Dr Leidner got there he found *Father Lavigny there before him*. Father Lavigny tells his story of seeing a light. *But again we have only his word for it.*

'I begin to get curious about Father Lavigny. The other day when I make the suggestion that Father Lavigny may be Frederick Bosner, Dr Leidner pooh-poohs the suggestion. He says Father Lavigny is a well-known man. I advance the supposition that Frederick Bosner, who has had nearly twenty years to make a career for himself, under a new name, may very possibly *be* a well-known man by this time! All the same, I do not think that he has spent the intervening time in a religious community. A very much simpler solution presents itself.

'Did anyone at the expedition know Father Lavigny by sight

before he came? Apparently not. Why then should not it be *someone impersonating the good Father*? I found out that a telegram had been sent to Carthage on the sudden illness of Dr Byrd, who was to have accompanied the expedition. To intercept a telegram, what could be easier? As to the work, there was no other epigraphist attached to the expedition. With a smattering of knowledge a clever man *might* bluff his way through. There had been very few tablets and inscriptions so far, and already I gathered that Father Lavigny's pronouncements had been felt to be somewhat unusual.

'It looked very much as though Father Lavigny were an *imposter*.

'But was he Frederick Bosner?

'Somehow, affairs did not seem to be shaping themselves that way. The truth seemed likely to lie in quite a different direction.

'I had a lengthy conversation with Father Lavigny. I am a practising Catholic and I know many priests and members of religious communities. Father Lavigny struck me as not ringing quite true to his role. But he struck me, on the other hand, as familiar in quite a different capacity. I *had* met men of his type quite frequently – but they were not members of a religious community. Far from it!

'I began to send off telegrams.

'And then, unwittingly, Nurse Leatheran gave me a valuable clue. We were examining the gold ornaments in the antika-room and she mentioned a trace of wax having been found adhering to a gold cup. Me, I say, "Wax?" and Father Lavigny, he said "Wax?" and his tone was enough! I knew in a flash exactly what he was doing here.'

Poirot paused and addressed himself directly to Dr Leidner.

'I regret to tell you, monsieur, that the gold cup in the antika-room, the gold dagger, the hair ornaments and several other things *are not the genuine articles found by you*. They are very clever electrotypes. Father Lavigny, I have just learned by this last answer to my telegrams, is none other than Raoul Menier, one of the cleverest thieves known to the French police. He specializes in thefts from museums of *objets d'art* and such like. Associated with him is Ali Yusuf, a semi-Turk, who is a first-class working jeweller. Our first knowledge of Menier was when certain objects in the Louvre were found not to be genuine – in every case it was discovered that a distinguished archaeologist *not known previously by sight to the director* had recently had the handling of the spurious articles when paying a visit to the Louvre. On inquiry all these distinguished gentlemen denied having paid a visit to the Louvre at the times stated!

'I have learned that Menier was in Tunis preparing the way for a theft from the Holy Fathers when your telegram arrived. Father Lavigny, who was in ill-health, was forced to refuse, but Menier managed to get hold of the telegram and substitute one of acceptance. He was quite safe in doing so. Even if the monks should read in some paper (in itself an unlikely thing) that Father Lavigny was in Iraq they would only think that the newspapers had got hold of a half-truth as so often happens.

'Menier and his accomplice arrived. The latter is seen when he is reconnoitring the antika-room from outside. The plan is for Father Lavigny to take wax impressions. Ali then makes clever duplicates. There are always certain collectors who are willing to pay a good price for genuine antiques and will ask no embarrassing questions. Father Lavigny will effect the substitution of the fake for the genuine article – preferably at night.

'And that is doubtless what he was doing when Mrs Leidner heard him and gave the alarm. What can he do? He hurriedly makes up a story of having seen a light in the antika-room.

'That "went down", as you say, very well. But Mrs Leidner was no fool. She may have remembered the trace of wax she had noticed and then put two and two together. And if she did, what will she do then? Would it not be *dans son caractère* to do nothing at once, but enjoy herself by letting hints slip to the discomfiture of Father Lavigny? She will let him see that she suspects – but not that she *knows*. It is, perhaps, a dangerous game, but she enjoys a dangerous game.

'And perhaps she plays that game too long. Father Lavigny sees the truth, and strikes before she realizes what he means to do.

'Father Lavigny is Raoul Menier – a thief. Is he also – a *murderer*?'

Poirot paced the room. He took out a handkerchief, wiped his forehead and went on: 'That was my position this morning. There were eight distinct possibilities and I did not know which of these possibilities was the right one. I still did not know *who was the murderer.*

'But murder is a habit. The man or woman who kills once will kill again.

'And by the second murder, the murderer was delivered into my hands.

'All along it was ever present in the back of my mind that some one of these people might have knowledge that they had kept back – knowledge incriminating the murderer.

'If so, that person would be in danger.

'My solicitude was mainly on account of Nurse Leatheran. She had an energetic personality and a brisk inquisitive mind. I was terrified of her finding out more than it was safe for her to know.

'As you all know, a second murder did take place. But the victim was not Nurse Leatheran – it was Miss Johnson.

'I like to think that I should have reached the correct solution anyway by pure reasoning, but it is certain that Miss Johnson's murder helped me to it much quicker.

'To begin with, one suspect was eliminated – Miss Johnson herself – for I did not for a moment entertain the theory of suicide.

'Let us examine now the facts of this second murder.

'Fact One: On Sunday evening Nurse Leatheran finds Miss Johnson in tears, and that same evening Miss Johnson burns a fragment of a letter which nurse believes to be in the same handwriting as that of the anonymous letters.

'Fact Two: The evening before her death Miss Johnson is found by Nurse Leatheran standing on the roof in a state that nurse describes as one of incredulous horror. When nurse questions her she says, "I've seen how someone could come in from outside – and no one would ever guess." She won't say any more. Father Lavigny is crossing the courtyard and Mr Reiter is at the door of the photographic-room.

'Fact Three: Miss Johnson is found dying. The only words she can manage to articulate are "the window – the window –"

'Those are the facts, and these are the problems with which we are faced:

'What is the truth of the letters?

'What did Miss Johnson see from the roof?

'What did she mean by "the window – the window"?

'*Eh bien*, let us take the second problem first as the easiest of solution. I went up with Nurse Leatheran and I stood where Miss Johnson had stood. From there she could see the courtyard and the archway and the north side of the building and two members of the staff. Had her words anything to do with either Mr Reiter or Father Lavigny?

'Almost at once a possible explanation leaped to my brain. If a stranger came in from *outside* he could only do so in *disguise*. And there was only *one* person whose general appearance lent itself to such an impersonation. Father Lavigny! With a sun helmet, sun glasses, black beard and a monk's long woollen robe, a stranger could pass in without the servants *realising* that a stranger had entered.

'Was *that* Miss Johnson's meaning? Or had she gone further? Did she realize that Father Lavigny's whole *personality* was a disguise? That he was someone other than he pretended to be?

'Knowing what I did know about Father Lavigny, I was inclined to call the mystery solved. Raoul Menier was the murderer. He had killed Mrs Leidner to silence her before she could give him away. Now *another person lets him see that she has penetrated his secret*. She, too, must be removed.

'And so everything is explained! The second murder. Father Lavigny's flight – minus robe and beard. (He and his friend are doubtless careering through Syria with excellent passports as two commercial travellers.) His action in placing the blood-stained quern under Miss Johnson's bed.

'As I say, I was almost satisfied – but not quite. For the perfect solution must explain *everything* – and this does not do so.

'It does not explain, for instance, why Miss Johnson should say "the window", as she was dying. It does not explain her fit of weeping over the letter. It does not explain her mental attitude on the roof – her incredulous horror and her refusal to tell Nurse Leatheran what it was that *she now suspected or knew*.

'It was a solution that fitted the *outer* facts, but it did not satisfy the *psychological* requirements.

'And then, as I stood on the roof, going over in my mind those three points: the letters, the roof, the window, I *saw* – just as Miss Johnson had seen!

'*And this time what I saw explained everything!*'

180

CHAPTER 28

JOURNEY'S END

Poirot looked round. Every eye was now fixed upon him. There had been a certain relaxation – a slackening of tension. Now the tension suddenly returned.

There was something coming . . . something . . .

Poirot's voice, quiet and unimpassioned, went on: 'The letters, the roof, "the window" . . . Yes, everything was explained – everything fell into place.

'I said just now that three men had alibis for the time of the crime. Two of those alibis I have shown to be worthless. I saw now my great – my amazing mistake. The third alibi was worthless too. Not only *could* Dr Leidner have committed the murder – but I was convinced that he *had* committed it.'

There was a silence, a bewildered, uncomprehending silence. Dr Leidner said nothing. He seemed lost in his far-away world still. David Emmott, however, stirred uneasily and spoke.

'I don't know what you mean to imply, M. Poirot. I told you that Dr Leidner never left the roof until at least a quarter to three. That is the absolute truth. I swear it solemnly. I am not lying. And it would have been quite impossible for him to have done so without my seeing him.'

Poirot nodded.

'Oh, I believe you. *Dr Leidner did not leave the roof.* That is an undisputed fact. But what I saw – and what Miss Johnson had seen – was *that Dr Leidner could murder his wife from the roof without leaving it.*'

We all stared.

'The *window*,' cried Poirot. '*Her* window! That is what I realized – just as Miss Johnson realized it. Her window was directly underneath, on the side away from the courtyard. And Dr Leidner was alone up there with no one to witness his actions. And those heavy stone querns and grinders were up there all ready to his hand. So simple, so very simple, granted one thing – *that the murderer had the opportunity to move the body before anyone else saw it* . . . Oh, it is beautiful – of an unbelievable simplicity!

'Listen – it went like this:

'Dr Leidner is on the roof working with the pottery. He calls you up, Mr Emmott, and while he holds you in talk he notices that, as usually happens, the small boy takes advantage of your absence to leave his work and go outside the courtyard. He keeps you with him ten minutes, then he lets you go and as soon as you are down below shouting to the boy he sets his plan in operation.

'He takes from his pocket the plasticine-smeared mask with which he has already scared his wife on a former occasion and dangles it over the edge of the parapet till it taps on his wife's window.

'That, remember, is the window giving on the countryside facing the opposite direction to the courtyard.

'Mrs Leidner is lying on her bed half asleep. She is peaceful and happy. Suddenly the mask begins tapping on the window and attracts her attention. But it is not dusk now – it is broad daylight – there is nothing terrifying about it. She recognizes it for what it is – a crude form of trickery! She is not frightened but indignant. She does what any other woman would do in her place. Jumps off the bed, opens the window, passes her head through the bars and turns her face upward to see who is playing the trick on her.

'Dr Leidner is waiting. He has in his hands, poised and ready, a heavy quern. At the psychological moment *he drops it* . . .

'With a faint cry (heard by Miss Johnson) Mrs Leidner collapses on the rug underneath the window.

'Now there is a hole in this quern, and through that Dr Leidner had previously passed a cord. He has now only to haul in the cord and bring up the quern. He replaces the latter neatly, bloodstained side down, amongst the other objects of that kind on the roof.

'Then he continues his work for an hour or more till he judges the moment has come for the second act. He descends the stairs, speaks to Mr Emmott and Nurse Leatheran, crosses the courtyard and enters his wife's room. This is the explanation he himself gives of his movements there:

'"*I saw my wife's body in a heap by the bed. For a moment or two I felt paralysed as though I couldn't move. Then at last I went and knelt down by her and lifted up her head. I saw she was dead . . . At last I got up. I felt dazed and as though I were drunk. I managed to get to the door and call out.*"

'A perfectly possible account of the actions of a grief-dazed man. Now listen to what I believe to be the truth. Dr Leidner enters the room, hurries to the window, and, having pulled on a pair of gloves, closes and fastens it, then picks up his wife's body and transports it to a position between the bed and the door. Then he notices a slight stain on the window-side rug. He cannot change it with the other rug, they are a different size, but he does the next best thing. He puts the stained rug in front of the washstand and the rug from the washstand under the window. If the stain is noticed, it will be connected with the *washstand* – not with the *window* – a very important point. There must be no suggestion that the window played any part in the business. Then he comes to the door and acts the part of the overcome husband, and that, I imagine, is not difficult. For he *did* love his wife.'

'My good man,' cried Dr Reilly impatiently, 'if he loved her, why did he kill her? Where's the motive? Can't you speak, Leidner? Tell him he's mad.'

Dr Leidner neither spoke nor moved.

Poirot said: 'Did I not tell you all along that this was a *crime passionnel*? Why did her first husband, Frederick Bosner, threaten to kill her? Because he loved her . . . And in the end, you see, he made his boast good . . .

'*Mais oui – mais oui – once I realize that it is Dr Leidner who did the killing*, everything falls into place . . .

'For the second time, I recommence my journey from the beginning – Mrs Leidner's first marriage – the threatening letters – her second marriage. The letters prevented her marrying any other man – but they did not prevent her marrying Dr Leidner. How simple that is – *if Dr Leidner is actually Frederick Bosner*.

'Once more let us start our journey – from the point of view this time of young Frederick Bosner.

'To begin with, he loves his wife Louise with an overpowering passion such as only a woman of her kind can evoke. She betrays him. He is sentenced to death. He escapes. He is involved in a railway accident but he manages to emerge with a second personality – *that of a young Swedish archaeologist, Eric Leidner*, whose body is badly disfigured and who will be conveniently buried as Frederick Bosner.

'What is the new Eric Leidner's attitude to the woman who was willing to send him to his death? First and most important, *he still loves her*. He sets to work to build up his new life. He is a man of great ability, his profession is congenial to him and he makes a success of it. *But he never forgets the ruling passion of his life.* He keeps himself informed of his wife's movements. Of one thing he is cold-bloodedly determined (remember Mrs Leidner's own description of him to Nurse Leatheran – gentle and kind but ruthless), *she shall belong to no other man.* Whenever he judges it necessary he despatches a letter. He imitates some of the peculiarities of her handwriting in case she should think of taking his letters to the police. Women who write sensational anonymous letters to themselves are such a common phenomenon that the police will be sure to jump to that solution given the likeness of the handwriting. At the same time he leaves her in doubt as to whether he is really alive or not.

'At last, after many years, he judges that the time has arrived; he re-enters her life. All goes well. His wife never dreams of his real identity. He is a well-known man. The upstanding, good-looking young fellow is now a middle-aged man with a beard and stooping shoulders. And so we see history repeating itself. As before, Frederick is able to dominate Louise. For the second time she consents to marry him. *And no letter comes to forbid the banns.*

'But *afterwards* a letter *does* come. Why?

'I think that Dr Leidner was taking no chances. The intimacy of marriage *might* awaken a memory. He wishes to impress on his wife, once and for all, *that Eric Leidner and Frederick Bosner are two different people.* So much so that a threatening letter comes from the former on account of the latter. The rather puerile gas poisoning business follows – arranged by Dr Leidner, of course. Still with the same object in view.

'After that he is satisfied. No more letters need come. They can settle down to happy married life together.

'And then, after nearly two years, *the letters recommence.*

'*Why? Eh bien,* I think I know. *Because the threat underlying the letters was always a genuine threat.* (That is why Mrs Leidner has always been frightened. She *knew* her Frederick's gentle but ruthless nature.) *If she belongs to any other man but him he would kill her. And she has given herself to Richard Carey.*

'And so, having discovered this, cold-bloodedly, calmly, Dr Leidner prepares the scene for murder.

'You see now the important part played by Nurse Leatheran? Dr Leidner's rather curious conduct (it puzzled me at the very first) in securing her services for his wife is explained. It was vital that a reliable professional witness should be able to state incontrovertibly that Mrs Leidner had been dead *over an hour* when her body was found – that is, that she had been killed at a time when *everybody could swear her husband was on the roof*. A suspicion *might* have arisen that he had killed her when he entered the room and found the body – but that was out of the question when a trained hospital nurse would assert positively that she had already been dead an hour.

'Another thing that is explained is the curious state of tension and strain that had come over the expedition this year. I never from the first thought that that could be attributed solely to *Mrs* Leidner's influence. For several years this particular expedition had had a reputation for happy good-fellowship. In my opinion, the state of mind of a community is always directly due to the influence of the man at the top. Dr Leidner, quiet though he was, was a man of great personality. It was due to his tact, to his judgment, to his sympathetic manipulation of human beings that the atmosphere had always been such a happy one.

'If there was a change, therefore, the change must be due to the man at the top – in other words, to Dr Leidner. It was *Dr* Leidner, not Mrs Leidner, who was responsible for the tension and uneasiness. No wonder the staff felt the change without understanding it. The kindly, genial Dr Leidner, outwardly the same, was only playing the part of himself. The real man was an obsessed fanatic plotting to kill.

'And now we will pass on to the second murder – that of Miss Johnson. In tidying up Dr Leidner's papers in the office (a job she took on herself unasked, craving for something to do) she must have come on some unfinished draft of one of the anonymous letters.

'It must have been both incomprehensible and extremely upsetting to her! Dr Leidner has been deliberately terrorizing his wife! She cannot understand it – but it upsets her badly. It is in this mood that Nurse Leatheran discovers her crying.

'I do not think at the moment that she suspected Dr Leidner of being the murderer, but my experiments with sounds in Mrs Leidner's and Father Lavigny's rooms are not lost upon her. She realizes that if it *was* Mrs Leidner's cry she heard, *the window in her room must have been open, not shut*. At the moment that conveys nothing vital to her, *but she remembers it.*

'Her mind goes on working – ferreting its way towards the truth. Perhaps she makes some reference to the letters which Dr Leidner understands and his manner changes. She may see that he is, suddenly, afraid.

'But Dr Leidner *cannot* have killed his wife! He was on the *roof* all the time.

'And then, one evening, as she herself is on the roof puzzling about it, the truth comes to her in a flash. Mrs Leidner has been killed from up *here*, through the open window.

'It was at that minute that Nurse Leatheran found her.

'And immediately, her old affection reasserting itself, she puts up a quick camouflage. Nurse Leatheran must not guess the horrifying discovery she has just made.

'She looks deliberately in the opposite direction (towards the courtyard) and makes a remark suggested to her by Father Lavigny's appearance as he crosses the courtyard.

'She refuses to say more. She has got to "think things out".

'And Dr Leidner, who has been watching her anxiously, *realizes that she knows the truth.* She is not the kind of woman to conceal her horror and distress from him.

'It is true that as yet she has not given him away – but how long can he depend upon her?

'Murder is a habit. That night he substitutes a glass of acid for her glass of water. There is just a chance she may be believed to have deliberately poisoned herself. There is even a chance she may be considered to have done the first murder and has now been overcome with remorse. To strengthen the latter idea he takes the quern from the roof and puts it under her bed.

'No wonder that poor Miss Johnson, in her death agony, could only try desperately to impart her hard-won information. Through "the window", *that* is how Mrs Leidner was killed, *not* through the door – through the *window* . . .

'And so thus, everything is explained, everything falls into place . . . Psychologically perfect.

'But there is no proof . . . No proof at all . . .'

None of us spoke. We were lost in a sea of horror . . . Yes, and not only horror. Pity, too.

Dr Leidner had neither moved nor spoken. He sat just as he had done all along. A tired, worn elderly man.

At last he stirred slightly and looked at Poirot with gentle, tired eyes.

'No,' he said, 'there is no proof. But that does not matter. You knew that I would not deny truth . . . I have never denied truth . . . I think – really – I am rather glad . . . I'm so tired . . .'

Then he said simply: 'I'm sorry about Anne. That was bad – senseless – it wasn't *me*! And she suffered, too, poor soul. Yes, that wasn't me. It was fear . . .'

A little smile just hovered on his pain-twisted lips.

'You would have made a good archaeologist, M. Poirot. You have the gift of re-creating the past.

'It was all very much as you said.

'I loved Louise and I killed her . . . if you'd known Louise you'd have understood . . . No, I think you understand anyway . . .'

CHAPTER 29
L'ENVOI

There isn't really any more to say about things.

They got 'Father' Lavigny and the other man just as they were going to board a steamer at Beyrouth.

Sheila Reilly married young Emmott. I think that will be good for her. He's no door-mat – he'll keep her in her place. She'd have ridden roughshod over poor Bill Coleman.

I nursed him, by the way, when he had appendicitis a year ago. I got quite fond of him. His people were sending him out to farm in South Africa.

I've never been out East again. It's funny – sometimes I wish I could. I think of the noise the water-wheel made and the women washing, and that queer haughty look that camels give you – and I get quite a homesick feeling. After all, perhaps dirt isn't really so unhealthy as one is brought up to believe!

Dr Reilly usually looks me up when he's in England, and as I said, it's he who's got me into this. 'Take it or leave it,' I said to him. 'I know the grammar's all wrong and it's not properly written or anything like that – but there it is.'

And he took it. Made no bones about it. It will give me a queer feeling if it's ever printed.

M. Poirot went back to Syria and about a week later he went home on the Orient Express and got himself mixed up in another murder. He was clever, I don't deny it, but I shan't forgive him in a hurry for pulling my leg the way he did. Pretending to think I might be mixed up in the crime and not a real hospital nurse at all!

Doctors are like that sometimes. Will have their joke, some of them will, and never think of *your* feelings!

I've thought and thought about Mrs Leidner and what she was really like . . . Sometimes it seems to me she was just a terrible woman – and other times I remember how nice she was to me and how soft her voice was – and her lovely fair hair and everything – and I feel that perhaps, after all, she was more to be pitied than blamed . . .

And I can't help but pity Dr Leidner. I know he was a murderer twice over, but it doesn't seem to make any difference. He was so dreadfully fond of her. It's awful to be fond of anyone like that.

Somehow, the more I get older, and the more I see of people and sadness and illness and everything, the sorrier I get for everyone. Sometimes, I declare, I don't know what's becoming of the good, strict principles my aunt brought me up with. A very religious woman she was, and most particular. There wasn't one of our neighbours whose faults she didn't know backwards and forwards . . .

Oh, dear, it's quite true what Dr Reilly said. How does one stop writing? If I could find a really good telling phrase.

I must ask Dr Reilly for some Arab one.

Like the one M. Poirot used.

In the name of Allah, the Merciful, the Compassionate . . .

Something like that.

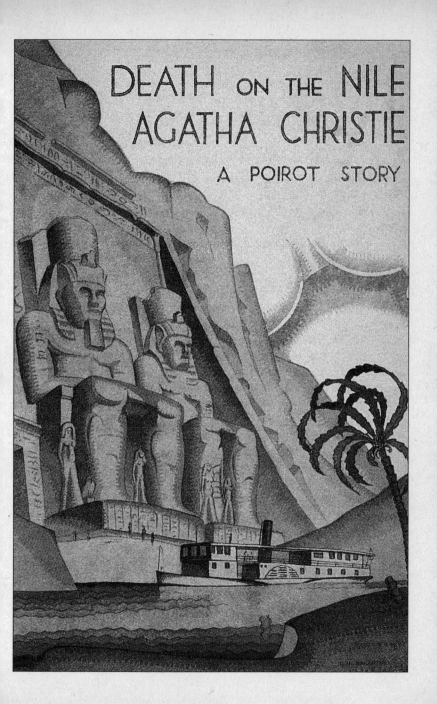

DEATH ON THE NILE
AGATHA CHRISTIE
A POIROT STORY

To my old friend Sybil Bennett
who also loves wandering about the world

CHAPTER I

'Linnet Ridgeway!'

'That's *her*!' said Mr Burnaby, the landlord of the Three Crowns.

He nudged his companion.

The two men stared with round bucolic eyes and slightly open mouths.

A big scarlet Rolls-Royce had just stopped in front of the local post office.

A girl jumped out, a girl without a hat and wearing a frock that looked (but only *looked*) simple. A girl with golden hair and straight autocratic features – a girl with a lovely shape – a girl such as was seldom seen in Malton-under-Wode.

With a quick imperative step she passed into the post office.

'That's her!' said Mr Burnaby again. And he went on in a low awed voice: 'Millions she's got . . . Going to spend thousands on the place. Swimming-pools there's going to be, and Italian gardens and a ballroom and half of the house pulled down and rebuilt . . .'

'She'll bring money into the town,' said his friend. He was a lean, seedy-looking man. His tone was envious and grudging.

Mr Burnaby agreed.

'Yes, it's a great thing for Malton-under-Wode. A great thing it is.'

Mr Burnaby was complacent about it.

'Wake us all up proper,' he added.

'Bit of difference from Sir George,' said the other.

'Ah, it was the 'orses did for him,' said Mr Burnaby indulgently. 'Never 'ad no luck.'

'What did he get for the place?'

'A cool sixty thousand, so I've heard.'

The lean man whistled.

Mr Burnaby went on triumphantly: 'And they say she'll have spent another sixty thousand before she's finished!'

'Wicked!' said the lean man. 'Where'd she *get* all that money from?'

'America, so I've heard. Her mother was the only daughter of one of those millionaire blokes. Quite like the pictures, isn't it?'

The girl came out of the post office and climbed into the car. As she drove off, the lean man followed her with his eyes. He muttered:

'It seems all wrong to me – her looking like that. Money *and* looks – it's too much! If a girl's as rich as that she's no right to be a good-looker as well. And she *is* a good-looker . . . Got everything, that girl has. Doesn't seem fair . . .'

II

Extract from the Social column of the *Daily Blague*.

Among those supping at Chez Ma Tante I noticed beautiful Linnet Ridgeway. She was with the Hon. Joanna Southwood, Lord Windlesham and Mr Toby Bryce. Miss Ridgeway, as everyone knows, is the daughter of Melhuish Ridgeway who married Anna Hartz. She inherits from her grandfather, Leopold Hartz, an immense fortune. The lovely Linnet is the sensation of the moment and it is rumoured that an engagement may be announced shortly. Certainly Lord Windlesham seemed very épris!!

III

The Hon. Joanna Southwood said:

'Darling, I think it's going to be all perfectly *marvellous*!'

She was sitting in Linnet Ridgeway's bedroom at Wode Hall.

From the window the eye passed over the gardens to open country with blue shadows of woodlands.

'It's rather perfect, isn't it?' said Linnet.

She leaned her arms on the window sill. Her face was eager, alive, dynamic. Beside her, Joanna Southwood seemed, somehow, a little dim – a tall thin young woman of twenty-seven, with a long clever face and freakishly plucked eyebrows.

'And you've done so much in the time! Did you have lots of architects and things?'

'Three.'

'What are architects like? I don't think I've ever seen any.'

'They were all right. I found them rather unpractical some-times.'

'Darling, you soon put *that* right! You are the *most* practical creature!'

Joanna picked up a string of pearls from the dressing table.

'I suppose these are real, aren't they, Linnet?'

'Of course.'

'I know it's "of course" to you, my sweet, but it wouldn't be to most people. Heavily cultured or even Woolworth! Darling, they really are *incredible*, so exquisitely matched. They must be worth the *most* fabulous sum!'

'Rather vulgar, you think?'

'No, not at all – just pure beauty. What *are* they worth?'

'About fifty thousand.'

'What a lovely lot of money! Aren't you afraid of having them stolen?'

'No, I always wear them – and anyway they're insured.'

'Let me wear them till dinner-time, will you, darling? It would give me such a thrill.'

Linnet laughed.

'Of course, if you like.'

'You know, Linnet, I really do envy you. You've simply got *everything*. Here you are at twenty, your own mistress, with any amount of money, looks, superb health. You've even got *brains*! When are you twenty-one?'

'Next June. I shall have a grand coming-of-age party in London.'

'And then are you going to marry Charles Windlesham? All the dreadful little gossip writers are getting so excited about it. And he really is frightfully devoted.'

Linnet shrugged her shoulders.

'I don't know. I don't really want to marry anyone yet.'

'Darling, how right you are! It's never quite the same after-wards, is it?'

The telephone shrilled and Linnet went to it.

'Yes? Yes?'

The butler's voice answered her:

'Miss de Bellefort is on the line. Shall I put her through?'

'Bellefort? Oh, of course, yes, put her through.'

A click and a voice, an eager, soft, slightly breathless voice: 'Hullo, is that Miss Ridgeway? *Linnet!*'

'*Jackie darling*! I haven't heard anything of you for ages and *ages*!'

'I know. It's awful. Linnet, I want to see you terribly.'

'Darling, can't you come down here? My new toy. I'd love to show it to you.'

'That's just what I want to do.'

'Well, jump into a train or a car.'

'Right, I will. A frightfully dilapidated two-seater. I bought it for fifteen pounds, and some days it goes beautifully. But it has moods. If I haven't arrived by tea-time you'll know it's had a mood. So long, my sweet.'

Linnet replaced the receiver. She crossed back to Joanna.

'That's my oldest friend, Jacqueline de Bellefort. We were together at a convent in Paris. She's had the most terrible bad luck. Her father was a French Count, her mother was American – a Southerner. The father went off with some woman, and her mother lost all her money in the Wall Street crash. Jackie was left absolutely broke. I don't know how she's managed to get along the last two years.'

Joanna was polishing her deep-blood-coloured nails with her friend's nail pad. She leant back with her head on one side scrutinizing the effect.

'Darling,' she drawled, 'won't that be rather *tiresome*? If any misfortunes happen to my friends I always drop them *at once*! It sounds heartless, but it saves such a lot of trouble later! They always want to borrow money off you, or else they start a dressmaking business and you have to get the most terrible clothes from them. Or they paint lampshades, or do batik scarves.'

'So, if I lost all my money, you'd drop me tomorrow?'

'Yes, darling, I would. You can't say I'm not honest about it! I only like successful people. And you'll find that's true of nearly everybody – only most people won't admit it. They just say that really they can't put up with Mary or Emily or Pamela any more! "Her troubles have made her so *bitter* and peculiar, poor dear!"'

'How beastly you are, Joanna!'

'I'm only on the make, like everyone else.'

'*I'm* not on the make!'

'For obvious reasons! You don't have to be sordid when good-looking, middle-aged American trustees pay you over a vast allowance every quarter.'

'And you're wrong about Jacqueline,' said Linnet. 'She's not a sponge. I've wanted to help her, but she won't let me. She's as proud as the devil.'

'What's she in such a hurry to see you for? I'll bet she wants something! You just wait and see.'

'She sounded excited about something,' admitted Linnet. 'Jackie always did get frightfully worked up over things. She once stuck a penknife into someone!'

'Darling, how thrilling!'

'A boy was teasing a dog. Jackie tried to get him to stop. He wouldn't. She pulled him and shook him, but he was much stronger than she was, and at last she whipped out a penknife and plunged it right into him. There was the *most* awful row!'

'I should think so. It sounds most uncomfortable!'

Linnet's maid entered the room. With a murmured word of apology, she took down a dress from the wardrobe and went out of the room with it.

'What's the matter with Marie?' asked Joanna. 'She's been crying.'

'Poor thing! You know I told you she wanted to marry a man who has a job in Egypt. She didn't know much about him, so I thought I'd better make sure he was all right. It turned out that he had a wife already – and three children.'

'What a lot of enemies you must make, Linnet.'

'Enemies?' Linnet looked surprised.

Joanna nodded and helped herself to a cigarette.

'Enemies, my sweet. You're so devastatingly efficient. And you're so frightfully good at doing the right thing.'

Linnet laughed.

'Why, I haven't got an enemy in the world.'

IV

Lord Windlesham sat under the cedar tree. His eyes rested on the graceful proportions of Wode Hall. There was nothing to mar its old-world beauty; the new buildings and additions were out of sight round the corner. It was a fair and peaceful sight bathed in the autumn sunshine. Nevertheless, as he gazed, it was no longer Wode Hall that Charles Windlesham saw. Instead, he seemed to see a more imposing Elizabethan mansion, a long sweep of park, a more bleak background . . . It was his own family seat,

Charltonbury, and in the foreground stood a figure – a girl's figure, with bright golden hair and an eager confident face . . . Linnet as mistress of Charltonbury!

He felt very hopeful. That refusal of hers had not been at all a definite refusal. It had been little more than a plea for time. Well, he could afford to wait a little . . .

How amazingly suitable the whole thing was! It was certainly advisable that he should marry money, but not such a matter of necessity that he could regard himself as forced to put his own feelings on one side. And he loved Linnet. He would have wanted to marry her even if she had been practically penniless, instead of one of the richest girls in England. Only, fortunately, she *was* one of the richest girls in England . . .

His mind played with attractive plans for the future. The Mastership of the Roxdale perhaps, the restoration of the west wing, no need to let the Scotch shooting . . .

Charles Windlesham dreamed in the sun.

V

It was four o'clock when the dilapidated little two-seater stopped with a sound of crunching gravel. A girl got out of it – a small slender creature with a mop of dark hair. She ran up the steps and tugged at the bell.

A few minutes later she was being ushered into the long stately drawing-room, and an ecclesiastical butler was saying with the proper mournful intonation: 'Miss de Bellefort.'

'Linnet!'

'Jackie!'

Windlesham stood a little aside, watching sympathetically as this fiery little creature flung herself open-armed upon Linnet.

'Lord Windlesham – Miss de Bellefort – my best friend.'

A pretty child, he thought – not really pretty but decidedly attractive, with her dark curly hair and her enormous eyes. He murmured a few tactful nothings and then managed unobtrusively to leave the two friends together.

Jacqueline pounced – in a fashion that Linnet remembered as being characteristic of her.

'Windlesham? Windlesham? *That's* the man the papers always say you're going to marry! Are you, Linnet? *Are* you?'

Linnet murmured: 'Perhaps.'

'Darling – I'm so glad! He looks nice.'

'Oh, don't make up your mind about it – I haven't made up my own mind yet.'

'Of course not! Queens always proceed with due deliberation to the choosing of a consort!'

'Don't be ridiculous, Jackie.'

'But you *are* a queen, Linnet! You always were. *Sa Majesté, la reine Linette. Linette la blonde*! And I – I'm the Queen's confidante! The trusted Maid of Honour.'

'What nonsense you talk, Jackie darling! Where have you been all this time? You just disappear. And you never write.'

'I hate writing letters. Where have I been? Oh, about three parts submerged, darling. In JOBS, you know. Grim jobs with grim women!'

'Darling, I wish you'd –'

'Take the Queen's bounty? Well, frankly, darling, that's what I'm here for. No, not to borrow money. It's not got to that yet! But I've come to ask a great big important favour!'

'Go on.'

'If you're going to marry the Windlesham man, you'll understand, perhaps.'

Linnet looked puzzled for a minute; then her face cleared.

'Jackie, do you mean –?'

'Yes, darling, *I'm engaged*!'

'So that's it! I thought you were looking particularly alive somehow. You always do, of course, but even more than usual.'

'That's just what I feel like.'

'Tell me all about him.'

'His name's Simon Doyle. He's big and square and incredibly simple and boyish and utterly adorable! He's poor – got no money. He's what you call "county" all right – but very impoverished county – a younger son and all that. His people come from Devonshire. He loves the country and country things. And for the last five years he's been in the City in a stuffy office. And now they're cutting down and he's out of a job. Linnet, I shall *die* if I can't marry him! I shall die! I shall die! I shall *die* . . .'

'Don't be ridiculous, Jackie.'

'I shall die, I tell you! I'm crazy about him. He's crazy about me. We can't live without each other.'

'Darling, you *have* got it badly!'

'I know. It's awful, isn't it? This love business gets hold of you and you can't do anything about it.'

She paused for a minute. Her dark eyes dilated, looked suddenly tragic. She gave a little shiver.

'It's – even frightening sometimes! Simon and I were made for each other. I shall never care for anyone else. And *you've* got to help us, Linnet. I heard you'd bought this place and it put an idea into my head. Listen, you'll have to have a land agent – perhaps two. I want you to give the job to Simon.'

'Oh!' Linnet was startled.

Jacqueline rushed on: 'He's got all that sort of thing at his finger-tips. He knows all about estates – was brought up on one. And he's got his business training too. Oh, Linnet, you will give him a job, won't you, for love of me? If he doesn't make good, sack him. But he will. And we can live in a little house, and I shall see lots of you, and everything in the garden will be too, too divine.'

She got up.

'Say you will, Linnet. Say you will. Beautiful Linnet! Tall golden Linnet! My own very special Linnet! Say you will!'

'Jackie –'

'You will?'

Linnet burst out laughing.

'Ridiculous Jackie! Bring along your young man and let me have a look at him and we'll talk it over.'

Jackie darted at her, kissing her exuberantly.

'*Darling Linnet* – you're a real friend! I knew you were. You wouldn't let me down – ever. You're just the loveliest thing in the world. Goodbye.'

'But, Jackie, you're *staying*.'

'Me? No, I'm not. I'm going back to London, and tomorrow I'll come back and bring Simon and we'll settle it all up. You'll adore him. He really is a *pet*.'

'But can't you wait and just have tea?'

'No, I can't wait, Linnet. I'm too excited. I must get back and tell Simon. I know I'm mad, darling, but I can't help it. Marriage will cure me, I expect. It always seems to have a very sobering effect on people.'

She turned at the door, stood a moment, then rushed back for a last quick birdlike embrace.

'Dear Linnet – there's no one like you.'

M. Gaston Blondin, the propriotor of that modish little restaurant Chez Ma Tante, was not a man who delighted to honour many of his clientèle. The rich, the beautiful, the notorious, and the well-born might wait in vain to be singled out and paid special attention. Only in the rarest cases did M. Blondin, with gracious condescension, greet a guest, accompany him to a privileged table, and exchange with him suitable and apposite remarks.

On this particular night, M. Blondin had exercised his royal prerogative three times – once for a Duchess, once for a famous racing peer, and once for a little man of comical appearance with immense black moustaches, who, a casual onlooker would have thought, could bestow no favour on Chez Ma Tante by his presence there.

M. Blondin, however, was positively fulsome in his attentions. Though clients had been told for the last half hour that a table was not to be had, one now mysteriously appeared, placed in a most favourable position. M. Blondin conducted the client to it with every appearance of *empressement*.

'But naturally, for *you* there is *always* a table, Monsieur Poirot! How I wish that you would honour us oftener!'

Hercule Poirot smiled, remembering that past incident wherein a dead body, a waiter, M. Blondin, and a very lovely lady had played a part.

'You are too amiable, Monsieur Blondin,' he said.

'And you are alone, Monsieur Poirot?'

'Yes, I am alone.'

'Oh, well, Jules here will compose for you a little meal that will be a poem – positively a poem! Women, however charming, have this disadvantage: they distract the mind from food! You will enjoy your dinner, Monsieur Poirot; I promise you that. Now as to wine –'

A technical conversation ensued, Jules, the *maître d'hotel*, assisting.

Before departing, M. Blondin lingered a moment, lowering his voice confidentially.

'You have grave affairs on hand?'

Poirot shook his head.

'I am, alas, a man of leisure,' he said softly. 'I have made the economies in my time and I have now the means to enjoy the life of idleness.'

'I envy you.'

'No, no, you would be unwise to do so. I can assure you, it is not so gay as it sounds.' He sighed. 'How true is the saying that man was forced to invent work in order to escape the strain of having to think.'

M. Blondin threw up his hands.

'But there is so much! There is travel!'

'Yes, there is travel. Already I have not done so badly. This winter I shall visit Egypt, I think. The climate, they say, is superb! One will escape from the fogs, the greyness, the monotony of the constantly falling rain.'

'Ah! Egypt,' breathed M. Blondin.

'One can even voyage there now, I believe, by train, escaping all sea travel except the Channel.'

'Ah, the sea, it does not agree with you?'

Hercule Poirot shook his head and shuddered slightly.

'I, too,' said M. Blondin with sympathy. 'Curious the effect it has upon the stomach.'

'But only upon certain stomachs! There are people on whom the motion makes no impression whatever. They actually *enjoy* it!'

'An unfairness of the good God,' said M. Blondin.

He shook his head sadly, and, brooding on the impious thought, withdrew.

Smooth-footed, deft-handed waiters ministered to the table. Toast Melba, butter, an ice pail, all the adjuncts to a meal of quality.

The Negro orchestra broke into an ecstasy of strange discordant noises. London danced.

Hercule Poirot looked on, registered impressions in his neat orderly mind.

How bored and weary most of the faces were! Some of those stout men, however, were enjoying themselves . . . whereas a patient endurance seemed to be the sentiment exhibited on their partners' faces. The fat woman in purple was looking radiant . . . Undoubtedly the fat had certain compensations in life . . . a zest – a gusto – denied to those of more fashionable contours.

A good sprinkling of young people – some vacant-looking – some bored – some definitely unhappy. How absurd to call youth the time of happiness – youth, the time of greatest vulnerability!

His glance softened as it rested on one particular couple. A well-matched pair – tall broad-shouldered man, slender delicate girl. Two bodies that moved in perfect rhythm of happiness. Happiness in the place, the hour, and in each other.

The dance stopped abruptly. Hands clapped and it started again. After a second *encore* the couple returned to their table close by Poirot. The girl was flushed, laughing. As she sat, he could study her face, lifted laughing to her companion.

There was something else beside laughter in her eyes. Hercule Poirot shook his head doubtfully.

'She cares too much, that little one,' he said to himself. It is not safe. No, it is not safe.'

And then a word caught his ear, 'Egypt.'

Their voices came to him clearly – the girl's young, fresh, arrogant, with just a trace of soft-sounding foreign R's, and the man's pleasant, low-toned, well-bred English.

'I'm *not* counting my chickens before they're hatched, Simon. I tell you Linnet won't let us down!'

'*I* might let *her* down.'

'Nonsense – it's just the right job for you.'

'As a matter of fact I think it is . . . I haven't really any doubts as to my capability. And I mean to make good – for *your* sake!'

The girl laughed softly, a laugh of pure happiness.

'We'll wait three months – to make sure you don't get the sack – and then –'

'And then I'll endow thee with my worldly goods – that's the hang of it, isn't it?'

'And, as I say, we'll go to Egypt for our honeymoon. Damn the expense! I've always wanted to go to Egypt all my life. The Nile and the Pyramids and the sand . . .'

He said, his voice slightly indistinct: 'We'll see it together, Jackie . . . together. Won't it be marvellous?'

'I wonder. Will it be as marvellous to you as it is to me? Do you really care – as much as I do?'

Her voice was suddenly sharp – her eyes dilated – almost with fear.

The man's answer came quickly crisp: 'Don't be absurd, Jackie.'

But the girl repeated: 'I wonder . . .'

Then she shrugged her shoulders. 'Let's dance.'

Hercule Poirot murmured to himself:

'*Une qui aime et un qui se laisse aimer.* Yes, I wonder too.'

VII

Joanna Southwood said: 'And suppose he's a terrible tough?'

Linnet shook her head. 'Oh, he won't be. I can trust Jacqueline's taste.'

Joanna murmured: 'Ah, but people don't run true to form in love affairs.'

Linnet shook her head impatiently. Then she changed the subject.

'I must go and see Mr Pierce about those plans.'

'Plans?'

'Yes, some dreadful insanitary old cottages. I'm having them pulled down and the people moved.'

'How sanitary and public-spirited of you, darling!'

'They'd have had to go anyway. Those cottages would have overlooked my new swimming pool.'

'Do the people who live in them like going?'

'Most of them are delighted. One or two are being rather stupid about it – really tiresome in fact. They don't seem to realize how vastly improved their living conditions will be!'

'But you're being quite high-handed about it, I presume.'

'My dear Joanna, it's to their advantage really.'

'Yes, dear. I'm sure it is. Compulsory benefit.'

Linnet frowned. Joanna laughed.

'Come now, you *are* a tyrant, admit it. A beneficent tyrant if you like!'

'I'm not the least bit of a tyrant.'

'But you like your own way!'

'Not especially.'

'Linnet Ridgeway, can you look me in the face and tell me of *any one occasion* on which you've failed to do exactly as you wanted?'

'Heaps of times.'

'Oh, yes, "heaps of times" – just like that – but no concrete example. And you simply can't think up one, darling, however hard you try! The triumphal progress of Linnet Ridgeway in her golden car.'

Linnet said sharply: 'You think I'm selfish?'

'No – just irresistible. The combined effect of money and charm. Everything goes down before you. What you can't buy with cash you buy with a smile. Result: Linnet Ridgeway, the Girl Who Has Everything.'

'Don't be ridiculous, Joanna!'

'Well, haven't you got everything?'

'I suppose I have . . . It sounds rather disgusting, somehow!'

'Of course it's disgusting, darling! You'll probably get terribly bored and blasé by and by. In the meantime, enjoy the triumphal progress in the golden car. Only I wonder, I really do wonder, what will happen when you want to go down a street which has a board saying "No Thoroughfare".'

'Don't be idiotic, Joanna.' As Lord Windlesham joined them, Linnet said, turning to him: 'Joanna is saying the nastiest things to me.'

'All spite, darling, all spite,' said Joanna vaguely as she got up from her seat.

She made no apology for leaving them. She had caught the glint in Windlesham's eye.

He was silent for a minute or two. Then he went straight to the point.

'Have you come to a decision, Linnet?'

Linnet said slowly: 'Am I being a brute? I suppose, if I'm not sure, I ought to say "No" –'

He interrupted her:

'Don't say it. You shall have time – as much time as you want. But I think, you know, we should be happy together.'

'You see,' Linnet's tone was apologetic, almost childish, 'I'm enjoying myself so much – especially with all this.' She waved a hand. 'I wanted to make Wode Hall into my real ideal of a country house, and I do think I've got it nice, don't you?'

'It's beautiful. Beautifully planned. Everything perfect. You're very clever, Linnet.'

He paused a minute and went on: 'And you like Charltonbury, don't you? Of course it wants modernizing and all that – but you're so clever at that sort of thing. You enjoy it.'

'Why, of course, Charltonbury's divine.'

She spoke with ready enthusiasm, but inwardly she was conscious of a sudden chill. An alien note had sounded, disturbing her complete satisfaction with life. She did not analyse the feeling at the moment, but later, when Windlesham had left her, she tried to probe the recesses of her mind.

Charltonbury – yes, that was it – she had resented the mention of Charltonbury. But why? Charltonbury was modestly famous. Windlesham's ancestors had held it since the time of Elizabeth. To be mistress of Charltonbury was a position unsurpassed in society. Windlesham was one of the most desirable peers in England.

Naturally he couldn't take Wode seriously . . . It was not in any way to be compared with Charltonbury.

Ah, but Wode was *hers*! She had seen it, acquired it, rebuilt and re-dressed it, lavished money on it. It was her own possession – her kingdom.

But in a sense it wouldn't count if she married Windlesham. What would they want with two country places? And of the two, naturally Wode Hall would be the one to be given up.

She, Linnet Ridgeway, wouldn't exist any longer. She would be Countess of Windlesham, bringing a fine dowry to Charltonbury and its master. She would be queen consort, not queen any longer.

'I'm being ridiculous,' said Linnet to herself.

But it was curious how she did hate the idea of abandoning Wode . . .

And wasn't there something else nagging at her?

Jackie's voice with that queer blurred note in it saying: 'I shall *die* if I can't marry him! I shall die. I shall die . . .'

So positive, so earnest. Did she, Linnet, feel like that about Windlesham? Assuredly she didn't. Perhaps she could never feel like that about anyone. It must be – rather wonderful – to feel like that . . .

The sound of a car came through the open window.

Linnet shook herself impatiently. That must be Jackie and her young man. She'd go out and meet them.

She was standing in the open doorway as Jacqueline and Simon Doyle got out of the car.

'Linnet!' Jackie ran to her. 'This is Simon. Simon, here's Linnet. She's just the most wonderful person in the world.'

Linnet saw a tall, broad-shouldered young man, with very dark blue eyes, crisply curling brown hair, a square chin, and a boyish, appealing, simple smile . . .

She stretched out a hand. The hand that clasped hers was firm and warm . . . She liked the way he looked at her, the naïve genuine admiration.

Jackie had told him she was wonderful, and he clearly thought that she was wonderful . . .

A warm sweet feeling of intoxication ran through her veins.

'Isn't this all lovely?' she said. 'Come in, Simon, and let me welcome my new land agent properly.'

And as she turned to lead the way she thought: 'I'm frightfully – frightfully happy. I like Jackie's young man . . . I like him enormously . . .'

And then a sudden pang: 'Lucky Jackie . . .'

VIII

Tim Allerton leant back in his wicker chair and yawned as he looked out over the sea. He shot a quick sidelong glance at his mother.

Mrs Allerton was a good-looking, white-haired woman of fifty. By imparting an expression of pinched severity to her mouth every time she looked at her son, she sought to disguise the fact of her intense affection for him. Even total strangers were seldom deceived by this device and Tim himself saw through it perfectly.

He said: 'Do you really like Majorca, Mother?'

'Well,' Mrs Allerton considered, 'it's cheap.'

'And cold,' said Tim with a slight shiver.

He was a tall, thin young man, with dark hair and a rather narrow chest. His mouth had a very sweet expression: his eyes were sad and his chin was indecisive. He had long delicate hands.

Threatened by consumption some years ago, he had never displayed a really robust physique. He was popularly supposed 'to write', but it was understood among his friends that inquiries as to literary output were not encouraged.

'What are you thinking of, Tim?'

Mrs Allerton was alert. Her bright, dark-brown eyes looked suspicious.

Tim Allerton grinned at her:

'I was thinking of Egypt.'

'Egypt?' Mrs Allerton sounded doubtful.

'Real warmth, darling. Lazy golden sands. The Nile. I'd like to go up the Nile, wouldn't you?'

'Oh, I'd *like* it.' Her tone was dry. 'But Egypt's expensive, my dear. Not for those who have to count the pennies.'

Tim laughed. He rose, stretched himself. Suddenly he looked alive and eager. There was an excited note in his voice.

'The expense will be my affair. Yes, darling. A little flutter on the Stock Exchange. With thoroughly satisfactory results. I heard this morning.'

'This morning?' said Mrs Allerton sharply. 'You only had one letter and that –'

She stopped and bit her lip.

Tim looked momentarily undecided whether to be amused or annoyed. Amusement gained the day.

'And that was from Joanna,' he finished coolly. 'Quite right, Mother. What a queen of detectives you'd make! The famous Hercule Poirot would have to look to his laurels if you were about.'

Mrs Allerton looked rather cross.

'I just happened to see the handwriting –'

'And knew it wasn't that of a stockbroker? Quite right. As a matter of fact it was yesterday I heard from them. Poor Joanna's handwriting *is* rather noticeable – sprawls about all over the envelope like an inebriated spider.'

'What does Joanna say? Any news?'

Mrs Allerton strove to make her voice sound casual and ordinary. The friendship between her son and his second cousin, Joanna Southwood, always irritated her. Not, as she put it to herself, that there was 'anything in it'. She was quite sure there wasn't. Tim had never manifested a sentimental interest in Joanna, nor she in him. Their mutual attraction seemed to be founded on gossip and the possession of a large number of friends and acquaintances in common. They both liked people and discussing people. Joanna had an amusing if caustic tongue.

It was not because Mrs Allerton feared that Tim might fall in love with Joanna that she found herself always becoming a little stiff in manner if Joanna were present or when letters from her arrived.

It was some other feeling hard to define – perhaps an un-acknowledged jealousy in the unfeigned pleasure Tim always seemed to take in Joanna's society. He and his mother were such perfect companions that the sight of him absorbed and interested in another woman always startled Mrs Allerton slightly. She fancied, too, that her own presence on these occasions set some barrier between the two members of the younger generation. Often she had come upon them eagerly absorbed in some conversation and, at sight of her, their talk had wavered, had seemed to include her rather too purposefully and as if duty bound. Quite definitely, Mrs Allerton did not like Joanna Southwood. She thought her insincere, affected, and essentially superficial. She found it very hard to prevent herself saying so in unmeasured tones.

In answer to her question, Tim pulled the letter out of his pocket and glanced through it. It was quite a long letter, his mother noted.

'Nothing much,' he said. 'The Devenishes are getting a divorce. Old Monty's been had up for being drunk in charge of a car. Windlesham's gone to Canada. Seems he was pretty badly hit when Linnet Ridgeway turned him down. She's definitely going to marry this land agent person.'

'How extraordinary! Is he very dreadful?'

'No, no, not at all. He's one of the Devonshire Doyles. No money, of course – and he was actually engaged to one of Linnet's best friends. Pretty thick, that.'

'I don't think it's at all nice,' said Mrs Allerton, flushing.

Tim flashed her a quick affectionate glance.

'I know, darling. You don't approve of snaffling other people's husbands and all that sort of thing.'

'In my day we had our standards,' said Mrs Allerton. 'And a very good thing too! Nowadays young people seem to think they can just go about doing anything they choose.'

Tim smiled. 'They don't only think it. They do it. *Vide* Linnet Ridgeway!'

'Well, I think it's horrid!'

Tim twinkled at her.

'Cheer up, you old die-hard! Perhaps I agree with you. Anyway, *I* haven't helped myself to anyone's wife or fiancée yet.'

'I'm sure you'd never do such a thing,' said Mrs Allerton. She added with spirit, 'I've brought you up properly.'

'So the credit is yours, not mine.'

He smiled teasingly at her as he folded the letter and put it away again. Mrs Allerton let the thought just flash across her mind: 'Most letters he shows to me. He only reads me snippets from Joanna's.'

But she put the unworthy thought away from her, and decided, as ever, to behave like a gentlewoman.

'Is Joanna enjoying life?' she asked.

'So so. Says she thinks of opening a delicatessen shop in Mayfair.'

'She always talks about being hard up,' said Mrs Allerton with a tinge of spite, 'but she goes about everywhere and her clothes must cost her a lot. She's always beautifully dressed.'

'Ah, well,' said Tim, 'she probably doesn't pay for them. No, mother, I don't mean what your Edwardian mind suggests to you. I just mean quite literally that she leaves her bills unpaid.'

Mrs Allerton sighed.

'I never know how people manage to do that.'

'It's a kind of special gift,' said Tim. 'If only you have sufficiently extravagant tastes, and absolutely no sense of money values, people will give you any amount of credit.'

'Yes, but you come to the Bankruptcy Court in the end like poor Sir George Wode.'

'You have a soft spot for that old horse coper – probably because he called you a rosebud in eighteen seventy-nine at a dance.'

'I wasn't born in eighteen seventy-nine,' Mrs Allerton retorted with spirit. 'Sir George has charming manners, and I won't have you calling him a horse coper.'

'I've heard funny stories about him from people that know.'

'You and Joanna don't mind what you say about people; anything will do so long as it's sufficiently ill-natured.'

Tim raised his eyebrows.

'My dear, you're quite heated. I didn't know old Wode was such a favourite of yours.'

'You don't realize how hard it was for him, having to sell Wode Hall. He cared terribly about that place.'

Tim suppressed the easy retort. After all, who was he to judge? Instead he said thoughtfully:

'You know, I think you're not far wrong there. Linnet asked

him to come down and see what she'd done to the place, and he refused quite rudely.'

'Of course. She ought to have known better than to ask him.'

'And I believe he's quite venomous about her – mutters things under his breath whenever he sees her. Can't forgive her for having given him an absolutely top price for the worm-eaten family estate.'

'And you can't understand that?' Mrs Allerton spoke sharply.

'Frankly,' said Tim calmly, 'I can't. Why live in the past? Why cling on to things that have been?'

'What are you going to put in their place?'

He shrugged his shoulders. 'Excitement, perhaps. Novelty. The joy of never knowing what may turn up from day to day. Instead of inheriting a useless tract of land, the pleasure of making money for yourself – by your own brains and skill.'

'A successful deal on the Stock Exchange, in fact!'

He laughed. 'Why not?'

'And what about an equal *loss* on the Stock Exchange?'

'That, dear, is rather tactless. And quite inappropriate today . . . What about this Egypt plan?'

'Well –'

He cut in smiling at her: 'That's settled. We've both always wanted to see Egypt.'

'When do you suggest?'

'Oh, next month. January's about the best time there. We'll enjoy the delightful society in this hotel a few weeks longer.'

'Tim,' said Mrs Allerton reproachfully. Then she added guiltily: 'I'm afraid I promised Mrs Leech that you'd go with her to the police station. She doesn't understand any Spanish.'

Tim made a grimace.

'About her ring? The blood-red ruby of the horse-leech's daughter? Does she still persist in thinking it's been stolen? I'll go if you like, but it's a waste of time. She'll only get some wretched chambermaid into trouble. I distinctly saw it on her finger when she went into the sea that day. It came off in the water and she never noticed.'

'She says she is quite sure she took it off and left it on her dressing-table.'

'Well, she didn't. I saw it with my own eyes. The woman's a fool. Any woman's a fool who goes prancing into the sea in December, pretending the water's quite warm just because the sun happens to be shining rather brightly at the moment. Stout women oughtn't to be allowed to bathe anyway; they look so revolting in bathing dresses.'

Mrs Allerton murmured, 'I really feel I ought to give up bathing.'

Tim gave a shout of laughter.

'You? You can give most of the young things points and to spare.'

Mrs Allerton sighed and said, 'I wish there were a few more young people for you here.'

Tim Allerton shook his head decidedly.

'I don't. You and I get along rather comfortably without outside distractions.'

'You'd like it if Joanna were here.'

'I wouldn't.' His tone was unexpectedly resolute. 'You're all wrong there. Joanna amuses me, but I don't really like her, and to have her around much gets on my nerves. I'm thankful she isn't here. I should be quite resigned if I were never to see Joanna again.'

He added, almost below his breath, 'There's only one woman in the world I've got a real respect and admiration for, and I think, Mrs Allerton, you know very well who that woman is.'

His mother blushed and looked quite confused.

Tim said gravely: 'There aren't very many really nice women in the world. You happen to be one of them.'

IX

In an apartment overlooking Central Park in New York Mrs Robson exclaimed: 'If that isn't just too lovely! You really are the luckiest girl, Cornelia.'

Cornelia Robson flushed responsively. She was a big clumsy looking girl with brown doglike eyes.

'Oh, it will be wonderful!' she gasped.

Old Miss Van Schuyler inclined her head in a satisfied fashion at this correct attitude on the part of poor relations. 'I've always dreamed of a trip to Europe,' sighed Cornelia, 'but I just didn't feel I'd ever get there.'

'Miss Bowers will come with me as usual, of course,' said Miss Van Schuyler, 'but as a social companion I find her limited –

very limited. There are many little things that Cornelia can do for me.'

'I'd just love to, Cousin Marie,' said Cornelia eagerly.

'Well, well, then that's settled,' said Miss Van Schuyler. 'Just run and find Miss Bowers, my dear. It's time for my eggnog.'

Cornelia departed. Her mother said: 'My dear Marie, I'm really *most* grateful to you! You know I think Cornelia suffers a lot from not being a social success. It makes her feel kind of mortified. If I could afford to take her to places – but you know how it's been since Ned died.'

'I'm very glad to take her,' said Miss Van Schuyler. 'Cornelia has always been a nice handy girl, willing to run errands, and not so selfish as some of these young people nowadays.'

Mrs Robson rose and kissed her rich relative's wrinkled and slightly yellow face.

'I'm just ever so grateful,' she declared.

On the stairs she met a tall capable-looking woman who was carrying a glass containing a yellow foamy liquid.

'Well, Miss Bowers, so you're off to Europe?'

'Why, yes, Mrs Robson.'

'What a lovely trip!'

'Why, yes, I should think it would be very enjoyable.'

'But you've been abroad before?'

'Oh, yes, Mrs Robson. I went over to Paris with Miss Van Schuyler last fall. But I've never been to Egypt before.'

Mrs Robson hesitated.

'I do hope – there won't be any – trouble.'

She had lowered her voice. Miss Bowers, however, replied in her usual tone:

'Oh, *no*, Mrs Robson; I shall take good care of *that*. I keep a very sharp look-out always.'

But there was still a faint shadow on Mrs Robson's face as she slowly continued down the stairs.

X

In his office down town Mr Andrew Pennington was opening his personal mail. Suddenly his fist clenched itself and came down on his desk with a bang; his face crimsoned and two big veins stood out on his forehead. He pressed a buzzer on his desk and a smart-looking stenographer appeared with commendable promptitude.

'Tell Mr Rockford to step in here.'

'Yes, Mr Pennington.'

A few minutes later, Sterndale Rockford, Pennington's partner, entered the office. The two men were not unlike – both tall, spare, with greying hair and clean-shaven, clever faces.

'What's up, Pennington?'

Pennington looked up from the letter he was re-reading. He said. 'Linnet's married . . .'

'*What?*'

'You heard what I said! Linnet Ridgeway's *married*!'

'How? When? Why didn't we hear about it?'

Pennington glanced at the calendar on his desk.

'She wasn't married when she wrote this letter, but she's married now. Morning of the fourth. That's today.'

Rockford dropped into a chair.

'Whew! No warning! Nothing? Who's the man?'

Pennington referred again to the letter.

'Doyle. Simon Doyle.'

'What sort of a fellow is he? Ever heard of him?'

'No. She doesn't say much . . .' He scanned the lines of clear, upright handwriting. 'Got an idea there's something hole-and-corner about this business . . . That doesn't matter. The whole point is, she's married.'

The eyes of the two men met. Rockford nodded.

'This needs a bit of thinking out,' he said quietly.

'What are we going to do about it?'

'I'm asking you.'

The two men sat silent. Then Rockford asked, 'Got any plan?'

Pennington said slowly: 'The *Normandie* sails today. One of us could just make it.'

'You're crazy! What's the big idea?'

Pennington began: 'Those British lawyers –' and stopped.

'What about 'em. Surely you're not going over to tackle 'em? You're mad!'

'I'm not suggesting that you – or I – should go to England.'

'What's the big idea, then?'

Pennington smoothed out the letter on the table.

'Linnet's going to Egypt for her honeymoon. Expects to be there a month or more . . .'

'Egypt – eh?'

Rockford considered. Then he looked up and met the other's glance.

'Egypt,' he said; '*that's* your idea!'

'Yes – a chance meeting. Over on a trip. Linnet and her husband – honeymoon atmosphere. It might be done.'

Rockford said doubtfully: 'She's sharp, Linnet is . . . but –'

Pennington went on softly: 'I think there might be ways of – managing it.'

Again their eyes met. Rockford nodded.

'All right, big boy.'

Pennington looked at the clock.

'We'll have to hustle – whichever of us is going.'

'You go,' said Rockford promptly. 'You always made a hit with Linnet. "Uncle Andrew." That's the ticket!'

Pennington's face had hardened. He said: 'I hope I can pull it off.'

'You've got to pull it off,' his partner said. 'The situation's critical . . .'

XI

William Carmichael said to the thin, weedy youth who opened the door inquiringly: 'Send Mr Jim to me, please.'

Jim Fanthorp entered the room and looked inquiringly at his uncle. The older man looked up with a nod and a grunt.

'Humph, there you are.'

'You asked for me?'

'Just cast an eye over this.'

The young man sat down and drew the sheaf of papers towards him. The elder man watched him.

'Well?'

The answer came promptly. 'Looks fishy to me, sir.'

Again the senior partner of Carmichael, Grant & Carmichael uttered his characteristic grunt.

Jim Fanthorp re-read the letter which had just arrived by air mail from Egypt:

. . . It seems wicked to be writing business letters on such a day. We have spent a week at Mena House and made an expedition to the Fayum. The day after tomorrow we are going up the Nile to Luxor and Assuan by steamer, and perhaps on to Khartoum. When we went into Cook's this morning to see about our tickets who do you think was the first person I saw? – my American trustee, Andrew Pennington. I think you met him two years ago when he was over. I had no idea he was in Egypt and he had no idea that I was! Nor that I was married! My letter, telling him of my marriage, must just have missed him. He is actually going up the Nile on the same trip that we are. Isn't it a coincidence? Thank you so much for all you have done in this busy time. I –

As the young man was about to turn the page, Mr Carmichael took the letter from him.

'That's all,' he said. 'The rest doesn't matter. Well, what do you think?'

His nephew considered for a moment – then he said:

'Well – I think – not a coincidence . . .'

The other nodded approval.

'Like a trip to Egypt?' he barked out.

'You think that's advisable?'

'I think there's no time to lose.'

'But, why me?'

'Use your brains, boy; use your brains. Linnet Ridgeway has never met you; no more has Pennington. If you go by air you may get there in time.'

'I – I don't like it.'

'Perhaps not – but you've got to do it.'

'It's – necessary?'

'In my opinion,' said Mr Carmichael, 'it's absolutely vital.'

XII

Mrs Otterbourne, readjusting the turban of native material that she wore draped round her head, said fretfully:

'I really don't see why we shouldn't go on to Egypt. I'm sick and tired of Jerusalem.'

As her daughter made no reply, she said, 'You might at least answer when you're spoken to.'

Rosalie Otterbourne was looking at a newspaper reproduction of a face. Below it was printed:

Mrs Simon Doyle, who before her marriage was the well-known society beauty, Miss Linnet Ridgeway. Mr and Mrs Doyle are spending their holiday in Egypt.

Rosalie said, 'You'd like to move on to Egypt, Mother?'

'Yes, I would,' Mrs Otterbourne snapped. 'I consider they've treated us in a most cavalier fashion here. My being here is an advertisement – I ought to get a special reduction in terms. When I hinted as much, I consider they were most impertinent – *most* impertinent. I told them exactly what I thought of them.'

The girl sighed. She said: 'One place is very like another. I wish we could get right away.'

'And this morning,' went on Mrs Otterbourne, 'the manager actually had the impertinence to tell me that all the rooms had been booked in advance and that he would require ours in two days' time.'

'So we've got to go somewhere.'

'Not at all. I'm quite prepared to fight for my rights.'

Rosalie murmured: 'I suppose we might as well go on to Egypt. It doesn't make any difference.'

'It's certainly not a matter of life or death,' agreed Mrs Otterbourne.

But there she was quite wrong – for a matter of life and death was exactly was it was.

CHAPTER 2

'That's Hercule Poirot, the detective,' said Mrs Allerton.

She and her son were sitting in brightly painted scarlet basket chairs outside the Cataract Hotel in Assuan. They were watching the retreating figures of two people – a short man dressed in a white silk suit and a tall slim girl.

Tim Allerton sat up in an unusually alert fashion.

'That funny little man?' he asked incredulously.

'That funny little man!'

'What on earth's he doing here?' Tim asked.

His mother laughed. 'Darling, you sound quite excited. Why do men enjoy crime so much? I hate detective stories and never read them. But I don't think Monsieur Poirot is here with any ulterior motive. He's made a good deal of money and he's seeing life, I fancy.'

'Seems to have an eye for the best-looking girl in the place.'

Mrs Allerton tilted her head a little on one side as she considered the retreating backs of M. Poirot and his companion.

The girl by his side overtopped him by some three inches. She walked well, neither stiffly nor sloughingly.

'I suppose she *is* quite good-looking,' said Mrs Allerton. She shot a little glance sideways at Tim. Somewhat to her amusement the fish rose at once.

'She's more than quite. Pity she looks so bad-tempered and sulky.'

'Perhaps that's just expression, dear.'

'Unpleasant young devil, I think. But she's pretty enough.'

The subject of these remarks was walking slowly by Poirot's side. Rosalie Otterbourne was twirling an unopened parasol, and her expression certainly bore out what Tim had just said. She looked both sulky and bad-tempered. Her eyebrows were drawn together in a frown, and the scarlet line of her mouth was drawn downward.

They turned to the left out of the hotel gate and entered the cool shade of the public gardens.

Hercule Poirot was prattling gently, his expression that of beatific good humour. He wore a white silk suit, carefully pressed, and a panama hat, and carried a highly ornamental fly whisk with a sham amber handle.

'– it enchants me,' he was saying. 'The black rocks of Elephantine, and the sun, and the little boats on the river. Yes, it is good to be alive.'

He paused and then added: 'You do not find it so, Mademoiselle?'

Rosalie Otterbourne said shortly: 'It's all right, I suppose. I think Assuan's a gloomy sort of place. The hotel's half empty, and everyone's about a hundred –'

She stopped – biting her lip.

Hercule Poirot's eyes twinkled.

'It is true, yes, I have one leg in the grave.'

'I – I wasn't thinking of you,' said the girl. 'I'm sorry. That sounded rude.'

'Not at all. It is natural you should wish for companions of your own age. Ah, well, there is *one* young man, at least.'

'The one who sits with his mother all the time? I like *her* – but I think he looks dreadful – so conceited!'

Poirot smiled.

'And I – am I conceited?'

'Oh, I don't think so.'

She was obviously uninterested – but the fact did not seem to annoy Poirot. He merely remarked with placid satisfaction:

'My best friend says that I am very conceited.'

'Oh, well,' said Rosalie vaguely, 'I suppose you have something to be conceited about. Unfortunately crime doesn't interest me in the least.'

Poirot said solemnly, 'I am delighted to learn that you have no guilty secret to hide.'

Just for a moment the sulky mask of her face was transformed as she shot him a swift questioning glance. Poirot did not seem to notice it as he went on:

'Madame, your mother, was not at lunch today. She is not indisposed, I trust?'

'This place doesn't suit her,' said Rosalie briefly. 'I shall be glad when we leave.'

'We are fellow passengers, are we not? We both make the excursion up to Wadi Halfa and the Second Cataract?'

'Yes.'

They came out from the shade of the gardens on to a dusty stretch of road bordered by the river. Five watchful bead-sellers, two vendors of postcards, three sellers of plaster scarabs, a couple of donkey boys and some detached but hopeful infantile riff-raff closed in upon them.

'You want beads, sir? Very good, sir. Very cheap . . .'

'Lady, you want scarab? Look – great queen – very lucky . . .'

'You look, sir – real lapis. Very good, very cheap . . .'

'You want ride donkey, sir? This very good donkey. This donkey Whiskey and Soda, sir . . .'

'You want to go granite quarries, sir? This very good donkey. Other donkey very bad, sir, that donkey fall down . . .'

'You want postcard – very cheap – very nice . . .'

'Look, lady . . . Only ten piastres – very cheap – lapis – this ivory . . .'

217

'This very good fly whisk – this all-amber . . .'

'You go out in boat, sir? I got very good boat, sir . . .'

'You go back to hotel, lady? This first-class donkey . . .'

Hercule Poirot made vague gestures to rid himself of this human cluster of flies. Rosalie stalked through them like a sleep-walker.

'It's best to pretend to be deaf and blind,' she remarked.

The infantile riff-raff ran alongside murmuring plaintively: 'Bakshish? Bakshish? Hip hip hurrah – very good, very nice . . .'

Their gaily coloured rags trailed picturesquely, and the flies lay in clusters on their eyelids. They were the most persistent. The others fell back and launched a fresh attack on the next corner.

Now Poirot and Rosalie only ran the gauntlet of the shops – suave, persuasive accents here . . .

'You visit my shop today, sir?' 'You want that ivory crocodile, sir?' 'You not been in my shop yet, sir? I show you very beautiful things.'

They turned into the fifth shop and Rosalie handed over several rolls of film – the object of the walk.

Then they came out again and walked towards the river's edge.

One of the Nile steamers was just mooring. Poirot and Rosalie looked interestedly at the passengers.

'Quite a lot, aren't there?' commented Rosalie.

She turned her head as Tim Allerton came up and joined them. He was a little out of breath as though he had been walking fast.

They stood there for a moment or two, and then Tim spoke.

'An awful crowd as usual, I suppose,' he remarked dispar-agingly, indicating the disembarking passengers.

'They're usually quite terrible,' agreed Rosalie.

All three wore the air of superiority assumed by people who are already in a place when studying new arrivals.

'Hullo!' exclaimed Tim, his voice suddenly excited. 'I'm damned if that isn't Linnet Ridgeway.'

If the information left Poirot unmoved, it stirred Rosalie's interest. She leaned forward and her sulkiness quite dropped from her as she asked: 'Where? That one in white?'

'Yes, there with the tall man. They're coming ashore now. He's the new husband, I suppose. Can't remember his name now.'

'Doyle,' said Rosalie. 'Simon Doyle. It was in all the newspapers. She's simply rolling, isn't she?'

'Only about the richest girl in England,' replied Tim cheerfully.

The three lookers-on were silent watching the passengers come ashore. Poirot gazed with interest at the subject of the remarks of his companions. He murmured: 'She is beautiful.'

'Some people have got everything,' said Rosalie bitterly.

There was a queer grudging expression on her face as she watched the other girl come up the gangplank.

Linnet Doyle was looking as perfectly turned out as if she were stepping on to the centre of the stage of a revue. She had something too of the assurance of a famous actress. She was used to being looked at, to being admired, to being the centre of the stage wherever she went.

She was aware of the keen glances bent upon her – and at the same time almost unaware of them; such tributes were part of her life.

She came ashore playing a role, even though she played it unconsciously. The rich beautiful society bride on her honeymoon. She turned, with a little smile and a light remark, to the tall man by her side. He answered, and the sound of his voice seemed to interest Hercule Poirot. His eyes lit up and he drew his brows together.

The couple passed close to him. He heard Simon Doyle say:

'We'll try and make time for it, darling. We can easily stay a week or two if you like it here.'

His face was turned towards her, eager, adoring, a little humble.

Poirot's eyes ran over him thoughtfully – the square shoulders, the bronzed face, the dark blue eyes, the rather childlike simplicity of the smile.

'Lucky devil,' said Tim after they had passed. 'Fancy finding an heiress who hasn't got adenoids and flat feet!'

'They look frightfully happy,' said Rosalie with a note of envy in her voice. She added suddenly, but so low that Tim did not catch the words, 'It isn't fair.'

Poirot heard, however. He had been frowning somewhat perplexedly, but now he flashed a quick glance towards her.

Tim said: 'I must collect some stuff for my mother now.'

He raised his hat and moved off. Poirot and Rosalie retraced their steps slowly in the direction of the hotel, waving aside fresh proffers of donkeys.

'So it is not fair, Mademoiselle?' asked Poirot gently.

The girl flushed angrily.

'I don't know what you mean.'

'I am repeating what you said just now under your breath. Oh, yes, you did.'

Rosalie Otterbourne shrugged her shoulders.

'It really seems a little too much for one person. Money, good looks, marvellous figure and –'

She paused and Poirot said:

'And love? Eh? And love? But you do not know – she may have been married for her money!'

'Didn't you see the way he looked at her?'

'Oh, yes, Mademoiselle. I saw all there was to see – indeed I saw something that you did not.'

'What was that?'

Poirot said slowly: 'I saw, Mademoiselle, dark lines below a woman's eyes. I saw a hand that clutched a sun-shade so tight that the knuckles were white . . .'

Rosalie was staring at him.

'What do you mean?'

'I mean that all is not the gold that glitters. I mean that, though this lady is rich and beautiful and beloved, there is all the same *something* that is not right. And I know something else.'

'Yes?'

'I know,' said Poirot, frowning, 'that somewhere, at some time, I have heard that voice before – the voice of Monsieur Doyle – and I wish I could remember where.'

But Rosalie was not listening. She had stopped dead. With the point of her sunshade she was tracing patterns in the loose sand. Suddenly she broke out fiercely:

'I'm odious. I'm quite odious. I'm just a beast through and through. I'd like to tear the clothes off her back and stamp on her lovely, arrogant, self-confident face. I'm just a jealous cat – but that's what I feel like. She's so horribly successful and poised and assured.'

Hercule Poirot looked a little astonished by the outburst. He took her by the arm and gave her a friendly little shake.

'*Tenez* – you will feel better for having said that!'

'I just hate her! I've never hated anyone so much at first sight.'

'Magnificent!'

Rosalie looked at him doubtfully. Then her mouth twitched and she laughed.

'*Bien*,' said Poirot, and laughed too.

They proceeded amicably back to the hotel.

'I must find Mother,' said Rosalie, as they came into the cool dim hall.

Poirot passed out on the other side on to the terrace overlooking the Nile. Here were little tables set for tea, but it was early still. He stood for a few moments looking at the river, then strolled down through the garden.

Some people were playing tennis in the hot sun. He paused to watch them for a while, then went on down the steep path. It was here, sitting on a bench overlooking the Nile, that he came upon the girl of Chez Ma Tante. He recognized her at once. Her face, as he had seen it that night, was securely etched upon his memory. The expression on it now was very different. She was paler, thinner, and there were lines that told of a great weariness and misery of spirit.

He drew back a little. She had not seen him, and he watched her for a while without her suspecting his presence. Her small foot tapped impatiently on the ground. Her eyes, dark with a kind of smouldering fire, had a queer kind of suffering dark triumph in them. She was looking out across the Nile where the white-sailed boats glided up and down the river.

A face – and a voice. He remembered them both. This girl's face and the voice he had heard just now, the voice of a newly made bridegroom . . .

And even as he stood there considering the unconscious girl, the next scene in the drama was played.

Voices sounded above. The girl on the seat started to her feet. Linnet Doyle and her husband came down the path. Linnet's voice was happy and confident. The look of strain and tenseness of muscle had quite disappeared, Linnet was happy.

The girl who was standing there took a step or two forward. The other two stopped dead.

'Hullo, Linnet,' said Jacqueline de Bellefort. 'So here you are!

221

We never seem to stop running into each other. Hullo, Simon, how are you?'

Linnet Doyle had shrunk back against the rock with a little cry. Simon Doyle's good-looking face was suddenly convulsed with rage. He moved forward as though he would have liked to strike the slim girlish figure.

With a quick birdlike turn of her head she signalled her realization of a stranger's presence. Simon turned his head and noticed Poirot. He said awkwardly: 'Hullo, Jacqueline; we didn't expect to see you here.'

The words were unconvincing in the extreme.

The girl flashed white teeth at them.

'Quite a surprise?' she asked. Then, with a little nod, she walked up the path.

Poirot moved delicately in the opposite direction. As he went, he heard Linnet Doyle say:

'Simon – for God's sake! Simon – what can we do?'

CHAPTER 3

Dinner was over. The terrace outside the Cataract Hotel was softly lit. Most of the guests staying at the hotel were sitting at little tables.

Simon and Linnet Doyle came out, a tall, distinguished looking grey-haired man, with a keen, clean-shaven American face, beside them. As the little group hesitated in the doorway, Tim Allerton rose from his chair nearby and came forward.

'You don't remember me I'm sure,' he said pleasantly to Linnet, 'but I'm Joanna Southwood's cousin.'

'Of course – how stupid of me! You're Tim Allerton. This is my husband' – a faint tremor in the voice, pride, shyness? – 'and this is my American trustee, Mr Pennington.'

Tim said: 'You must meet my mother.'

A few minutes later they were sitting together in a party – Linnet in the corner, Tim and Pennington each side of her, both talking to her, vying for her attention. Mrs Allerton talked to Simon Doyle.

The swing doors revolved. A sudden tension came into the beautiful upright figure sitting in the corner between the two men. Then it relaxed as a small man came out and walked across the terrace.

Mrs Allerton said: 'You're not the only celebrity here, my dear. That funny little man is Hercule Poirot.'

She had spoken lightly, just out of instinctive social tact to bridge an awkward pause, but Linnet seemed struck by the information.

'Hercule Poirot? Of course – I've heard of him . . .'

She seemed to sink into a fit of abstraction. The two men on either side of her were momentarily at a loss.

Poirot had strolled across to the edge of the terrace, but his attention was immediately solicited.

'Sit down, Monsieur Poirot. What a lovely night!'

He obeyed.

'*Mais oui, Madame*, it is indeed beautiful.'

He smiled politely at Mrs Otterbourne. What draperies of black ninon and that ridiculous turban effect! Mrs Otterbourne went on in her high complaining voice:

'Quite a lot of notabilities here now, aren't there? I expect we shall see a paragraph about it in the papers soon. Society beauties, famous novelists –'

She paused with a slight mock-modest laugh.

Poirot felt, rather than saw, the sulky frowning girl opposite him flinch and set her mouth in a sulkier line than before.

'You have a novel on the way at present, Madame?' he inquired.

Mrs Otterbourne gave her little self-conscious laugh again.

'I'm being dreadfully lazy. I really must set to. My public is getting terribly impatient – and my publisher, poor man! Appeals by every post! Even cables!'

Again he felt the girl shift in the darkness.

'I don't mind telling you, Monsieur Poirot, I am partly here for local colour. *Snow on the Desert's Face* – that is the title of my new book. Powerful – suggestive. Snow – on the desert – melted in the first flaming breath of passion.'

Rosalie got up, muttering something, and moved away down into the dark garden.

'One must be strong,' went on Mrs Otterbourne, wagging the turban emphatically. 'Strong meat – that is what my books are – all important. Libraries banned – no matter! I speak the truth.

Sex – ah! Monsieur Poirot – why is everyone so afraid of sex? The pivot of the universe! You have read my books?'

'Alas, Madame! You comprehend, I do not read many novels. My work –'

Mrs Otterbourne said firmly: 'I must give you a copy of *Under the Fig Tree*. I think you will find it significant. It is outspoken – but it is *real*!'

'That is most kind of you, Madame. I will read it with pleasure.'

Mrs Otterbourne was silent a minute or two. She fidgeted with a long chain of beads that was wound twice round her neck. She looked swiftly from side to side.

'Perhaps – I'll just slip up and get it for you now.'

'Oh, Madame, pray do not trouble yourself. Later –'

'No, no. It's no trouble.' She rose. 'I'd like to show you –'

'What is it, Mother?'

Rosalie was suddenly at her side.

'Nothing, dear. I was just going up to get a book for Monsieur Poirot.'

'The *Fig Tree*? I'll get it.'

'You don't know where it is, dear. I'll go.'

'Yes, I do.'

The girl went swiftly across the terrace and into the hotel.

'Let me congratulate you, Madame, on a very lovely daughter,' said Poirot, with a bow.

'Rosalie? Yes, yes – she is good-looking. But she's very *hard*, Monsieur Poirot. And no sympathy with illness. She always thinks she knows best. She imagines she knows more about my health than I do myself –'

Poirot signalled to a passing waiter.

'A liqueur, Madame? A chartreuse? A crème de menthe?'

Mrs Otterbourne shook her head vigorously.

'No, no. I am practically a teetotaller. You may have noticed I never drink anything but water – or perhaps lemonade. I cannot bear the taste of spirits.'

'Then may I order you a lemon squash, Madame?'

He gave the order – one lemon squash and one Benedictine.

The swing door revolved. Rosalie passed through and came towards them, a book in her hand.

224

'Here you are,' she said. Her voice was quite expressionless – almost remarkably so.

'Monsieur Poirot has just ordered me a lemon squash,' said her mother.

'And you, Mademoiselle, what will you take?'

'Nothing.' She added, suddenly conscious of the curtness: 'Nothing, thank you.'

Poirot took the volume which Mrs Otterbourne held out to him. It still bore its original jacket, a gaily coloured affair representing a lady, with smartly shingled hair and scarlet fingernails, sitting on a tiger skin, in the traditional costume of Eve. Above her was a tree with the leaves of an oak, bearing large and improbably coloured apples.

It was entitled *Under the Fig Tree*, by Salome Otterbourne. On the inside was a publisher's blurb. It spoke enthusiastically of the superb courage and realism of this study of a modern woman's love life. 'Fearless, unconventional, realistic,' were the adjectives used.

Poirot bowed and murmured: 'I am honoured, Madame.'

As he raised his head, his eyes met those of the authoress's daughter. Almost involuntarily he made a little movement. He was astonished and grieved at the eloquent pain they revealed.

It was at that moment that the drinks arrived and created a welcome diversion.

Poirot lifted his glass gallantly.

'*A votre santé, Madame – Mademoiselle.*'

Mrs Otterbourne, sipping her lemonade, murmured, 'So refreshing – delicious!'

Silence fell on the three of them. They looked down to the shining black rocks in the Nile. There was something fantastic about them in the moonlight. They were like vast prehistoric monsters lying half out of the water. A little breeze came up suddenly and as suddenly died away. There was a feeling in the air of hush – of expectancy.

Hercule Poirot brought his gaze back to the terrace and its occupants. Was he wrong, or was there the same hush of expectancy there? It was like a moment on the stage when one is waiting for the entrance of the leading lady.

And just at that moment the swing doors began to revolve once more. This time it seemed as though they did so with a special air of importance. Everyone had stopped talking and was looking towards them.

A dark slender girl in a wine-coloured evening frock came through. She paused for a minute, then walked deliberately across the terrace and sat down at an empty table. There was nothing flaunting, nothing out of the way about her demeanour, and yet it had somehow the studied effect of a stage entrance.

'Well,' said Mrs Otterbourne. She tossed her turbaned head. 'She seems to think she is somebody, that girl!'

Poirot did not answer. He was watching. The girl had sat down in a place where she could look deliberately across at Linnet Doyle. Presently, Poirot noticed, Linnet Doyle leant forward and said something and a moment later got up and changed her seat. She was now sitting facing in the opposite direction.

Poirot nodded thoughtfully to himself.

It was about five minutes later that the other girl changed her seat to the opposite side of the terrace. She sat smoking and smiling quietly, the picture of contented ease. But always, as though unconsciously, her meditative gaze was on Simon Doyle's wife.

After a quarter of an hour Linnet Doyle got up abruptly and went into the hotel. Her husband followed her almost immediately.

Jacqueline de Bellefort smiled and twisted her chair round. She lit a cigarette and stared out over the Nile. She went on smiling to herself.

CHAPTER 4

'Monsieur Poirot.'

Poirot got hastily to his feet. He had remained sitting out on the terrace alone after everyone else had left. Lost in meditation he had been staring at the smooth shiny black rocks when the sound of his name recalled him to himself.

It was a well-bred, assured voice, a charming voice, although perhaps a trifle arrogant.

Hercule Poirot, rising quickly, looked into the commanding eyes of Linnet Doyle. She wore a wrap of rich purple velvet over her white satin gown and she looked more lovely and more regal than Poirot had imagined possible.

'You are Monsieur Hercule Poirot?' said Linnet.

It was hardly a question.

'At your service, Madame.'

'You know who I am, perhaps?'

'Yes, Madame. I have heard your name. I know exactly who you are.'

Linnet nodded. That was only what she had expected. She went on, in her charming autocratic manner: 'Will you come with me into the card room, Monsieur Poirot? I am very anxious to speak to you.'

'Certainly, Madame.'

She led the way into the hotel. He followed. She led him into the deserted card room and motioned him to close the door. Then she sank down on a chair at one of the tables and he sat down opposite her.

She plunged straightaway into what she wanted to say. There were no hesitations. Her speech came flowingly.

'I have heard a great deal about you, Monsieur Poirot, and I know that you are a very clever man. It happens that I am urgently in need of someone to help me – and I think very possibly that you are the man who would do it.'

Poirot inclined his head.

'You are very amiable, Madame, but you see, I am on holiday, and when I am on holiday I do not take cases.'

'That could be arranged.'

It was not offensively said – only with the quiet confidence of a young woman who had always been able to arrange matters to her satisfaction.

Linnet Doyle went on: 'I am the subject, Monsieur Poirot, of an intolerable persecution. That persecution has got to stop! My own idea was to go to the police about it, but my – my husband seems to think that the police would be powerless to do anything.'

'Perhaps – if you would explain a little further?' murmured Poirot politely.

'Oh, yes, I will do so. The matter is perfectly simple.'

There was still no hesitation – no faltering. Linnet Doyle had a clear-cut businesslike mind. She only paused a minute so as to present the facts as concisely as possible.

'Before I met my husband, he was engaged to a Miss de Bellefort. She was also a friend of mine. My husband broke off his engagement to her – they were not suited in any way. She, I am sorry to say, took it rather hard . . . I – am very sorry about that – but these things cannot be helped. She made certain – well, threats – to which I paid very little attention, and which, I may say, she has not attempted to carry out. But instead she has adopted the extraordinary course of – of following us about wherever we go.'

Poirot raised his eyebrows.

'Ah – rather an unusual – er – revenge.'

'Very unusual – and very ridiculous! But also – annoying.'

She bit her lip.

Poirot nodded.

'Yes, I can imagine that. You are, I understand, on your honeymoon?'

'Yes. It happened – the first time – at Venice. She was there – at Danielli's. I thought it was just coincidence. Rather embarrassing, but that was all. Then we found her on board the boat at Brindisi. We – we understood that she was going on to Palestine. We left her, as we thought, on the boat. But – but when we got to Mena House she was there – waiting for us.'

Poirot nodded.

'And now?'

'We came up the Nile by boat. I – I was half expecting to find her on board. When she wasn't there I thought she had stopped being so – so childish. But when we got here – she – she was here – waiting.'

Poirot eyed her keenly for a moment. She was still perfectly composed, but the knuckles of the hand that was gripping the table were white with the force of her grip.

He said: 'And you are afraid this state of things may continue?'

'Yes.' She paused. 'Of course the whole thing is idiotic! Jacqueline is making herself utterly ridiculous. I am surprised she hasn't got more pride – more dignity.'

Poirot made a slight gesture.

'There are times, Madame, when pride and dignity – they go by the board! There are other – stronger emotions.'

'Yes, possibly.' Linnet spoke impatiently. 'But what on earth can she hope to *gain* by all this?'

'It is not always a question of gain, Madame.'

Something in his tone struck Linnet disagreeably. She flushed and said quickly: 'You are right. A discussion of motives is beside the point. The crux of the matter is that this has got to be stopped.'

'And how do you propose that that should be accomplished, Madame?' Poirot asked.

'Well – naturally – my husband and I cannot continue being subjected to this annoyance. There must be some kind of legal redress against such a thing.'

She spoke impatiently. Poirot looked at her thoughtfully as he asked: 'Has she threatened you in actual words in public? Used insulting language? Attempted any bodily harm?'

'No.'

'Then, frankly, Madame, I do not see what you can do. If it is a young lady's pleasure to travel in certain places, and those places are the same where you and your husband find themselves – *eh bien* – what of it? The air is free to all! There is no question of her forcing herself upon your privacy? It is always in public that these encounters take place?'

'You mean there is nothing that I can do about it?' Linnet sounded incredulous.

Poirot said placidly: 'Nothing at all, as far as I can see. Mademoiselle de Bellefort is within her rights.'

'But – but it is maddening! It is *intolerable* that I should have to put up with this!'

Poirot said dryly: 'I must sympathize with you, Madame – especially as I imagine that you have not often had to put up with things.'

Linnet was frowning.

'There *must* be some way of stopping it,' she murmured.

Poirot shrugged his shoulders.

'You can always leave – move on somewhere else,' he suggested.

'Then she will follow!'

'Very possibly – yes.'

'It's absurd!'

'Precisely.'

'Anyway, why should I – we – run away? As though – as though –'

She stopped.

'Exactly, Madame. As though –! It is all there, is it not?'

Linnet lifted her head and stared at him.

'What do you mean?'

Poirot altered his tone. He leant forward; his voice was confidential, appealing. He said very gently: 'Why do you mind so much, Madame?'

'Why? But it's maddening! Irritating to the last degree! I've told you why!'

Poirot shook his head.

'Not altogether.'

'What do you mean?' Linnet asked again.

Poirot leant back, folded his arms and spoke in a detached impersonal manner.

'*Ecoutez*, Madame. I will recount to you a little history. It is that one day, a month or two ago, I am dining in a restaurant in London. At the table next to me are two people, a man and a girl. They are very happy, so it seems, very much in love. They talk with confidence of the future. It is not that I listen to what is not meant for me; they are quite oblivious of who hears them and who does not. The man's back is to me, but I can watch the girl's face. It is very intense. She is in love – heart, soul, and body – and she is not of those who love lightly and often. With her it is clearly the life and the death. They are engaged to be married, these two; that is what I gather; and they talk of where they shall pass the days of their honeymoon. They plan to go to Egypt.'

He paused. Linnet said sharply: 'Well?'

Poirot went on: 'That is a month or two ago, but the girl's face – I do not forget it. I know that I shall remember if I see it again. And I remember too the man's voice. And I think you can guess, Madame, when it is I see the one and hear the other again. It is here in Egypt. The man is on his honeymoon, yes – but he is on his honeymoon with another woman.'

Linnet said sharply: 'What of it? I had already mentioned the facts.'

'The facts – yes.'

'Well then?'

Poirot said slowly: 'The girl in the restaurant mentioned a friend – a friend who, she was very positive, would not let her down. That friend, I think, was you, Madame.'

'Yes. I told you we had been friends.'

Linnet flushed.

'And she trusted you?'

'Yes.'

She hesitated for a moment, biting her lip impatiently; then, as Poirot did not seem disposed to speak, she broke out:

'Of course the whole thing was very unfortunate. But these things happen, Monsieur Poirot.'

'Ah! yes, they happen, Madame.' He paused. 'You are of the Church of England, I presume?'

'Yes.' Linnet looked slightly bewildered.

'Then you have heard portions of the Bible read aloud in church. You have heard of King David and of the rich man who had many flocks and herds and the poor man who had one ewe lamb – and of how the rich man took the poor man's one ewe lamb. That was something that happened, Madame.'

Linnet sat up. Her eyes flashed angrily.

'I see perfectly what you are driving at, Monsieur Poirot! You think, to put it vulgarly, that I stole my friend's young man. Looking at the matter sentimentally – which is, I suppose, the way people of your generation cannot help looking at things – that is possibly true. But the real hard truth is different. I don't deny that Jackie was passionately in love with Simon, but I don't think you take into account that he may not have been equally devoted to her. He was very fond of her, but I think that even before he met me he was beginning to feel that he had made a mistake. Look at it clearly, Monsieur Poirot. Simon discovers that it is I he loves, not Jackie. What is he to do? Be heroically noble and marry a woman he does not care for – and thereby probably ruin three lives – for it is doubtful whether he could make Jackie happy under those circumstances? If he were actually married to her when he met me I agree that it *might* be his duty to stick to her – though I'm not really sure of that. If one person is unhappy the other suffers too. But an engagement is not really binding. If a mistake has been made, then surely it is better to face the fact before it is too late. I admit that it was very hard on Jackie, and I'm very sorry about it – but there it is. It was inevitable.'

'I wonder.'

She stared at him.

'What do you mean?'

'It is very sensible, very logical – all that you say! But it does not explain one thing.'

'What is that?'

'Your own attitude, Madame. See you, this pursuit of you, you might take it in two ways. It might cause you annoyance – yes, or it might stir your pity – that your friend should have been so deeply hurt as to throw all regard for the conventions aside. But that is not the way you react. No, to you this persecution is *intolerable* – and why? It can be for one reason only – that you feel a sense of guilt.'

Linnet sprang to her feet.

'How dare you? Really, Monsieur Poirot, this is going too far.'

'But I do dare, Madame! I am going to speak to you quite frankly. I suggest to you that, although you may have endeavoured to gloss over the fact to yourself, you did deliberately set about taking your husband from your friend. I suggest that you felt strongly attracted to him at once. But I suggest that there was a moment when you hesitated, when you realized that there was a *choice* – that you could refrain or go on. I suggest that the initiative rested with *you* – not with Monsieur Doyle. You are beautiful, Madame; you are rich; you are clever; intelligent – and you have charm. You could have exercised that charm or you could have restrained it. You had everything, Madame, that life can offer. Your friend's life was bound up in one person. You knew that, but, though you hesitated, you did not hold your hand. You stretched it out and, like the rich man in the Bible, you took the poor man's one ewe lamb.'

There was a silence. Linnet controlled herself with an effort and said in a cold voice: 'All this is quite beside the point!'

'No, it is not beside the point. I am explaining to you just why the unexpected appearances of Mademoiselle de Bellefort have upset you so much. It is because though she may be unwomanly and undignified in what she is doing, you have the inner conviction that she has right on her side.'

'That's not true.'

Poirot shrugged his shoulders.

'You refuse to be honest with yourself.'

'Not at all.'

Poirot said gently: 'I should say, Madame, that you have had a happy life, that you have been generous and kindly in your attitude towards others.'

'I have tried to be,' said Linnet. The impatient anger died out of her face. She spoke simply – almost forlornly.

'And that is why the feeling that you have deliberately caused injury to someone upsets you so much, and why you are so reluctant to admit the fact. Pardon me if I have been impertinent, but the psychology, it is the most important fact in a case.'

Linnet said slowly: 'Even supposing what you say were true – and I don't admit it, mind – what can be done about it now? One can't alter the past; one must deal with things as they are.'

Poirot nodded.

'You have the clear brain. Yes, one cannot go back over the past. One must accept things as they are. And sometimes, Madame, that is all one can do – accept the consequences of one's past deeds.'

'You mean,' asked Linnet incredulously, 'that I can do nothing – *nothing?*'

'You must have courage, Madame; that is what it seems like to me.'

Linnet said slowly:

'Couldn't you – talk to Jackie – to Miss de Bellefort? Reason with her?'

'Yes, I could do that. I will do that if you would like me to do so. But do not expect much result. I fancy that Mademoiselle de Bellefort is so much in the grip of a fixed idea that nothing will turn her from it.'

'But surely we can do *something* to extricate ourselves?'

'You could, of course, return to England and establish yourselves in your own house.'

'Even then, I suppose, Jacqueline is capable of planting herself in the village, so that I should see her every time I went out of the grounds.'

'True.'

'Besides,' said Linnet slowly, 'I don't think that Simon would agree to run away.'

'What is his attitude in this?'

'He's furious – simply furious.'

Poirot nodded thoughtfully.

Linnet said appealingly, 'You will – talk to her?'

'Yes, I will do that. But it is my opinion that I shall not be able to accomplish anything.'

Linnet said violently: 'Jackie is extraordinary! One can't tell what she will do!'

'You spoke just now of certain threats she had made. Would you tell me what those threats were?'

Linnet shrugged her shoulders.

'She threatened to – well – kill us both. Jackie can be rather – Latin sometimes.'

'I see.' Poirot's tone was grave.

Linnet turned to him appealingly.

'You will act for me?'

'No, Madame.' His tone was firm. 'I will not accept a commission from you. I will do what I can in the interests of humanity. That, yes. There is here a situation that is full of difficulty and danger. I will do what I can to clear it up – but I am not very sanguine as to my chance of success.'

Linnet Doyle said slowly: 'But you will not act for *me*?'

'No, Madame,' said Hercule Poirot.

CHAPTER 5

Hercule Poirot found Jacqueline de Bellefort sitting on the rocks directly overlooking the Nile. He had felt fairly certain that she had not retired for the night and that he would find her somewhere about the grounds of the hotel.

She was sitting with her chin cupped in the palms of her hands, and she did not turn her head or look around at the sound of his approach.

'Mademoiselle de Bellefort?' asked Poirot. 'You permit that I speak to you for a little moment?'

Jacqueline turned her head slightly. A faint smile played round her lips.

'Certainly,' she said. 'You are Monsieur Hercule Poirot, I think? Shall I make a guess? You are acting for Mrs Doyle, who has promised you a large fee if you succeed in your mission.'

Poirot sat down on the bench near her.

'Your assumption is partially correct,' he said, smiling. 'I have just come from Madame Doyle, but I am not accepting any fee from her and, strictly speaking, I am not acting for her.'

'Oh!'

Jacqueline studied him attentively.

'Then why have you come?' she asked abruptly.

Hercule Poirot's reply was in the form of another question.

'Have you ever seen me before, Mademoiselle?'

She shook her head.

'No, I do not think so.'

'Yet I have seen you. I sat next to you once at Chez Ma Tante. You were there with Monsieur Simon Doyle.'

A strange masklike expression came over the girl's face. She said, 'I remember that evening . . .'

'Since then,' said Poirot, 'many things have occurred.'

'As you say, many things have occurred.'

Her voice was hard with an undertone of desperate bitterness.

'Mademoiselle, I speak as a friend. Bury your dead!'

She looked startled.

'What do you mean?'

'Give up the past! Turn to the future! What is done is done. Bitterness will not undo it.'

'I'm sure that that would suit dear Linnet admirably.'

Poirot made a gesture.

'I am not thinking of her at this moment! I am thinking of *you*. You have suffered – yes – but what you are doing now will only prolong the suffering.'

She shook her head.

'You're wrong. There are times when I almost enjoy myself.'

'And that, Mademoiselle, is the worst of all.'

She looked up swiftly.

'You're not stupid,' she said. She added slowly, 'I believe you mean to be kind.'

'Go home, Mademoiselle. You are young; you have brains, the world is before you.'

Jacqueline shook her head slowly.

'You don't understand – or you won't. Simon is my world.'

'Love is not everything, Mademoiselle,' Poirot said gently. 'It is only when we are young that we think it is.'

But the girl still shook her head.

'You don't understand.' She shot him a quick look. 'You know all about it, of course? You've talked to Linnet? And you were in the restaurant that night . . . Simon and I loved each other.'

'I know that you loved him.'

She was quick to perceive the inflection of his words. She repeated with emphasis:

'*We loved each other*. And I loved Linnet . . . I trusted her. She was my best friend. All her life Linnet has been able to buy everything she wanted. She's never denied herself anything. When she saw Simon she wanted him – and she just took him.'

'And he allowed himself to be – bought?'

Jacqueline shook her dark head slowly.

'No, it's not quite like that. If it were, I shouldn't be here now . . . You're suggesting that Simon isn't worth caring for . . . If he'd married Linnet for her money, that would be true. But he didn't marry her for her money. It's more complicated than that. There's such a thing as *glamour*, Monsieur Poirot. And money helps that. Linnet had an "atmosphere", you see. She was the queen of a kingdom – the young princess – luxurious to her fingertips. It was like a stage setting. She had the world at her feet, one of the richest and most sought-after peers in England wanting to marry her. And she stoops instead to the obscure Simon Doyle . . . Do you wonder it went to his head?' She made a sudden gesture. 'Look at the moon up there. You see her very plainly, don't you? She's very real. But if the sun were to shine you wouldn't be able to see her at all. It was rather like that. I was the moon . . . When the sun came out, Simon couldn't see me any more . . . He was dazzled. He couldn't see anything but the sun – Linnet.'

She paused and then she went on: 'So you see it was – glamour. She went to his head. And then there's her complete assurance – her habit of command. She's so sure of herself that she makes other people sure. Simon was weak, perhaps, but then he's a very simple person. He would have loved me and me only if Linnet hadn't come along and snatched him up in her golden chariot. And I know – I know perfectly – that he wouldn't ever have fallen in love with her if she hadn't made him.'

'That is what you think – yes.'

'I *know* it. He loved me – he will always love me.'

Poirot said: 'Even now?'

A quick answer seemed to rise to her lips, then be stifled. She looked at Poirot and a deep burning colour spread over her face. She looked away; her head dropped down. She said in a low stifled voice: 'Yes, I know. He hates me now. Yes, hates me . . . He'd better be careful!'

With a quick gesture she fumbled in a little silk bag that lay on the seat. Then she held out her hand. On the palm of it was a small pearl-handled pistol – a dainty toy it looked.

'Nice little thing, isn't it? she said. 'Looks too foolish to be real, but it is real! One of those bullets would kill a man or a woman. And I'm a good shot.' She smiled a faraway, reminiscent smile.

'When I went home as a child with my mother, to South Carolina, my grandfather taught me to shoot. He was the old-fashioned kind that believes in shooting – especially where honour is concerned. My father, too, he fought several duels as a young man. He was a good swordsman. He killed a man once. That was over a woman. So you see, Monsieur Poirot' – she met his eyes squarely – 'I've hot blood in me! I bought this when it first happened. I meant to kill one or other of them – the trouble was I couldn't decide which. Both of them would have been unsatisfactory. If I'd thought Linnet would have looked afraid – but she's got plenty of physical courage. She can stand up to physical action. And then I thought I'd – wait! That appealed to me more and more. After all, I could do it any time; it would be more fun to wait and – think about it! And then this idea came to my mind – to follow them! Whenever they arrived at some faraway spot and were together and happy, they should see *Me*! And it worked. It got Linnet badly – in a way nothing else could have done! It got right under her skin . . . That was when I began to enjoy myself . . . And there's nothing she can do about it! I'm always perfectly pleasant and polite! There's not a word they can take hold of! It's poisoning everything – everything – for them.' Her laugh rang out, clear and silvery.

Poirot grasped her arm.

'Be quiet. Quiet, I tell you.'

Jacqueline looked at him.

'Well?' she asked. Her smile was definitely challenging.

'Mademoiselle, I beseech you, do not do what you are doing.'

'Leave dear Linnet alone, you mean!'

'It is deeper than that. Do not open your heart to evil.'

Her lips fell apart; a look of bewilderment came into her eyes.

Poirot went on gravely: 'Because – if you do – evil will come . . . Yes, very surely evil will come . . . It will enter in and make its home within you, and after a little while it will no longer be possible to drive it out.'

Jacqueline stared at him. Her glance seemed to waver, to flicker uncertainly.

She said: 'I – don't know –' Then she cried out definitely, 'You can't stop me.'

'No,' said Hercule Poirot. 'I cannot stop you.' His voice was sad.

'Even if I were to – kill her, you couldn't stop me.'

'No – not if you were willing to pay the price.'

Jacqueline de Bellefort laughed.

'Oh, I'm not afraid of death! What have I got to live for, after all? I suppose you believe it's very wrong to kill a person who has injured you – even if they've taken away everything you had in the world?'

Poirot said steadily: 'Yes, Mademoiselle. I believe it is the unforgivable offence – to kill.'

Jacqueline laughed again.

'Then you ought to approve of my present scheme of revenge; because, you see, as long as it works, I shan't use that pistol . . . But I'm afraid – yes, afraid sometimes – it all goes red – I want to hurt her – to stick a knife into her, to put my dear little pistol close against her head and then – just press with my finger – *Oh!*'

The exclamation startled him.

'What is it, Mademoiselle!'

She turned her head and was staring into the shadows.

'Someone – standing over there. He's gone now.'

Hercule Poirot looked round sharply.

The place seemed quite deserted.

'There seems no one here but ourselves, Mademoiselle.' He got up. 'In any case I have said all I came to say. I wish you good night.'

Jacqueline got up too. She said almost pleadingly, 'You do understand – that I can't do what you ask me to do?'

Poirot shook his head.

'No – for you could do it! There is always a moment! Your friend Linnet – there was a moment, too, in which she could have held her hand . . . She let it pass by. And if one does that, then

238

one is committed to the enterprise and there comes no second chance.'

'No second chance . . .' said Jacqueline de Bellefort.

She stood brooding for a moment; then she lifted her head defiantly.

'Good night, Monsieur Poirot.'

He shook his head sadly and followed her up the path to the hotel.

CHAPTER 6

On the following morning Simon Doyle joined Hercule Poirot as the latter was leaving the hotel to walk down to the town.

'Good morning, Monsieur Poirot.'

'Good morning, Monsieur Doyle.'

'You going to the town? Mind if I stroll along with you?'

'But certainly. I shall be delighted.'

The two men walked side by side, passed out through the gateway and turned into the cool shade of the gardens. Then Simon removed his pipe from his mouth and said, 'I understand, Monsieur Poirot, that my wife had a talk with you last night?'

'That is so.'

Simon Doyle was frowning a little. He belonged to that type of men of action who find it difficult to put thoughts into words and who have trouble in expressing themselves clearly.

'I'm glad of one thing,' he said. 'You've made her realize that we're more or less powerless in the matter.'

'There is clearly no legal redress,' agreed Poirot.

'Exactly. Linnet didn't seem to understand that.' He gave a faint smile. 'Linnet's been brought up to believe that every annoyance can automatically be referred to the police.'

'It would be pleasant if such were the case,' said Poirot.

There was a pause. Then Simon said suddenly, his face going very red as he spoke:

'It's – it's infamous that she should be victimized like this! She's done nothing! If anyone likes to say I behaved like a cad, they're welcome to say so! I suppose I did. But I won't have the whole thing visited on Linnet. She had nothing whatever to do with it.'

Poirot bowed his head gravely but said nothing.

'Did you – er – have you – talked to Jackie – Miss de Bellefort?'

'Yes, I have spoken with her.'

'Did you get her to see sense?'

'I'm afraid not.'

Simon broke out irritably: 'Can't she see what an ass she's making of herself? Doesn't she realize that no decent woman would behave as she is doing? Hasn't she got any pride or self-respect?'

Poirot shrugged his shoulders.

'She has only a sense of – injury, shall we say?' he replied.

'Yes, but damn it all, man, decent girls don't behave like this! I admit I was entirely to blame. I treated her damned badly and all that. I should quite understand her being thoroughly fed up with me and never wishing to see me again. But this following me round – it's – it's *indecent*! Making a show of herself! What the devil does she hope to get out of it?'

'Perhaps – revenge!'

'Idiotic! I'd really understand better if she'd tried to do something melodramatic – like taking a pot shot at me.'

'You think that would be more like her – yes?'

'Frankly I do. She's hot-blooded – and she's got an ungovernable temper. I shouldn't be surprised at her doing anything while she was in a white-hot rage. But this spying business –' He shook his head.

'It is more subtle – yes! It is intelligent!'

Doyle stared at him.

'You don't understand. It's playing hell with Linnet's nerves.'

'And yours?'

Simon looked at him with momentary surprise.

'Me? I'd like to wring the little devil's neck.'

'There is nothing, then, of the old feeling left?'

'My dear Monsieur Poirot – how can I put it? It's like the moon when the sun comes out. You don't know it's there any more. When once I'd met Linnet – Jackie didn't exist.'

'*Tiens, c'est drôle, ça!*' muttered Poirot.

'I beg your pardon?'

'Your simile interested me, that is all.'

Again flushing, Simon said: 'I suppose Jackie told you that I'd only married Linnet for her money? Well, that's a damned lie!

240

I wouldn't marry any woman for money! What Jackie doesn't understand is that it's difficult for a fellow when – when – a woman cares for him as she cared for me.'

'Ah?'

Poirot looked up sharply.

Simon blundered on: 'It – it – sounds a caddish thing to say, but Jackie was *too* fond of me!'

'*Une qui aime et un qui se laisse aimer,*' murmured Poirot.

'Eh? What's that you say? You see, a man doesn't want to feel that a woman cares more for him than he does for her.' His voice grew warm as he went on. 'He doesn't want to feel *owned*, body and soul. It's the damned *possessive* attitude! This man is *mine* – he *belongs* to me! That's the sort of thing I can't stick – no man could stick! He wants to get away – to get free. He wants to own his woman; he doesn't want *her* to own *him*.'

He broke off, and with fingers that trembled slightly he lit a cigarette.

Poirot said: 'And it is like that that you felt with Mademoiselle Jacqueline?'

'Eh?' Simon stared and then admitted: 'Er – yes – well, yes, as a matter of fact I did. She doesn't realize that, of course. And it's not the sort of thing I could ever tell her. But I *was* feeling restless – and then I met Linnet, and she just swept me off my feet! I'd never seen anything so lovely. It was all so amazing. Everyone kowtowing to her – and then her singling out a poor chump like me.'

His tone held boyish awe and astonishment.

'I see,' said Poirot. He nodded thoughtfully. 'Yes – I see.'

'Why can't Jackie take it like a man?' demanded Simon resentfully.

A very faint smile twitched Poirot's upper lip.

'Well, you see, Monsieur Doyle, to begin with she is *not* a man.'

'No, no – but I meant take it like a good sport! After all, you've got to take your medicine when it comes to you. The fault's mine, I admit. But there it is! If you no longer care for a girl, it's simply madness to marry her. And, now that I see what Jackie's really like and the lengths she is likely to go to, I feel I've had rather a lucky escape.'

'The lengths she is likely to go to,' Poirot repeated thoughtfully. 'Have you an idea, Monsieur Doyle, what those lengths are?'

Simon looked at him rather startled.

'No – at least, what do you mean?'

'You know she carries a pistol about with her?'

Simon frowned, then shook his head.

'I don't believe she'll use that – now. She might have done so earlier. But I believe it's got past that. She's just spiteful now – trying to take it out of us both.'

Poirot shrugged his shoulders.

'It may be so,' he said doubtfully.

'It's Linnet I'm worrying about,' declared Simon, somewhat unnecessarily.

'I quite realize that,' said Poirot.

'I'm not really afraid of Jackie doing any melodramatic shooting stuff, but this spying and following business has absolutely got Linnet on the raw. I'll tell you the plan I've made, and perhaps you can suggest improvements on it. To begin with, I've announced fairly openly that we're going to stay here ten days. But tomorrow the steamer *Karnak* starts from Shellal to Wadi Halfa. I propose to book passages on that under an assumed name. Tomorrow we'll go on an excursion to Philae. Linnet's maid can take the luggage. We'll join the *Karnak* at Shellal. When Jackie finds we don't come back, it will be too late – we shall be well on our way. She'll assume we have given her the slip and gone back to Cairo. In fact I might even bribe the porter to say so. Inquiry at the tourist offices won't help her, because our names won't appear. How does that strike you?'

'It is well imagined, yes. And suppose she waits here till you return?'

'We may not return. We would go on to Khartoum and then perhaps by air to Kenya. She can't follow us all over the globe.'

'No; there must come a time when financial reasons forbid. She has very little money, I understand.'

Simon looked at him with admiration.

'That's clever of you. Do you know, I hadn't thought of that. Jackie's as poor as they make them.'

'And yet she has managed to follow you so far?'

Simon said doubtfully:

'She's got a small income, of course. Something under two

hundred a year, I imagine. I suppose – yes, I suppose she must have sold out the capital to do what she's doing.'

'So that the time will come when she has exhausted her resources and is quite penniless?'

'Yes . . .'

Simon wriggled uneasily. The thought seemed to make him uncomfortable. Poirot watched him attentively.

'No,' he remarked. 'No, it is not a pretty thought . . .'

Simon said rather angrily, 'Well, *I* can't help it!' Then he added, 'What do you think of my plan?'

'I think it may work, yes. But it is, of course, a *retreat*.'

Simon flushed.

'You mean, we're running away? Yes, that's true . . . But Linnet –'

Poirot watched him, then gave a short nod.

'As you say, it may be the best way. But remember, Mademoiselle de Bellefort has brains.'

Simon said sombrely: 'Some day, I feel, we've got to make a stand and fight it out. Her attitude isn't reasonable.'

'Reasonable, *mon Dieu!*' cried Poirot.

'There's no reason why women shouldn't behave like rational beings,' Simon asserted stolidly.

Poirot said dryly: 'Quite frequently they do. That is even more upsetting!' He added, 'I, too, shall be on the *Karnak*. It is part of my itinerary.

'Oh!' Simon hesitated, then said, choosing his words with some embarrassment: 'That isn't – isn't – er – on our account in any way? I mean I wouldn't like to think –'

Poirot disabused him quickly:

'Not at all. It was all arranged before I left London. I always make my plans well in advance.'

'You don't just move on from place to place as the fancy takes you? Isn't the latter really pleasanter?'

'Perhaps. But to succeed in life every detail should be arranged well beforehand.'

Simon laughed and said: 'That is how the more skilful murderer behaves, I suppose.'

'Yes – though I must admit that the most brilliant crime I remember and one of the most difficult to solve was committed on the spur of the moment.'

Simon said boyishly: 'You must tell us something about your cases on board the *Karnak*.'

'No, no; that would be to talk – what do you call it? – the shop.'

'Yes, but your kind of shop is rather thrilling. Mrs Allerton thinks so. She's longing to get a chance to cross-question you.'

'Mrs Allerton? That is the charming grey-haired woman who has such a devoted son?'

'Yes. She'll be on the *Karnak* too.'

'Does she know that you –?'

'Certainly not,' said Simon with emphasis. 'Nobody knows. I've gone on the principle that it's better not to trust anybody.'

'An admirable sentiment – and one which I always adopt. By the way, the third member of your party, the tall grey-haired man –'

'Pennington?'

'Yes. He is travelling with you?'

Simon said grimly: 'Not very usual on a honeymoon, you were thinking? Pennington is Linnet's American trustee. We ran across him by chance in Cairo.'

'*Ah, vraiment*! You permit a question? She is of age, Madame your wife?'

Simon looked amused.

'She isn't actually twenty-one yet – but she hadn't got to ask anyone's consent before marrying me. It was the greatest surprise to Pennington. He left New York on the *Carmanic* two days before Linnet's letter got there telling him of our marriage, so he knew nothing about it.'

'The *Carmanic* –' murmured Poirot.

'It was the greatest surprise to him when we ran into him at Shepheard's in Cairo.'

'That was indeed the coincident!'

'Yes, and we found that he was coming on this Nile trip – so naturally we foregathered; couldn't have done anything else decently. Besides that, it's been – well, a relief in some ways.' He looked embarrassed again. 'You see, Linnet's been all strung up – expecting Jackie to turn up anywhere and everywhere. While we were alone together, the subject kept coming up. Andrew Pennington's a help that way, we have to talk of outside matters.'

'Your wife has not confided in Mr Pennington?'

'No.' Simon's jaw looked aggressive. 'It's nothing to do with anyone else. Besides, when we started on this Nile trip we thought we'd seen the end of the business.'

Poirot shook his head.

'You have not seen the end of it yet. No – the end is not yet at hand. I am very sure of that.'

'I say, Monsieur Poirot, you're not very encouraging.'

Poirot looked at him with a slight feeling of irritation. He thought to himself: 'The Anglo-Saxon, he takes nothing seriously but playing games! He does not grow up.'

Linnet Doyle – Jacqueline de Bellefort – both of them took the business seriously enough. But in Simon's attitude he could find nothing but male impatience and annoyance. He said: 'You will permit me an impertinent question? Was it your idea to come to Egypt for your honeymoon?'

Simon flushed.

'No, of course not. As a matter of fact I'd rather have gone anywhere else, but Linnet was absolutely set upon it. And so – and so –'

He stopped rather lamely.

'Naturally,' said Poirot gravely.

He appreciated the fact that, if Linnet Doyle was set upon anything, that thing had to happen.

He thought to himself: 'I have now heard three separate accounts of the affair – Linnet Doyle's, Jacqueline de Bellefort's, Simon Doyle's. Which of them is nearest to the truth?'

CHAPTER 7

Simon and Linnet Doyle set off on their expedition to Philae about eleven o'clock the following morning. Jacqueline de Bellefort, sitting on the hotel balcony, watched them set off in the picturesque sailing-boat. What she did not see was the departure of the car – laden with luggage, and in which sat a demure-looking maid – from the front door of the hotel. It turned to the right in the direction of Shellal.

Hercule Poirot decided to pass the remaining two hours before lunch on the island of Elephantine, immediately opposite the hotel.

245

He went down to the landing-stage. There were two men just stepping into one of the hotel boats, and Poirot joined them. The men were obviously strangers to each other. The younger of them had arrived by train the day before. He was a tall, dark-haired young man, with a thin face and a pugnacious chin. He was wearing an extremely dirty pair of grey flannel trousers and a high-necked polo jumper singularly unsuited to the climate. The other was a slightly podgy middle-aged man who lost no time in entering into conversation with Poirot in idiomatic but slightly broken English. Far from taking part in the conversation, the younger man merely scowled at them both and then deliberately turned his back on them and proceeded to admire the agility with which the Nubian boatman steered the boat with his toes as he manipulated the sail with his hands.

It was very peaceful on the water, the great smooth slippery black rocks gliding by and the soft breeze fanning their faces. Elephantine was reached very quickly and on going ashore Poirot and his loquacious acquaintance made straight for the museum. By this time the latter had produced a card which he handed to Poirot with a little bow. It bore the inscription: 'Signor Guido Richetti, Archeologo.'

Not to be outdone, Poirot returned the bow and extracted his own card. These formalities completed, the two men stepped into the Museum together, the Italian pouring forth a stream of erudite information. They were by now conversing in French.

The young man in the flannel trousers strolled listlessly round the Museum, yawning from time to time, and then escaped to the outer air.

Poirot and Signor Richetti at last found him. The Italian was energetic in examining the ruins, but presently Poirot, espying a green-lined sunshade which he recognized on the rocks down by the river, escaped in that direction.

Mrs Allerton was sitting on a large rock, a sketch-book by her side and a book on her lap.

Poirot removed his hat politely and Mrs Allerton at once entered into conversation.

'Good morning,' she said. 'I suppose it would be quite impossible to get rid of some of these awful children.'

A group of small black figures surrounded her, all grinning

and posturing and holding out imploring hands as they lisped 'Bakshish' at intervals, hopefully.

'I thought they'd get tired of me,' said Mrs Allerton sadly. 'They've been watching me for over two hours now – and they close in on me little by little; and then I yell "Imshi" and brandish my sunshade at them and they scatter for a minute or two. And then they come back and stare and stare, and their eyes are simply disgusting, and so are their noses, and I don't believe I really like children – not unless they're more or less washed and have the rudiments of manners.'

She laughed ruefully.

Poirot gallantly attempted to disperse the mob for her, but without avail. They scattered and then reappeared, closing in once more.

'If there were only any peace in Egypt, I should like it better,' said Mrs Allerton. 'But you can never be alone anywhere. Someone is always pestering you for money, or offering you donkeys, or beads, or expeditions to native villages, or duck shooting.'

'It is the great disadvantage, that is true,' said Poirot.

He spread his handkerchief cautiously on the rock and sat somewhat gingerly upon it.

'Your son is not with you this morning?' he went on.

'No, Tim had some letters to get off before we leave. We're doing the trip to the Second Cataract, you know.'

'I, too.'

'I'm so glad. I want to tell you that I'm quite thrilled to meet you. When we were in Majorca, there was a Mrs Leech there, and she was telling us the most wonderful things about you. She'd lost a ruby ring bathing, and she was just lamenting that you weren't there to find it for her.

'Ah, *parbleu*, but I am not the diving seal!'

They both laughed.

Mrs Allerton went on.

'I saw you from my window walking down the drive with Simon Doyle this morning. Do tell me what you make of him! We're so excited about him.'

'Ah? Truly?'

'Yes. You know his marriage to Linnet Ridgeway was the greatest surprise. She was supposed to be going to marry Lord

Windlesham and then suddenly she gets engaged to this man no one had ever heard of!'

'You know her well, Madame?'

'No, but a cousin of mine, Joanna Southwood, is one of her best friends.'

'Ah, yes, I have read that name in the papers.' He was silent a moment and then went on, 'She is a young lady very much in the news, Mademoiselle Joanna Southwood.'

'Oh, she knows how to advertise herself all right,' snapped Mrs Allerton.

'You do not like her, Madame?'

'That was a nasty remark of mine.' Mrs Allerton looked penitent. 'You see I'm old-fashioned. I don't like her much. Tim and she are the greatest of friends, though.'

'I see,' said Poirot.

His companion shot a quick look at him. She changed the subject.

'How very few young people there are out here! That pretty girl with the chestnut hair and the appalling mother in the turban is almost the only young creature in the place. You have talked to her a good deal, I notice. She interests me, that child.'

'Why is that, Madame?'

'I feel sorry for her. You can suffer so much when you are young and sensitive. I think she is suffering.'

'Yes, she is not happy, poor little one.'

'Tim and I call her the "sulky girl". I've tried to talk to her once or twice, but she's snubbed me on each occasion. However, I believe she's going on this Nile trip too, and I expect we'll have to be more or less all matey together, shan't we?'

'It is a possible contingency, Madame.'

'I'm very matey really – people interest me enormously. All the different types.' She paused, then said: 'Tim tells me that that dark girl – her name is de Bellefort – is the girl who was engaged to Simon Doyle. It's rather awkward for them – meeting like this.'

'It is awkward – yes,' agreed Poirot.

'You know, it may sound foolish, but she almost frightened me. She looked so – intense.'

Poirot nodded his head slowly.

'You were not far wrong, Madame. A great force of emotion is always frightening.'

'Do people interest you too, Monsieur Poirot? Or do you reserve your interest for potential criminals?'

'Madame – that category would not leave many people outside it.'

Mrs Allerton looked a trifle startled.

'Do you really mean that?'

'Given the particular incentive, that is to say,' Poirot added.

'Which would differ?'

'Naturally.'

Mrs Allerton hesitated – a little smile on her lips.

'Even I perhaps?'

'Mothers, Madame, are particularly ruthless when their children are in danger.'

She said gravely, 'I think that's true – yes, you're quite right.'

She was silent a minute or two, then she said, smiling: I'm trying to imagine motives for crime suitable for everyone in the hotel. It's quite entertaining. Simon Doyle, for instance?'

Poirot said, smiling: 'A very simple crime – a direct short-cut to his objective. No subtlety about it.'

'And therefore very easily detected?'

'Yes; he would not be ingenious.'

'And Linnet?'

'That would be like the Queen in your *Alice in Wonderland*, "Off with her head."'

'Of course. The divine right of monarchy! Just a little bit of the Naboth's vineyard touch. And the dangerous girl – Jacqueline de Bellefort – could *she* do a murder?'

Poirot hesitated for a minute or two, then he said doubtfully, 'Yes, I think she could.'

'But you're not sure?'

'No. She puzzles me, that little one.'

'I don't think Mr Pennington could do one, do you? He looks so desiccated and dyspeptic – with no red blood in him.'

'But possibly a strong sense of self-preservation.'

'Yes, I suppose so. And poor Mrs Otterbourne in her turban?'

'There is always vanity.'

'As a motive for murder?' Mrs Allerton asked doubtfully.

'Motives for murder are sometimes very trivial, Madame.'

'What are the most usual motives, Monsieur Poirot?'

'Most frequent – money. That is to say, gain in its various ramifications. Then there is revenge – and love, and fear, and pure hate, and beneficence –'

'Monsieur Poirot!'

'Oh, yes, Madame. I have known of – shall we say A? – being removed by B solely in order to benefit C. Political murders often come under the same heading. Someone is considered to be harmful to civilization and is removed on that account. Such people forget that life and death are the affair of the good God.'

He spoke gravely.

Mrs Allerton said quietly: 'I am glad to hear you say that. All the same, God chooses his instruments.'

'There is a danger in thinking like that, Madame.'

She adopted a lighter tone.

'After this conversation, Monsieur Poirot, I shall wonder that there is anyone left alive!'

She got up.

'We must be getting back. We have to start immediately after lunch.'

When they reached the landing-stage they found the young man in the polo jumper just taking his place in the boat. The Italian was already waiting. As the Nubian boatman cast the sail loose and they started, Poirot addressed a polite remark to the stranger.

'There are very wonderful things to be seen in Egypt, are there not?'

The young man was now smoking a somewhat noisome pipe. He removed it from his mouth and remarked briefly and very emphatically, in astonishingly well-bred accents: 'They make me sick.'

Mrs Allerton put on her pince-nez and surveyed him with pleasurable interest.

'Indeed? And why is that?' Poirot asked.

'Take the Pyramids. Great blocks of useless masonry, put up to minister to the egoism of a despotic bloated king. Think of the sweated masses who toiled to build them and died doing it. It makes me sick to think of the suffering and torture they represent.'

Mrs Allerton said cheerfully: 'You'd rather have no Pyramids, no Parthenon, no beautiful tombs or temples – just the solid satisfaction of knowing that people got three meals a day and died in their beds.'

The young man directed his scowl in her direction.

'I think human beings matter more than stones.'

'But they do not endure as well,' remarked Hercule Poirot.

'I'd rather see a well fed worker than any so-called work of art. What matters is the future – not the past.'

This was too much for Signor Richetti, who burst into a torrent of impassioned speech not too easy to follow.

The young man retorted by telling everybody exactly what he thought of the capitalist system. He spoke with the utmost venom.

When the tirade was over they had arrived at the hotel landing-stage.

Mrs Allerton murmured cheerfully: 'Well, well,' and stepped ashore. The young man directed a baleful glance after her.

In the hall of the hotel Poirot encountered Jacqueline de Bellefort. She was dressed in riding clothes. She gave him an ironical little bow.

'I'm going donkey-riding. Do you recommend the native villages, Monsieur Poirot?'

'Is that your excursion today, Mademoiselle? *Eh bien*, they are picturesque – but do not spend large sums on native curios.'

'Which are shipped here from Europe? No, I am not so easy to deceive as that.'

With a little nod she passed out into the brilliant sunshine.

Poirot completed his packing – a very simple affair, since his possessions were always in the most meticulous order. Then he repaired to the dining-room and ate an early lunch.

After lunch the hotel bus took the passengers for the Second Cataract to the station where they were to catch the daily express from Cairo to Shellal – a ten-minute run.

The Allertons, Poirot, the young man in the dirty flannel trousers and the Italian were the passengers. Mrs Otterbourne and her daughter had made the expedition to the Dam and to Philae and would join the steamer at Shellal.

The train from Cairo and Luxor was about twenty minutes late. However, it arrived at last, and the usual scenes of wild activity occurred. Native porters taking suitcases out of the train collided with other porters putting them in.

Finally, somewhat breathless, Poirot found himself, with an assortment of his own, the Allertons', and some totally unknown luggage, in one compartment, while Tim and his mother were elsewhere with the remains of the assorted baggage.

The compartment in which Poirot found himself was occupied by an elderly lady with a very wrinkled face, a stiff white stock, a good many diamonds and an expression of reptilian contempt for the majority of mankind.

She treated Poirot to an aristocratic glare and retired behind the pages of an American magazine. A big, rather clumsy young woman of under thirty was sitting opposite her. She had eager brown eyes, rather like a dog's, untidy hair, and a terrific air of willingness to please. At intervals the old lady looked over the top of her magazine and snapped an order at her.

'Cornelia, collect the rugs.' 'When we arrive look after my dressing-case. On no account let anyone else handle it.' 'Don't forget my paper-cutter.'

The train run was brief. In ten minutes' time they came to rest on the jetty where the S.S. *Karnak* was awaiting them. The Otterbournes were already on board.

The *Karnak* was a smaller steamer than the *Papyrus* and the *Lotus*, the First Cataract steamers, which are too large to pass through the locks of the Assuan dam. The passengers went on board and were shown their accommodation. Since the boat was not full, most of the passengers had accommodation on the promenade deck. The entire forward part of this deck was occupied by an observation saloon, all glass-enclosed, where the passengers could sit and watch the river unfold before them. On the deck below were a smoking-room and a small drawing-room and on the deck below that, the dining-saloon.

Having seen his possessions disposed in his cabin, Poirot came out on the deck again to watch the process of departure. He joined Rosalie Otterbourne, who was leaning over the side.

'So now we journey into Nubia. You are pleased, Mademoiselle?'

The girl drew a deep breath.

'Yes. I feel that one's really getting away from things at last.'

She made a gesture with her hand. There was a savage aspect about the sheet of water in front of them, the masses of rock without vegetation that came down to the water's edge – here and

252

there a trace of houses, abandoned and ruined as a result of the damming up of the waters. The whole scene had a melancholy, almost sinister charm.

'Away from *people*,' said Rosalie Otterbourne.

'Except those of our own number, Mademoiselle?'

She shrugged her shoulders. Then she said: 'There's something about this country that makes me feel – wicked. It brings to the surface all the things that are boiling inside one. Everything's so unfair – so unjust.'

'I wonder. You cannot judge by material evidence.'

Rosalie muttered: 'Look at – at some people's mothers – and look at mine. There is no God but Sex, and Salome Otterbourne is its Prophet.' She stopped. 'I shouldn't have said that, I suppose.'

Poirot made a gesture with his hands.

'Why not say it – to me? I am one of those who hear many things. If, as you say, you boil inside – like the jam – *eh bien*, let the scum come to the surface, and then one can take it off with a spoon, so.'

He made a gesture of dropping something into the Nile.

'Then, it has gone.'

'What an extraordinary man you are!' Rosalie said. Her sulky mouth twisted into a smile. Then she suddenly stiffened as she exclaimed: 'Well, here are Mrs Doyle and her husband! I'd no idea *they* were coming on this trip!'

Linnet had just emerged from a cabin half-way down the deck. Simon was behind her. Poirot was almost startled by the look of her – so radiant, so assured. She looked positively arrogant with happiness. Simon Doyle, too, was a transformed being. He was grinning from ear to ear and looking like a happy schoolboy.

'This is grand,' he said as he too leaned on the rail. 'I'm really looking forward to this trip, aren't you, Linnet? It feels, somehow, so much less touristy – as though we were really going into the heart of Egypt.'

His wife responded quickly: 'I know. It's so much – wilder, somehow.'

Her hand slipped through his arm. He pressed it close to his side.

'We're off, Lin,' he murmured.

The steamer was drawing away from the jetty. They had

started on their seven-day journey to the Second Cataract and back.

Behind them a light silvery laugh rang out. Linnet whipped round.

Jacqueline de Bellefort was standing there. She seemed amused.

'Hullo, Linnet! I didn't expect to find *you* here. I thought you said you were staying in Assuan another ten days. This is a surprise!'

'You – you didn't –' Linnet's tongue stammered. She forced a ghastly conventional smile. 'I – I didn't expect to see you either.'

'No?'

Jacqueline moved away to the other side of the boat. Linnet's grasp on her husband's arm tightened.

'Simon – Simon –'

All Doyle's good-natured pleasure had gone. He looked furious. His hands clenched themselves in spite of his effort at self-control.

The two of them moved a little away. Without turning his head Poirot caught scraps of disjointed words:

'. . . turn back . . . impossible . . . we could . . .' and then, slightly louder, Doyle's voice, despairing but grim: 'We can't run away for ever, Lin. We've got to go through with it now . . .'

It was some hours later. Daylight was just fading. Poirot stood in the glass-enclosed saloon looking straight ahead. The *Karnak* was going through a narrow gorge. The rocks came down with a kind of sheer ferocity to the river flowing deep and swift between them. They were in Nubia now.

He heard a movement and Linnet Doyle stood by his side. Her fingers twisted and untwisted themselves; she looked as he had never yet seen her look. There was about her the air of a bewildered child. She said:

'Monsieur Poirot, I'm afraid – I'm afraid of everything. I've never felt like this before. All these wild rocks and the awful grimness and starkness. Where are we going? What's going to happen? I'm afraid, I tell you. Everyone hates me. I've never felt like that before. I've always been nice to people – I've done things for them – and they hate me – lots of people hate me. Except for Simon, I'm surrounded by enemies . . . It's terrible to feel – that there are people who hate you . . .'

'But what is all this, Madame?'

She shook her head.

'I suppose – it's nerves . . . I just feel that – everything's unsafe all round me.'

She cast a quick nervous glance over his shoulder. Then she said abruptly: 'How will all this end? We're caught here. Trapped! There's no way out. We've got to go on. I – I don't know where I am.'

She slipped down on to a seat. Poirot looked down on her gravely; his glance was not untinged with compassion.

'How did she know we were coming on this boat?' she said. 'How could she have known?'

Poirot shook his head as he answered: 'She has brains, you know.'

'I feel as though I shall never escape from her.'

Poirot said: 'There is one plan you might have adopted. In fact I am surprised that it did not occur to you. After all, with you, Madame, money is no object. Why did you not engage in your own private dahabiyeh?'

'If we'd known about all this – but you see we didn't – then. And it was difficult . . .' She flashed out with sudden impatience: 'Oh! you don't understand half my difficulties. I've got to be careful with Simon . . . He's – he's absurdly sensitive – about money. About my having so much! He wanted me to go to some little place in Spain with him – he – he wanted to pay all our honeymoon expenses himself. As if it *mattered*! Men are stupid! He's got to get used to – to – living comfortably. The mere idea of a dahabiyeh upset him – the – the needless expense. I've got to educate him – gradually.'

She looked up, bit her lip vexedly, as though feeling that she had been led into discussing her difficulties rather too unguardedly.

She got up.

'I must change. I'm sorry, Monsieur Poirot. I'm afraid I've been talking a lot of foolish nonsense.'

Mrs Allerton, looking quiet and distinguished in her simple black lace evening gown, descended two decks to the dining-room. At the door of it her son caught her up.

'Sorry, darling. I thought I was going to be late.'

'I wonder where we sit.' The saloon was dotted with little tables. Mrs Allerton paused till the steward, who was busy seating a party of people, could attend to them.

'By the way,' she added, 'I asked little Hercule Poirot to sit at our table.'

'Mother, you didn't!' Tim sounded really taken aback and annoyed.

His mother stared at him in surprise. Tim was usually so easy-going.

'My dear, do you mind?'

'Yes, I do. He's an unmitigated little bounder!'

'Oh, no, Tim! I don't agree with you.'

'Anyway, what do we want to get mixed up with an outsider for? Cooped up like this on a small boat, that sort of thing is always a bore. He'll be with us morning, noon and night.'

'I'm sorry, dear.' Mrs Allerton looked distressed. 'I thought really it would amuse you. After all, he must have had a varied experience. And you love detective stories.'

Tim grunted.

'I wish you wouldn't have these bright ideas, Mother. We can't get out of it now, I suppose?'

'Really, Tim, I don't see how we can.'

'Oh, well, we shall have to put up with it, I suppose.'

The steward came to them at this minute and led them to a table. Mrs Allerton's face wore rather a puzzled expression as she followed him. Tim was usually so easy-going and good-tempered. This outburst was quite unlike him. It wasn't as though he had the ordinary Britisher's dislike – and mistrust – of foreigners. Tim was very cosmopolitan. Oh, well – she sighed. Men were incomprehensible! Even one's nearest and dearest had unsuspected reactions and feelings.

As they took their places, Hercule Poirot came quickly and silently into the dining-saloon. He paused with his hand on the back of the third chair.

'You really permit, Madame, that I avail myself of your kind suggestion?'

'Of course. Sit down, Monsieur Poirot.'

'You are most amiable.'

She was uneasily conscious that, as he seated himself, he shot a swift glance at Tim, and that Tim had not quite succeeded in masking a somewhat sullen expression.

Mrs Allerton set herself to produce a pleasant atmosphere. As they drank their soup, she picked up the passenger list which had been placed beside her plate.

'Let's try and identify everybody,' she suggested cheerfully. 'I always think that's rather fun.'

She began reading: 'Mrs Allerton, Mr T. Allerton. That's easy enough! Miss de Bellefort. They've put her at the same table as the Otterbournes, I see. I wonder what she and Rosalie will make of each other. Who comes next? Dr Bessner. Dr Bessner? Who can identify Dr Bessner?'

She bent her glance on a table at which four men sat together.

'I think he must be the fat one with the closely shaved head and the moustache. A German, I should imagine. He seems to be enjoying his soup very much.' Certain succulent noises floated across to them.

Mrs Allerton continued: 'Miss Bowers? Can we make a guess at Miss Bowers? There are three or four women – no, we'll leave her for the present. Mr and Mrs Doyle. Yes, indeed, the lions of this trip. She really is very beautiful, and what a perfectly lovely frock she is wearing.'

Tim turned round in his chair. Linnet and her husband and Andrew Pennington had been given a table in the corner. Linnet was wearing a white dress and pearls.

'It looks frightfully simple to me,' said Tim. 'Just a length of stuff with a kind of cord round the middle.'

'Yes, darling,' said his mother. 'A very nice manly description of an eighty-guinea model.'

'I can't think why women pay so much for their clothes,' Tim said. 'It seems absurd to me.'

Mrs Allerton proceeded with her study of her fellow passengers.

'Mr Fanthorp must be one of the four at that table. The

intensely quiet young man who never speaks. Rather a nice face, cautious and intelligent.'

Poirot agreed.

'He is intelligent – yes. He does not talk, but he listens very attentively, and he also watches. Yes, he makes good use of his eyes. Not quite the type you would expect to find travelling for pleasure in this part of the world. I wonder what he is doing here.'

'Mr Ferguson,' read Mrs Allerton. 'I feel that Ferguson must be our anti-capitalist friend. Mrs Otterbourne, Miss Otterbourne. We know all about them. Mr Pennington? Alias Uncle Andrew. He's a good-looking man, I think –'

'Now, Mother,' said Tim.

'I think he's very good-looking in a dry sort of way,' said Mrs Allerton. 'Rather a ruthless jaw. Probably the kind of man one reads about in the paper, who operates on Wall Street – or is it *in* Wall Street? I'm sure he must be extremely rich. Next – Monsieur Hercule Poirot – whose talents are really being wasted. Can't you get up a crime for Monsieur Poirot, Tim?'

But her well-meant banter only seemed to annoy her son anew. He scowled and Mrs Allerton hurried on: 'Mr Richetti. Our Italian archaeological friend. Then Miss Robson and last of all Miss Van Schuyler. The last's easy. The very ugly old American lady who is clearly going to be very exclusive and speak to nobody who doesn't come up to the most exacting standards! She's rather marvellous, isn't she, really? A kind of period piece. The two women with her must be Miss Bowers and Miss Robson – perhaps a secretary, the thin one with pince-nez, and a poor relation, the rather pathetic young woman who is obviously enjoying herself in spite of being treated like a black slave. I think Robson's the secretary woman and Bowers is the poor relation.'

'Wrong, Mother,' said Tim, grinning. He had suddenly recovered his good humour.

'How do you know?'

'Because I was in the lounge before dinner and the old bean said to the companion woman: "Where's Miss Bowers? Fetch her at once, Cornelia." And away trotted Cornelia like an obedient dog.'

'I shall have to talk to Miss Van Schuyler,' mused Mrs Allerton.

Tim grinned again.

'She'll snub you, Mother.'

'Not at all. I shall pave the way by sitting near her and conversing, in low (but penetrating), well-bred tones, about any titled relations and friends I can remember. I think a casual mention of your second cousin, once removed, the Duke of Glasgow, would probably do the trick.'

'How unscrupulous you are, Mother!'

Events after dinner were not without their amusing side to a student of human nature.

The socialistic young man (who turned out to be Mr Ferguson as deduced) retired to the smoking-room, scorning the assemblage of passengers in the observation saloon on the top deck.

Miss Van Schuyler duly secured the best and most undraughty position there by advancing firmly on a table at which Mrs Otterbourne was sitting and saying, 'You'll excuse me, I am sure, but I *think* my knitting was left here!'

Fixed by a hypnotic eye, the turban rose and gave ground. Miss Van Schuyler established herself and her suite. Mrs Otterbourne sat down nearby and hazarded various remarks, which were met with such chilling politeness that she soon gave up. Miss Van Schuyler then sat in glorious isolation. The Doyles sat with the Allertons. Dr Bessner retained the quiet Mr Fanthorp as a companion. Jacqueline de Bellefort sat by herself with a book. Rosalie Otterbourne was restless. Mrs Allerton spoke to her once or twice and tried to draw her into their group, but the girl responded ungraciously.

M. Hercule Poirot spent his evening listening to an account of Mrs Otterbourne's mission as a writer.

On his way to his cabin that night he encountered Jacqueline de Bellefort. She was leaning over the rail and, as she turned her head, he was struck by the look of acute misery on her face. There was now no insouciance, no malicious defiance, no dark flaming triumph.

'Good night, Mademoiselle.'

'Good night, Monsieur Poirot.' She hesitated, then said: 'You were surprised to find me here?'

'I was not so much surprised as sorry – very sorry . . .'

He spoke gravely.

'You mean sorry – for *me*?'

'That is what I meant. You have chosen, Mademoiselle, the dangerous course . . . As we here in this boat have embarked on a journey, so you too have embarked on your own private journey – a journey on a swift moving river, between dangerous rocks, and heading for who knows what currents of disaster . . .'

'Why do you say this?'

'Because it is true . . . You have cut the bonds that moored you to safety. I doubt now if you could turn back if you would.'

She said very slowly: 'That is true . . .'

Then she flung her head back.

'Ah, well – one must follow one's star, wherever it leads.'

'Beware, Mademoiselle, that it is not a false star . . .'

She laughed and mimicked the parrot cry of the donkey boys:

'That very bad star, sir! That star fall down . . .'

He was just dropping off to sleep when the murmur of voices awoke him. It was Simon Doyle's voice he heard, repeating the same words he had used when the steamer left Shellal.

'We've got to go through with it now . . .'

'Yes,' thought Hercule Poirot to himself, 'we have got to go through with it now . . .'

He was not happy.

CHAPTER 9

The steamer arrived early next morning at Ez-Zebua.

Cornelia Robson, her face beaming, a large flapping hat on her head, was one of the first to hurry on shore. Cornelia was not good at snubbing people. She was of an amiable disposition and disposed to like all her fellow creatures.

The sight of Hercule Poirot, in a white suit, pink shirt, large black bow tie and a white topee, did not make her wince as the aristocratic Miss Van Schuyler would assuredly have winced. As they walked together up an avenue of sphinxes, she responded readily to his conventional opening, 'Your companions are not coming ashore to view the temple?'

'Well, you see, Cousin Marie – that's Miss Van Schuyler – never gets up very early. She has to be very, very careful of her health. And of course she wanted Miss Bowers, that's her hospital nurse, to do things for her. And she said, too, that this isn't one of the best temples – but she was frightfully kind and said it would be quite all right for me to come.'

'That was very gracious of her,' said Poirot dryly.

The ingenuous Cornelia agreed unsuspectingly.

'Oh, she's very kind. It's simply wonderful of her to bring me on this trip. I do feel I'm a lucky girl. I just could hardly believe it when she suggested to Mother that I should come too.'

'And you have enjoyed it – yes?'

'Oh, it's been wonderful! I've seen Italy – Venice and Padua and Pisa – and then Cairo – only cousin Marie wasn't very well in Cairo, so I couldn't get round much, and now this wonderful trip up the Wadi Halfa and back.'

Poirot said, smiling, 'You have the happy nature, Mademoiselle.'

He looked thoughtfully from her to silent, frowning Rosalie, who was walking ahead by herself.

'She's very nice-looking, isn't she?' said Cornelia, following his glance. 'Only kind of scornful-looking. She's very English, of course. She's not as lovely as Mrs Doyle. I think Mrs Doyle's the loveliest, the most elegant woman I've ever seen! And her husband just worships the ground she walks on, doesn't he? I think that grey-haired lady is kind of distinguished-looking, don't you? She's a cousin of a Duke, I believe. She was talking about him right near us last night. But she isn't actually titled herself, is she?'

She prattled on until the dragoman in charge called a halt and began to intone: 'This temple was dedicated to Egyptian God Amun and the Sun God Re-Harakhte – whose symbol was hawk's head . . .'

It droned on. Dr Bessner, Baedeker in hand, mumbled to himself in German. He preferred the written word.

Tim Allerton had not joined the party. His mother was breaking the ice with the reserved Mr Fanthorp. Andrew Pennington, his arm through Linnet Doyle's, was listening attentively, seemingly most interested in the measurements as recited by the guide.

'Sixty-five feet high, is that so? Looks a little less to me. Great fellow, this Rameses. An Egyptian live wire.'

'A big business man, Uncle Andrew.'

Andrew Pennington looked at her appreciatively.

'You look fine this morning, Linnet. I've been a mite worried about you lately. You've looked kind of peaky.'

Chatting together, the party returned to the boat. Once more the *Karnak* glided up the river. The scenery was less stern now. There were palms, cultivation.

It was as though the change in the scenery had relieved some secret oppression that had brooded over the passengers. Tim Allerton had got over his fit of moodiness. Rosalie looked less sulky. Linnet seemed almost light-hearted.

Pennington said to her: 'It's tactless to talk business to a bride on her honeymoon, but there are just one or two things –'

'Why, of course, Uncle Andrew.' Linnet at once became businesslike. 'My marriage has made a difference, of course.'

'That's just it. Some time or other I want your signature to several documents.'

'Why not now?'

Andrew Pennington glanced round. Their corner of the observation saloon was quite untenanted. Most of the people were outside on the deck space between the observation saloon and the cabin. The only occupants of the saloon were Mr Ferguson – who was drinking beer at a small table in the middle, his legs, encased in their dirty flannel trousers, stuck out in front of him, whilst he whistled to himself in the intervals of drinking – M. Hercule Poirot, who was sitting before him, and Miss Van Schuyler, who was sitting in a corner reading a book on Egypt.

'That's fine,' said Andrew Pennington. He left the saloon.

Linnet and Simon smiled at each other – a slow smile that took a few minutes to come to full fruition.

'All right, sweet?' he asked.

'Yes, still all right . . . Funny how I'm not rattled any more.'

Simon said with deep conviction in his tone: 'You're marvellous.'

Pennington came back. He brought with him a sheaf of closely written documents.

'Mercy!' cried Linnet. 'Have I got to sign all these?'

Andrew Pennington was apologetic.

'It's tough on you, I know, but I'd just like to get your affairs put in proper shape. First of all there's the lease of the Fifth Avenue property . . . then there are the Western Land

Concessions . . .' He talked on, rustling and sorting the papers. Simon yawned.

The door to the deck swung open and Mr Fanthorp came in. He gazed aimlessly round, then strolled forward and stood by Poirot looking out at the pale blue water and the yellow enveloping sands . . .

'– you sign just there,' concluded Pennington, spreading a paper before Linnet and indicating a space.

Linnet picked up the document and glanced through it. She turned back once to the first page, then, taking up the fountain pen Pennington had laid beside her, she signed her name *Linnet Doyle* . . .

Pennington took away the paper and spread out another.

Fanthorp wandered over in their direction. He peered out through the side window at something that seemed to interest him on the bank they were passing.

'That's just the transfer,' said Pennington. 'You needn't read it.'

But Linnet took a brief glance through it. Pennington laid down a third paper. Again Linnet perused it carefully.

'They're all quite straightforward,' said Andrew. 'Nothing of interest. Only legal phraseology.'

Simon yawned again.

'My dear girl, you're not going to read the whole lot through, are you? You'll be at it till lunch-time and longer.'

'I always read everything through,' said Linnet. 'Father taught me to do that. He said there might be some clerical error.'

Pennington laughed rather harshly.

'You're a grand woman of business, Linnet.'

'She's much more conscientious than I'd be,' said Simon, laughing. 'I've never read a legal document in my life. I sign where they tell me to sign on the dotted line – and that's that.'

'That's frightfully slipshod,' said Linnet disapprovingly.

'I've no business head,' declared Simon cheerfully. 'Never had. A fellow tells me to sign – I sign. It's much the simplest way.'

Andrew Pennington was looking at him thoughtfully. He said dryly, stroking his upper lip, 'A little risky sometimes, Doyle?'

'Nonsense,' replied Simon. 'I'm not one of those people who believe the whole world is out to do one down. I'm a trusting kind of fellow – and it pays, you know. I've hardly ever been let down.'

Suddenly, to everyone's surprise, the silent Mr Fanthorp swung around and addressed Linnet.

'I hope I'm not butting in, but you must let me say how much I admire your businesslike capacity. In my profession – er – I am a lawyer – I find ladies sadly unbusinesslike. Never to sign a document unless you read it through is admirable – altogether admirable.'

He gave a little bow. Then, rather red in the face, he turned once more to contemplate the banks of the Nile.

Linnet looked rather uncertainly: 'Er – thank you . . .' She bit her lip to repress a giggle. The young man had looked so preternaturally solemn.

Andrew Pennington looked seriously annoyed.

Simon Doyle looked uncertain whether to be annoyed or amused.

The backs of Mr Fanthorp's ears were bright crimson.

'Next, please,' said Linnet, smiling up at Pennington.

But Pennington looked decidedly ruffled.

'I think perhaps some other time would be better,' he said stiffly. 'As – er – Doyle says, if you have to read through all these we shall be here till lunch-time. We mustn't miss enjoying the scenery. Anyway those first two papers were the only urgent ones. We'll settle down to business later.'

'It's frightfully hot in here,' Linnet said. 'Let's go outside.'

The three of them passed through the swing door. Hercule Poirot turned his head. His gaze rested thoughtfully on Mr Fanthorp's back; then it shifted to the lounging figure of Mr Ferguson who had his head thrown back and was still whistling softly to himself.

Finally Poirot looked over at the upright figure of Miss Van Schuyler in her corner. Miss Van Schuyler was glaring at Mr Ferguson.

The swing door on the port side opened and Cornelia Robson hurried in.

'You've been a long time,' snapped the old lady. 'Where've you been?'

'I'm so sorry, Cousin Marie. The wool wasn't where you said it was. It was in another case altogther –'

'My dear child, you are perfectly hopeless at finding anything! You are willing, I know, my dear, but you must try to be a little cleverer and quicker. It only needs *concentration.*'

'I'm so sorry, Cousin Marie. I'm afraid I am very stupid.'

'Nobody need be stupid if they *try*, my dear. I have brought you on this trip, and I expect a little attention in return.'

Cornelia flushed.

'I'm very sorry, Cousin Marie.'

'And where is Miss Bowers? It was time for my drops ten minutes ago. Please go and find her at once. The doctor said it was most important –'

But at this stage Miss Bowers entered, carrying a small medicine glass.

'Your drops, Miss Van Schuyler.'

'I should have had them at eleven,' snapped the old lady. 'If there's one thing I detest it's unpunctuality.'

'Quite,' said Miss Bowers. She glanced at her wristwatch. 'It's exactly half a minute to eleven.'

'By my watch it's ten past.'

'I think you'll find my watch is right. It's a perfect time-keeper. It never loses or gains.' Miss Bowers was quite imperturbable.

Miss Van Schuyler swallowed the contents of the medicine glass.

'I feel definitely worse,' she snapped.

'I'm sorry to hear that, Miss Van Schuyler.'

Miss Bowers did not sound sorry. She sounded completely uninterested. She was obviously making the correct reply mechanically.

'It's too hot in here,' snapped Miss Van Schuyler. 'Find me a chair on the deck, Miss Bowers. Cornelia, bring my knitting. Don't be clumsy or drop it. And then I shall want you to wind some wool.'

The procession passed out.

Mr Ferguson sighed, stirred his legs and remarked to the world at large, 'Gosh, I'd like to scrag that dame.'

Poirot asked interestedly: 'She is a type you dislike, eh?'

'Dislike? I should say so. What good has that woman ever been to anyone or anything? She's never worked or lifted a finger. She's just battened on other people. She's a parasite – and a damned unpleasant parasite. There are a lot of people on this boat I'd say the world could do without.'

'Really?'

'Yes. That girl in here just now, signing share transfers and throwing her weight about. Hundreds and thousands of wretched workers slaving for a mere pittance to keep her in silk stockings and useless luxuries. One of the richest women in England, so someone told me – and never done a hand's turn in her life.'

'Who told you she was one of the richest women in England?'

Mr Ferguson cast a belligerent eye at him.

'A man you wouldn't be seen speaking to! A man who works with his hands and isn't ashamed of it! Not one of your dressed-up, foppish good-for-nothings.'

His eye rested unfavourably on the bow tie and pink shirt.

'Me, I work with my brains and am not ashamed of it,' said Poirot, answering the glance.

Mr Ferguson merely snorted.

'Ought to be shot – the lot of them!' he asserted.

'My dear young man,' said Poirot, 'what a passion you have for violence!'

'Can you tell me of any good that can be done without it? You've got to break down and destroy before you can build up.'

'It is certainly much easier and much noisier and much more spectacular.'

'What do *you* do for a living? Nothing at all, I bet. Probably call yourself a middle man.'

'I am not a middle man. I am a top man,' declared Hercule Poirot with a slight arrogance.

'What *are* you?'

'I am a detective,' said Hercule Poirot with the modest air of one who says 'I am a king.'

'Good God!' The young man seemed seriously taken aback. 'Do you mean that girl actually totes about a dumb dick? Is she as careful of her precious skin as *that*?'

'I have no connection whatever with Monsieur and Madame Doyle,' said Poirot stiffly. 'I am on holiday.'

'Enjoying a vacation – eh?'

'And you? Is it not that you are on holiday also?'

'Holiday!' Mr Ferguson snorted. Then he added cryptically: 'I'm studying conditions.'

'Very interesting,' murmured Poirot and moved gently out on to the deck.

Miss Van Schuyler was established in the best corner. Cornelia knelt in front of her, her arms outstretched with a skein of grey wool upon them. Miss Bowers was sitting very upright reading the *Saturday Evening Post*.

Poirot wandered gently onward down the starboard deck. As he passed round the stern of the boat he almost ran into a woman who turned a startled face towards him – a dark, piquant, Latin face. She was neatly dressed in black and had been standing talking to a big burly man in uniform – one of the engineers, by the look of him. There was a queer expression on both their faces – guilt and alarm. Poirot wondered what they had been talking about.

He rounded the stern and continued his walk along the port side. A cabin door opened and Mrs Otterbourne emerged and nearly fell into his arms. She was wearing a scarlet satin dressing-gown.

'So sorry,' she apologized. 'Dear Mr Poirot – so very sorry. The motion – just the motion, you know. Never did have any sea legs. If the boat would only keep still . . .' She clutched at his arm. 'It's the pitching I can't stand . . . Never really happy at sea . . . And left all alone here hour after hour. That girl of mine – no sympathy – no understanding of her poor old mother who's done everything for her . . .' Mrs Otterbourne began to weep. 'Slaved for her I have – worn myself to the bone – to the bone. A *grande amoureuse* – that's what I might have been – a *grande amoureuse* – sacrificed everything – everything . . . And nobody cares! But I'll tell everyone – I'll tell them now – how she neglects me – how hard she is – making me come on this journey – bored to death . . . I'll go and tell them now –'

She surged forward. Poirot gently repressed the action.

'I will send her to you, Madame. Re-enter your cabin. It is best that way –'

'No. I want to tell everyone – everyone on the boat –'

'It is too dangerous, Madame. The sea is too rough. You might be swept overboard.'

Mrs Otterbourne looked at him doubtfully.

'You think so. You really think so?'

'I do.'

267

He was successful. Mrs Otterbourne wavered, faltered and re-entered her cabin.

Poirot's nostrils twitched once or twice. Then he nodded and walked on to where Rosalie Otterbourne was sitting between Mrs Allerton and Tim.

'Your mother wants you, Mademoiselle.'

She had been laughing quite happily. Now her face clouded over. She shot a quick suspicious look at him and hurried along the deck.

'I can't make that child out,' said Mrs Allerton. 'She varies so. One day she's friendly; the next day, she's positively rude.'

'Thoroughly spoilt and bad-tempered,' said Tim.

Mrs Allerton shook her head.

'No. I don't think it's that. I think she's unhappy.'

Tim shrugged his shoulders.

'Oh, well, I suppose we've all got our private troubles.' His voice sounded hard and curt.

A booming noise was heard.

'Lunch,' cried Mrs Allerton delightedly. 'I'm starving.'

II

That evening, Poirot noticed that Mrs Allerton was sitting talking to Miss Van Schuyler. As he passed, Mrs Allerton closed one eye and opened it again. She was saying, 'Of course at Calfries Castle – the dear Duke –'

Cornelia, released from her attendance, was out on the deck. She was listening to Dr Bessner, who was instructing her somewhat ponderously in Egyptology as culled from the pages of Baedeker. Cornelia listened with rapt attention.

Leaning over the rail Tim Allerton was saying: 'Anyhow, it's a rotten world . . .'

Rosalie Otterbourne answered: 'It's unfair; some people have everything.'

Poirot sighed. He was glad that he was no longer young.

On the Monday morning various expressions of delight and appreciation were heard on the deck of the *Karnak*. The steamer was moored to the bank and a few hundred yards away, the morning sun just striking it, was a great temple carved out of the face of the rock. Four colossal figures, hewn out of the cliff, look out eternally over the Nile and face the rising sun.

Cornelia Robson said incoherently: 'Oh, Monsieur Poirot, isn't it wonderful? I mean they're so big and peaceful – and looking at them makes one feel that one's so small – and rather like an insect – and that nothing matters very much really, does it?'

Mr Fanthorp, who was standing near by, murmured, 'Very – er – impressive.'

'Grand, isn't it?' said Simon Doyle, strolling up. He went on confidentially to Poirot: 'You know, I'm not much of a fellow for temples and sight-seeing and all that, but a place like this sort of gets you, if you know what I mean. Those old Pharaohs must have been wonderful fellows.'

The other had drifted away. Simon lowered his voice.

'I'm no end glad we came on this trip. It's – well, it's cleared things up. Amazing why it should – but there it is. Linnet's got her nerve back. She say's it's because shes actually *faced* the business at last.'

'I think that is very probable,' said Poirot.

'She says that when she actually saw Jackie on the boat she felt terrible – and then, suddenly, it didn't matter any more. We're both agreed that we won't try to dodge her any more. We'll just meet her on her own ground and show her that this ridiculous stunt of hers doesn't worry us a bit. It's just damned bad form – that's all. She thought she'd got us badly rattled, but now, well, we just aren't rattled any more. That ought to show her.'

'Yes,' said Poirot thoughtfully.

'So that's splendid, isn't it?'

'Oh, yes, yes.'

Linnet came along the deck. She was dressed in a soft shade of apricot linen. She was smiling. She greeted Poirot with no particular enthusiasm, just gave him a cool nod and then drew her husband away.

Poirot realized with a momentary flicker of amusement that he had not made himself popular by his critical attitude. Linnet was used to unqualified admiration of all she was or did. Hercule Poirot had sinned noticeably against this creed.

Mrs Allerton, joining him, murmured:

'What a difference in that girl! She looked worried and not very happy at Assuan. Today she looks so happy that one might almost be afraid she was fey.'

Before Poirot could respond as he meant, the party was called to order. The official dragoman took charge and the party was led ashore to visit Abu Simbel.

Poirot himself fell into step with Andrew Pennington.

'It is your first visit to Egypt – yes?' he asked.

'Why, no, I was here in nineteen twenty-three. That is to say I was in Cairo. I've never been this trip up the Nile before.'

'You came over on the *Carmanic*, I believe – at least so Madame Doyle was telling me.'

Pennington shot a shrewd glance in his direction.

'Why, yes, that is so,' he admitted.

'I wondered if you had happened to come across some friends of mine who were aboard – the Rushington Smiths.'

'I can't recall anyone of that name. The boat was full and we had bad weather. A lot of passengers hardly appeared, and in any case the voyage is so short one doesn't get to know who is on board and who isn't.'

'Yes, that is very true. What a pleasant surprise your running into Madame Doyle and her husband. You had no idea they were married?'

'No. Mrs Doyle had written me, but the letter was forwarded on and I only received it some days after our unexpected meeting in Cairo.'

'You have known her for many years, I understand?'

'Why, I should say I have, Monsieur Poirot. I've known Linnet Ridgeway since she was just a cute little thing so high –' He made an illustrating gesture. 'Her father and I were lifelong friends. A very remarkable man, Melhuish Ridgeway – and a very successful one.'

'His daughter comes into a considerable fortune, I understand . . . Ah, *pardon* – perhaps it is not delicate what I say there.'

Andrew Pennington seemed slightly amused.

'Oh, that's pretty common knowledge. Yes, Linnet's a wealthy woman.'

'I suppose, though, that the recent slump is bound to affect any stocks, however sound they may be?'

Pennington took a moment or two to answer. He said at last: 'That, of course, is true to a certain extent. The position is very difficult in these days.'

Poirot murmured: 'I should imagine, however, that Madame Doyle has a keen business head.'

'That is so. Yes, that is so. Linnet is a clever practical girl.'

They came to a halt. The guide proceeded to instruct them on the subject of the temple built by the great Rameses. The four colossi of Rameses himself, one pair on each side of the entrance, hewn out of the living rock, looked down on the little straggling party of tourists.

Signor Richetti, disdaining the remarks of the dragoman, was busy examining the reliefs of Negro and Syrian captives on the bases of the colossi on either side of the entrance.

When the party entered the temple, a sense of dimness and peace came over them. The still vividly coloured reliefs on some of the inner walls were pointed out, but the party tended to break up into groups.

Dr Bessner read sonorously in German from a Baedeker, pausing every now and then to translate for the benefit of Cornelia, who walked in a docile manner beside him. This was not to continue, however. Miss Van Schuyler, entering on the arm of the phlegmatic Miss Bowers, uttered a commanding: 'Cornelia, come here,' and the instruction had perforce to cease. Dr Bessner beamed after her vaguely through his thick lenses.

'A very nice maiden, that,' he announced to Poirot. 'She does not look so starved as some of these young women. No, she has the nice curves. She listens too very intelligently; it is a pleasure to instruct her.'

It fleeted across Poirot's mind that it seemed to be Cornelia's fate either to be bullied or instructed. In any case she was always the listener, never the talker.

Miss Bowers, momentarily released by the peremptory summons

of Cornelia, was standing in the middle of the temple, looking about her with her cool, incurious gaze. Her reaction to the wonders of the past was succinct.

'The guide says the name of one of these gods or goddesses was Mut. Can you beat it?'

There was an inner sanctuary where sat four figures eternally presiding, stangely dignified in their dim aloofness.

Before them stood Linnet and her husband. Her arm was in his, her face lifted – a typical face of the new civilization, intelligent, curious, untouched by the past.

Simon said suddenly: 'Let's get out of here. I don't like these four fellows – especially the one in the high hat.'

'That's Amon, I suppose. And that one is Rameses. Why don't you like them? I think they're very impressive.'

'They're a damned sight too impressive; there's something uncanny about them. Come out into the sunlight.'

Linnet laughed but yielded.

They came out of the temple into the sunshine with the sand yellow and warm about their feet. Linnet began to laugh. At their feet in a row, presenting a momentarily gruesome appearance as though sawn from their bodies, were the heads of half a dozen Nubian boys. The eyes rolled, the heads moved rhythmically from side to side, the lips chanted a new invocation:

'Hip, hip *hurray*! Hip, hip *hurray*! Very good, very nice. Thank you very much.'

'How absurd! How do they do it? Are they really buried very deep?'

Simon produced some small change.

'Very good, very nice, very expensive,' he mimicked.

Two small boys in charge of the 'show' picked up the coins neatly.

Linnet and Simon passed on. They had no wish to return to the boat, and they were weary of sight-seeing. They settled themselves with their backs to the cliff and let the warm sun bake them through.

'How lovely the sun is,' thought Linnet. 'How warm – how safe . . . How lovely it is to be happy . . . How lovely to be me – me . . . me : . . Linnet . . .'

Her eyes closed. She was half asleep, half awake, drifting in the midst of thought that was like the sand drifting and blowing.

Simon's eyes were open. They too held contentment. What a fool he'd been to be rattled that first night . . . There was nothing to be rattled about . . . Everything was all right . . . After all, one could trust Jackie –

There was a shout – people running towards him waving their arms – shouting . . .

Simon stared stupidly for a moment. Then he sprang to his feet and dragged Linnet with him.

Not a minute too soon. A big boulder hurtling down the cliff crashed past them. If Linnet had remained where she was she would have been crushed to atoms.

White-faced they clung together. Hercule Poirot and Tim Allerton ran up to them.

'*Ma foi*, Madame, that was a near thing.'

All four instinctively looked up at the cliff. There was nothing to be seen. But there was a path along the top. Poirot remembered seeing some natives walking along there when they had first come ashore.

He looked at the husband and wife. Linnet looked dazed still – bewildered. Simon, however, was inarticulate with rage.

'God damn her!' he ejaculated.

He checked himself with a quick glance at Tim Allerton.

The latter said: 'Phew, that was near! Did some fool bowl that thing over, or did it get detached on its own?'

Linnet was very pale. She said with difficulty: 'I think – some fool must have done it.'

'Might have crushed you like an eggshell. Sure you haven't got an enemy, Linnet?'

Linnet swallowed twice and found a difficulty in answering the light-hearted raillery.

'Come back to the boat, Madame,' Poirot said quickly. 'You must have a restorative.'

They walked quickly, Simon still full of pent-up rage, Tim trying to talk cheerfully and distract Linnet's mind from the danger she had run, Poirot with a grave face.

And then, just as they reached the gangplank, Simon stopped dead. A look of amazement spread over his face.

Jacqueline de Bellefort was just coming ashore. Dressed in blue gingham, she looked childish this morning.

'Good God!' said Simon under his breath. 'So it *was* an accident, after all.'

The anger went out of his face. An overwhelming relief showed so plainly that Jacqueline noticed something amiss.

'Good morning,' she said. 'I'm afraid I'm a little on the late side.'

She gave them all a nod and stepped ashore and proceeded in the direction of the temple.

Simon clutched Poirot's arm. The other two had gone on.

'My God, that's a relief. I thought – I thought –'

Poirot nodded. 'Yes, yes, I know what you thought.' But he himself still looked grave and preoccupied. He turned his head and noted carefully what had become of the rest of the party from the ship.

Miss Van Schuyler was slowly returning on the arm of Miss Bowers.

A little farther away Mrs Allerton was standing laughing at the little Nubian row of heads. Mrs Otterbourne was with her.

The others were nowhere in sight.

Poirot shook his head as he followed Simon slowly on to the boat.

CHAPTER II

'Will you explain to me, Madame, the meaning of the word "fey"?'

Mrs Allerton looked slightly surprised. She and Poirot were toiling slowly up to the rock overlooking the Second Cataract. Most of the others had gone up on camels, but Poirot had felt that the motion of the camel was slightly reminiscent of that of a ship. Mrs Allerton had put it on the grounds of personal indignity.

They had arrived at Wadi Halfa the night before. This morning two launches had conveyed all the party to the Second Cataract, with the exception of Signor Richetti, who had insisted on making an excursion of his own to a remote spot called Semna, which, he explained, was of paramount interest as being the gateway of Nubia in the time of Amenemhet III, and where there was a stele recording the fact that on entering Egypt Negroes must pay customs duties. Everything had been done to discourage this example of individuality, but with no avail. Signor Richetti was determined and had waved aside each objection: (1) that the expedition was not worth making, (2) that the expedition could not be made, owing to the impossibility of getting a car there, (3) that no car could be obtained to do the trip, (4) that a car would be a prohibitive price. Having scoffed at (1), expressed incredulity at (2), offered to find a car himself to (3), and bargained fluently in Arabic for (4), Signor Richetti had at last departed – his departure being arranged in a secret and furtive manner, in case some of the other tourists should take it into their heads to stray from the appointed paths of sight-seeing.

'Fey?' Mrs Allerton put her head on one side as she considered her reply. 'Well, it's a Scotch word, really. It means the kind of exalted happiness that comes before disaster. You know – it's too good to be true.'

She enlarged on the theme. Poirot listened attentively.

'I thank you, Madame. I understand now. It is odd that you should have said that yesterday – when Madame Doyle was to escape death so shortly afterwards.'

Mrs Allerton gave a little shiver.

'It must have been a very near escape. Do you think some of these little black wretches rolled it over for fun? It's the sort of thing boys might do all over the world – not perhaps really meaning any harm.'

Poirot shrugged his shoulders.

'It may be, Madame.'

He changed the subject, talking of Majorca and asking various practical questions from the point of view of a possible visit.

Mrs Allerton had grown to like the little man very much – partly perhaps out of a contradictory spirit. Tim, she felt, was always trying to make her less friendly to Hercule Poirot, whom he summarized firmly as 'the worst kind of bounder'. But she herself did not call him a bounder; she supposed it was his somewhat foreign exotic clothing which roused her son's prejudices. She herself found him an intelligent and stimulating companion. He was also extremely sympathetic. She found herself suddenly confiding in him her dislike of Joanna Southwood. It eased her to talk of the matter. And after all, why not? He did not know Joanna – would probably never meet her. Why should she not ease herself of that constantly borne burden of jealous thought?

At the same moment Tim and Rosalie Otterbourne were talking of her. Tim had just been half jestingly abusing his luck. His rotten health, never bad enough to be really interesting, yet not good enough for him to have led the life he would have chosen. Very little money, no congenial occupation.

'A thoroughly lukewarm, tame existence,' he finished discontentedly.

Rosalie said abruptly, 'You've got something heaps of people would envy you.'

'What's that?'

'Your mother.'

Tim was surprised and pleased.

'Mother? Yes, of course she is quite unique. It's nice of you to see it.'

'I think she's marvellous. She looks so lovely – so composed and calm – as though nothing could ever touch her, and yet – and yet somehow she's always ready to be funny about things too . . .'

Rosalie was stammering slightly in her earnestness.

Tim felt a rising warmth to the girl. He wished he could return the compliment, but lamentably, Mrs Otterbourne was his idea of the world's greatest menace. The inability to respond in kind made him embarrassed.

Miss Van Schuyler had stayed in the launch. She could not risk the ascent either on a camel or on her legs. She had said snappily:

'I'm sorry to have to ask you to stay with me, Miss Bowers. I intended you to go and Cornelia to stay, but girls are so selfish. She rushed off without a word to me. And I actually saw her talking to that very unpleasant and ill-bred young man, Ferguson. Cornelia has disappointed me sadly. She has absolutely no social sense.'

Miss Bowers replied in her usual matter-of-fact fashion:

'That's quite all right, Miss Van Schuyler. It would have been a hot walk up there, and I don't fancy the look of those saddles on the camels. Fleas, as likely as not.'

She adjusted her glasses, screwed up her eyes to look at the party descending the hill and remarked: 'Miss Robson isn't with that young man any more. She's with Dr Bessner.'

Miss Van Schuyler grunted.

Since she had discovered that Dr Bessner had a large clinic in Czechoslovakia and a European reputation as a fashionable physician, she was disposed to be gracious to him. Besides she might need his professional services before the journey was over.

When the party returned to the *Karnak* Linnet gave a cry of surprise.

'A telegram for me.'

She snatched it off the board and tore it open.

'Why – I don't understand – potatoes, beetroots – what does it mean, Simon?'

Simon was just coming to look over her shoulder when a furious voice said: 'Excuse me, that telegram is for me,' and Signor Richetti snatched it rudely from her hand, fixing her with a furious glare as he did so.

Linnet stared in surprise for a moment, then turned over the envelope.

'Oh, Simon, what a fool I am! It's Richetti – not Ridgeway – and anyway of course my name isn't Ridgeway now. I must apologize.'

She followed the little archaeologist up to the stern of the boat.

'I am so sorry, Signor Richetti. You see my name was Ridgeway before I married, and I haven't been married very long, and so . . .'

She paused, her face dimpled with smiles, inviting him to smile upon a young bride's *faux pas*.

But Richetti was obviously 'not amused'. Queen Victoria at her most disapproving could not have looked more grim. 'Names should be read carefully. It is inexcusable to be careless in these matters.'

Linnet bit her lip and her colour rose. She was not accustomed to have her apologies received in this fashion. She turned away and, rejoining Simon, said angrily, 'These Italians are really insupportable.'

'Never mind, darling; let's go and look at that big ivory crocodile you liked.'

They went ashore together.

Poirot, watching them walk up the landing-stage, heard a sharp indrawn breath. He turned to see Jacqueline de Bellefort at his side. Her hands were clenched on the rail. The expression on her face, as she turned it towards him, quite startled him. It was no longer gay or malicious. She looked devoured by some inner consuming fire.

'They don't care any more.' The words came low and fast. 'They've got beyond me. I can't reach them . . . They don't mind if I'm here or not . . . I can't – I can't hurt them any more . . .'

Her hands on the rail trembled.

'Mademoiselle –'

She broke in: 'Oh, it's too late now – too late for warnings . . . You were right. I ought not to have come. Not on this journey. What did you call it? A journey of the soul? I can't go back; I've got to go on. And I'm going on. They shan't be happy together; they shan't. I'd kill him sooner . . .'

She turned abruptly away. Poirot, staring after her, felt a hand on his shoulder.

'Your girl friend seems a trifle upset, Monsieur Poirot.' Poirot turned. He stared in surprise, seeing an old acquaintance.

'Colonel Race.'

The tall bronzed man smiled.

'Bit of a surprise, eh?'

Hercule Poirot had come across Colonel Race a year previously in London. They had been fellow guests at a very strange dinner party – a dinner party that had ended in death for that strange man, their host.

Poirot knew that Race was a man of unadvertised goings and comings. He was usually to be found in one of the outposts of Empire where trouble was brewing.

'So you are here at Wadi Halfa,' he remarked thoughtfully.

'I am here on this boat.'

'You mean?'

'That I am making the return journey with you to Shellal.'

Hercule Poirot's eyebrows rose.

'That is very interesting. Shall we, perhaps, have a little drink?'

They went into the observation saloon, now quite empty. Poirot ordered a whisky for the Colonel and a double orangeade full of sugar for himself.

'So you make the return journey with us,' said Poirot as he sipped. 'You would go faster, would you not, on the Government steamer, which travels by night as well as day?'

Colonel Race's face creased appreciatively.

'You're right on the spot as usual, Monsieur Poirot,' he said pleasantly.

'It is, then, the passengers?'

'One of the passengers.'

'Now which one, I wonder?' Hercule Poirot asked of the ornate ceiling.

'Unfortunately I don't know myself,' said Race ruefully.

Poirot looked interested.

Race said: 'There's no need to be mysterious to you. We've had a good deal of trouble out here – one way and another. It isn't the people who ostensibly lead the rioters that we're after. It's the men who very cleverly put the match to the gunpowder. There were three of them. One's dead. One's in prison. I want the third man – a man with five or six cold-blooded murders to his credit. He's one of the cleverest paid agitators that ever existed . . . He's on this boat. I know that from a passage in a letter that passed through our hands. Decoded it said: "X will be on the *Karnak* trip seventh to thirteenth." It didn't say under what name X would be passing.'

'Have you any description of him?'

'No. American, Irish, and French descent. Bit of a mongrel. That doesn't help us much. Have you got any ideas?'

'An idea – it is all very well,' said Poirot meditatively.

Such was the understanding between them that Race pressed him no further. He knew Hercule Poirot did not ever speak unless he was sure.

Poirot rubbed his nose and said unhappily: 'There passes itself something on this boat that causes me much inquietude.'

Race looked at him inquiringly.

'Figure to yourself,' said Poirot, 'a person A who has grievously wronged a person B. The person B desires the revenge. The person B makes the threats.'

'A and B being both on this boat?'

Poirot nodded. 'Precisely.'

'And B, I gather, being a woman?'

'Exactly.'

Race lit a cigarette.

'I shouldn't worry. People who go about talking of what they are going to do don't usually do it.'

'And particularly is that the case with *les femmes*, you would say! Yes, that is true.'

But he still did not look happy.

'Anything else?' asked Race.

'Yes, there is something. Yesterday the person A had a very near escape from death, the kind of death that might very conveniently be called an accident.'

'Engineered by B?'

'No, that is just the point. B could have had nothing to do with it.'

'Then it *was* an accident.'

'I suppose so – but I don't like such accidents.'

'You're quite sure B could have had no hand in it?'

'Absolutely.'

'Oh, well, coincidences do happen. Who is A, by the way? A particularly disagreeable person?'

'On the contrary. A is a charming, rich, and beautiful young lady.'

Race grinned.

'Sounds quite like a novelette.'

'*Peut-être.* But I tell you, I am not happy, my friend. If I am right, and after all I am constantly in the habit of being right' – Race smiled into his moustache at this typical utterance – 'then there is matter for grave inquietude. And now, *you* come to add yet another complication. You tell me that there is a man on the *Karnak* who kills.'

'He doesn't usually kill charming young ladies.'

Poirot shook his head in a dissatisfied manner.

'I am afraid, my friend,' he said. 'I am afraid . . . Today, I advised this lady, Madame Doyle, to go with her husband to Khartoum, not to return on this boat. But they would not agree. I pray to Heaven that we may arrive at Shellal without catastrophe.'

'Aren't you taking rather a gloomy view?'

Poirot shook his head.

'I am afraid,' he said simply. 'Yes, I, Hercule Poirot, I'm afraid . . .'

Cornelia Robson stood inside the temple of Abu Simbel. It was the evening of the following day – a hot still evening. The *Karnak* was anchored once more at Abu Simbel to permit a second visit to be made to the temple, this time by artificial light. The difference this made was considerable, and Cornelia commented wonderingly on the fact to Mr Ferguson, who was standing by her side.

'Why, you see it ever so much better now!' she exclaimed. 'All those enemies having their heads cut off by the King – they just stand right out. That's a cute kind of castle there that I never noticed before. I wish Dr Bessner was here, he'd tell me what it was.'

'How you can stand that old fool beats me,' said Ferguson gloomily.

'Why, he's just one of the kindest men I've ever met.'

'Pompous old bore.'

'I don't think you ought to speak that way.'

The young man gripped her suddenly by the arm. They were just emerging from the temple into the moonlight.

'Why do you stick being bored by fat old men – and bullied and snubbed by a vicious old harridan?'

'Why, Mr Ferguson!'

'Haven't you got any spirit? Don't you know you're just as good as she is?'

'But I'm not!' Cornelia spoke with honest conviction.

'You're not as rich; that's all you mean.'

'No, it isn't. Cousin Marie's very cultured, and –'

'Cultured!' The young man let go of her arm as suddenly as he had taken it. 'That word makes me sick.'

Cornelia looked at him in alarm.

'She doesn't like you talking to me, does she?' asked the young man.

Cornelia blushed and looked embarrassed.

'Why? Because she thinks I'm not her social equal! Pah! Doesn't that make you see red?'

Cornelia faltered out: 'I wish you wouldn't get so mad about things.'

'Don't you realize – and you an American – that everyone is born free and equal?'

'They're not,' said Cornelia with calm certainty.

'My good girl, it's part of your constitution!'

'Cousin Marie says politicians aren't gentlemen,' said Cornelia. 'And of course people aren't equal. It doesn't make sense. I know I'm kind of homely-looking, and I used to feel mortified about it sometimes, but I've got over that. I'd like to have been born elegant and beautiful like Mrs Doyle, but I wasn't, so I guess it's no use worrying.'

'Mrs Doyle!' exclaimed Ferguson with deep contempt. 'She's the sort of woman who ought to be shot as an example.'

Cornelia looked at him anxiously.

'I believe it's your digestion,' she said kindly. 'I've got a special kind of pepsin that Cousin Marie tried once. Would you like to try it?'

Mr Ferguson said: 'You're impossible!'

He turned and strode away. Cornelia went on towards the boat. Just as she was crossing the gangway he caught her up once more.

'You're the nicest person on the boat,' he said. 'And mind you remember it.'

Blushing with pleasure Cornelia repaired to the observation saloon. Miss Van Schuyler was conversing with Dr Bessner – an agreeable conversation dealing with certain royal patients of his.

Cornelia said guiltily: 'I do hope I haven't been a long time, Cousin Marie.'

Glancing at her watch, the old lady snapped: 'You haven't exactly hurried, my dear. And what have you done with my velvet stole?'

Cornelia looked round.

'Shall I see if it's in the cabin, Cousin Marie?'

'Of course it isn't! I had it just after dinner in here, and I haven't moved out of the place. It was on that chair.'

Cornelia made a desultory search.

'I can't see it anywhere, Cousin Marie.'

'Nonsense!' said Miss Van Schuyler. 'Look about.' It was an order such as one might give to a dog, and in her doglike fashion Cornelia obeyed. The quiet Mr Fanthorp, who was sitting at a table near by, rose and assisted her. But the stole could not be found.

The day had been such an unusually hot and sultry one that

most people had retired early after going ashore to view the temple. The Doyles were playing bridge with Pennington and Race at a table in a corner. The only other occupant of the saloon was Hercule Poirot, who was yawning his head off at a small table near the door.

Miss Van Schuyler, making a Royal Progress bedward, with Cornelia and Miss Bowers in attendance, paused by his chair. He sprang politely to his feet, stifling a yawn of gargantuan dimensions.

Miss Van Schuyler said: 'I have only just realized who you are, Monsieur Poirot. I may tell you that I have heard of you from my old friend Rufus Van Aldin. You must tell me about your cases sometime.'

Poirot, his eyes twinkling a little through their sleepiness, bowed in an exaggerated manner. With a kindly but condescending nod, Miss Van Schuyler passed on.

Poirot yawned once more. He felt heavy and stupid with sleep and could hardly keep his eyes open. He glanced over at the bridge players, absorbed in their game, then at young Fanthorp, who was deep in a book. Apart from them the saloon was empty.

He passed through the swing door out on to the deck. Jacqueline de Bellefort, coming precipitately along the deck, almost collided with him.

'Pardon, Mademoiselle.'

She said: 'You look sleepy, Monsieur Poirot.'

He admitted it frankly:

'*Mais oui* – I am consumed with sleep. I can hardly keep my eyes open. It has been a day very close and oppressive.'

'Yes.' She seemed to brood over it. 'It's been the sort of day when things – snap! Break! When one can't go on . . .'

Her voice was low and charged with passion. She looked not at him, but towards the sandy shore. Her hands were clenched, rigid . . .

Suddenly the tension relaxed. She said: 'Good night, Monsieur Poirot.'

'Good night, Mademoiselle.'

Her eyes met his, just for a swift moment. Thinking it over the next day, he came to the conclusion that there had been appeal in that glance. He was to remember it afterwards.

Then he passed on to his cabin and she went towards the saloon.

II

Cornelia, having dealt with Miss Van Schuyler's many needs and fantasies, took some needlework with her back to the saloon. She herself did not feel in the least sleepy. On the contrary she felt wide awake and slightly excited.

The bridge four were still at it. In another chair the quiet Fanthorp read a book. Cornelia sat down to her needlework.

Suddenly the door opened and Jacqueline de Bellefort came in. She stood in the doorway, her head thrown back. Then she pressed a bell and sauntered across to Cornelia and sat down.

'Been ashore?' she asked.

'Yes. I thought it was just fascinating in the moonlight.'

Jacqueline nodded.

'Yes, lovely night . . . A real honeymoon night.'

Her eyes went to the bridge table – rested a moment on Linnet Doyle.

The boy came in answer to the bell. Jacqueline ordered a double gin. As she gave the order Simon Doyle shot a quick glance at her. A faint line of anxiety showed between his eyebrows.

His wife said: 'Simon, we're waiting for you to call.'

Jacqueline hummed a little tune to herself. When the drink came, she picked it up, said: 'Well, here's to crime,' drank it off and ordered another.

Again Simon looked across from the bridge table. His calls became slightly absent-minded. His partner, Pennington, took him to task.

Jacqueline began to hum again, at first under her breath, then louder:

'*He was her man and he did her wrong . . .*'

'Sorry,' said Simon to Pennington. 'Stupid of me not to return your lead. That gives 'em rubber.'

Linnet rose to her feet.

'I'm sleepy. I think I'll go to bed.'

'About time to turn in,' said Colonel Race.

'I'm with you,' agreed Pennington.

'Coming, Simon?'

Doyle said slowly: 'Not just yet. I think I'll have a drink first.'

Linnet nodded and went out. Race followed her. Pennington finished his drink and then followed suit.

Cornelia began to gather up her embroidery.

'Don't go to bed, Miss Robson,' said Jacqueline. 'Please don't. I feel like making a night of it. Don't desert me.'

Cornelia sat down again.

'We girls must stick together,' said Jacqueline.

She threw back her head and laughed – a shrill laugh without merriment.

The second drink came.

'Have something,' said Jacqueline.

'No, thank you very much,' replied Cornelia.

Jacqueline tilted back her chair. She hummed now loudly: '*He was her man and he did her wrong . . .*'

Mr Fanthorp turned a page of *Europe from Within*.

Simon Doyle picked up a magazine.

'Really, I think I'll go to bed,' said Cornelia. 'It's getting very late.'

'You can't go to bed yet,' Jacqueline declared. 'I forbid you to. Tell me about yourself.'

'Well – I don't know. There isn't much to tell,' Cornelia faltered. 'I've just lived at home, and I haven't been around much. This is my first trip to Europe. I'm just loving every minute of it.'

Jacqueline laughed.

'You're a happy sort of person, aren't you? God, I'd like to be you.'

'Oh, would you? But I mean – I'm sure –'

Cornelia felt flustered. Undoubtedly Miss de Bellefort was drinking too much. That wasn't exactly a novelty to Cornelia. She had seen plenty of drunkenness during Prohibition years. But there was something else . . . Jacqueline de Bellefort was talking to her – was looking at her – and yet, Cornelia felt, it was as though, somehow, she was talking to someone else . . .

But there were only two other people in the room, Mr Fanthorp and Mr Doyle. Mr Fanthorp seemed quite absorbed in his book. Mr Doyle was looking rather odd – a queer sort of watchful look on his face.

Jacqueline said again: 'Tell me all about yourself.'

Always obedient, Cornelia tried to comply. She talked, rather heavily, going into unnecessary small details about her daily life. She was so unused to being the talker. Her role was so constantly that of the listener. And yet Miss de Bellefort seemed to want to know. When Cornelia faltered to a standstill, the other girl was quick to prompt her.

'Go on – tell me more.'

And so Cornelia went on ('Of course, Mother's very delicate – some days she touches nothing but cereals –') unhappily conscious that all she said was supremely uninteresting, yet flattered by the other girl's seeming interest. But was she interested? Wasn't she, somehow, listening to something else – or, perhaps, *for* something else? She was looking at Cornelia, yes, but wasn't there *someone else*, sitting in the room?

'And of course we get very good art classes, and last winter I had a course of –'

(How late was it? Surely very late. She had been talking and talking. If only something definite would happen –)

And immediately, as though in answer to her wish, something did happen. Only, at that moment, it seemed very natural.

Jacqueline turned her head and spoke to Simon Doyle.

'Ring the bell, Simon. I want another drink.'

Simon Doyle looked up from his magazine and said quietly: 'The stewards have gone to bed. It's after midnight.'

'I tell you I want another drink.'

Simon said: 'You've had quite enough to drink, Jackie.'

She swung round at him.

'What damned business is it of yours?'

He shrugged his shoulders, 'None.'

She watched him for a minute or two. Then she said: 'What's the matter, Simon? Are you afraid?'

Simon did not answer. Rather elaborately he picked up his magazine again.

Cornelia murmured: 'Oh, dear – as late as that – I – must –'

She began to fumble, dropped a thimble . . .

Jacqueline said: 'Don't go to bed. I'd like another woman here – to support me.' She began to laugh again. 'Do you know what Simon over there is afraid of? He's afraid *I'm* going to tell you the story of *my* life.'

'Oh, really?'

Cornelia was the prey of conflicting emotions. She was deeply embarrassed but at the same time pleasurably thrilled. How – how *black* Simon Doyle was looking.

'Yes, it's a very sad story,' said Jacqueline; her soft voice was low and mocking. 'He treated me rather badly, didn't you, Simon?'

Simon Doyle said brutally: 'Go to bed, Jackie. You're drunk.'

'If you're embarrassed, Simon dear, you'd better leave the room.'

Simon Doyle looked at her. The hand that held the magazine shook a little, but he spoke bluntly.

'I'm staying,' he said.

Cornelia murmured for the third time, 'I really must – it's so late –'

'You're not to go,' said Jacqueline. Her hand shot out and held the other girl in her chair. 'You're to stay and hear what I've go to say.'

'Jackie,' said Simon sharply, 'you're making a fool of yourself! For God's sake, go to bed.'

Jacqueline sat up suddenly in her chair. Words poured from her rapidly in a soft hissing stream.

'You're afraid of a scene, aren't you? That's because you're so English – so reticent! You want me to behave "decently", don't you? But I don't care whether I behave decently or not! You'd better get out of here quickly – because I'm going to talk – a lot.'

Jim Fanthorp carefully shut his book, yawned, glanced at his watch, got up and strolled out. It was a very British and utterly unconvincing performance.

Jacqueline swung round in her chair and glared at Simon.

'You damned fool,' she said thickly, 'do you think you can treat me as you have done and get away with it?'

Simon Doyle opened his lips, then shut them again. He sat quite still as though he were hoping that her outburst would exhaust itself if he said nothing to provoke her further.

Jacqueline's voice came thick and blurred. It fascinated Cornelia, totally unused to naked emotions of any kind.

'I told you,' said Jacqueline, 'that I'd kill you sooner than see you go to another woman ... You don't think I meant that? *You're wrong*. I've only been – waiting! You're my man! Do you hear? You belong to me ...'

Still Simon did not speak. Jacqueline's hand fumbled a moment or two on her lap. She leant forward.

'I told you I'd kill you and I meant it . . .' Her hand came up suddenly with something in it that flashed and gleamed. 'I'll shoot you like a dog – like the dirty dog you are . . .'

Now at last Simon acted. He sprang to his feet, but at the same moment she pulled the trigger . . .

Simon fell twisted – fell across a chair . . . Cornelia screamed and rushed to the door. Jim Fanthorp was on the deck leaning over the rail. She called to him.

'Mr Fanthorp . . . Mr Fanthorp . . .'

He ran to her; she clutched at him incoherently . . .

'She's shot him – Oh! she's shot him . . .'

Simon Doyle still lay as he had fallen half into and across a chair . . . Jacqueline stood as though paralysed. She was trembling violently, and her eyes, dilated and frightened, were staring at the crimson stain slowly soaking through Simon's trouser leg just below the knee where he held a handkerchief close against the wound.

She stammered out:

'I didn't mean . . . Oh, my God, I didn't really mean . . .'

The pistol dropped from her nervous fingers with a clatter on the floor. She kicked it away with her foot. It slid under one of the settees.

Simon, his voice faint, murmured: 'Fanthorp, for heaven's sake – there's someone coming . . . Say it's all right – an accident – something. There mustn't be a scandal over this.'

Fanthorp nodded in quick comprehension. He wheeled round to the door where a startled Nubian face showed. He said: 'All right – all right! Just fun!'

The black face looked doubtful, puzzled, then reassured. The teeth showed in a wide grin. The boy nodded and went off.

Fanthorp turned back.

'That's all right. Don't think anybody else heard. Only sounded like a cork, you know. Now the next thing –'

He was startled. Jacqueline suddenly began to weep hysterically.

'Oh, God, I wish I were dead . . . I'll kill myself. I'll be better dead . . . Oh, what have I done – what have I done?'

Cornelia hurried to her.

'Hush, dear, hush.'

Simon, his brow wet, his face twisted with pain, said urgently:

'Get her away. For God's sake, get her out of here! Get her to her cabin, Fanthorp. Look here, Miss Robson, get that hospital nurse of yours.' He looked appealingly from one to the other of them. 'Don't leave her. Make quite sure she's safe with the nurse looking after her. Then get hold of old Bessner and bring him here. For God's sake, don't let any news of this get to my wife.'

Jim Fanthorp nodded comprehendingly. The quiet young man was cool and competent in an emergency.

Between them he and Cornelia got the weeping, struggling girl out of the saloon and along the deck to her cabin. There they had more trouble with her. She fought to free herself; her sobs redoubled.

'I'll drown myself . . . I'll drown myself . . . I'm not fit to live . . . Oh, Simon – Simon!'

Fanthorp said to Cornelia: 'Better get hold of Miss Bowers. I'll stay while you get her.'

Cornelia nodded and hurried out.

As soon as she left, Jacqueline clutched Fanthorp.

'His leg – it's bleeding – broken . . . He may bleed to death. I must go to him . . . Oh, Simon – Simon – how could I?'

Her voice rose. Fanthorp said urgently: 'Quietly – quietly . . . He'll be all right.'

She began to struggle again.

'Let me go! Let me throw myself overboard . . . Let me kill myself!'

Fanthorp holding her by the shoulders forced her back on to the bed.

'You must stay here. Don't make a fuss. Pull yourself together. It's all right, I tell you.'

To his relief, the distraught girl did manage to control herself a little, but he was thankful when the curtains were pushed aside and the efficient Miss Bowers, neatly dressed in a hideous kimono, entered, accompanied by Cornelia.

'Now then,' said Miss Bowers briskly, 'what's all this?'

She took charge without any sign of surprise and alarm.

Fanthorp thankfully left the overwrought girl in her capable hands and hurried along to the cabin occupied by Dr Bessner. He knocked and entered on top of the knock.

'Dr Bessner?'

A terrific snore resolved itself, and a startled voice asked: 'So? What is it?'

By this time Fanthorp had switched the light on. The doctor blinked up at him, looking rather like a large owl.

'It's Doyle. He's been shot. Miss de Bellefort shot him. He's in the saloon. Can you come?'

The stout doctor reacted promptly. He asked a few curt questions, pulled on his bedroom slippers and a dressing-gown, picked up a little case of necessaries and accompanied Fanthorp to the lounge.

Simon had managed to get the window beside him open. He was leaning his head against it, inhaling the air. His face was a ghastly colour.

Dr Bessner came over to him.

'Ha? So? What have we here?'

A handkerchief sodden with blood lay on the carpet, and on the carpet itself was a dark stain.

The doctor's examination was punctuated with Teutonic grunts and exclamations.

'Yes, it is bad this . . . The bone is fractured. And a big loss of blood. Herr Fanthorp, you and I must get him to my cabin. So – like this. He cannot walk. We must carry him, thus.'

As they lifted him Cornelia appeared in the doorway. Catching sight of her, the doctor uttered a grunt of satisfaction.

'Ach, it is you? Goot. Come with us. I have need of assistance. You will be better than my friend here. He looks a little pale already.'

Fanthorp emitted a rather sickly smile.

'Shall I get Miss Bowers?' he asked.

'You will do very well, young lady,' he announced. 'You will not faint or be foolish, hein?'

'I can do what you tell me,' said Cornelia eagerly.

Bessner nodded in a satisfied fashion.

The procession passed along the deck.

The next ten minutes were purely surgical and Mr Jim Fanthorp did not enjoy it at all. He felt secretly ashamed of the superior fortitude exhibited by Cornelia.

'So, that is the best I can do,' announced Dr Bessner at last. 'You have been a hero, my friend.' He patted Simon approvingly on the shoulder. Then he rolled up his sleeve and produced a hypodermic needle.

'And now I will give you something to make you sleep. Your wife, what about her?'

Simon said weakly: 'She needn't know till the morning . . .' He went on: 'I – you mustn't blame Jackie . . . It's been all my fault. I treated her disgracefully . . . poor kid – she didn't know what she was doing . . .'

Dr Bessner nodded comprehendingly.

'Yes, yes – I understand . . .'

'My fault –' Simon urged. His eyes went to Cornelia. 'Someone – ought to stay with her. She might – hurt herself –'

Dr Bessner injected the needle. Cornelia said, with quiet competence: It's all right, Mr Doyle. Miss Bowers is going to stay with her all night . . .'

A grateful look flashed over Simon's face. His body relaxed. His eyes closed. Suddenly he jerked them open. 'Fanthorp?'

'Yes, Doyle.'

'The pistol . . . ought not to leave it . . . lying about. The boys will find it in the morning . . .'

Fanthorp nodded. 'Quite right. I'll go and get hold of it now.'

He went out of the cabin and along the deck. Miss Bowers appeared at the door of Jacqueline's cabin.

'She'll be all right now,' she announced. 'I've given her a morphine injection.'

'But you'll stay with her?'

'Oh, yes. Morphia excites some people. I shall stay all night.'

Fanthorp went on to the lounge.

Some three minutes later there was a tap on Bessner's cabin door.

'Dr Bessner?'

'Yes?' The stout man appeared.

Fanthorp beckoned him out on the deck.

'Look here – I can't find that pistol . . .'

'What is that?'

'The pistol. It dropped out of the girl's hand. She kicked it away and it went under a settee. It isn't under that settee now.'

They stared at each other.

'But who can have taken it?'

Fanthorp shrugged his shoulders.

Bessner said: 'It is curious, that. But I do not see what we can do about it.'

Puzzled and vaguely alarmed, the two men separated.

CHAPTER 13

Hercule Poirot was just wiping the lather from his freshly shaved face when there was a quick tap on the door, and hard on top of it Colonel Race entered unceremoniously. He closed the door behind him.

He said: 'Your instinct was quite correct. It's happened.'

Poirot straightened up and asked sharply: 'What has happened?'

'Linnet Doyle's dead – shot through the head last night.'

Poirot was silent for a minute, two memories vividly before him – a girl in a garden at Assuan saying in a hard breathless voice: 'I'd like to put my dear little pistol against her head and just press the trigger,' and another more recent memory, the same voice saying: 'One feels one can't go on – the kind of day when something breaks' – and that strange momentary flash of appeal in her eyes. What had been the matter with him not to respond to that appeal? He had been blind, deaf, stupid with his need for sleep . . .

Race went on: 'I've got some slight official standing; they sent for me, put it in my hands. The boat's due to start in half an hour, but it will be delayed till I give the word. There's a possibility, of course, that the murderer came from the shore.'

Poirot shook his head.

Race acquiesced in the gesture.

'I agree. One can pretty well rule that out. Well, man, it's up to you. This is your show.'

Poirot had been attiring himself with a neat-fingered celerity. He said now: 'I am at your disposal.'

The two men stepped out on the deck.

Race said: 'Bessner should be there by now. I sent the steward for him.'

There were four cabins de luxe, with bathrooms, on the boat. Of the two on the port side one was occupied by Dr Bessner, the

292

other by Andrew Pennington. On the starboard side the first was occupied by Miss Van Schuyler, and the one next to it by Linnet Doyle. Her husband's dressing cabin was next door.

A white-faced steward was standing outside the door of Linnet Doyle's cabin. He opened the door for them and they passed inside. Dr Bessner was bending over the bed. He looked up and grunted as the other two entered.

'What can you tell us, Doctor, about this business?' asked Race.

Bessner rubbed his unshaven jaw meditatively.

'Ach! She was shot – shot at close quarters. See – here just above the ear – that is where the bullet entered. A very little bullet – I should say a twenty-two. The pistol, it was held close against her head, see, there is blackening here, the skin is scorched.'

Again in a sick wave of memory Poirot thought of those words uttered in Assuan.

Bessner went on: 'She was asleep; there was no struggle; the murderer crept up in the dark and shot her as she lay there.'

'Ah! *non!*' Poirot cried out. His sense of psychology was outraged. Jacqueline de Bellefort creeping into a darkened cabin, pistol in hand – no, it did not 'fit', that picture.

Bessner stared at him with his thick lenses.

'But that is what happened, I tell you.'

'Yes, yes. I did not mean what you thought. I was not contradicting you.'

Bessner gave a satisfied grunt.

Poirot came up and stood beside him. Linnet Doyle was lying on her side. Her attitude was natural and peaceful. But above the ear was a tiny hole with an incrustation of dried blood round it.

Poirot shook his head sadly.

Then his gaze fell on the white painted wall just in front of him and he drew in his breath sharply. Its white neatness was marred by a big wavering letter J scrawled in some brownish-red medium.

Poirot stared at it, then he leaned over the dead girl and very gently picked up her right hand. One finger of it was stained a brownish-red.

'*Non d'un nom d'un nom!*' ejaculated Hercule Poirot.

'Eh? What is that?'

Dr Bessner looked up.

'Ach! *That.*'

Race said: 'Well, I'm damned. What do you make of that, Poirot?'

Poirot swayed a little on his toes.

'You ask me what I make of it. *Eh bien,* it is very simple, is it not? Madame Doyle is dying; she wishes to indicate her murderer, and so she writes with her finger, dipped in her own blood, the initial letter of her murderer's name. Oh, yes, it is astonishingly simple.'

'Ach, but –'

Dr Bessner was about to break out, but a peremptory gesture from Race silenced him.

'So it strikes you that?' he asked slowly.

Poirot turned round on him nodding his head.

'Yes, yes. It is, as I say, of an astonishing simplicity! It is so familiar, is it not? It has been done so often, in the pages of the romance of crime! It is now, indeed, a little *vieux jeu*! It leads one to suspect that our murderer is – old-fashioned!'

'*C'est de l'enfantillage,*' agreed Poirot.

'But it was done with a purpose,' suggested Race.

'That – naturally,' agreed Poirot, and his face was grave.

'What does J stand for?' asked Race.

Poirot replied promptly: 'J stands for Jacqueline de Bellefort, a young lady who declared to me less than a week ago that she would like nothing better than to –' he paused and then deliberately quoted, '"to put my dear little pistol close against her head and then just press with my finger –"'

'*Gott im Himmel*' exclaimed Dr Bessner.

There was a momentary silence. Then Race drew a deep breath and said: 'Which is just what was done here?'

Bessner nodded.

'That is so, yes. It was a pistol of very small calibre – as I say, probably a twenty-two. The bullet has got to be extracted, of course, before we can say definitely.'

Race nodded in swift comprehension. Then he asked: 'What about time of death?'

Bessner stroked his jaw again. His fingers made a rasping sound.

'I would not care to be too precise. It is now eight o'clock. I will say, with due regard to the temperature last night, that she has been dead certainly six hours and probably not longer than eight.'

'That puts it between midnight and two a.m.'

'That is so.'

There was a pause. Race looked around.

'What about her husband? I suppose he sleeps in the cabin next door.'

'At the moment,' said Dr Bessner, 'he is asleep in my cabin.' Both men looked very surprised.

Bessner nodded his head several times.

'Ach, so. I see you have not been told about that. Mr Doyle was shot last night in the saloon.'

'Shot? By whom?'

'By the young lady, Jacqueline de Bellefort.'

Race asked sharply, 'Is he badly hurt?'

'Yes, the bone is splintered. I have done all that is possible at the moment, but it is necessary, you understand, that the fracture should be X-rayed as soon as possible and proper treatment given such as is impossible on this boat.'

Poirot murmured: 'Jacqueline de Bellefort.'

His eyes went again to the J on the wall.

Race said abruptly: 'If there is nothing more we can do here for the moment, let's go below. The management has put the smoking-room at our disposal. We must get the details of what happened last night.'

They left the cabin. Race locked the door and took the key with him.

'We can come back later,' he said. 'The first thing to do is to get all the facts clear.'

They went down to the deck below, where they found the manager of the *Karnak* waiting uneasily in the doorway of the smoking-room. The poor man was terribly upset and worried over the whole business, and was eager to leave everything in Colonel Race's hands.

'I feel I can't do better than leave it to you, sir, seeing your official position. I'd had orders to put myself at your disposal in the – er – other matter. If you will take charge, I'll see that everything is done as you wish.'

'Good man! To begin with I'd like this room kept clear for me and Monsieur Poirot during this inquiry.'

'Certainly, sir.'

'That's all at present. Go on with your own work. I know where to find you.'

Looking slightly relieved, the manager left the room.

Race said, 'Sit down, Bessner, and let's have the whole story of what happened last night.'

They listened in silence to the doctor's rumbling voice.

'Clear enough,' said Race, when he had finished. 'The girl worked herself up, helped by a drink or two, and finally took a pot shot at the man with a twenty-two pistol. Then she went along to Linnet Doyle's cabin and shot her as well.'

But Dr Bessner was shaking his head.

'No, no, I do not think so. I do not think that was *possible*. For one thing she would not write her own initial on the wall; it would be ridiculous, *nicht wahr?*'

'She might,' Race declared, 'if she were as blindly mad and jealous as she sounds; she might want to – well – sign her name to the crime, so to speak.'

Poirot shook his head. 'No, no, I do not think she would be as – as *crude* as that.'

'Then there's only one reason for that J. It was put there by someone else deliberately to throw suspicion on her.'

Bessner nodded. 'Yes, and the criminal was unlucky, because, you see, it is not only *unlikely* that the young Fräulein did the murder; it is also I think *impossible*.'

'How's that?'

Bessner explained Jacqueline's hysterics and the circumstances which had led Miss Bowers to take charge of her.

'And I think – I am sure – that Miss Bowers stayed with her all night.'

Race said: 'If that's so, it's going to simplify matters very much.'

'Who discovered the crime?' Poirot asked.

'Mrs Doyle's maid, Louise Bourget. She went to call her mistress as usual, found her dead, and came out and flopped into the steward's arms in a dead faint. He went to the manager, who came to me. I got hold of Bessner and then came for you.'

Poirot nodded.

Race said: 'Doyle's got to know. You say he's asleep still?'

Bessner nodded. 'Yes, he's still asleep in my cabin. I gave him a strong opiate last night.'

Race turned to Poirot.

'Well,' he said, 'I don't think we need detain the doctor any longer, eh? Thank you, Doctor.'

Bessner rose. 'I will have my breakfast, yes. And then I will go back to my cabin and see if Mr Doyle is ready to wake.'

'Thanks.'

Bessner went out. The two men looked at each other.

'Well, what about it, Poirot?' Race asked. 'You're the man in charge. I'll take my orders from you. You say what's to be done.'

Poirot bowed.

'*Eh bien!*' he said, 'we must hold the court of inquiry. First of all, I think we must verify the story of the affair last night. That is to say, we must question Fanthorp and Miss Robson, who were the actual witnesses of what occurred. The disappearance of the pistol is very significant.'

Race rang a bell and sent a message by the steward.

Poirot sighed and shook his head. 'It is bad, this,' he murmured. 'It is bad.'

'Have you any ideas?' asked Race curiously.

'My ideas conflict. They are not well arranged; they are not orderly. There is, you see, the big fact that this girl hated Linnet Doyle and wanted to kill her.'

'You think she's capable of it?'

'I think so – yes.' Poirot sounded doubtful.

'But not in this way? That's what's worrying you, isn't it? Not to creep into her cabin in the dark and shoot her while she was sleeping. It's the cold-bloodedness that strikes you as not ringing true.'

'In a sense, yes.'

'You think that this girl, Jacqueline de Bellefort, is incapable of a premeditated cold-blooded murder?'

Poirot said slowly: 'I am not sure, you see. She would have the brains – yes. But I doubt if, physically, she could bring herself to do the *act* . . .'

Race nodded. 'Yes, I see . . . Well, according to Bessner's story, it would also have been physically impossible.'

'If that is true it clears the ground considerably. Let us hope it is true.' Poirot paused and then added simply: 'I shall be glad if it is so, for I have for that little one much sympathy.'

The door opened and Fanthorp and Cornelia came in. Bessner followed them.

Cornelia gasped out: 'Isn't this just awful? Poor, poor Mrs Doyle! And she was so lovely too. It must have been a real *fiend* who could hurt her! And poor Mr Doyle; he'll go half crazy when he knows! Why, even last night he was so frightfully worried lest she should hear about his accident.'

'That is just what we want you to tell us about, Miss Robson,' said Race. 'We want to know exactly what happened last night.'

Cornelia began a little confusedly, but a question or two from Poirot helped matters.

'Ah, yes, I understand. After the bridge, Madame Doyle went to her cabin. Did she really go to her cabin, I wonder?'

'She did,' said Race. 'I actually saw her. I said good night to her at the door.'

'And the time?'

'Mercy, I couldn't say,' replied Cornelia.

'It was twenty past eleven,' said Race.

'*Bien*. Then at twenty past eleven, Madame Doyle was alive and well. At that moment there was, in the saloon, who?'

Fanthorp answered: 'Doyle was there. And Miss de Bellefort. Myself and Miss Robson.'

'That's so,' agreed Cornelia. 'Mr Pennington had a drink and then went off to bed.'

'That was how much later?'

'Oh, about three or four minutes.'

'Before half-past eleven, then?'

'Oh, yes.'

'So that there were left in the saloon you, Mademoiselle Robson, Mademoiselle de Bellefort, Monsieur Doyle and Monsieur Fanthorp. What were you all doing?'

'Mr Fanthorp was reading a book. I'd got some embroidery. Miss de Bellefort was – she was –'

Fanthorp came to the rescue. 'She was drinking pretty heavily.'

'Yes,' agreed Cornelia. 'She was talking to me mostly and asking me about things at home. And she kept saying things – to me mostly, but I think they were kind of meant for Mr Doyle.

298

He was getting kind of mad at her, but he didn't say anything. I think he thought if he kept quiet she might simmer down.

'But she didn't?'

Cornelia shook her head.

'I tried to go once or twice, but she made me stay, and I was getting very, very uncomfortable. And then Mr Fanthorp got up and went out –'

'It was a little embarrassing,' said Fanthorp. 'I thought I'd make an unobtrusive exit. Miss de Bellefort was clearly working up for a scene.'

'And then she pulled out the pistol,' went on Cornelia, 'and Mr Doyle jumped up to try and get it away from her, and it went off and shot him through the leg; and then she began to sob and cry – and I was scared to death and ran out after Mr Fanthorp, and he came back with me, and Mr Doyle said not to make a fuss, and one of the Nubian boys heard the noise of the shot and came along, but Mr Fanthorp told him it was all right; and then we got Jacqueline away to her cabin, and Mr Fanthorp stayed with her while I got Miss Bowers.' Cornelia paused breathless.

'What time was this?' asked Race.

Cornelia said again, 'Mercy, I don't know,' but Fanthorp answered promptly:

'It must have been about twenty minutes past twelve. I know that it was actually half-past twelve when I finally got to my cabin.'

'Now let me be quite sure on one or two points,' said Poirot. 'After Madame Doyle left the saloon, did any of you four leave it?'

'No.'

'You are quite certain Mademoiselle de Bellefort did not leave the saloon at all?'

Fanthorp answered promptly: 'Positive. Neither Doyle, Miss de Bellefort, Miss Robson, nor myself left the saloon.'

'Good. That establishes the fact that Mademoiselle de Bellefort could not possibly have shot Madame Doyle before – let us say – twenty past twelve. Now, Mademoiselle Robson, you went to fetch Mademoiselle Bowers. Was Mademoiselle de Bellefort alone in her cabin during that period?'

'No. Mr Fanthorp stayed with her.'

'Good! So far, Mademoiselle de Bellefort has a perfect alibi.

Mademoiselle Bowers is the next person to interview, but, before I send for her, I should like to have your opinion on one or two points. Monsieur Doyle, you say, was very anxious that Mademoiselle de Bellefort should not be left alone. Was he afraid, do you think, that she was contemplating some further rash act?'

'That is my opinion,' said Fanthorp.

'He was definitely afraid she might attack Madame Doyle?'

'No.' Fanthorp shook his head. 'I don't think that was his idea at all. I think he was afraid she might – er – do something rash to herself.'

'Suicide?'

'Yes. You see, she seemed completely sobered and heart-broken at what she had done. She was full of self-reproach. She kept saying she would be better dead.'

Cornelia said timidly: 'I think he was rather upset about her. He spoke – quite nicely. He said it was all his fault – that he'd treated her badly. He – he was really very nice.'

Hercule Poirot nodded thoughtfully. 'Now about that pistol,' he went on. 'What happened to that?'

'She dropped it,' said Cornelia.

'And afterwards?'

Fanthorp explained how he had gone back to search for it, but had not been able to find it.

'Aha!' said Poirot. 'Now we begin to arrive. Let us, I pray you, be very precise. Describe to me exactly what happened.'

'Miss de Bellefort let it fall. Then she kicked it away from her with her foot.'

'She sort of hated it,' explained Cornelia. 'I know just what she felt.'

'And it went under a settee, you say. Now be very careful. Mademoiselle de Bellefort did not recover that pistol before she left the saloon?'

Both Fanthorp and Cornelia were positive on that point.

'*Précisément.* I seek only to be very exact, you comprehend. Then we arrive at this point. When Mademoiselle de Bellefort leaves the saloon the pistol is under the settee, and, since Mad-emoiselle de Bellefort is not left alone – Monsieur Fanthorp, Mademoiselle Robson or Mademoiselle Bowers being with her – she has no opportunity to get back the pistol after she left the saloon. What time was it, Monsieur Fanthorp, when you went back to look for it?'

'It must have been just before half-past twelve.'

'And how long would have elapsed between the time you and Dr Bessner carried Monsieur Doyle out of the saloon until you returned to look for the pistol?'

'Perhaps five minutes – perhaps a little more.'

'Then in that five minutes someone removes that pistol from where it lay out of sight under the settee. That someone was *not* Mademoiselle de Bellefort. Who was it? It seems highly probable that the person who removed it was the murderer of Madame Doyle. We may assume, too, that the person had overheard or seen something of the events immediately preceeding.'

'I don't see how you make that out,' objected Fanthorp.

'Because,' said Hercule Poirot, 'you have just told us that the pistol was out of sight under the settee. Therefore it is hardly credible that it was discovered by *accident*. It was taken by someone who knew it was there. Therefore that someone must have assisted at the scene.'

Fanthorp shook his head. 'I saw no one when I went out on the deck just before the shot was fired.'

'Ah, but you went out by the door on the starboard side.'

'Yes. The same side as my cabin.'

'Then if there had been anybody at the port door looking through the glass you would not have seen him?'

'No,' admitted Fanthorp.

'Did anyone hear the shot except the Nubian boy?'

'Not as far as I know.'

Fanthorp went on: 'You see, the windows in here were all closed. Miss Van Schuyler felt a draught earlier in the evening. The swing doors were shut. I doubt if the shot would be clearly heard. It would only sound like the pop of a cork.'

Race said: 'As far as I know, no one seems to have heard the other shot – the shot that killed Mrs Doyle.'

'That we will inquire into presently,' said Poirot. 'For the moment we still concern ourselves with Mademoiselle de Bellefort. We must speak to Mademoiselle Bowers. But first, before you go' – he arrested Fanthorp and Cornelia with a gesture – 'you will give me a little information about yourselves. Then it will not be necessary to call you again later. You first, Monsieur – your full name.'

'James Lechdale Fanthorp.'

'Address?'

'Glasmore House, Market Donnington, Northamptonshire.'

'Your profession?'

'I am a lawyer.'

'And your reasons for visiting this country?'

There was a pause. For the first time the impassive Mr Fanthorp seemed taken aback. He said at last, almost mumbling the words, 'Er – pleasure.'

'Aha!' said Poirot. 'You take the holiday; that is it, yes?'

'Er – yes.'

'Very well, Monsieur Fanthorp. Will you give me a brief account of your own movements last night after the events we have just been narrating?'

'I went straight to bed.'

'That was at –?'

'Just after half-past twelve.'

'Your cabin is number twenty-two on the starboard side – the one nearest the saloon.'

'Yes.'

'I will ask you one more question. Did you hear anything – anything at all – after you went to your cabin?'

Fanthorp considered.

'I turned in very quickly. I *think* I heard a kind of splash just as I was dropping off to sleep. Nothing else.'

'You heard a kind of splash? Near at hand?'

Fanthorp shook his head.

'Really, I couldn't say. I was half asleep.'

'And what time would that be?'

'It might have been about one o'clock. I can't really say.'

'Thank you, Monsieur Fanthorp. That is all.'

Poirot turned his attention to Cornelia.

'And now, Mademoiselle Robson. Your full name?'

'Cornelia Ruth. And my address is The Red House, Bellfield, Connecticut.'

'What brought you to Egypt?'

'Cousin Marie, Miss Van Schuyler, brought me along on a trip.'

'Had you ever met Madame Doyle previous to this journey?'

'No, never.'

'And what did you do last night?'

'I went right to bed after helping Dr Bessner with Mr Doyle's leg.'

'Your cabin is –?'

'Forty-three on the port side – right next door to Miss de Bellefort.'

'And did you hear anything?'

Cornelia shook her head. 'I didn't hear a thing.'

'No splash?'

'No, but then I wouldn't, because the boat's against the bank on my side.'

Poirot nodded. 'Thank you, Mademoiselle Robson. Now perhaps you will be so kind as to ask Mademoiselle Bowers to come here.'

Fanthorp and Cornelia went out.

'That seems clear enough,' said Race. 'Unless three independent witnesses are lying, Jacqueline de Bellefort couldn't have got hold of the pistol. But somebody did. And somebody overheard the scene. And somebody was B.F. enough to write a big J on the wall.'

There was a tap on the door and Miss Bowers entered. The hospital nurse sat down in her usual composed efficient manner. In answer to Poirot she gave her name, address, and qualifications, adding: 'I've been looking after Miss Van Schuyler for over two years now.'

'Is Mademoiselle Van Schuyler's health very bad?'

'Why, no, I wouldn't say that,' replied Miss Bowers. 'She's not very young, and she's nervous about herself, and she likes to have a nurse around handy. There's nothing serious the matter with her. She just likes plenty of attention, and she's willing to pay for it.'

Poirot nodded comprehendingly. Then he said: 'I understand that Mademoiselle Robson fetched you last night?'

'Why, yes, that's so.'

'Will you tell me exactly what happened?'

'Well, Miss Robson just gave me a brief outline of what had occurred, and I came along with her. I found Miss de Bellefort in a very excited, hysterical condition.'

'Did she utter any threats against Madame Doyle?'

'No, nothing of that kind. She was in a condition of morbid

self-reproach. She'd taken a good deal of alcohol, I should say, and she was suffering from reaction. I didn't think she ought to be left. I gave her a shot of morphia and sat with her.'

'Now, Mademoiselle Bowers, I want you to answer this. Did Mademoiselle de Bellefort leave her cabin at all?'

'No, she did not.'

'And you yourself?'

'I stayed with her until early this morning.'

'You are quite sure of that?'

'Absolutely sure.'

'Thank you, Mademoiselle Bowers.'

The nurse went out. The two men looked at each other.

Jacqueline de Bellefort was definitely cleared of the crime. Who then had shot Linnet Doyle?

CHAPTER 14

Race said: 'Someone pinched the pistol. It wasn't Jacqueline de Bellefort. Someone knew enough to feel that his crime would be attributed to her. But that someone did not know that a hospital nurse was going to give her morphia and sit up with her all night. And one thing more. Someone had already attempted to kill Linnet Doyle by rolling a boulder over the cliff; that someone was *not* Jacqueline de Bellefort. Who was it?'

Poirot said: 'It will be simpler to say who it could not have been. Neither Monsieur Doyle, Madame Allerton, Monsieur Allerton, Mademoiselle Van Schuyler, nor Mademoiselle Bowers could have had anything to do with it. They were all within my sight.'

'H'm,' said Race; 'that leaves rather a large field. What about motive?

'That is where I hope Monsieur Doyle may be able to help us. There have been several incidents –'

The door opened and Jacqueline de Bellefort entered. She was very pale and she stumbled a little as she walked.

'I didn't do it,' she said. Her voice was that of a frightened child. 'I didn't do it. Oh, please believe me. Everyone will think I did it – but I didn't – I didn't. It's – it's awful. I wish it hadn't happened. I might have killed Simon last night; I was mad, I think. But I didn't do the other . . .'

She sat down and burst into tears.

Poirot patted her on the shoulder.

'There, there. We know that you did not kill Madame Doyle. It is proved – yes, proved, *mon enfant*. It was not you.'

Jackie sat up suddenly, her wet handkerchief clasped in her hand.

'But who did?'

'That,' said Poirot, 'is just the question we are asking ourselves. You cannot help us there, my child?'

Jacqueline shook her head.

'I don't know . . . I can't imagine . . . No, I haven't the faintest idea.' She frowned deeply. 'No,' she said at last. 'I can't think of anyone who wanted her dead.' Her voice faltered a little. 'Except me.'

Race said: 'Excuse me a minute – just thought of something.' He hurried out of the room.

Jacqueline de Bellefort sat with her head downcast, nervously twisting her fingers. She broke out suddenly: 'Death's horrible – horrible! I – hate the thought of it.'

Poirot said: 'Yes. It is not pleasant to think, is it, that now, at this very moment, someone is rejoicing at the successful carrying out of his or her plan.'

'Don't – don't!' cried Jackie. 'It sounds horrible, the way you put it.'

Poirot shrugged his shoulders. 'It is true.'

Jackie said in a low voice: 'I – I wanted her dead – and she *is* dead . . . And, what is worse . . . she died – just like I said.'

'Yes, Mademoiselle. She was shot through the head.'

She cried out: 'Then I was right, that night at the Cataract Hotel. There *was* someone listening!'

'Ah!' Poirot nodded his head. 'I wondered if you would remember that. Yes, it is altogether too much of a coincidence – that Madame Doyle should be killed in just the way you described.'

Jackie shuddered.

'That man that night – who can he have been?'

Poirot was silent for a minute or two, then he said in quite a different tone of voice: 'You are sure it was a man, Mademoiselle?'

Jackie looked at him in surprise.

'Yes, of course. At least –'

'Well, Mademoiselle?'

She frowned, half closing her eyes in an effort to remember. She said slowly: 'I *thought* it was a man . . .'

'But now you are not so sure?'

Jackie said slowly: 'No, I can't be certain. I just assumed it was a man – but it was really just a – a figure – a shadow . . .'

She paused and then, as Poirot did not speak, she added: 'You think it must have been a woman? But surely none of the women on this boat can have wanted to kill Linnet?'

Poirot merely moved his head from side to side.

The door opened and Bessner appeared.

'Will you come and speak with Mr Doyle, please, Monsieur Poirot? He would like to see you.'

Jackie sprang up. She caught Bessner by the arm.

'How is he? Is he – all right?'

'Naturally he is not all right,' replied Dr Bessner reproachfully. 'The bone is fractured, you understand.'

'But he's not going to die?' cried Jackie.

'Ach, who said anything about dying? We will get him to civilization and there we will have an X-ray and proper treatment.'

'Oh!' The girl's hands came together in convulsive pressure. She sank down again on a chair.

Poirot stepped out on to the deck with the doctor and at that moment Race joined them. They went up to the promenade deck and along to Bessner's cabin.

Simon Doyle was lying propped with cushions and pillows, an improvised cage over his leg. His face was ghastly in colour, the ravages of pain with shock on top of it. But the predominant expression on his face was bewilderment – the sick bewilderment of a child.

He muttered: 'Please come in. The doctor's told me – told me – about Linnet . . . I can't believe it. I simply can't believe it's true.'

'I know. It's a bad knock,' said Race.

Simon stammered: 'You know – Jackie didn't do it. I'm certain Jackie didn't do it! It looks black against her, I dare say, but she *didn't* do it. She – she was a bit tight last night, and all worked up, and that's why she went for me. But she wouldn't – she wouldn't do *murder* . . . not cold-blooded murder . . .'

Poirot said gently: 'Do not distress yourself, Monsieur Doyle. Whoever shot your wife, it was not Mademoiselle de Bellefort.'

Simon looked at him doubtfully.

'Is that on the square?'

'But since it was not Mademoiselle de Bellefort,' continued Poirot, 'can you give us any idea of who it might have been?'

Simon shook his head. The look of bewilderment increased.

'It's crazy – impossible. Apart from Jackie nobody could have wanted to do her in.'

'Reflect, Monsieur Doyle. Had she no enemies? Is there no one who had a grudge against her?'

Again Simon shook his head with the same hopeless gesture.

'It sounds absolutely fantastic. There's Windlesham, of course. She more or less chucked him to marry me – but I can't see a polite stick like Windlesham committing murder, and anyway he's miles away. Same thing with old Sir George Wode. He'd got a down on Linnet over the house – disliked the way she was pulling it about; but he's miles away in London, and anyway to think of murder in such a connection would be fantastic.'

'Listen, Monsieur Doyle.' Poirot spoke very earnestly. 'On the first day we came on board the *Karnak* I was impressed by a little conversation which I had with Madame your wife. She was very upset – very distraught. She said – mark this well – that *everybody* hated her. She said she felt afraid – unsafe – as though *everyone* round her were an enemy.'

'She was pretty upset at finding Jackie aboard. So was I,' said Simon.

'That is true, but it does not quite explain those words. When she said she was surrounded by enemies, she was almost certainly exaggerating, but all the same she did mean more than one person.'

'You might be right there,' admitted Simon. 'I think I can explain that. It was a name in the passenger list that upset her.'

'A name in the passenger list? What name?'

'Well, you see, she didn't actually tell me. As a matter of fact I wasn't even listening very carefully. I was going over the Jacqueline business in my mind. As far as I remember, Linnet said something about doing people down in business, and that it made her uncomfortable to meet anyone who had a grudge against her family. You see, although I don't really know the family history very well, I gather that Linnet's mother was a millionaire's daughter. Her father was only just ordinary plain wealthy, but after his marriage he naturally began playing the markets or whatever you call it. And as a result of that, of course, several people got it in the neck. You know, affluence one day, the gutter the next. Well, I gather there was someone on board whose father had got up against Linnet's father and taken a pretty hard knock. I remember Linnet saying: "It's pretty awful when people hate you without even knowing you."'

'Yes,' said Poirot thoughtfully. 'That would explain what she said to me. For the first time she was feeling the burden of her inheritance and not its advantages. You are quite sure, Monsieur Doyle, that she did not mention this man's name?'

Simon shook his head ruefully.

'I didn't really pay much attention. Just said: "Oh, nobody minds what happened to their fathers nowadays. Life goes too fast for that." Something of that kind.'

Bessner said dryly: 'Ach, but I can have a guess. There is certainly a young man with a grievance on board.'

'You mean Ferguson?' said Poirot.

'Yes. He spoke against Mrs Doyle once or twice. I myself have heard him.'

'What can we do to find out?' asked Simon.

Poirot replied: 'Colonel Race and I must interview all the passengers. Until we have got their stories it would be unwise to form theories. Then there is the maid. We ought to interview her first of all. It would, perhaps, be as well if we did that here. Monsieur Doyle's presence might be helpful.'

'Yes, that's a good idea,' said Simon.

'Had she been with Mrs Doyle long?'

'Just a couple of months, that's all.'

'Only a couple of months!' exclaimed Poirot.

'Why, you don't think –'

'Had Madame any valuable jewellery?'

'There were her pearls,' said Simon. 'She once told me they were worth forty or fifty thousand.' He shivered. 'My God, do you think those damned pearls –?'

'Robbery is a possible motive,' said Poirot. 'All the same it seems hardly credible . . . Well, we shall see. Let us have the maid here.'

Louise Bourget was that same vivacious Latin brunette who Poirot had seen one day and noticed.

She was anything but vivacious now. She had been crying and looked frightened. Yet there was a kind of sharp cunning apparent in her face which did not prepossess the two men favourably towards her.

'You are Louise Bourget?'

'Yes, Monsieur.'

'When did you last see Madame Doyle alive?'

'Last night, Monsieur. I was in her cabin to undress her.'

'What time was that?'

'It was some time after eleven, Monsieur. I cannot say exactly when. I undress Madame and put her to bed, and then I leave.'

'How long did all that take?'

'Ten minutes, Monsieur. Madame was tired. She told me to put the lights out when I went.'

'And when you had left her, what did you do?'

'I went to my own cabin, Monsieur, on the deck below.'

'And you heard or saw nothing more that can help us?'

'How could I, Monsieur?'

'That, Mademoiselle, is for you to say, not for us,' Hercule Poirot retorted.

She stole a sideways glance at him.

'But, Monsieur, I was nowhere near . . . What could I have seen or heard? I was on the deck below. My cabin, it was on the other side of the boat, even. It is impossible that I should have heard anything. Naturally if I had been unable to sleep, if I had mounted the stairs, *then* perhaps I might have seen the assassin, this monster, enter or leave Madame's cabin, but as it is –'

She threw out her hands appealingly to Simon.

'Monsieur, I implore you – you see how it is? What can I say?'

'My good girl,' said Simon harshly, 'don't be a fool. Nobody thinks you saw or heard anything. You'll be quite all right. I'll look after you. Nobody's accusing you of anything.'

Louise murmured, 'Monsieur is very good,' and dropped her eyelids modestly.

'We take it, then, that you saw and heard nothing?' asked Race impatiently.

'That is what I said, Monsieur.'

'And you know of no one who had a grudge against your mistress?'

To the surprise of the listeners Louise nodded her head vigorously.

'Oh, yes. That I do know. To that question I can answer Yes most emphatically.'

Poirot said, 'You mean Mademoiselle de Bellefort?'

'She, certainly. But it is not of her I speak. There was someone else on this boat who disliked Madame, who was very angry because of the way Madame had injured him.'

'Good lord!' Simon exclaimed. 'What's all this?'

Louise went on, still emphatically nodding her head with the utmost vigour.

'Yes, yes, yes, it is as I say! It concerns the former maid of Madame – my predecessor. There was a man, one of the engineers on this boat, who wanted her to marry him. And my predecessor, Marie her name was, she would have done so. But Madame Doyle, she made inquiries and she discovered that this Fleetwood already had a wife – a wife of colour you understand, a wife of this country. She had gone back to her own people, but he was still married to her, you understand. And so Madame she told all this to Marie, and Marie was very unhappy and she would not see Fleetwood any more. And this Fleetwood, he was infuriated, and when he found out that this Madame Doyle had formerly been Mademoiselle Linnet Ridgeway he tells me that he would like to kill her! Her interference ruined his life, he said.'

Louise paused triumphantly.

'This is interesting,' said Race.

Poirot turned to Simon.

'Had you any idea of this?'

'None whatever,' Simon replied with patent sincerity. 'I doubt if Linnet even knew the man was on the boat. She had probably forgotten all about the incident.'

He turned sharply to the maid.

'Did you say anything to Mrs Doyle about this?'

'No, Monsieur, of course not.'

Poirot asked: 'Do you know anything about your mistress's pearls?'

'Her pearls? Louise's eyes opened very wide. 'She was wearing them last night.'

'You saw them when she came to bed?'

'Yes, Monsieur.'

'Where did she put them?'

'On the table by the side as always.'

'That is where you last saw them?'

'Yes, Monsieur.'

'Did you see them there this morning?'

A startled look came into the girl's face.

'*Mon Dieu*! I did not even look. I come up to the bed, I see – I see Madame; and then I cry out and rush out of the door, and I faint.'

Hercule Poirot nodded his head.

'You did not look. But I, I have the eyes which notice, and there were no pearls on the table beside the bed this morning.'

CHAPTER 15

Hercule Poirot's observation had not been at fault. There were no pearls on the table by Linnet Doyle's bed.

Louise Bourget was bidden to make a search among Linnet's belongings. According to her, all was in order. Only the pearls had disappeared.

As they emerged from the cabin a steward was waiting to tell them that breakfast had been served in the smoking-room. As they passed along the deck, Race paused to look over the rail.

'Aha! I see you have had an idea, my friend.'

'Yes. It suddenly came to me, when Fanthorp mentioned thinking he had heard a splash. It's perfectly possible that after the murder, the murderer threw the pistol overboard.'

Poirot said slowly: 'You really think that is possible, my friend?' Race shrugged his shoulders.

'It's a suggestion. After all, the pistol wasn't anywhere in the cabin. First thing I looked for.'

'All the same,' said Poirot, 'it is incredible that it should have been thrown overboard.'

Race asked: 'Where is it then?'

Poirot replied thoughtfully, 'If it is not in Madame Doyle's cabin, there is, logically, only one other place where it could be.'

'Where's that?'

'In Mademoiselle de Bellefort's cabin.'

Race said thoughtfully: 'Yes. I see –'

He stopped suddenly.

'She's out of her cabin. Shall we go and have a look now?'

Poirot shook his head. 'No, my friend, that would be precipitate. It may not yet have been put there.'

'What about an immediate search of the whole boat.'

'That way we should show our hand. We must work with great care. It is very delicate, our position, at the moment. Let us discuss the situation as we eat.'

Race agreed. They went into the smoking-room.

'Well,' said Race as he poured himself out a cup of coffee, 'we've got two definite leads. There's the disappearance of the pearls. And there's the man Fleetwood. As regards the pearls, robbery seems indicated, but – I don't know whether you'll agree with me –'

Poirot said quickly: 'But it was an odd moment to choose?'

'Exactly. To steal the pearls at such a moment invites a close search of everybody on board. How then could the thief hope to get away with his booty?'

'He might have gone ashore and dumped it.'

'The company always has a watchman on the bank.'

'Then that is not feasible. Was the murder committed to divert attention from the robbery? No, that does not make sense; it is profoundly unsatisfactory. But supposing that Madame Doyle woke up and caught the thief in the act?'

'And therefore the thief shot her? But she was shot whilst she slept.'

'So that does not make sense . . . You know, I have a little idea about those pearls – and yet – no – it is impossible. Because if my idea was right the pearls would not have disappeared. Tell me, what did you think of the maid?'

'I wondered,' said Race slowly, 'if she knew more than she said.'

'Ah, you too had that impression?'

'Definitely not a nice girl,' said Race.

Hercule Poirot nodded. 'Yes, I would not trust her.'

'You think she had something to do with the murder?'

'No. I would not say that.'

'With the theft of the pearls, then?'

'That is more probable. She had only been with Madame Doyle a very short time. She may be a member of a gang that specializes in jewel robberies. In such a case there is often a maid with excellent references. Unfortunately we are not in a position to seek information on these points. And yet that explanation does not quite satisfy me ... Those pearls – ah, *sacré*, my little idea *ought* to be right. And yet nobody would be so imbecile –' He broke off.

'What about the man Fleetwood?'

'We must question him. It may be that we have there the solution. If Louise Bourget's story is true, he had a definite motive for revenge. He could have overheard the scene between Jacqueline and Monsieur Doyle, and when they had left the saloon he could have darted in and secured the gun. Yes, it is all quite possible. And that letter J scrawled in blood. That, too, would accord with a simple, rather crude nature.'

'In fact, he's just the person we are looking for?'

'Yes – only –' Poirot rubbed his nose. He said with a slight grimace: 'See you, I recognize my own weaknesses. It has been said of me that I like to make a case difficult. This solution that you put to me – it is too simple, too easy. I cannot feel that it really happened. And yet, that may be the sheer prejudice on my part.'

'Well, we'd better have the fellow here.'

Race rang the bell and gave the order. Then he asked, 'Any other – possibilities?'

'Plenty, my friend. There is, for example, the American trustee.'

'Pennington?'

'Yes, Pennington. There was a curious little scene in here the other day.' He narrated the happenings to Race. 'You see – it is significant. Madame, she wanted to read all the papers before signing. So he makes the excuse of another day. And then, the husband, he makes a very significant remark.'

'What was that?'

'He says – "I never read anything. I sign where I am told to sign." You perceive the significance of that. Pennington did. I saw it in his eye. He looked at Doyle as though an entirely new idea had come into his head. Just imagine, my friend, that you

313

have been left trustee to the daughter of an intensely wealthy man. You use, perhaps, that money to speculate with. I know it is so in all detective novels – but you read of it too in the newspapers. It happens, my friend, it *happens*.'

'I don't dispute it,' said Race.

'There is, perhaps, still time to make good by speculating wildly. Your ward is not yet of age. And then – she marries! The control passes from your hands into hers at a moment's notice! A disaster! But there is still a chance. She is on a honeymoon. She will perhaps be careless about business. A casual paper, slipped in among others, signed without reading . . . But Linnet Doyle was not like that. Honeymoon or no honeymoon, she is a business woman. And then her husband makes a remark, and a new idea comes to that desperate man who is seeking a way out from ruin. If Linnet Doyle were to die, her fortune would pass to her husband – and he would be easy to deal with; he would be a child in the hands of an astute man like Andrew Pennington. *Mon cher Colonel*, I tell you I *saw* the thought pass through Andrew Pennington's head. "If only it were *Doyle* I had got to deal with . . ." That is what he was thinking.'

'Quite possible, I daresay,' said Race dryly, 'but you've no evidence.'

'Alas, no.'

'Then there's young Ferguson,' said Race. 'He talks bitterly enough. Not that I go by talk. Still, he *might* be the fellow whose father was ruined by old Ridgeway. It's a little far-fetched but it's *possible*. People do brood over bygone wrongs sometimes.' He paused a minute and then said: 'And there's my fellow.'

'Yes, there is "your fellow" as you call him.'

'He's a killer,' said Race. 'We know that. On the other hand, I can't see any way in which he could have come up against Linnet Doyle. Their orbits don't touch.'

Poirot said slowly: 'Unless, accidentally, she had become possessed of evidence showing his identity.'

'That's possible, but it seems highly unlikely.' There was a knock at the door. 'Ah, here's our would-be bigamist.'

Fleetwood was a big, truculent-looking man. He looked suspiciously from one to the other of them as he entered the room. Poirot recognized him as the man he had seen talking to Louise Bourget.

Fleetwood asked suspiciously: 'You wanted to see me?'

'We did,' said Race. 'You probably know that a murder was committed on this boat last night?'

Fleetwood nodded.

'And I believe it is true that you had reason to feel anger against the woman who was killed.'

A look of alarm sprang up in Fleetwood's eyes.

'Who told you that?'

'You considered that Mrs Doyle had interfered between you and a young woman.'

'I know who told you that – that lying French hussy. She's a liar through and through, that girl.'

'But this particular story happens to be true.'

'It's a dirty lie!'

'You say that, although you don't know what it is yet.'

The shot told. The man flushed and gulped.

'It is true, is it not, that you were going to marry the girl Marie, and that she broke it off when she discovered that you were a married man already?'

'What business was it of hers?'

'You mean, what business was it of Mrs Doyle's? Well, you know, bigamy is bigamy.'

'It wasn't like that. I married one of the locals out here. It didn't answer. She went back to her people. I've not seen her for a half a dozen years.'

'Still you were married to her.'

The man was silent. Race went on: 'Mrs Doyle, or Miss Ridgeway as she then was, found out all this?'

'Yes, she did, curse her! Nosing about where no one ever asked her to. I'd have treated Marie right. I'd have done anything for her. And she'd never have known about the other, if it hadn't been for that meddlesome young lady of hers. Yes, I'll say it, I *did* have a grudge against the lady, and I felt bitter about it when I saw her on this boat, all dressed up in pearls and diamonds and lording it all over the place, with never a thought that she'd broken up a man's life for him! I felt bitter all right, but if you think I'm a dirty murderer – if you think I went and shot her with a gun, well, that's a damned lie! I never touched her. And that's God's truth.'

He stopped. The sweat was rolling down his face.

'Where were you last night between the hours of twelve and two?'

'In my bunk asleep – and my mate will tell you so.'

'We shall see,' said Race. He dismissed him with a curt nod. 'That'll do.'

'*Eh bien?*' inquired Poirot as the door closed behind Fleetwood.

Race shrugged his shoulders. 'He tells quite a straight story. He's nervous, of course, but not unduly so. We'll have to investigate his alibi – though I don't suppose it will be decisive. His mate was probably asleep, and this fellow could have slipped in and out if he wanted to. It depends whether anyone else saw him.'

'Yes, one must inquire as to that.'

'The next thing, I think,' said Race, 'is whether anyone heard anything which might give a clue as to the time of the crime. Bessner places it as having occurred between twelve and two. It seems reasonable to hope that someone among the passengers may have heard the shot – even if they did not recognize it for what it was. I didn't hear anything of the kind myself. What about you?'

Poirot shook his head.

'Me, I slept absolutely like the log. I heard nothing – but nothing at all. I might have been drugged, I slept so soundly.'

'A pity,' said Race. 'Well, let's hope we have a bit of luck with the people who have cabins on the starboard side. Fanthorp we've done. The Allertons come next. I'll send the steward to fetch them.'

Mrs Allerton came in briskly. She was wearing a soft grey striped silk dress. Her face looked distressed.

'It's too horrible,' she said as she accepted the chair that Poirot placed for her. 'I can hardly believe it. That lovely creature, with everything to live for – dead. I almost feel I can't believe it.'

'I know how you feel, Madame,' said Poirot sympathetically.

'I'm glad *you* are on board,' said Mrs Allerton simply. 'You'll be able to find out who did it. I'm so glad it isn't that poor tragic girl.'

'You mean Mademoiselle de Bellefort. Who told you she did not do it?'

'Cornelia Robson,' replied Mrs Allerton, with a faint smile. 'You know, she's simply thrilled by it all. It's probably the only exciting thing that has ever happened to her, and probably the only exciting thing that ever will happen to her. But she's so nice that she's terribly ashamed of enjoying it. She thinks it's awful of her.'

Mrs Allerton gave a look at Poirot and then added: 'But I mustn't chatter. You want to ask me questions.'

'If you please. You went to bed at what time, Madame?'

'Just after half past ten.'

'And you went to sleep at once?'

'Yes. I was sleepy.'

'And did you hear anything – anything at all – during the night?'

Mrs Allerton wrinkled her brows.

'Yes, I think I heard a splash and someone running – or was it the other way about? I'm rather hazy. I just had a vague idea that someone had fallen overboard at sea – a dream, you know – and then I woke up and listened, but it was all quite quiet.'

'Do you know what time that was?'

'No, I'm afraid I don't. But I don't think it was very long after I went to sleep. I mean it was within the first hour or so.'

'Alas, Madame, that is not very definite.'

'No, I know it isn't. But it's no good trying to guess, is it, when I haven't really the vaguest idea?'

'And that is all you can tell us, Madame?'

'I'm afraid so.'

'Had you ever actually met Madame Doyle before?'

'No, Tim had met her. And I'd heard a good deal about her – through a cousin of ours, Joanna Southwood, but I'd never spoken to her till we met at Assuan.'

'I have one other question, Madame, if you will pardon me for asking.'

Mrs Allerton murmured with a faint smile, 'I should love to be asked an indiscreet question.'

'It is this. Did you, or your family, ever suffer any financial loss through the operations of Madame Doyle's father, Melhuish Ridgeway?'

Mrs Allerton looked throughly astonished.

'Oh, no! The family finances have never suffered except by dwindling . . . you know, everything paying less interest than it used to. There's never been anything melodramatic about our poverty. My husband left very little money, but what he left I still have, though it doesn't yield as much as it used to yield.'

'I thank you, Madame. Perhaps you will ask your son to come to us.'

Tim said lightly, when his mother came: 'Ordeal over? My turn now! What sort of things did they ask you?'

'Only whether I heard anything last night,' said Mrs Allerton. 'And unluckily I didn't hear anything at all. I can't think why not. After all, Linnet's cabin is only one away from mine. I should think I'd have been bound to hear the shot. Go along, Tim; they're waiting for you.'

To Tim Allerton Poirot repeated his previous questions.

Tim answered: 'I went to bed early, half-past ten or so. I read for a bit. Put out my light just after eleven.'

'Did you hear anything after that?'

'Heard a man's voice saying good night, I think, not far away.'

'That was me saying good night to Mrs Doyle,' said Race.

'Yes. After that I went to sleep. Then, later, I heard a kind of hullabaloo going on, somebody calling Fanthorp, I remember.'

'Mademoiselle Robson when she ran out from the observation saloon.'

'Yes, I suppose that was it. And then a lot of different voices. And then somebody running along the deck. And then a splash. And then I heard old Bessner booming out something about "Careful now" and "Not too quick."'

'You heard a splash.'

'Well, something of that kind.'

'You are sure it was not a *shot* you heard?'

'Yes, I suppose it might have been . . . I did hear a cork pop. Perhaps that was the shot. I may have imagined the splash from connecting the idea of the cork with liquid pouring into a glass . . . I know my foggy idea was that there was some kind of party on, and I wished they'd all go to bed and shut up.'

'Anything more after that?'

Tim shrugged his shoulders. 'After that – oblivion.'

'You heard nothing more?'

'Nothing whatever.'

'Thank you, Monsieur Allerton.'

Tim got up and left the cabin.

CHAPTER 16

Race pored thoughtfully over a plan of the promenade deck of the *Karnak*.

'Fanthorp, young Allerton, Mrs Allerton. Then an empty cabin – Simon Doyle's. Now who's on the other side of Mrs Doyle's? The old American dame. If anyone heard anything she would have done. If she's up we'd better have her along.'

Miss Van Schuyler entered the room. She looked even older and yellower than usual this morning. Her small dark eyes had an air of venomous displeasure in them.

Race rose and bowed.

'We're very sorry to trouble you, Miss Van Schuyler. It's very good of you. Please sit down.'

Miss Van Schuyler said sharply: 'I dislike being mixed up in this. I resent it very much. I do not wish to be associated in any way with this – er – very unpleasant affair.'

'Quite – quite. I was just saying to Monsieur Poirot that the sooner we took your statement the better, as then you need have no further trouble.'

Miss Van Schuyler looked at Poirot with something approaching favour.

'I'm glad you both realize my feelings. I am not accustomed to anything of this kind.'

Poirot said soothingly: 'Precisely, Mademoiselle. That is why we wish to free you from unpleasantness as quickly as possible. Now you went to bed last night – at what time?'

'Ten o'clock is my usual time. Last night I was rather later, as Cornelia Robson, very inconsiderately, kept me waiting.'

'*Très bien*, Mademoiselle. Now what did you hear after you had retired?'

Miss Van Schuyler said: 'I sleep very lightly.'

'A *merveille*! That is very fortunate for us.'

'I was awakened by that rather flashy young woman, Mrs Doyle's maid, who said, "*Bonne nuit, Madame*" in what I cannot but think an unnecessarily loud voice.'

'And after that?'

'I went to sleep again. I woke up thinking someone was in my cabin, but I realized that it was someone in the cabin next door.'

'In Madame Doyle's cabin?'

'Yes. Then I heard someone outside on the deck and then a splash.'

'You have no idea what time this was?'

'I can tell you the time exactly. It was ten minutes past one.'

'You are sure of that?'

'Yes. I looked at my little clock that stands by my bed.'

'You did not hear a shot?'

'No, nothing of the kind.'

'But it might possibly have been a shot that awakened you?'

Miss Van Schuyler considered the question, her toadlike head on one side.

'It might,' she admitted rather grudgingly.

'And you have no idea what might have caused the splash you heard?'

'Not at all – I know perfectly.'

Colonel Race sat up alertly. 'You know?'

'Certainly. I did not like this sound of prowling around. I got up and went to the door of my cabin. Miss Otterbourne was leaning over the side. She had just dropped something into the water.'

'Miss Otterbourne?' Race sounded really surprised.

'Yes.'

'You are quite sure it was Miss Otterbourne?'

'I saw her face distinctly.'

'She did not see you?'

'I do not think so.'

Poirot leaned forward.

'And what did her face look like, Mademoiselle?'

'She was in a condition of considerable emotion.'

Race and Poirot exchanged a quick glance.

'And then?' Race prompted.

'Miss Otterbourne went away round the stern of the boat and I returned to bed.'

There was a knock at the door and the manager entered. He carried in his hand a dripping bundle.

'We've got it, Colonel.'

Race took the package. He unwrapped fold after fold of sodden velvet. Out of it fell a coarse handkerchief, faintly stained with pink, wrapped round a small pearl-handled pistol.

Race gave Poirot a glance of slightly malicious triumph.

'You see,' he said, 'my idea was right. It *was* thrown over-board.'

He held the pistol out on the palm of his hand.

'What do you say, Monsieur Poirot? Is this the pistol you saw at the Cataract Hotel that night?'

Poirot examined it carefully; then he said quietly: 'Yes – that is it. There is the ornamental work on it – and the initials J.B. It is an *article de luxe*, a very feminine production, but it is none the less a lethal weapon.'

'Twenty-two,' murmured Race. He took out the clip. 'Two bullets fired. Yes, there doesn't seem much doubt about it.'

Miss Van Schuyler coughed significantly.

'And what about my stole?' she demanded.

'Your stole, Mademoiselle?'

'Yes, that is my velvet stole you have there.'

Race picked up the dripping folds of material.

'This is yours, Miss Van Schuyler?'

'Certainly it's mine!' the old lady snapped. 'I missed it last night. I was asking everyone if they'd seen it.'

Poirot questioned Race with a glance, and the latter gave a slight nod of assent.

'Where did you see it last, Miss Van Schuyler?'

'I had it in the saloon yesterday evening. When I came to go to bed I could not find it anywhere.'

Race said quickly: 'You realize what it's been used for?' He spread it out, indicating with a finger the scorching and several small holes. 'The murderer wrapped it round the pistol to deaden the noise of the shot.'

'Impertinence!' snapped Miss Van Schuyler. The colour rose in her wizened cheeks.

Race said: 'I shall be glad, Miss Van Schuyler, if you will tell me the extent of your previous acquaintance with Mrs Doyle.'

'There was no previous acquaintance.'

'But you knew of her?'

'I knew who she was, of course.'

'But your families were not acquainted?'

'As a family we have always prided ourselves on being exclu-sive, Colonel Race. My dear mother would never have dreamed of calling upon any of the Hartz family, who, outside their wealth, were nobodies.'

'That is all you have to say, Miss Van Schuyler?'

'I have nothing to add to what I have told you. Linnet Ridgeway was brought up in England and I never saw her till I came aboard this boat.'

She rose. Poirot opened the door and she marched out.

The eyes of the two men met.

'That's her story,' said Race, 'and she's going to stick to it! It may be true. I don't know. But – Rosalie Otterbourne? I hadn't expected that.'

Poirot shook his head in a perplexed manner. Then he brought down his hand on the table with a sudden bang.

'But it does not make sense,' he cried. '*Nom d'un nom d'un nom!* It does not make sense.'

Race looked at him.

'What do you mean exactly?'

'I mean that up to a point it is all the clear sailing. Someone wished to kill Linnet Doyle. Someone overheard the scene in the saloon last night. Someone sneaked in there and retrieved the pistol – Jacqueline de Bellefort's pistol, remember. Somebody shot Linnet Doyle with that pistol and wrote the letter J on the wall . . . All so clear, is it not? All pointing to Jacqueline de Bellefort as the murderess. And then what does the murderer do? Leave the pistol – the damning pistol – Jacqueline de Bellefort's pistol, for everyone to find? No, he – or she – throws the pistol, that particularly damning bit of evidence, overboard. Why, my friend, why?'

Race shook his head. 'It's odd.'

'It is more than odd – it is *impossible*!'

'Not impossible, since it happened!'

'I do not mean that. I mean the sequence of events is impossible. Something is wrong.'

Colonel Race glanced curiously at his colleague. He respected – he had reason to respect – the brain of Hercule Poirot. Yet for the moment he did not follow the other's process of thought. He asked no question, however. He seldom did ask questions. He proceeded straightforwardly with the matter in hand.

'What's the next thing to be done? Question the Otterbourne girl?'

'Yes, that may advance us a little.'

Rosalie Otterbourne entered ungraciously. She did not look nervous or frightened in any way – merely unwilling and sulky.

'Well,' she asked, 'what is it?'

Race was the spokesman.

'We're investigating Mrs Doyle's death,' he explained.

Rosalie nodded.

'Will you tell me what you did last night?'

Rosalie reflected a minute.

'Mother and I went to bed early – before eleven. We didn't hear anything in particular, except a bit of fuss outside Dr Bessner's cabin. I heard the old man's German voice booming away. Of course I didn't know what it was all about till this morning.'

'You didn't hear a shot?'

'No.'

'Did you leave your cabin at all last night?'

'No.'

'You are quite sure of that?'

Rosalie stared at him.

'What do you mean? Of course I'm sure of it.'

'You did not, for instance, go round to the starboard side of the boat and throw something overboard?'

The colour rose in her face.

'Is there any rule against throwing things overboard?'

'No, of course not. Then you did?'

'No, I didn't. I never left my cabin, I tell you.'

'Then if anyone says that they saw you –?'

She interrupted him. 'Who says they saw me?'

'Miss Van Schuyler.'

323

'Miss Van Schuyler?' She sounded genuinely astonished.

'Yes. Miss Van Schuyler says she looked out of her cabin and saw you throw something over the side.'

Rosalie said clearly, 'That's a damned lie.' Then, as though struck by a sudden thought, she asked: 'What time was this?'

It was Poirot who answered.

'It was ten minutes past one, Mademoiselle.'

She nodded her head thoughtfully. 'Did she see anything else?'

Poirot looked at her curiously. He stroked his chin.

'See – no,' he replied, 'but she heard something.'

'What did she hear?'

'Someone moving about in Madame Doyle's cabin.'

'I see,' muttered Rosalie.

She was pale now – deadly pale.

'And you persist in saying that you threw nothing overboard, Mademoiselle?'

'What on earth should I run about throwing things overboard for in the middle of the night?'

'There might be a reason – an innocent reason.'

'Innocent?' repeated the girl sharply.

'That's what I said. You see, Mademoiselle, something *was* thrown overboard last night – something that was not innocent.'

Race silently held out the bundle of stained velvet, opening it to display its contents.

Rosalie Otterbourne shrank back. 'Was that – what – she was killed with?'

'Yes, Mademoiselle.'

'And you think that I – I did it? What utter nonsense! Why on earth should I want to kill Linnet Doyle? I don't even know her!'

She laughed and stood up scornfully. 'The whole thing is too ridiculous.'

'Remember, Miss Otterbourne,' said Race, 'that Miss Van Schuyler is prepared to swear she saw your face quite clearly in the moonlight.'

Rosalie laughed again. 'That old cat? She's probably half blind anyway. It wasn't me she saw.' She paused. 'Can I go now?'

Race nodded and Rosalie Otterbourne left the room.

The eyes of the two men met. Race lit a cigarette.

'Well, that's that. Flat contradiction. Which of 'em do we believe?'

Poirot shook his head. 'I have a little idea that neither of them was being quite frank.'

'That's the worst of our job,' said Race despondently. 'So many people keep back the truth for positively futile reasons. What's our next move? Get on with the questioning of the passengers?'

'I think so. It is always well to proceed with order and method.'

Race nodded.

Mrs Otterbourne, dressed in floating batik material, succeeded her daughter. She corroborated Rosalie's statement that they had both gone to bed before eleven o'clock. She herself had heard nothing of interest during the night. She could not say whether Rosalie had left their cabin or not. On the subject of the crime she was inclined to hold forth.

'The *crime passionel*!' she exclaimed. 'The primitive instinct – to kill! So closely allied to the sex instinct. That girl, Jacqueline, half Latin, hot-blooded, obeying the deepest instincts of her being, stealing forth, revolver in hand –'

'But Jacqueline de Bellefort did not shoot Madame Doyle. That we know for certain. It is proved,' explained Poirot.

'Her husband, then,' said Mrs Otterbourne, rallying from the blow. 'The blood lust and the sex instinct – a sexual crime. There are many well-known instances.'

'Mr Doyle was shot through the leg and he was quite unable to move – the bone was fractured,' explained Colonel Race. 'He spent the night with Dr Bessner.'

Mrs Otterbourne was even more disappointed. She searched her mind hopefully.

'Of course!' she said. 'How foolish of me! Miss Bowers!'

'Miss Bowers?'

'Yes. Naturally. It's so *clear* psychologically. Repression! The repressed virgin! Maddened by the sight of these two – a young husband and wife passionately in love with each other. Of course it was her! She's just the type – sexually unattractive, innately respectable. In my book, *The Barren Vine* –'

Colonel Race interrupted tactfully: 'Your suggestions have been most helpful, Mrs Otterbourne. We must get on with our job now. Thank you so much.'

He escorted her gallantly to the door and came back wiping his brow.

'What a poisonous woman! Whew! Why didn't somebody murder *her*!'

'It may yet happen,' Poirot consoled him.

'There might be some sense in that. Whom have we got left? Pennington – we'll keep him for the end, I think. Richetti – Ferguson.'

Signor Richetti was very voluble, very agitated.

'But what a horror, what an infamy – a woman so young and so beautiful – indeed an inhuman crime!'

Signor Richetti's hands flew expressively up in the air.

His answers were prompt. He had gone to bed early – very early. In fact immediately after dinner. He had read for a while – a very interesting pamphlet lately published – *Prähistorische Forschung in Kleinasien* – throwing an entirely new light on the painted pottery of the Anatolian foothills.

He had put out his light some time before eleven. No, he had not heard any shot. Not any sound like the pop of a cork. The only thing he had heard – but that was later, in the middle of the night – was a splash, a big splash, just near his porthole.

'Your cabin is on the lower deck, on the starboard side, is it not?'

'Yes, yes, that is so. And I heard the big splash.' His arms flew up once more to describe the bigness of the splash.

'Can you tell me at all what time that was?'

Signor Richetti reflected.

'It was one, two, three hours after I go to sleep. Perhaps two hours.'

'About ten minutes past one, for instance?'

'It might very well be, yes. Ah! But what a terrible crime – how inhuman . . . So charming a woman . . .'

Exit Signor Richetti, still gesticulating freely.

Race looked at Poirot. Poirot raised his eyebrows expressively, then shrugged his shoulders. They passed on to Mr Ferguson.

Ferguson was difficult. He sprawled insolently in a chair.

'Grand to-do about this business!' he sneered. 'What's it really matter? Lots of superfluous women in the world!'

Race said coldly: 'Can we have an account of your movements last night, Mr Ferguson?'

'Don't see why you should, but I don't mind. I mooched around a good bit. Went ashore with Miss Robson. When she went back to the boat I mooched around by myself for a while. Came back and turned in round about midnight.'

'Your cabin is on the lower deck, starboard side?'

'Yes. I'm up among the nobs.'

'Did you hear a shot? It might only have sounded like the popping of a cork.'

Ferguson considered. 'Yes, I think I did hear something like a cork . . . Can't remember when – before I went to sleep. But there was still a lot of people about then – commotion, running about on the deck above.'

'That was probably the shot fired by Miss de Bellefort. You didn't hear another?'

Ferguson shook his head.

'Nor a splash?'

'A splash? Yes, I believe I did hear a splash. But there was so much row going on I can't be sure about it.'

'Did you leave your cabin during the night?'

Ferguson grinned. 'No, I didn't. And I didn't participate in the good work, worse luck.'

'Come, come, Mr Ferguson, don't behave childishly.'

The young man reacted angrily.

'Why shouldn't I say what I think? I believe in violence.'

'But you don't practice what you preach?' murmured Poirot. 'I wonder.'

He leaned forward.

'It was the man, Fleetwood, was it not, who told you that Linnet Doyle was one of the richest women in England?'

'What's Fleetwood got to do with this?'

'Fleetwood, my friend, had an excellent motive for killing Linnet Doyle. He had a special grudge against her.'

Mr Ferguson came up out of his seat like a jack-in-the-box.

'So that's your dirty game, is it?' he demanded wrathfully. 'Put it on to a poor devil like Fleetwood, who can't defend himself, who's got no money to hire lawyers. But I tell you this – if you try and saddle Fleetwood with this business you'll have me to deal with.'

'And who exactly are you?' asked Poirot sweetly.

Mr Ferguson got rather red.

'I can stick by my friends anyway,' he said gruffly.

'Well, Mr Ferguson, I think that's all we need for the present,' said Race.

As the door closed behind Ferguson he remarked unexpectedly: 'Rather a likeable young cub, really.'

'You don't think he is the man *you* are after?' asked Poirot.

'I hardly think so. I suppose he *is* on board. The information was very precise. Oh, well, one job at a time. Let's have a go at Pennington.'

CHAPTER 18

Andrew Pennington displayed all the conventional reactions of grief and shock. He was, as usual, carefully dressed. He had changed into a black tie. His long clean-shaven face bore a bewildered expression.

'Gentlemen,' he said sadly, 'this business has got me right down! Little Linnet – why, I remember her as the cutest little thing you can imagine. How proud of her Melhuish Ridgeway used to be, too! Well, there's no point in going into that. Just tell me what I can do; that's all I ask.'

Race said: 'To begin with, Mr Pennington, did you hear anything last night?'

'No, sir, I can't say I did. I have the cabin right next to Dr Bessner's number forty – forty-one, and I heard a certain commotion going on in there round about midnight or so. Of course I didn't know what it was at the time.'

'You heard nothing else? No shots?'

Andrew Pennington shook his head.

'Nothing whatever of that kind.'

'And you went to bed at what time?'

'Must have been some time after eleven.'

He leant forward.

'I don't suppose it's news to you to know that there's plenty of rumours going about the boat. That half-French girl – Jacqueline de Bellefort – there was something fishy there, you know. Linnet didn't tell me anything, but naturally I wasn't born blind and deaf. There'd been some affair between her and Simon, some time, hadn't there – *Cherchez la femme* – that's a pretty good sound rule, and I should say you wouldn't have to *cherchez* far.'

'You mean that in your belief Jacqueline de Bellefort shot Madame Doyle?' Poirot asked.

'That's what it looks like to me. Of course I don't *know* anything . . .'

'Unfortunately we *do* know something!'

'Eh?' Mr Pennington looked startled.

'We know that it is quite impossible for Mademoiselle de Bellefort to have shot Madame Doyle.'

He explained carefully the circumstances. Pennington seemed reluctant to accept them.

'I agree it looks all right on the face of it – but this hospital nurse woman, I'll bet she didn't stay awake all night. She dozed off and the girl slipped out and in again.'

'Hardly likely, Monsieur Pennington. She had administered a strong opiate, remember. And anyway a nurse is in the habit of sleeping lightly and waking when her patient wakes.'

'It all sounds rather fishy to me,' declared Pennington.

Race said in a gently authoritative manner: 'I think you must take it from me, Mr Pennington, that we have examined all the possibilities very carefully. The result is quite definite – Jacqueline de Bellefort did not shoot Mrs Doyle. So we are forced to look elsewhere. That is where we hope you may be able to help us.'

'I?' Pennington gave a nervous start.

'Yes. You were an intimate friend of the dead woman. You know the circumstances of her life, in all probability, much better than her husband does, since he only made her acquaintance a few months ago. You would know, for instance, of anyone who had a grudge against her. You would know, perhaps, whether there was anyone who had a motive for desiring her death.'

Andrew Pennington passed his tongue over rather dry-looking lips.

'I assure you, I have no idea . . . You see Linnet was brought up in England. I know very little of her surroundings and associations.'

'And yet,' mused Poirot, 'there was someone on board who was interested in Madame's removal. She had a near escape before, you remember, at this very place, when that boulder crashed down – ah! but you were not there, perhaps?'

'No. I was inside the temple at the time. I heard about it afterwards, of course. A very near escape. But possibly an accident, don't you think?'

Poirot shrugged his shoulders.

'One thought so at the time. Now – one wonders.'

'Yes – yes, of course.' Pennington wiped his face with a fine silk handkerchief.

Colonel Race went on: 'Mr Doyle happened to mention someone being on board who bore a grudge – not against her personally, but against her family. Do you know who that could be?'

Pennington looked genuinely astonished.

'No, I've no idea.'

'She didn't mention the matter to you?'

'No.'

'You were an intimate friend of her father's – you cannot remember any business operations of his that might have resulted in ruin for some business opponent?'

Pennington shook his head helplessly. 'No outstanding case. Such operations were frequent, of course, but I can't recall anyone who uttered threats – nothing of that kind.'

'In short, Mr Pennington, you cannot help us?'

'It seems so. I deplore my inadequacy, gentlemen.'

Race interchanged a glance with Poirot, then he said: 'I'm sorry too. We'd had hopes.'

He got up as a sign the interview was at an end.

Andrew Pennington said: 'As Doyle's laid up, I expect he'd like me to see to things. Pardon me, Colonel, but what exactly are the arrangements?'

'When we leave here we shall make a non-stop run to Shellal, arriving there tomorrow morning.'

'And the body?'

'Will be removed to one of the cold storage chambers.'

Andrew Pennington bowed his head. Then he left the room.

Poirot and Race again interchanged a glance.

'Mr Pennington,' said Race, lighting a cigarette, 'was not at all comfortable.'

Poirot nodded. 'And,' he said, 'Mr Pennington was sufficiently perturbed to tell a rather stupid lie. He was *not* in the temple of

Abu Simbel when that boulder fell. I – *moi qui vous parle* – can swear to that. I had just come from there.'

'A very stupid lie,' said Race, 'and a very revealing one.'

Again Poirot nodded.

'But for the moment,' he said, and smiled, 'we handle him with the gloves of kid, is it not so?'

'That was the idea,' agreed Race.

'My friend, you and I understand each other to a marvel.'

There was a faint grinding noise, a stir beneath their feet. The *Karnak* had started on her homeward journey to Shellal.

'The pearls,' said Race. 'That is the next thing to be cleared up.'

'You have a plan?'

'Yes.' He glanced at his watch. 'It will be lunch time in half an hour. At the end of the meal I propose to make an announcement – just state the fact that the pearls have been stolen, and that I must request everyone to stay in the dining-saloon while a search is conducted.'

Poirot nodded approvingly.

'It is well imagined. Whoever took the pearls still has them. By giving no warning beforehand, there will be no chance of their being thrown overboard in a panic.'

Race drew some sheets of paper towards him. He murmured apologetically: 'I'd like to make a brief précis of the facts as I go along. It keeps one's mind free of confusion.'

'You do well. Method and order, they are everything,' replied Poirot.

Race wrote for some minutes in his small neat script. Finally he pushed the result of his labours towards Poirot.

'Anything you don't agree with there?'

Poirot took up the sheets. They were headed:

MURDER OF MRS LINNET DOYLE

Mrs Doyle was last seen alive by her maid, Louise Bourget. Time: 11.30 (approx.).

From 11.30–12.20 following have alibis: Cornelia Robson, James Fanthorp, Simon Doyle, Jacqueline de Bellefort – *nobody else* – but crime almost certainly committed *after* that time, since it is practically certain that pistol used was Jacqueline de Bellefort's, which was then in her handbag. That her pistol was used is not *absolutely* certain until after post mortem and expert evidence re bullet – but it may be taken as overwhelmingly probable.

Probable course of events: X (murderer) was witness of scene between Jacqueline and Simon Doyle in observation saloon and noted where pistol went under settee. After the saloon was vacant, X procured pistol – his or her idea being that Jacqueline de Bellefort would be thought guilty of crime. On this theory certain people are automatically cleared of suspicion:

Cornelia Robson, since she had no opportunity to take pistol before James Fanthorp returned to search for it.

Miss Bowers – same.

Dr Bessner – same.

N.B. – Fanthorp is not definitely excluded from suspicion, since he could actually have pocketed pistol while declaring himself unable to find it.

Any other person could have taken the pistol during that ten minutes' interval.

Possible motives for the murder:

Andrew Pennington. This is on the assumption that he has been guilty of fraudulent practices. There is a certain amount of evidence in favour of that assumption, but not enough to justify making out a case against him. If it was he who rolled down the boulder, he is a man who can seize a chance when it presents itself. The crime, clearly, was not premeditated except in a *general* way. Last night's shooting scene was an ideal opportunity.

Objections to the theory of Pennington's guilt: *why did he throw the pistol overboard, since it constituted a valuable clue against J.B.?*

Fleetwood. Motive, revenge. Fleetwood considered himself injured by Linnet Doyle. Might have overheard scene and noted position of pistol. He may have taken pistol because it was a handy weapon, rather than with the idea of throwing guilt on Jacqueline. This would fit in with throwing it overboard. *But if that were the case, why did he write J in blood on the wall?*

N.B. – Cheap handkerchief found with pistol more likely to have belonged to a man like Fleetwood than to one of the well-to-do passengers.

Rosalie Otterbourne. Are we to accept Miss Van Schuyler's evidence or Rosalie's denial? Something *was* thrown overboard at the time and that something was presumably the pistol wrapped up in the velvet stole.

Points to be noted. Had Rosalie any motive? She may have disliked Linnet Doyle and even been envious of her – but as a motive for murder that seems grossly inadequate. The evidence against her can be convincing only if we discover an adequate motive. As far as we know, there is no previous knowledge or link between Rosalie Otterbourne and Linnet Doyle.

Miss Van Schuyler. The velvet stole in which pistol was wrapped belonged to Miss Van Schuyler. According to her own statement she last saw it in the observation saloon. She drew attention to its loss during the evening, and a search was made for it without success.

How did the stole come into the possession of X? Did X purloin it some time early in the evening? But if so, why? Nobody could tell, in advance, that there was going to be a scene between Jacqueline and Simon. Did X find the stole in the saloon when he went to get the pistol from under the settee? But if so, why was it not found when the search for it was made? Did it never leave Miss Van Schuyler's possession? That is to say: Did Miss Van Schuyler murder Linnet Doyle? Is her accusation of Rosalie Otterbourne a deliberate lie? If she did murder her, what was her motive?

Other possibilities:

Robbery as a motive. Possible, since the pearls have disappeared, and Linnet Doyle was certainly wearing them last night.

Someone with a grudge against the Ridgeway family. Possible – again no evidence.

We know that there is a dangerous man on board – a killer. Here we have a killer and a death. May not the two be connected? But we should have to show that Linnet Doyle possessed dangerous knowledge concerning this man.

Conclusions: We can group the persons on board into two classes – those who had a possible motive or against whom there is definite evidence, and those who, as far as we know, are free of suspicion.

Group I	Group II
Andrew Pennington	Mrs Allerton
Fleetwood	Tim Allerton
Rosalie Otterbourne	Cornelia Robson
Miss Van Schuyler	Miss Bowers
Louise Bourget (Robbery?)	Dr Bessner
Ferguson (Political?)	Signor Richetti
	Mrs Otterbourne
	James Fanthorp

Poirot pushed the paper back.

'It is very just, very exact, what you have written there.'

'You agree with it?'

'Yes.'

'And now what is your contribution?'

Poirot drew himself up in an important manner.

'Me, I pose myself one question: "*Why* was the pistol thrown overboard?"'

'That's all?'

'At the moment, yes. Until I can arrive at a satisfactory answer to that question, there is not sense anywhere. That is – that *must* be the starting point. You will notice, my friend, that, in your summary of where we stand, you have not attempted to answer that point.'

Race shrugged his shoulders.

'Panic.'

Poirot shook his head perplexedly. He picked up the sodden velvet wrap and smoothed it out, wet and limp, on the table. His fingers traced the scorched marks and the burnt holes.

'Tell me, my friend,' he said suddenly. 'You are more convers-ant with firearms than I am. Would such a thing as this, wrapped round a pistol, make much difference in muffling the sound?'

'No, it wouldn't. Not like a silencer, for instance.'

Poirot nodded. He went on: 'A man – certainly a man who had had much handling of firearms – would know that. But a woman – a woman would *not* know.'

Race looked at him curiously. 'Probably not.'

'No. She would have read the detective stories where they are not always very exact as to details.'

Race flicked the little pearl-handled pistol with his finger.

'This little fellow wouldn't make much noise anyway,' he said. 'Just a pop, that's all. With any other noise around, ten to one you wouldn't notice it.'

'Yes, I have reflected as to that.'

Poirot picked up the handkerchief and examined it.

'A man's handkerchief – but not a gentleman's handkerchief. *Ce cher* Woolworth, I imagine. Threepence at most.'

'The sort of handkerchief a man like Fleetwood would own.'

'Yes. Andrew Pennington, I notice, carries a very fine silk handkerchief.'

'Ferguson?' suggested Race.

'Possibly. As a gesture. But then it ought to be a bandana.'

'Used it instead of a glove, I suppose, to hold the pistol and obviate fingerprints.' Race added, with slight facetiousness, '"The Clue of the Blushing Handkerchief."'

'Ah, yes. Quite a *jeune fille* colour, is it not?' He laid it down and returned to the stole, once more examining the powder marks.

'All the same,' he murmured, 'it is odd . . .'

'What's that?'

Poirot said gently: '*Cette pauvre* Madame Doyle. Lying there so peacefully . . . with the little hole in her head. You remember how she looked?'

Race looked at him curiously. 'You know,' he said, 'I've got an idea you're trying to tell me something – but I haven't the faintest idea what it is.'

CHAPTER 19

There was a tap on the door.

'Come in,' Race called.

A steward entered.

'Excuse me, sir,' he said to Poirot, 'but Mr Doyle is asking for you.'

'I will come.'

Poirot rose. He went out of the room and up the companionway to the promenade deck and along it to Dr Bessner's cabin.

Simon, his face flushed and feverish, was propped up with pillows. He looked embarrassed.

'Awfully good of you to come along, Monsieur Poirot. Look here, there's something I want to ask you.'

'Yes?'

Simon got still redder in the face.

'It's – it's about Jackie. I want to see her. Do you think – would you mind – would she mind, d'you think, if you asked her to come along here? You know I've been lying here thinking . . . That wretched kid – she is only a kid after all – and I treated her damn' badly – and –' He stammered to silence.

Poirot looked at him with interest.

'You desire to see Mademoiselle Jacqueline? I will fetch her.'

'Thanks. Awfully good of you.'

Poirot went on his quest. He found Jacqueline de Bellefort sitting huddled up in a corner of the observation saloon. There was an open book on her lap but she was not reading.

Poirot said gently: 'Will you come with me, Mademoiselle? Monsieur Doyle wants to see you.'

She started up. Her face flushed – then paled. She looked bewildered.

'Simon? He wants to see me – to see *me*?'

He found her incredulity moving.

'Will you come, Mademoiselle?'

She went with him in a docile fashion, like a child, but like a puzzled child.

'I – yes, of course I will.'

Poirot passed into the cabin.

'Here is Mademoiselle.'

She stepped in after him, wavered, stood still . . . standing there mute and dumb, her eyes fixed on Simon's face.

'Hullo, Jackie.' He, too, was embarrassed. He went on: 'Awfully good of you to come. I wanted to say – I mean – what I mean is –'

She interrupted him then. Her words came out in a rush – breathless, desperate.

'Simon – I didn't kill Linnet. You know I didn't do that . . . I – I – was mad last night. Oh, can you ever forgive me?'

Words came more easily to him now.

'Of course. That's all right! Absolutely all right! That's what I wanted to say. Thought you might be worrying a bit, you know . . .'

'*Worrying? A bit?* Oh! Simon!'

'That's what I wanted to see you about. It's quite all right, see, old girl? You just got a bit rattled last night – a shade tight. All perfectly natural.'

'Oh, Simon! I might have killed you!'

'Not you. Not with a rotten little peashooter like that . . .'

'And your leg! Perhaps you'll never walk again . . .'

'Now, look here, Jackie, don't be maudlin. As soon as we get to Assuan they're going to put the X-ray to work, and dig out that tin-pot bullet, and everything will be as right as rain.'

Jacqueline gulped twice, then she rushed forward and knelt down by Simon's bed, burying her face and sobbing. Simon patted her awkwardly on the head. His eyes met Poirot's and, with a reluctant sigh, the latter left the cabin.

He heard broken murmurs as he went:

'How could I be such a devil? Oh, Simon! . . . I'm so dreadfully sorry.'

Outside Cornelia Robson was leaning over the rail. She turned her head.

'Oh, it's you, Monsieur Poirot. It seems so awful somehow that it should be such a lovely day.'

Poirot looked up at the sky.

'When the sun shines you cannot see the moon,' he said. 'But when the sun is gone – ah, when the sun is gone.'

Cornelia's mouth fell open.

'I beg your pardon?'

'I was saying, Mademoiselle, that when the sun has gone down, we shall see the moon. That is so, is it not?'

'Why – why, yes – certainly.'

She looked at him doubtfully.

Poirot laughed gently.

'I utter the imbecilities,' he said. 'Take no notice.'

He strolled gently towards the stern of the boat. As he passed the next cabin he paused for a minute. He caught fragments of speech from within.

'Utterly ungrateful – after all I've done for you – no consideration for your wretched mother – no idea of what I suffer . . .'

Poirot's lips stiffened as he pressed them together. He raised a hand and knocked.

'Is Mademoiselle Rosalie there?'

Rosalie appeared in the doorway. Poirot was shocked at her appearance. There were dark circles under her eyes and drawn lines round her mouth.

'What's the matter?' she said ungraciously. 'What do you want?'

'The pleasure of a few minutes' conversation with you, Mademoiselle. Will you come?'

Her mouth went sulky at once. She shot him a suspicious look.

'Why should I?'

'I entreat you, Mademoiselle.'

'Oh, I suppose –'

She stepped out on the deck, closing the door behind her.

'Well?'

Poirot took her gently by the arm and drew her along the deck, still in the direction of the stern. They passed the bathrooms and round the corner. They had the stern part of the deck to themselves. The Nile flowed away behind them.

Poirot rested his elbows on the rail. Rosalie stood up straight and stiff.

'Well?' she asked again, and her voice held the same ungracious tone.

Poirot spoke slowly, choosing his words. 'I could ask you certain questions, Mademoiselle, but I do not think for one moment that you would consent to answer them.'

'Seems rather a waste to bring me along here then.'

Poirot drew a finger slowly along the wooden rail.

'You are accustomed, Mademoiselle, to carrying your own burdens . . . But you can do that too long. The strain becomes too great. For you, Mademoiselle, the strain is becoming too great.'

'I don't know what you are talking about,' said Rosalie.

'I am talking about facts, Mademoiselle – plain ugly facts. Let us call the spade the spade and say it in one little short sentence. Your mother drinks, Mademoiselle.'

Rosalie did not answer. Her mouth opened; then she closed it again. For once she seemed at a loss.

'There is no need for you to talk, Mademoiselle. I will do all the talking. I was interested at Assuan in the relations existing between you. I saw at once that, in spite of your carefully studied unfilial remarks, you were in reality passionately protecting her from something. I very soon knew what that something was. I knew it long before I encountered your mother one morning in an unmistakable state of intoxication. Moreover, her case, I could see, was one of secret bouts of drinking – by far the most difficult kind of case with which to deal. You were coping with it manfully. Nevertheless, she had all the secret drunkard's cunning. She managed to get hold of a secret supply of spirits and to keep it successfully hidden from you. I should not be surprised if you discovered its hiding place only yesterday. Accordingly, last night, as soon as your mother was really soundly asleep, you stole out with the contents of the *cache*, went round to the other side of the boat (since your own side was up against the bank) and cast it overboard into the Nile.'

He paused.

'I am right, am I not?'

'Yes – you're quite right.' Rosalie spoke with sudden passion. 'I was a fool not to say so, I suppose! But I didn't want everyone to know. It would go all over the boat. And it seemed so – so silly – I mean – that I –'

Poirot finished the sentence for her.

'So silly that you should be suspected of committing a murder?'

Rosalie nodded.

Then she burst out again: 'I've tried so hard to – keep everyone from knowing . . . It isn't really her fault. She got discouraged. Her books didn't sell any more. People are tired of all that cheap sex stuff . . . It hurt her – it hurt her dreadfully. And so she began to – to drink. For a long time I didn't know why she was so queer. Then, when I found out, I tried to – to stop it. She'd be all right for a bit, and then, suddenly, she'd start, and there would be dreadful quarrels and rows with people. It was awful.' She shuddered. 'I had always to be on the watch – to get her away . . .'

'And then – she began to dislike me for it. She – she's turned right against me. I think she almost hates me sometimes.'

'*Pauvre petite*,' said Poirot.

She turned on him vehemently.

'Don't be sorry for me. Don't be kind. It's easier if you're not.' She sighed – a long heartrending sigh. 'I'm so tired . . . I'm so deadly, deadly tired.'

'I know,' said Poirot.

'People think I'm awful. Stuck-up and cross and bad-tempered. I can't help it. I've forgotten how to be – to be nice.'

'That is what I said to you; you have carried your burden by yourself too long.'

Rosalie said slowly. 'It's a relief – to talk about it. You – you've always been kind to me, Monsieur Poirot. I'm afraid I've been rude to you often.'

'*La politesse*, it is not necessary between friends.'

The suspicion came back to her face suddenly.

'Are you – are you going to tell everyone? I suppose you must, because of those damned bottles I threw overboard.'

'No, no, it is not necessary. Just tell me what I want to know. At what time was this? Ten minutes past one?'

'About that, I should think. I don't remember exactly.'

'Now tell me, Mademoiselle. Mademoiselle Van Schuyler saw *you*, did you see *her*?'

Rosalie shook her head.

'No, I didn't.'

'She says that she looked out of the door of her cabin.'

'I don't think I should have seen her. I just looked along the deck and then out to the river.'

Poirot nodded.

'And did you see anyone – anyone at all, when you looked down the deck?'

There was a pause – quite a long pause. Rosalie was frowning. She seemed to be thinking earnestly.

At last she shook her head quite decisively.

'No,' she said. 'I saw nobody.'

Hercule Poirot slowly nodded his head. But his eyes were grave.

CHAPTER 20

People crept into the dining-saloon by ones and twos in a very subdued manner. There seemed a general feeling that to sit down eagerly to food displayed an unfortunate heartlessness. It was with an almost apologetic air that one passenger after another came and sat down at their tables.

Tim Allerton arrived some few minutes after his mother had taken her seat. He was looking in a thoroughly bad temper.

'I wish we'd never come on this blasted trip,' he growled.

Mrs Allerton shook her head sadly.

'Oh, my dear, so do I. That beautiful girl! It all seems such a *waste*. To think that anyone could shoot her in cold blood. It seems awful to me that anyone could do such a thing. And that other poor child.'

'Jacqueline?'

'Yes; my heart aches for her. She looks so dreadfully unhappy.'

'Teach her not to go round loosing off toy firearms,' said Tim unfeelingly as he helped himself to butter.

'I expect she was badly brought up.'

'Oh, for God's sake, Mother, don't go all maternal about it.'

'You're in a shocking bad temper, Tim.'

'Yes I am. Who wouldn't be?'

'I don't see what there is to be cross about. It's just frightfully sad.'

Tim said crossly: 'You're taking the romantic point of view! What you don't seem to realize is that it's no joke being mixed up in a murder case.'

Mrs Allerton looked a little startled.

'But surely –'

'That's just it. There's no "But surely" about it. Everyone on this damned boat is under suspicion – you and I as well as the rest of them.'

Mrs Allerton demurred. 'Technically we are, I suppose – but actually it's ridiculous!'

'There's nothing ridiculous where murder's concerned! You may sit there, darling, just exuding virtue and conscious rectitude, but a lot of unpleasant policeman at Shellal or Assuan won't take you at your face value.'

'Perhaps the truth will be known before then.'

'Why should it be?'

'Monsieur Poirot may find out.'

'That old mountebank? He won't find out anything. He's all talk and moustaches.'

'Well, Tim,' said Mrs Allerton. 'I daresay everything you say is true, but, even if it is, we've got to go through with it, so we might as well make up our minds to it and go through with it as cheerfully as we can.'

But her son showed no abatement of gloom.

'There's this blasted business of the pearls being missing, too.'

'Linnet's pearls?'

'Yes. It seems somebody must have pinched 'em.'

'I suppose that was the motive for the crime,' said Mrs Allerton.

'Why should it be? You're mixing up two perfectly different things.'

'Who told you that they were missing?'

'Ferguson. He got it from his tough friend in the engine room, who got it from the maid.'

'They were lovely pearls,' declared Mrs Allerton.

Poirot sat down at the table, bowing to Mrs Allerton.

'I am a little late,' he said.

'I expect you have been busy,' Mrs Allerton replied.

'Yes, I have been much occupied.'

He ordered a fresh bottle of wine from the waiter.

'We're very catholic in our tastes,' said Mrs Allerton. 'You drink wine always; Tim drinks whisky and soda, and I try all the different brands of mineral water in turn.'

'*Tiens*!' said Poirot. He stared at her for a moment. He murmured to himself: 'It is an idea, that . . .'

Then, with an impatient shrug of his shoulders, he dismissed the sudden preoccupation that had distracted him and began to chat lightly of other matters.

'Is Mr Doyle badly hurt?' asked Mrs Allerton.

'Yes, it is a fairly serious injury. Dr Bessner is anxious to reach Assuan so that his leg can be X-rayed and the bullet removed. But he hopes there will be no permanent lameness.'

'Poor Simon,' said Mrs Allerton. 'Only yesterday he looked such a happy boy, with everything in the world he wanted. And now his beautiful wife killed and he himself laid up and helpless. I do hope, though –'

'What do you hope, Madame?' asked Poirot as Mrs Allerton paused.

'I hope he's not too angry with that poor child.'

'With Mademoiselle Jacqueline? Quite the contrary. He was full of anxiety on her behalf.'

He turned to Tim.

'You know, it is a pretty little problem of psychology, that. All the time that Mademoiselle Jacqueline was following them from place to place, he was absolutely furious; but now, when she has actually shot him, and wounded him dangerously – perhaps made him lame for life – all his anger seems to have evaporated. Can you understand that?'

'Yes,' said Tim thoughtfully, 'I think I can. The first thing made him feel a fool –'

Poirot nodded. 'You are right. It offended his male dignity.'

'But now – if you look at it a certain way, it's *she* who's made a fool of herself. Everyone's down on her, and so –'

'He can be generously forgiving,' finished Mrs Allerton. 'What children men are!'

'A profoundly untrue statement that women always make,' murmured Tim.

Poirot smiled. Then he said to Tim: 'Tell me, Madame Doyle's cousin, Miss Joanna Southwood, did she resemble Madame Doyle?'

'You've got it a little wrong, Monsieur Poirot. She was our cousin and Linnet's friend.'

'Ah, pardon – I was confused. She is a young lady much in the news, that. I have been interested in her for some time.'

'Why?' asked Tim sharply.

Poirot half rose to bow to Jacqueline de Bellefort, who had just come in and passed their table on the way to her own. Her cheeks were flushed and her eyes bright, and her breath came a little unevenly. As he resumed his seat Poirot seemed to have forgotten Tim's question. He murmured vaguely: 'I wonder if all young ladies with valuable jewels are as careless as Madame Doyle was?'

'It is true, then, that they were stolen?' asked Mrs Allerton.

'Who told you so, Madame?'

'Ferguson said so,' Tim volunteered.

Poirot nodded gravely.

'It is quite true.'

'I suppose,' Mrs Allerton nervously, 'that this will mean a lot of unpleasantness for all of us. Tim says it will.'

Her son scowled, but Poirot had turned to him.

'Ah! You have had previous experience, perhaps? You have been in a house where there was a robbery?'

'Never,' said Tim.

'Oh, yes, darling, you were at the Portarlingtons' that time – when that awful woman's diamonds were stolen.'

'You always get things hopelessly wrong, Mother. I was there when it was discovered that the diamonds she was wearing round her fat neck were only paste! The actual substitution was probably done months earlier. As a matter of fact, of lot of people said she'd had it done herself!'

'Joanna said so, I expect.'

'Joanna wasn't there.'

'But she knew them quite well. And it's very like her to make that kind of suggestion.'

'You're always down on Joanna, Mother.'

Poirot hastily changed the subject. He had it in mind to make a really big purchase at one of the Assuan shops. Some very attractive purple and gold material at one of the Indian merchants. There would, of course, be the duty to pay, but –

'They tell me that they can – how do you say – expedite it for me. And that the charges will not be too high. How think you, will it arrive all right?'

Mrs Allerton said that many people, so she had heard, had had things sent straight to England from the shops in question and that everything had arrived safely.

'*Bien.* Then I will do that. But the trouble one has, when one is abroad, if a parcel comes out from England! Have you had experience of that? Have you had any parcels arrive since you have been on your travels?'

'I don't think we have, have we, Tim? You get books some-times, but of course there is never any trouble about them.'

'Ah, no, books are different.'

Dessert had been served. Now, without any previous warning, Colonel Race stood up and made his speech.

He touched on the circumstances of the crime and announced the theft of the pearls. A search of the boat was about to be instituted, and he would be obliged if all the passengers would remain in the saloon until this was completed. Then, after that, if the passengers agreed, as he was sure they would, they themselves would be kind enough to submit to a search.

Poirot slipped nimbly along to his side. There was a little buzz and hum all round them. Voices doubtful, indignant, excited . . .

344

Poirot reached Race's side and murmured something in his ear just as the latter was about to leave the dining-saloon.

Race listened, nodded assent, and beckoned a steward. He said a few brief words to him; then, together with Poirot, he passed out on to the deck, closing the door behind him.

They stood for a minute or two by the rail. Race lit a cigarette.

'Not a bad idea of yours,' he said. 'We'll soon see if there's anything in it. I'll give 'em three minutes.'

The door of the dining-saloon opened and the same steward to whom they had spoken came out. He saluted Race and said: 'Quite right, sir. There's a lady who says it's urgent she should speak to you at once without delay.'

'Ah!' Race's face showed satisfaction. 'Who is it?'

'Miss Bowers, sir, the hospital nurse lady.'

A slight shade of surprise showed on Race's face. He said, 'Bring her to the smoking-room. Don't let anyone else leave.'

'No, sir – the other steward will attend to that.'

He went back into the dining-room. Poirot and Race went to the smoking-room.

'Bowers, eh?' muttered Race.

They had hardly got inside the smoking-room before the steward reappeared with Miss Bowers. He ushered her in and left, shutting the door behind him.

'Well, Miss Bowers?' Colonel Race looked at her inquiringly. 'What's all this?'

Miss Bowers looked her usual composed, unhurried self. She displayed no particular emotion.

'You'll excuse me, Colonel Race,' she said, 'but under the circumstances I thought the best thing to do would be to speak to you at once' – she opened her neat black handbag – 'and to return you these.'

She took out a string of pearls and laid them on the table.

If Miss Bowers had been the kind of woman who enjoyed creating a sensation, she would have been richly repaid by the result of her action.

A look of utter astonishment passed over Colonel Race's face as he picked up the pearls from the table.

'This is most extraordinary,' he said. 'Will you kindly explain, Miss Bowers?'

'Of course. That's what I've come to do.' Miss Bowers settled herself comfortably in a chair. 'Naturally it was a little difficult for me to decide what it was best for me to do. The family would naturally be averse to scandal of any kind, and they trusted my discretion, but the circumstances are so very unusual that it really leaves me no choice. Of course, when you didn't find anything in the cabins, your next move would be a search of the passengers, and, if the pearls were then found in my possession, it would be rather an awkward situation and the truth would come out just the same.'

'And just what is the truth? Did you take these pearls from Mrs Doyle's cabin?'

'Oh, no, Colonel Race, of course not. Miss Van Schuyler did.'

'Miss Van Schuyler?'

'Yes. She can't help it, you know, but she does – er – take things. Especially jewellery. That's really why I'm always with her. It's not her health at all; it's this little idiosyncrasy. I keep on the alert, and fortunately there's never been any trouble since I've been with her. It just means being watchful, you know. And she always hides the things she takes in the same place – rolled up in a pair of stockings – so that it makes it very simple. I look each morning. Of course I'm a light sleeper, and I always sleep next door to her, and with the communicating door open if it's in a hotel, so that I usually hear. Then I go after her and persuade her to go back to bed. Of course it's been rather more difficult on a boat. But she doesn't usually do it at night. It's more just picking up things that she sees left about. Of course, pearls have a great attraction for her always.'

Miss Bowers ceased speaking.

Race asked: 'How did you discover they had been taken?'

'They were in her stockings this morning. I knew whose they were, of course. I've often noticed them. I went along to put them back, hoping that Mrs Doyle wasn't up yet and hadn't discovered her loss. But there was a steward standing there, and he told me about the murder and that no one could go in. So then, you see, I was in a regular quandary. But I still hoped to slip them back in the cabin later, before their absence had been noticed. I can assure you I've passed a very unpleasant morning wondering what was the best thing to do. You see, the Van Schuyler family is so *very* particular and exclusive. It would never do if this got into the newspapers. But that won't be necessary, will it?'

Miss Bowers really looked worried.

'That depends on circumstances,' said Colonel Race cautiously.

'But we shall do our best for you, of course. What does Miss Van Schuyler say to this?'

'Oh, she'll deny it, of course. She always does. Says some wicked person has put it there. She never admits taking anything. That's why if you catch her in time she goes back to bed like a lamb. Says she just went out to look at the moon. Something like that.'

'Does Miss Robson know about this – er – failing?'

'No, she doesn't. Her mother knows, but she's a very simple kind of girl and her mother thought it best she should know nothing about it. I was quite equal to dealing with Miss Van Schuyler,' added the competent Miss Bowers.

'We have to thank you, Mademoiselle, for coming to us so promptly,' said Poirot.

Miss Bowers stood up.

'I'm sure I hope I acted for the best.'

'Be assured that you have.'

'You see, what with there being a murder as well –'

Colonel Race interrupted her. His voice was grave.

'Miss Bowers, I am going to ask you a question, and I want to impress upon you that it has got to be answered truthfully. Miss Van Schuyler is unhinged mentally to the extent of being a kleptomaniac. Has she also a tendancy to homicidal mania?'

Miss Bowers' answer came immediately: 'Oh, dear me, no!

347

Nothing of that kind. You can take my word for it absolutely. The old lady wouldn't hurt a fly.'

The reply came with such positive assurance that there seemed nothing more to be said. Nevertheless Poirot did interpolate one mild inquiry.

'Does Miss Van Schuyler suffer at all from deafness?'

'As a matter of fact she does, Monsieur Poirot. Not so that you'd notice in any way, not if you were speaking to her, I mean. But quite often she doesn't hear you when you come into a room. Things like that.'

'Do you think she would have heard anyone moving about in Mrs Doyle's cabin, which is next door to her own?'

'Oh, I shouldn't think so – not for a minute. You see, the bunk is the other side of the cabin, not even against the partition wall. No, I don't think she would have heard anything.'

'Thank you, Miss Bowers.'

Race said: 'Perhaps you will now go back to the dining-saloon and wait with the others?'

He opened the door for her and watched her go down the staircase and enter the saloon. Then he shut the door and came back to the table. Poirot had picked up the pearls.

'Well,' said Race grimly, 'that reaction came pretty quickly. That's a very cool-headed and astute young woman – perfectly capable of holding out on us and still further if she thinks it suits her book. What about Miss Marie Van Schuyler now? I don't think we can eliminate her from the possible suspects. You know, she *might* have committed murder to get hold of those jewels. We can't take the nurse's word for it. She's all out to do the best for the family.'

Poirot nodded in agreement. He was very busy with the pearls, running them through his fingers, holding them up to his eyes.

He said: 'We may take it, I think, that part of the old lady's story to us is true. She *did* look out of her cabin and she *did* see Rosalie Otterbourne. But I don't think she *heard* anything or anyone in Linnet Doyle's cabin. I think she was just peering out from *her* cabin preparatory to slipping along and purloining the pearls.'

'The Otterbourne girl was there, then?'

'Yes. Throwing her mother's secret *cache* of drink overboard.'

Colonel Race shook his head sympathetically.

'So that's it! Tough on a young 'un.'

'Yes, her life has not been very gay, *cette pauvre petite Rosalie*.'

'Well, I'm glad that's been cleared up. *She* didn't see or hear anything?'

'I asked her that. She responded – after a lapse of quite twenty seconds – that she saw nobody.'

'Oh?' Race looked alert.

'Yes, it is suggestive, that.'

Race said slowly: 'If Linnet Doyle was shot round about ten minutes past one, or indeed any time after the boat had quieted down, it has seemed amazing to me that no one heard the shot. I grant you that a little pistol like that wouldn't make much noise, but all the same the boat would be deadly quiet, and any noise, even a little pop, should have been heard. But I begin to understand better now. The cabin on the forward side of hers was unoccupied – since her husband was in Dr Bessner's cabin. The one aft was occupied by the Van Schuyler woman, who was deaf. That leaves only –'

He paused and looked expectantly at Poirot, who nodded.

'The cabin next to her on the other side of the boat. In other words – Pennington. We always seem to come back to Pennington.'

'We will come back to him presently with the kid gloves removed! Ah, yes, I am promising myself that pleasure.'

'In the meantime we'd better get on with our search of the boat. The pearls still make a convenient excuse, even though they have been returned – but Miss Bowers is not likely to advertise the fact.'

'Ah, these pearls!' Poirot held them up against the light once more. He stuck out his tongue and licked them; he even gingerly tried one of them between his teeth. Then, with a sigh, he threw them down on the table.

'Here are more complications, my friend,' he said. 'I am not an expert on precious stones, but I have had a good deal to do with them in my time and I am fairly certain of what I say. These pearls are only a clever imitation.'

CHAPTER 22

Colonel Race swore hastily.

'This damned case gets more and more involved.' He picked up the pearls. 'I suppose you've not made a mistake? They look all right to me.'

'They are a very good imitation – yes.'

'Now where does that lead us? I suppose Linnet Doyle didn't deliberately have an imitation made and bring it aboard with her for safety. Many women do.'

'I think, if that were so, her husband would know about it.'

'She may not have told him.'

Poirot shook his head in a dissatisfied manner.

'No, I do not think that is so. I was admiring Madame Doyle's pearls the first evening on the boat – their wonderful sheen and lustre. I am sure that she was wearing the genuine ones then.'

'That brings us up against two possibilities. First, that Miss Van Schuyler only stole the imitation string after the real ones had been stolen by someone else. Second, that the whole kleptomaniac story is a fabrication. Either Miss Bowers is a thief, and quickly invented the story and allayed suspicion by handing over the false pearls, or else that whole party is in it together. That is to say, they are a gang of clever jewel thieves masquerading as an exclusive American family.'

'Yes,' Poirot murmured. 'It is difficult to say. But I will point out to you one thing – to make a perfect and exact copy of the pearls, clasp and all, good enough to stand a chance of deceiving Madame Doyle, is a highly skilled technical performance. It could not be done in a hurry. Whoever copied those pearls must have had a good opportunity of studying the original.'

Race rose to his feet.

'Useless to speculate about it any further now. Let's get on with the job. We've got to find the real pearls. And at the same time we'll keep our eyes open.'

They disposed of the cabins occupied on the lower deck. That of Signor Richetti contained various archaeological works in different languages, a varied assortment of clothing, hair lotions of a highly scented kind and two personal letters – one from an archaeological expedition in Syria, and one from, apparently, a sister in Rome. His handkerchiefs were all of coloured silk.

They passed on to Ferguson's cabin.

There was a sprinkling of communistic literature, a good many snapshots, Samuel Butler's *Erewhon* and a cheap edition of Pepys' *Diary*. His personal possessions were not many. Most of what outer clothing there was was torn and dirty; the underclothing, on the other hand, was of really good quality. The handkerchiefs were expensive linen ones.

'Some interesting discrepancies,' murmured Poirot.

Race nodded. 'Rather odd that there are absolutely no personal papers, letters, etc.'

'Yes; that gives one to think. An odd young man, Monsieur Ferguson.' He looked thoughtfully at a signet ring he held in his hand, before replacing it in the drawer where he had found it.

They went along to the cabin occupied by Louise Bourget. The maid had her meals after the other passengers, but Race had sent word that she was to be taken to join the others. A cabin steward met them.

'I'm sorry, sir,' he apologized, 'but I've not been able to find the young woman anywhere. I can't think where she can have got to.'

Race glanced inside the cabin. It was empty.

They went up to the promenade deck and started on the starboard side. The first cabin was that occupied by James Fanthorp. Here all was in meticulous order. Mr Fanthorp travelled light, but all that he had was of good quality.

'No letters,' said Poirot thoughtfully. 'He is careful, our Mr Fanthorp, to destroy his correspondence.'

They passed on to Tim Allerton's cabin, next door.

There were evidences here of an Anglo-Catholic turn of mind – an exquisite little triptych, and a big rosary of intricately carved wood. Besides personal clothing, there was a half completed manuscript, a good deal annotated and scribbled over, and a good collection of books, most of them recently published. There were also a quantity of letters thrown carelessly into a drawer. Poirot, never in the least scrupulous about reading other people's correspondence, glanced through them. He noted that amongst them there were no letters from Joanna Southwood. He picked up a tube of Seccotine, fingered it absently for a minute or two, then said: 'Let us pass on.'

'No Woolworth handkerchiefs,' reported Race, rapidly replacing the contents of a drawer.

Mrs Allerton's cabin was the next. It was exquisitely neat, and a faint old-fashioned smell of lavender hung about it. The two men's search was soon over. Race remarked as they left it: 'Nice woman, that.'

The next cabin was that which had been used as a dressing-room by Simon Doyle. His immediate necessities – pyjamas, toilet things, etc. – had been moved to Bessner's cabin, but the remainder of his possessions were still there – two good-sized leather suitcases and a kitbag. There were also some clothes in the wardrobe.

'We will look carefully here, my friend,' said Poirot, 'for it is possible that the thief hid the pearls here.'

'You think it is likely?'

'But yes, indeed. Consider! The thief, whoever he or she may be, must know that sooner or later a search will be made, and therefore a hiding-place in his or her own cabin would be injudicious in the extreme. The public rooms present other difficulties. But here is a cabin belonging to a man who cannot possibly visit it himself so that, if the pearls are found here, it tells us nothing at all.' But the most meticulous search failed to reveal any trace of the missing necklace.

Poirot murmured '*Zut!*' to himself and they emerged once more on the deck.

Linnet Doyle's cabin had been locked after the body was removed, but Race had the key with him. He unlocked the door and the two men stepped inside.

Except for the removal of the girl's body, the cabin was exactly as it had been that morning.

'Poirot,' said Race, 'if there's anything to be found here, for God's sake go ahead and find it. You can if anyone can – I know that.'

'This time you do not mean the pearls, *mon ami*?'

'No. The murder's the main thing. There may be something I overlooked this morning.'

Quietly, deftly, Poirot went about his search. He went down on his knees and scrutinized the floor inch by inch. He examined the bed. He went rapidly through the wardrobe and chest of drawers. He went through the wardrobe trunk and the two costly suitcases. He looked through the expensive gold-fitted dressing-case. Finally he turned his attention to the washstand. There were various creams, powders, face lotions. But the only thing that seemed to interest Poirot were two little bottles labelled Nailex. He picked them up at last and brought them to the dressing-table. One, which bore the inscription Nailex Rose, was empty but for a drop or two of dark red fluid at the bottom. The other, the same size, but labelled Nailex Cardinal, was nearly full. Poirot uncorked first the empty, then the full one, and sniffed them both delicately.

An odour of peardrops billowed into the room. With a slight grimace he recorked them.

'Get anything?' asked Race.

Poirot replied by a French proverb: '*On no prend pas les mouches avec le vinaigre.*' Then he said with a sigh: 'My friend, we have not been fortunate. The murderer has not been obliging. He has not dropped for us the cuff link, the cigarette end, the cigar ash – or, in the case of the woman, the handkerchief, the lipstick, or the hair slide.'

'Only the bottle of nail polish?'

Poirot shrugged his shoulders. 'I must ask the maid. There is something – yes – a little curious there.'

'I wonder where the devil the girl's got to?' said Race.

They left the cabin, locking the door behind them, and passed on to that of Miss Van Schuyler.

Here again were all the appurtenances of wealth, expensive toilet fittings, good luggage, a certain number of private letters and papers all perfectly in order.

The next cabin was the double one occupied by Poirot, and beyond it that of Race. 'Hardly like to hide 'em in either of these,' said the Colonel.

Poirot demurred. 'It might be. Once, on the Orient Express, I investigated a murder. There was a little matter of a scarlet kimono. It had disappeared, and yet it must be on the train. I found it – where do you think? In my own locked suitcase! Ah! It was an impertinence, that!'

'Well, let's see if anybody has been impertinent with you or me this time.'

But the thief of the pearls had not been impertinent with Hercule Poirot or with Colonel Race.

Rounding the stern they made a very careful search of Miss Bowers' cabin but could find nothing of a suspicious nature. Her handkerchiefs were of plain linen with an initial.

The Otterbournes' cabin came next. Here, again, Poirot made a very meticulous search, but with no result.

The next cabin was Bessner's. Simon Doyle lay with an untasted tray of food beside him.

'Off my feed,' he said apologetically.

He was looking feverish and very much worse than earlier in the day. Poirot appreciated Bessner's anxiety to get him as swiftly as possible to hospital and skilled appliances. The little Belgian explained what the two of them were doing, and Simon nodded approval. On learning that the pearls had been restored by Miss Bowers, but proved to be merely imitation, he expressed the most complete astonishment.

'You are quite sure, Monsieur Doyle, that your wife did not have an imitation string which she brought aboard with her instead of the real ones?'

Simon shook his head decisively.

'Oh, no. I'm quite sure of that. Linnet loved those pearls and she wore 'em everywhere. They were insured against every possible risk, so I think that made her a bit careless.'

'Then we must continue our search.'

He started opening drawers. Race attacked a suitcase.

Simon stared. 'Look here, you surely don't suspect old Bessner pinched them?'

Poirot shrugged his shoulders.

'It might be so. After all, what do we know of Dr Bessner? Only what he himself gives out.'

'But he couldn't have hidden them in here without my seeing him.'

'He could not have hidden anything *today* without your having seen him. But we do not know when the substitution took place. He may have effected the exchange some days ago.'

'I never thought of that.'

But the search was unavailing.

The next cabin was Pennington's. The two men spent some time in their search. In particular, Poirot and Race examined carefully a case full of legal and business documents, most of them requiring Linnet's signature.

Poirot shook his head gloomily. 'These seem all square and aboveboard. You agree?'

'Absolutely. Still, the man isn't a born fool. If there *had* been a compromising document there – a power of attorney or something of that kind – he'd be pretty sure to have destroyed it first thing.'

'That is so, yes.'

Poirot lifted a heavy Colt revolver out of the top drawer of the chest of drawers, looked at it and put it back.

'So it seems there are still some people who travel with revolvers,' he murmured.

'Yes, a little suggestive, perhaps. Still, Linnet Doyle wasn't shot with a thing that size.' Race paused and then said: 'You know, I've thought of a possible answer to your point about the pistol being thrown overboard. Supposing that the actual murderer did leave it in Linnet Doyle's cabin, and that someone else – some second person – took it away and threw it into the river?'

'Yes, that is possible. I have thought of it. But it opens up a whole string of questions. Who was that second person? What interest had they in endeavouring to shield Jacqueline de Bellefort by taking away the pistol? What was the second person doing there? The only other person we know of who went into the cabin was Mademoiselle Van Schuyler. Was it conceivably Mademoiselle Van Schuyler who removed it? Why should *she* wish to shield Jacqueline de Bellefort? And yet – what other reason can there be for the removal of the pistol?'

Race suggested, 'She may have recognized the stole as hers, got the wind up, and thrown the whole bag of tricks over on that account.'

'The stole, perhaps, but would she have got rid of the pistol, too? Still, I agree that it is a possible solution. But it is always – *bon Dieu*! it is clumsy. And you still have not appreciated one point about the stole –'

As they emerged from Pennington's cabin Poirot suggested that Race should search the remaining cabins, those occupied by Jacqueline, Cornelia and two empty ones at the end, while he himself had a few words with Simon Doyle. Accordingly he retraced his steps along the deck and re-entered Bessner's cabin.

Simon said: 'Look here, I've been thinking. I'm perfectly sure that those pearls were all right yesterday.'

'Why is that, Monsieur Doyle?'

'Because Linnet' – he winced as he uttered his wife's name – 'was passing them through her hands just before dinner and talking about them. She knew something about pearls. I feel certain she'd have known if they were a fake.'

'They were a very good imitation, though. Tell me, was Madame Doyle in the habit of letting those pearls out of her hands? Did she ever lend them to a friend for instance?'

Simon flushed with slight embarrassment.

'You see, Monsieur Poirot, it's difficult for me to say . . . I – I – well, you see, I hadn't known Linnet very long.'

'Ah, no, it was a quick romance – yours.'

Simon went on. 'And so – really – I shouldn't know a thing like that. But Linnet was awfully generous with her things. I should think she might have done.'

'She never, for instance' – Poirot's voice was very smooth – 'she never, for instance, lent them to Mademoiselle de Bellefort?'

'What d'you mean?' Simon flushed brick-red, tried to sit up and, wincing, fell back. 'What are you getting at? That Jackie stole the pearls? She didn't. I'll swear she didn't. Jackie's as straight as a die. The mere idea of her being a thief is ridiculous – absolutely ridiculous.'

Poirot looked at him with gently twinkling eyes. 'Oh, la! la! la!' he said unexpectedly. 'That suggestion of mine, it has indeed stirred up the nest of hornets.'

Simon repeated doggedly, unmoved by Poirot's lighter note, 'Jackie's straight!'

Poirot remembered a girl's voice by the Nile in Assuan saying, 'I love Simon – and he loves me . . .'

He had wondered which of the three statements he had heard that night was the true one. It seemed to him that it had turned out to be Jacqueline who had come closest to the truth.

The door opened and Race came in.

'Nothing,' he said brusquely. 'Well, we didn't expect it. I see the stewards coming along with their report as to the searching of the passengers.'

A steward and stewardess appeared in the doorway. The former spoke first. 'Nothing, sir.'

'Any of the gentlemen make any fuss?'

'Only the Italian gentleman, sir. He carried on a good deal.

Said it was a dishonour – something of that kind. He'd got a gun on him, too.'

'What kind of a gun?'

'Mauser automatic twenty-five, sir.'

'Italians are pretty hot-tempered,' said Simon. 'Richetti got in no end of a stew at Wadi Halfa just because of a mistake over a telegram. He was darned rude to Linnet over it.'

Race turned to the stewardess. She was a big handsome-looking woman.

'Nothing on any of the ladies, sir. They made a good deal of fuss – except for Mrs Allerton, who was as nice as nice could be. Not a sign of the pearls. By the way, the young lady, Miss Rosalie Otterbourne, had a little pistol in her handbag.'

'What kind?'

'It was a very small one, sir, with a pearl handle. A kind of toy.'

Race stared. 'Devil take this case,' he muttered. 'I thought we'd got *her* cleared of suspicion, and now – Does every girl on this blinking boat carry around pearl-handled toy pistols?'

He shot a question at the stewardess. 'Did she show any feeling over your finding it?'

The woman shook her head. 'I don't think she noticed. I had my back turned whilst I was going through the handbag.'

'Still, she must have known you'd come across it. Oh, well, it beats me. What about the maid?'

'We've looked all over the boat, sir. We can't find her anywhere.'

'What's this?' asked Simon.

'Mrs Doyle's maid – Louise Bourget. She's disappeared.'

'*Disappeared?*'

Race said thoughtfully: 'She might have stolen the pearls. she is the one person who had ample opportunity to get a replica made.'

'And then, when she found a search was being instituted, she threw herself overboard?' Simon suggested.

'Nonsense,' replied Race, irritably. 'A woman can't throw herself overboard in broad daylight, from a boat like this, without somebody realizing the fact. She's bound to be somewhere on board.' He addressed the stewardess once more. 'When was she last seen?'

'About half an hour before the bell went for lunch, sir.'

'We'll have a look at her cabin anyway,' said Race. 'That may tell us something.'

He led the way to the deck below. Poirot followed him. They unlocked the door of the cabin and passed inside.

Louise Bourget, whose trade it was to keep other people's belongings in order, had taken a holiday where her own were concerned. Odds and ends littered the top of the chest of drawers; a suitcase gaped open, with clothes hanging out of the side of it and preventing it shutting; underclothing hung limply over the sides of the chairs.

As Poirot, with swift neat fingers, opened the drawers of the dressing-chest, Race examined the suitcase.

Louise's shoes were lined along by the bed. One of them, a black patent leather, seemed to be resting at an extraordinary angle, almost unsupported. The appearance of it was so odd that it attracted Race's attention.

He closed the suitcase and bent over the line of shoes. Then he uttered a sharp exclamation.

'*Qu'est-ce qu'ily a?*'

Race said grimly: 'She hasn't disappeared. She's here – under the bed . . .'

CHAPTER 23

The body of the dead woman, who in life had been Louise Bourget, lay on the floor of her cabin. The two men bent over it.

Race straightened himself first.

'Been dead close on an hour, I should say. We'll get Bessner on to it. Stabbed to the heart. Death pretty well instantaneous, I should imagine. She doesn't look pretty, does she?'

'No.'

Poirot shook his head with a slight shudder.

The dark feline face was convulsed, as though with surprise and fury, the lips drawn back from the teeth.

Poirot bent again gently and picked up the right hand. Something just showed within the fingers. He detached it and held it out to Race, a little sliver of flimsy paper coloured a pale mauvish pink.

'You see what it is?'

'Money,' said Race.

'The corner of a thousand-franc note, I fancy.'

'Well, it's clear what happened,' said Race. 'She knew some-thing – and she was blackmailing the murderer with her know-ledge. We thought she wasn't being quite straight this morning.'

Poirot cried out: 'We have been idiots – fools! We should have known – then. What did she say? "What could I have seen or heard? I was on the deck below. Naturally, if I had been unable to sleep, if I had mounted the stairs, *then* perhaps I might have seen this assassin, this monster, enter or leave Madame's cabin, but as it is –" Of course, that is what did happen! She did come up. She did see someone gliding into Linnet Doyle's cabin – or coming out of it. And, because of her greed, her insensate greed, she lies here –'

'And we are no nearer to knowing who killed her,' finished Race disgustedly.

Poirot shook his head. 'No, no. We know much more now. We know – we know almost everything. Only what we know seems incredible . . . Yet it must be so. Only I do not see. Pah! what a fool I was this morning! We felt – both of us felt – that she was keeping something back, and yet we never realized that logical reason, blackmail.'

'She must have demanded hush money straight away,' said Race. 'Demanded it with threats. The murderer was forced to accede to that request and paid her in French notes. Anything there?'

Poirot shook his head thoughtfully. 'I hardly think so. Many people take a reserve of money with them when travelling – sometimes five-pound notes, sometimes dollars, but very often French notes as well. Possibly the murderer paid her all he had in a mixture of currencies. Let us continue our reconstruction.'

'The murderer comes to her cabin, gives her the money, and then –'

'And then,' said Poirot, 'she counts it. Oh, yes, I know that class. She would count the money, and while she counted it she was completely off her guard. The murderer struck. Having done so successfully, he gathered up the money and fled – not noticing that the corner of one of the notes was torn.'

'We may get him that way,' suggested Race doubtfully.

'I doubt it,' said Poirot. 'He will examine those notes, and will probably notice the tear. Of course if he were of a parsimonious disposition he would not be able to bring himself to destroy a *mille* note – but I very much fear that his temperament is just the opposite.'

'How do you make that out?'

'Both this crime and the murder of Madame Doyle demanded certain qualities – courage, audacity, bold execution, lightning action; those qualities do not accord with a saving, prudent disposition.'

Race shook his head sadly. 'I'd better get Bessner down,' he said.

The stout doctor's examination did not take long. Accompanied by a good many *Ach's* and *So's*, he went to work.

'She has been dead not more than an hour,' he announced. 'Death it was very quick – at once.'

'And what weapon do you think was used?'

'Ach, it is interesting that. It was something very sharp, very thin, very delicate. I could show you the kind of thing.'

Back again in his cabin he opened a case and extracted a long, delicate, surgical knife.

'It was something like that, my friend; it was not a common table knife.'

'I suppose,' suggested Race smoothly, 'that none of your own knives are – er – missing, Doctor?'

Bessner stared at him; then his face grew red with indignation.

'What is that you say? Do you think I – I, Carl Bessner – who is so well-known all over Austria – I with my clients, my highly born patients – I have killed a miserable little *femme de chambre*? Ah, but it is ridiculous – absurd, what you say! None of my knives are missing – not one, I tell you. They are all here, correct, in their places. You can see for yourself. And this insult to my profession I will not forget.'

Dr Bessner closed his case with a snap, flung it down and stamped out on to the deck.

'Whew!' said Simon. 'You've put the old boy's back up.'

Poirot shrugged his shoulders. 'It is regrettable.'

'You're on the wrong tack. Old Bessner's one of the best, even though he is a kind of Boche.'

Dr Bessner reappeared suddenly.

'Will you be so kind as to leave me now my cabin? I have to do the dressing of my patient's leg.'

Miss Bowers had entered with him and stood, brisk and professional, waiting for the others to go.

Race and Poirot crept out meekly. Race muttered something and went off. Poirot turned to his left. He heard scraps of girlish conversation, a little laugh. Jacqueline and Rosalie were together in the latter's cabin.

The door was open and the two girls were standing near it. As his shadow fell on them they looked up. He saw Rosalie Otterbourne smile at him for the first time – a shy welcoming smile – a little uncertain in its lines, as of one who does a new and unfamiliar thing.

'You talk the scandal, Mesdemoiselles?' he accused them.

'No, indeed,' said Rosalie. 'As a matter of fact we were just comparing lipsticks.'

Poirot smiled. '*Les chiffons d'aujourd'hui*,' he murmured.

But there was something a little mechanical about his smile, and Jacqueline de Bellefort, quicker and more observant than Rosalie, saw it. She dropped the lipstick she was holding and came out upon the deck.

'Has something – what has happened now?'

'It is as you guess, Mademoiselle; something has happened.'

'What?' Rosalie came out too.

'Another death,' said Poirot.

Rosalie caught her breath sharply. Poirot was watching her narrowly. He saw alarm and something more – consternation – show for a minute or two in her eyes.

'Madame Doyle's maid has been killed,' he told them bluntly.

'Killed?' cried Jacqueline. '*Killed*, do you say?'

'Yes, that is what I said.' Though his answer was nominally to her, it was Rosalie whom he watched. It was Rosalie to whom he spoke as he went on: 'You see, this maid she saw something she was not intended to see. And so – she was silenced, in case she should not hold her tongue.'

'What was it she saw?'

Again it was Jacqueline who asked, and again Poirot's answer was to Rosalie. It was an odd little three-cornered scene.

'There is, I think, very little doubt what it was she saw,' said

361

Poirot. 'She saw someone enter and leave Linnet Doyle's cabin on that fatal night.'

His ears were quick. He heard the sharp intake of breath and saw the eyelids flicker. Rosalie Otterbourne had reacted just as he intended she should.

'Did she say who it was she saw?' Rosalie asked.

Gently – regretfully – Poirot shook his head.

Footsteps pattered up the deck. It was Cornelia Robson, her eyes wide and startled.

'Oh, Jacqueline,' she cried, 'something awful has happened! Another dreadful thing!'

Jacqueline turned to her. The two moved a few steps forward. Almost unconsciously Poirot and Rosalie Otterbourne moved in the other direction.

Rosalie said sharply: 'Why do you look at me? What have you got in your mind?'

'That is two questions you ask me. I will ask you only one in return. Why do you not tell me all the truth, Mademoiselle?'

'I don't know what you mean. I told you – everything – this morning.'

'No, there were things you did not tell me. You did not tell me that you carry about in your handbag a small-calibre pistol with a pearl handle. You did not tell me all that you saw last night.'

She flushed. Then she said sharply: 'It's quite untrue. I haven't got a revolver.'

'I did not say a revolver. I said a small pistol that you carry about in your handbag.'

She wheeled round, darted into her cabin and out again and thrust her grey leather handbag into his hands.

'You're talking nonsense. Look for yourself if you like.'

Poirot opened the bag. There was no pistol inside.

He handed the bag back to her, meeting her scornful triumphant glance.

'No,' he said pleasantly. 'It is not there.'

'You see. You're not always right, Monsieur Poirot. And you're wrong about that other ridiculous thing you said.'

'No, I do not think so.'

'You're infuriating!' She stamped an angry foot. 'You get an idea into your head, and you go on and on and on about it.'

'Because I want you to tell me the truth.'

'What is the truth? You seem to know it better than I do.'

Poirot said: 'You want me to tell what it was you saw? If I am right, will you admit that I am right? I will tell you my little idea. I think that when you came round the stern of the boat you stopped involuntarily because you saw a man come out of a cabin about half-way down the deck – Linnet Doyle's cabin, as you realized next day. You saw him come out, close the door behind him, and walk away from you down the deck and – perhaps – enter one of the two end cabins. Now, then, am I right, Mademoiselle?'

She did not answer.

Poirot said: 'Perhaps you think it is wiser not to speak. Perhaps you are afraid that, if you do, you too will be killed.'

For a moment he thought she had risen to the easy bait, that the accusation against her courage would succeed where more subtle arguments would have failed.

Her lips opened – trembled – then, 'I saw no one,' said Rosalie Otterbourne.

CHAPTER 24

Miss Bowers came out of Dr Bessner's cabin, smoothing her cuffs over her wrists.

Jacqueline left Cornelia abruptly and accosted the hospital nurse.

'How is he?' she demanded.

Poirot came up in time to hear the answer. Miss Bowers was looking rather worried.

'Things aren't going too badly,' she said.

Jacqueline cried: 'You mean, he's worse?'

'Well, I must say I shall be relieved when we get in and can get a proper X-ray done and the whole thing cleaned up under an anaesthetic. When do you think we shall get to Shellal, Monsieur Poirot?'

'Tomorrow morning.'

Miss Bowers pursed her lips and shook her head.

'It's very fortunate. We are doing all we can, but there's always such a danger of septicæmia.'

Jacqueline caught Miss Bowers' arm and shook it.

'Is he going to die? Is he going to die?'

'Dear me, no, Miss de Bellefort. That is, I hope not, I'm sure. The wound in itself isn't dangerous, but there's no doubt it ought to be X-rayed as soon as possible. And then, of course poor Mr Doyle ought to have been kept absolutely quiet today. He's had far too much worry and excitement. No wonder his temperature is rising. What with the shock of his wife's death, and one thing and another –'

Jacqueline relinquished her grasp of the nurse's arm and turned away. She stood leaning over the side, her back to the other two.

'What I say is, we've got to hope for the best always,' said Miss Bowers. 'Of course Mr Doyle has a very strong constitution – one can see that – probably never had a day's illness in his life. So that's in his favour. But there's no denying that this rise in temperature is a nasty sign and –'

She shook her head, adjusted her cuffs once more, and moved briskly away.

Jacqueline turned and walked gropingly, blinded by tears, towards her cabin. A hand below her elbow steadied and guided her. She looked up through the tears to find Poirot by her side. She leaned on him a little and he guided her through the cabin door.

She sank down on the bed and the tears came more freely, punctuated by great shuddering sobs.

'He'll die! He'll die! I know he'll die . . . And I shall have killed him. Yes, I shall have killed him . . .'

Poirot shrugged his shoulders. He shook his head a little, sadly. 'Mademoiselle, what is done is done. One cannot take back the accomplished action. It is too late to regret.'

She cried out more vehemently: 'I shall have killed him! And I love him so . . . I love him so.'

Poirot sighed. 'Too much . . .'

It had been his thought long ago in the restaurant of M. Blondin. It was his thought again now.

He said, hesitating a little: 'Do not, at all events, go by what Miss Bowers says. Hospital nurses, me, I find them always gloomy! The night nurse, always, she is astonished to find her patient alive in the evening; the day nurse, always, she is surprised to find him alive in the morning! They know too much, you see, of the possibilities that may arise. When one is motoring one might easily say to oneself: "If a car came out from that cross-road – or if that lorry backed suddenly – or if the wheel came off the car that is approaching – or if a dog jumped off the hedge on to my driving arm – *eh bien*, I should probably be killed!" But one assumes, and usually rightly, that none of these things *will* happen, and that one will get to one's journey's end. But if, of course, one has been in an accident, or seen one or more accidents, then one is inclined to take the opposite point of view.'

Jacqueline asked, half smiling through her tears: 'Are you trying to console me, Monsieur Poirot?'

'The *bon Dieu* knows what I am trying to do! You should not have come on this journey.'

'No – I wish I hadn't. It's been – so awful. But – it will be soon over now.'

'*Mais oui – mais oui.*'

'And Simon will go to the hospital, and they'll give the proper treatment and everything will be all right.'

'You speak like the child! "And they lived happily ever afterward." That is it, is it not?'

She flushed suddenly scarlet.

'Monsieur Poirot, I never meant – never –'

'It is too soon to think of such a thing! That is the proper hypocritical thing to say, is it not? But you are partly a Latin, Mademoiselle Jacqueline. You should be able to admit facts even if they do not sound very decorous. *Le roi est mort – vive le roi!* The sun has gone and the moon rises. That is so, is it not?'

'You don't understand. He's just sorry for me – awfully sorry for me, because he knows how terrible it is for me to know I've hurt him so badly.'

'Ah, well,' said Poirot. 'The pure pity, it is a very lofty sentiment.'

He looked at her half mockingly, half with some other emotion.

He murmured softly under his breath words in French:

'La vie est vaine.
Un peu d'amour,
Un peu de haine,
Et puis bonjour.

La vie est brève.
Un peu d'espoir,
Un peu de rêve,
Et puis bonsoir.'

He went out again on to the deck. Colonel Race was striding along the deck and hailed him at once.

'Poirot. Good man! I want you. I've got an idea.'

Thrusting his arm through Poirot's he walked him up the deck.

'Just a chance remark of Doyle's. I hardly noticed it at the time. Something about a telegram.'

'*Tiens – c'est vrai.'*

'Nothing in it, perhaps, but one can't leave any avenue unexplored. Damn it all, man, two murders, and we're still in the dark.'

Poirot shook his head. 'No, not in the dark. In the light.'

Race looked at him curiously. 'You have an idea?'

'It is more than an idea now. *I am sure.'*

'Since – when?'

'Since the death of the maid, Louise Bourget.'

'Damned if I see it!'

'My friend, it is so clear – so clear. Only there are difficulties – embarrassments – impediments! See you, around a person like Linnet Doyle there is so much – so many conflicting hates and jealousies and envies and meannesses. It is like a cloud of flies, buzzing, buzzing . . .'

'But you think you know?' The other looked at him curiously. 'You wouldn't say so unless you were sure. Can't say I've any real light, myself. I've suspicions, of course . . .'

Poirot stopped. He laid an impressive hand on Race's arm.

'You are a great man, *mon Colonel* . . . You do not say: "Tell me. What is it that you think?" You know that if I could speak now I would. But there is much to be cleared away first. But think, think for a moment along the lines that I shall indicate. There are certain points . . . There is the statement of Mademoiselle de Bellefort that someone overheard our conversation that night in the garden at Assuan. There is the statement of Monsieur Tim Allerton as to what he heard and did on the night of the crime. There are Louise Bourget's significant answers to our questions this morning. There is the fact that Madame Allerton drinks water, that her son drinks whisky and soda and that I drink wine. Add to that the fact of two bottles of nail polish and the proverb I quoted. And finally we come to the crux of the whole business, the fact that the pistol was wrapped up in a cheap handkerchief and a velvet stole and thrown overboard . . .'

Race was silent a minute or two, then he shook his head.

'No,' he said. 'I don't see it. Mind, I've got a faint idea what you're driving at, but as far as I can see, it doesn't work.'

'But yes . . . but yes. You are seeing only half the truth. And remember this – we must start again from the beginning, since our first conception was entirely wrong.'

Race made a slight grimace.

'I'm used to that. It often seems to me that's all detective work is, wiping out your false starts and beginning again.'

'Yes, it is very true, that. And it is just what some people will not do. They conceive a certain theory, and everything has to fit into that theory. If one little fact will not fit it, they throw it aside. But it is always the facts that will not fit in that are significant. All along I have realized the significance of that pistol being removed from the scene of the crime. I knew that it meant something, but what that something was I only realized one little half hour ago.'

'And I still don't see it!'

'But you will! Only reflect along the lines I indicated. And now let us clear up this matter of a telegram. That is, if the Herr Doktor will admit us.'

Dr Bessner was still in a very bad humour. In answer to their knock he disclosed a scowling face.

'What is it? Once more you wish to see my patient? But I tell you it is not wise. He has fever. He has had more than enough excitement today.'

'Just one question,' said Race. 'Nothing more, I assure you.'

With an unwilling grunt the doctor moved aside and the two men entered the cabin. Dr Bessner, growling to himself, pushed past them.

'I return in three minutes,' he said. 'And then – positively – you go!'

They heard him stumping down the deck.

Simon Doyle looked from one to the other of them inquiringly.

'Yes,' he said, 'what is it?'

'A very little thing,' Race replied. 'Just now, when the stewards were reporting to me, they mentioned that Signor Richetti had been particularly troublesome. You said that that didn't surprise you, as you knew he had a bad temper, and that he had been rude to your wife over some matter of a telegram. Now can you tell me about the incident?'

'Easily. It was at Wadi Halfa. We'd just come back from the Second Cataract. Linnet thought she saw a telegram for her sticking up on the board. She'd forgotten, you see, that she wasn't called Ridgeway any longer, and Richetti and Ridgeway do look rather alike when written in an atrocious handwriting. So she tore it open, couldn't make head or tail of it, and was puzzling over it when this fellow Richetti came along, fairly tore it out of her hand and gibbered with rage. She went after him to apologize and he was frightfully rude to her about it.'

Race drew a deep breath. 'And do you know at all, Mr Doyle, what was in that telegram?'

'Yes. Linnet read part of it out aloud. It said –'

He paused. There was a commotion outside. A high-pitched voice was rapidly approaching.

'Where are Monsieur Poirot and Colonel Race? I must see them *immediately*! It is most important. I have vital information. I – Are they with Mr Doyle?'

Bessner had not closed the door. Only the curtain hung across the open doorway. Mrs Otterbourne swept it to one side and entered like a tornado. Her face was suffused with colour, her gait slightly unsteady, her command of words not quite under her control.

'Mr Doyle,' she said dramatically, 'I know who killed your wife!'

'What?'

Simon stared at her. So did the other two.

Mrs Otterbourne swept all three of them with a triumphant glance. She was happy – superbly happy.

'Yes,' she said. 'My theories are completely vindicated. The deep, primeval, primordial urges – it may appear impossible – fantastic – but it is the truth!'

Race said sharply: 'Do I understand that you have evidence in your possession to show who killed Mrs Doyle?'

Mrs Otterbourne sat down in a chair and leaned forward, nodding her head vigorously.

'Certainly I have. You will agree, will you not, that whoever killed Louise Bourget also killed Linnet Doyle – that the two crimes were committed by one and the same hand?'

'Yes, yes,' said Simon impatiently. 'Of course. That stands to reason. Go on.'

'Then my assertion holds. I know who killed Louise Bourget; therefore I know who killed Linnet Doyle.'

'You mean, you have a theory as to who killed Louise Bourget,' suggested Race sceptically.

Mrs Otterbourne turned on him like a tiger.

'No, I have exact knowledge. I *saw* the person with my own eyes.'

Simon, fevered, shouted out: 'For God's sake, start at the beginning. You know the person who killed Louise Bourget, you say.'

Mrs Otterbourne nodded.

'I will tell you exactly what occurred.'

Yes, she was very happy – no doubt of it! This was her moment, her triumph! What of it if her books were failing to sell, if the stupid public that once had bought them and devoured them voraciously now turned to newer favourites? Salome Otterbourne would once again be notorious. Her name would be in all the papers. She would be principal witness for the prosecution at the trial.

She took a deep breath and opened her mouth.

'It was when I went down to lunch. I hardly felt like eating – all the horror of the recent tragedy – Well, I needn't go into that. Half-way down I remembered that I had – er – left something in my cabin. I told Rosalie to go on without me. She did.'

Mrs Otterbourne paused a minute.

The curtain across the door moved slightly as though lifted by the wind, but none of the three men noticed it.

'I – er –' Mrs Otterbourne paused. Thin ice to skate over here, but it must be done somehow. 'I – er – had an arrange-ment with one of the – er – *personnel* of the ship. He was to – er – get me something I needed, but I did not wish my daughter to know of it. She is inclined to be tiresome in certain ways –'

Not too good, this, but she could think of something that sounded better before it came to telling the story in court.

Race's eyebrows lifted as his eyes asked a question of Poirot.

Poirot gave an infinitesimal nod. His lips formed the word: 'Drink.'

The curtain across the door moved again. Between it and the door itself something showed with a faint steel-blue gleam.

Mrs Otterbourne continued: 'The arrangement was that I should go round to the stern on the deck below this, and there I should find the man waiting for me. As I went along the deck a cabin door opened and somebody looked out. It was this girl – Louise Bourget, or whatever her name is. She seemed to be expecting someone. When she saw it was me, she looked disappointed and went abruptly inside again. I didn't think anything of it, of course. I went along just as I had said I would and got the – the stuff from the man. I paid him and – er – just had a word with him. Then I started back. Just as I came around the corner I saw someone knock on the maid's door and go into the cabin.'

Race said, 'And that person was –?'

Bang!

The noise of the explosion filled the cabin. There was an acrid sour smell of smoke. Mrs Otterbourne turned slowly sideways, as though in supreme inquiry, then her body slumped forward and she fell to the ground with a crash. From just behind her ear the blood flowed from a round neat hole.

There was a moment's stupefied silence. Then both the able-bodied men jumped to their feet. The woman's body hindered their movements a little. Race bent over her while Poirot made a catlike jump for the door and the deck.

The deck was empty. On the ground just in front of the sill lay a big Colt revolver.

Poirot glanced in both directions. The deck was empty. He then sprinted towards the stern. As he rounded the corner he ran into Tim Allerton, who was coming full tilt from the opposite direction.

'What the devil was that?' cried Tim breathlessly.

Poirot said sharply: 'Did you meet anyone on your way here?'

'Meet anyone? No.'

'Then come with me.' He took the young man by the arm and retraced his steps. A little crowd had assembled by now. Rosalie,

Jacqueline, and Cornelia had rushed out of their cabins. More people were coming along the deck from the saloon – Ferguson, Jim Fanthorp, and Mrs Allerton.

Race stood by the revolver. Poirot turned his head and said sharply to Tim Allerton: 'Got any gloves in your pocket?'

Tim fumbled.

'Yes, I have.'

Poirot seized them from him, put them on, and bent to examine the revolver. Race did the same. The others watched breathlessly.

Race said: 'He didn't go the other way. Fanthorp and Ferguson were sitting on this deck lounge; they'd have seen him.'

Poirot responded, 'And Mr Allerton would have met him if he'd gone aft.'

Race said, pointing to the revolver: 'Rather fancy we've seen this not so very long ago. Must make sure, though.'

He knocked on the door of Pennington's cabin. There was no answer. The cabin was empty. Race strode to the right-hand drawer of the chest and jerked it open. The revolver was gone.

'Settles that,' said Race. 'Now then, where's Pennington himself?'

They went out again on deck. Mrs Allerton had joined the group. Poirot moved swiftly over to her.

'Madame, take Miss Otterbourne with you and look after her. Her mother has been' – he consulted Race with an eye and Race nodded – 'killed.'

Dr Bessner came bustling along.

'*Gott im Himmel!* What is there now?'

They made way for him. Race indicated the cabin. Ressner went inside.

'Find Pennington,' said Race. 'Any fingerprints on that revolver?'

'None,' said Poirot.

They found Pennington on the deck below. He was sitting in the little drawing-room writing letters. He lifted a handsome, clean-shaven face.

'Anything new?' he asked.

'Didn't you hear a shot?'

'Why – now you mention it – I believe I did hear a kind of a bang. But I never dreamed – Who's been shot?'

'Mrs Otterbourne.'

'*Mrs Otterbourne?*' Pennington sounded quite astounded. 'Well, you do surprise me. Mrs Otterbourne.' He shook his head. 'I can't see that at all.' He lowered his voice. 'Strikes me, gentlemen, we've got a homicidal maniac aboard. We ought to organize a defence system.'

'Mr Pennington,' said Race, 'how long have you been in this room?'

'Why, let me see.' Mr Pennington gently rubbed his chin. 'I should say a matter of twenty minutes or so.'

'And you haven't left it?'

'Why no – certainly not.'

He looked inquiringly at the two men.

'You see, Mr Pennington,' said Race, 'Mrs Otterbourne was shot with your revolver.'

CHAPTER 25

Mr Pennington was shocked. Mr Pennington could hardly believe it.

'Why, gentlemen,' he said, 'this is a very serious matter. Very serious indeed.'

'Extremely serious for you, Mr Pennington.'

'For me?' Pennington's eyebrows rose in startled surprise. 'But, my dear sir, I was sitting quietly writing in here when that shot was fired.'

'You have, perhaps, a witness to prove that?'

Pennington shook his head.

'Why, no – I wouldn't say that. But it's clearly impossible that I should have gone to the deck above, shot this poor woman (and why should I shoot her anyway?) and come down again with no one seeing me. There are always plenty of people on the deck lounge this time of day.'

'How do you account for your pistol being used?'

'Well – I'm afraid I may be to blame there. Quite soon after getting aboard there was a conversation in the saloon one evening, I remember, about firearms, and I mentioned then that I always carried a revolver with me when I travel.'

'Who was there?'

'Well, I can't remember exactly. Most people, I think. Quite a crowd, anyway.'

He shook his head gently.

'Why, yes,' he said. 'I am certainly to blame there.'

He went on: 'First Linnet, then Linnet's maid, and now Mrs Otterbourne. There seems no reason in it all!'

'There *was* reason,' said Race.

'There was?'

'Yes. Mrs Otterbourne was on the point of telling us that she had seen a certain person go into Louise's cabin. Before she could name that person she was shot dead.'

Andrew Pennington passed a fine silk handkerchief over his brow.

'All this is terrible,' he murmured.

Poirot said: 'Monsieur Pennington, I would like to discuss certain aspects of the case with you. Will you come to my cabin in half an hour's time?'

'I should be delighted.'

Pennington did not sound delighted. He did not look delighted either. Race and Poirot exchanged glances and then abruptly left the room.

'Cunning old devil,' said Race, 'but he's afraid. Eh?'

Poirot nodded. 'Yes, he is not happy, our Monsieur Pennington.'

As they reached the promenade deck again, Mrs Allerton came out of her cabin and, seeing Poirot, beckoned him imperiously.

'Madame?'

'That poor child! Tell me, Monsieur Poirot, is there a double cabin somewhere that I could share with her? She oughtn't to go back to the one she shared with her mother, and mine is only a single one.'

'That can be arranged, Madame. It is very good of you.'

'It's mere decency. Besides, I'm very fond of the girl. I've always liked her.'

'Is she very upset?'

'Terribly. She seems to have been absolutely devoted to that odious woman. That is what is so pathetic about it all. Tim says he believes she drank. Is that true?'

Poirot nodded.

'Oh, well, poor woman, one must not judge her, I suppose; but that girl must have had a terrible life.'

'She did, Madame. She is very proud and she was very loyal.'

'Yes, I like that – loyalty, I mean. It's out of fashion nowadays. She's an odd character, that girl – proud, reserved, stubborn, and terribly warm-hearted underneath, I fancy.'

'I see that I have given her into good hands, Madame.'

'Yes, don't worry. I'll look after her. She's inclined to cling to me in the most pathetic fashion.'

Mrs Allerton went back into the cabin. Poirot returned to the scene of the tragedy.

Cornelia was still standing on the deck, her eyes wide. She said: 'I don't understand, Monsieur Poirot. How did the person who shot her get away without our seeing him?'

'Yes, how?' echoed Jacqueline.

'Ah,' said Poirot, 'it was not quite such a disappearing trick as you think, Mademoiselle. There were three distinct ways the murderer might have gone.'

Jacqueline looked puzzled. She said, 'Three?'

'He might have gone to the right, or he might have gone to the left, but I don't see any other way,' puzzled Cornelia.

Jacqueline too frowned. Then her brow cleared.

She said: 'Of course. He could move in two directions on one plane, but he could go at right angles to that plane too. That is, he couldn't go *up* very well, but he could go *down*.'

Poirot smiled. 'You have brains, Mademoiselle.'

Cornelia said: 'I know I'm just a plain mutt, but I still don't see.'

Jacqueline said: 'Monsieur Poirot means, darling, that he could swing himself over the rail and down on to the deck below.'

'My!' gasped Cornelia. 'I never thought of that. He'd have to be mighty quick about it, though. I suppose he could just do it?'

'He could do it easily enough,' said Tim Allerton. 'Remember, there's always a minute of shock after a thing like this. One hears a shot and one's too paralysed to move for a second or two.'

'That was your experience, Monsieur Allerton?'

'Yes, it was. I just stood like a dummy for quite five seconds. Then I fairly sprinted round the deck.'

Race came out of Bessner's cabin and said authoritatively: 'Would you mind all clearing off? We want to bring out the body.'

Everyone moved away obediently. Poirot went with them. Cornelia said to him with sad earnestness: 'I'll never forget this trip as long as I live. Three deaths . . . It's just like living in a nightmare.'

Ferguson overheard her. He said aggressively: 'That's because you're over-civilized. You should look on death as the Oriental does. It's a mere incident – hardly noticeable.'

'That's all very well,' Cornelia said. 'They're not educated, poor creatures.'

'No, and a good thing too. Education has devitalized the white races. Look at America – goes in for an orgy of culture. Simply disgusting.'

'I think you're talking nonsense,' said Cornelia, flushing. 'I attend lectures every winter on Greek Art and the Renaissance, and I went to some on famous Women of History.'

Mr Ferguson groaned in agony: 'Greek Art; Renaissance! Famous Women of History! It makes me quite sick to hear you. It's the *future* that matters, woman, not the past. Three women are dead on this boat. Well, what of it? They're no loss! Linnet Doyle and her money! The French maid – a domestic parasite. Mrs Otterbourne – a useless fool of a woman. Do you think anyone really cares whether they're dead or not? *I* don't. I think it's a damned good thing!'

'Then you're wrong!' Cornelia blazed out at him. 'And it makes me sick to hear you talk and talk, as though nobody mattered but *you*. I didn't like Mrs Otterbourne much, but her daughter was ever so fond of her, and she's all broken up over her mother's death. I don't know much about the French maid, but I expect somebody was fond of her somewhere; and as for Linnet Doyle – well, apart from everything else, she was just lovely! She was so beautiful when she came into a room that it made a lump come in your throat. I'm homely myself, and that makes me appreciate beauty a lot more. She was as beautiful – just as a woman – as anything in Greek Art. And when anything beautiful's dead, it's a loss to the world. So there!'

Mr Ferguson stepped back a pace. He caught hold of his hair with both hands and tugged at it vehemently.

'I give it up,' he said. 'You're unbelievable. Just haven't got a bit of natural female spite in you anywhere.' He turned to Poirot. 'Do you know, sir, that Cornelia's father was practically ruined by Linnet Ridgeway's old man? But does the girl gnash her teeth when she sees the heiress sailing about in pearls and Paris models? No, she just bleats out: "Isn't she beautiful?" like a blessed Baa Lamb. I don't believe she even felt sore at her.'

Cornelia flushed. 'I did – just for a minute. Poppa kind of died of discouragement, you know, because he hadn't made good.'

'Felt sore for a minute! I ask you.'

Cornelia flashed round on him.

'Well, didn't you say just now it was the future that mattered, not the past? All that was in the past, wasn't it? It's over.'

'Got me there,' said Ferguson. 'Cornelia Robson, you're the only nice woman I've ever come across. Will you marry me?'

'Don't be absurd.'

'It's a genuine proposal – even if it is made in the presence of Old Man Sleuth. Anyway, you're a witness, Monsieur Poirot. I've deliberately offered marriage to this female – against all my principles, because I don't believe in legal contracts between the sexes; but I don't think she'd stand for anything else, so marriage it shall be. Come on, Cornelia, say yes.'

'I think you're utterly ridiculous,' said Cornelia, flushing.

'Why won't you marry me?'

'You're not serious,' said Cornelia.

'Do you mean not serious in proposing or do you mean not serious in character?'

'Both, but I really meant character. You laugh at all sorts of serious things. Education and Culture – and – and Death. You wouldn't be *reliable*.'

She broke off, flushed again, and hurried along into her cabin.

Ferguson stared after her. 'Damn the girl! I believe she really means it. She wants a man to be reliable. *Reliable* – ye gods!' He paused and then said curiously: 'What's the matter with you, Monsieur Poirot? You seem very deep in thought.'

Poirot roused himself with a start.

'I reflect, that is all. I reflect.'

'Meditation on Death. Death, the Recurring Decimal, by Hercule Poirot. One of his well-known monographs.'

'Monsieur Ferguson,' said Poirot, 'you are a very impertinent young man.'

'You must excuse me. I like attacking established institutions.'

'And I am an established institution?'

'Precisely. What do you think of that girl?'

'Of Miss Robson?'

'Yes.'

'I think that she has a great deal of character.'

'You're right. She's got spirit. She looks meek, but she isn't. She's got guts. She's – oh, damn it, I want that girl. It mightn't be a bad move if I tackled the old lady. If I could once get her thoroughly against me, it might cut some ice with Cornelia.'

He wheeled and went into the observation saloon. Miss Van Schuyler was seated in her usual corner. She looked even more arrogant than usual. She was knitting. Ferguson strode up to her. Hercule Poirot, entering unobtrusively, took a seat a discreet distance away and appeared to be absorbed in a magazine.

'Good afternoon, Miss Van Schuyler.'

Miss Van Schuyler raised her eyes for a bare second, dropped them again and murmured frigidly, 'Er – good afternoon.'

'Look here, Miss Van Schuyler, I want to talk to you about something pretty important. It's just this. I want to marry your cousin.'

Miss Van Schuyler's ball of wool dropped on to the ground and ran wildly across the saloon.

She said in a venomous tone: 'You must be out of your senses, young man.'

'Not at all. I'm determined to marry her. I've asked her to marry me!'

Miss Van Schuyler surveyed him coldly, with the kind of speculative interest she might have accorded to an odd sort of beetle.

'Indeed? And I presume she sent you about your business.'

'She refused me.'

'Naturally.'

'Not "naturally" at all. I'm going to go on asking her till she agrees.'

'I can assure you, sir, that I shall take steps to see that my young cousin is not subjected to any such persecution,' said Miss Van Schuyler in a biting tone.

'What have you got against me?'

Miss Van Schuyler merely raised her eyebrows and gave a vehement tug to her wool, preparatory to regaining it and closing the interview.

'Come now,' persisted Mr Ferguson, 'what have you got against me?'

'I should think that was quite obvious, Mr – er – I don't know your name.'

'Ferguson.'

'Mr Ferguson.' Miss Van Schuyler uttered the name with definite distaste. 'Any such idea is quite out of the question.'

'You mean,' said Ferguson, 'that I'm not good enough for her?'

'I should think that would have been obvious to you.'

'In what way am I not good enough?'

Miss Van Schuyler again did not answer.

'I've got two legs, two arms, good health, and quite reasonable brains. What's wrong with that?'

'There is such a thing as social position, Mr Ferguson.'

'Social position is bunk!'

The door swung open and Cornelia came in. She stopped dead on seeing her redoubtable Cousin Marie in conversation with her would-be suitor.

The outrageous Mr Ferguson turned his head, grinned broadly and called out: 'Come along, Cornelia. I'm asking for your hand in marriage in the best conventional manner.'

'Cornelia,' said Miss Van Schuyler, and her voice was truly awful in quality, '*have you encouraged this young man?*'

'I – no, of course not – at least – not exactly – I mean –'

'What do you mean?'

'She hasn't encouraged me,' said Mr Ferguson helpfully. 'I've done it all. She hasn't actually pushed me in the face, because she's got too kind a heart. Cornelia, your cousin says I'm not good enough for you. That, of course, is true, but not in the way she means it. My moral nature certainly doesn't equal yours, but her point is that I'm hopelessly below you socially.'

'That I think, is equally obvious to Cornelia,' said Miss Van Schuyler.

'Is it?' Mr Ferguson looked at her searchingly. 'Is that why you won't marry me?'

'No, it isn't.' Cornelia flushed. 'If – if I liked you, I'd marry you no matter who you were.'

'But you don't like me?'

'I – I think you're just outrageous. The way you say things . . .

The *things* you say . . . I – I've never met anyone the least like you. I –'

Tears threatened to overcome her. She rushed from the room.

'On the whole,' said Mr Ferguson, 'that's not too bad for a start.' He leaned back in his chair, gazed at the ceiling, whistled, crossed his disreputable knees and remarked: 'I'll be calling you Cousin yet.'

Miss Van Schuyler trembled with rage. 'Leave this room at once, sir, or I'll ring for the steward.'

'I've paid for my ticket,' said Mr Ferguson. 'They can't possibly turn me out of the public lounge. But I'll humour you.' He sang softly, 'Yo ho ho, and a bottle of rum.' Rising, he sauntered nonchalantly to the door and passed out.

Choking with anger Miss Van Schuyler struggled to her feet. Poirot, discreetly emerging from retirement behind his magazine, sprang up and retrieved the ball of wool.

'Thank you, Monsieur Poirot. If you would send Miss Bowers to me – I feel quite upset – that insolent young man.'

'Rather eccentric, I'm afraid,' said Poirot. 'Most of that family are. Spoilt, of course. Always inclined to tilt at windmills.' He added carelessly, 'You recognized him, I suppose?'

'Recognized him?'

'Calls himself Ferguson and won't use his title because of his advanced ideas.'

'His *title*?' Miss Van Schuyler's tone was sharp.

'Yes, that's young Lord Dawlish. Rolling in money, of course, but he became a communist when he was at Oxford.'

Miss Van Schuyler, her face a battleground of contradictory emotions, said: 'How long have you known this, Monsieur Poirot?'

Poirot shrugged his shoulders.

'There was a picture in one of these papers – I noticed the resemblance. Then I found a signet ring with a coat of arms on it. Oh, there's no doubt about it, I assure you.'

He quite enjoyed reading the conflicting expressions that succeeded each other on Miss Van Schuyler's face. Finally, with a gracious inclination of the head, she said, 'I am very much obliged to you, Monsieur Poirot.'

Poirot looked after her and smiled as she went out of the saloon. Then he sat down and his face grew grave once more. He was following out a train of thought in his mind. From time to time he nodded his head.

'*Mais oui*,' he said at last. 'It all fits in.'

Race found him still sitting there.

'Well, Poirot, what about it? Pennington's due in ten minutes. I'm leaving this in your hands.'

Poirot rose quickly to his feet. 'First, get hold of young Fanthorp.'

'Fanthorp?' Race looked surprised.

'Yes. Bring him to my cabin.'

Race nodded and went off. Poirot went along to his cabin. Race arrived with young Fanthorp a minute or two afterward.

Poirot indicated chairs and offered cigarettes.

'Now, Monsieur Fanthorp,' he said, 'to our business! I perceive that you wear the same tie that my friend Hastings wears.'

Jim Fanthorp looked down at his neckwear with some bewilderment.

'It's an O.E. tie,' he said.

'Exactly. You must understand that, though I am a foreigner, I know something of the English point of view. I know, for instance, that there are "things which are done" and "things which are not done."'

Jim Fanthorp grinned.

'We don't say that sort of thing much nowadays, sir.'

'Perhaps not, but the custom, it still remains. The Old School Tie is the Old School Tie, and there are certain things (I know this from experience) that the Old School Tie does not do! One of those things, Monsieur Fanthorp, is to butt into a private conversation unasked when one does not know the people who are conducting it.'

Fanthorp stared.

Poirot went on: 'But the other day, Monsieur Fanthorp, that is exactly what you did do. Certain persons were quietly transacting some private business in the observation saloon. You strolled near them, obviously in order to overhear what it was that was in progress, and presently you actually turned round and

380

congratulated a lady – Madame Simon Doyle – on the soundness of her business methods.'

Jim Fanthorp's face got very red. Poirot swept on, not waiting for a comment.

'Now that, Monsieur Fanthorp, was not at all the behaviour of one who wears a tie similar to that worn by my friend Hastings! Hastings is all delicacy, would die of shame before he did such a thing! Therefore, taking that action of yours in conjunction with the fact that you are a very young man to be able to afford an expensive holiday, that you are a member of a country solicitor's firm, and therefore probably not extravagantly well off, and that you show no signs of recent illness such as might necessitate a prolonged visit abroad, I ask myself – and am now asking you – what is the reason for your presence on this boat?'

Jim Fanthorp jerked his head back.

'I decline to give you any information whatever, Monsieur Poirot. I really think you must be mad.'

'I am not mad. I am very, very sane. Where is your firm? In Northampton; that is not very far from Wode Hall. What conversation did you try to overhear? One concerning legal documents. What was the object of your remark – a remark which you uttered with obvious embarrassment and *malaise*? Your object was to prevent Madame Doyle from signing any document unread.'

He paused.

'On this boat we have had a murder, and following that murder two other murders in rapid succession. If I further give you the information that the weapon which killed Madame Otterbourne was a revolver owned by Monsieur Andrew Pennington, then perhaps you will realize that it is actually your duty to tell us all you can.'

Jim Fanthorp was silent for some minutes. At last he said: 'You have rather an odd way of going about things, Monsieur Poirot, but I appreciate the points you have made. The trouble is that I have no exact information to lay before you.'

'You mean that it is a case, merely, of suspicion.'

'Yes.'

'And therefore you think it injudicious to speak? That may be true, legally speaking. But this is not a court of law. Colonel Race and myself are endeavouring to track down a murderer. Anything that can help us to do so may be valuable.'

Again Jim Fanthorp reflected. Then he said: 'Very well. What is it you want to know?'

'Why did you come on this trip?'

'My uncle, Mr Carmichael, Mrs Doyle's English solicitor, sent me. He handled a good many of her affairs. In this way, he was often in correspondence with Mr Andrew Pennington, who was Mrs Doyle's American trustee. Several small incidents (I cannot enumerate them all) made my uncle suspicious that all was not quite as it should be.'

'In plain language,' said Race, 'your uncle suspected that Pennington was a crook?'

Jim Fanthorp nodded, a faint smile on his face.

'You put it rather more bluntly than I should, but the main idea is correct. Various excuses made by Pennington, certain plausible explanations of the disposal of funds, aroused my uncle's distrust.

'While these suspicions of his were still nebulous, Miss Ridgeway married unexpectedly and went off on her honeymoon to Egypt. Her marriage relieved my uncle's mind, as he knew that on her return to England the estate would have to be formally settled and handed over.

'However, in a letter she wrote him from Cairo, she mentioned casually that she had unexpectedly run across Andrew Pennington. My uncle's suspicions became acute. He felt sure that Pennington, perhaps by now in a desperate position, was going to try and obtain signatures from her which would cover his own defalcations. Since my uncle had no definite evidence to lay before her, he was in a most difficult position. The only thing he could think of was to send me out here, travelling by air, with instruction to discover what was in the wind. I was to keep my eyes open and act summarily if necessary – a most unpleasant mission, I can assure you. As a matter of fact, on the occasion you mention I had to behave more or less as a cad! It was awkward, but on the whole I was satisfied with the result.'

'You mean you put Madame Doyle on her guard?' asked Race.

'Not so much that, but I think I put the wind up Pennington. I felt convinced he wouldn't try any more funny business for some time, and by then I hoped to have got intimate enough with Mr and Mrs Doyle to convey some kind of a warning. As a matter of fact I hoped to do so through Doyle. Mrs Doyle was so attached to Mr Pennington that it would have been a bit awkward to suggest things to her about him. It would have been easier for me to approach the husband.'

Race nodded.

Poirot asked: 'Will you give me a candid opinion on one point, Monsieur Fanthorp? If you were engaged in putting a swindle over, would you choose Madame Doyle or Monsieur Doyle as a victim?'

Fanthorp smiled faintly.

'Mr Doyle, every time. Linnet Doyle was very shrewd in business matters. Her husband, I should fancy, is one of those trustful fellows who know nothing of business and are always ready to "sign on the dotted line" as he himself put it.'

'I agree,' said Poirot. He looked at Race. 'And there's your motive.'

Jim Fanthorp said: 'But this is all pure conjecture. It isn't *evidence.*'

Poirot replied, easily: '*Ah, bah!* we will get evidence!'

'How?'

'Possibly from Mr Pennington himself.'

Fanthorp looked doubtful.

'I wonder. I very much wonder.'

Race glanced at his watch. 'He's about due now.'

Jim Fanthorp was quick to take the hint. He left them.

Two minutes later Andrew Pennington made his appearance. His manner was all smiling urbanity. Only the taut line of his jaw and the wariness of his eyes betrayed the fact that a thoroughly experienced fighter was on his guard.

'Well, gentlemen,' he said, 'here I am.'

He sat down and looked at them inquiringly.

'We asked you to come here, Monsieur Pennington,' began Poirot, 'because it is fairly obvious that you have a very special and immediate interest in the case.'

Pennington raised his eyebrows slightly.

'Is that so?'

Poirot said gently: 'Surely. You have known Linnet Ridgeway, I understand, since she was quite a child.'

'Oh! that –' His face altered, became less alert. 'I beg pardon,

I didn't quite get you. Yes, as I told you this morning, I've known Linnet since she was a cute little thing in pinafores.'

'You were on terms of close intimacy with her father?'

'That's so. Melhuish Ridgeway and I were very close – very close.'

'You were so intimately associated that on his death he appointed you business guardian to his daughter and trustee to the vast fortune she inherited?'

'Why, roughly, that is so.' The wariness was back again. The note was more cautious. 'I was not the only trustee, naturally; others were associated with me.'

'Who have since died?'

'Two of them are dead. The other, Mr Sterndale Rockford, is alive.'

'Your partner?'

'Yes.'

'Mademoiselle Ridgeway, I understand, was not yet of age when she married?'

'She would have been twenty-one next July.'

'And in the normal course of events she would have come into control of her fortune then?'

'Yes.'

'But her marriage precipitated matters?'

Pennington's jaw hardened. He shot out his chin at them aggressively.

'You'll pardon me, gentlemen, but what exact business is all this of yours?'

'If you dislike answering the question –'

'There's no dislike about it. I don't mind what you ask me. But I don't see the relevance of all this.'

'Oh, but surely, Monsieur Pennington' – Poirot leaned forward, his eyes green and catlike – 'there is the question of motive. In considering that, financial considerations must always be taken into account.'

Pennington said sullenly: 'By Ridgeway's will, Linnet got control of her dough when she was twenty-one or when she married.'

'No conditions of any kind?'

'No conditions.'

'And it is a matter, I am credibly assured, of millions.'

384

'Millions it is.'

Poirot said softly: 'Your responsibility, Mr Pennington, and that of your partner, has been a very grave one.'

Pennington replied curtly: 'We're used to responsibility. Doesn't worry us any.'

'I wonder.'

Something in his tone flicked the other man on the raw. He asked angrily: 'What the devil do you mean?'

Poirot replied with an air of engaging frankness: 'I was wondering, Mr Pennington, whether Linnet Ridgeway's sudden marriage caused any – consternation, in your office?'

'Consternation?'

'That was the word I used.'

'What the hell are you driving at?'

'Something quite simple. Are Linnet Doyle's affairs in the perfect order they should be?'

Pennington rose to his feet.

'That's enough. I'm through.' He made for the door.

'But you will answer my question first?'

Pennington snapped: 'They're in perfect order.'

'You were not so alarmed when the news of Linnet Ridgeway's marriage reached you that you rushed over to Europe by the first boat and staged an apparently fortuitous meeting in Egypt?'

Pennington came back towards them. He had himself under control once more.

'What you are saying is absolute balderdash! I didn't even know that Linnet was married till I met her in Cairo. I was utterly astonished. Her letter must have missed me by a day in New York. It was forwarded and I got it about a week later.'

'You came over by the *Carmanic*, I think you said.'

'That's right.'

'And the letter reached New York after the *Carmanic* sailed?'

'How many times have I got to repeat it?'

'It is strange,' said Poirot.

'What's strange?'

'That on your luggage there are no labels of the *Carmanic*. The only recent labels of transatlantic sailing are the *Normandie*. The *Normandie*, I remember, sailed two days after the *Carmanic*.'

For a moment the other was at a loss. His eyes wavered.

Colonel Race weighed in with telling effect.

'Come now, Mr Pennington,' he said. 'We've several reasons for believing that you came over on the *Normandie* and not by the *Carmanic*, as you said. In that case, you received Mrs Doyle's letter before you left New York. It's no good denying it, for it's the easiest thing in the world to check up the steamship companies.'

Andrew Pennington felt absent-mindedly for a chair and sat down. His face was impassive – a poker face. Behind that mask his agile brain looked ahead to the next move.

'I'll have to hand it to you, gentlemen. You've been too smart for me. But I had my reasons for acting as I did.'

'No doubt.' Race's tone was curt.

'If I give them to you, it must be understood I do so in confidence.'

'I think you can trust us to behave fittingly. Naturally I cannot give assurances blindly.'

'Well –' Pennington sighed. 'I'll come clean. There was some monkey business going on in England. It worried me. I couldn't do much about it by letter. The only thing was to come over and see for myself.'

'What do you mean by monkey business?'

'I'd good reason to believe that Linnet was being swindled.'

'By whom?'

'Her British lawyer. Now that's not the kind of accusation you can fling around anyhow. I made up my mind to come over right away and see into matters myself.'

'That does great credit to your vigilance, I am sure. But why the little deception about not having received the letter?'

'Well, I ask you –' Pennington spread out his hands. 'You can't butt in on a honeymoon couple without more or less coming down to brass tacks and giving your reasons. I thought it best to make the meeting accidental. Besides, I didn't know anything about the husband. He might have been mixed up in the racket for all I knew.'

'In fact all your actions were actuated by pure disinterestedness,' said Colonel Race dryly.

'You've said it, Colonel.'

There was a pause. Race glanced at Poirot. The little man leant forward.

'Monsieur Pennington, we do not believe a word of your story.'

'The hell you don't! And what the hell do you believe?'

'We believe that Linnet Ridgeway's unexpected marriage put you in a financial quandary. That you came over posthaste to try and find some way out of the mess you were in – that is to say, some way of gaining time. That, with that end in view, you endeavoured to obtain Madame Doyle's signature to certain documents and failed. That on the journey up the Nile, when walking along the cliff top at Abu Simbel, you dislodged a boulder which fell and only very narrowly missed its object –'

'You're crazy.'

'We believe that the same kind of circumstances occurred on the return journey. That is to say, an opportunity presented itself of putting Madame Doyle out of the way at a moment when her death would be almost certainly ascribed to the action of another person. We not only believe, but *know*, that it was your revolver which killed a woman who was about to reveal to us the name of the person who she had reason to believe killed both Linnet Doyle and the maid Louise –'

'Hell!' The forcible ejaculation broke forth and interrupted Poirot's stream of eloquence. 'What are you getting at? Are you crazy? What motive had I to kill Linnet? I wouldn't get her money; that goes to her husband. Why don't you pick on him? *He's* the one to benefit – not me.'

Race said coldly: 'Doyle never left the lounge on the night of the tragedy till he was shot at and wounded in the leg. The impossibility of his walking a step after that is attested to by a doctor and a nurse – both independent and reliable witnesses. Simon Doyle could not have killed his wife. He could not have killed Louise Bourget. He most definitely did not kill Mrs Otterbourne. You know that as well as we do.'

'I know he didn't kill her.' Pennington sounded a little calmer. 'All I say is, why pick on me when I don't benefit by her death?'

'But, my dear sir,' Poirot's voice came soft as a purring cat, 'that is rather a matter of opinion. Madame Doyle was a keen woman of business, fully conversant with her own affairs and very quick to spot any irregularity. As soon as she took up the control of her property, which she would have done on her return to England, her suspicions were bound to be aroused. But now that she is dead and that her husband, as you have just pointed out, inherits, the whole thing is different. Simon Doyle knows nothing whatever of his wife's affairs except that she was a rich woman. He is of a simple, trusting disposition. You will find it easy to place complicated statements before him, to involve the real issue in a net of figures, and to delay settlement with pleas of legal formalities and the recent depression. I think that it makes a very considerable difference to you whether you deal with the husband or the wife.'

Pennington shrugged his shoulders.

'Your ideas are – fantastic.'

'Time will show.'

'What did you say?'

'I said, "Time will show!" This is a matter of three deaths – three murders. The law will demand the most searching investigation into the condition of Madame Doyle's estate.'

He saw the sudden sag in the other's shoulders and knew that he had won. Jim Fanthorp's suspicions were well founded.

Poirot went on: 'You've played – and lost. Useless to go on bluffing.'

'You don't understand,' Pennington muttered. 'It's all square enough really. It's been this damned slump – Wall Street's been crazy. But I'd staged a comeback. With luck everything will be O.K. by the middle of June.'

With shaking hands he took a cigarette, tried to light it, failed.

'I suppose,' mused Poirot, 'that the boulder was a sudden temptation. You thought nobody saw you.'

'That was an accident. I swear it was an accident!' The man leant forward, his face working, his eyes terrified. 'I stumbled and fell against it. I swear it was an accident . . .'

The two men said nothing.

Pennington suddenly pulled himself together. He was still a wreck of a man, but his fighting spirit had returned in a certain measure. He moved towards the door.

'You can't pin that on me, gentlemen. It was an accident. And it wasn't I who shot her. D'you hear? You can't pin that on me either – and you never will.'

He went out.

CHAPTER 27

As the door closed behind him, Race gave a deep sigh.

'We got more than I thought we should. Admission of fraud. Admission of attempted murder. Further than that it's impossible to go. A man will confess, more or less, to attempted murder, but you won't get him to confess to the real thing.'

'Sometimes it can be done,' said Poirot. His eyes were dreamy – catlike.

Race looked at him curiously.

'Got a plan?'

Poirot nodded. Then he said, ticking off the items on his fingers: 'The garden at Assuan. Mr Allerton's statement. The two bottles of nail polish. My bottle of wine. The velvet stole. The stained handkerchief. The pistol that was left on the scene of the crime. The death of Louise. The death of Madame Otterbourne. Yes, it's all there. Pennington didn't do it, Race!'

'What?' Race was startled.

'Pennington didn't do it. He had the motive, yes. He had the *will* to do it, yes. He got as far as *attempting* to do it. *Mais c'est tout.* For this crime, something was wanted that Pennington hadn't got! This is a crime that needed audacity, swift and faultless execution, courage, indifference to danger, and a resourceful, calculating brain. Pennington hasn't got those attributes. He couldn't do a crime unless he knew it to be safe. This crime wasn't safe! It hung on a razor edge. It needed boldness. Pennington isn't bold. He's only astute.'

Race looked at him with the respect one able man gives to another.

'You've got it all well taped,' he said.

'I think so, yes. There are one or two things – that telegram for instance, that Linnet Doyle read. I should like to get that cleared up.'

'By Jove, we forgot to ask Doyle. He was telling us when poor old Ma Otterbourne came along. We'll ask him again.'

'Presently. First, I have someone else to whom I wish to speak.'

'Who's that?'

'Tim Allerton.'

Race raised his eyebrows.

'Allerton? Well, we'll get him here.'

He pressed a bell and sent the steward with a message.

Tim Allerton entered with a questioning look.

'Steward said you wanted to see me?'

'That is right, Monsieur Allerton. Sit down.'

Tim sat. His face was attentive but very slightly bored.

'Anything I can do?' His tone was polite but not enthusiastic.

Poirot said: 'In a sense, perhaps. What I really require is for you to listen.'

Tim's eyebrows rose in polite surprise.

'Certainly. I'm the world's best listener. Can be relied on to say "Ooer!" at the right moments.'

'That is very satisfactory. "Oo-er!" will be very expressive. *Eh bien*, let us commence. When I met you and your mother at Assuan, Monsieur Allerton, I was attracted to your company very strongly. To begin with, I thought your mother was one of the most charming people I had ever met –'

The weary face flickered for a moment; a shade of expression came into it.

'She is – unique,' he said.

'But the second thing that interested me was your mention of a certain lady.'

'Really?'

'Yes, a Mademoiselle Joanna Southwood. You see, I had recently been hearing that name.'

He paused and went on: 'For the last three years there have been certain jewel robberies that have been worrying Scotland Yard a good deal. They are what may be described as Society robberies. The method is usually the same – the substitution of an imitation piece of jewellery for an original. My friend, Chief Inspector Japp, came to the conclusion that the robberies were not the work of one person, but of two people working in with each other very cleverly. He was convinced, from the considerable inside knowledge displayed, that the robberies were the work of people in a good social position. And finally his attention became riveted on Mademoiselle Joanna Southwood.

'Every one of the victims had been either a friend or acquaintance of hers, and in each case she had either handled or been lent the piece of jewellery in question. Also, her style of living was far in excess of her income. On the other hand it was quite clear that the actual robbery – that is to say the substitution – had *not* been accomplished by her. In some cases she had been out of England during the period when the jewellery must have been replaced.

'So gradually a little picture grew up in Chief Inspector Japp's mind. Mademoiselle Southwood was at one time associated with a Guild of Modern Jewellery. He suspected that she handled the jewels in question, made accurate drawings of them, got them copied by some humble but dishonest working jeweller and that the third part of the operation was the successful substitution by another person – somebody who could have been proved never to have handled the jewels and never to have had anything to do with copies or imitations of precious stones. Of the identity of this other person Japp was ignorant.

'Certain things that fell from you in conversation interested me. A ring that disappeared when you were in Majorca, the fact that you had been in a house-party where one of these fake substitutions had occurred, your close association with Mademoiselle Southwood. There was also the fact that you obviously resented my presence and tried to get your mother to be less friendly towards me. That might, of course, have been just personal dislike, but I thought not. You were too anxious to try and hide your distaste under a genial manner.

'*Eh bien!* after the murder of Linnet Doyle, it is discovered that her pearls are missing. You comprehend, at once I think of you! But I am not quite satisfied. For if you are working, as I suspect, with Mademoiselle Southwood (who was an intimate friend of Madame Doyle's), then substitution would be the method employed – not barefaced theft. But then, the pearls quite unexpectedly are returned, and what do I discover? That they are not genuine, but imitation.

'I know then who the real thief is. It was the imitation string which was stolen and returned – an imitation which you had previously substituted for the real necklace.'

He looked at the young man in front of him. Tim was white under his tan. He was not so good a fighter as Pennington; his stamina was bad. He said, with an effort to sustain his mocking manner: 'Indeed? And if so, what did I do with them?'

'That I know also.'

The young man's face changed – broke up.

Poirot went on slowly: 'There is only one place where they can be. I have reflected, and my reason tells me that that is so. Those pearls, Monsieur Allerton, are concealed in a rosary that hangs in your cabin. The beads of it are very elaborately carved. I think you had it made specially. Those beads unscrew, though you would never think so to look at them. Inside each is a pearl, stuck with Seccotine. Most police searchers respect religious symbols unless there is something obviously queer about them. You counted on that. I endeavoured to find out how Mademoiselle Southwood sent the imitation necklace out to you. She must have done so, since you came here from Majorca on hearing that Madame Doyle would be here for her honeymoon. My theory is that it was sent in a book – a square hole being cut out of the pages in the middle. A book goes with the ends open and is practically never opened in the post.'

There was a pause – a long pause. Then Tim said quietly: 'You win! It's been a good game, but it's over at last. There's nothing for it now, I suppose, but to take my medicine.'

Poirot nodded gently.

'Do you realize that you were seen that night?'

'Seen?' Tim started.

'Yes, on the night that Linnet Doyle died, someone saw you leave her cabin just after one in the morning.'

Tim said: 'Look here – you aren't thinking . . . it wasn't I who killed her! I'll swear that! I've been in the most awful stew. To have chosen that night of all others . . . God, it's been awful!'

Poirot said: 'Yes, you must have had uneasy moments. But, now that the truth has come out, you may be able to help us. Was Madame Doyle alive or dead when you stole the pearls?'

'I don't know,' Tim said hoarsely. 'Honest to God, Monsieur Poirot, I don't know! I'd found out where she put them at night – on the little table by the bed. I crept in, felt very softly on the table and grabbed 'em, put down the others and crept out again. I assumed, of course, that she was asleep.'

'Did you hear her breathing? Surely you would have listened for that?'

Tim thought earnestly.

'It was very still – very still indeed. No, I can't remember actually hearing her breathe.'

'Was there any smell of smoke lingering in the air, as there would have been if a firearm had been discharged recently?'

'I don't think so. I don't remember it.'

Poirot sighed.

'Then we are no further.'

Tim asked curiously, 'Who was it saw me?'

'Rosalie Otterbourne. She came round from the other side of the boat and saw you leave Linnet Doyle's cabin and go to your own.'

'So it was she who told you.'

Poirot said gently, 'Excuse me; she did not tell me.'

'But then, how do you know?'

'Because I am Hercule Poirot I do not need to be told. When I taxed her with it, do you know what she said? She said: "I saw nobody." And she lied.'

'But why?'

Poirot said in a detached voice: 'Perhaps because she thought the man she saw was the murderer. It looked like that, you know.'

'That seems to me all the more reason for telling you.'

Poirot shrugged his shoulders. 'She did not think so, it seems.'

Tim said, a queer note in his voice: 'She's an extraordinary sort of a girl. She must have been through a pretty rough time with that mother of hers.'

'Yes, life has not been easy for her.'

'Poor kid,' Tim muttered. Then he looked towards Race.

'Well, sir, where do we go from here? I admit taking the pearls from Linnet's cabin and you'll find them just where you say they are. I'm guilty all right. But as far as Miss Southwood is concerned, I'm not admitting anything. You've no evidence whatever against her. How I got hold of the fake necklace is my own business.'

Poirot murmured: 'A very correct attitude.'

Tim said with a flash of humour: 'Always the gentleman!' He added: 'Perhaps you can imagine how annoying it was to me to find my mother cottoning on to you! I'm not a sufficiently hardened criminal to enjoy sitting cheek by jowl with a successful detective just before bringing off a rather risky coup! Some people might get a kick out of it. I didn't. Frankly, it gave me cold feet.'

'But it did not deter you from making your attempt?'

Tim shrugged his shoulders.

'I couldn't funk it to that extent. The exchange had to be made sometime and I'd got a unique opportunity on this boat – a cabin only two doors off, and Linnet herself so preoccupied with her own troubles that she wasn't likely to detect the change.'

'I wonder if that was so –'

Tim looked up sharply. 'What do you mean?'

Poirot pressed the bell. 'I am going to ask Miss Otterbourne if she will come here for a minute.'

Tim frowned but said nothing. A steward came, received the order and went away with the message.

Rosalie came after a few minutes. Her eyes, reddened with recent weeping, widened a little at seeing Tim, but her old attitude of suspicion and defiance seemed entirely absent. She sat down and with a new docility looked from Race to Poirot.

'We're very sorry to bother you, Miss Otterbourne,' said Race gently. He was slightly annoyed with Poirot.

'It doesn't matter,' the girl said in a low voice.

Poirot said: 'It is necessary to clear up one or two points. When I asked you whether you saw anyone on the starboard deck at one-ten this morning, your answer was that you saw nobody. Fortunately I have been able to arrive at the truth without your help. Monsieur Allerton has admitted that he was in Linnet Doyle's cabin last night.'

She flashed a swift glance at Tim. Tim, his face grim and set, gave a curt nod.

'The time is correct, Monsieur Allerton?'

Allerton replied, 'Quite correct.'

Rosalie was staring at him. Her lips trembled – fell apart . . .

'But you didn't – you didn't –'

He said quickly: 'No, I didn't kill her. I'm a thief, not a murderer. It's all going to come out, so you might as well know. I was after her pearls.'

Poirot said, 'Mr Allerton's story is that he went to her cabin last night and exchanged a string of fake pearls for the real ones.'

'Did you?' asked Rosalie. Her eyes, grave, sad, child-like, questioned his.

'Yes,' said Tim.

There was a pause. Colonel Race shifted restlessly.

Poirot said in a curious voice: 'That, as I say, is Monsieur Allerton's story, partially confirmed by your evidence. That is to say, there is evidence that he did visit Linnet Doyle's cabin last night, but there is no evidence to show why he did so.'

Tim stared at him. 'But you know!'

'What do I know?'

'Well – you know I've got the pearls.'

'*Mais oui – mais oui!* I know you have the pearls, but I do not know when you got them. It may have been *before* last night . . . You said just now that Linnet Doyle would not have noticed the substitution. I am not so sure of that. Supposing she *did* notice it . . . Supposing, even, she knew who did it . . . Supposing that last night she threatened to expose the whole business, and that you knew she meant to do so . . . and supposing that you overheard the scene in the saloon between Jacqueline de Bellefort and Simon Doyle and, as soon as the saloon was empty, you slipped in and secured the pistol, and then, an hour later, when the boat had quieted down, you crept along to Linnet Doyle's cabin and made quite sure that no exposure would come . . .'

'My God!' said Tim. Out of his ashen face, two tortured, agonized eyes gazed dumbly at Hercule Poirot.

The latter went on: 'But somebody else saw you – the girl Louise. The next day she came to you and blackmailed you. You must pay her handsomely or she would tell what she knew. You realized that to submit to blackmail would be the beginning of the end. You pretended to agree, made an appointment to come to her cabin just before lunch with the money. Then, when she was counting the notes, you stabbed her.

'But again luck was against you. Somebody saw you go to her cabin' – he half turned to Rosalie – 'your mother. Once again you had to act – dangerously, foolhardily – but it was the only chance. You had heard Pennington talk about his revolver. You rushed into his cabin, got hold of it, listened outside Dr Bessner's cabin door and shot Madame Otterbourne before she could reveal your name.'

'No-o!' cried Rosalie. 'He didn't! He didn't!'

'After that, you did the only thing you could do – rushed round the stern. And when I rushed after you, you had turned and pretended to be coming in the *opposite* direction. You had handled the revolver in gloves; those gloves were in your pocket when I asked for them . . .'

Tim said, 'Before God, I swear it isn't true – not a word of it.' But his voice, ill-assured and trembling, failed to convince.

It was then that Rosalie Otterbourne surprised them.

'Of course it isn't true! And Monsieur Poirot knows it isn't! He's saying it for some reason of his own.'

Poirot looked at her. A faint smile came to his lips. He spread out his hands in token surrender.

'Mademoiselle is too clever . . . But you agree – it was a good case?'

'What the devil –' Tim began with rising anger, but Poirot held up a hand.

'There is a very good case against you, Monsieur Allerton. I wanted you to realize that. Now I will tell you something more pleasant. I have not yet examined that rosary in your cabin. It may be that, when I do, I shall find nothing there. And then, since Mademoiselle Otterbourne sticks to it that she saw no one on the deck last night, *eh bien*! there is no case against you at all. The pearls were taken by a kleptomaniac who has since returned them. They are in a little box on the table by the door, if you would like to examine them with Mademoiselle.'

Tim got up. He stood for a moment unable to speak. When he did, his words seemed inadequate, but it is possible that they satisfied his listeners.

'Thanks!' he said. 'You won't have to give me another chance!'

He held the door open for the girl; she passed out and, picking up the little cardboard box, he followed her.

Side by side they went. Tim opened the box, took out the sham string of pearls and hurled it far from him into the Nile.

'There!' he said. 'That's gone. When I return the box to Poirot the real string will be in it. What a damned fool I've been!'

Rosalie said in a low voice: 'Why did you come to do it in the first place?'

'How did I come to start, do you mean? Oh, I don't know. Boredom – laziness – the fun of the thing. Such a much more attractive way of earning a living than just pegging away at a job. Sounds pretty sordid to you, I expect, but you know there was an attraction about it – mainly the risk, I suppose.'

'I think I understand.'

'Yes, but you wouldn't ever do it.'

Rosalie considered for a moment or two, her grave young head bent.

'No,' she said simply. 'I wouldn't.'

He said: 'Oh, my dear – you're so lovely . . . so utterly lovely. Why wouldn't you say you'd seen me last night?'

'I thought – they might suspect you,' Rosalie said.

'Did you suspect me?'

'No. I couldn't believe that you'd kill anyone.'

'No. I'm not the strong stuff murderers are made of. I'm only a miserable sneak-thief.'

She put out a timid hand and touched his arm.

'Don't say that.'

He caught her hand in his.

'Rosalie, would you – you know what I mean? Or would you always despise me and throw it in my teeth?'

She smiled faintly. 'There are things you could throw in my teeth, too . . .'

'Rosalie – darling . . .'

But she held back a minute longer.

'This – Joanna?'

Tim gave a sudden shout.

'Joanna? You're as bad as Mother. I don't care a damn about Joanna. She's got a face like a horse and a predatory eye. A most unattractive female.'

Presently Rosalie said: 'Your mother need never know about you.'

'I'm not sure,' Tim said thoughtfully. 'I think I shall tell her. Mother's got plenty of stuffing, you know. She can stand up to things. Yes, I think I shall shatter her maternal illusions about me. She'll be so relieved to know that my relations with Joanna were purely of a business nature that she'll forgive me everything else.'

They had come to Mrs Allerton's cabin and Tim knocked firmly on the door. It opened and Mrs Allerton stood on the threshold.

'Rosalie and I –' began Tim. He paused.

'Oh, my dears,' said Mrs Allerton. She folded Rosalie in her arms. 'My dear, dear child. I always hoped – but Tim was so tiresome – and pretended he didn't like you. But of course I saw through *that*!'

Rosalie said in a broken voice: 'You've been so sweet to me – always. I used to wish – to wish –'

She broke off and sobbed happily on Mrs Allerton's shoulder.

As the door closed behind Tim and Rosalie, Poirot looked somewhat apologetically at Colonel Race. The Colonel was looking rather grim.

'You will consent to my little arrangement, yes?' Poirot pleaded. 'It is irregular – I know it is irregular, yes – but I have a high regard for human happiness.'

'You've none for mine,' said Race.

'That *jeune fille*. I have a tenderness towards her, and she loves that young man. It will be an excellent match; she has the stiffening he needs; the mother likes her; everything thoroughly suitable.'

'In fact the marriage has been arranged by heaven and Hercule Poirot. All I have to do is to compound a felony.'

'But, *mon ami*, I told you, it was all conjecture on my part.'

Race grinned suddenly.

'It's all right by me,' he said. 'I'm not a damned policeman, thank God! I daresay the young fool will go straight enough now. The girl's straight all right. No, what I'm complaining of is your treatment of *me*! I'm a patient man, but there are limits to patience! *Do* you know who committed the three murders on this boat or *don't* you?'

'I do.'

'Then why all this beating about the bush?'

'You think that I am just amusing myself with side issues? And it annoys you? But it is not that. Once I went professionally to an archæological expedition – and I learnt something there. In the course of an excavation, when something comes up out of the ground, everything is cleared away very carefully all around it. You take away the loose earth, and you scrape here and there with a knife until finally your object is there, all alone, ready to be drawn and photographed with no extraneous matter confusing it. That is what I have been seeking to do – clear away the extraneous matter so that we can see the truth – the naked shining truth.'

'Good,' said Race. 'Let's have this naked shining truth. It wasn't Pennington. It wasn't young Allerton. I presume it wasn't Fleetwood. Let's hear who it was for a change.'

'My friend, I am just about to tell you.'

There was a knock on the door. Race uttered a muffled curse. It was Dr Bessner and Cornelia. The latter was looking upset.

'Oh, Colonel Race,' she exclaimed, 'Miss Bowers has just told me about Cousin Marie. It's been the most dreadful shock. She said she couldn't bear the responsibility all by herself any longer, and that I'd better know, as I was one of the family. I just couldn't believe it at first, but Dr Bessner here has been just wonderful.'

'No, no,' protested the doctor modestly.

'He's been so kind, explaining it all, and how people really can't help it. He's had kleptomaniacs in his clinic. And he's explained to me how it's very often due to a deep-seated neurosis.'

Cornelia repeated the words with awe.

'It's planted very deeply in the subconscious; sometimes it's just some little thing that happened when you were a child. And he's cured people by getting them to think back and remember what that little thing was.'

Cornelia paused, drew a deep breath, and started off again.

'But it's worrying me dreadfully in case it all gets out. It would be too, too terrible in New York. Why, all the tabloids would have it. Cousin Marie and Mother and everybody – they'd never hold up their heads again.'

Race sighed. 'That's all right,' he said. 'This is Hush Hush House.'

'I beg your pardon, Colonel Race?'

'What I was endeavouring to say was that anything short of murder is being hushed up.'

'Oh!' Cornelia clasped her hands. 'I'm *so* relieved. I've just been worrying and worrying.'

'You have the heart too tender,' said Dr Bessner, and patted her benevolently on the shoulder. He said to the others: 'She has a very sensitive and beautiful nature.'

'Oh, I haven't really. You're too kind.'

Poirot murmured, 'Have you seen any more of Mr Ferguson?' Cornelia blushed.

'No – but Cousin Marie's been talking about him.'

'It seems the young man is highly born,' said Dr Bessner. 'I must confess he does not look it. His clothes are terrible. Not for a moment does he appear a well-bred man.'

'And what do you think, Mademoiselle?'

'I think he must be just plain crazy,' said Cornelia.

Poirot turned to the doctor. 'How is your patient?'

'Ach, he is going on splendidly. I have just reassured the Fräulein de Bellefort. Would you believe it, I found her in despair. Just because the fellow had a bit of a temperature this afternoon! But what could be more natural? It is amazing that he is not in a high fever now. But no, he is like some of our peasants; he has a magnificent constitution, the constitution of an ox. I have seen them with deep wounds that they hardly notice. It is the same with Mr Doyle. His pulse is steady, his temperature only slightly above normal. I was able to pooh-pooh the little lady's fears. All the same, it is ridiculous, *nicht wahr*? One minute you shoot a man; the next you are in hysterics in case he may not be doing well.'

Cornelia said: 'She loves him terribly, you see.'

'Ach! but it is not sensible, that. If *you* loved a man, would you try and shoot him? No, you are sensible.'

'I don't like things that go off with bangs anyway,' said Cornelia.

'Naturally you do not. You are very feminine.'

Race interrupted this scene of heavy approval. 'Since Doyle is all right there's no reason I shouldn't come along and resume our talk of this afternoon. He was just telling me about a telegram.'

Dr Bessner's bulk moved up and down appreciatively.

'Ho, ho, ho, it was very funny that! Doyle, he tells me about it. It was a telegram all about vegetables – potatoes, artichokes, leeks – Ach! pardon?'

With a stifled exclamation, Race had sat up in his chair.

'My God,' he said. 'So that's it! Richetti!'

He looked round on three uncomprehending faces.

'A new code – it was used in the South African rebellion. Potatoes mean machine guns, artichokes are high explosives – and so on. Richetti is no more an archæologist than I am! He's a very dangerous agitator, a man who's killed more than once, and I'll swear that he's killed once again. Mrs Doyle opened that telegram by mistake, you see. If she were ever to repeat what was in it before me, he knew his goose would be cooked!'

He turned to Poirot. 'Am I right?' he asked. 'Is Richetti the man?'

'He is *your* man,' said Poirot. 'I always thought there was something wrong about him. He was almost too word-perfect in his rôle; he was all archæologist, not enough human being.'

He paused and then said: 'But it was not Richetti who killed Linnet Doyle. For some time now I have known what I may express as the "first half" of the murderer. Now I know the "second half" also. The picture is complete. But you understand that, although I know what must have happened, I have no proof that it happened. Intellectually the case is satisfying. Actually it is profoundly unsatisfactory. There is only one hope – a confession from the murderer.'

Dr Bessner raised his shoulders sceptically. 'Ah! but that – it would be a miracle.'

'I think not. Not under the circumstances.'

Cornelia cried out: 'But who is it? Aren't you going to tell us?'

Poirot's eyes ranged quietly over the three of them. Race, smiling sardonically, Bessner, still looking sceptical, Cornelia, her mouth hanging a little open, gazing at him with eager eyes.

'*Mais oui*,' he said. 'I like an audience, I must confess. I am vain, you see. I am puffed up with conceit. I like to say: "See how clever is Hercule Poirot!"'

Race shifted a little in his chair.

'Well,' he asked gently, 'just how clever *is* Hercule Poirot?'

Shaking his head sadly from side to side Poirot said: 'To begin with I was stupid – incredibly stupid. To me the stumbling block was the pistol – Jacqueline de Bellefort's pistol. Why had that pistol not been left on the scene of the crime? The idea of the murderer was quite plainly to incriminate her. Why then did the murderer take it away? I was so stupid that I thought of all sorts of fantastic reasons. The real one was very simple. The murderer took it away because he *had* to take it away – because he had no choice in the matter.'

'You and I, my friend,' Poirot leaned towards Race, 'started our investigation with a preconceived idea. That idea was that the crime was committed on the spur of the moment, without any preliminary planning. Somebody wished to remove Linnet Doyle and had seized their opportunity to do so at a moment when the crime would almost certainly be attributed to Jacqueline de Bellefort. It therefore followed that the person in question had overheard the scene between Jacqueline and Simon Doyle and had obtained possession of the pistol after the others had left the saloon.

'But, my friends, if that preconceived idea was wrong, the whole aspect of the case altered. And it *was* wrong! This was no spontaneous crime committed on the spur of the moment. It was, on the contrary, very carefully planned and accurately timed, with all the details meticulously worked out beforehand, even to the drugging of Hercule Poirot's bottle of wine on the night in question!

'But yes, that is so! I was put to sleep so that there should be no possibility of my participating in the events of the night. It did just occur to me as a possibility. I drink wine; my two companions at table drink whisky and mineral water respectively. Nothing easier than to slip a dose of harmless narcotic into my bottle of wine – the bottles stand on the tables all day. But I dismissed the thought. It had been a hot day; I had been unusually tired; it was not really extraordinary that I should for once have slept heavily instead of lightly as I usually do.

'You see, I was still in the grip of the preconceived idea. If I had been drugged, that would have implied premeditation, it would mean that before seven-thirty, when dinner is served, the crime had already been decided upon; and that (always from the point of view of the preconceived idea) was absurd.

'The first blow to the preconceived idea was when the pistol was recovered from the Nile. To begin with, if we were right in our assumptions, the pistol ought never to have been thrown overboard at all . . . And there was more to follow.'

Poirot turned to Dr Bessner.

'You, Dr Bessner, examined Linnet Doyle's body. You will remember that the wound showed signs of scorching – that is to say, that the pistol had been placed close against the head before being fired.'

Bessner nodded. 'So. That is exact.'

'But when the pistol was found it was wrapped in a velvet stole, and that velvet showed definite signs that a pistol had been fired through its folds, presumably under the impression that that would deaden the sound of the shot. But if the pistol had been fired through the velvet, there would have been no signs of burning on the victim's skin. Therefore, the shot fired by Jacqueline de Bellefort at Simon Doyle? Again no, for there had been two witnesses of that shooting, and we knew all about it. It appeared, therefore, as though a *third* shot had been fired – one we knew nothing about. But only two shots had been fired from the pistol, and there was no hint or suggestion of another shot.

'Here we were face to face with a very curious unexplained circumstance. The next interesting point was the fact that in Linnet Doyle's cabin I found two bottles of coloured nail polish. Now ladies very often vary the colour of their nails, but so far Linnet Doyle's nails had always been the shade called Cardinal – a deep dark red. The other bottle was labelled Rose, which is a shade of pale pink, but the few drops remaining in the bottle were not pale pink but a bright red. I was sufficiently curious to take out the stopper and sniff. Instead of the usual strong odour of peardrops, the bottle smelt of vinegar! That is to say, it suggested that the drop or two of fluid in it was red ink. Now there is no reason why Madame Doyle should not have had a bottle of red ink, but it would have been more natural if she had had red ink in a red ink bottle and not in a nail-polish bottle. It suggested a link with the faintly stained handkerchief which had been wrapped round the pistol. Red ink washes out quickly but always leaves a pale pink stain.

'I should perhaps have arrived at the truth with these slender indications, but an event occurred which rendered all doubt superfluous. Louise Bourget was killed in circumstances which pointed unmistakably to the fact that she had been blackmailing the murderer. Not only was a fragment of a *mille* franc note still clasped in her hand, but I remembered some very significant words she had used this morning.

'Listen carefully, for here is the crux of the whole matter. When

403

I asked her if she had seen anything the previous night she gave this very curious answer: "Naturally, if I had been unable to sleep, if I had mounted the stairs, *then* perhaps I might have seen this assassin, this monster enter or leave Madame's cabin . . ." Now what exactly did that tell us?'

Bessner, his nose wrinkling with intellectual interest, replied promptly: 'It told you that she *had* mounted the stairs.'

'No, no; you fail to see the point. Why should she have said that, to *us*?'

'To convey a hint.'

'But why *hint* to us? If she knows who the murderer is, there are two courses open to her – to tell us the truth, or to hold her tongue and demand money for her silence from the person concerned! But she does neither. She neither says promptly: "I saw nobody. I was asleep." Nor does she say: "Yes, I saw someone, and it was so and so." Why use that significant indeterminate rigmarole of words? *Parbleu*, there can be only one reason! She is hinting to the murderer; therefore the murderer must have been present at the time. But, besides myself and Colonel Race, only two people were present – Simon Doyle and Dr Bessner.'

The doctor sprang up with a roar.

'Ach! what is that you say? You accuse me? Again? But it is ridiculous – beneath contempt.'

Poirot said sharply: 'Be quiet. I am telling you what I thought at the time. Let us remain impersonal.'

'He doesn't mean he thinks it's you now,' said Cornelia soothingly.

Poirot went on quickly: 'So it lay there – between Simon Doyle and Dr Bessner. But what reason has Bessner to kill Linnet Doyle? None, so far as I know. Simon Doyle, then? But that was impossible! There were plenty of witnesses who could swear that Doyle never left the saloon that evening until the quarrel broke out. After that he was wounded and it would then have been physically impossible for him to have done so. Had I good evidence on both those points? Yes, I had the evidence of Mademoiselle Robson, of Jim Fanthorp, and of Jacqueline de Bellefort as to the first, and I had the skilled testimony of Dr Bessner and of Mademoiselle Bowers as to the other. No doubt was possible.

'So Dr Bessner *must* be the guilty one. In favour of this theory there was the fact that the maid had been stabbed with a surgical knife. On the other hand Bessner had deliberately called attention to this fact.

'And then, my friends, a second perfectly indisputable fact became apparent to me. Louise Bourget's hint could not have been intended for Dr Bessner, because she could perfectly well have spoken to him in private at any time she liked. There was one person, *and one person only*, who corresponded to her necessity – Simon Doyle! Simon Doyle was wounded, was constantly attended by a doctor, was in that doctor's cabin. It was to him therefore that she risked saying those ambiguous words, in case she might not get another chance. And I remember how she had gone on, turning to him: "Monsieur, I implore you – you see how it is? What can I say?" And this answer: "My good girl, don't be a fool. Nobody thinks you saw or heard anything. You'll be quite all right. I'll look after you. Nobody's accusing you of anything." That was the assurance she wanted, and she got it!'

Bessner uttered a colossal snort.

'Ach! it is foolish, that! Do you think a man with a fractured bone and a splint on his leg could go walking about the boat and stabbing people? I tell you, it was *impossible* for Simon Doyle to leave his cabin.'

Poirot said gently: 'I know. That is quite true. The thing was impossible. It was impossible, but it was also true! There could be only one logical meaning behind Louise Bourget's words.

'So I returned to the beginning and reviewed the crime in the light of this new knowledge. Was it possible that in the period preceding the quarrel Simon Doyle had left the saloon and the others had forgotten or not noticed it? I could not see that that was possible. Could the skilled testimony of Dr Bessner and Mademoiselle Bowers be disregarded? Again I felt sure it could not. But, I remembered, there was a gap between the two. Simon Doyle had been alone in the saloon for a period of five minutes, and the skilled testimony of Dr Bessner only applied to the time after that period. For that period we had only the evidence of visual appearance, and, though apparently that was perfectly sound, it was no longer certain. What had actually been *seen* – leaving assumption out of the question?

'Mademoiselle Robson had seen Mademoiselle de Bellefort fire her pistol, had seen Simon Doyle collapse on to a chair, had seen him clasp a handkerchief to his leg and seen that handkerchief gradually soak through red. What had Monsieur Fanthorp heard and seen? He heard a shot, he found Doyle with a red-stained handkerchief clasped to his leg. What had happened then? Doyle had been very insistent that Mademoiselle de Bellefort should be got away, that she should not be left alone. After that, he suggested that Fanthorp should get hold of the doctor.

'Accordingly Mademoiselle Robson and Monsieur Fanthorp got out with Mademoiselle de Bellefort and for the next five minutes they are busy, on the port side of the deck. Mademoiselle Bowers', Dr Bessner's and Mademoiselle de Bellefort's cabins are all on the port side. Two minutes are all that Simon Doyle needs. He picks up the pistol from under the sofa, slips out of his shoes, runs like a hare silently along the starboard deck, enters his wife's cabin, creeps up to her as she lies asleep, shoots her through the head, puts the bottle that has contained the red ink on her washstand (it mustn't be found on him), runs back, gets hold of Mademoiselle Van Schuyler's velvet stole, which he has quietly stuffed down the side of a chair in readiness, muffles it round the pistol and fires a bullet into his leg. His chair into which he falls (in genuine agony this time) is by a window. He lifts the window and throws the pistol (wrapped up with the tell-tale handkerchief in the velvet stole) into the Nile.'

'Impossible!' said Race.

'No, my friend, not *impossible*. Remember the evidence of Tim Allerton. He heard a pop – *followed* by a splash. And he heard something else – the footsteps of a man running – a man running past his door. But nobody could have been running along the starboard side of the deck. What he heard was the stockinged feet of Simon Doyle running past his cabin.'

Race said: 'I still say it's impossible. No man could work out the whole caboodle like that in a flash – especially a chap like Doyle who is slow in his mental processes.'

'But very quick and deft in his physical actions!'

'That, yes. But he wouldn't be capable of thinking the whole thing out.'

'But he did not think it out himself, my friend. That is where we were all wrong. It looked like a crime committed on the spur of the moment, but it was *not* a crime committed on the spur of the moment. As I say, it was a very cleverly planned and well thought out piece of work. It could not be *chance* that Simon Doyle had a bottle of red ink in his pocket. No, it must be *design*. It was not *chance* that Jacqueline de Bellefort's foot kicked the pistol under the settee, where it would be out of sight and unremembered until later.'

'Jacqueline?'

'Certainly. The two halves of the murder. What gave Simon his alibi? The shot fired by Jacqueline. What gave Jacqueline *her* alibi? The insistence of Simon which resulted in a hospital nurse remaining with her all night. There, between the two of them, you get all the qualities you require – the cool, resourceful, planning brain, Jacqueline de Bellefort's brain, and the man of action to carry it out with incredible swiftness and timing.'

'Look at it the right way, and it answers every question. Simon Doyle and Jacqueline had been lovers. Realize that they are still lovers, and it is all clear. Simon does away with his rich wife, inherits her money, and in due course will marry his old love. It was all very ingenious. The persecution of Madame Doyle by Jacqueline, all part of the plan. Simon's pretended rage . . . And yet – there were lapses. He held forth to me once about possessive women – held forth with real bitterness. It ought to have been clear to me that it was his wife he was thinking about – not Jacqueline. Then his manner to his wife in public. An ordinary, inarticulate Englishman, such as Simon Doyle, is very embarrassed at showing any affection. Simon was not a really good actor. He overdid the devoted manner. That conversation I had with Mademoiselle Jacqueline, too, when she pretended that somebody had overheard, *I* saw no one. And there *was* no one! But it was to be a useful red herring later. Then one night on this boat I thought I heard Simon and Linnet outside my cabin. He was saying, "We've got to go through with it now." It was Doyle all right, but it was to Jacqueline he was speaking.

'The final drama was perfectly planned and timed. There was a sleeping draught for me, in case I might put an inconvenient finger in the pie. There was the selection of Mademoiselle Robson as a witness – the working up of the scene, Mademoiselle de Bellefort's exaggerated remorse and hysterics. She made a good deal of noise, in case the shot should be heard. *En vérité*, it was an extraordinarily clever idea. Jacqueline says she has shot Doyle;

407

Mademoiselle Robson says so; Fanthorp says so – and when Simon's leg is examined he *has* been shot. It looks unanswerable! For both of them there is a perfect alibi – at the cost, it is true, of a certain amount of pain and risk to Simon Doyle, but it is necessary that his wound should definitely disable him.

'And then the plan goes wrong. Louise Bourget has been wakeful. She has come up the stairway and she has seen Simon Doyle run along to his wife's cabin and come back. Easy enough to piece together what has happened the following day. And so she makes her greedy bit for hush money, and in so doing signs her death warrant.'

'But Mr Doyle couldn't have killed *her*?' Cornelia objected.

'No, the other partner did that murder. As soon as he can, Simon Doyle asks to see Jacqueline. He even asks me to leave them alone together. He tells her then of the new danger. They must act at once. He knows where Bessner's scalpels are kept. After the crime the scalpel is wiped and returned, and then, very late and rather out of breath, Jacqueline de Bellefort hurries in to lunch.

'And still all is not well, for Madame Otterbourne has seen Jacqueline go into Louise Bourget's cabin. And she comes hot-foot to tell Simon about it. Jacqueline is the murderess. Do you remember how Simon shouted at the poor woman? Nerves, we thought. But the door was open and he was trying to convey the danger to his accomplice. She heard and she acted – acted like lightning. She remembered Pennington had talked about a revolver. She got hold of it, crept up outside the door, listened and, at the critical moment, fired. She boasted once that she was a good shot, and her boast was not an idle one.

'I remarked after that third crime that there were three ways the murderer could have gone. I meant that he could have gone aft (in which case Tim Allerton was the criminal), he could have gone over the side (very improbable) or he could have gone into a cabin. Jacqueline's cabin was just two away from Dr Bessner's. She had only to throw down the revolver, bolt into the cabin, ruffle her hair and fling herself down on the bunk. It was risky, but it was the only possible chance.'

There was a silence, then Race asked: 'What happened to the first bullet fired at Doyle by the girl?'

'I think it went into the table. There is a recently made hole there. I think Doyle had time to dig it out with a penknife and fling it through the window. He had, of course, a spare cartridge, so that it would appear that only two shots had been fired.'

Cornelia sighed. 'They thought of everything,' she said. 'It's – horrible!'

Poirot was silent. But it was not a modest silence. His eyes seemed to be saying: 'You are wrong. They didn't allow for Hercule Poirot.'

Aloud he said, 'And now, Doctor, we will go and have a word with your patient.'

CHAPTER 30

It was very much later that evening that Hercule Poirot came and knocked on the door of a cabin.

A voice said 'Come in' and he entered.

Jacqueline de Bellefort was sitting in a chair. In another chair, close against the wall, sat the big stewardess.

Jacqueline's eyes surveyed Poirot thoughtfully. She made a gesture towards the stewardess.

'Can she go?'

Poirot nodded to the woman and she went out. Poirot drew up her chair and sat down near Jacqueline. Neither of them spoke. Poirot's face was unhappy.

In the end it was the girl who spoke first.

'Well,' she said, 'it is all over! You were too clever for us, Monsieur Poirot.'

Poirot sighed. He spread out his hands. He seemed strangely dumb.

'All the same,' said Jacqueline reflectively, 'I can't really see that you had much proof. You were quite right, of course, but if we'd bluffed you out –'

'In no other way, Mademoiselle, could the thing have happened.'

'That's proof enough for a logical mind, but I don't believe it would have convinced a jury. Oh, well – it can't be helped. You sprang it all on Simon, and he went down like a ninepin. He just lost his head utterly, poor lamb, and admitted everything.' She shook her head. 'He's a bad loser.'

'But you, Mademoiselle, are a good loser.'

She laughed suddenly – a queer, gay, defiant little laugh.

'Oh, yes, I'm a good loser all right.' She looked at him.

She said suddenly and impulsively: 'Don't mind so much, Monsieur Poirot! About me, I mean. You do mind, don't you?'

'Yes, Mademoiselle.'

'But it wouldn't have occurred to you to let me off?'

Hercule Poirot said quietly, 'No.'

She nodded her head in quiet agreement.

'No, it's no use being sentimental. I might do it again . . . I'm not a safe person any longer. I can feel that myself . . .' She went on broodingly: 'It's so dreadfully easy – killing people. And you begin to feel that it doesn't matter . . . that it's only *you* that matters! It's dangerous – that.'

She paused, then said with a little smile: 'You did your best for me, you know. That night at Assuan – you told me not to open my heart to evil . . . Did you realize then what was in my mind?'

He shook his head.

'I only knew that what I said was true.'

'It was true. I could have stopped, then, you know. I nearly did . . . I could have told Simon that I wouldn't go on with it . . . But then perhaps –'

She broke off. She said: 'Would you like to hear about it? From the beginning?'

'If you care to tell me, Mademoiselle.'

'I think I want to tell you. It was all very simple really. You see, Simon and I loved each other . . .'

It was a matter-of-fact statement, yet, underneath the lightness of her tone, there were echoes . . .

Poirot said simply: 'And for you love would have been enough, but not for him.'

'You might put it that way, perhaps. But you don't quite understand Simon. You see, he's always wanted money so dreadfully. He liked all the things you get with money – horses and yachts and sport – nice things all of them, things a man ought to be keen about. And he'd never been able to have any of them. He's awfully simple, Simon is. He wants things just as a child wants them – you know – terribly.

'All the same he never tried to marry anybody rich and horrid. He wasn't that sort. And then we met – and – and that sort of settled things. Only we didn't see when we'd be able to marry. He'd had rather a decent job, but he'd lost it. In a way it was his own fault. He tried to do something smart over money, and got found out at once. I don't believe he really meant to be dishonest. He just thought it was the sort of thing people did in the City.'

A flicker passed over her listener's face, but he guarded his tongue.

'There we were, up against it; and then I thought of Linnet and her new country house, and I rushed off to her. You know, Monsieur Poirot, I loved Linnet, really I did. She was my best friend, and I never dreamed that anything would ever come between us. I just thought how lucky it was she was rich. It might make all the difference to me and Simon if she'd give him a job. And she was awfully sweet about it and told me to bring Simon down to see her. It was about then you saw us that night at Chez Ma Tante. We were making whoopee, although we couldn't really afford it.'

She paused, sighed, then went on: 'What I'm going to say now is quite true, Monsieur Poirot. Even though Linnet is dead, it doesn't alter the truth. That's why I'm not really sorry about her, even now. She went all out to get Simon away from me. That's the absolute truth! I don't think she even hesitated for more than about a minute. I was her friend, but she didn't care. She just went baldheaded for Simon . . .

'And Simon didn't care a damn about her! I talked a lot to you about glamour, but of course that wasn't true. He didn't want Linnet. He thought her good-looking but terribly bossy, and he hated bossy women! The whole thing embarrassed him frightfully. But he did like the thought of her money.

'Of course I saw that . . . and at last I suggested to him that it might be a good thing if he – got rid of me and married Linnet. But he scouted the idea. He said, money or no money, it would be hell to be married to her. He said his idea of having money was to have it himself – not to have a rich wife holding the purse strings. "I'd be a kind of damned Prince Consort," he said to me. He said, too, that he didn't want anyone but me . . .

'I think I know when the idea came into his head. He said one day: "If I'd any luck, I'd marry her and she'd die in about a year and leave me all the boodle." And then a queer startled look came into his eyes. That was when he first thought of it . . .

411

'He talked about it a good deal, one way and another – about how convenient it would be if Linnet died. I said it was an awful idea, and then he shut up about it. Then, one day, I found him reading up all about arsenic. I taxed him with it then, and he laughed and said: "Nothing venture, nothing have! It's about the only time in my life I shall be near to touching a far lot of money."

'After a bit I saw that he'd made up his mind. And I was terrified – simply terrified. Because, you see, I realized that he'd never pull it off. He's so childishly simple. He'd have no kind of subtlety about it – and he's got no imagination. He would probably have just bunged arsenic into her and assumed the doctor would say she'd died of gastritis. He always thought things would go right.

'So I had to come into it, too, to look after him . . .'

She said it very simply but in complete good faith. Poirot had no doubt whatever that her motive had been exactly what she said it was. She herself had not coveted Linnet Ridgeway's money, but she had loved Simon Doyle, had loved him beyond reason and beyond rectitude and beyond pity.

'I thought and I thought – trying to work out a plan. It seemed to me that the basis of the idea ought to be a kind of two-handed alibi. You know – if Simon and I could somehow or other give evidence against each other, but actually that evidence would clear us of everything. It would be easy enough for me to pretend to hate Simon. It was quite a likely thing to happen under the circumstances. Then, if Linnet was killed, I should probably be suspected, so it would be better if I was suspected right away. We worked out details little by little. I wanted it to be so that, if anything went wrong, they'd get me and not Simon. But Simon was worried about me.

'The only thing I was glad about was that I hadn't got to do *it*. I simply couldn't have! Not go along in cold blood and kill her when she was asleep! You see, I hadn't forgiven her – I think I could have killed her face to face, but not the other way . . .

'We worked everything out carefully. Even then, Simon went and wrote a J in blood which was a silly melodramatic thing to do. It's just the sort of thing he *would* think of! But it went off all right.'

Poirot nodded.

'Yes. It was not your fault that Louise Bourget could not sleep that night . . . And afterwards, Mademoiselle?'

She met his eyes squarely.

'Yes,' she said 'it's rather horrible isn't it? I can't believe that I – did that! I know now what you meant by opening your heart to evil . . . You know pretty well how it happened. Louise made it clear to Simon that she knew. Simon got you to bring me to him. As soon as we were alone together he told me what had happened. He told me what I'd got to do. I wasn't even horrified. I was so afraid – so deadly afraid . . . That's what murder does to you. Simon and I were safe – quite safe – except for this miserable blackmailing French girl. I took her all the money we could get hold of. I pretended to grovel. And then, when she was counting the money, I – did it! It was quite easy. That's what's so horribly, horribly frightening about it . . . It's so terribly easy . . .

'And even then we weren't safe. Mrs Otterbourne had seen me. She came triumphantly along the deck looking for you and Colonel Race. I'd no time to think. I just acted like a flash. It was almost exciting. I knew it was touch or go that time. That seemed to make it better . . .'

She stopped again.

'Do you remember when you came into my cabin afterwards? You said you were not sure why you had come. I was so miserable – so terrified. I thought Simon was going to die . . .'

'And I – was hoping it,' said Poirot.

Jacqueline nodded.

'Yes, it would have been better for him that way.'

'That was not my thought.'

Jacqueline looked at the sternness of his face.

She said gently: 'Don't mind so much for me, Monsieur Poirot. After all, I've lived hard always, you know. If we'd won out, I'd have been very happy and enjoyed things and probably should never have regretted anything. As it is – well, one goes through with it.'

She added: 'I suppose the stewardess is in attendance to see I don't hang myself or swallow a miraculous capsule of prussic acid as people always do in books. You needn't be afraid! I shan't do that. It will be easier for Simon if I'm standing by.'

Poirot got up. Jacqueline rose also. She said with a sudden smile: 'Do you remember when I said I must follow my star?

You said it might be a false star. And I said: "That very bad star, that star fall down."'

He went out to the deck with her laughter ringing in his ears.

CHAPTER 31

It was early dawn when they came into Shellal. The rocks came down grimly to the water's edge.

Poirot murmured: '*Quel pays sauvage!*'

Race stood beside him. 'Well,' he said, 'we've done our job. I've arranged for Richetti to be taken ashore first. Glad we've got him. He's been a slippery customer, I can tell you. Given us the slip dozens of times.'

He went on: 'We must get hold of a stretcher for Doyle. Remarkable how he went to pieces.'

'Not really,' said Poirot. 'That boyish type of criminal is usually intensely vain. Once prick the bubble of their self-esteem and it is finished! They go to pieces like children.'

'Deserves to be hanged,' said Race. 'He's a cold-blooded scoundrel. I'm sorry for the girl – but there's nothing to be done about it.'

Poirot shook his head.

'People say love justifies everything, but that is not true . . . Women who care for men as Jacqueline cares for Simon Doyle are very dangerous. It is what I said when I saw her first. "She cares too much, that little one!" It is true.'

Cornelia Robson came up beside him.

'Oh,' she said, 'we're nearly in.' She paused a minute or two, then added, 'I've been with her.'

'With Mademoiselle de Bellefort?'

'Yes. I felt it was kind of awful for her boxed up with that stewardess. Cousin Marie's very angry, though, I'm afraid.'

Miss Van Schuyler was progressing slowly down the deck towards them. Her eyes were venomous.

'Cornelia,' she snapped, 'you've behaved outrageously. I shall send you straight home.'

Cornelia took a deep breath. 'I'm sorry, Cousin Marie, but I'm not going home. I'm going to get married.'

'So you've seen sense at last,' snapped the old lady.

Ferguson came striding round the corner of the deck. He said: 'Cornelia, what's this I hear? It's not true!'

'It's quite true,' said Cornelia. 'I'm going to marry Dr Bessner. He asked me last night.'

'And why are you going to marry him?' asked Ferguson furiously. 'Simply because he's rich?'

'No, I'm not,' said Cornelia indignantly. 'I like him. He's kind, and he knows a lot. And I've always been interested in sick folks and clinics, and I shall have just a wonderful life with him.'

'Do you mean to say,' asked Mr Ferguson incredulously, 'that you'd rather marry that disgusting old man than Me?'

'Yes, I would. You're not reliable! You wouldn't be at all a comfortable sort of person to live with. And he's *not* old. He's not fifty yet.'

'He's got a stomach,' said Mr Ferguson venomously.

'Well, I've got round shoulders,' retorted Cornelia. 'What one looks like doesn't matter. He says I really could help him in his work, and he's going to teach me all about neurosis.'

She moved away.

Ferguson said to Poirot: 'Do you think she really means that?'

'Certainly.'

'She prefers that pompous old bore to me?'

'Undoubtedly.'

'The girl's mad,' declared Ferguson.

Poirot's eyes twinkled.

'She is a woman of an original mind,' he said. 'It is probably the first time you have met one.'

The boat drew in to the landing-stage. A cordon had been drawn round the passengers. They had been asked to wait before disembarking.

Richetti, dark-faced and sullen, was marched ashore by two engineers.

Then, after a certain amount of delay, a stretcher was brought. Simon Doyle was carried along the deck to the gangway.

He looked a different man – cringing, frightened, all his boyish insouciance vanished.

Jacqueline de Bellefort followed. A stewardess walked beside her. She was pale but otherwise looked much as usual. She came up to the stretcher.

'Hullo, Simon!' she said.

He looked up at her quickly. The old boyish look came back to his face for a moment.

'I messed it up,' he said. 'Lost my head and admitted everything! Sorry, Jackie. I've let you down.'

She smiled at him then. 'It's all right, Simon,' she said. 'A fool's game, and we've lost. That's all.'

She stood aside. The bearers picked up the handles of the stretcher. Jacqueline bent down and tied the lace of her shoe. Then her hand went to her stocking top and she straightened up with something in her hand.

There was a sharp explosive 'pop'.

Simon Doyle gave one convulsed shudder and then lay still.

Jacqueline de Bellefort nodded. She stood for a minute, pistol in hand. She gave a fleeting smile at Poirot.

Then, as Race jumped forward, she turned the little glittering toy against her heart and pressed the trigger.

She sank down in a soft huddled heap.

Race shouted: 'Where the devil did she get that pistol?'

Poirot felt a hand on his arm. Mrs Allerton said softly, 'You – knew?'

He nodded. 'She had a pair of these pistols. I realized that when I heard that one had been found in Rosalie Otterbourne's handbag the day of the search. Jacqueline sat at the same table as they did. When she realized that there was going to be a search, she slipped it into the other girl's handbag. Later she went to Rosalie's cabin and got it back, after having distracted her attention with a comparison of lipsticks. As both she and her cabin had been searched yesterday, it wasn't thought necessary to do it again.'

Mrs Allerton said: 'You wanted her to take that way out?'

'Yes. But she would not take it alone. That is why Simon Doyle has died an easier death than he deserved.'

Mrs Allerton shivered. 'Love can be a very frightening thing.'

'That is why most great love stories are tragedies.'

Mrs Allerton's eyes rested upon Tim and Rosalie, standing side by side in the sunlight, and she said suddenly and passionately: 'But thank God, there is happiness in the world.'

'As you say, Madame, thank God for it.'

Presently the passengers went ashore.

Later the bodies of Louise Bourget and Mrs Otterbourne were carried off the *Karnak*.

Lastly the body of Linnet Doyle was brought ashore, and all over the world wires began to hum, telling the public that Linnet Doyle, who had been Linnet Ridgeway, the famous, the beautiful, the wealthy Linnet Doyle was dead.

Sir George Wode read about it in his London club, and Sterndale Rockford in New York, and Joanna Southwood in Switzerland, and it was discussed in the bar of the Three Crowns in Malton-under-Wode.

And Mr Burnaby said acutely: 'Well, it doesn't seem to have done her much good, poor lass.'

But after a while they stopped talking about her and discussed instead who was going to win the Grand National. For, as Mr Ferguson was saying at that minute in Luxor, it is not the past that matters but the future.

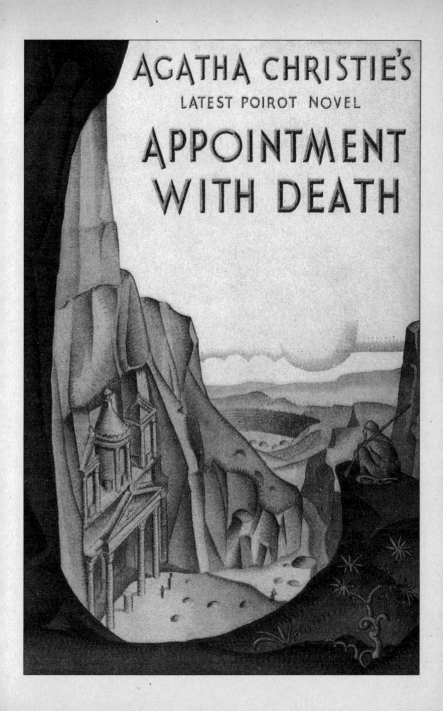

AGATHA CHRISTIE'S
LATEST POIROT NOVEL
APPOINTMENT
WITH DEATH

To Richard and Myra Mallock
to remind them of their journey
to Petra

PART I

....

CHAPTER I

'*You do see, don't you, that she's got to be killed?*'

The question floated out into the still night air, seemed to hang there a moment and then drift away down into the darkness towards the Dead Sea.

Hercule Poirot paused a minute with his hand on the window catch. Frowning, he shut it decisively, thereby excluding any injurious night air! Hercule Poirot had been brought up to believe that all outside air was best left outside, and that night air was especially dangerous to the health.

As he pulled the curtains neatly over the window and walked to his bed, he smiled tolerantly to himself.

'*You do see, don't you, that she's got to be killed?*'

Curious words for one Hercule Poirot, detective, to overhear on his first night in Jerusalem.

'Decidedly, wherever I go, there is something to remind me of crime!' he murmured to himself.

His smile continued as he remembered a story he had once heard concerning Anthony Trollope the novelist. Trollope was crossing the Atlantic at the time and had overheard two fellow passengers discussing the last published instalment of one of his novels.

'Very good,' one man had declared. 'But he ought to kill off that tiresome old woman.'

With a broad smile the novelist had addressed them:

'Gentlemen, I am much obliged to you! I will go and kill her immediately!'

Hercule Poirot wondered what had occasioned the words he had just overheard. A collaboration, perhaps, over a play or a book.

He thought, still smiling: 'Those words might be remembered, one day, and given a more sinister meaning.'

There had been, he now recollected, a curious nervous intensity in the voice – a tremor that spoke of some intense emotional strain. A man's voice – or a boy's . . .

Hercule Poirot thought to himself as he turned out the light by his bed: '*I should know that voice again . . .*'

II

Their elbows on the window-sill, their heads close together, Raymond and Carol Boynton gazed out into the blue depths of the night. Nervously, Raymond repeated his former words: 'You do see, don't you, that she's got to be killed?'

Carol Boynton stirred slightly. She said, her voice deep and hoarse: 'It's horrible . . .'

'It's not more horrible than *this*!'

'I suppose not . . .'

Raymond said violently: 'It can't go on like this – it can't . . . We *must* do something . . . And there isn't anything else we *can* do . . .'

Carol said – but her voice was unconvincing and she knew it: 'If we could get away somehow –?'

'We can't.' His voice was empty and hopeless. 'Carol, you know we can't . . .'

The girl shivered. 'I know, Ray – I know.'

He gave a sudden short, bitter laugh.

'People would say we were crazy – not to be able just to walk out –'

Carol said slowly: 'Perhaps we – are crazy!'

'I dare say. Yes, I dare say we are. Anyway, we soon shall be . . . I suppose some people would say we are already – here we are calmly planning, in cold blood, to kill our own mother!'

Carol said sharply: 'She isn't our own mother!'

'No, that's true.'

There was a pause and then Raymond said, his voice now quietly matter-of-fact: 'You do agree, Carol?'

Carol answered steadily: 'I think she ought to die – yes . . .'

Then she broke out suddenly: 'She's mad . . . I'm quite sure she's mad . . . She – she couldn't torture us like she does if she were sane. For years we've been saying: "*This can't go on!*" and it *has* gone on! We've said, "*She'll die some time*" – but she hasn't died! I don't think she ever will die unless –'

Raymond said steadily: '*Unless we kill her . . .*'

'Yes.'

She clenched her hands on the window-sill in front of her.

Her brother went on in a cool, matter-of-fact tone, with just a slight tremor denoting his deep underlying excitement.

'You see why it's got to be one of us, don't you? With Lennox, there's Nadine to consider. And we couldn't bring Jinny into it.'

Carol shivered.

'Poor Jinny . . . I'm so afraid . . .'

'I know. It's getting pretty bad, isn't it? That's why something's got to be done quickly – before she goes right over the edge.'

Carol stood up suddenly, pushing back the tumbled chestnut hair from her forehead.

'Ray,' she said, 'you don't think it's really *wrong*, do you?'

He answered in that same would-be dispassionate tone. 'No. I think it's just like killing a mad dog – something that's doing harm in the world and must be stopped. This is the only way of stopping it.'

Carol murmured: 'But they'd – they'd send us to the chair just the same . . . I mean we couldn't explain what she's like . . . It would sound fantastic . . . In a way, you know, it's all in our own *minds*!'

Raymond said: 'Nobody will ever know. I've got a plan. I've thought it all out. We shall be quite safe.'

Carol turned suddenly round on him.

'Ray – somehow or another – you're different. Something's *happened* to you . . . What's put all this into your head?'

'Why should you think anything's happened to me?'

He turned his head away, staring out into the night.

'Because it has . . . Ray, was it that girl on the train?'

'No, of course not – why should it be? Oh, Carol, don't talk nonsense. Let's get back again to – to –'

'To your plan? Are you sure it's a – good plan?'

'Yes. I think so . . . We must wait for the right opportunity, of course. And then – if it goes all right – we shall be free – all of us.'

'Free?' Carol gave a little sigh. She looked up at the stars. Then suddenly she shook from head to foot in a sudden storm of weeping.

'Carol, what's the matter?'

She sobbed out brokenly: 'It's so lovely – the night and the blueness and the stars. If only we could be part of it all . . . If only we could be like other people instead of being as we are – all queer and warped and *wrong*.'

'But we shall be – all right – when she's dead!'

'Are you *sure*? Isn't it too late? Shan't we always be queer and different?'

'No, no, no.'

'I wonder –'

'Carol, if you'd rather not –'

She pushed his comforting arm aside.

'No, I'm with you – definitely I'm with you! Because of the others – especially Jinny. We *must* save Jinny!'

Raymond paused a moment. 'Then – we'll go on with it?'

'Yes!'

'Good. I'll tell you my plan . . .'

He bent his head to hers.

CHAPTER 2

Miss Sarah King, M.B., stood by the table in the writing-room of the Solomon Hotel in Jerusalem, idly turning over the papers and magazines. A frown contracted her brows and she looked preoccupied.

The tall middle-aged Frenchman who entered the room from the hall watched her for a moment or two before strolling up to the opposite side of the table. When their eyes met, Sarah made a little gesture of smiling recognition. She remembered that this man had come to help her when travelling from Cairo and had carried one of her suitcases at a moment when no porter appeared to be available.

'You like Jerusalem, yes?' asked Dr Gerard after they had exchanged greetings.

'It's rather terrible in some ways,' said Sarah, and added: 'Religion is very odd!'

The Frenchman looked amused.

'I know what you mean.' His English was very nearly perfect. 'Every imaginable sect squabbling and fighting!'

'And the awful things they've built, too!' said Sarah.

424

'Yes, indeed.'

Sarah sighed.

'They turned me out of one place today because I had on a sleeveless dress,' she said ruefully. 'Apparently the Almighty doesn't like my arms in spite of having made them.'

Dr Gerard laughed. Then he said: 'I was about to order some coffee. You will join me, Miss –?'

'King, my name is. Sarah King.'

'And mine – permit me.' He whipped out a card. Taking it, Sarah's eyes widened in delighted awe.

'Dr Theodore Gerard? Oh! I *am* excited to meet you. I've read all your works, of course. Your views on schizophrenia are frightfully interesting.'

'*Of course?*' Gerard's eyebrows rose inquisitively.

Sarah explained rather diffidently.

'You see – I'm by way of being a doctor myself. Just got my M.B.'

'Ah! I see.'

Dr Gerard ordered coffee and they sat down in a corner of the lounge. The Frenchman was less interested in Sarah's medical achievements than in the black hair that rippled back from her forehead and the beautifully shaped red mouth. He was amused at the obvious awe with which she regarded him.

'You are staying here long?' he asked conversationally.

'A few days. That is all. Then I want to go to Petra.'

'Aha! I, too, was thinking of going there if it does not take too long. You see, I have to be back in Paris on the four-teenth.'

'It takes about a week, I believe. Two days to go, two days there and two days back again.'

'I must go to the travel bureau in the morning and see what can be arranged.'

A party of people entered the lounge and sat down. Sarah watched them with some interest. She lowered her voice.

'Those people who have just come in, did you notice them on the train the other night? They left Cairo the same time as we did.'

Dr Gerard screwed in an eyeglass and directed his glance across the room. 'Americans?'

Sarah nodded.

'Yes. An American family. But – rather an unusual one, I think.'

'Unusual? How unusual?'

'Well, look at them. Especially at the old woman.'

Dr Gerard complied. His keen professional glance flitted swiftly from face to face.

He noticed first a tall rather loose-boned man – age about thirty. The face was pleasant but weak and his manner seemed oddly apathetic. Then there were two good-looking youngsters – the boy had almost a Greek head. 'Something the matter with him, too,' thought Dr Gerard. 'Yes – a definite state of nervous tension.' The girl was clearly his sister, a strong resemblance, and she also was in an excitable condition. There was another girl younger still – with golden-red hair that stood out like a halo; her hands were very restless, they were tearing and pulling at the handkerchief in her lap. Yet another woman, young, calm, dark-haired with a creamy pallor, a placid face not unlike a Luini Madonna. Nothing jumpy about *her*! And the centre of the group – 'Heavens!' thought Dr Gerard, with a Frenchman's candid repulsion. 'What a horror of a woman!' Old, swollen, bloated, sitting there immovable in the midst of them – a distorted old Buddha – a gross spider in the centre of a web!

To Sarah he said: '*La Maman*, she is not beautiful, eh?' And he shrugged his shoulders.

'There's something rather – sinister about her, don't you think?' asked Sarah.

Dr Gerard scrutinized her again. This time his eye was professional, not aesthetic.

'Dropsy – cardiac –' he added a glib medical phrase.

'Oh, yes, *that*!' Sarah dismissed the medical side.

'But there is something odd in their attitude to her, don't you think?'

'Who are they, do you know?'

'Their name is Boynton. Mother, married son, his wife, one younger son and two younger daughters.'

Dr Gerard murmured: '*La famille Boynton* sees the world.'

'Yes, but there's something odd about the *way* they're seeing it. They never speak to anyone else. And none of them can do anything unless the old woman says so!'

'She is of the matriarchal type,' said Gerard thoughtfully.

426

'She's a complete tyrant, I think,' said Sarah.

Dr Gerard shrugged his shoulders and remarked that the American woman ruled the earth – that was well known.

'Yes, but it's more than just that.' Sarah was persistent. 'She's – oh, she's got them all so *cowed* – so positively under her thumb – that it's – it's indecent!'

'To have too much power is bad for women,' Gerard agreed with sudden gravity. He shook his head.

'It is difficult for a woman not to abuse power.'

He shot a quick sideways glance at Sarah. She was watching the Boynton family – or rather she was watching one particular member of it. Dr Gerard smiled a quick comprehending Gallic smile. Ah! So it was like that, was it?

He murmured tentatively: 'You have spoken with them – yes?'

'Yes – at least with one of them.'

'The young man – the younger son?'

'Yes. On the train coming here from Kantara. He was standing in the corridor. I spoke to him.'

There was no self-consciousness in her attitude to life. She was interested in humanity and was of a friendly though impatient disposition.

'What made you speak to him?' asked Gerard.

Sarah shrugged her shoulders.

'Why not? I often speak to people travelling. I'm interested in people – in what they do and think and feel.'

'You put them under the microscope, that is to say.'

'I suppose you might call it that,' the girl admitted.

'And what were your impressions in this case?'

'Well,' she hesitated, 'it was rather odd . . . To begin with, the boy flushed right up to the roots of his hair.'

'Is that so remarkable?' asked Gerard drily.

Sarah laughed.

'You mean that he thought I was a shameless hussy making advances to him? Oh, no, I don't think he thought that. Men can always tell, can't they?'

She gave him a frank questioning glance. Dr Gerard nodded his head.

'I got the impression,' said Sarah, speaking slowly and frowning a little, 'that he was – how shall I put it? – both excited and appalled. Excited out of all proportion – and quite absurdly apprehensive at the same time. Now that's odd, isn't it? Because I've always found Americans unusually self-possessed. An American boy of twenty, say, has infinitely more knowledge of the world and far more *savoir-faire* than an English boy of the same age. And this boy must be over twenty.'

'About twenty-three or four, I should say.'

'As much as that?'

'I should think so.'

'Yes . . . perhaps you're right . . . Only, somehow, he seems very young . . .'

'Maladjustment mentally. The "child" factor persists.'

'Then I *am* right? I mean, there *is* something not quite normal about him?'

Dr Gerard shrugged his shoulders, smiling a little at her earnestness.

'My dear young lady, are any of us quite normal? But I grant you that there is probably a neurosis of some kind.'

'Connected with that horrible old woman, I'm sure.'

'You seem to dislike her very much,' said Gerard, looking at her curiously.

'I do. She's got a – oh, a malevolent eye!'

Gerard murmured: 'So have many mothers when their sons are attracted to fascinating young ladies!'

Sarah shrugged an impatient shoulder. Frenchmen were all alike, she thought, obsessed by sex! Though, of course, as a conscientious psychologist she herself was bound to admit that there was always an underlying basis of sex to most phenomena. Sarah's thoughts ran along a familiar psychological track.

She came out of her meditations with a start. Raymond Boynton was crossing the room to the centre table. He selected a magazine. As he passed her chair on his return journey she looked at him and spoke.

'Have you been busy sightseeing today?'

She selected her words at random, her real interest was to see how they would be received.

Raymond half stopped, flushed, shied like a nervous horse and his eyes went apprehensively to the centre of his family group. He muttered: 'Oh – oh, yes – why, yes, certainly. I –'

Then, as suddenly as though he had received the prick of

a spur, he hurried back to his family, holding out the magazine.

The grotesque Buddha-like figure held out a fat hand for it, but as she took it her eyes, Dr Gerard noticed, were on the boy's face. She gave a grunt, certainly no audible thanks. The position of her head shifted very slightly. The doctor saw that she was now looking hard at Sarah. Her face was quite impassive, it had no expression in it. Impossible to tell what was passing in the woman's mind.

Sarah looked at her watch and uttered an exclamation.

'It's much later than I thought.' She got up. 'Thank you so much, Dr Gerard, for standing me coffee. I must write some letters now.'

He rose and took her hand.

'We shall meet again, I hope,' he said.

'Oh, yes! Perhaps you will come to Petra?'

'I shall certainly try to do so.'

Sarah smiled at him and turned away. Her way out of the room led her past the Boynton family.

Dr Gerard, watching, saw Mrs Boynton's gaze shift to her son's face. He saw the boy's eyes meet hers. As Sarah passed, Raymond Boynton half turned his head – not towards her, but away from her . . . It was a slow, unwilling motion and conveyed the idea that old Mrs Boynton had pulled an invisible string.

Sarah King noticed the avoidance, and was young enough and human enough to be annoyed by it. They had had such a friendly talk together in the swaying corridor of the wagons-lits. They had compared notes on Egypt, had laughed at the ridiculous language of the donkey boys and street touts. Sarah had described how a camel man when he had started hopefully and impudently, 'You English lady or American?' had received the answer: 'No, Chinese.' And her pleasure in seeing the man's complete bewilderment as he stared at her. The boy had been, she thought, like a nice eager schoolboy – there had been, perhaps, something almost pathetic about his eagerness. And now, for no reason at all, he was shy, boorish – positively rude.

'I shan't take any more trouble with him,' said Sarah indignantly.

For Sarah, without being unduly conceited, had a fairly good opinion of herself. She knew herself to be definitely attractive to the opposite sex, and she was not one to take a snubbing lying down!

She had been, perhaps, a shade over-friendly to this boy because, for some obscure reason, she had felt sorry for him.

But now, it was apparent, he was merely a rude, stuck-up, boorish young American!

Instead of writing the letters she had mentioned, Sarah King sat down in front of her dressing-table, combed the hair back from her forehead, looked into a pair of troubled hazel eyes in the glass, and took stock of her situation in life.

She had just passed through a difficult emotional crisis. A month ago she had broken off her engagement to a young doctor some four years her senior. They had been very much attracted to each other, but had been too much alike in temperament. Disagreements and quarrels had been of common occurrence. Sarah was of too imperious a temperament herself to brook a calm assertion of autocracy. Like many high-spirited women, Sarah believed herself to admire strength. She had always told herself that she wanted to be mastered. When she met a man capable of mastering her she found that she did not like it at all! To break off her engagement had cost her a good deal of heart-burning, but she was clear-sighted enough to realize that mere mutual attraction was not a sufficient basis on which to build a lifetime of happiness. She had treated herself deliberately to an interesting holiday abroad in order to help on forgetfulness before she went back to start working in earnest.

Sarah's thoughts came back from the past to the present.

'I wonder,' she thought, 'if Dr Gerard will let me talk to him about his work. He's done such marvellous work. If only he'll take me seriously . . . Perhaps – if he comes to Petra –'

Then she thought again of the strange boorish young American.

She had no doubt that it was the presence of his family which had caused him to react in such a peculiar manner, but she felt slightly scornful of him, nevertheless. To be under the thumb of one's family like that – it was really rather ridiculous – especially for a *man*!

And yet . . .

A queer feeling passed over her. Surely there was something a little *odd* about it all?

She said suddenly out loud: 'That boy wants rescuing! I'm going to see to it!'

CHAPTER 3

When Sarah had left the lounge, Dr Gerard sat where he was for some minutes. Then he strolled to the table, picked up the latest number of *Le Matin* and strolled with it to a chair a few yards away from the Boynton family. His curiosity was aroused.

He had at first been amused by the English girl's interest in this American family, shrewdly diagnosing that it was inspired by interest in one particular member of the family. But now something out of the ordinary about this family party awakened in him the deeper, more impartial interest of the scientist. He sensed that there was something here of definite psychological interest.

Very discreetly, under the cover of his paper, he took stock of them. First the boy in whom that attractive English girl took such a decided interest. Yes, thought Gerard, definitely the type to appeal to her temperamentally. Sarah King had strength – she possessed well-balanced nerves, cool wits and a resolute will. Dr Gerard judged the young man to be sensitive, perceptive, diffident and intensely suggestible. He noted with a physician's eye the obvious fact that the boy was at the moment in a state of high nervous tension. Dr Gerard wondered why. He was puzzled. Why should a young man whose physical health was obviously good, who was abroad ostensibly enjoying himself, be in such a condition that nervous breakdown was imminent?

The doctor turned his attention to the other members of the party. The girl with the chestnut hair was obviously Raymond's sister. They were of the same racial type, small-boned, well-shaped, aristocratic looking. They had the same slender well-formed hands, the same clean line of jaw, and the same poise of the head on a long, slender neck. And the girl, too, was nervous . . . She made slight involuntary nervous movements, her eyes were deeply shadowed underneath and over bright. Her voice, when she spoke, was too quick and a shade breathless. She was watchful – alert – unable to relax.

'And she is afraid, too,' decided Dr Gerard. 'Yes, she is afraid!'

He overheard scraps of conversation – a very ordinary normal conversation.

'We might go to Solomon's Stables?' 'Would that be too much for Mother?' 'The Wailing Wall in the morning?' 'The Temple, of course – the Mosque of Omar they call it – I wonder why?' 'Because it's been made into a Moslem mosque, of course, Lennox.'

Ordinary commonplace tourist's talk. And yet, somehow, Dr Gerard felt a queer conviction that these overheard scraps of dialogue were all singularly unreal. They were a mask – a cover for something that surged and eddied underneath – something too deep and formless for words . . . Again he shot a covert glance from behind the shelter of *Le Matin*.

Lennox? That was the elder brother. The same family likeness could be traced, but there was a difference. Lennox was not so highly strung; he was, Gerard decided, of a less nervous temperament. But about him, too, there seemed something odd. There was no sign of muscular tension about him as there was about the other two. He sat relaxed, limp. Puzzling, searching among memories of patients he had seen sitting like that in hospital wards, Gerard thought:

'He is *exhausted* – yes, exhausted with suffering. That look in the eyes – the look you see in a wounded dog or a sick horse – dumb bestial endurance . . . It is odd, that . . . Physically there seems nothing wrong with him . . . Yet there is no doubt that lately he has been through much suffering – mental suffering – now he no longer suffers – he endures dumbly – waiting, I think, for the blow to fall . . . What blow? Am I fancying all this? No, the man is waiting for something, for the end to come. So cancer patients lie and wait, thankful that an anodyne dulls the pain a little . . .'

Lennox Boynton got up and retrieved a ball of wool that the old lady had dropped.

'Here you are, Mother.'

'Thank you.'

What was she knitting, this monumental impassive old woman? Something thick and coarse. Gerard thought: 'Mittens for inhabitants of a workhouse!' And smiled at his own fantasy.

He turned his attention to the youngest member of the party – the girl with the golden-red hair. She was, perhaps, nineteen.

Her skin had the exquisite clearness that often goes with red hair. Although over thin, it was a beautiful face. She was sitting smiling to herself – smiling into space. There was something a little curious about that smile. It was so far removed from the Solomon Hotel, from Jerusalem . . . It reminded Dr Gerard of something . . . Presently it came to him in a flash. It was the strange unearthly smile that lifts the lips of the Maidens in the Acropolis at Athens – something remote and lovely and a little inhuman . . . The magic of the smile, her exquisite stillness gave him a little pang.

And then with a shock, Dr Gerard noticed her hands. They were concealed from the group round her by the table, but he could see them clearly from where he sat. In the shelter of her lap they were picking – picking – tearing a delicate handkerchief into tiny shreds.

It gave him a horrible shock. The aloof remote smile – the still body – and the busy destructive hands . . .

CHAPTER 4

There was a slow asthmatic wheezing cough – then the monumental knitting woman spoke.

'Ginevra, you're tired, you'd better go to bed.'

The girl started, her fingers stopped their mechanical action. 'I'm not tired, Mother.'

Gerard recognized appreciatively the musical quality of her voice. It had the sweet singing quality that lends enchantment to the most commonplace utterances.

'Yes, you are. I always know. I don't think you'll be able to do any sightseeing tomorrow.'

'Oh! but I shall. I'm quite all right.'

In a thick hoarse voice – almost a grating voice, her mother said: 'No, you're not. You're going to be ill.'

'I'm not! I'm not!'

The girl began trembling violently.

A soft, calm voice said: 'I'll come up with you, Jinny.'

The quiet young woman with wide, thoughtful grey eyes and neatly-coiled dark hair rose to her feet.

Old Mrs Boynton said: 'No. Let her go up alone.'

The girl cried: 'I want Nadine to come!'

'Then of course I will.' The young woman moved a step forward.

The old woman said: 'The child prefers to go by herself – don't you, Jinny?'

There was a pause – a pause of a moment, then Ginevra Boynton said, her voice suddenly flat and dull:

'Yes; I'd rather go alone. Thank you, Nadine.'

She moved away, a tall angular figure that moved with a surprising grace.

Dr Gerard lowered his paper and took a full satisfying gaze at old Mrs Boynton. She was looking after her daughter and her fat face was creased into a peculiar smile. It was, very faintly, a caricature of the lovely unearthly smile that had transformed the girl's face so short a time before.

Then the old woman transferred her gaze to Nadine. The latter had just sat down again. She raised her eyes and met her mother-in-law's glance. Her face was quite imperturbable. The old woman's glance was malicious.

Dr Gerard thought: 'What an absurdity of an old tyrant!'

And then, suddenly, the old woman's eyes were full on him, and he drew in his breath sharply. Small black smouldering eyes they were, but something came from them, a power, a definite force, a wave of evil malignancy. Dr Gerard knew something about the power of personality. He realized that this was no spoilt tyrannical invalid indulging petty whims. This old woman was a definite force. In the malignancy of her glare he felt a resemblance to the effect produced by a cobra. Mrs Boynton might be old, infirm, a prey to disease, but she was not powerless. She was a woman who knew the meaning of power, who had exercised a lifetime of power and who had never once doubted her own force. Dr Gerard had once met a woman who performed a most dangerous and spectacular act with tigers. The great slinking brutes had crawled to their places and performed their degrading and humiliating tricks. Their eyes and subdued snarls told of hatred, bitter fanatical hatred, but they had obeyed, cringed. That had been a young woman, a woman with an arrogant dark beauty, but the look had been the same.

'*Une dompteuse*,' said Dr Gerard to himself.

And he understood now what that undercurrent to the harmless family talk had been. It was hatred – a dark eddying stream of hatred.

He thought: 'How fanciful and absurd most people would think me! Here is a commonplace devoted American family revelling in Palestine – and I weave a story of black magic round it!'

Then he looked with interest at the quiet young woman who was called Nadine. There was a wedding ring on her left hand, and as he watched her he saw her give one swift betraying glance at the fair-haired, loose-limbed Lennox. He knew, then . . .

They were man and wife, those two. But it was a mother's glance rather than a wife's – a true mother's glance – protecting, anxious. And he knew something more. He knew that, alone out of that group, Nadine Boynton was unaffected by her mother-in-law's spell. She may have disliked the old woman, but she was not afraid of her. The power did not touch her.

She was unhappy, deeply concerned about her husband, but she was free.

Dr Gerard said to himself: 'All this is very interesting.'

CHAPTER 5

Into these dark imaginings a breath of the commonplace came with almost ludicrous effect.

A man came into the lounge, caught sight of the Boyntons and came across to them. He was a pleasant middle-aged American of a strictly conventional type. He was carefully dressed, with a long clean-shaven face and he had a slow, pleasant, somewhat monotonous voice.

'I was looking around for you all,' he said.

Meticulously he shook hands with the entire family. 'And how do you find yourself, Mrs Boynton? Not too tired by the journey?'

Almost graciously, the old lady wheezed out: 'No, thank you. My health's never good, as you know –'

'Why, of course, too bad – too bad.'

'But I'm certainly no worse.'

Mrs Boynton added with a slow reptilian smile: 'Nadine, here, takes good care of me, don't you, Nadine?'

'I do my best.' Her voice was expressionless.

'Why, I bet you do,' said the stranger heartily. 'Well, Lennox, and what do you think of King David's city?'

'Oh, I don't know.'

Lennox spoke apathetically – without interest.

'Find it kind of disappointing, do you? I'll confess it struck me that way at first. But perhaps you haven't been around much yet?'

Carol Boynton said: 'We can't do very much because of Mother.'

Mrs Boynton explained: 'A couple of hours' sightseeing is about all I can manage every day.'

The stranger said heartily: 'I think it's wonderful you manage to do all you do, Mrs Boynton.'

Mrs Boynton gave a slow, wheezy chuckle; it had an almost gloating sound.

'I don't give in to my body! It's the mind that matters! Yes, it's the *mind* . . .'

Her voice died away. Gerard saw Raymond Boynton give a nervous jerk.

'Have you been to the Wailing Wall yet, Mr Cope?' he asked.

'Why, yes, that was one of the first places I visited. I hope to have done Jerusalem thoroughly in a couple more days, and I'm letting them get me out an itinerary at Cook's so as to do the Holy Land thoroughly – Bethlehem, Nazareth, Tiberias, the Sea of Galilee. It's all going to be mighty interesting. Then there's Jerash, there are some very interesting ruins there – Roman, you know. And I'd very much like to have a look at the Rose Red City of Petra, a most remarkable natural phenomenon, I believe that is – and right off the beaten track – but it takes the best part of a week to get there and back, and do it properly.'

Carol said: 'I'd love to go there. It sounds marvellous.'

'Why, I should say it was definitely worth seeing – yes, definitely worth seeing.' Mr Cope paused, shot a somewhat dubious glance at Mrs Boynton, and then went on in a voice that to the listening Frenchman was palpably uncertain:

'I wonder now if I couldn't persuade some of you people to come with me? Naturally I know *you* couldn't manage it, Mrs Boynton, and naturally some of your family would want to remain with you, but if you were to divide forces, so to speak –'

He paused. Gerard heard the even click of Mrs Boynton's knitting needles. Then she said:

'I don't think we'd care to divide up. We're a very homey group.' She looked up. 'Well, children, what do you say?'

There was a queer ring in her voice. The answers came promptly. 'No, Mother.' 'Oh, no.' 'No, of course not.'

Mrs Boynton said, smiling that very odd smile of hers: 'You see – they won't leave me. What about you, Nadine? You didn't say anything.'

'No, thank you, Mother, not unless Lennox cares about it.'

Mrs Boynton turned her head slowly towards her son.

'Well, Lennox, what about it, why don't you and Nadine go? She seems to want to.'

He started – looked up. 'I – well – no, I – I think we'd better all stay together.'

Mr Cope said genially: 'Well, you *are* a devoted family!' But something in his geniality rang a little hollow and forced.

'We keep to ourselves,' said Mrs Boynton. She began to wind up her ball of wool. 'By the way, Raymond, who was that young woman who spoke to you just now?'

Raymond started nervously. He flushed, then went white.

'I – I don't know her name. She – she was on the train the other night.'

Mrs Boynton began slowly to try to heave herself out of her chair.

'I don't think we'll have much to do with her,' she said.

Nadine rose and assisted the old woman to struggle out of her chair. She did it with a professional deftness that attracted Gerard's attention.

'Bedtime,' said Mrs Boynton. 'Good night, Mr Cope.'

'Good night, Mrs Boynton. Good night, Mrs Lennox.'

They went off – a little procession. It did not seem to occur to any of the younger members of the party to stay behind.

Mr Cope was left looking after them. The expression on his face was an odd one.

As Dr Gerard knew by experience, Americans are disposed to be a friendly race. They have not the uneasy suspicion of the travelling Briton. To a man of Dr Gerard's tact making

437

the acquaintance of Mr Cope presented few difficulties. The American was lonely and was, like most of his race, disposed to friendliness. Dr Gerard's card-case was again to the fore.

Reading the name on it, Mr Jefferson Cope was duly impressed.

'Why, surely, Dr Gerard, you were over in the States not very long ago?'

'Last autumn. I was lecturing at Harvard.'

'Of course. Yours, Dr Gerard, is one of the most distinguished names in your profession. You're pretty well at the head of your subject in Paris.'

'My dear sir, you are far too kind! I protest.'

'No, no, this is a great privilege – meeting you like this. As a matter of fact, there are several very distinguished people here in Jerusalem just at present. There's yourself and there's Lord Welldon, and Sir Gabriel Steinbaum, the financier. Then there's the veteran English archaeologist, Sir Manders Stone. And there's Lady Westholme, who's very prominent in English politics. And there's that famous Belgian detective Hercule Poirot.'

'Little Hercule Poirot? Is he here?'

'I read his name in the local paper as having lately arrived. Seems to me all the world and his wife are at the Solomon Hotel. A mighty fine hotel it is, too. And very tastefully decorated.'

Mr Jefferson Cope was clearly enjoying himself. Dr Gerard was a man who could display a lot of charm when he chose. Before long the two men had adjourned to the bar.

After a couple of highballs Gerard said: 'Tell me, is that a typical American family to whom you were talking?'

Jefferson Cope sipped his drink thoughtfully. Then he said: 'Why, no, I wouldn't say it was exactly typical.'

'No? A very devoted family, I thought.'

Mr Cope said slowly: 'You mean they all seem to revolve round the old lady? That's true enough. She's a very remarkable old lady, you know.'

'Indeed?'

Mr Cope needed very little encouragement. The gentle invitation was enough.

'I don't mind telling you, Dr Gerard, I've been having that family a good deal on my mind lately. I've been thinking about them a lot. If I may say so, it would ease my mind to talk to you about the matter. If it won't bore you, that is?'

Dr Gerard disclaimed boredom. Mr Jefferson Cope went on slowly, his pleasant clean-shaven face creased with perplexity.

'I'll tell you straight away that I'm just a little worried. Mrs Boynton, you see, is an old friend of mine. That is to say, not the old Mrs Boynton, the young one, Mrs Lennox Boynton.'

'Ah, yes, that very charming dark-haired young lady.'

'That's right. That's Nadine. Nadine Boynton, Dr Gerard, is a very lovely character. I knew her before she was married. She was in hospital then, working to be a trained nurse. Then she went for a vacation to stay with the Boyntons and she married Lennox.'

'Yes?'

Mr Jefferson Cope took another sip of highball and went on:

'I'd like to tell you, Dr Gerard, just a little of the Boynton family history.'

'Yes? I should be most interested.'

'Well, you see, the late Elmer Boynton – he was quite a well-known man and a very charming personality – was twice married. His first wife died when Carol and Raymond were tiny toddlers. The second Mrs Boynton, so I've been told, was a handsome woman when he married her, though not very young. Seems odd to think she can ever have been handsome to look at her now, but that's what I've been told on very good authority. Anyway, her husband thought a lot of her and adopted her judgement on almost every point. He was an invalid for some years before he died, and she practically ruled the roost. She's a very capable woman with a fine head for business. A very conscientious woman, too. After Elmer died, she devoted herself absolutely to these children. There's one of her own, too, Ginevra – pretty red-haired girl, but a bit delicate. Well, as I was telling you, Mrs Boynton devoted herself entirely to her family. She just shut out the outside world entirely. Now I don't know what you think, Dr Gerard, but I don't think that's always a very sound thing.'

'I agree with you. It is most harmful to developing mentalities.'

'Yes, I should say that just about expresses it. Mrs Boynton shielded these children from the outside world and never let them make any outside contacts. The result of that is that they've grown up – well, kind of nervy. They're jumpy, if you know what I mean. Can't make friends with strangers. It's bad, that.'

'It is very bad.'

'I've no doubt Mrs Boynton meant well. It was just over-devotion on her part.'

'They all live at home?' asked the doctor.

'Yes.'

'Do neither of the sons work?'

'Why, no. Elmer Boynton was a rich man. He left all his money to Mrs Boynton for her lifetime – but it was understood that it was for the family upkeep generally.'

'So they are dependent on her financially?'

'That is so. And she's encouraged them to live at home and not go out and look for jobs. Well, maybe that's all right, there's plenty of money, they don't need to take a job, but I think for the male sex, anyway, work's a good tonic. Then, there's another thing – they've none of them got any hobbies. They don't play golf. They don't belong to any country club. They don't go around to dances or do anything with the other young people. They live in a great barrack of a house way down in the country miles from anywhere. I tell you, Dr Gerard, it seems all wrong to me.'

'I agree with you,' said Dr Gerard.

'Not one of them has got the least social sense. The community spirit – that's what's lacking! They may be a very devoted family, but they're all bound up in themselves.'

'There has never been any question of one or other of them branching out for him or herself?'

'Not that I've heard of. They just sit around.'

'Do you put the blame for that on them or on Mrs Boynton?'

Jefferson Cope shifted uneasily.

'Well, in a sense, I feel she is more or less responsible. It's bad bringing-up on her part. All the same, when a young fellow comes to maturity it's up to him to kick over the traces of his own accord. No boy ought to keep on being tied to his mother's apron strings. He ought to choose to be independent.'

Dr Gerard said thoughtfully: 'That might be impossible.'

'Why impossible?'

'There are methods, Mr Cope, of preventing a tree from growing.'

Cope stared. 'They're a fine healthy lot, Dr Gerard.'

'The mind can be stunted and warped as well as the body.'

'They're bright mentally, too.'

Jefferson Cope went on: 'No, Dr Gerard, take it from me, a man has got the control of his own destiny right there in his own hands. A man who respects himself strikes out on his own and makes something of his life. He doesn't just sit round and twiddle his thumbs. No woman ought to respect a man who does that.'

Gerard looked at him curiously for a minute or two. Then he said: 'You refer particularly, I think, to Mr Lennox Boynton?'

'Why, yes, it was Lennox I was thinking of. Raymond's only a boy still. But Lennox is just on thirty. Time he showed he was made of something.'

'It is a difficult life, perhaps, for his wife?'

'Of course it's a difficult life for her! Nadine is a very fine girl. I admire her more than I can say. She's never let drop one word of complaint. *But she's not happy*, Dr Gerard. She's just as unhappy as she can be.'

Gerard nodded his head.

'Yes, I think that well might be.'

'I don't know what you think about it, Dr Gerard, but *I* think that there's a limit to what a woman ought to put up with! If I were Nadine I'd put it to young Lennox straight. Either he sets to and proves what he's made of, or else –'

'Or else, you think, she should leave him?'

'She's got her own life to live, Dr Gerard. If Lennox doesn't appreciate her as she ought to be appreciated – well, there are other men who will.'

'There is – yourself, for instance?'

The American flushed. Then he looked straight at the other with a certain simple dignity.

'That's so,' he said. 'I'm not ashamed of my feeling for that lady. I respect her and I am very deeply attached to her. All I want is her happiness. If she were happy with Lennox, I'd sit right back and fade out of the picture.'

'But as it is?'

'But as it is I'm standing by! If she wants me, *I'm here!*'

'You are, in fact, the *parfait gentil* knight,' murmured Gerard.

'Pardon?'

'My dear sir, chivalry only lives nowadays in the American nation! You are content to serve your lady without hope of

441

reward! It is most admirable, that! What exactly do you hope to be able to do for her?'

'My idea is to be right here at hand if she needs me.'

'And what, may I ask, is the older Mrs Boynton's attitude towards you?'

Jefferson Cope said slowly: 'I'm never quite sure about that old lady. As I've told you, she isn't fond of making outside contacts. But she's been different to me, she's always very gracious and treats me quite like one of the family.'

'In fact, she approves of your friendship with Mrs Lennox?'

'She does.'

Dr Gerard shrugged his shoulders.

'That is, perhaps, a little odd?'

Jefferson Cope said stiffly: 'Let me assure you, Dr Gerard, there is nothing dishonourable in that friendship. It is purely platonic.'

'My dear sir, I am quite sure of that. I repeat, though, that for Mrs Boynton to encourage that friendship is a curious action on her part. You know, Mr Cope, Mrs Boynton interests me – she interests me greatly.'

'She is certainly a remarkable woman. She has great force of character – a most prominent personality. As I say, Elmer Boynton had the greatest faith in her judgement.'

'So much so that he was content to leave his children completely at her mercy from the financial point of view. In my country, Mr Cope, it is impossible by law to do such a thing.'

Mr Cope rose. 'In America,' he said, 'we're great believers in absolute freedom.'

Dr Gerard rose also. He was unimpressed by the remark. He had heard it made before by people of many different nationalities. The illusion that freedom is the prerogative of one's own particular race is fairly widespread.

Dr Gerard was wiser. He knew that no race, no country and no individual could be described as free. But he also knew that there were different degrees of bondage.

He went up to bed thoughtful and interested.

Sarah King stood in the precincts of the Temple – the Haramesh-Sherif. Her back was to the Dome of the Rock. The splashing of fountains sounded in her ears. Little groups of tourists passed by without disturbing the peace of the oriental atmosphere.

Strange, thought Sarah, that once a Jebusite should have made this rocky summit into a threshing floor and that David should have purchased it for six hundred shekels of gold and made it a Holy Place. And now the loud chattering tongues of sightseers of all nations could be heard.

She turned and looked at the Mosque which now covered the shrine and wondered if Solomon's temple would have looked half as beautiful.

There was a clatter of footsteps and a little party came out from the interior of the Mosque. It was the Boyntons escorted by a voluble dragoman. Mrs Boynton was supported between Lennox and Raymond. Nadine and Mr Cope walked behind. Carol came last. As they were moving off, the latter caught sight of Sarah.

She hesitated, then, on a sudden decision, she wheeled round and ran swiftly and noiselessly across the courtyard.

'Excuse me,' she said breathlessly. 'I must – I – I felt I must speak to you.'

'Yes?' said Sarah.

Carol was trembling violently. Her face was quite white.

'It's about – my brother. When you – you spoke to him last night you must have thought him very rude. But he didn't mean to be – he – he couldn't help it. Oh, do please believe me.'

Sarah felt that the whole scene was ridiculous. Both her pride and her good taste were offended. Why should a strange girl suddenly rush up and tender a ridiculous apology for a boorish brother?

An off-hand reply trembled on her lips – and then, quickly, her mood changed.

There was something out of the ordinary here. This girl was in deadly earnest. That something in Sarah which had led her to adopt a medical career reacted to the girl's need. Her instinct told her there was something badly wrong.

She said encouragingly: 'Tell me about it.'

'He spoke to you on the train, didn't he?' began Carol.

Sarah nodded. 'Yes; at least, I spoke to him.'

'Oh, of course. It would be that way round. But, you see, last night Ray was afraid –'

She stopped.

'Afraid?'

Carol's white face crimsoned.

'Oh, I know it sounds absurd – mad. You see, my mother – she's – she's not well – and she doesn't like us making friends outside. But – but I know Ray would – would like to be friends with you.'

Sarah was interested. Before she could speak, Carol went on: 'I – I know what I'm saying sounds very silly, but we are – rather an odd family.' She cast a quick look round – it was a look of fear.

'I – I mustn't stay,' she murmured. 'They may miss me.'

Sarah made up her mind. She spoke.

'Why shouldn't you stay – if you want to? We might walk back together.'

'Oh, no.' Carol drew back. 'I – I couldn't do that.'

'Why not?' said Sarah.

'I couldn't really. My mother would be – would be –'

Sarah said clearly and calmly:

'I know it's awfully difficult sometimes for parents to realize that their children are grown up. They will go on trying to run their lives for them. But it's a pity, you know, to give in! One must stand up for one's rights.'

Carol murmured: 'You don't understand – you don't understand in the least . . .'

Her hands twisted together nervously.

Sarah went on: 'One gives in sometimes because one is afraid of rows. Rows are very unpleasant, but I think freedom of action is always worth fighting for.'

'Freedom?' Carol stared at her. 'None of us have ever been free. We never will be.'

'Nonsense!' said Sarah clearly.

Carol leaned forward and touched her arm.

'Listen. I *must* try and make you understand! Before her marriage my mother – she's my stepmother really – was a wardress in a prison. My father was the Governor and he married her. Well, *it's been like that ever since*. She's gone on being a wardress – *to us*. That's why our life is just – being in prison!'

Her head jerked round again.

'They've missed me. I – I must go.'

Sarah caught her by the arm as she was darting off.

'One minute. We must meet again and talk.'

'I can't. I shan't be able to.'

'Yes, you can.' She spoke authoritatively. 'Come to my room after you go to bed. It's 319. Don't forget, 319.'

She released her hold. Carol ran off after her family.

Sarah stood staring after her. She awoke from her thoughts to find Dr Gerard by her side.

'Good morning, Miss King. So you've been talking to Miss Carol Boynton?'

'Yes, we had the most extraordinary conversation. Let me tell you.'

She repeated the substance of her conversation with the girl. Gerard pounced on one point.

'Wardress in a prison, was she, that old hippopotamus? That is significant, perhaps.'

Sarah said:

'You mean that that is the cause of her tyranny? It is the habit of her former profession.'

Gerard shook his head.

'No, that is approaching it from the wrong angle. There is some deep underlying compulsion. She does not love tyranny *because she has been a wardress*. Let us rather say that *she became a wardress because she loved tyranny*. In my theory it was a secret desire for power over other human beings that led her to adopt that profession.'

His face was very grave.

'There are such strange things buried down in the unconscious. A lust for power – a lust for cruelty – a savage desire to tear and rend – all the inheritance of our past racial memories . . . They are all there, Miss King, all the cruelty and savagery and lust . . . We shut the door on them and deny them conscious life, but sometimes – they are too strong.'

Sarah shivered. 'I know.'

Gerard continued: 'We see it all round us today – in political creeds, in the conduct of nations. A reaction from humanitarianism – from pity – from brotherly good-will. The creeds sound well sometimes – a wise régime – a beneficent government – but imposed by *force* – resting on a basis of cruelty and fear. They are opening the door, these apostles of violence, they are letting up the old savagery, the old delight in cruelty *for its own sake*! Oh, it is difficult – Man is an animal very delicately balanced. He has one prime necessity – to survive. To advance too quickly is as fatal as to lag behind. He must survive! He must, perhaps, retain some of the old savagery, but he must not – no definitely he must not – *deify* it!'

There was a pause. Then Sarah said:

'You think old Mrs Boynton is a kind of sadist?'

'I am almost sure of it. I think she rejoices in the infliction of pain – mental pain, mind you, not physical. That is very much rarer and very much more difficult to deal with. She likes to have control of other human beings and she likes to make them suffer.'

'It's pretty beastly,' said Sarah.

Gerard told her of his conversation with Jefferson Cope. 'He doesn't realize what is going on?' she said thoughtfully.

'How should he? He is not a psychologist.'

'True. He hasn't got our disgusting minds!'

'Exactly. He has a nice, upright, sentimental, normal American mind. He believes in good rather than evil. He sees that the atmosphere of the Boynton family is all wrong, but he credits Mrs Boynton with misguided devotion rather than active maleficence.'

'That should amuse her,' said Sarah.

'I should imagine it does!'

Sarah said impatiently:

'But why don't they break away? They could.'

Gerard shook his head.

'No, there you are wrong. *They cannot.* Have you ever seen the old experiment with a cock? You chalk a line on the floor and put the cock's beak on it. The cock believes he is tied there. He cannot raise his head. So with these unfortunates. She has worked on them, remember, since they were children. And her dominance has been mental. She has hypnotized them to believe that *they cannot disobey her*. Oh, I know most people would say that was nonsense – but you and I know better. She has made them believe that utter dependence on her is inevitable. They have been in prison so long that if the prison door stands open they would no longer notice! One of them, at least, no longer even wants to be free! And they would all be *afraid* of freedom.'

Sarah asked practically: 'What will happen when she dies?'

Gerard shrugged his shoulders.

'It depends. On how soon that happens. If it happened *now* – well, I think it might not be too late. The boy and girl – they are still young – impressionable. They would become, I believe, normal human beings. With Lennox, possibly, it has gone too far. He looks to me like a man who has parted company with hope – he lives and endures like a brute beast.'

Sarah said impatiently: 'His wife ought to have done something! She ought to have yanked him out of it.'

'I wonder. She may have tried – and failed.'

'Do you think she's under the spell, too?'

Gerard shook his head.

'No. I don't think the old lady has any power over her, and for that reason she hates her with a bitter hatred. Watch her eyes.'

Sarah frowned. 'I can't make her out – the young one, I mean. Does she know what is going on?'

'I think she must have a pretty shrewd idea.'

'H'm,' said Sarah. 'That old woman ought to be murdered! Arsenic in her early morning tea would be my prescription.'

Then she said abruptly:

'What about the youngest girl – the red-haired one with the rather fascinating vacant smile?'

Gerard frowned. 'I don't know. There is something queer there. Ginevra Boynton is the old woman's own daughter, of course.'

'Yes. I suppose that would be different – or wouldn't it?'

Gerard said slowly: 'I do not believe that when once the mania for power (and the lust for cruelty) has taken possession of a human being it can spare *anybody* – not even its nearest and dearest.'

He was silent for a moment, then he said: 'Are you a Christian, mademoiselle?'

Sarah said slowly: 'I don't know. I used to think that I wasn't anything. But now – I'm not sure. I feel – oh, I feel that if I could sweep all this away' – she made a violent gesture – 'all the buildings and the sects and the fierce squabbling churches – that – that I might see Christ's quiet figure riding into Jerusalem on a donkey – and believe in Him.'

Dr Gerard said gravely: 'I believe at least in one of the chief tenets of the Christian faith – *contentment with a lowly place*. I am a doctor and I know that ambition – the desire to succeed – to have power – leads to most ills of the human soul. If the desire is realized it leads to arrogance, violence and final satiety – and if it is denied – ah! if it is denied – let all the asylums for the insane rise up and give their testimony! They are filled with human beings who were unable to face being mediocre, insignificant, ineffective and who therefore created for themselves ways of escape from reality so as to be shut off from life itself for ever.'

Sarah said abruptly: 'It's a pity the old Boynton woman isn't in an asylum.'

Gerard shook his head.

'No – her place is not there among the failures. It is worse than that. She has succeeded, you see! She has accomplished her dream.'

Sarah shuddered.

She cried passionately: 'Such things ought not to be!'

CHAPTER 7

Sarah wondered very much whether Carol Boynton would keep her appointment that night.

On the whole she rather doubted it. She was afraid that Carol would have a sharp reaction after her semi-confidences of the morning.

Nevertheless she made her preparations, slipping on a blue satin dressing-gown and getting out her little spirit lamp and boiling up water.

She was just on the point of giving Carol up (it was after one o'clock) and going to bed, when there was a tap on her door. She opened it and drew quickly back to let Carol come in.

The latter said breathlessly: 'I was afraid you might have gone to bed . . .'

Sarah's manner was carefully matter-of-fact.

'Oh, no, I was waiting for you. Have some tea, will you? It's real Lapsang Souchong.'

She brought over a cup. Carol had been nervous and uncertain of herself. Now she accepted the cup and a biscuit and her manner became calmer.

'This is rather fun,' said Sarah, smiling.

Carol looked a little startled.

'Yes,' she said doubtfully. 'Yes, I suppose it is.'

'Rather like the midnight feasts we used to have at school,' went on Sarah. 'I suppose you didn't go to school?'

Carol shook her head.

'No, we never left home. We had a governess – different governesses. They never stayed long.'

'Did you never go away at all?'

'No. We've lived always in the same house. This coming abroad is the first time I've ever been away.'

Sarah said casually: 'It must have been a great adventure.'

'Oh, it was. It – it's all been like a dream.'

'What made your – your stepmother decide to come abroad?'

At the mention of Mrs Boynton's name, Carol had flinched. Sarah said quickly:

'You know, I'm by way of being a doctor. I've just taken my M.B. Your mother – or stepmother rather – is very interesting to me – as a case, you know. I should say she was quite definitely a pathological case.'

Carol stared. It was clearly a very unexpected point of view to her. Sarah had spoken as she had with deliberate intent. She realized that to her family Mrs Boynton loomed as a kind of powerful obscene idol. It was Sarah's object to rob her of her more terrifying aspect.

'Yes,' she said. 'There's a kind of disease of – of grandeur – that gets hold of people. They get very autocratic and insist on everything being done exactly as they say and are altogether very difficult to deal with.'

Carol put down her cup.

'Oh,' she cried, 'I'm so glad to be talking to you. Really, you know, I believe Ray and I have been getting quite – well, quite queer. We'd get terribly worked up about things.'

'Talking with an outsider is always a good thing,' said Sarah.

'Inside a family one is apt to get too intense.' Then she asked casually: 'If you are unhappy, haven't you ever thought of leaving home?'

Carol looked startled. 'Oh, no! How could we? I – I mean Mother would never allow it.'

'But she couldn't stop you,' said Sarah gently. 'You're over age.'

'I'm twenty-three.'

'Exactly.'

'But still, I don't see how – I mean, I wouldn't know where to go and what to do.'

Her tone seemed bewildered.

'You see,' she said, 'we haven't got any money.'

'Haven't you any friends you could go to?'

'Friends?' Carol shook her head. 'Oh, no, we don't know anyone!'

'Did none of you ever think of leaving home?'

'No – I don't think so. Oh – oh – we couldn't.'

Sarah changed the subject. She found the girl's bewilderment pitiful.

She said: 'Are you fond of your stepmother?'

Slowly Carol shook her head. She whispered in a low scared voice: 'I hate her. So does Ray . . . We've – we've often wished she would die.'

Again Sarah changed the subject.

'Tell me about your elder brother.'

'Lennox? I don't know what's the matter with Lennox. He hardly ever speaks now. He goes about in a kind of daydream. Nadine's terribly worried about him.'

'You are fond of your sister-in-law?'

'Yes, Nadine is different. She's always kind. But she's very unhappy.'

'About your brother?'

'Yes.'

'Have they been married long?'

'Four years.'

'And they've always lived at home?'

'Yes.'

Sarah asked: 'Does your sister-in-law like that?'

'No.'

450

There was a pause. Then Carol said:

'There was an awful fuss just over four years ago. You see, as I told you, none of us ever go outside the house at home. I mean we go into the grounds, but nowhere else. But Lennox did. He got out at night. He went into Fountain Springs – there was a sort of dance going on. Mother was frightfully angry when she found out. It was terrible. And then, after that, she asked Nadine to come and stay. Nadine was a very distant cousin of Father's. She was very poor and was training to be a hospital nurse. She came and stayed with us for a month. I can't tell you how exciting it was to have someone to stay! And she and Lennox fell in love with each other. And Mother said they'd better be married quickly and live on with us.'

'And was Nadine willing to do that?'

Carol hesitated.

'I don't think she wanted to do that very much, but she didn't really *mind*. Then, later, she wanted to go away – with Lennox, of course –'

'But they didn't go?' asked Sarah.

'No, Mother wouldn't hear of it.'

Carol paused, and then said:

'I don't think – she likes Nadine any longer. Nadine is – funny. You never know what she's thinking. She tries to help Jinny and Mother doesn't like it.'

'Jinny is your youngest sister?'

'Yes. Ginevra is her real name.'

'Is she – unhappy, too?'

Carol shook her head doubtfully.

'Jinny's been very queer lately. I don't understand her. You see, she's always been rather delicate – and – and Mother fusses about her and – and it makes her worse. And lately Jinny has been very queer indeed. She – she frightens me sometimes. She – she doesn't always know what she's doing.'

'Has she seen a doctor?'

'No, Nadine wanted her to, but Mother said no – and Jinny got very hysterical and screamed, and said she wouldn't see a doctor. But I'm worried about her.'

Suddenly Carol rose.

'I mustn't keep you up. It's – it's very good of you letting me come and talk to you. You must think us very odd as a family.'

'Oh, everybody's odd, really,' said Sarah lightly. 'Come again, will you? And bring your brother, if you like.'

'May I really?'

'Yes; we'll do some secret plotting. I'd like you to meet a friend of mine, too, a Dr Gerard, an awfully nice Frenchman.'

The colour came into Carol's cheeks.

'Oh, what fun it sounds. If only Mother doesn't find out!'

Sarah suppressed her original retort and said instead, 'Why should she? Good night. Shall we say tomorrow night at the same time?'

'Oh, yes. The day after, you see, we may be going away.'

'Then let's have a definite date for tomorrow. Good night.'

'Good night – and thank you.'

Carol went out of the room and slipped noiselessly along the corridor. Her own room was on the floor above. She reached it, opened the door – and stood appalled on the threshold. Mrs Boynton was sitting in an armchair by the fireplace in a crimson wool dressing-gown.

A little cry escaped from Carol's lips. 'Oh!'

A pair of black eyes bored into hers.

'Where have you been, Carol?'

'I – I –'

'Where have you been?'

A soft, husky voice with that queer menacing undertone in it that always made Carol's heart beat with unreasoning terror.

'To see a Miss King – Sarah King.'

'The girl who spoke to Raymond the other evening?'

'Yes, Mother.'

'Have you made any plans to see her again?'

Carol's lips moved soundlessly. She nodded assent. Fright – great sickening waves of fright . . .

'When?'

'Tomorrow night.'

'You are not to go. You understand?'

'Yes, Mother.'

'You promise?'

'Yes – yes.'

Mrs Boynton struggled to get up. Mechanically Carol came forward and helped her. Mrs Boynton walked slowly across the room, supporting herself on her stick. She paused in the doorway and looked back at the cowering girl.

'You are to have nothing more to do with this Miss King. You understand?'

'Yes, Mother.'

'Repeat it.'

'I am to have nothing more to do with her.'

'Good.'

Mrs Boynton went out and shut the door.

Stiffly, Carol moved across the bedroom. She felt sick, her whole body felt wooden and unreal. She dropped on to the bed and suddenly she was shaken by a storm of weeping.

It was as though a vista had opened before her – a vista of sunlight and trees and flowers . . .

Now the black walls had closed round her once more.

CHAPTER 8

'Can I speak to you a minute?'

Nadine Boynton turned in surprise, staring into the dark eager face of an entirely unknown young woman.

'Why, certainly.'

But as she spoke, almost unconsciously she threw a quick nervous glance over her shoulder.

'My name is Sarah King,' went on the other.

'Oh, yes?'

'Mrs Boynton, I'm going to say something rather odd to you. I talked to your sister-in-law for quite a long time the other evening.'

A faint shadow seemed to ruffle the serenity of Nadine Boynton's face.

'You talked to Ginevra?'

'No, not to Ginevra – to Carol.'

The shadow lifted.

'Oh, I see – to Carol.'

Nadine Boynton seemed pleased, but very much surprised. 'How did you manage that?'

Sarah said: 'She came to my room – quite late.'

She saw the faint raising of the pencilled brows on the white forehead. She said with some embarrassment: 'I'm sure this must seem very odd to you.'

'No,' said Nadine Boynton. 'I am very glad. Very glad indeed. It is very nice for Carol to have a friend to talk to.'

'We – we got on very well together.' Sarah tried to choose her words carefully. 'In fact we arranged to – to meet again the following night.'

'Yes.'

'But Carol didn't come.'

'Didn't she?'

Nadine's voice was cool – reflective. Her face, so quiet and gentle, told Sarah nothing.

'No. Yesterday she was passing through the hall. I spoke to her and she didn't answer. Just looked at me once, and then away again, and hurried on.'

'I see.'

There was a pause. Sarah found it difficult to go on. Nadine Boynton said presently: 'I'm – very sorry. Carol is – rather a nervous girl.'

Again that pause. Sarah took her courage in both hands. 'You know, Mrs Boynton, I'm by way of being a doctor. I think – I think it would be good for your sister-in-law not to – not to shut herself away too much from people.'

Nadine Boynton looked thoughtfully at Sarah.

She said: 'I see. You're a doctor. That makes a difference.'

'You see what I mean?' Sarah urged.

Nadine bent her head. She was still thoughtful.

'You are quite right, of course,' she said after a minute or two. 'But there are difficulties. My mother-in-law is in bad health and she has what I can only describe as a morbid dislike of any outsiders penetrating into her family circle.'

Sarah said mutinously: 'But Carol is a grown-up woman.'

Nadine Boynton shook her head.

'Oh, no,' she said. 'In body, but not in mind. If you talked to her you must have noticed that. In an emergency she would always behave like a frightened child.'

'Do you think that's what happened? Do you think she became – afraid?'

'I should imagine, Miss King, that my mother-in-law insisted on Carol having nothing more to do with you.'

'And Carol gave in?'

Nadine Boynton said quietly: 'Can you really imagine her doing anything else?'

The eyes of the two women met. Sarah felt that behind the mask of conventional words they understood each other. Nadine, she felt, understood the position. But she was clearly not prepared to discuss it in any way.

Sarah felt discouraged. The other evening it had seemed to her as though half the battle were won. By means of secret meetings she would imbue Carol with the spirit of revolt – yes, and Raymond, too. (Be honest now, wasn't it Raymond really she had had in mind all along?) And now, in the very first round of the battle she had been ignominiously defeated by that hulk of shapeless flesh with her evil, gloating eyes. Carol had capitulated without a struggle.

'It's all *wrong*!' cried Sarah.

Nadine did not answer. Something in her silence went home to Sarah like a cold hand laid on her heart. She thought: 'This woman knows the hopelessness of it much better than I do. She's *lived* with it!'

The lift gates opened. The older Mrs Boynton emerged. She leaned on a stick and Raymond supported her on the other side.

Sarah gave a slight start. She saw the old woman's eyes sweep from her to Nadine and back again. She had been prepared for dislike in those eyes – for hatred even. She was not prepared for what she saw – a triumphant and malicious enjoyment. Sarah turned away. Nadine went forward and joined the other two.

'So there you are, Nadine,' said Mrs Boynton. 'I'll sit down and rest a little before I go out.'

They settled her in a high-backed chair. Nadine sat down beside her.

'Who were you talking to, Nadine?'

'A Miss King.'

'Oh, yes. The girl who spoke to Raymond the other night. Well, Ray, why don't you go and speak to her now? She's over there at the writing-table.'

The old woman's mouth widened into a malicious smile as she looked at Raymond. His face flushed. He turned his head away and muttered something.

'What's that you say, son?'

'I don't want to speak to her.'

'No, I thought not. You won't speak to her. You couldn't however much you wanted to!'

She coughed suddenly – a wheezing cough.

'I'm enjoying this trip, Nadine,' she said. 'I wouldn't have missed it for anything.'

'No?'

Nadine's voice was expressionless.

'Ray.'

'Yes, Mother?'

'Get me a piece of notepaper – from the table over there in the corner.'

Raymond went off obediently. Nadine raised her head. She watched, not the boy, but the old woman. Mrs Boynton was leaning forward, her nostrils dilated as though with pleasure. Ray passed close by Sarah. She looked up, a sudden hope showing in her face. It died down as he brushed past her, took some notepaper from the case and went back across the room.

There were little beads of sweat on his forehead as he rejoined them, and his face was dead white.

Very softly Mrs Boynton murmured: 'Ah . . .' as she watched his face.

Then she saw Nadine's eyes fixed on her. Something in them made her own snap with sudden anger.

'Where's Mr Cope this morning?' she said.

Nadine's eyes dropped again. She answered in her gentle, expressionless voice:

'I don't know. I haven't seen him.'

'I like him,' said Mrs Boynton. 'I like him very much. We must see a good deal of him. You'll like that, won't you?'

'Yes,' said Nadine. 'I, too, like him very much.'

'What's the matter with Lennox lately? He seems very dull and quiet. Nothing wrong between you, is there?'

'Oh, no. Why should there be?'

'I wondered. Married people don't always hit it off. Perhaps you'd be happier living in a home of your own?'

Nadine did not answer.

'Well, what do you say to the idea? Does it appeal to you?'

456

Nadine shook her head. She said, smiling: 'I don't think it would appeal to *you*, Mother.'

Mrs Boynton's eyelids flickered. She said sharply and venomously, 'You've always been against me, Nadine.'

The younger woman replied evenly:

'I'm sorry you should think that.'

The old woman's hand closed on her stick. Her face seemed to get a shade more purple.

She said, with a change of tone: 'I forgot my drops. Get them for me, Nadine.'

'Certainly.'

Nadine got up and crossed the lounge to the lift. Mrs Boynton looked after her. Raymond sat limply in a chair, his eyes glazed with dull misery.

Nadine went upstairs and along the corridor. She entered the sitting-room of their suite. Lennox was sitting by the window. There was a book in his hand, but he was not reading. He roused himself as Nadine came in. 'Hallo, Nadine.'

'I've come up for Mother's drops. She forgot them.'

She went on into Mrs Boynton's bedroom. From a bottle on the washstand she carefully measured a dose into a small medicine glass, filling it up with water. As she passed through the sitting-room again she paused.

'Lennox.'

It was a moment or two before he answered her. It was as though the message had a long way to travel.

Then he said: 'I beg your pardon. What is it?'

Nadine Boynton set down the glass carefully on the table. Then she went over and stood beside him.

'Lennox, look at the sunshine – out there, through the window. Look at life. It's beautiful. We might be out in it – instead of being here looking through a window.'

Again there was a pause. Then he said: 'I'm sorry. Do you want to go out?'

She answered him quickly: 'Yes, I want to go out – *with you* – out into the sunshine – out into life – and live – the two of us together.'

He shrank back into his chair. His eyes looked restless, hunted.

'Nadine, my dear – must we go into all this again?'

'Yes, we must. Let us go away and lead our own life some-where.'

'How can we? We've no money.'

'We can earn money.'

'How could we? What could we do? I'm untrained. Thousands of men – qualified men – trained men – are out of a job as it is. We couldn't manage it.'

'I would earn money for both of us.'

'My dear child, you'd never even completed your training. It's hopeless – impossible.'

'No, what is hopeless and impossible is our present life.'

'You don't know what you are talking about. Mother is very good to us. She gives us every luxury.'

'Except freedom. Lennox, make an effort. Come with me now – today –'

'Nadine, I think you're quite mad.'

'No, I'm sane. Absolutely and completely sane. I want a life of my own, with you, in the sunshine – not stifled in the shadow of an old woman who is a tyrant and who delights in making you unhappy.'

'Mother may be rather an autocrat –'

'Your mother is mad! She's insane!'

He answered mildly: 'That's not true. She's got a remarkably good head for business.'

'Perhaps – yes.'

'And you must realize, Nadine, she can't live for ever. She's getting old and she's in very bad health. At her death my father's money is divided equally among us share and share alike. You remember, she read us the will?'

'When she dies,' said Nadine, 'it may be too late.'

'Too late?'

'Too late for happiness.'

Lennox murmured: 'Too late for happiness.' He shivered suddenly. Nadine went closer to him. She put her hand on his shoulder.

'Lennox, I love you. It's a battle between me and your mother. Are you going to be on her side or mine?'

'On yours – on yours!'

'Then do what I ask.'

'It's impossible!'

'No, it's not impossible. Think, Lennox, we could have children . . .'

'Mother wants us to have children. She has said so.'

'I know, but I won't bring children into the world to live in the shadow you have all been brought up in. Your mother can influence you, but she's no power over me.'

Lennox murmured: 'You make her angry sometimes, Nadine; it isn't wise.'

'She is only angry because she knows that she can't influence my mind or dictate my thoughts!'

'I know you are always polite and gentle with her. You're wonderful. You're too good for me. You always have been. When you said you would marry me it was like an unbelievable dream.'

Nadine said quietly: 'I was wrong to marry you.'

Lennox said hopelessly: 'Yes, you were wrong.'

'You don't understand. What I mean is that if I had gone away then and asked you to follow me you would have done so. Yes, I really believe you would . . . I was not clever enough then to understand your mother and what she wanted.'

She paused, then she said: 'You refuse to come away? Well, I can't make you. But *I* am free to go! I think – I think I *shall* go . . .'

He stared up at her incredulously. For the first time his reply came quickly, as though at last the sluggish current of his thoughts was accelerated. He stammered: 'But – but – you can't do that. Mother – Mother would never hear of it.'

'She couldn't stop me.'

'You've no money.'

'I could make, borrow, beg or steal it. Understand, Lennox, your mother has no power over me! I can go or stay at my will. I am beginning to feel that I have borne this life long enough.'

'Nadine – don't leave me – don't leave me . . .'

She looked at him thoughtfully – quietly – with an inscrutable expression.

'Don't leave me, Nadine.'

He spoke like a child. She turned her head away, so that he should not see the sudden pain in her eyes.

She knelt down beside him.

459

'*Then come with me.* Come with me! You can. Indeed you can if you only will!'

He shrank back from her.

'I can't. I can't, I tell you. I haven't – God help me – *I haven't the courage* . . .'

CHAPTER 9

Dr Gerard walked into the office of Messrs Castle, the tourist agents, and found Sarah King at the counter.

She looked up.

'Oh, good morning. I'm fixing up my tour to Petra. I've just heard you are going after all.'

'Yes, I find I can just manage it.'

'How nice.'

'Shall we be a large party, I wonder?'

'They say just two other women – and you and me. One car load.'

'That will be delightful,' said Gerard, with a little bow. Then he, in turn, attended to his business.

Presently, holding his mail in his hands, he joined Sarah as she stepped out of the office. It was a crisp, sunny day, with a slight cold tang in the air.

'What news of our friends, the Boyntons?' asked Dr Gerard. 'I have been to Bethlehem and Nazareth and other places – a tour of three days.'

Slowly and rather unwillingly, Sarah narrated her abortive efforts to establish contact.

'Anyhow, I failed,' she finished. 'And they're leaving today.'

'Where are they going?'

'I've no idea.'

She went on vexedly: 'I feel, you know, that I've made rather a fool of myself!'

'In what way?'

'Interfering in other people's business.'

Gerard shrugged his shoulders.

'That is a matter of opinion.'

'You mean whether one should interfere or not?'

'Yes.'

'Do you?'

The Frenchman looked amused.

'You mean, is it my habit to concern myself with other people's affairs? I will say to you frankly: No.'

'Then you think I'm wrong to have tried butting in?'

'No, no, you misunderstand me.' Gerard spoke quickly and energetically. 'It is, I think, a moot question. Should one, if one sees a wrong being done, attempt to put it right? One's interference may do good – but it may do incalculable harm! It is impossible to lay down any ruling on the subject. Some people have a genius for interference – they do it well! Some people do it clumsily and had therefore better leave it alone! Then there is, too, the question of *age*. Young people have the courage of their ideals and convictions – their values are more theoretical than practical. They have not experienced, as yet, that fact contradicts theory! If you have a belief in yourself and in the rightness of what you are doing, you can often accomplish things that are well worth while! (Incidentally, you often do a good deal of harm!) On the other hand, the middle-aged person has experience – he has found that harm as well as, and perhaps more often than, good comes of trying to interfere and so – very wisely, he refrains! So the result is even – the earnest young do both harm and good – the prudent middle-aged do neither!'

'All that isn't very helpful,' objected Sarah.

'Can one person ever be helpful to another? It is *your* problem, not mine.'

'You mean *you* are not going to do anything about the Boyntons?'

'No. For me, there would be no chance of success.'

'Then there isn't for me, either?'

'For you, there might be.'

'Why?'

'Because you have special qualifications. The appeal of your youth and sex.'

'Sex? Oh, I see.'

'One comes always back to sex, does one not? You have failed with the girl. It does not follow that you would fail with her brother. What you have just told me (what the girl Carol told you) shows very clearly the one menace to Mrs Boynton's autocracy. The eldest son, Lennox, defied her in the force of

461

his young manhood. He played truant from home, went to local dances. The desire of a man for a mate was stronger than the hypnotic spell. But the old woman was quite aware of the power of sex. (She will have seen something of it in her career.) She dealt with it very cleverly – brought a pretty but penniless girl into the house – encouraged a marriage. And so acquired yet another slave.'

Sarah shook her head.

'I don't think young Mrs Boynton is a slave.'

Gerard agreed.

'No, perhaps not. I think that, because she was a quiet, docile young girl, old Mrs Boynton underestimated her force of will and character. Nadine Boynton was too young and inexperienced at the time to appreciate the true position. She appreciates it now, but it is too late.'

'Do you think she has given up hope?'

Dr Gerard shook his head doubtfully.

'If she has plans no one would know about them. There are, you know, certain possibilities where Cope is concerned. Man is a naturally jealous animal – and jealousy is a strong force. Lennox Boynton might still be roused from the inertia in which he is sinking.'

'And you think' – Sarah purposely made her tone very business-like and professional – 'that there's a chance I might be able to do something about Raymond?'

'I do.'

Sarah sighed.

'I suppose I might have tried. Oh, well, it's too late now, anyway. And – and I don't like the idea.'

Gerard looked amused.

'That is because you are English! The English have a complex about sex. They think it is "not quite nice".'

Sarah's indignant response failed to move him.

'Yes, yes; I know you are very modern – that you use freely in public the most unpleasant words you can find in the dictionary – that you are professional and entirely uninhibited! *Tout de même*, I repeat, you have the same facial characteristics as your mother and your grandmother. You are still the blushing English Miss although you do not blush!'

'I never heard such rubbish!'

Dr Gerard, a twinkle in his eye, and quite unperturbed, added: 'And it makes you very charming.'

This time Sarah was speechless.

Dr Gerard hastily raised his hat. 'I take my leave,' he said, 'before you have time to begin to say all that you think.' He escaped into the hotel.

Sarah followed him more slowly.

There was a good deal of activity going on. Several cars loaded with luggage were in the process of departing. Lennox and Nadine Boynton and Mr Cope were standing by a big saloon car superintending arrangements. A fat dragoman was standing talking to Carol with quite unintelligible fluency.

Sarah passed them and went into the hotel.

Mrs Boynton, wrapped in a thick coat, was sitting in a chair, waiting to depart. Looking at her, a queer revulsion of feeling swept over Sarah. She had felt that Mrs Boynton was a sinister figure, an incarnation of evil malignancy.

Now, suddenly, she saw the old woman as a pathetic ineffectual figure. To be born with such a lust for power, such a desire for dominion – and to achieve only a petty domestic tyranny! If only her children could see her as Sarah saw her that minute – an object of pity – a stupid, malignant, pathetic, posturing old woman. On an impulse Sarah went up to her.

'Goodbye, Mrs Boynton,' she said. 'I hope you'll have a nice trip.'

The old lady looked at her. Malignancy struggled with outrage in those eyes.

'You've wanted to be very rude to me,' said Sarah.

(Was she crazy, she wondered, what on earth was urging her on to talk like this?)

'You've tried to prevent your son and daughter making friends with me. Don't you think, really, that that is all very silly and childish? You like to make yourself out a kind of ogre, but really, you know, you're just pathetic and rather ludicrous. If I were you I'd give up all this silly play-acting. I expect you'll hate me for saying this, but I mean it – and some of it may stick. You know you could have a lot of fun still. It's really much better to be friendly – and kind. You could be if you tried.'

There was a pause.

Mrs Boynton had frozen into a deadly immobility. At last she passed her tongue over her dry lips, her mouth opened . . . Still for a moment, no words came.

'Go on,' said Sarah encouragingly. 'Say it! It doesn't matter what you say to me. But think over what I've said to you.'

The words came at last – in a soft, husky, but penetrating voice. Mrs Boynton's basilisk eyes looked, not at Sarah, but oddly over her shoulder. She seemed to address, not Sarah, but some familiar spirit.

'*I never forget,*' she said. '*Remember that. I've never forgotten anything – not an action, not a name, not a face . . .*'

There was nothing in the words themselves, but the venom with which they were spoken made Sarah retreat a step. And then Mrs Boynton laughed – it was, definitely, rather a horrible laugh.

Sarah shrugged her shoulders. 'You poor old thing,' she said.

She turned away. As she went towards the lift she almost collided with Raymond Boynton. On an impulse she spoke quickly.

'Goodbye. I hope you'll have a lovely time. Perhaps we'll meet again some day.' She smiled at him, a warm, friendly smile, and passed quickly on.

Raymond stood as though turned to stone. So lost in his own thoughts was he that a small man with big moustaches, endeavouring to pass out of the lift, had to speak several times.

'*Pardon.*'

At last it penetrated. Raymond stepped aside.

'So sorry,' he said. 'I – I was thinking.'

Carol came towards him.

'Ray, get Jinny, will you? She went back to her room. We're going to start.'

'Right. I'll tell her she's got to come straight away.'

Raymond walked into the lift.

Hercule Poirot stood for a moment looking after him, his eyebrows raised, his head a little on one side as though he was listening.

Then he nodded his head as though in agreement. Walking through the lounge, he took a good look at Carol, who had joined her mother.

Then he beckoned the head waiter who was passing.

'*Pardon.* Can you tell me the name of those people over there?'

'The name is Boynton, monsieur; they are Americans.'

'Thank you,' said Hercule Poirot.

On the third floor Dr Gerard, going to his room, passed Raymond Boynton and Ginevra walking towards the waiting lift. Just as they were about to get into it, Ginevra said: 'Just a minute, Ray, wait for me in the lift.'

She ran back, turned a corner, caught up with the walking man. 'Please – I must speak to you.'

Dr Gerard looked up in astonishment.

The girl came up close to him and caught his arm.

'They're taking me away! They may be going to kill me . . . I don't really belong to them, you know. My name isn't really Boynton . . .'

She hurried on, her words coming fast and tumbling over each other.

'I'll trust you with the secret. I'm – I'm *royal*, really! I'm the heiress to a throne. That's why – there are enemies all round me. They try to poison me – all sorts of things . . . If you could help me – to get away –'

She broke off. Footsteps. 'Jinny –'

Beautiful in her sudden startled gesture, the girl put a finger to her lips, threw Gerard an imploring glance, and ran back.

'I'm coming, Ray.'

Dr Gerard walked on with his eyebrows raised. Slowly he shook his head and frowned.

CHAPTER 10

It was the morning of the start to Petra.

Sarah came down to find a big masterful woman with a rocking-horse nose, whom she had already noticed in the hotel, outside the main entrance, objecting fiercely to the size of the car.

'A great deal too small! Four passengers? *And* a dragoman? Then, of course, we must have a much larger saloon. Please take that car away and return with one of an adequate size.'

In vain did the representative of Messrs Castle raise his voice in explanation. That was the size of car always provided. It was really a most comfortable car. A larger car was not suitable for desert travel. The large woman, metaphorically speaking, rolled over him like a large steamroller.

Then she turned her attention to Sarah.

'Miss King? I am Lady Westholme. I am sure you agree with me that that car was grossly inadequate as to size?'

'Well,' said Sarah cautiously, 'I agree that a larger one *would* be more comfortable!'

The young man from Castle's murmured that a larger car would add to the price.

'The price,' said Lady Westholme firmly, 'is inclusive, and I shall certainly refuse to sanction any addition to it. Your prospectus distinctly states "in comfortable saloon car". You will keep to the terms of your agreement.'

Recognizing defeat, the young man from Castle's murmured something about seeing what he could do and wilted away from the spot.

Lady Westholme turned to Sarah, a smile of triumph on her weather-beaten countenance, her large red rocking-horse nostrils dilated exultantly.

Lady Westholme was a very well-known figure in the English political world. When Lord Westholme, a middle-aged, simple-minded peer whose only interests in life were hunting, shooting and fishing, was returning from a trip to the United States, one of his fellow passengers was a Mrs Vansittart. Shortly afterwards Mrs Vansittart became Lady Westholme. The match was often cited as one of the examples of the danger of ocean voyages. The new Lady Westholme lived entirely in tweeds and stout brogues, bred dogs, bullied the villagers and forced her husband pitilessly into public life. It being borne in upon her, however, that politics were not Lord Westholme's *métier* in life and never would be, she graciously allowed him to resume his sporting activities and herself stood for Parliament. Being elected with a substantial majority, Lady Westholme threw herself with vigour into political life, being especially active at Question Time. Cartoons of her soon began to appear (always a sure sign of success). As a public figure she stood for the old-fashioned values of family life, welfare work amongst women, and was an ardent supporter of the League of Nations. She had decided views on questions of Agriculture, Housing and Slum Clearance. She was much respected and almost universally disliked! It was highly possible that she would be given an under-secretaryship when her party returned to power. At the moment a Liberal Government (owing to a split in the National Government between Labour and Conservatives) was somewhat unexpectedly in power.

Lady Westholme looked with grim satisfaction after the departing car. 'Men always think they can impose upon women,' she said.

Sarah thought that it would be a brave man who thought he could impose upon Lady Westholme! She introduced Dr Gerard, who had just come out of the hotel.

'Your name is, of course, familiar to me,' said Lady Westholme, shaking hands. 'I was talking to Professor Chantereau the other day in Paris. I have been taking up the question of the treatment of pauper lunatics very strongly lately. Very strongly indeed. Shall we come inside while we wait for a better car to be obtained?'

A vague little middle-aged lady with wisps of grey hair who was hovering nearby turned out to be Miss Amabel Pierce, the fourth member of the party. She, too, was swept into the lounge under Lady Westholme's protecting wing.

'You are a professional woman, Miss King?'

'I've just taken my M.B.'

'Good,' said Lady Westholme with condescending approval. 'If anything is to be accomplished, mark my words, it is women who will do it.'

Uneasily conscious for the first time of her sex, Sarah followed Lady Westholme meekly to a seat.

There, as they sat waiting, Lady Westholme informed them that she had refused an invitation to stay with the High Commissioner during her stay in Jerusalem. 'I did not want to be hampered by officialdom. I wished to look into things by myself.'

'What things?' Sarah wondered.

Lady Westholme went on to explain that she was staying at the Solomon Hotel so as to remain unhampered. She added that she had made several suggestions to the manager for the more competent running of his hotel.

'Efficiency,' said Lady Westholme, 'is my watchword.'

It certainly seemed to be! In a quarter of an hour a large and extremely comfortable car arrived and in due course – after advice from Lady Westholme as to how the luggage should be stowed – the party set off.

Their first halt was the Dead Sea. They had lunch at Jericho. Afterwards when Lady Westholme, armed with a Baedeker, had gone off with Miss Pierce, the doctor and the fat dragoman, to do a tour of old Jericho, Sarah remained in the garden of the hotel.

Her head ached slightly and she wanted to be alone. A deep depression weighed her down – a depression for which she found it hard to account. She felt suddenly listless and uninterested, disinclined for sightseeing, bored by her companions. She wished at this moment that she had never committed herself to this Petra tour. It was going to be very expensive and she felt quite sure she wasn't going to enjoy it! Lady Westholme's booming voice, Miss Pierce's endless twitterings, and the anti-Zionist lamentation of the dragoman, were already fraying her nerves to a frazzle. She disliked almost as much Dr Gerard's amused air of knowing exactly how she was feeling.

She wondered where the Boyntons were now – perhaps they had gone on to Syria – they might be at Baalbek or Damascus. Raymond – she wondered what Raymond was doing. Strange how clearly she could see his face – its eagerness – its diffidence – its nervous tension . . .

Oh, hell! Why go on thinking of people she would probably never see again? That scene the other day with the old woman – what could have possessed her to march up to the old lady and spurt out a lot of nonsense. Other people must have heard some of it. She fancied that Lady Westholme had been quite close by. Sarah tried to remember exactly what it was she had said. Something that probably sounded quite absurdly hysterical. Goodness, what a fool she had made of herself! But it wasn't her fault really; it was old Mrs Boynton's. There was something about her that made you lose your sense of proportion.

Dr Gerard entered and plumped down in a chair, wiping his hot forehead.

'Phew! That woman should be poisoned!' he declared.

Sarah started. 'Mrs Boynton?'

'Mrs Boynton! No, I meant that Lady Westholme! It is incredible to me that she has had a husband for many years and that he has not already done so. What can he be made of, that husband?'

Sarah laughed.

'Oh, he's the "huntin', fishin', shootin'" kind,' she explained.

'Psychologically that is very sound! He appeases his lust to kill on the (so-called) lower creations.'

'I believe he is very proud of his wife's activities.'

The Frenchman suggested:

'Because they take her a good deal away from home? That is understandable.' Then he went on, 'What did you say just now? Mrs Boynton? Undoubtedly it would be a very good idea to poison her, too. Undeniably the simplest solution of that family problem! In fact a great many women would be better poisoned. All women who have grown old and ugly.'

He made an expressive face.

Sarah cried out, laughing:

'Oh, you Frenchmen! You've got no use for any woman who isn't young and attractive.'

Gerard shrugged his shoulders.

'We are more honest about it, that is all. Englishmen, they do not get up in tubes and trains for ugly women – no, no.'

'How depressing life is,' said Sarah with a sigh.

'There is no need for *you* to sigh, mademoiselle.'

'Well, I feel thoroughly disgruntled today.'

'Naturally.'

'What do you mean – naturally?' snapped Sarah.

'You could find the reason very easily if you examine your state of mind honestly.'

'I think it's our fellow travellers who depress me,' said Sarah. 'It's awful, isn't it, but I do hate women! When they're inefficient and idiotic like Miss Pierce, they infuriate me – and, when they're efficient like Lady Westholme, they annoy me more still.'

'It is, I should say, unavoidable that these two people should annoy you. Lady Westholme is exactly fitted to the life she leads and is completely happy and successful. Miss Pierce has worked for years as a nursery governess and has suddenly come into a small legacy which has enabled her to fulfil her life-long wish and travel. So far, travel has lived up to her expectations. Consequently you, who have just been thwarted in obtaining what you want, naturally resent the existence of people who have been more successful in life than you are.'

'I suppose you're right,' said Sarah gloomily. 'What a horribly accurate mind-reader you are. I keep trying to humbug myself and you won't let me.'

At this moment the others returned. The guide seemed the most exhausted of the three. He was quite subdued and hardly exuded any information on the way to Amman. He did not even mention the Jews. For which everyone was profoundly grateful. His voluble and frenzied account of their iniquities had done much to try everyone's temper on the journey from Jerusalem.

Now the road wound upward from the Jordan, twisting and turning, with clumps of oleanders showing rose-coloured flowers.

They reached Amman late in the afternoon and after a short visit to the Graeco-Roman theatre went to bed early. They were to make an early start the next morning as it was a full day's motor run across the desert to Ma'an.

They left soon after eight o'clock. The party was inclined to be silent. It was a hot airless day and by noon when a halt was made for a picnic lunch to be eaten, it was really stiflingly hot. The irritation of a hot day of being boxed up closely with three other human beings had got a little on everyone's nerves.

Lady Westholme and Dr Gerard had a somewhat irritable argument over the League of Nations. Lady Westholme was a fervent supporter of the League. The Frenchman, on the other hand, chose to be witty at the League's expense. From the attitude of the League concerning Abyssinia and Spain they passed to the Litvania boundary dispute of which Sarah had never heard and from there to the activities of the League in suppressing dope gangs.

'You must admit they have done wonderful work. Wonderful!' snapped Lady Westholme.

Dr Gerard shrugged his shoulders.

'Perhaps. And at wonderful expense too!'

'The matter is a very serious one. Under the Dangerous Drugs Act –' The argument waged on.

Miss Pierce twittered to Sarah: 'It is really *most* interesting travelling with Lady Westholme.'

Sarah said acidly: 'Is it?' but Miss Pierce did not notice the acerbity and twittered happily on.

'I've so *often* seen her name in the papers. So *clever* of women

470

to go into public life and hold their own. I'm always so *glad* when a *woman* accomplishes something!'

'Why?' demanded Sarah ferociously.

Miss Pierce's mouth fell open and she stammered a little.

'Oh, because – I mean – just because – well – it's so nice that women are *able* to do things!'

'I don't agree,' said Sarah. 'It's nice when *any* human being is able to accomplish something worth while! It doesn't matter a bit whether it's a man or a woman. Why should it?'

'Well, of course –' said Miss Pierce. 'Yes, I confess – of course, looking at it in that light –'

But she looked slightly wistful. Sarah said more gently:

'I'm sorry, but I do hate this differentiation between the sexes. *"The modern girl has a thoroughly business-like attitude towards life."* That sort of thing. It's not a bit true! Some girls are business-like and some aren't. Some men are sentimental and muddle-headed, others are clear-headed and logical. There are just different types of brains. Sex only matters where sex is directly concerned.'

Miss Pierce flushed a little at the word sex and adroitly changed the subject.

'One can't help wishing that there were a little shade,' she murmured. 'But I do think all this emptiness is so wonderful, don't you?'

Sarah nodded.

Yes, she thought, the emptiness was marvellous . . . Healing . . . Peaceful . . . No human beings to agitate one with their tiresome inter-relationships . . . No burning personal problems! Now, at last, she felt, she was free of the Boyntons. Free of that strange compelling wish to interfere in the lives of people whose orbit did not remotely touch her own. She felt soothed and at peace. Here was loneliness, emptiness, spaciousness . . . In fact, peace . . .

Only, of course, one wasn't alone to enjoy it. Lady Westholme and Dr Gerard had finished with drugs and were now arguing about guileless young women who were exported in a sinister manner to Argentinian cabarets. Dr Gerard had displayed throughout the conversation a levity which Lady Westholme, who, being a true politician, had no sense of humour, found definitely deplorable.

'We go on now, yes?' announced the tarbrushed dragoman, and began to talk about the iniquities of Jews again.

It was about an hour off sunset when they reached Ma'an at last. Strange wild-faced men crowded round the car. After a short halt they went on.

Looking over the flat desert country, Sarah was at a loss as to where the rocky stronghold of Petra could be. Surely they could see for miles and miles all round them? There were no mountains, no hills anywhere. Were they, then, still many miles from their journey's end?

They reached the village of Ain Musa where the cars were to be left. Here horses were waiting for them – sorry-looking thin beasts. The inadequacy of her striped washing-frock disturbed Miss Pierce greatly. Lady Westholme was sensibly attired in riding breeches, not perhaps a particularly becoming style to her type of figure, but certainly practical.

The horses were led out of the village along a slippery path with loose stones. The ground fell away and the horses zig-zagged down. The sun was close on setting.

Sarah was very tired with the long, hot journey in the car. Her senses felt dazed. The ride was like a dream. It seemed to her afterwards that it was like the pit of Hell opening at one's feet. The way wound down – down into the ground. The shapes of rock rose up round them – down, down into the bowels of the earth, through a labyrinth of red cliffs. They towered now on either side. Sarah felt stifled – menaced by the ever-narrowing gorge.

She thought confusedly to herself: 'Down into the valley of death – down into the valley of death . . .'

On and on. It grew dark – the vivid red of the walls faded – and still on, winding in and out, imprisoned, lost in the bowels of the earth.

She thought: 'It's fantastic and unbelievable . . . a dead city.'

And again like a refrain came the words: '*The valley of death* . . .'

Lanterns were lit now. The horses wound along through the narrow ways. Suddenly they came out into a wide space – the cliffs receded. Far ahead of them was a cluster of lights.

'That is camp!' said the guide.

The horses quickened their pace a little – not very much – they were too starved and dispirited for that, but they showed just a shade of enthusiasm. Now the way ran along a gravelly water-bed. The lights grew nearer.

They could see a cluster of tents, a higher row up against the face of a cliff. Caves, too, hollowed out in the rock.

They were arriving. Bedouin servants came running out.

Sarah stared up at one of the caves. It held a sitting figure. What was it? An idol? A gigantic squatting image?

No, that was the flickering lights that made it loom so large. But it *must* be an idol of some kind, sitting there immovable, brooding over the place . . .

And then, suddenly her heart gave a leap of recognition.

Gone was the feeling of peace – of escape – that the desert had given her. She had been led from freedom back into captivity. She had ridden down into this dark winding valley and here, like an archpriestess of some forgotten cult, like a monstrous swollen female Buddha, sat Mrs Boynton . . .

CHAPTER 11

Mrs Boynton was here, at Petra!

Sarah answered mechanically questions that were addressed to her. Would she have dinner straight away – it was ready – or would she like to wash first? Would she prefer to sleep in a tent or a cave?

Her answer to that came quickly. A tent. She flinched at the thought of a cave, the vision of that monstrous squatting figure recurred to her. (Why was it that something about the woman seemed hardly human?)

Finally she followed one of the native servants. He wore khaki breeches, much patched, and untidy puttees and a ragged coat very much the worse for wear. On his head the native headdress, the *cheffiyah*, its long folds protecting the neck and secured in place with a black silk twist fitting tightly to the crown of his head. Sarah admired the easy swing with which he walked – the careless proud carriage of his head. Only the European part of his costume seemed tawdry and wrong. She thought: 'Civilization *is* all wrong – *all* wrong! But for civilization there wouldn't be a Mrs Boynton! In savage tribes they'd probably have killed and eaten her years ago!'

She realized, half-humorously, that she was over-tired and on edge. A wash in hot water and a dusting of powder over her face and she felt herself again – cool, poised, and ashamed of her recent panic.

She passed a comb through her thick black hair, squinting sideways at her reflection in the wavering light of a small oil-lamp in a very inadequate glass.

Then she pushed aside the tent-flap and came out into the night prepared to descend to the big marquee below.

'You – here?'

It was a low cry – dazed, incredulous.

She turned to look straight into Raymond Boynton's eyes. So amazed they were! And something in them held her silent and almost afraid. Such an unbelievable joy . . . It was as though he had seen a vision of Paradise – wondering, dazed, thankful, humble! Never, in all her life, was Sarah to forget that look. So might the damned look up and see Paradise . . .

He said again: '*You* . . .'

It did something to her – that low, vibrant tone. It made her heart turn over in her breast. It made her feel shy, afraid, humble and yet suddenly arrogantly glad. She said quite simply: 'Yes.'

He came nearer – still dazed – still only half believing.

Then suddenly he took her hand.

'It *is* you,' he said. 'You're real. I thought at first you were a ghost – because I'd been thinking about you so much.' He paused and then said, 'I love you, you know . . . I have from the moment I saw you in the train. I know that now. And I want you to know it so that – so that you'll know it isn't me – the real me – who – who behaves so caddishly. You see I can't answer for myself even now. I might do – anything! I might pass you by or cut you, but I do want you to know that it isn't me – the real me – who is responsible for that. It's my nerves. I can't depend on them . . . When She tells me to do things – I do them! My nerves make me! You will understand, won't you? Despise me if you have to –'

She interrupted him. Her voice was low and unexpectedly sweet. 'I won't despise you.'

'All the same, I'm pretty despicable! I ought to – to be able to behave like a man.'

It was partly an echo of Gerard's advice, but more out of her own knowledge and hope that Sarah answered – and behind the sweetness of her voice there was a ring of certainty and conscious authority.

'You will now.'

'Shall I?' His voice was wistful. 'Perhaps . . .'

'You'll have courage now. I'm sure of it.'

He drew himself up – flung back his head.

'Courage? Yes, that's all that's needed. Courage!'

Suddenly he bent his head, touched her hand with his lips. A minute later he had left her.

CHAPTER 12

Sarah went down to the big marquee. She found her three fellow travellers there. They were sitting at table eating. The guide was explaining that there was another party here.

'They came two days ago. Go day after tomorrow. Americans. The mother, very fat, very difficult get here! Carried in chair by bearers – they say very hard work – they get very hot – yes.'

Sarah gave a sudden spurt of laughter. Of course, take it properly, the whole thing was funny!

The fat dragoman looked at her gratefully. He was not finding his task too easy. Lady Westholme had contradicted him out of Baedeker three times that day and had now found fault with the type of bed provided. He was grateful to the one member of his party who seemed to be unaccountably in a good temper.

'Ha!' said Lady Westholme. 'I think these people were at the Solomon. I recognized the old mother as we arrived here. I think I saw you talking to her at the hotel, Miss King.'

Sarah blushed guiltily, hoping Lady Westholme had not over-heard much of that conversation.

'Really, what possessed me!' she thought to herself in an agony.

In the meantime Lady Westholme had made a pronouncement. 'Not interesting people at all. Very provincial,' she said.

Miss Pierce made eager sycophantish noises and Lady Westholme embarked on a history of various interesting and prominent Americans whom she had met recently.

The weather being so unusually hot for the time of year, an early start was arranged for the morrow.

The four assembled for breakfast at six o'clock. There were no signs of any of the Boynton family. After Lady Westholme had commented unfavourably on the absence of fruit, they consumed tea, tinned milk, and fried eggs in a generous allowance of fat flanked by extremely salty bacon.

Then they started forth, Lady Westholme and Dr Gerard discussing with animation on the part of the former the exact value of vitamins in diet and the proper nutrition of the working classes.

Then there was a sudden hail from the camp and they halted to allow another person to join the party. It was Mr Jefferson Cope who hurried after them, his pleasant face flushed with the exertion of running.

'Why, if you don't mind, I'd like to join your party this morning. Good morning, Miss King. Quite a surprise meeting you and Dr Gerard here. What do you think of it?'

He made a gesture indicating the fantastic red rocks that stretched in every direction.

'I think it's rather wonderful and just a little horrible,' said Sarah. 'I always thought of it as romantic and dream-like – the "rose-red city". But it's much more *real* than that – it's as real as – as raw beef.'

'And very much the colour of it,' agreed Mr Cope.

'But it's marvellous, too,' admitted Sarah.

The party began to climb. Two Bedouin guides accompanied them. Tall men, with an easy carriage, they swung upward unconcernedly in their hobnailed boots completely footsure on the slippery slope. Difficulties soon began. Sarah had a good head for heights and so had Dr Gerard. But both Mr Cope and Lady Westholme were far from happy, and the unfortunate Miss Pierce had to be almost carried over the precipitous places, her eyes shut, her face green, while her voice rose ceaselessly in a perpetual wail.

'I never could look down places. Never – from a child!'

Once she declared her intention of going back, but on turning to face the descent, her skin assumed an even greener tinge, and she reluctantly decided that to go on was the only thing to be done.

Dr Gerard was kind and reassuring. He went up behind her, holding a stick between her and the sheer drop like a balustrade and she confessed that the illusion of a rail did much to conquer the feeling of vertigo.

Sarah, panting a little, asked the dragoman, Mahmoud, who, in spite of his ample proportions, showed no signs of distress:

'Don't you ever have trouble getting people up here? Elderly ones, I mean.'

'Always – always we have trouble,' agreed Mahmoud serenely.

'Do you always try and take them?'

Mahmoud shrugged his thick shoulders.

'They like to come. They have paid money to see these things. They wish to see them. The Bedouin guides are very clever – very sure-footed – always they manage.'

They arrived at last at the summit. Sarah drew a deep breath.

All around and below stretched the blood-red rocks – a strange and unbelievable country unparalleled anywhere. Here in the exquisite pure morning air they stood like gods, surveying a baser world – a world of flaring violence.

Here was, as the guide told them, the 'Place of Sacrifice' – the 'High Place'. He showed them the trough cut in the flat rock at their feet.

Sarah strayed away from the rest, from the glib phrases that flowed so readily from the dragoman's tongue. She sat on a rock, pushed her hands through her thick black hair, and gazed down on the world at her feet. Presently she was aware of someone standing by her side. Dr Gerard's voice said:

'You appreciate the appositeness of the devil's temptation in the New Testament. Satan took Our Lord up to the summit of a mountain and showed Him the world. "All these things will I give thee, if thou wilt fall down and worship me." How much greater the temptation up on high to be a God of Material Power.'

Sarah assented, but her thoughts were so clearly elsewhere that Gerard observed her in some surprise.

'You are pondering something very deeply,' he said.

'Yes, I am.' She turned a perplexed face to him. 'It's a wonderful idea – to have a place of sacrifice up here. I think sometimes, don't you, that a sacrifice is *necessary* . . . I mean, one can have too much regard for life. Death isn't really so important as we make out.'

'If you feel that, Miss King, you should not have adopted our profession. To us, Death is and must always be – the Enemy.'

Sarah shivered.

'Yes, I suppose you're right. And yet, so often death might solve a problem. It might mean, even, fuller life . . .'

'It is expedient for us that one man should die for the people!' quoted Gerard gravely.

Sarah turned a startled face on him.

'I didn't mean –' She broke off. Jefferson Cope was approaching them.

'Now this is really a most remarkable spot,' he declared. 'Most remarkable, and I'm only too pleased not to have missed it. I don't mind confessing that though Mrs Boynton is certainly a most remarkable woman – I greatly admire her pluck in being determined to come here – it does certainly complicate matters travelling with her. Her health is poor, and I suppose it naturally makes her a little inconsiderate of other people's feelings, but it does not seem to occur to her that her family might like occasionally to go on excursions without her. She's just so used to them clustering round her that I suppose she doesn't think –'

Mr Cope broke off. His nice kindly face looked a little disturbed and uncomfortable.

'You know,' he said, 'I heard a piece of information about Mrs Boynton that disturbed me greatly.'

Sarah was lost in her own thoughts again – Mr Cope's voice just flowed pleasantly in her ears like the agreeable murmur of a remote stream, but Dr Gerard said:

'Indeed? What was it?'

'My informant was a lady I came across in the hotel at Tiberias. It concerned a servant girl who had been in Mrs Boynton's employ. The girl, I gather, was – had –'

Mr Cope paused, glanced delicately at Sarah and lowered his voice. 'She was going to have a child. The old lady, it seemed, discovered this, but was apparently quite kind to the girl. Then a few weeks before the child was born she turned her out of the house.'

Dr Gerard's eyebrows went up.

478

'Ah,' he said reflectively.

'My informant seemed very positive of her facts. I don't know whether you agree with me, but that seems to me a very cruel and heartless thing to do. I cannot understand –'

Dr Gerard interrupted him.

'You should try to. That incident, I have no doubt, gave Mrs Boynton a good deal of quiet enjoyment.'

Mr Cope turned a shocked face on him.

'No, sir,' he said with emphasis. 'That I cannot believe. Such an idea is quite inconceivable.'

Softly Dr Gerard quoted:

'*So I returned and did consider all the oppressions done beneath the sun. And there was weeping and wailing from those that were oppressed and had no comfort; for with their oppressors there was power, so that no one came to comfort them. Then I did praise the dead which are already dead, yea, more than the living which linger still in life; yea, he that is not is better than dead or living; for he doth not know of the evil that is wrought for ever on earth . . .*'

He broke off and said:

'My dear sir, I have made a life's study of the strange things that go on in the human mind. It is no good turning one's face only to the fairer side of life. Below the decencies and conventions of everyday life, there lies a vast reservoir of strange things. There is such a thing, for instance, as delight in cruelty for its own sake. But when you have found that, there is something deeper still. The desire, profound and pitiful, to be appreciated. If that is thwarted, if through an unpleasing personality a human being is unable to get the response it needs, it turns to other methods – it must be *felt* – it must *count* – and so to innumerable strange perversions. The habit of cruelty, like any other habit, can be cultivated, can take hold of one –'

Mr Cope coughed. 'I think, Dr Gerard, that you are slightly exaggerating. Really, the air up here is too wonderful . . .'

He edged away. Gerard smiled a little. He looked again at Sarah. She was frowning – her face was set in a youthful sternness. She looked, he thought, like a young judge delivering sentence . . .

He turned as Miss Pierce tripped unsteadily towards him.

'We are going down now,' she fluttered. 'Oh dear! I am sure I shall never manage it, but the guide says the way down is quite a different route and much easier. I do hope so, because from a child I never have been able to look down from heights . . .'

The descent was down the course of a waterfall. Although there were loose stones which were a possible source of danger to ankles, it presented no dizzy vistas.

The party arrived back at the camp weary but in good spirits and with an excellent appetite for a late lunch. It was past two o'clock.

The Boynton family was sitting round the big table in the marquee. They were just finishing their meal.

Lady Westholme addressed a gracious sentence to them in her most condescending manner.

'Really a most interesting morning,' she said. 'Petra is a wonderful spot.'

Carol, to whom the words seemed addressed, shot a quick look at her mother and murmured:

'Oh, yes – yes, it is,' and relapsed into silence.

Lady Westholme, feeling she had done her duty, addressed herself to her food.

As they ate, the four discussed plans for the afternoon.

'I think I shall rest most of the afternoon,' said Miss Pierce. 'It is important, I think, not to do too much.'

'I shall go for a walk and explore,' said Sarah. 'What about you, Dr Gerard?'

'I will go with you.'

Mrs Boynton dropped a spoon with a ringing clatter and everyone jumped.

'I think,' said Lady Westholme, 'that I shall follow your example, Miss Pierce. Perhaps half an hour with a book, then I shall lie down and take an hour's rest at least. After that, perhaps, a short stroll.'

Slowly, with the help of Lennox, old Mrs Boynton struggled to her feet. She stood for a moment and then spoke.

'You'd better all go for a walk this afternoon,' she said with unexpected amiability.

It was, perhaps, slightly ludicrous to see the startled faces of her family.

'But, Mother, what about you?'

'I don't need any of you. I like sitting alone with my book. Jinny had better not go. She'll lie down and have a sleep.'

'Mother, I'm not tired. I want to go with the others.'

'You *are* tired. You've got a headache! You must be careful of yourself. Go and lie down and sleep. I know what's best for you.'

'I – I –'

Her head thrown back, the girl stared rebelliously. Then her eyes dropped – faltered . . .

'Silly child,' said Mrs Boynton. 'Go to your tent.'

She stumped out of the marquee – the others followed.

'Dear me,' said Miss Pierce. 'What very peculiar people. Such a very odd colour – the mother. Quite purple. Heart, I should imagine. The heat must be very trying to her.'

Sarah thought: 'She's letting them go free this afternoon. She knows Raymond wants to be with me. Why? Is it a trap?'

After lunch, when she had gone to her tent and had changed into a fresh linen dress, the thought still worried her. Since last night her feeling towards Raymond had swelled into a passion of protective tenderness. This, then, was love – this agony on another's behalf – this desire to avert, at all costs, pain from the beloved . . . Yes, she loved Raymond Boynton. It was St George and the Dragon reversed. It was she who was the rescuer and Raymond who was the chained victim.

And Mrs Boynton was the Dragon. A dragon whose sudden amiability was, to Sarah's suspicious mind, definitely sinister.

It was about a quarter-past three when Sarah strolled down to the marquee.

Lady Westholme was sitting on a chair. Despite the heat of the day she was still wearing her serviceable Harris tweed skirt. On her lap was the report of a Royal Commission. Dr Gerard was talking to Miss Pierce, who was standing by her tent holding a book entitled *The Love Quest* and described on its wrapper as a thrilling tale of passion and misunderstanding.

'I don't think it's wise to lie down too soon after lunch,' explained Miss Pierce. 'One's digestion, you know. Quite cool and pleasant in the shadow of the marquee. Oh dear, do you think that old lady is wise to sit in the sun up there?'

They all looked at the ridge in front of them. Mrs Boynton was sitting as she had sat last night, a motionless Buddha in the door of her cave. There was no other human creature in sight. All the camp personnel were asleep. A short distance away, following the line of the valley, a little group of people walked together.

'For once,' said Dr Gerard, 'the good Mamma permits them to enjoy themselves without her. A new devilment on her part, perhaps?'

'Do you know,' said Sarah, 'that's just what I thought.'

'What suspicious minds we have. Come, let us join the truants.'

Leaving Miss Pierce to her exciting reading, they set off. Once round the bend of the valley, they caught up the other party who were walking slowly. For once, the Boyntons looked happy and carefree.

Lennox and Nadine, Carol and Raymond, Mr Cope with a broad smile on his face and the last arrivals, Gerard and Sarah, were soon all laughing and talking together.

A sudden wild hilarity was born. In everyone's mind was the feeling that this was a snatched pleasure – a stolen joy to enjoy to the full. Sarah and Raymond did not draw apart. Instead, Sarah walked with Carol and Lennox. Dr Gerard chatted to Raymond close behind them. Nadine and Jefferson Cope walked a little apart.

It was the Frenchman who broke up the party. His words had been coming spasmodically for some time. Suddenly he stopped.

'A thousand excuses. I fear I must go back.'

Sarah looked at him. 'Anything the matter?'

He nodded. 'Yes, fever. It's been coming on ever since lunch.'

Sarah scrutinized him. 'Malaria?'

'Yes. I'll go back and take quinine. Hope this won't be a bad attack. It is a legacy from a visit to the Congo.'

'Shall I come with you?' asked Sarah.

'No, no. I have my case of drugs with me. A confounded nuisance. Go on, all of you.'

He walked quickly back in the direction of the camp.

Sarah looked undecidedly after him for a minute, then she met Raymond's eyes, smiled at him, and the Frenchman was forgotten.

For a time the six of them, Carol, herself, Lennox, Mr Cope, Nadine and Raymond, kept together.

Then, somehow or other, she and Raymond had drifted apart.

They walked on, climbing up rocks, turning ledges, and rested at last in a shady spot.

There was a silence – then Raymond said:

'What's your name? It's King, I know. But your other name.'

'Sarah.'

'Sarah. May I call you that?'

'Of course.'

'Sarah, will you tell me something about yourself?'

Leaning back against the rocks, she talked, telling him of her life at home in Yorkshire, of her dogs and the aunt who had brought her up.

Then, in his turn, Raymond told her a little, disjointedly, of his own life.

After that there was a long silence. Their hands strayed together. They sat, like children, hand in hand, strangely content.

Then, as the sun grew lower, Raymond stirred.

'I'm going back now,' he said. 'No, not with you. I want to go back by myself. There's something I have to say and do. Once that's done, once I've proved to myself that I'm not a coward – then – then – I shan't be ashamed to come to you and ask you to help me. I shall need help, you know, I shall probably have to borrow money from you.'

Sarah smiled.

'I'm glad you're a realist. You can count on me.'

'But first I've got to do this alone.'

'Do what?'

The young boyish face grew suddenly stern. Raymond Boynton said: 'I've got to prove my courage. It's now or never.'

Then, abruptly, he turned and strode away.

Sarah leant back against the rock and watched his receding figure. Something in his words had vaguely alarmed her. He had seemed so intense – so terribly in earnest and strung up. For a moment she wished she had gone with him . . .

But she rebuked herself sternly for that wish. Raymond had desired to stand alone, to test his new-found courage. That was his right.

But she prayed with all her heart that that courage would not fail . . .

The sun was setting when Sarah came once more in sight of the camp. As she came nearer in the dim light she could make out the grim figure of Mrs Boynton still sitting in the mouth of the cave. Sarah shivered a little at the sight of that grim, motionless figure . . .

She hurried past on the path below and came into the lighted marquee.

Lady Westholme was sitting knitting a navy-blue jumper, a skein of wool hung round her neck. Miss Pierce was embroidering a table-mat with anaemic blue forget-me-nots, and being instructed on the proper reform of the Divorce Laws.

The servants came in and out preparing for the evening meal. The Boyntons were at the far end of the marquee in deck-chairs reading. Mahmoud appeared, fat and dignified, and was plaintively reproachful. Very nice after-tea ramble had been arranged to take place, but everyone absent from camp . . . The programme was now entirely thrown out . . . Very instructive visit to Nabataen architecture.

Sarah said hastily that they had all enjoyed themselves very much.

She went off to her tent to wash for supper. On the way back she paused by Dr Gerard's tent, calling in a low voice: 'Dr Gerard.'

There was no answer. She lifted the flap and looked in. The doctor was lying motionless on his bed. Sarah withdrew noiselessly, hoping he was asleep.

A servant came to her and pointed to the marquee. Evidently supper was ready. She strolled down again. Everyone else was assembled there round the table with the exception of Dr Gerard and Mrs Boynton. A servant was dispatched to tell the old lady dinner was ready. Then there was a sudden commotion outside. Two frightened servants rushed in and spoke excitedly to the dragoman in Arabic.

Mahmoud looked round him in a flustered manner and went outside. On an impulse Sarah joined him.

'What's the matter?' she asked.

Mahmoud replied: 'The old lady. Abdul says she is ill – cannot move.'

'I'll come and see.'

Sarah quickened her step. Following Mahmoud, she climbed the rock and walked along until she came to the squat figure in the chair, touched the puffy hand, felt for the pulse, bent over her . . .

When she straightened herself she was paler.

She retraced her steps back to the marquee. In the doorway she paused a minute looking at the group at the far end of the table. Her voice when she spoke sounded to herself brusque and unnatural.

'I'm so sorry,' she said. She forced herself to address the head of the family, Lennox. '*Your mother is dead, Mr Boynton.*'

And curiously, as though from a great distance, she watched the faces of five people to whom that announcement meant freedom . . .

PART II

Colonel Carbury smiled across the table at his guest and raised his glass. 'Well, here's to crime!'

Hercule Poirot's eyes twinkled in acknowledgement of the aptness of the toast.

He had come to Amman with a letter of introduction to Colonel Carbury from Colonel Race.

Carbury had been interested to see this world-famous person to whose gifts his old friend and ally in the Intelligence had paid such unstinting tribute.

'As neat a bit of psychological deduction as you'll ever find!' Race had written of the solution of the Shaitana murder.

'We must show you all we can of the neighbourhood,' said Carbury, twisting a somewhat ragged brindled moustache. He was an untidy stocky man of medium height with a semibald head and vague, mild, blue eyes. He did not look in the least like a soldier. He did not look even particularly alert. He was not in the least one's idea of a disciplinarian. Yet in Transjordania he was a power.

'There's Jerash,' he said. 'Care about that sort of thing?'

'I am interested in everything!'

'Yes,' said Carbury. 'That's the only way to react to life.' He paused.

'Tell me, d'you ever find your own special job has a way of following you round?'

'*Pardon?*'

'Well – to put it plainly – do you come to places expecting a holiday from crime – and find instead bodies cropping up?'

'It has happened, yes; more than once.'

'H'm,' said Colonel Carbury and looked particularly abstracted.

Then he roused himself with a jerk. 'Got a body now I'm not very happy about,' he said.

486

'Indeed?'

'Yes. Here in Amman. Old American woman. Went to Petra with her family. Trying journey, unusual heat for time of year, old woman suffered from heart trouble, difficulties of the journey a bit harder for her than she imagined, extra strain on heart – she popped off!'

'Here – in Amman?'

'No, down at Petra. They brought the body here today.'

'Ah!'

'All quite natural. Perfectly possible. Likeliest thing in the world to happen. Only –'

'Yes? Only –?'

Colonel Carbury scratched his bald head.

'I've got the idea,' he said, 'that her family did her in!'

'Aha! And what makes you think that?'

Colonel Carbury did not reply to that question directly.

'Unpleasant old woman, it seems. No loss. General feeling all round that her popping off was a good thing. Anyway, very difficult to prove anything so long as the family stick together and if necessary lie like hell. One doesn't want complications – or international unpleasantness. Easiest thing to do – let it go! Nothing really to go upon. Knew a doctor chap once. He told me – often had suspicions in cases of his patients – hurried into the next world a little ahead of time! *He* said – best thing to do to keep quiet unless you really had something damned good to go upon! Otherwise beastly stink, case not proved, black mark against an earnest hard-working G.P. Something in that. All the same –' He scratched his head again. 'I'm a tidy man,' he said unexpectedly.

Colonel Carbury's tie was under his left ear, his socks were wrinkled, his coat stained and torn. Yet Hercule Poirot did not smile. He saw, clearly enough, the inner neatness of Colonel Carbury's mind, his neatly docketed facts, his carefully sorted impressions.

'Yes. I'm a tidy man,' said Carbury. He waved a vague hand. 'Don't like a mess. When I come across a mess I want to clear it up. See?'

Hercule Poirot nodded gravely. He saw.

'There was no doctor down there?' he asked.

'Yes, two. One of 'em was down with malaria, though. The

other's a girl – just out of the medical student stage. Still, she knows her job, I suppose. There wasn't anything odd about the death. Old woman had got a dicky heart. She'd been taking heart medicine for some time. Nothing really surprising about her conking out suddenly like she did.'

'Then what, my friend, is worrying you?' asked Poirot gently.

Colonel Carbury turned a harassed blue eye on him.

'Heard of a Frenchman called Gerard? Theodore Gerard?'

'Certainly. A very distinguished man in his own line.'

'Loony bins,' confirmed Colonel Carbury. 'Passion for a charwoman at the age of four makes you insist you're the Archbishop of Canterbury when you're thirty-eight. Can't see why and never have, but these chaps explain it very convincingly.'

'Dr Gerard is certainly an authority on certain forms of deep-seated neurosis,' agreed Poirot, with a smile. 'Is – er – are – er – his views on the happening at Petra based on that line of argument?'

Colonel Carbury shook his head vigorously.

'No, no. Shouldn't have worried about them if they had been! Not, mind you, that I don't believe it's all true. It's just one of those things I don't understand – like one of my Bedouin fellows who can get out of a car in the middle of a flat desert, feel the ground with his hand and tell you to within a mile or two where you are. It isn't magic, but it looks like it. No, Dr Gerard's story is quite straightforward. Just plain facts. I think, if you're interested – you *are* interested?'

'Yes, yes.'

'Good man. Then I think I'll just phone over and get Gerard along here, and you can hear his story for yourself.'

When the Colonel had dispatched an orderly on this quest, Poirot said:

'Of what does this family consist?'

'Name's Boynton. There are two sons, one of 'em married. His wife's a nice-looking girl – the quiet, sensible kind. And there are two daughters. Both of 'em quite good-looking in totally different styles. Younger one a bit nervy – but that may be just shock.'

'Boynton,' said Poirot. His eyebrows rose. 'That is curious – very curious.'

Carbury cocked an inquiring eye at him. But as Poirot said nothing more, he himself went on:

'Seems pretty obvious Mother was a pest! Had to be waited on hand and foot and kept the whole lot of them dancing attendance. And she held the purse strings. None of them had a penny of their own.'

'Aha! All very interesting. Is it known how she left her money?'

'I did just slip that question in – casual like, you know. It gets divided equally between the lot of them.'

Poirot nodded his head. Then he asked:

'You are of the opinion that they are all in it?'

'Don't know. That's where the difficulty's going to lie. Whether it was a concerted effort, or whether it was one bright member's idea – I don't know. Maybe the whole thing's a mare's nest! What it comes to is this: I'd like to have your professional opinion. Ah, here comes Gerard.'

CHAPTER 2

The Frenchman came in with a quick yet unhurried tread. As he shook hands with Colonel Carbury he shot a keen, interested glance at Poirot. Carbury said:

'This is M. Hercule Poirot. Staying with me. Been talking to him about this business down at Petra.'

'Ah, yes?' Gerard's quick eyes looked Poirot up and down. 'You are interested?'

Hercule Poirot threw up his hands.

'Alas! one is always incurably interested in one's own subject.'

'True,' said Gerard.

'Have a drink?' said Carbury.

He poured out a whisky and soda and placed it by Gerard's elbow. He held up the decanter inquiringly, but Poirot shook his head. Colonel Carbury set it down again and drew his chair a little nearer.

'Well,' he said, 'where are we?'

'I gather,' said Poirot to Gerard, 'that Colonel Carbury is not satisfied.'

Gerard made an expressive gesture.

'And that,' he said, 'is my fault! And I may be wrong. Remember that, Colonel Carbury, I may be entirely wrong.'

Carbury gave a grunt.

'Give Poirot the facts,' he said.

Dr Gerard began by a brief recapitulation of the events preceding the journey to Petra. He gave a short sketch of the various members of the Boynton family and described the condition of emotional strain under which they were labouring.

Poirot listened with interest.

Then Gerard proceeded to the actual events of their first day at Petra, describing how he had returned to the camp.

'I was in for a bad bout of malaria – cerebral type,' he explained. 'For that I proposed to treat myself by an intravenous injection of quinine. That is the usual method.'

Poirot nodded his comprehension.

'The fever was on me badly. I fairly staggered into my tent. I could not at first find my case of drugs, someone had moved it from where I had originally placed it. Then, when I had found that, I could not find my hypodermic syringe. I hunted for it for some time, then gave it up and took a large dose of quinine by the mouth and flung myself on my bed.'

Gerard paused, then went on:

'Mrs Boynton's death was not discovered until after sunset. Owing to the way in which she was sitting and the support the chair gave to her body, no change occurred in her position and it was not until one of the boys went to summon her to dinner at six-thirty that it was noticed that anything was wrong.'

He explained in full detail the position of the cave and its distance away from the big marquee.

'Miss King, who is a qualified doctor, examined the body. She did not disturb me, knowing that I had fever. There was, indeed, nothing that could be done. Mrs Boynton was dead – and had been dead for some little time.'

Poirot murmured: 'How long exactly?'

Gerard said slowly:

'I do not think that Miss King gave much attention to that point. She did not, I presume, think it of any importance.'

'One can say, at least, when she was last definitely known to be alive?' said Poirot.

Colonel Carbury cleared his throat and referred to an official-looking document.

'Mrs Boynton was spoken to by Lady Westholme and Miss

Pierce shortly after 4 p.m. Lennox Boynton spoke to his mother about four-thirty. Mrs Lennox Boynton had a long conversation with her about five minutes later. Carol Boynton had a word with her mother at a time she is unable to state precisely – but which from the evidence of others would seem to have been about ten minutes past five.

'Jefferson Cope, an American friend of the family, returning to the camp with Lady Westholme and Miss Pierce, saw her asleep. He did not speak to her. That was about twenty to six. Raymond Boynton, the younger son, seems to have been the last person to see her alive. On his return from a walk he went and spoke to her at about ten minutes to six. The discovery of the body was made at six-thirty when a servant went to tell her dinner was ready.'

'Between the time that Mr Raymond Boynton spoke to her and half-past six did no one go near her?' asked Poirot.

'I understand not.'

'But someone *might* have done so?' Poirot persisted.

'I don't think so. From close on six onwards servants were moving about the camp, people were going to and from their tents. No one can be found who saw anyone approaching the old lady.'

'Then Raymond Boynton was definitely the last person to see his mother alive?' said Poirot.

Dr Gerard and Colonel Carbury interchanged a quick glance. Colonel Carbury drummed on the table with his fingers.

'This is where we begin to get into deep waters,' he said. 'Go on, Gerard. This is your pigeon.'

'As I mentioned just now, Sarah King, when she examined Mrs Boynton, saw no reason for determining the exact time of death. She merely said that Mrs Boynton had been dead "some little time", but when, on the following day for reasons of my own, I endeavoured to narrow things down and happened to mention that Mrs Boynton was last seen alive by her son Raymond at a little before six, Miss King, to my great surprise, said point-blank that that was impossible – that at that time Mrs Boynton must already have been dead.'

Poirot's eyebrows rose. 'Odd. Extremely odd. And what does M. Raymond Boynton say to that?'

Colonel Carbury said abruptly: 'He swears that his mother was alive. He went up to her and said, "I'm back. Hope you have had a nice afternoon?" Something of that kind. He says she just grunted, "Quite all right," and he went on to his tent.'

Poirot frowned perplexedly.

'Curious,' he said. 'Extremely curious. Tell me, was it growing dusk by then?'

'The sun was just setting.'

'Curious,' said Poirot again. 'And you, Dr Gerard, when did you see the body?'

'Not until the following day. At 9 a.m. to be precise.'

'And your estimate of the time death had occurred?'

The Frenchman shrugged his shoulders.

'It is difficult to be exact after that length of time. There must necessarily be a margin of several hours. Were I giving evidence on oath I could only say that she had been dead certainly twelve hours and not longer than eighteen. You see, that does not help at all.'

'Go on, Gerard,' said Colonel Carbury. 'Give him the rest of it.'

'On getting up in the morning,' said Dr Gerard, 'I found my hypodermic syringe – it was behind a case of bottles on my dressing-table.'

He leaned forward.

'You may say, if you like, that I had overlooked it the day before. I was in a miserable state of fever and wretchedness, shaking from head to foot, and how often does one look for a thing that is there all the time and yet be unable to find it! I can only say that I am quite positive the syringe was *not* there then.'

'There's something more still,' said Carbury.

'Yes, two facts for what they are worth and they mean a great deal. There was a mark on the dead woman's wrist – a mark such as would be caused by the insertion of a hypodermic syringe. Her daughter, I may say, explains it as having been caused by the prick of a pin –'

Poirot stirred. 'Which daughter?'

'Her daughter Carol.'

'Yes, continue, I pray you.'

'And there is the last fact. Happening to examine my little case of drugs, I noticed that my stock of digitoxin was very much diminished.'

'Digitoxin,' said Poirot, 'is a heart poison, is it not?'

'Yes. It is obtained from *Digitalis purpurea* – the common foxglove. There are four active principles – *digitalin* – *digitonin* – *digitalein* – and *digitoxin*. Of these *digitoxin* is considered the most active poisonous constituent of digitalis leaves. According to Kopp's experiments it is from six to ten times stronger than *digitalin* or *digitalein*. It is official in France – but not in the British Pharmacopoeia.'

'And a large dose of digitoxin?'

Dr Gerard said gravely: 'A large dose of digitoxin thrown suddenly on the circulation by intravenous injection would cause sudden death by quick palsy of the heart. It has been estimated that four milligrams might prove fatal to an adult man.'

'And Mrs Boynton already suffered with heart trouble?'

'Yes, as a matter of fact she was actually taking a medicine containing digitalin.'

'That,' said Poirot, 'is extremely interesting.'

'D'you mean,' asked Colonel Carbury, 'that her death might have been attributed to an overdose of her own medicine?'

'That – yes. But I meant more than that.'

'In some senses,' said Dr Gerard, 'digitalin may be considered a cumulative drug. Moreover, as regards post-mortem appearance, the active principles of the digitalis may destroy life and leave no appreciable sign.'

Poirot nodded slow appreciation.

'Yes, that is clever – very clever. Almost impossible to prove satisfactorily to a jury. Ah, but let me tell you, gentlemen, if this is a murder, it is a very clever murder! The hypodermic replaced, the poison employed, a poison which the victim was already taking – the possibilities of a mistake – or accident – are overwhelming. Oh, yes, there are brains here. There is thought – care – genius.'

For a moment he sat in silence, then he raised his head. 'And yet, one thing puzzles me.'

'What is that?'

'The theft of the hypodermic syringe.'

'It was taken,' said Dr Gerard quickly.

'Taken – and returned?'

'Yes.'

'Odd,' said Poirot. 'Very odd. Otherwise everything fits so well . . .'

Colonel Carbury looked at him curiously.

'Well?' he said. 'What's your expert opinion? Was it murder – or wasn't it?'

Poirot held up a hand.

'One moment. We have not yet arrived at that point. There is still some evidence to consider.'

'What evidence? You've had it all.'

'Ah! but this is evidence *that I, Hercule Poirot*, bring to you.'

He nodded his head and smiled a little at their two astonished faces.

'Yes, it is droll, that! That I, to whom you tell the story, should in return present you with a piece of evidence about which you do not know. It was like this. In the Solomon Hotel, one night, I go to the window to make sure it is closed –'

'Closed – or open?' asked Carbury.

'Closed,' said Poirot firmly. 'It was open, so naturally I go to close it. But before I do so, as my hand is on the latch, I hear a voice speaking – an agreeable voice, low and clear with a tremor in it of nervous excitement. I say to myself it is a voice I will know again. And what does it say, this voice? It says these words, "*You do see, don't you, that she's got to be killed?*"'

'At the moment, *naturellement*, I do not take those words as referring to a killing of flesh and blood. I think it is an author or perhaps a playwright who speaks. But now – *I am not so sure.* That is to say I am sure it was nothing of the kind.'

Again he paused before saying: 'Messieurs, I will tell you this – *to the best of my knowledge and belief* those words were spoken by a young man whom I saw later in the lounge of the hotel and who was, so they told me on inquiring, a young man of the name of Raymond Boynton.'

CHAPTER 3

'Raymond Boynton said that!'

The exclamation broke from the Frenchman.

'You think it unlikely – psychologically speaking?' Poirot inquired placidly.

Gerard shook his head.

'No, I should not say that. I was surprised, yes. If you follow me,

I was surprised just because Raymond Boynton was so eminently fitted to be a suspect.'

Colonel Carbury sighed. 'These psychological fellers!' the sigh seemed to say.

'Question is,' he murmured, 'what are we going to do about it?'

Gerard shrugged his shoulders.

'I do not see what you can do,' he confessed. 'The evidence is bound to be inconclusive. You may know that murder has been done but it will be difficult to prove it.'

'I see,' said Colonel Carbury. 'We suspect that murder's been done and we just sit back and twiddle our fingers! Don't like it!' He added, as if in extenuation, his former odd plea, 'I'm a tidy man.'

'I know. I know.' Poirot nodded his head sympathetically. 'You would like to clear this up. You would like to know definitely, exactly what occurred and how it occurred. And you, Dr Gerard? You have said that there is nothing to be done – that the evidence is bound to be inconclusive? That is probably true. But are you satisfied that the matter should rest so?'

'She was a bad life,' said Gerard slowly. 'In any case, she might have died very shortly – a week – a month – a year.'

'So you are satisfied?' persisted Poirot.

Gerard went on:

'There is no doubt that her death was – how shall we put it? – beneficial to the community. It has brought freedom to her family. They will have scope to develop – they are all, I think, people of good character and intelligence. They will be – now – useful members of society! The death of Mrs Boynton, as I see it, has resulted in nothing but good.'

Poirot repeated for the third time: 'So you are satisfied?'

'No.' Gerard pounded a fist suddenly on the table. 'I am *not* "satisfied", as you put it! It is my instinct to preserve life – not to hasten death. Therefore, though my conscious mind may repeat that this woman's death was a good thing, my unconscious mind rebels against it! *It is not well, gentlemen, that a human being should die before her time has come.*'

Poirot smiled. He leaned back contented with the answer he had probed for so patiently.

Colonel Carbury said unemotionally: 'He don't like murder! Quite right! No more do I.'

He rose and poured himself out a stiff whisky and soda. His guests' glasses were still full.

'And now,' he said, returning to the subject, 'let's get down to brass tacks. *Is there anything to be done about it?* We don't like it – no! But we may have to lump it! No good making a fuss if you can't deliver the goods.'

Gerard leaned forward. 'What is your professional opinion, M. Poirot? You are the expert.'

Poirot took a little time to speak. Methodically he arranged an ash-tray or two and made a little heap of used matches. Then he said:

'You desire to know, do you not, Colonel Carbury, *who killed Mrs Boynton?* (That is if she *was* killed and did not die a natural death.) Exactly *how and when* she was killed – and in fact the whole truth of the matter?'

'I should like to know that, yes.' Carbury spoke unemotionally.

Hercule Poirot said slowly: 'I see no reason why you should not know it!'

Dr Gerard looked incredulous. Colonel Carbury looked mildly interested.

'Oh,' he said. 'So you don't, don't you? That's interestin'. How d'you propose to set about it?'

'By methodical sifting of the evidence, by a process of reasoning.'

'Suits me,' said Colonel Carbury.

'And by a study of the psychological possibilities.'

'Suits Dr Gerard, I expect,' said Carbury. 'And after that – after you've sifted the evidence and done some reasoning and paddled in psychology – *hey presto!* – you think you can produce the rabbit out of the hat?'

'I should be extremely surprised if I could not do so,' said Poirot calmly.

Colonel Carbury stared at him over the rim of his glass. Just for a moment the vague eyes were no longer vague – they measured – and appraised.

He put down his glass with a grunt.

'What do you say to that, Dr Gerard?'

'I admit that I am sceptical of success . . . Yes, I know that M. Poirot has great powers.'

'I am gifted – yes,' said the little man. He smiled modestly.

Colonel Carbury turned away his head and coughed.

Poirot said: 'The first thing to decide is whether this is a composite murder – planned and carried out by the Boynton family as a whole, or whether it is the work of one of them only. If the latter, which is the most likely member of the family to have attempted it.'

Dr Gerard said: 'There is your own evidence. One must, I think, consider first Raymond Boynton.'

'I agree,' said Poirot. 'The words I overheard and the discrepancy between his evidence and that of the young woman doctor puts him definitely in the forefront of the suspects.'

'He was the last person to see Mrs Boynton alive. That is his own story. Sarah King contradicts that. Tell me, Dr Gerard, is there – eh? – you know what I mean – a little *tendresse*, shall we say – there?'

The Frenchman nodded. 'Emphatically so.'

'Aha! Is she, this young lady, a brunette with hair that goes back from her forehead – so – and big hazel eyes and a manner very decided?'

Dr Gerard looked rather surprised.

'Yes, that describes her very well.'

'I think I have seen her – in the Solomon Hotel. She spoke to this Raymond Boynton and afterwards he remained *planté là* – in a dream – blocking the exit from the lift. Three times I had to say "Pardon" before he heard me and moved.'

He remained in thought for some moments. Then he said: 'So, to begin with, we will accept the medical evidence of Miss Sarah King with certain mental reservations. She is an interested party.'

He paused – then went on: 'Tell me, Dr Gerard, do you think Raymond Boynton is of the temperament that could commit murder easily?'

Gerard said slowly: 'You mean deliberate planned murder? Yes, I think it is possible – but only under conditions of intense emotional strain.'

'Those conditions were present?'

'Definitely. This journey abroad undoubtedly heightened the nervous and mental strain under which all these people were living. The contrast between their own lives and those of other people was more apparent to them. And in Raymond Boynton's case –'

'Yes?'

'There was the additional complication of being strongly attracted to Sarah King.'

'That would give him an additional motive? And an additional stimulus?'

'That is so.'

Colonel Carbury coughed.

'Like to butt in a moment. That sentence of his you overheard, "*You do see, don't you, that she's got to be killed?*" Must have been spoken to someone.'

'A good point,' said Poirot. 'I had not forgotten it. Yes, to whom was Raymond Boynton speaking? Undoubtedly to a member of his family. But which member? Can you tell us something, Doctor, of the mental condition of the other members of the family?'

Gerard replied promptly:

'Carol Boynton was, I should say, in very much the same state as Raymond – a state of rebellion accompanied by a severe nervous excitement, but uncomplicated in her case by the introduction of a sex factor. Lennox Boynton had passed the stage of revolt. He was sunk in apathy. He was finding it, I think, difficult to concentrate. His method of reaction to his surroundings was to retire further and further within himself. He was definitely an introvert.'

'And his wife?'

'His wife, though tired and unhappy, showed no signs of mental conflict. She was, I believe, hesitating on the brink of a decision.'

'Such a decision being?'

'Whether or not to leave her husband.'

He repeated the conversation he had held with Jefferson Cope. Poirot nodded in comprehension.

'And what of the younger girl – Ginevra her name is, is it not?'

The Frenchman's face was grave. He said:

'I should say that mentally she is in an extremely dangerous condition. She has already begun to display symptoms of schizophrenia. Unable to bear the suppression of her life, she is escaping into a realm of fantasy. She has advanced delusions of persecution – that is to say, she claims to be a royal personage – in danger – enemies surrounding her – all the usual things!'

'And that – is dangerous?'

'Very dangerous. It is the beginning of what is often homicidal mania. The sufferer kills – not for the lust of killing – but *in self-defence*. He or she kills in order not to be killed themselves. From their point of view it is eminently rational.'

'So you think that Ginevra Boynton might have killed her mother?'

'Yes. But I doubt if she would have had the knowledge or the constructiveness to do it the way it was done. The cunning of that class of mania is usually very simple and obvious. And I am almost certain she would have chosen a more spectacular method.'

'But she is a *possibility?*' Poirot insisted.

'Yes,' admitted Gerard.

'And afterwards – when the deed was done? *Do you think the rest of the family knew who had done it?*'

'They know!' said Colonel Carbury unexpectedly. 'If ever I came across a bunch of people who had something to hide – these are they! They're putting something over all right.'

'We will make them tell us what it is,' said Poirot.

'Third degree?' said Colonel Carbury.

'No.' Poirot shook his head. 'Just ordinary conversation. On the whole, you know, people tell you the truth. Because it is easier! Because it is less strain on the inventive faculties! You can tell one lie – or two lies – or three lies – or even four lies – *but you cannot lie all the time*. And so – the truth becomes plain.'

'Something in that,' agreed Carbury.

Then he said bluntly: 'You'll talk to them, you say? That means you're willing to take this on.'

Poirot bowed his head.

'Let us be very clear about this,' he said. 'What you demand, and what I undertake to supply, is the truth. But mark this, even when we have got the truth, there may be no *proof*. That is to say, no proof that would be accepted in a court of law. You comprehend?'

'Quite,' said Carbury. 'You satisfy me of what really happened. Then it's up to me to decide whether action is possible or not – having regard to the international aspects. Anyway, it will be cleared up – no mess. Don't like mess.'

Poirot smiled.

'One thing more,' said Carbury. 'I can't give you much time. Can't detain these people here indefinitely.'

Poirot said quietly:

'You can detain them twenty-four hours. You shall have the truth by tomorrow night.'

Colonel Carbury stared hard at him.

'Pretty confident, aren't you?' he asked.

'I know my own ability,' murmured Poirot.

Rendered uncomfortable by this un-British attitude, Colonel Carbury looked away and fingered his untidy moustaches.

'Well,' he mumbled, 'it's up to you.'

'And if you succeed, my friend,' said Dr Gerard, 'you are indeed a marvel!'

CHAPTER 4

Sarah King looked long and searchingly at Hercule Poirot. She noted the egg-shaped head, the gigantic moustaches, the dandified appearance and the suspicious blackness of his hair. A look of doubt crept into her eyes. 'Well, mademoiselle, are you satisfied?'

Sarah flushed as she met the amused ironical glance of his eyes.

'I beg your pardon,' she said awkwardly.

'*Du tout*! To use an expression I have recently learnt, you give me the once-over, is it not so?'

Sarah smiled a little. 'Well, at any rate, you can do the same to me,' she said.

'Assuredly. I have not neglected to do so.'

She glanced at him sharply. Something in his tone. But Poirot was twirling his moustaches complacently, and Sarah thought (for the second time), 'The man's a mountebank!'

Her self-confidence restored, she sat up a little straighter and said inquiringly: 'I don't think I quite understand the object of this interview?'

'The good Dr Gerard did not explain?'

Sarah said frowning: 'I don't understand Dr Gerard. He seems to think –'

'Something is rotten in the state of Denmark,' quoted Poirot. 'You see, I know your Shakespeare.'

Sarah waved aside Shakespeare.

'What exactly is all this fuss about?' she demanded.

'*Eh bien*, one wants, does one not, to get at the truth of this affair?'

'Are you talking about Mrs Boynton's death?'

'Yes.'

'Isn't it rather a fuss about nothing? You, of course, are a specialist, M. Poirot. It is natural for you –'

Poirot finished the sentence for her.

'It is natural for me to suspect crime whenever I can possibly find an excuse for doing so?'

'Well – yes – perhaps.'

'You have no doubt yourself as to Mrs Boynton's death?'

Sarah shrugged her shoulders.

'Really, M. Poirot, if you had been to Petra you would realize that the journey there was a somewhat strenuous business for an old woman whose cardiac condition was unsatisfactory.'

'It seems a perfectly straightforward business to you?'

'Certainly. I can't understand Dr Gerard's attitude. He didn't even know anything about it. He was down with fever. I'd bow to his superior medical knowledge naturally – in this case he had nothing whatever to go on. I suppose they can have a P.M. in Jerusalem if they like – if they're not satisfied with my verdict.'

Poirot was silent for a moment, then he said:

'There is a fact, Miss King, that you do not yet know. Dr Gerard has not told you of it.'

'What fact?' demanded Sarah.

'A supply of a drug – digitoxin – is missing from Dr Gerard's travelling medicine case.'

'Oh!' Quickly Sarah took in this new aspect of the case. Equally quickly she pounced on the one doubtful point.

'Is Dr Gerard quite sure of that?'

Poirot shrugged his shoulders.

'A doctor, as you should know, mademoiselle, is usually fairly careful in making his statements.'

'Oh, of course. That goes without saying. But Dr Gerard had malaria at the time.'

'That is so, of course.'

'Has he any idea when it could have been taken?'

'He had occasion to go to his case on the night of his arrival in

Petra. He wanted some phenacetin – as his head was aching badly. When he replaced the phenacetin the following morning and shut up the case he is almost certain that all the drugs were intact.'

'Almost –' said Sarah.

Poirot shrugged.

'Yes, there is a doubt! There is the doubt that any man, who is honest, would be likely to feel.'

Sarah nodded. 'Yes, I know. One always distrusts those people who are *over* sure. But all the same, M. Poirot, the evidence *is* very slight. It seems to me –' She paused. Poirot finished the sentence for her.

'It seems to you that an inquiry on my part is ill-advised!'

Sarah looked him squarely in the face.

'Frankly, it does. Are you sure, M. Poirot, that this is not a case of Roman Holiday?'

Poirot smiled. 'The private lives of a family upset and disturbed – so that Hercule Poirot can play a little game of detection to amuse himself?'

'I didn't mean to be offensive – but isn't it a little like that?'

'You, then, are on the side of the *famille* Boynton, mademoiselle?'

'I think I am. They've suffered a good deal. They – they oughtn't to have to stand any more.'

'And *la Maman*, she was unpleasant, tyrannical, disagreeable and decidedly better dead than alive? That also – *hein?*'

'When you put it like that –' Sarah paused, flushed, went on: 'One shouldn't, I agree, take that into consideration.'

'But all the same – one does! That is, *you* do, mademoiselle! I – do not! To me it is all the same. The victim may be one of the good God's saints – or, on the contrary – a monster of infamy. It moves me not. The fact is the same. A life – taken! I say it always – I do not approve of murder.'

'Murder?' Sarah drew in her breath sharply. 'But what evidence of that is there? The flimsiest imaginable! Dr Gerard himself cannot be sure!'

Poirot said quietly: 'But there is other evidence, mademoiselle.'

'What evidence?' Her voice was sharp.

'*The mark of a hypodermic puncture upon the dead woman's wrist.* And something more still – *some words that I overheard spoken in Jerusalem* on a clear, still night when I went to close my bedroom

502

window. Shall I tell you what those words were, Miss King? They were these. I heard Mr Raymond Boynton say: "*You do see, don't you, that she's got to be killed?*"'

He saw the colour drain slowly from Sarah's face.

She said: '*You heard that?*'

'Yes.'

The girl stared straight ahead of her.

She said at last: 'It would be you who heard it!'

He acquiesced.

'Yes, it would be me. These things happen. You see now why I think there should be an investigation?'

Sarah said quietly: 'I think you are quite right.'

'Ah! And you will help me?'

'Certainly.'

Her tone was matter-of-fact – unemotional. Her eyes met his coolly.

Poirot bowed. 'Thank you, mademoiselle. Now I will ask you to tell me in your own words exactly what you can remember of that particular day.'

Sarah considered for a moment.

'Let me see. I went on an expedition in the morning. None of the Boyntons were with us. I saw them at lunch. They were finishing as we came in. Mrs Boynton seemed in an unusually good temper.'

'She was not usually amiable, I understand.'

'Very far from it,' said Sarah with a slight grimace.

She then described how Mrs Boynton had released her family from attendance on her.

'That too, was unusual?'

'Yes. She usually kept them around her.'

'Do you think, perhaps, that she suddenly felt remorseful – that she had what is called – *un bon moment*?'

'No, I don't,' said Sarah bluntly.

'What did you think, then?'

'I was puzzled. I suspected it was something of the cat-and-mouse order.'

'If you would elaborate, mademoiselle?'

'A cat enjoys letting a mouse away – and then catching it again. Mrs Boynton had that kind of mentality. I thought she was up to some new devilry or other.'

'What happened next, mademoiselle?'

'The Boyntons started off –'

'All of them?'

'No, the youngest, Ginevra, was left behind. She was told to go and rest.'

'Did she wish to do so?'

'No. But that didn't matter. She did what she was told. The others started off. Dr Gerard and I joined them –'

'When was this?'

'About half-past three.'

'Where was Mrs Boynton then?'

'Nadine – young Mrs Boynton – had settled her in her chair outside her cave.'

'Proceed.'

'When we got round the bend, Dr Gerard and I caught up the others. We all walked together. Then, after a while, Dr Gerard turned back. He had been looking rather queer for some time. I could see he had fever. I wanted to go back with him, but he wouldn't hear of it.'

'What time was this?'

'Oh! about four, I suppose.'

'And the rest?'

'We went on.'

'Were you all together?'

'At first. Then we split up.' Sarah hurried on as though fore-seeing the next question. 'Nadine Boynton and Mr Cope went one way and Carol, Lennox, Raymond and I went another.'

'And you continued like that?'

'Well – no. Raymond Boynton and I separated from the others. We sat down on a slab of rock and admired the wildness of the scenery. Then he went off and I stayed where I was for some time longer. It was about half-past five when I looked at my watch and realized I had better get back. I reached the camp at six o'clock. It was just about sunset.'

'You passed Mrs Boynton on the way?'

'I noticed she was still in her chair up on the ridge.'

'That did not strike you as odd – that she had not moved?'

'No, because I had seen her sitting there the night before when we arrived.'

'I see. *Continuez.*'

'I went into the marquee. The others were all there – except Dr Gerard. I washed and then came back. They brought in dinner and one of the servants went to tell Mrs Boynton. He came running back to say she was ill. I hurried out. She was sitting in her chair just as she had been, but as soon as I touched her I realized she was dead.'

'You had no doubt at all as to her death being natural?'

'None whatever. I had heard that she suffered from heart trouble, though no specified disease had been mentioned.'

'You simply thought she had died sitting there in her chair?'

'Yes.'

'Without calling out for assistance?'

'Yes. It happens that way sometimes. She might even have died in her sleep. She was quite likely to have dozed off. In any case, all the camp was asleep most of the afternoon. No one would have heard her unless she had called very loud.'

'Did you form an opinion as to how long she had been dead?'

'Well, I didn't really think very much about it. She had clearly been dead some time.'

'What do you call some time?' asked Poirot.

'Well – over an hour. It might have been much longer. The refraction of the rock would keep her body from cooling quickly.'

'Over an hour? Are you aware, Mademoiselle King, that Raymond Boynton spoke to her only a little over half an hour earlier, and that she was then alive and well?'

Now her eyes no longer met his. But she shook her head. 'He must have made a mistake. It must have been earlier than that.'

'No, mademoiselle, it was not.'

She looked at him point-blank. He noticed again the firm set of her mouth.

'Well,' said Sarah, 'I'm young and I haven't got much experience of dead bodies – but I know enough to be quite sure of one thing. Mrs Boynton had been dead *at least* an hour when I examined her body!'

'That,' said Hercule Poirot unexpectedly, 'is your story and you are going to stick to it! Then can you explain *why* Mr Boynton should say his mother was alive when she was, in point of fact, dead?'

'I've no idea,' said Sarah. 'They're probably rather vague about times, all of them! They're a very nervy family.'

'On how many occasions, mademoiselle, have you spoken with them?'

Sarah was silent a moment, frowning a little.

'I can tell you exactly,' she said. 'I talked to Raymond Boynton in the wagons-lits corridor coming to Jerusalem. I had two conversations with Carol Boynton – one at the Mosque of Omar and one late that evening in my bedroom. I had a conversation with Mrs Lennox Boynton the following morning. That's all – up to the afternoon of Mrs Boynton's death, when we all went walking together.'

'You did not have any conversation with Mrs Boynton herself?'

Sarah flushed uncomfortably.

'Yes. I exchanged a few words with her on the day she left Jerusalem.' She paused and then blurted out: 'As a matter of fact, I made a fool of myself.'

'Ah?'

The interrogation was so patent that, stiffly and unwillingly, Sarah gave an account of the conversation.

Poirot seemed interested and cross-examined her closely.

'The mentality of Mrs Boynton – it is very important in this case,' he said. 'And you are an outsider – an unbiased observer. That is why your account of her is very significant.'

Sarah did not reply. She still felt hot and uncomfortable when she thought of that interview.

'Thank you, mademoiselle,' said Poirot. 'I will now converse with the other witnesses.'

Sarah rose. 'Excuse me, M. Poirot, but if I might make a suggestion –'

'Certainly. Certainly.'

'Why not postpone all this until an autopsy can be made and you discover whether or not your suspicions are justified? I think all this is rather like putting the cart before the horse.'

Poirot waved a grandiloquent hand. 'This is the method of Hercule Poirot,' he announced.

Pressing her lips together, Sarah left the room.

Lady Westholme entered the room with the assurance of a transatlantic liner coming into dock.

Miss Amabel Pierce, an indeterminate craft, followed in the liner's wake and sat down in an inferior make of chair slightly in the background.

'Certainly, M. Poirot,' boomed Lady Westholme. 'I shall be delighted to assist you by any means in my power. I have always considered that in matters of this kind one has a public duty to perform –'

When Lady Westholme's public duty had held the stage for some minutes, Poirot was adroit enough to get in a question.

'I have a perfect recollection of the afternoon in question,' replied Lady Westholme. 'Miss Pierce and I will do all we can to assist you.'

'Oh, yes,' sighed Miss Pierce, almost ecstatically. 'So tragic, was it not? Dead – just like that – in the twinkle of an eye!'

'If you will tell me exactly what occurred on the afternoon in question?'

'Certainly,' said Lady Westholme. 'After we had finished lunch I decided to take a brief siesta. The morning excursion had been somewhat fatiguing. Not that I was really tired – I seldom am. I do not really know what fatigue is. One has so often, on public occasions, no matter what one really feels –'

Again an adroit murmur from Poirot.

'As I say, I was in favour of a siesta. Miss Pierce agreed with me.'

'Oh, yes,' sighed Miss Pierce. 'And I was *terribly* tired after the morning. Such a *dangerous* climb – and although interesting, *most* exhausting. I'm afraid I'm not *quite* as strong as Lady Westholme.'

'Fatigue,' said Lady Westholme, 'can be conquered like every-thing else. I make a point of never giving in to my bodily needs.'

Poirot said:

'After lunch, then, you two ladies went to your tents?'

'Yes.'

'Mrs Boynton was then sitting at the mouth of her cave?'

'Her daughter-in-law assisted her there before she herself went off.'

'You could both see her?'

'Oh, yes,' said Miss Pierce. 'She was opposite, you know – only, of course, a little way along and up above.'

Lady Westholme elucidated the statement.

'The caves opened on to a ledge. Below that ledge were some tents. Then there was a small stream and across that stream was the big marquee and some other tents. Miss Pierce and I had tents near the marquee. She was on the right side of the marquee and I was on the left. The opening of our tents faced the ledge, but of course it was some distance away.'

'Nearly two hundred yards, I understand.'

'Possibly.'

'I have here a plan,' said Poirot, 'concocted with the help of the dragoman, Mahmoud.'

Lady Westholme remarked that in that case it was probably wrong!

'That man is grossly inaccurate. I have checked his statements from my Baedeker. Several times his information was definitely misleading.'

'According to my plan,' said Poirot, 'the cave next to Mrs Boynton's was occupied by her son, Lennox, and his wife. Raymond, Carol and Ginevra Boynton had tents just below but more to the right – in fact, almost opposite the marquee. On the right of Ginevra Boynton's was Dr Gerard's tent and next to that again that of Miss King. On the other side of the stream – next to the marquee on the left – you and Mr Cope had tents. Miss Pierce's, as you mentioned, was on the right of the marquee. Is that correct?'

Lady Westholme admitted grudgingly that as far as she knew it was.

'I thank you. That is perfectly clear. Pray continue, Lady Westholme.'

Lady Westholme smiled graciously on him and went on:

'At about quarter to four I strolled along to Miss Pierce's tent to see if she were awake yet and felt like a stroll. She was sitting in the doorway of the tent reading. We agreed to start in about half an hour when the sun was less hot. I went back to my tent and read for about twenty-five minutes. Then I went along and joined Miss Pierce. She was ready and we started out. Everyone in the camp seemed asleep – there was no one about, and seeing

Mrs Boynton sitting up there alone, I suggested to Miss Pierce that we should ask her if she wanted anything before we left.'

'Yes, you did. *Most* thoughtful of you, I considered,' murmured Miss Pierce.

'I felt it to be my duty,' said Lady Westholme with a rich complacency.

'And then for her to be so rude about it!' exclaimed Miss Pierce.

Poirot looked inquiring.

'Our path passed just under the ledge,' explained Lady Westholme, 'and I called up to her, saying that we were going for a stroll and could we do anything for her before we went. Do you know, M. Poirot, absolutely the only answer she gave us was a *grunt*! A grunt! She just looked at us as though we were – as though we were dirt!'

'Disgraceful it was!' said Miss Pierce, flushing.

'I must confess,' said Lady Westholme, reddening a little, 'that I made then a somewhat uncharitable remark.'

'I think you were quite justified,' said Miss Pierce. '*Quite* – under the circumstances.'

'What was this remark?' asked Poirot.

'I said to Miss Pierce that perhaps she *drank*! Really her manner was *most* peculiar. It had been all along. I thought it possible that drink might account for it. The evils of alcoholic indulgence, as I very well know –'

Dexterously, Poirot steered the conversation away from the drink question.

'Had her manner been very peculiar on this particular day? At lunch-time, for instance?'

'N-No,' said Lady Westholme, considering. 'No, I should say then that her manner had been fairly normal – for an American of that type, that is to say,' she added condescendingly.

'She was very abusive to that servant,' said Miss Pierce.

'Which one?'

'Not very long before we started out.'

'Oh! yes, I remember, she *did* seem extraordinarily annoyed with him! Of course,' went on Lady Westholme, 'to have servants about who cannot understand a word of English is very trying, but what I say is that when one is travelling one must make allowances.'

'What servant was this?' asked Poirot.

'One of the Bedouin servants attached to the camp. He went up to her – I think she must have sent him to fetch her something, and I suppose he brought the wrong thing – I don't really know what it was – but she was very angry about it. The poor man slunk away as fast as he could, and she shook her stick at him and called out.'

'What did she call out?'

'We were too far away to hear. At least I didn't hear anything distinctly, did you, Miss Pierce?'

'No, I didn't. I think she'd sent him to fetch something from her youngest daughter's tent – or perhaps she was angry with him for going into her daughter's tent – I couldn't say exactly.'

'What did he look like?'

Miss Pierce, to whom the question was addressed, shook her head vaguely.

'Really, I couldn't say. He was too far away. All these Arabs look alike to me.'

'He was a man of more than average height,' said Lady Westholme, 'and wore the usual native head-dress. He had on a pair of very torn and patched breeches – really disgraceful they were – and his puttees were wound most untidily – all anyhow! These men need *discipline*!'

'You could point the man out among the camp servants?'

'I doubt it. We didn't see his face – it was too far away. And, as Miss Pierce says, really these Arabs look all alike.'

'I wonder,' said Poirot thoughtfully, 'what it was he did to make Mrs Boynton so angry?'

'They are very trying to the patience sometimes,' said Lady Westholme. 'One of them took my shoes away, though I had expressly told him – by pantomime too – that I preferred to clean my shoes myself.'

'Always I do that, too,' said Poirot, diverted for a moment from his interrogation. 'I take everywhere my little shoe-cleaning outfit. Also, I take a duster.'

'So do I.' Lady Westholme sounded quite human.

'Because these Arabs they do not remove the dust from one's belongings –'

'Never! Of course one has to dust one's things three or four times a day –'

'But it is well worth it.'

'Yes, indeed. I cannot STAND dirt!'

Lady Westholme looked positively militant.

She added with feeling:

'The flies – in the bazaars – terrible!'

'Well, well,' said Poirot, looking slightly guilty. 'We can soon inquire from this man what it was that irritated Mrs Boynton. To continue with your story?'

'We strolled along slowly,' said Lady Westholme. 'And then we met Dr Gerard. He was staggering along and looked very ill. I could see at once he had fever.'

'He was shaking,' put in Miss Pierce. 'Shaking all over.'

'I saw at once he had an attack of malaria coming on,' said Lady Westholme. 'I offered to come back with him and get him some quinine, but he said he had his own supply with him.'

'Poor man,' said Miss Pierce. 'You know it always seems so dreadful to me to see a doctor ill. It seems all wrong somehow.'

'We strolled on,' continued Lady Westholme. 'And then we sat down on a rock.'

Miss Pierce murmured: 'Really – so tired after the morning's exertion – the climbing –'

'I never feel fatigue,' said Lady Westholme firmly. 'But there was no point in going farther. We had a very good view of all the surrounding scenery.'

'Were you out of sight of the camp?'

'No, we were sitting facing towards it.'

'So romantic,' murmured Miss Pierce. 'A camp pitched in the middle of a wilderness of rose-red rocks.'

She sighed and shook her head.

'That camp could be much better run than it is,' said Lady Westholme. Her rocking-horse nostrils dilated. 'I shall take up the matter with Castle's. I am not at all sure that the drinking water is boiled as well as filtered. It should be. I shall point that out to them.'

Poirot coughed and led the conversation quickly away from the subject of drinking water.

'Did you see any other members of the party?' he inquired.

'Yes. The elder Mr Boynton and his wife passed us on their way back to the camp.'

'Were they together?'

'No, Mr Boynton came first. He looked a little as though he had had a touch of the sun. He was walking as though he were slightly dizzy.'

'The back of the neck,' said Miss Pierce. 'One *must* protect the back of the neck! I always wear a thick silk handkerchief.'

'What did Mr Lennox Boynton do on his return to the camp?' asked Poirot.

For once Miss Pierce managed to get in first before Lady Westholme could speak.

'He went right up to his mother, but he didn't stay long with her.'

'How long?'

'Just a minute or two.'

'I should put it at just over a minute myself,' said Lady Westholme. 'Then he went on into his cave and after that he went down to the marquee.'

'And his wife?'

'She came along about a quarter of an hour later. She stopped a minute and spoke to us – quite civilly.'

'I think she's very nice,' said Miss Pierce. 'Very nice indeed.'

'She is not so impossible as the rest of the family,' allowed Lady Westholme.

'You watched her return to the camp?'

'Yes. She went up and spoke to her mother-in-law. Then she went into her cave and brought out a chair, and sat by her talking for some time – about ten minutes, I should say.'

'And then?'

'Then she took the chair back to the cave and went down to the marquee where her husband was.'

'What happened next?'

'That very peculiar American came along,' said Lady Westholme. 'Cope, I think his name is. He told us that there was a very good example of the debased architecture of the period just round the bend of the valley. He said we ought not to miss it. Accordingly, we walked there. Mr Cope had with him quite an interesting article on Petra and the Nabateans.'

'It was all *most* interesting,' declared Miss Pierce.

Lady Westholme continued:

'We strolled back to the camp, it being then about twenty

minutes to six. It was growing quite chilly.'

'Mrs Boynton was still sitting where you had left her?'

'Yes.'

'Did you speak to her?'

'No. As a matter of fact I hardly noticed her.'

'What did you do next?'

'I went to my tent, changed my shoes and got out my own packet of China tea. I then went to the marquee. The dragoman was there and I directed him to make some tea for Miss Pierce and myself with the tea I had brought and to make quite sure that the water with which it was made was boiling. He said that dinner would be ready in about half an hour – the boys were laying the table at the time – but I said that made no difference.'

'*I* always say a cup of tea makes *all* the difference,' murmured Miss Pierce vaguely.

'Was there anyone in the marquee?'

'Oh, yes. Mr and Mrs Lennox Boynton were sitting at one end reading. And Carol Boynton was there too.'

'And Mr Cope?'

'He joined us at our tea,' said Miss Pierce. 'Though he said tea-drinking wasn't an American habit.'

Lady Westholme coughed.

'I became just a little afraid that Mr Cope was going to be a nuisance – that he might fasten himself upon me. It is a little difficult sometimes to keep people at arm's length when one is travelling. I find they are inclined to presume. Americans, especially, are sometimes rather dense.'

Poirot murmured suavely:

'I am sure, Lady Westholme, that you are quite capable of dealing with situations of that kind. When travelling acquaintances are no longer of any use to you, I am sure you are an adept at dropping them.'

'I think I am capable of dealing with most situations,' said Lady Westholme complacently.

The twinkle in Poirot's eye was quite lost upon her.

'If you will just conclude your recital of the day's happenings?' murmured Poirot.

'Certainly. As far as I can remember, Raymond Boynton and the red-haired Boynton girl came in shortly afterwards. Miss

King arrived last. Dinner was then ready to be served. One of the servants was dispatched by the dragoman to announce the fact to old Mrs Boynton. The man came running back with one of his comrades in a state of some agitation and spoke to the dragoman in Arabic. There was some mention of Mrs Boynton being taken ill. Miss King offered her services. She went out with the dragoman. She came back and broke the news to the members of Mrs Boynton's family.'

'She did it very abruptly,' put in Miss Pierce. 'Just blurted it out. I think myself it ought to have been done more gradually.'

'And how did Mrs Boynton's family take the news?' asked Poirot.

For once both Lady Westholme and Miss Pierce seemed a little at a loss. The former said at last in a voice lacking its usual self-assurance:

'Well – really – it is difficult to say. They – they were very quiet about it.'

'Stunned,' said Miss Pierce.

She offered the word more as a suggestion than as a fact.

'They all went out with Miss King,' said Lady Westholme. 'Miss Pierce and I very sensibly remained where we were.'

A faintly wistful look was observable in Miss Pierce's eye at this point.

'I detest vulgar curiosity!' continued Lady Westholme.

The wistful look became more pronounced. It was clear that Miss Pierce had had perforce to hate vulgar curiosity, too!

'Later,' concluded Lady Westholme, 'the dragoman and Miss King returned. I suggested that dinner should be served immediately to the four of us, so that the Boynton family could dine later in the marquee without the embarrassment of strangers being present. My suggestion was adopted and immediately after the meal I retired to my tent. Miss King and Miss Pierce did the same. Mr Cope, I believe, remained in the marquee as he was a friend of the family and thought he might be of some assistance to them. That is all I know, M. Poirot.'

'When Miss King had broken the news, *all* the Boynton family accompanied her out of the marquee?'

'Yes – no, I believe, now that you come to mention it, that the red-haired girl stayed behind. Perhaps you can remember, Miss Pierce?'

'Yes, I think – I am quite sure she did.'

Poirot asked: 'What did she do?'

Lady Westholme stared at him.

'What did she *do*, M. Poirot? She did not do anything as far as I can remember.'

'I mean was she sewing – or reading – did she look anxious – did she say anything?'

'Well, really –' Lady Westholme frowned. 'She – er – she just sat there as far as I can remember.'

'She twiddled her fingers,' said Miss Pierce suddenly. 'I remember noticing – poor thing, I thought, it shows what she's feeling! Not that there was anything to show in her *face*, you know – just her hands turning and twisting.'

'Once,' went on Miss Pierce conversationally, 'I remember tearing up a pound note that way – not thinking of what I was doing. "Shall I catch the first train and go to her?" I thought (it was a great-aunt of mine – taken suddenly ill). "Or shall I *not*?" And I couldn't make up my mind one way or the other and there, I looked down, and instead of the telegram I was tearing up a pound note – *a pound note* – into tiny pieces!'

Miss Pierce paused dramatically.

Not entirely approving of this sudden bid for the limelight on the part of her satellite, Lady Westholme said coldly: 'Is there anything else, M. Poirot?'

With a start, Poirot seemed to come out of a brown study. 'Nothing – nothing – you have been most clear – most definite.'

'I have an excellent memory,' said Lady Westholme with satisfaction.

'One last little demand, Lady Westholme,' said Poirot. 'Please continue to sit as you are sitting – without looking round. Now would you be so kind as to describe to me just what Miss Pierce is wearing today – that is if Miss Pierce does not object?'

'Oh, no! not in the least!' twittered Miss Pierce.

'Really, M. Poirot, is there any *object* –'

'Please be so kind as to do as I ask, madame.'

Lady Westholme shrugged her shoulders and then said with a rather bad grace:

'Miss Pierce has on a striped brown and white cotton dress, and is wearing with it a Sudanese belt of red, blue and beige leather. She is wearing beige silk stockings and brown glacé strap shoes. There is a ladder in her left stocking. She has a necklace of cornelian beads and one of bright royal blue beads – and is wearing a brooch with a pearl butterfly on it. She has an imitation scarab ring on the third finger of her right hand. On her head she has a double terai of pink and brown felt.'

She paused – a pause of quiet competence. Then:

'Is there anything further?' she asked coldly.

Poirot spread out his hands in a wild gesture.

'You have my entire admiration, madame. Your observation is of the highest order.'

'Details rarely escape me.'

Lady Westholme rose, made a slight inclination of her head, and left the room. As Miss Pierce was following her, gazing down ruefully at her left leg, Poirot said:

'A little moment, please, mademoiselle?'

'Yes?' Miss Pierce looked up, a slightly apprehensive look upon her face.

Poirot leaned forward confidentially.

'You see this bunch of wild flowers on the table here?'

'Yes,' said Miss Pierce – staring.

'And you noticed that when you first came into the room I sneezed once or twice?'

'Yes?'

'Did you notice if I had just been sniffing those flowers?'

'Well – really – no – I couldn't say.'

'But you remember my sneezing?'

'Oh yes, I remember *that*!'

Ah, well – no matter. I wondered, you see, if these flowers might induce the hay fever. No matter!'

'Hay fever?' cried Miss Pierce. 'I remember a cousin of mine was a *martyr* to it! She always said that if you sprayed your nose daily with a solution of boracic –'

With some difficulty Poirot shelved the cousin's nasal treatment and got rid of Miss Pierce. He shut the door and came back into the room with his eyebrows raised.

'But I did not sneeze,' he murmured. 'So much for that. No, I did not sneeze.'

Lennox Boynton came into the room with a quick, resolute step. Had he been there, Dr Gerard would have been surprised at the change in the man. The apathy was gone. His bearing was alert – although he was plainly nervous. His eyes had a tendency to shift rapidly from point to point about the room.

'Good morning, M. Boynton.' Poirot rose and bowed ceremoniously. Lennox responded somewhat awkwardly. 'I much appreciate your giving me this interview.'

Lennox Boynton said rather uncertainly: 'Er – Colonel Carbury said it would be a good thing – advised it – some formalities – he said.'

'Please sit down, M. Boynton.'

Lennox sat down on the chair lately vacated by Lady Westholme. Poirot went on conversationally:

'This has been a great shock to you, I am afraid?'

'Yes, of course. Well, no, perhaps not . . . We always knew that my mother's heart was not strong.'

'Was it wise, under those circumstances, to allow her to undertake such an arduous expedition?'

Lennox Boynton raised his head. He spoke not without a certain sad dignity.

'My mother, M. – er – Poirot, made her own decisions. If she made up her mind to anything it was no good our opposing her.'

He drew in his breath sharply as he said the last words. His face suddenly went rather white.

'I know well,' admitted Poirot, 'that elderly ladies are sometimes headstrong.'

Lennox said irritably:

'What is the purpose of all this? That is what I want to know. Why have all these formalities arisen?'

'Perhaps you do not realize, Mr Boynton, that in cases of sudden and unexplained deaths, formalities must necessarily arise.'

Lennox said sharply: 'What do you mean by "unexplained"?'

Poirot shrugged his shoulders.

'There is always the question to be considered: Is a death natural – or might it perhaps be suicide?'

517

'Suicide?' Lennox Boynton stared.

Poirot said lightly:

'You, of course, would know best about such possibilities. Colonel Carbury, naturally, is in the dark. It is necessary for him to decide whether to order an inquiry – an autopsy – all the rest of it. As I was on the spot and as I have much experience of these matters, he suggested that I should make a few inquiries and advise him upon the matter. Naturally he does not wish to cause you inconvenience if it can be helped.'

Lennox Boynton said angrily: 'I shall wire to our Consul in Jerusalem.'

Poirot said non-committally: 'You are quite within your rights in doing so, of course.'

There was a pause. Then Poirot said, spreading out his hands:

'If you object to answering my questions –'

Lennox Boynton said quickly: 'Not at all. Only – it seems – all so unnecessary.'

'I comprehend. I comprehend perfectly. But it is all very simple, really. A matter, as they say, of routine. Now, on the afternoon of your mother's death, M. Boynton, I believe you left the camp at Petra and went for a walk?'

'Yes. We all went – with the exception of my mother and my youngest sister.'

'Your mother was then sitting in the mouth of her cave?'

'Yes, just outside it. She sat there every afternoon.'

'Quite so. You started – when?'

'Soon after three, I should say.'

'You returned from your walk – when?'

'I really couldn't say what time it was – four o'clock, five o'clock, perhaps.'

'About an hour or two hours after you set out?'

'Yes – about that, I should think.'

'Did you pass anyone on your way back?'

'Did I what?'

'Pass anyone. Two ladies sitting on a rock, for instance.'

'I don't know. Yes, I think I did.'

'You were, perhaps, too absorbed in your thoughts to notice?'

'Yes, I was.'

'Did you speak to your mother when you got back to the camp?'

'Yes – yes, I did.'

'She did not then complain of feeling ill?'

'No – no, she seemed perfectly all right.'

'May I ask what exactly passed between you?'

Lennox paused a minute.

'She said I had come back soon. I said, yes, I had.' He paused again in an effort of concentration. 'I said it was hot. She – she asked me the time – said her wrist-watch had stopped. I took it from her, wound it up, set it, and put it back on her wrist.'

Poirot interrupted gently: 'And what time was it?'

'Eh?' said Lennox.

'What time was it when you set the hands of the wrist-watch?'

'Oh, I see. It – it was twenty-five minutes to five.'

'So, you do know exactly the time you returned to the camp!' said Poirot gently.

Lennox flushed.

'Yes, what a fool I am! I'm sorry, M. Poirot, my wits are all astray, I'm afraid. All this worry –'

Poirot chimed in quickly: 'Oh! I understand – I understand perfectly! It is all of the most disquieting! And what happened next?'

'I asked my mother if she wanted anything. A drink – tea, coffee, etc. She said no. Then I went to the marquee. None of the servants seemed to be about, but I found some soda water and drank it. I was thirsty. I sat there reading some old numbers of the *Saturday Evening Post*. I think I must have dozed off.'

'Your wife joined you in the marquee?'

'Yes, she came in not long after.'

'And you did not see your mother again alive?'

'No.'

'She did not seem in any way agitated or upset when you were talking to her?'

'No, she was exactly as usual.'

'She did not refer to any trouble or annoyance with one of the servants?'

Lennox stared.

'No, nothing at all.'

'And that is all you can tell me?'

'I am afraid so – yes.'

'Thank you, Mr Boynton.'

Poirot inclined his head as a sign that the interview was over. Lennox did not seem very willing to depart. He stood hesitating by the door. 'Er – there's nothing else?'

'Nothing. Perhaps you would be so good as to ask your wife to come here?'

Lennox went slowly out. On the pad beside him Poirot wrote L.B. 4.35 p.m.

CHAPTER 7

Poirot looked with interest at the tall, dignified young woman who entered the room. He rose and bowed to her politely. 'Mrs Lennox Boynton? Hercule Poirot, at your service.'

Nadine Boynton sat down. Her thoughtful eyes were on Poirot's face.

'I hope you do not mind, madame, my intruding on your sorrow in this way?'

Her eyes did not waver. She did not reply at once. Her eyes remained steady and grave. At last she gave a sigh and said: 'I think it is best for me to be quite frank with you, M. Poirot.'

'I agree with you, madame.'

'You apologized for intruding upon my sorrow. That sorrow, M. Poirot, does not exist and it is idle to pretend that it does. I had no love for my mother-in-law and I cannot honestly say that I regret her death.'

'Thank you, madame, for your plain speaking.'

Nadine went on: 'Still, although I cannot pretend sorrow, I can admit to another feeling – remorse.'

'Remorse?' Poirot's eyebrows went up.

'Yes. Because, you see, it was I who brought about her death. For that I blame myself bitterly.'

'What is this you are saying, madame?'

'I am saying that *I* was the cause of my mother-in-law's death. I was acting, as I thought, honestly – but the result was unfortunate. To all intents and purposes, I killed her.'

Poirot leaned back in his chair. 'Will you be so kind as to elucidate this statement, madame?'

Nadine bent her head.

'Yes, that is what I wish to do. My first reaction, naturally, was to keep my private affairs to myself, but I see that the time has come when it would be better to speak out. I have no doubt, M. Poirot, that you have often received confidences of a somewhat intimate nature?'

'That, yes.'

'Then I will tell you quite simply what occurred. My married life, M. Poirot, has not been particularly happy. My husband is not entirely to blame for that – his mother's influence over him has been unfortunate – but I have been feeling for some time that my life was becoming intolerable.'

She paused and then went on:

'On the afternoon of my mother-in-law's death I came to a decision. I have a friend – a very good friend. He has suggested more than once that I should throw in my lot with him. On that afternoon I accepted his proposal.'

'You decided to leave your husband?'

'Yes.'

'Continue, madame.'

Nadine said in a lower voice:

'Having once made my decision, I wanted to – to establish it as soon as possible. I walked home to the camp by myself. My mother-in-law was sitting alone, there was no one about, and I decided to break the news to her there and then. I got a chair – sat down by her and told her abruptly what I had decided.'

'She was surprised?'

'Yes, I am afraid it was a great shock to her. She was both surprised and angry – very angry. She – she worked herself into quite a state about it! Presently I refused to discuss the matter any longer. I got up and walked away.' Her voice dropped. 'I – I never saw her again alive.'

Poirot nodded his head slowly. He said: 'I see.'

Then he said: 'You think her death was the result of the shock?'

'It seems to me almost certain. You see, she had already over-exerted herself considerably getting to this place. My news, and her anger at it, would do the rest . . . I feel additionally guilty because I have had a certain amount of training in illness and so I, more than anyone else, ought to have realized the possibility of such a thing happening.'

Poirot sat in silence for some minutes, then he said:

'What exactly did you do when you left her?'

'I took the chair I had brought out back into my cave, then I went down to the marquee. My husband was there.'

Poirot watched her closely as he said:

'Did you tell *him* of your decision? Or had you already told him?'

There was a pause, an infinitesimal pause, before Nadine said: 'I told him then.'

'How did he take it?'

She answered quietly: 'He was very upset.'

'Did he urge you to reconsider your decision?'

She shook her head.

'He – he didn't say very much. You see, we had both known for some time that something like this might happen.'

Poirot said: 'You will pardon me, but – the other man was, of course, Mr Jefferson Cope?'

She bent her head. 'Yes.'

There was a long pause, then, without any change of voice, Poirot asked: 'Do you own a hypodermic syringe, madame?'

'Yes – no.'

His eyebrows rose.

She explained: 'I have an old hypodermic amongst other things in a travelling medicine chest, but it is in our big luggage which we left in Jerusalem.'

'I see.'

There was a pause, then she said, with a shiver of uneasiness: 'Why did you ask me that, M. Poirot?'

He did not answer the question. Instead he put one of his own. 'Mrs Boynton was, I believe, taking a mixture containing digitalis?'

'Yes.'

He thought that she was definitely watchful now.

'That was for her heart trouble?'

'Yes.'

'Digitalis is, to some extent, a cumulative drug?'

'I believe it is. I do not know very much about it.'

'If Mrs Boynton had taken a big overdose of digitalis –'

She interrupted him quickly but with decision.

'She did not. She was always most careful. So was I if I measured the dose for her.'

'There might have been an overdose in this particular bottle. A mistake of the chemist who made it up?'

'I think that is very unlikely,' she replied quietly.

'Ah, well: the analysis will soon tell us.'

Nadine said: 'Unfortunately the bottle was broken.'

Poirot eyed her with sudden interest.

'Indeed. Who broke it?'

'I'm not quite sure. One of the servants, I think. In carrying my mother-in-law's body into her cave, there was a good deal of confusion and the light was very poor. A table got knocked over.'

Poirot eyed her steadily for a minute or two.

'That,' he said, 'is very interesting.'

Nadine Boynton shifted wearily in her chair.

'You are suggesting, I think, that my mother-in-law did not die of shock, but of an overdose of digitalis?' she said, and went on: 'That seems to me most improbable.'

Poirot leaned forward.

'*Even when I tell you that Dr Gerard, the French physician who was staying in the camp, had missed an appreciable quantity of a preparation of digitoxin from his medicine chest?*'

Her face grew very pale. He saw the clutch of her hand on the table. Her eyes dropped. She sat very still. She was like a Madonna carved in stone.

'Well, madame,' said Poirot at last, 'what have you to say to that?'

The seconds ticked on but she did not speak. It was quite two minutes before she raised her head, and he started a little when he saw the look in her eyes.

'M. Poirot, *I did not kill my mother-in-law.* That you know! She was alive and well when I left her. There are many people who can testify to that! Therefore, being innocent of the crime, I can venture to appeal to you. Why must you mix yourself up in this business? If I swear to you on my honour that justice and only justice has been done, will you not abandon this inquiry? There has been so much suffering – you do not know. Now that at last there is peace and the possibility of happiness, must you destroy it all?'

Poirot sat up very straight. His eyes shone with a green light. 'Let me be clear, madame; what are you asking me to do?'

'I am telling you that my mother-in-law died a natural death and I am asking you to accept that statement.'

'Let us be definite. *You believe that your mother-in-law was deliberately killed,* and you are asking me to condone *murder!*'

'I am asking you to have pity!'

'Yes – on someone who had no pity!'

'You do not understand – it was not like that.'

'Did you commit the crime yourself, madame, that you know so well?'

Nadine shook her head. She showed no signs of guilt. 'No,' she said quietly. 'She was alive when I left her.'

'And then – what happened? You *know* – or you *suspect*?'

Nadine said passionately:

'I have heard, M. Poirot, that once, in that affair of the Orient Express, you accepted an official verdict of what had happened?'

Poirot looked at her curiously. 'I wonder who told you that?'

'Is it true?'

He said slowly: 'That case was – different.'

'No. No, it was not different! The man who was killed was evil' – her voice dropped – 'as *she* was . . .'

Poirot said: 'The moral character of the victim has nothing to do with it! A human being who has exercised the right of private judgement and taken the life of another human being is not safe to exist amongst the community. *I* tell you that! I, Hercule Poirot!'

'How hard you are!'

'Madame, in some ways I am adamant. I will not condone murder! That is the final word of Hercule Poirot.'

She got up. Her dark eyes flashed with sudden fire.

'Then go on! Bring ruin and misery into the lives of innocent people! I have nothing more to say.'

'But I, I think, madame, that you have a lot to say . . .'

'No, nothing more.'

'But, yes. What happened, madame, *after* you left your mother-in-law? Whilst you and your husband were in the marquee together?'

She shrugged her shoulders. 'How should I know?'

'You *do* know – or you suspect.'

She looked him straight in the eyes. 'I know nothing, M. Poirot.'

Turning, she left the room.

After noting on his pad – N.B. 4.40 – Poirot opened the door and called to the orderly whom Colonel Carbury had left at his disposal, an intelligent man with a good knowledge of English. He asked him to fetch Miss Carol Boynton.

He looked with some interest at the girl as she entered, at the chestnut hair, the poise of the head on the long neck, the nervous energy of the beautifully shaped hands.

He said: 'Sit down, mademoiselle.'

She sat down obediently. Her face was colourless and expressionless. Poirot began with a mechanical expression of sympathy to which the girl acquiesced without any change of expression.

'And now, mademoiselle, will you recount to me how you spent the afternoon of the day in question?'

Her answer came promptly, raising the suspicion that it had already been well rehearsed.

'After luncheon we all went for a stroll. I returned to the camp –'

Poirot interrupted. 'A little minute. Were you all together until then?'

'No, I was with my brother Raymond and Miss King for most of the time. Then I strolled off on my own.'

'Thank you. And you were saying you returned to the camp. Do you know the approximate time?'

'I believe it was just about ten minutes past five.'

Poirot put down C.B. 5.10.

'And what then?'

'My mother was still sitting where she had been when we set out. I went up and spoke to her, and then went on to my tent.'

'Can you remember exactly what passed between you?'

'I just said it was very hot and that I was going to lie down. My mother said she would remain where she was. That was all.'

'Did anything in her appearance struck you as out of the ordinary?'

'No. At least that is –'

She paused doubtfully, staring at Poirot.

'It is not from me that you can get the answer, mademoiselle,' said Poirot quietly.

'I was just considering. I hardly noticed at the time, but now, looking back –'

'Yes?'

Carol said slowly: 'It is true – she was a funny colour – her face was very red – more so than usual.'

'She might, perhaps, have had a shock of some kind?' Poirot suggested.

'A shock?' she stared at him.

'Yes, she might have had, let us say, some trouble with one of the Arab servants.'

'Oh!' Her face cleared. 'Yes – she might.'

'She did not mention such a thing having happened?'

'N-o – no, nothing at all.'

Poirot went on: 'And what did you do next, mademoiselle?'

'I went to my tent and lay down for about half an hour. Then I went down to the marquee. My brother and his wife were there reading.'

'And what did you do?'

'Oh! I had some sewing to do. And then I picked up a magazine.'

'Did you speak to your mother again on your way to the marquee?'

'No. I went straight down. I don't think I even glanced in her direction.'

'And then?'

'I remained in the marquee until – until Miss King told us she was dead.'

'And that is all you know, mademoiselle?'

'Yes.'

Poirot leaned forward. His tone was the same, light and conversational.

'And what did you *feel*, mademoiselle?'

'What did I feel?'

'Yes – when you found that your mother – pardon – your

stepmother, was she not? – what did you feel when you found her dead?'

She stared at him.

'I don't understand what you mean!'

'I think you understand very well.'

Her eyes dropped. She said uncertainly:

'It was – a great shock.'

'Was it?'

The blood rushed to her face. She stared at him helplessly. Now he saw fear in her eyes.

'*Was* it such a great shock, mademoiselle? *Remembering a certain conversation you had with your brother Raymond one night in Jerusalem?*'

His shot proved right. He saw it in the way the colour drained out of her cheeks again.

'You know about that?' she whispered.

'Yes, I know.'

'But how – how?'

'Part of your conversation was overheard.'

'Oh!' Carol Boynton buried her face in her hands. Her sobs shook the table.

Hercule Poirot waited a minute, then he said quietly:

'You were planning together to bring about your stepmother's death.'

Carol sobbed out brokenly: 'We were mad – mad – that evening!'

'Perhaps.'

'It's impossible for you to understand the state we were in!' She sat up, pushing back the hair from her face. 'It would sound fantastic. It wasn't so bad in America – but travelling brought it home to us so.'

'Brought what home to you?' His voice was kind now, sympathetic.

'Our being different from – other people! We – we got desperate about it. And there was Jinny.'

'Jinny?'

'My sister. You haven't seen her. She was going – well, queer. And Mother was making her worse. She didn't seem to realize. We were afraid, Ray and I, that Jinny was going quite, quite mad! And we saw Nadine thought so, too, and that made us more afraid because Nadine knows about nursing and things like that.'

'Yes, yes?'

'That evening in Jerusalem things kind of boiled up! Ray was beside himself. He and I got all strung up and it seemed – oh, indeed, it did seem *right* to plan as we did! Mother – Mother *wasn't* sane. I don't know what you think, but it *can* seem quite *right* – almost noble – to kill someone!'

Poirot nodded his head slowly. 'Yes, it has seemed so, I know, to many. That is proved by history.'

'That's how Ray and I felt – that night . . .' She beat her hand on the table. 'But we didn't really do it. Of course we didn't do it! When daylight came the whole thing seemed absurd, melodramatic – oh, yes, and wicked too! Indeed, indeed, M. Poirot, Mother died perfectly naturally of heart failure. Ray and I had nothing to do with it.'

Poirot said quietly: 'Will you swear to me, mademoiselle, as you hope for salvation after death, that Mrs Boynton did not die as the result of any action of yours?'

She lifted her head. Her voice came steady and deep:

'I swear,' said Carol, 'as I hope for salvation, that I never harmed her . . .'

Poirot leaned back in his chair.

'So,' he said, 'that is that.'

There was silence. Poirot thoughtfully caressed his superb moustaches. Then he said: 'What exactly was your plan?'

'Plan?'

'Yes, you and you brother must have had a plan.'

In his mind he ticked off the seconds before her answer came. One, two, three.

'We had no plan,' said Carol at last. 'We never got as far as that.'

Hercule Poirot got up.

'That is all, mademoiselle. Will you be so good as to send your brother to me?'

Carol rose. She stood undecidedly for a minute.

'M. Poirot, you do – you do believe me?'

'Have I said,' asked Poirot, 'that I do not?'

'No, but –' She stopped.

He said: 'You will ask your brother to come here?'

'Yes.'

She went slowly towards the door. She stopped as she got to it, turning round passionately.

'I *have* told you the truth – I have!'

Hercule Poirot did not answer.

Carol Boynton went slowly out of the room.

Poirot noted the likeness between brother and sister as Raymond Boynton came into the room.

His face was stern and set. He did not seem nervous or afraid. He dropped into a chair, stared hard at Poirot, and said: 'Well?'

Poirot said gently: 'Your sister has spoken with you?'

Raymond nodded. 'Yes, when she told me to come here. Of course I realize that your suspicions are quite justified. If our conversation was overheard that night, the fact that my stepmother died rather suddenly certainly *would* seem suspicious! I can only assure you that the conversation was – the madness of an evening! We were, at the time, under an intolerable strain. This fantastic plan of killing my stepmother did – oh, how shall I put it? – it let off steam somehow!'

Hercule Poirot bent his head slowly.

'That,' he said, 'is possible.'

'In the morning, of course, it all seemed – rather absurd! I swear to you, M. Poirot, that I never thought of the matter again!'

Poirot did not answer.

Raymond said quickly:

'Oh, yes, I know that that is easy enough to *say*. I cannot expect you to believe me on my bare word. But consider the facts. I spoke to my mother just a little before six o'clock. She was certainly alive and well then. I went to my tent, had a wash and joined the others in the marquee. From that time onwards neither Carol nor I moved from the place. We were in full sight of everyone. You must see, M. Poirot, that my mother's death was natural – a case of heart failure – it couldn't be anything else! There were servants about, a lot of coming and going. Any other idea is absurd.'

Poirot said quietly: 'Do you know, Mr Boynton, that Miss King is of the opinion that when she examined the body – at six-thirty – death had occurred at least an hour and a half and probably *two hours* earlier?'

Raymond stared at him. He looked dumbfounded.

'Sarah said that?' he gasped.

Poirot nodded. 'What have you to say now?'

'But – it's impossible!'

'That is Miss King's testimony. Now *you* come and tell me that your mother was alive and well only forty minutes before Miss King examined the body.'

Raymond said: 'But she was!'

'Be careful, Mr Boynton.'

'Sarah *must* be mistaken! There must be some factor she didn't take into account. Refraction off the rock – something. I can assure you, M. Poirot, that my mother *was* alive at just before six and that I spoke to her.'

Poirot's face showed nothing.

Raymond leant forward earnestly.

'M. Poirot, I know how it must seem to you, but look at the thing fairly. You are a biased person. You are bound to be by the nature of things. You live in an atmosphere of crime. Every sudden death must seem to you a possible crime! Can't you realize that your sense of proportion is not to be relied upon? People die every day – especially people with weak hearts – and there is nothing in the least sinister about such deaths.'

Poirot sighed. 'So you would teach me my business, is that it?'

'No, of course not. But I do think that you are prejudiced – because of that unfortunate conversation. There is nothing really about my mother's death to awaken suspicion except that unlucky hysterical conversation between Carol and myself.'

Poirot shook his head. 'You are in error,' he said. 'There is something else. There is the poison taken from Dr Gerard's medicine chest.'

'Poison?' Ray stared at him. '*Poison?*' He pushed his chair back a little. He looked completely stupefied. 'Is *that* what you suspect?'

Poirot gave him a minute or two. Then he said quietly, almost indifferently: 'Your plan was different – eh?'

'Oh, yes.' Raymond answered mechanically. 'That's why – this changes everything . . . I – I can't think clearly.'

'What was *your* plan?'

'Our plan? It was –'

Raymond stopped abruptly. His eyes became alert, suddenly watchful.

'I don't think,' he said, 'that I'll say any more.'

'As you please,' said Poirot.

He watched the young man out of the room.

He drew his pad towards him and in small, neat characters made a final entry. R.B. 5.55?

Then, taking a large sheet of paper, he proceeded to write. His task completed, he sat back with his head on one side contemplating the result. It ran as follows:

Boyntons and Jefferson Cope leave the camp	3.5 (approx.)
Dr Gerard and Sarah King leave the camp	3.15 (approx.)
Lady Westholme and Miss Pierce leave the camp	4.15
Dr Gerard returns to camp	4.20 (approx.)
Lennox Boynton returns to camp	4.35
Nadine Boynton returns to camp and talks to Mrs Boynton	4.40
Nadine Boynton leaves her mother-in-law and goes to marquee	4.50 (approx.)
Carol Boynton returns to camp	5.10
Lady Westholme, Miss Pierce and Mr Jefferson Cope return to camp	5.40
Raymond Boynton returns to camp	5.50
Sarah King returns to camp	6.0
Body discovered	6.30

CHAPTER 10

'I wonder,' said Hercule Poirot. He folded up the list, went to the door and ordered Mahmoud to be brought to him. The stout dragoman was voluble. Words dripped from him in a rising flood.

'Always, always, I am blamed. When anything happens, say

always, my fault. Always my fault. When Lady Ellen Hunt sprain her ankle coming down from Place of Sacrifice it my fault, though she would go high-heeled shoes and she sixty at least – perhaps seventy. My life all one misery! Ah! what with miseries and iniquities, Jews do to us –'

At last Poirot succeeded in stemming the flood and in getting in his question.

'Half-past five o'clock, you say? No, I not think any of servants were about then. You see, lunch is late – two o'clock. And then to clear it away. After the lunch all afternoon sleep. Yes, Americans, they not take tea. We all settle sleep by half-past three. At five I who am soul of efficiency – always – always I watch for the comfort of ladies and gentlemen I serving, I come out knowing that time all English ladies want tea. But no one there. They all gone walking. For me, that is very well – better than usual. I can go back sleep. At quarter to six trouble begin – large English lady – very grand lady – come back and want tea although boys are now laying dinner. She makes quite fuss – says water must be boiling – I am to see myself. Ah, my good gentlemen! What a life – what a life! I do all I can – always I blamed – I –'

Poirot asked about the recriminations.

'There is another small matter. The dead lady was angry with one of the boys. Do you know which one it was and what it was about?'

Mahmoud's hands rose to heaven.

'Should I know? But naturally not. Old lady did not complain to me.'

'Could you find out?'

'No, my good gentlemen, that would be impossible. None of the boys admit it for a moment. Old lady angry, you say? Then naturally boys would not tell. Abdul say it Mohammed, and Mohammed say it Aziz and Aziz say it Aissa, and so on. They are all very stupid Bedouin – understand nothing.'

He took a breath and continued: 'Now I, I have advantage of Mission education. I recite to you Keats – Shelley – "Iadadoveandasweedovedied –"'

Poirot flinched. Though English was not his native tongue, he knew it well enough to suffer from the strange enunciation of Mahmoud.

'Superb!' he said hastily. 'Superb! Definitely I recommend you to all my friends.'

He contrived to escape from the dragoman's eloquence. Then he took his list to Colonel Carbury, whom he found in his office.

Carbury pushed his tie a little more askew and asked:

'Got anything?'

Poirot said: 'Shall I tell you a theory of mine?'

'If you like,' said Colonel Carbury and sighed. One way and another he heard a good many theories in the course of his existence.

'My theory is that criminology is the easiest science in the world! One has only to let the criminal talk – sooner or later he will tell you everything.'

'I remember you said something of the kind before. Who's been telling you things?'

'Everybody.' Briefly, Poirot retailed the interviews he had had that morning.

'H'm,' said Carbury. 'Yes, you've got hold of a pointer or two, perhaps. Pity of it is they all seem to point in opposite directions. Have we got a case, that's what I want to know?'

'No.'

Carbury sighed again. 'I was afraid not.'

'But before nightfall,' said Poirot, 'you shall have the truth!'

'Well, that's all you ever promised me,' said Colonel Carbury. 'And I rather doubted you getting that! Sure of it?'

'I am very sure.'

'Must be nice to feel like that,' commented the other.

If there was a faint twinkle in his eye, Poirot appeared unaware of it. He produced his list.

'Neat,' said Colonel Carbury approvingly.

He bent over it.

After a minute or two he said: 'Know what I think?'

'I should be delighted if you would tell me.'

'Young Raymond Boynton's out of it.'

'Ah! you think so?'

'Yes. Clear as a bell what *he* thought. We might have known he'd be out of it. Being, as in detective stories, the most likely person. Since you practically overheard him saying he was going to bump off the old lady – we might have known that meant he was innocent!'

'You read the detective stories, yes?'

'Thousands of them,' said Colonel Carbury. He added, and his tone was that of a wistful schoolboy: 'I suppose you couldn't do the things the detective does in books? Write a list of significant facts – things that don't seem to mean anything but are really frightfully important – that sort of thing.'

'Ah,' said Poirot kindly. 'You like that kind of detective story? But certainly, I will do it for you with pleasure.'

He drew a sheet of paper towards him and wrote quickly and neatly:

Significant points

1 Mrs Boynton was taking a mixture containing digitalis.
2 Dr Gerard missed a hypodermic syringe.
3 Mrs Boynton took definite pleasure in keeping her family from enjoying themselves with other people.
4 Mrs Boynton, on the afternoon in question, encouraged her family to go away and leave her.
5 Mrs Boynton was a mental sadist.
6 The distance from the marquee to the place where Mrs Boynton was sitting is (roughly) two hundred yards.
7 Mr Lennox Boynton said at first he did not know what time he returned to the camp, but later he admitted having set his mother's wrist-watch to the right time.
8 Dr Gerard and Miss Genevra Boynton occupied tents next door to each other.
9 At half-past six, when dinner was ready, a servant was dispatched to announce the fact to Mrs Boynton.

The Colonel perused this with great satisfaction.

'Capital!' he said. 'Just the thing! You've made it difficult – and seemingly irrelevant – absolutely the authentic touch! By the way, it seems to me there are one or two noticeable omissions. But that, I suppose, is what you tempt the mug with?'

Poirot's eyes twinkled a little, but he did not answer.

'Point two, for instance,' said Colonel Carbury tentatively. '*Dr Gerard missed a hypodermic syringe* – yes. He also missed a concentrated solution of digitalis – or something of that kind.'

'The latter point,' said Poirot, 'is not important in the way the absence of his hypodermic syringe is important.'

'Splendid!' said Colonel Carbury, his face irradiated with smiles. 'I don't get it at all. *I* should have said the digitalis was much more important than the syringe! And what about that servant motif that keeps cropping up – a servant being sent to tell her dinner was ready – and that story of her shaking her stick at a servant earlier in the afternoon? You're not going to tell me one of my poor desert mutts bumped her off after all? Because,' added Colonel Carbury sternly, 'if so, that would be *cheating.*'

Poirot smiled, but did not answer.

As he left the office he murmured to himself:

'Incredible! The English never grow up!'

Sarah King sat on a hill-top absently plucking up wild flowers. Dr Gerard sat on a rough wall of stones near her.

She said suddenly and fiercely: 'Why did you start all this? If it hadn't been for *you* –'

Dr Gerard said slowly: 'You think I should have kept silence?'

'Yes.'

'Knowing what I knew?'

'You didn't *know*,' said Sarah.

The Frenchman sighed. 'I did know. But I admit one can never be absolutely sure.'

'Yes, one can,' said Sarah uncompromisingly.

The Frenchman shrugged his shoulders. 'You, perhaps!'

Sarah said: 'You had fever – a high temperature – you couldn't be clear-headed about the business. The syringe was probably there all the time. And you may have made a mistake about the digitoxin or one of the servants may have meddled with the case.'

Gerard said cynically: 'You need not worry! The evidence is almost bound to be inconclusive. You will see, your friends the Boyntons will get away with it!'

Sarah said fiercely: 'I don't want that, either.'

He shook his head. 'You are illogical!'

'Wasn't it you –' Sarah demanded, 'in Jerusalem – who said a great deal about not interfering? And now look!'

'I have not interfered. I have only told what I know!'

'And I say you don't *know* it. Oh dear, there we are, back again! I'm arguing in a circle.'

Gerard said gently: 'I am sorry, Miss King.'

Sarah said in a low voice:

'You see, after all, *they haven't escaped* – any of them! *She's* still there! Even from her grave she can still reach out and hold them. There was something – terrible about her – she's just as terrible now she's dead! I feel – I feel she's *enjoying* all this!'

She clenched her hands. Then she said in an entirely different tone, a light everyday voice: 'That little man's coming up the hill.'

Dr Gerard looked over his shoulder.

'Ah! he comes in search of us, I think.'

'Is he as much of a fool as he looks?' asked Sarah.

Dr Gerard said gravely: 'He is not a fool at all.'

'I was afraid of that,' said Sarah King.

With sombre eyes she watched the uphill progress of Hercule Poirot.

He reached them at last, uttered a loud 'ouf' and wiped his forehead. Then he looked sadly down at his patent leather shoes.

'Alas!' he said. 'This stony country! My poor shoes.'

'You can borrow Lady Westholme's shoe-cleaning apparatus,' said Sarah unkindly. 'And her duster. She travels with a kind of patent housemaid's equipment.'

'That will not remove the scratches, mademoiselle,' Poirot shook his head sadly.

'Perhaps not. Why on earth do you wear shoes like that in this sort of country?'

Poirot put his head a little on one side.

'I like to have the appearance *soigné*,' he said.

'I should give up trying for that in the desert,' said Sarah.

'Women do not look their best in the desert,' said Dr Gerard dreamily. 'But Miss King here, yes – she always looks neat and well-turned out. But that Lady Westholme in her great thick coats and skirts and those terrible unbecoming riding breeches and boots – *quelle horreur de femme*! And the poor Miss Pierce – her clothes so limp, like faded cabbage leaves, and the chains and the beads that clink! Even young Mrs Boynton, who is a good-looking woman, is not what you call *chic*! Her clothes are uninteresting.'

536

Sarah said restively: 'Well, I don't suppose M. Poirot climbed up here to talk about clothes!'

'True,' said Poirot. 'I came to consult Dr Gerard – his opinion should be of value to me – and yours, too, mademoiselle – you are young and up to date in your psychology. I want to know, you see, all that you can tell me of Mrs Boynton.'

'Don't you know all that by heart now?' asked Sarah.

'No. I have a feeling – more than a feeling – a certainty that the mental equipment of Mrs Boynton is very important in this case. Such types as hers are no doubt familiar to Dr Gerard.'

'From my point of view she was certainly an interesting study,' said the doctor.

'Tell me.'

Dr Gerard was nothing loath. He described his own interest in the family group, his conversation with Jefferson Cope, and the latter's complete misreading of the situation.

'He is a sentimentalist, then,' said Poirot.

'Oh, essentially! He has ideals – based, really, on a deep instinct of laziness. To take human nature at its best, and the world as a pleasant place is undoubtedly the easiest course in life! Jefferson Cope has, consequently, not the least idea what people are really like.'

'That might be dangerous sometimes,' said Poirot.

Dr Gerard went on: 'He persisted in regarding what I may describe as "the Boynton situation" as a case of mistaken devotion. Of the underlying hate, rebellion, slavery and misery he had only the faintest notion.'

'It is stupid, that,' Poirot commented.

'All the same,' went on Dr Gerard, 'even the most wilfully obtuse of sentimental optimists cannot be quite blind. I think, on the journey to Petra, Mr Jefferson Cope's eyes were being opened.'

And he described the conversation he had had with the American on the morning of Mrs Boynton's death.

'That is an interesting story, that story of a servant girl,' said Poirot thoughtfully. 'It throws light on the old woman's methods.'

Gerard said: 'It was altogether an odd strange morning, that! You have not been to Petra, M. Poirot. If you go you must certainly climb to the Place of Sacrifice. It has an – how shall I

537

say? – an atmosphere!' He described the scene in detail, adding: 'Mademoiselle here sat like a young judge, speaking of the sacrifice of one to save many. You remember, Miss King?'

Sarah shivered. 'Don't! Don't let's talk of that day.'

'No, no,' said Poirot. 'Let us talk of events further back in the past. I am interested, Dr Gerard, in your sketch of Mrs Boynton's mentality. What I do not quite understand is this, having brought her family into absolute subjection, why did she then arrange this trip abroad where surely there was danger of outside contacts and of her authority being weakened?'

Dr Gerard leaned forward excitedly.

'But, *mon vieux*, that is just it! Old ladies are the same all the world over. They get bored! If their speciality is playing patience, they sicken of the patience they know too well. They want to learn a new patience. And it is just the same with an old lady whose recreation (incredible as it may sound) is the dominating and tormenting of human creatures! Mrs Boynton – to speak of her as *une dompteuse* – had tamed her tigers. There was perhaps some excitement as they passed through the stage of adolescence. Lennox's marriage to Nadine was an adventure. But then, suddenly, all was stale. Lennox is so sunk in melancholy that it is practically impossible to wound or distress him. Raymond and Carol show no signs of rebellion. Ginevra – ah! *la pauvre Ginevra* – she, from her mother's point of view, gives the poorest sport of all. For Ginevra has found a way of escape! She escapes from reality into fantasy. The more her mother goads her, the more easily she gets a secret thrill out of being a persecuted heroine! From Mrs Boynton's point of view it is all deadly dull. She seeks, like Alexander, new worlds to conquer. And so she plans the voyage abroad. There will be the danger of her tamed beasts rebelling, there will be opportunities for inflicting fresh pain! It sounds absurd, does it not, but it was so! She wanted a new thrill.'

Poirot took a deep breath. 'It is perfect, that. Yes, I see exactly what you mean. *It was so*. It all fits in. She chose to live dangerously, *la maman* Boynton – and she paid the penalty!'

Sarah leaned forward, her pale, intelligent face very serious. 'You mean,' she said, 'that she drove her victims too far and – and they turned on her – or – or one of them did?'

Poirot bowed his head.

Sarah said, and her voice was a little breathless:

'*Which of them?*'

Poirot looked at her, at her hands clenched fiercely on the wild flowers, at the pale rigidity of her face.

He did not answer – was indeed saved from answering, for at that moment Gerard touched his shoulder and said: 'Look.'

A girl was wandering along the side of the hill. She moved with a strange rhythmic grace that somehow gave the impression that she was not quite real. The gold red of her hair shone in the sunlight, a strange secretive smile lifted the beautiful corners of her mouth. Poirot drew in his breath.

He said: 'How beautiful . . . How strangely movingly beautiful . . . That is how Ophelia should be played – like a young goddess straying from another world, happy because she has escaped out of the bondage of human joys and griefs.'

'Yes, yes, you are right,' said Gerard. 'It is a face to dream of, is it not? *I* dreamt of it. In my fever I opened my eyes and saw that face – with its sweet, unearthly smile . . . It was a good dream. I was sorry to wake . . .'

Then, with a return to his commonplace manner:

'That is Ginevra Boynton,' he said.

CHAPTER 12

In another minute the girl had reached them.

Dr Gerard performed the introduction.

'Miss Boynton, this is M. Hercule Poirot.'

'Oh.' She looked at him uncertainly. Her fingers joined together, twined themselves uneasily in and out. The enchanted nymph had come back from the country of enchantment. She was now just an ordinary awkward girl, slightly nervous and ill at ease.

Poirot said: 'It is a piece of good fortune meeting you here, mademoiselle. I tried to see you in the hotel.'

'Did you?'

Her smile was vacant. Her fingers began plucking at the belt of her dress. He said gently:

'Will you walk with me a little way?'

She moved docilely enough, obedient to his whim.

Presently she said, rather unexpectedly, in a queer, hurried voice:

539

'You are – you are a detective, aren't you?'

'Yes, mademoiselle.'

'A very well-known detective?'

'The best detective in the world,' said Poirot, stating it as a simple truth, no more, no less.

Ginevra Boynton breathed very softly:

'You have come here to protect me?'

Poirot stroked his moustaches thoughtfully. He said:

'Are you, then, in danger, mademoiselle?'

'Yes, yes.' She looked round with a quick, suspicious glance. 'I told Dr Gerard about it in Jerusalem. He was very clever. He gave no sign at the time. But he followed me – to that terrible place with the red rocks.' She shivered. 'They meant to kill me there. I have to be continually on my guard.'

Poirot nodded gently and indulgently.

Ginevra Boynton said: 'He is kind – and good. He is in love with me!'

'Yes?'

'Oh, yes. He says my name in his sleep . . .' Her voice softened – again a kind of trembling, unearthly beauty hovered there. 'I saw him – lying there turning and tossing – and saying my name . . . I stole away quietly.' She paused. 'I thought, perhaps, *he* had sent for you? I have a terrible lot of enemies, you know. They are all round me. Sometimes they are *disguised*.'

'Yes, yes,' said Poirot gently. 'But you are safe here – with all your family round you.'

She drew herself up proudly.

'They are *not* my family! I have nothing to do with them. I cannot tell you who I really am – that is a great secret. It would surprise you if you knew.'

He said gently: 'Was your mother's death a great shock to you, mademoiselle?'

Ginevra stamped her feet.

'I tell you – she *wasn't* my mother! My enemies paid her to pretend she was and to see I did not escape!'

'Where were you on the afternoon of her death?'

'I was in the tent . . . It was hot in there, but I didn't dare come out . . . *They* might have got me . . .' She gave a little quiver. 'One of them – looked into my tent. He was disguised but I knew him. I pretended to be asleep. The Sheikh had sent him. The Sheikh wanted to kidnap me, of course.'

For a few moments Poirot walked in silence, then he said: 'They are very pretty, these histories you recount to yourself?'

She stopped. She glared at him. 'They're *true*. They're all *true*.' Again she stamped an angry foot.

'Yes,' said Poirot, 'they are certainly ingenious.'

She cried out: 'They are true – *true* –'

Then, angrily, she turned from him and ran down the hillside. Poirot stood looking after her. In a minute or two he heard a voice close behind him.

'What did you say to her?'

Poirot turned to where Dr Gerard, a little out of breath, stood beside him. Sarah was coming towards them both, but she came at a more leisurely pace.

Poirot answered Gerard's question.

'I told her,' he said, 'that she had imagined to herself some pretty stories.'

The doctor nodded his head thoughtfully.

'And she was angry? That is a good sign. It shows, you see, that she has not yet completely passed through the door. She still knows that it is *not* the truth! I shall cure her.'

'Ah, you are undertaking a cure?'

'Yes. I have discussed the matter with young Mrs Boynton and her husband. Ginevra will come to Paris and enter one of my clinics. Afterwards she will have her training for the stage.'

'The stage?'

'Yes – there is a possibility there for her of great success. And that is what she needs – what she *must* have! In many essentials she has the same nature as her mother.'

'No!' cried Sarah, revolted.

'It seems impossible to you, but certain fundamental traits are the same. They were both born with a great yearning for importance; they both demand that their personality shall impress! This poor child has been thwarted and suppressed at every turn; she has been given no outlet for her fierce ambition, for her love of life, for the expression of her vivid romantic personality.' He gave a little laugh. '*Nous allons changer tout ça!*'

Then, with a little bow, he murmured: 'You will excuse me?' And he hurried down the hill after the girl.

Sarah said: 'Dr Gerard is tremendously keen on his job.'

'I perceive his keenness,' said Poirot.

Sarah said, with a frown: 'All the same, I can't bear his comparing her to that horrible old woman – although, once – I felt sorry for Mrs Boynton myself.'

'When was that, mademoiselle?'

'That time I told you about in Jerusalem. I suddenly felt as though I'd got the whole business wrong. You know that feeling one has sometimes when just for a short time you see everything the other way round? I got all het-up about it and went and made a fool of myself!'

'Oh, no – not that!'

Sarah, as always when she remembered her conversation with Mrs Boynton, was blushing acutely.

'I felt all exalted as though I had a mission! And then later, when Lady W. fixed a fishy eye on me and said she had seen me talking to Mrs Boynton, I thought she had probably overheard, and I felt the *most* complete ass.'

Poirot said: 'What exactly was it that old Mrs Boynton said to you? Can you remember the exact words?'

'I think so. They made rather an impression on me. "*I never forget*," that's what she said. "*Remember that. I've never forgotten anything – not an action, not a name, not a face.*"' Sarah shivered. 'She said it so *malevolently* – not even looking at me. I feel – I feel as if, even now, I can hear her . . .'

Poirot said gently: 'It impressed you very much?'

'Yes. I'm not easily frightened – but sometimes I dream of her saying just those words and her evil, leering triumphant face. Ugh!' She gave a quick shiver. Then she turned suddenly to him.

'M. Poirot, perhaps I ought not to ask, but have you come to a conclusion about this business? Have you found out anything definite?'

'Yes.'

He saw her lips tremble as she asked, 'What?'

'I have found out to whom Raymond Boynton spoke that night in Jerusalem. It was to his sister Carol.'

'Carol – of course!'

Then she went on: 'Did you tell him – did you ask him –'

It was no use. She could not go on. Poirot looked at her gravely and compassionately. He said quietly:

'It means – so much to you, mademoiselle?'

'It means just everything!' said Sarah. Then she squared her shoulders. 'But I've got to *know*.'

Poirot said quietly: 'He told me that it was a hysterical outburst – no more! That he and his sister were worked up. He told me that in daylight such an idea appeared fantastic to them both.'

'I see . . .'

Poirot said gently: 'Miss Sarah, will you not tell me what it is you fear?'

Sarah turned a white despairing face upon him.

'That afternoon – we were together. And he left me saying – saying he wanted to do something *now* – while he had the courage. I thought he meant just to – to tell her. But supposing he meant . . .'

Her voice died away. She stood rigid, fighting for control.

CHAPTER 13

Nadine Boynton came out of the hotel. As she hesitated uncertainly, a waiting figure sprang forward.

Mr Jefferson Cope was immediately at his lady's side.

'Shall we walk up this way? I think it's the pleasantest.'

She acquiesced.

They walked along and Mr Cope talked. His words came freely if a trifle monotonously. It is not certain whether he perceived that Nadine was not listening. As they turned aside on to the stony flower-covered hill-side, she interrupted him.

'Jefferson, I'm sorry. I've got to talk to you.'

Her face had grown pale.

'Why, certainly, my dear. Anything you like, but don't distress yourself.'

She said: 'You're cleverer than I thought. You know, don't you, what I'm going to say?'

'It is undoubtedly true,' said Mr Cope, 'that circumstances alter cases. I do feel, very profoundly, that in the present circumstances decisions may have to be reconsidered.' He sighed. 'You've got to go right ahead, Nadine, and do just what you feel.'

She said with real emotion: 'You're so *good*, Jefferson. So patient! I feel I've treated you very badly. I really have been downright mean to you.'

'Now, look here, Nadine, let's get this right. I've always known what my limitations were where you were concerned. I've had the deepest affection and respect for you ever since I've known you. All I want is your happiness. That's all I've ever wanted. Seeing you unhappy has very nearly driven me crazy. And I may say that I've blamed Lennox. I've felt that he didn't deserve to keep you if he didn't value your happiness a little more than he seemed to do.'

Mr Cope took a breath and went on:

'Now I'll admit that after travelling with you to Petra, I felt that perhaps Lennox wasn't quite so much to blame as I thought. He wasn't so much selfish where you were concerned, as too unselfish where his mother was concerned. I don't want to say anything against the dead, but I do think that your mother-in-law was perhaps an unusually difficult woman.'

'Yes, I think you may say that,' murmured Nadine.

'Anyway,' went on Mr Cope, 'you came to me yesterday and told me that you'd definitely decided to leave Lennox. I applaud your decision. It wasn't right – the life you were leading. You were quite honest with me. You didn't pretend to be more than just mildly fond of me. Well, that was all right with me. All I asked was the chance to look after you and treat you as you should be treated. I may say that afternoon was one of the happiest afternoons in my life.'

Nadine cried out: 'I'm sorry – I'm sorry.'

'No, my dear, because all along I had a kind of feeling that it wasn't real. I felt it was quite on the cards that you would have changed your mind by the next morning. Well, things are different now. You and Lennox can lead a life of your own.'

Nadine said quietly: 'Yes. I can't leave Lennox. Please forgive me.'

'Nothing to forgive,' declared Mr Cope. 'You and I will go back to being old friends. We'll just forget about that afternoon.'

Nadine placed a gentle hand on his arm. 'Dear Jefferson, thank you. I'm going to find Lennox now.'

She turned and left him. Mr Cope went on alone.

Nadine found Lennox sitting at the top of the Graeco-Roman theatre. He was in such a brown study that he hardly noticed her till she sank breathless at his side. 'Lennox.'

'Nadine.' He half turned.

She said: 'We haven't been able to talk until now. But you know, don't you, that I am not leaving you?'

He said gravely: 'Did you ever really mean to, Nadine?'

She nodded. 'Yes. You see, it seemed to be the only possible thing left to do. I hoped – I hoped that you would come after me. Poor Jefferson, how mean I have been to him.'

Lennox gave a sudden curt laugh.

'No, you haven't. Anyone who is as unselfish as Cope ought to be given full scope for his nobility! And you were right, you know, Nadine. When you told me that you were going away with him you gave me the shock of my life! You know, honestly, I think I must have been going queer or something lately. Why the hell didn't I snap my fingers in Mother's face and go off with you when you wanted me to?'

She said gently: 'You couldn't, my dear, you couldn't.'

Lennox said musingly: 'Mother was a damned queer character . . . I believe she'd got us all half hypnotized.'

'She had.'

Lennox mused a minute or two longer. Then he said: 'When you told me that afternoon – it was just like being hit a crack on the head! I walked back half dazed, and then, suddenly I saw what a damned fool I'd been! I realized that there was only one thing to be done if I didn't want to lose you.'

He felt her stiffen. His tone became grimmer.

'I went and –'

'Don't . . .'

He gave her a quick glance.

'I went and – argued with her.' He spoke with a complete change of tone – careful and rather toneless. 'I told her that I got to choose between her and you – and that I chose you.'

There was a pause.

He repeated, in a tone of curious self-approval:

'Yes, that's what I said to her.'

CHAPTER 14

Poirot met two people on his way home. The first was Mr Jefferson Cope.

'M. Hercule Poirot? My name's Jefferson Cope.'

The two men shook hands ceremoniously.

Then, falling into step beside Poirot, Mr Cope explained: 'It's just got round to me that you're making a kind of routine inquiry into the death of my old friend Mrs Boynton. That certainly was a shocking business. Of course, mind you, the old lady ought never to have undertaken such a fatiguing journey. But she was headstrong, M. Poirot. Her family could do nothing with her. She was by way of being a household tyrant – had had her own way too long, I guess. It certainly is true what she said went. Yes, sir, that certainly was true.'

There was a momentary pause.

'I'd just like to tell you, M. Poirot, that I'm an old friend of the Boynton family. Naturally they're all a good deal upset over this business; they're a trifle nervous and highly strung, too, you know, so if there are any arrangements to be made – necessary formalities, arrangements for the funeral – transport of the body to Jerusalem, why, I'll take as much trouble as I can off their hands. Just call upon me for anything that needs doing.'

'I am sure the family will appreciate your offer,' said Poirot. He added, 'You are, I think, a special friend of young Mrs Boynton's.'

Mr Jefferson Cope went a little pink.

'Well, we won't say much about that, M. Poirot. I hear you had an interview with Mrs Lennox Boynton this morning, and she may have given you a hint how things were between us, but that's all over now. Mrs Boynton is a very fine woman and she feels that her first duty is to her husband in his sad bereavement.'

There was a pause. Poirot received the information by a delicate gesture of the head. Then he murmured:

'It is the desire of Colonel Carbury to have a clear statement concerning the afternoon of Mrs Boynton's death. Can you give me an account of that afternoon?'

'Why, certainly. After our luncheon and a brief rest we set out for a kind of informal tour round. We escaped, I'm glad to say, without that pestilential dragoman. That man's just crazy on the subject of the Jews. I don't think he's quite sane on that point. Anyway, as I was saying, we set out. It was then that I had my interview with Nadine. Afterwards she wished to be alone with her husband to discuss matters with him. I went off on my own, working gradually back towards the camp. About half-way there I met the two English ladies who had been on the morning expedition – one of them's an English peeress, I understand?'

Poirot said that such was the case.

'Ah, she's a fine woman, a very powerful intellect and very well informed. The other seemed to me rather a weak sister – and she looked about dead with fatigue. That expedition in the morning was very strenuous for an elderly lady, especially when she doesn't like heights. Well, as I was saying, I met these two ladies and was able to give them some information on the subject of the Nabateans. We went around a bit and got back to the camp about six. Lady Westholme insisted on having tea and I had the pleasure of having a cup with her – the tea was kind of weak, but it had an interesting flavour. Then the boys laid the table for supper and sent out to the old lady only to find that she was sitting there dead in her chair.'

'Did you notice her as you walked home?'

'I did notice she was there – it was her usual seat in the afternoon and evening, but I didn't pay special attention. I was just explaining to Lady Westholme the conditions of our slump. I had to keep an eye on Miss Pierce, too. She was so tired she kept turning her ankles.'

'Thank you, Mr Cope. May I be so indiscreet as to ask if Mrs Boynton is likely to have left a large fortune?'

'A very considerable one. That is to say, strictly speaking, it was not hers to leave. She had a life interest in it and at her death it is divided between the late Elmer Boynton's children. Yes, they will all be very comfortably off now.'

'Money,' murmured Poirot, 'makes a lot of difference. How many crimes have been committed for it?'

Mr Cope looked a little startled.

'Why, that's so, I suppose,' he admitted.

Poirot smiled sweetly and murmured: 'But there are so many motives for murder, are there not? Thank you, Mr Cope, for your kind co-operation.'

'You're welcome, I'm sure,' said Mr Cope. 'Do I see Miss King sitting up there? I think I'll go and have a word with her.'

Poirot continued to descend the hill.

He met Miss Pierce fluttering up it.

She greeted him breathlessly.

'Oh, M. Poirot, I'm so glad to meet you. I've been talking to that very odd girl – the youngest one, you know. She has been saying the strangest things – about enemies, and some sheikh that wanted to kidnap her and how she has spies all round her. Really, it sounded *most* romantic! Lady Westholme says it is all nonsense and that she once had a red-headed kitchenmaid who told lies just like that, but I think sometimes that Lady Westholme is rather *hard*. And after all, it might be true, mightn't it, M. Poirot? I read some years ago that one of the Czar's daughters was not killed in the Revolution in Russia, but escaped secretly to America. The Grand Duchess Tatiana, I think it was. If so, this *might* be her daughter, mightn't it? She *did* hint at something royal – and she has a look, don't you think? Rather Slavonic – those cheek-bones. How thrilling it would be!'

Poirot said somewhat sententiously: 'It is true that there are many strange things in life.'

'I didn't really take in this morning who you were,' said Miss Pierce, clasping her hands. 'Of course you are that *very* famous detective! I read *all* about the ABC case. It was so *thrilling*. I had actually a post as governess near Doncaster at the time.'

Poirot murmured something. Miss Pierce went on with growing agitation.

'That is why I felt perhaps – I had been wrong – this morning. One must always tell *everything*, must one not? Even the *smallest* detail, however unrelated it may *seem*. Because, of course, if you are mixed up in this, poor Mrs Boynton *must* have been murdered! I see that now! I suppose Mr Mah Mood – I cannot remember his name – but the dragoman, I mean – I suppose he could not be a *Bolshevik agent?* Or even, perhaps, Miss King? I believe many *quite* well-brought-up girls of *good* family belong to these dreadful Communists! That's why I wondered if I *ought* to tell you – because, you see, it was rather *peculiar* when one comes to think of it.'

'Precisely,' said Poirot. 'And therefore you will tell me all about it.'

'Well, it's not really anything very much. It's only that on the next morning after the discovery I was up rather early – and I looked out of my tent to see the effect of the sunrise you know (only, of course, it wasn't actually sunrise because the sun must have risen quite an hour before). But it was *early* –'

'Yes, yes. And you saw?'

'That's the curious thing – at least, at the time it didn't *seem* much. It was only that I saw that Boynton girl come out of her tent and fling something right out into the stream – nothing in *that*, of course, but it *glittered* – in the sunlight! As it went through the air. It *glittered*, you know.'

'Which Boynton girl was it?'

'I think it was the one they call Carol – a very nice-looking girl – so like her brother – really they might be *twins*. Or, of course, it *might* have been the youngest one. The sun was in my eyes, so I couldn't quite see. But I don't think the hair was red – just bronze. I'm so fond of that coppery-bronze hair! Red hair always says *carrots* to me!' She tittered.

'And she threw away a brightly glittering object?' said Poirot.

'Yes. And of course, as I said, I didn't think much of it *at the time*. But later I walked along the stream and Miss King was there. And there amongst a lot of other very unsuitable things – even a tin or two – I saw a little bright metal box – not an exact square – a sort of long square, if you understand what I mean –'

'But yes, I understand perfectly. About so long?'

'Yes, how *clever* of you! And I thought to myself, "I suppose *that's* what the Boynton girl threw away, but it's a nice little box." And just out of curiosity I picked it up and opened it. It had a kind of syringe inside – the same thing they stuck into my arm when I was being inoculated for typhoid. And I thought how curious to throw it away like that because it didn't seem broken or anything. But just as I was wondering, Miss King spoke behind me. I hadn't heard her come up. And she said, "Oh, thank you – that's my hypodermic. I was coming to look for it." So I gave it to her, and she went back to the camp with it.'

Miss Pierce paused and then went on hurriedly:

'And, of course, I expect there is *nothing in it* – only it *did* seem a little curious that Carol Boynton should throw away Miss King's syringe. I mean, it was odd, if you know what I mean. Though, of course, I expect there is a very good explanation.'

She paused, looking expectantly at Poirot.

His face was grave. 'Thank you, mademoiselle. What you have told me may not be important in itself, but I will tell you this! It completes my case! Everything is now clear and in order.'

'Oh, really?' Miss Pierce looked as flushed and pleased as a child.

Poirot escorted her to the hotel.

Back in his own room he added one line to his memorandum. Point No. 10. '*I never forget. Remember that. I've never forgotten anything . . .*'

'*Mais oui,*' he said. 'It is all clear now!'

CHAPTER 15

'My preparations are complete,' said Hercule Poirot.

With a little sigh he stepped back a pace or two and contemplated his arrangement of one of the unoccupied hotel bedrooms.

Colonel Carbury, leaning inelegantly against the bed which had been pushed against the wall, smiled as he puffed at his pipe. 'Funny feller, aren't you, Poirot?' he said. 'Like to dramatize things.'

'Perhaps – that is true,' admitted the little detective. 'But indeed it is not all self-indulgence. If one plays a comedy, one must first set the scene.'

'Is this a comedy?'

'Even if it is a tragedy – there, too, the *décor* must be correct.'

Colonel Carbury looked at him curiously.

'Well,' he said, 'it's up to you! I don't know what you're driving at. I gather, though, that you've *got* something.'

'I shall have the honour to present to you what you asked me for – the truth!'

'Do you think we can get a conviction?'

'That, my friend, I did not promise you.'

'True enough. Maybe I'm glad you haven't. It depends.'

'My arguments are mainly psychological,' said Poirot.

Colonel Carbury sighed. 'I was afraid they might be.'

'But they will convince you,' Poirot reassured him. 'Oh, yes, they will convince you. The truth, I have always thought, is curious and beautiful.'

'Sometimes,' said Colonel Carbury, 'it's damned unpleasant.'

'No, no.' Poirot was earnest. 'You take there the personal view. Take instead the abstract, the detached point of vision. Then the absolute logic of events is fascinating and orderly.'

'I'll try to look on it that way,' said the Colonel.

Poirot glanced at his watch, a large grotesque turnip of a watch.

'But yes, indeed, it belonged to my grandfather.'

'Thought it might have done.'

'It is time to commence our proceedings,' said Poirot. 'You, *mon Colonel*, will sit here behind this table in an official position.'

'Oh, all right,' Carbury grunted. 'You don't want me to put my uniform on, do you?'

'No, no. If you would permit that I straightened your tie.' He suited the action to the word. Colonel Carbury grinned again, sat down in the chair indicated and a moment later, unconsciously, tweaked his tie round under his left ear again.

'Here,' continued Poirot, slightly altering the position of the chairs, 'we place *la famille Boynton*.

'And over here,' he went on, 'we will place the three outsiders who have a definite stake in the case. Dr Gerard, on whose evidence the case for the prosecution depends. Miss Sarah King, who has two separate interests in the case, a personal one, and that of medical examiner. Also Mr Jefferson Cope, who was on intimate terms with the Boyntons and so may be definitely described as an interested party.'

He broke off. 'Aha – here they come.'

He opened the door to admit the party.

Lennox Boynton and his wife came in first. Raymond and Carol followed. Ginevra walked by herself, a faint, faraway smile on her lips. Dr Gerard and Sarah King brought up the rear. Mr Jefferson Cope was a few minutes late and came in with an apology.

When he had taken his place Poirot stepped forward.

'Ladies and gentlemen,' he said, 'this is an entirely informal gathering. It has come about through the accident of my presence in Amman. Colonel Carbury did me the honour to consult me –'

Poirot was interrupted. The interruption came from what was seemingly the most unlikely quarter. Lennox Boynton said suddenly and pugnaciously:

'Why? Why the devil should he bring you into this business?'

Poirot waved a hand gracefully.

'Me, I am often called in in cases of sudden death.'

Lennox Boynton said: 'Doctors send for you whenever there is a case of heart failure?'

Poirot said gently: 'Heart failure is such a very loose and unscientific term.'

Colonel Carbury cleared his throat. It was an official noise. He spoke in an official tone.

'Best to make it quite clear. Circumstance of death reported to me. Very natural occurrence. Weather unusually hot – journey a very trying one for an elderly lady in bad health. So far all quite clear. But Dr Gerard came to me and volunteered a statement –'

He looked inquiringly at Poirot. Poirot nodded.

'Dr Gerard is a very eminent physician with a world-wide reputation. Any statement he makes is bound to be received with attention. Dr Gerard's statement was as follows. On the morning after Mrs Boynton's death he noted that a certain quantity of a powerful drug acting on the heart was missing from his medical supplies. On the previous afternoon he had noticed the disappearance of a hypodermic syringe. Syringe was returned during the night. Final point – there was a puncture on the dead woman's wrist corresponding to the mark of a hypodermic syringe.'

Colonel Carbury paused.

'In these circumstances I considered that it was the duty of those in authority to inquire into the matter. M. Hercule Poirot was my guest and very considerately offered his highly specialized services. I gave him full authority to make any investigations he pleased. We are assembled here now to hear his report on the matter.'

There was silence – a silence so acute that you could have heard – as the saying is – a pin drop. Actually someone did drop what was probably a shoe in the next room. It sounded like a bomb in the hushed atmosphere.

Poirot cast a quick glance at the little group of three people on his right, then turned his gaze to the five people huddled together on his left – a group of people with frightened eyes.

Poirot said quietly: 'When Colonel Carbury mentioned this business to me, I gave him my opinion as an expert. I told him that it might not be possible to bring proof – such proof as would be admissible in a court of law – but I told him very definitely that I was sure I could arrive at the truth – simply by questioning the people concerned. For let me tell you this, my friends, to investigate a crime it is only necessary to let the guilty party or parties *talk* – always, in the end, they tell you what you want to know!' He paused.

'So, in this case, although you have lied to me, you have also, unwittingly, told me the truth.'

He heard a faint sigh, the scrape of a chair on the floor to his right, but he did not look round. He continued to look at the Boyntons.

'First, I examined the possibility of Mrs Boynton having died a natural death – and I decided against it. The missing drug – the hypodermic syringe – and above all, the attitude of the dead lady's family all convinced me that that supposition could not be entertained.

'Not only was Mrs Boynton killed in cold blood – but every member of her family was aware of the fact! Collectively they reacted as guilty parties.

'But there are degrees in guilt. I examined the evidence carefully with a view to ascertaining whether the murder – yes, it was *murder* – had been committed by the old lady's family *acting on a concerted plan*.

'There was, I may say, overwhelming motive. One and all stood to gain by her death – both in the financial sense – for they would at once attain financial independence and indeed enjoy very considerable wealth – and also in the sense of being freed from what had become an almost insupportable tyranny.

'To continue: I decided, almost immediately, that the concerted theory would not hold water. The stories of the Boynton family did not dovetail neatly into each other, and no system of workable alibis had been arranged. The facts seemed more to suggest that one – or possibly two – members of the family had acted in collusion and that the others were accessories after the fact. I next considered which particular member or members – were indicated. Here, I may say, I was inclined to be biased by a certain piece of evidence known only to myself.'

Here Poirot recounted his experience in Jerusalem.

'Naturally, that pointed very strongly to Mr Raymond Boynton as the prime mover in the affair. Studying the family, I came to the conclusion that the most likely recipient of his confidences that night would be his sister Carol. They strongly resembled each other in appearance and temperament, and so would have a keen bond of sympathy and they also possessed the nervous rebellious temperament necessary for the conception of such an act. That their motive was partly unselfish – to free the whole family and particularly their younger sister – only made the planning of the deed more plausible.' Poirot paused a minute.

Raymond Boynton half opened his lips, then shut them again. His eyes looked steadily at Poirot with a kind of dumb agony in them.

'Before I go into the case against Raymond Boynton, I would like to read to you a list of significant points which I drew up and submitted to Colonel Carbury this afternoon.

Significant points

1 Mrs Boynton was taking a mixture containing digitalin.
2 Dr Gerard missed a hypodermic syringe.
3 Mrs Boynton took definite pleasure in keeping her family from enjoying themselves with other people.
4 Mrs Boynton, on the afternoon in question, encouraged her family to go away and leave her.
5 Mrs Boynton is a mental sadist.
6 The distance from the marquee to the place where Mrs Boynton was sitting is (roughly) two hundred yards.
7 Mr Lennox Boynton said at first he did not know what time he returned to the camp, but later he admitted having set his mother's wrist-watch to the right time.
8 Dr Gerard and Miss Genevra Boynton occupied tents next door to each other.
9 At half-past six, when dinner was ready, a servant was dispatched to announce the fact to Mrs Boynton.
10 Mrs Boynton, in Jerusalem, used these words: "I never forget. Remember that. I've never forgotten anything."

'Although I have numbered the points separately, occasionally they can be bracketed in pairs. That is the case, for instance, with the first two. *Mrs Boynton taking a mixture containing digitalis. Dr Gerard had missed a hypodermic syringe*. Those two points were the first thing that struck me about the case, and I may say to you that I found them most extraordinary – and quite irreconcilable. You do not see what I mean? No matter. I will return to the point presently. Let it suffice that I noticed those two points as something that had definitely got to be explained satisfactorily.

'I will conclude now with my study of the possibility of Raymond Boynton's guilt. The following are the facts. He had been heard to discuss the possibility of taking Mrs Boynton's life. He was in a condition of great nervous excitement. He had – mademoiselle will forgive me' – he bowed apologetically to Sarah – 'just passed through a moment of great emotional crisis. That is, he had fallen in love. The exaltation of his feelings might lead him to act in one of several ways. He might feel mellowed and softened towards the world in general, including his stepmother – he might feel the courage at last to defy her and shake off her influence – or he might find just the additional spur to turn his crime from theory to practice. That is the psychology! Let us now examine the *facts*.

'Raymond Boynton left the camp with the others about three-fifteen. Mrs Boynton was then alive and well. Before long Raymond and Sarah King had a *tête-à-tête* interview. Then he left her. According to him, he returned to the camp at ten minutes to six. He went up to his mother, exchanged a few words with her, then went to his tent and afterwards down to the marquee. He says that at ten minutes to six, *Mrs Boynton was alive and well*.

'But we now come to a fact which directly contradicts that statement. At half-past six Mrs Boynton's death was discovered by a servant. Miss King, who holds a medical degree, examined her body and she swears definitely that at that time, though she did not pay any special attention to the time when death had occurred, it had *most certainly and decisively* taken place at least an hour (and probably *a good deal more*) before six o'clock.

'We have here, you see, two conflicting statements. Setting aside the possibility that Miss King may have made a mistake –'

Sarah interrupted him. 'I don't make mistakes. That is, if I had, I would admit to it.'

Her tone was hard and clear.

Poirot bowed to her politely.

'Then there are only two possibilities – either Miss King or Mr Boynton is lying! Let us examine Raymond Boynton's reasons for so doing. Let us assume that Miss King was *not* mistaken and *not* deliberately lying. What, then, was the sequence of events? Raymond Boynton returns to the camp, sees his mother sitting at the mouth of her cave, goes up to her and finds she is dead. What does he do? Does he call for help? Does he immediately inform the camp of what has happened? No, he waits a minute or two, then passes on to his tent and joins his family in the marquee and *says nothing*. Such conduct is exceedingly curious, is it not?'

Raymond said in a nervous, sharp voice:

'It would be idiotic, of course. That ought to show you that my mother was alive and well as I've said. Miss King was flustered and upset and made a mistake.'

'One asks oneself,' said Poirot, calmly sweeping on, 'whether there could possibly be a reason for such conduct? It seems, on the face of it, that Raymond Boynton *cannot be guilty*, since at the only time he was known to approach his stepmother that afternoon *she had already been dead for some time*. Now, supposing, therefore, that Raymond Boynton is *innocent*, can we explain his conduct?

'And I say, that on the assumption that he is innocent, we can! For I remember that fragment of conversation I overheard. "*You do see, don't you, that she's got to be killed?*" He comes back from his walk and finds her dead and at once his guilty memory envisages a certain possibility. The plan has been carried out – not by him – but by his fellow planner. *Tout simplement* – he suspects that his sister, Carol Boynton, is guilty.'

'It's a lie,' said Raymond in a low, trembling voice.

Poirot went on: 'Let us now take the possibility of Carol Boynton being the murderess. What is the evidence against her? She has the same highly-strung temperament – the kind of temperament that might see such a deed coloured with heroism. It was she to whom Raymond Boynton was talking that night in Jerusalem. Carol Boynton returned to the camp at ten minues past five. According to her own story she went up and spoke to her mother. No one saw her do so. The camp was deserted – the boys were asleep. Lady Westholme, Miss Pierce and Mr

556

Cope were exploring caves out of sight of the camp. There was no witness of Carol Boynton's possible action. The time would agree well enough. The case, then, against Carol Boynton is a perfectly possible one.' He paused. Carol had raised her head. Her eyes looked steadily and sorrowfully into his.

'There is one other point. The following morning, very early, Carol Boynton was seen to throw something into the stream. There is reason to believe that that something was a hypodermic syringe.'

'*Comment?*' Dr Gerard looked up surprised. 'But my hypodermic was *returned*. Yes, yes, I have it now.'

Poirot nodded vigorously.

'Yes, yes. This second hypodermic, it is very curious – very interesting. I have been given to understand that this hypodermic belonged to Miss King. Is that so?'

Sarah paused for a fraction of a second.

Carol spoke quickly: 'It was not Miss King's syringe,' she said. 'It was mine.'

'Then you admit throwing it away, mademoiselle?'

She hesitated just a second.

'Yes, of course. Why shouldn't I?'

'Carol!' It was Nadine. She leaned forward, her eyes wide and distressed. 'Carol . . . Oh, I don't understand . . .'

Carol turned and looked at her. There was something hostile in her glance.

'There's nothing to understand! I threw away an old hypodermic. I never touched the – the poison.'

Sarah's voice broke in: 'It is quite true what Miss Pierce told you, M. Poirot. It *was* my syringe.'

Poirot smiled.

'It is very confusing, this affair of the hypodermic – and yet, I think, it could be explained. Ah, well, we have now two cases made out – the case for the innocence of Raymond Boynton – the case for the guilt of his sister Carol. But me, I am scrupulously fair. I look always on both sides. Let us examine what occurred if Carol Boynton was innocent.

'She returns to the camp, she goes up to her stepmother, and she finds her – shall we say – dead! What is the first thing she will think? She will suspect that her brother Raymond may have killed her. She does not know what to do. So she says nothing.

And presently, about an hour later, Raymond Boynton returns and having presumably spoken to his mother, *says nothing of anything being amiss*. Do you not think that then her suspicions would become certainties? Perhaps she goes to his tent and finds there a hypodermic syringe. Then, indeed, she is *sure*! She takes it quickly and hides it. Early in the morning she flings it as far away as she can.

'There is one more indication that Carol Boynton is innocent. She assures me when I question her that she and her brother never seriously intended to carry out their plan. I ask her to swear – and she swears immediately and with the utmost solemnity that she is not guilty of the crime! You see, that is the way she puts it. She does not swear that *they* are not guilty. She swears for *herself*, not her brother – and thinks that I will not pay special attention to the pronoun.

'*Eh bien*, that is the case for the innocence of Carol Boynton. And now let us go back a step and consider not the innocence but the possible guilt of Raymond. Let us suppose that Carol is speaking the truth, that Mrs Boynton was alive at five-ten. Under what circumstances can Raymond be guilty? We can suppose that he killed his mother at ten minutes to six when he went up to speak to her. There were boys about the camp, true, but the light was fading. It might have been managed, but it then follows that Miss King lied. Remember, she came back to the camp only five minutes after Raymond. From the distance she would see him go up to his mother. Then, when later she is found dead, Miss King realizes that *Raymond has killed her*, and to save him, she lies – knowing that Dr Gerard is down with fever and cannot expose her lie!'

'I did *not* lie!' said Sarah clearly.

'There is yet another possibility. Miss King, as I have said, reached the camp a few minutes after Raymond. If Raymond Boynton found his mother alive, it may have been *Miss King* who administered the fatal injection. She believed that Mrs Boynton was fundamentally evil. She may have seen herself as a just executioner. That would equally well explain her lying about the time of death.'

Sarah had grown very pale. She spoke in a low, steady voice.

'It is true that I spoke of the expediency of one person dying to save many. It was the Place of Sacrifice that suggested the idea to me. But I can swear to you that I never harmed that disgusting old woman – nor would the idea of doing so ever have entered my head!'

'And yet,' said Poirot softly, 'one of you two *must be lying*.'

Raymond Boynton shifted in his chair. He cried out impetuously:

'You win, M. Poirot! I'm the liar. Mother was dead when I went up to her. It – it quite knocked me out. I'd been going, you see, to have it out with her. To tell her that from henceforth I was a free agent. I was – all set, you understand. And there she was – dead! Her hand all cold and flabby. And I thought – just what you said. I thought maybe Carol – you see, there was the mark on her wrist –'

Poirot said quickly: 'That is the one point on which I am not completely informed. What was the method you counted on employing? You *had* a method – and it was connected with a hypodermic syringe. That much I know. If you want me to believe you, you must tell me the rest.'

Raymond said hurriedly: 'It was a way I read in a book – an English detective story – you stuck an empty hypodermic syringe into someone and it did the trick. It sounded perfectly scientific. I – I thought we'd do it that way.'

'Ah,' said Poirot. 'I comprehend. And you purchased a syringe?'

'No. As a matter of fact I pinched Nadine's.'

Poirot shot a quick look at her. 'The syringe that is in your baggage in Jerusalem?' he murmured.

A faint colour showed in the young woman's face.

'I – I wasn't sure what had become of it,' she murmured. Poirot murmured: 'You are so quick-witted, madame.'

CHAPTER 16

There was a pause. Then clearing his throat with a slightly affected sound, Poirot went on:

'We have now solved the mystery of what I might term *the second hypodermic*. That belonged to Mrs Lennox Boynton, was taken by Raymond Boynton before leaving Jerusalem, was taken from Raymond by Carol after the discovery of Mrs Boynton's dead body, was thrown away by her, found by Miss Pierce, and claimed by Miss King as hers. I presume Miss King has it now.'

'I have,' said Sarah.

'So that when you said it was yours just now, you were doing what you told us you do not do – you told a lie.'

Sarah said calmly: 'That's a different kind of lie. It isn't – it isn't a *professional* lie.'

Gerard nodded appreciation.

'Yes, it is a point that. I understand you perfectly, mademoiselle.'

'Thanks,' said Sarah.

Again Poirot cleared his throat.

'Let us now review our time-table. Thus:

Boyntons and Jefferson Cope leave the camp	3.5 (approx.)
Dr Gerard and Sarah King leave the camp	3.15 (approx.)
Lady Westholme and Miss Pierce leave the camp	4.15
Dr Gerard returns to camp	4.20 (approx.)
Lennox Boynton returns to camp	4.35
Nadine Boynton returns to camp and talks to Mrs Boynton	4.40
Nadine Boynton leaves her mother-in-law and goes to marquee	4.50 (approx.)
Carol Boynton returns to camp	5.10
Lady Westholme, Miss Pierce and Mr Jefferson Cope return to camp	5.40
Raymond Boynton returns to camp	5.50
Sarah King returns to camp	6.0
Body discovered	6.30

'There is, you will notice, a gap of twenty minutes between four-fifty when Nadine Boynton left her mother-in-law and five-ten when Carol returned. Therefore, if Carol is speaking the truth, Mrs Boynton must have been killed in that twenty minutes.

'Now who could have killed her? At that time Miss King and Raymond Boynton were together. Mr Cope (not that he had any perceivable motive for killing her) has an alibi. He was with Lady Westholme and Miss Pierce. Lennox Boynton was with his wife in the marquee. Dr Gerard was groaning with fever in his tent. The camp is deserted, the boys are asleep. It is a suitable moment for a crime! Was there a person who could have committed it?'

His eyes went thoughtfully to Ginevra Boynton.

'*There was one person.* Ginevra Boynton was in her tent all the afternoon. That is what we have been told – but actually there is evidence that she was *not* in her tent all the time. Ginevra Boynton made a very significant remark. She said that Dr Gerard spoke her name in his fever. And Dr Gerard has also told us that he dreamt in his fever of Ginevra Boynton's face. But it was not a dream! It was actually her face he saw, standing there by his bed. He thought it an effect of fever – but it was the truth. Ginevra was in Dr Gerard's tent. Is it not possible that she had come to put back the hypodermic syringe after using it?'

Ginevra Boynton raised her head with its crown of red-gold hair. Her wide beautiful eyes stared at Poirot. They were singularly expressionless. She looked like a vague saint.

'*Ah, ça non!*' cried Dr Gerard.

'Is it, then, so psychologically impossible?' inquired Poirot.

The Frenchman's eyes dropped.

Nadine Boynton said sharply: 'It's quite impossible!'

Poirot's eyes came quickly round to her.

'Impossible, madame?'

'Yes.' She paused, bit her lip, then went on, 'I will not hear of such a disgraceful accusation against my young sister-in-law. We – all of us – know it to be impossible.'

Ginevra moved a little on her chair. The lines of her mouth relaxed into a smile – the touching, innocent half-unconscious smile of a very young girl.

Nadine said again: 'Impossible.'

Her gentle face had hardened into lines of determination. The eyes that met Poirot's were hard and unflinching.

Poirot leaned forward in what was half a bow.

'Madame is very intelligent,' he said.

Nadine said quietly: 'What do you mean by that, M. Poirot?'

'I mean, madame, that all along I have realized that you have what I believe is called an "excellent headpiece".'

'You flatter me.'

'I think not. All along you have envisaged the situation calmly and collectively. You have remained on outwardly good terms

561

with your husband's mother, deeming that the best thing to be done, but inwardly you have judged and condemned her. I think that some time ago you realized that the only chance for your husband's happiness was for him to make an effort to leave home – strike out on his own no matter how difficult and penurious such a life might be. You were willing to take all risks and you endeavoured to influence him to exactly that course of action. But you failed, madame. Lennox Boynton had no longer *the will to freedom*. He was content to sink into a condition of apathy and melancholy.

'Now I have no doubt at all, madame, but that you love your husband. Your decision to leave him was not actuated by a greater love for another man. It was, I think, a desperate venture undertaken as a last hope. A woman in your position could only try three things. She could try appeal. That, as I have said, failed. She could threaten to leave herself. But it is possible that even that threat would not have moved Lennox Boynton. It would plunge him deeper in misery, but it would not cause him to rebel. There was one last desperate throw. *You could go away with another man*. Jealousy and the instinct of possession is one of the most deeply rooted fundamental instincts in man. You showed your wisdom in trying to reach that deep underground savage instinct. If Lennox Boynton would let you go without an effort to another man – then he must indeed be beyond human aid, and you might as well then try to make a new life for yourself elsewhere.

'But let us suppose that even that last desperate remedy failed. Your husband was terribly upset at your decision, but in spite of that he did not, as you had hoped, react as a primitive man might have done with an uprush of the possessive instinct. Was there anything at all that could save your husband from his own rapidly failing mental condition? Only one thing. *If his stepmother were to die*, it might not be too late. He might be able to start life anew as a free man, building up in himself independence and manliness once more.'

Poirot paused, then repeated gently: 'If your mother-in-law were to die . . .'

Nadine's eyes were still fixed on him. In an unmoved gentle voice she said: 'You are suggesting that I helped to bring that event about, are you not? But you cannot do so, M. Poirot.

After I had broken the news of my impending departure to Mrs Boynton, I went straight to the marquee and joined Lennox. I did not leave it again until my mother-in-law was found dead. Guilty of her death I may be, in the sense that I gave her a shock – that, of course, presupposes a natural death. But if, as you say (though so far you have no direct evidence of it and cannot have until an autopsy has taken place) she was deliberately killed, then *I* had no opportunity of doing so.'

Poirot said: 'You did not leave the marquee again until your mother-in-law was found dead. That is what you have just said. That, Mrs Boynton, was one of the points I found curious about this case.'

'What do you mean?'

'It is here on my list. Point nine. At half-past six, when dinner was ready, a servant was dispatched to announce the fact to Mrs Boynton.'

Raymond said: 'I don't understand.'

Carol said: 'No more do I.'

Poirot looked from one to the other of them.

'You do not, eh? "A servant was sent" – why a *servant*? Were you not, all of you, most assiduous in your attendance on the old lady as a general rule? Did not one or other of you always escort her to meals? She was infirm. It was difficult for her to rise from a chair without assistance. Always one or other of you was at her elbow. I suggest then, that on dinner being announced the natural thing would have been for one or other of her family to go out and help her. But not one of you offered to do so. You all sat there, paralysed, watching each other, wondering, perhaps, why no one went.'

Nadine said sharply: 'All this is absurd, M. Poirot! We were all tired that evening. We ought to have gone, I admit, but – on that evening – we just didn't!'

'Precisely – precisely – *on that particular evening!* You, madame, did perhaps more waiting on her than anyone else. It was one of the duties that you accepted mechanically. But that evening you did not offer to go out to help her in. Why? That is what I asked myself – why? And I tell you my answer. *Because you knew quite well that she was dead . . .*

'No, no, do not interrupt me, madame.' He raised an impassioned hand. 'You will now listen to me – Hercule Poirot! There were witnesses to your conversation with your mother-in-law. Witnesses who could *see* but could not *hear*! Lady Westholme and Miss Pierce were a long way away. They saw you *apparently* having a conversation with your mother-in-law, but what actual evidence is there of what occurred? I will propound to you instead a little theory. You have brains, madame. If in your quiet unhurried fashion you have decided on – shall we say the *elimination* of your husband's mother – you will carry it out with intelligence and with due preparation. You have access to Dr Gerard's tent during his absence on the morning excursion. You are fairly sure that you will find a suitable drug. Your nursing training helps you there. You choose digitoxin – the same kind of drug that the old lady is taking – you also take his hypodermic syringe since, to your annoyance, your own has disappeared. You hope to replace the syringe before the doctor notices its absence.'

'Before proceeding to carry out your plan, you make one last attempt to stir your husband into action. You tell him of your intention to marry Jefferson Cope. Though your husband is terribly upset he does not react as you had hoped – so you are forced to put your plan of murder into action. You return to the camp exchanging a pleasant natural word with Lady Westholme and Miss Pierce as you pass. You go up to where your mother-in-law is sitting. You have the syringe with the drug in it ready. It is easy to seize her wrist and – proficient as you are with your nurse's training – force home the plunger. It is done before your mother-in-law realizes what you are doing. From far down the valley the others only see you talking to her, bending over her. Then deliberately you go and fetch a chair and sit there apparently engaged in an amicable conversation for some minutes. Death must have been almost instantaneous. It is a dead woman to whom you sit talking, but who shall guess that? Then you put away the chair and go down to the marquee, where you find your husband reading a book. And you are careful not to leave that marquee! Mrs Boynton's death, you are sure, will be put down to heart trouble. (It will, indeed, be *due* to heart trouble.) In only one thing have your plans gone astray. You cannot return the syringe to Dr Gerard's tent because the doctor is in there shivering with malaria – and although you do not know it, he has *already missed the syringe.* That, madame, was the flaw in an otherwise perfect crime.'

There was silence – a moment's dead silence – then Lennox Boynton sprang to his feet.

'No,' he shouted. 'That's a damned lie. Nadine did nothing. She couldn't have done anything. My mother – my mother was already dead.'

'Ah?' Poirot's eyes came gently round to him. 'So, after all, it was *you* who killed her, Mr Boynton.'

Again a moment's pause – then Lennox dropped back into his chair and raised trembling hands to his face.

'Yes – that's right – I killed her.'

'You took the digitoxin from Dr Gerard's tent?'

'Yes.'

'When?'

'As – as – you said – in the morning.'

'And the syringe?'

'The syringe? Yes.'

'Why did you kill her?'

'Can you ask?'

'I *am* asking, Mr Boynton!'

'But you *know* – my wife was leaving me – with Cope –'

'Yes, but you only learnt that in the *afternoon.*'

Lennox stared at him. 'Of course. When we were out –'

'But you took the poison and the syringe in the *morning – before* you knew?'

'Why the hell do you badger me with questions?' He paused and passed a shaking hand across his forehead. 'What does it matter, anyway?'

'It matters a great deal. I advise you, Mr Lennox Boynton, to tell me the truth.'

'The truth?' Lennox stared at him.

'That is what I said – the truth.'

'By God, I will,' said Lennox suddenly. 'But I don't know whether you will believe me.' He drew a deep breath. 'That afternoon, when I left Nadine, I was absolutely all to pieces. I'd never dreamed she'd go from me to someone else. I was – I was nearly mad! I felt as though I was drunk or recovering from a bad illness.'

Poirot nodded. He said: 'I noted Lady Westholme's description of your gait when you passed her. That is why I knew your wife was not speaking the truth when she said she told you *after* you were both back at the camp. Continue, Mr Boynton.'

'I hardly knew what I was doing . . . But as I got near, my brain seemed to clear. It flashed over me that I had only myself to blame! I'd been a miserable worm! I ought to have defied my stepmother and cleared out years ago. And it came to me that it mightn't be too late even now. There she was, the old devil, sitting up like an obscene idol against the red cliffs. I went right up to have it out with her. I meant to tell her just what I thought and to announce that I was clearing out. I had a wild idea I might get away at once that evening – clear out with Nadine and get as far as Ma'an, anyway, that night.'

'Oh, Lennox – my dear –'

It was a long, soft sigh.

He went on: 'And then, my God – you could have struck me down with a touch! She was dead. Sitting there – dead . . . I – I didn't know what to do – I was dumb – dazed – everything I was going to shout out at her bottled up inside me – turning to lead – I can't explain . . . Stone – that's what it felt like – being turned to stone. I did something mechanically – I picked up her wrist-watch – it was lying in her lap – and put it round her wrist – her horrid limp dead wrist . . .'

He shuddered. 'God – it was awful . . . Then I stumbled down, went into the marquee. I ought to have called someone, I suppose – but I couldn't. I just sat there, turning the pages – waiting . . .'

He stopped.

'You won't believe that – you can't. Why didn't I call someone? Tell Nadine? I don't know.'

Dr Gerard cleared his throat.

'Your statement is perfectly plausible, Mr Boynton,' he said. 'You were in a bad nervous condition. Two severe shocks administered in rapid succession would be quite enough to put you in the condition you have described. It is the Weissenhalter reaction – best exemplified in the case of a bird that has dashed its head against a window. Even after its recovery it refrains instinctively from all action – giving itself time to readjust the nerve centres – I do not express myself well in English, but what I mean is this: *You could not have acted any other way.* Any decisive action of any kind would have been quite impossible for you! You passed through a period of mental paralysis.'

He turned to Poirot.

'I assure you, my friend, that is so!'

'Oh, I do not doubt it,' said Poirot. 'There was a little fact I had already noted – the fact that Mr Boynton had replaced his mother's wrist-watch – that was capable of two explanations – it might have been a cover for the actual deed, or it might have been observed and misinterpreted by Mrs Boynton. She returned only five minutes after her husband. She must therefore have seen that action. When she got up to her mother-in-law and found her dead with a mark of a hypodermic syringe on her wrist she would naturally jump to the conclusion that her husband had committed the deed – that her announcement of her decision to leave him had produced a reaction in him different from that for which she had hoped. Briefly, Nadine Boynton believed that she had inspired her husband to commit murder.'

He looked at Nadine. 'That is so, madame?'

She bowed her head. Then she asked:

'Did you *really* suspect me, M. Poirot?'

'I thought you were a possibility, madame.'

She leaned forward.

'And now? *What really happened, M. Poirot?*'

CHAPTER 17

'What really happened?' Poirot repeated.

He reached behind him, drew forward a chair and sat down. His manner was now friendly – informal.

'It is a question, is it not? For the digitoxin *was* taken – the syringe *was* missing – there *was* the mark of a hypodermic on Mrs Boynton's wrist.

'It is true that in a few days' time we shall know definitely – the autopsy will tell us – whether Mrs Boynton died of an overdose of digitalis or not. But then it may be too late! It would be better to reach the truth tonight – while the murderer is here under our hand.'

Nadine raised her head sharply.

'You mean that you still believe – that one of us – here in this room . . .' Her voice died away.

Poirot was slowly nodding to himself.

'The truth, that is what I promised Colonel Carbury. And so, having cleared our path we are back again where I was earlier in the day, writing down a list of printed facts and being faced straightway with two glaring inconsistencies.'

Colonel Carbury spoke for the first time. 'Suppose, now, we hear what they are?' he suggested.

Poirot said with dignity: 'I am about to tell you. We will take once more those first two facts on my list. *Mrs Boynton was taking a mixture of digitalis and Dr Gerard missed a hypodermic syringe.* Take those facts and set them against the undeniable fact (with which I was immediately confronted) that the Boynton family showed unmistakably guilty reactions. It would seem, therefore, certain that one of the Boynton family *must* have committed the crime! And yet, those two facts I mentioned were all *against* the theory. For, you see, to take a concentrated solution of digitalis – that, yes, it is a clever idea, because Mrs Boynton was already taking the drug. But what would a member of her family do then? *Ah, ma foi!* there was only one sensible thing to do. Put the poison *into her bottle of medicine*! That is what anyone, anyone with a grain of sense *and who had access to the medicine* would certainly do!

'Sooner or later Mrs Boynton takes a dose and dies – and even if the digitalis is discovered in the bottle it may be set down as a mistake of the chemist who made it up. Certainly nothing can be proved!

'Why, then, *the theft of the hypodermic needle?*

'There can be only two explanations of that – either Dr Gerard overlooked the syringe and it was never stolen, or else the syringe was taken because the murderer had *not* got access to the medicine – that is to say the murderer was *not* a member of the Boynton family. Those two first facts point overwhelmingly to an *outsider* as having committed the crime!

'I saw that – but I was puzzled, as I say, by the strong evidences of guilt displayed by the Boynton family. Was it possible that, *in spite of that consciousness of guilt,* the Boynton family were *innocent*? I set out to prove – not the guilt – but the *innocence* of those people!

'That is where we stand now. The murder was committed by an

568

outsider – that is, *by someone who was not sufficiently intimate with Mrs Boynton to enter her tent or to handle her medicine bottle.*'

He paused.

'There are three people in this room who are, technically, outsiders, but who have a definite connection with the case.

'Mr Cope, whom we will consider first, has been closely associated with the Boynton family for some time. Can we discover motive and opportunity on his part? It seems not. Mrs Boynton's death has affected him adversely – since it has brought about the frustration of certain hopes. Unless Mr Cope's motive was an almost fanatical desire to benefit others, we can find no reason for his desiring Mrs Boynton's death. (Unless, of course, there is a motive about which we are entirely in the dark. We do not know what Mr Cope's dealings with the Boynton family have been.)'

Mr Cope said with dignity: 'This seems to me a little farfetched, M. Poirot. You must remember I had absolutely no opportunity for committing this deed and, in any case I hold very strong views as to the sanctity of human life.'

'Your position certainly seems impeccable,' said Poirot with gravity. 'In a work of fiction you would be strongly suspected on that account.'

He turned a little in his chair. 'We now come to Miss King. Miss King had a certain amount of motive and she had the necessary medical knowledge and is a person of character and determination, but since she left the camp before three-thirty with the others and did not return to it until six o'clock, it seems difficult to see where she could have got her opportunity.

'Next we must consider Dr Gerard. Now here we must take into account the actual time that the murder was committed. According to Mr Lennox Boynton's last statement, his mother was dead at four thirty-five. According to Lady Westholme and Miss Pierce, she was alive at four-sixteen when they started on their walk. That leaves *exactly twenty minutes* unaccounted for. Now, as these two ladies walked *away* from the camp, Dr Gerard passed them going to it. There is no one to say *what Dr Gerard's movements were when he reached the camp* because the two ladies' backs were towards it. They were walking *away* from it. *Therefore it is perfectly possible for Dr Gerard to have committed the crime.* Being a doctor, he could easily counterfeit the appearance of malaria. There is, I should say, a possible motive. Dr Gerard might have wished to save a certain person whose reason (perhaps more vital a loss than loss of life) was in danger, and he may have considered the sacrifice of an old and worn-out life worth it!'

'Your ideas,' said Dr Gerard, 'are fantastic!'

Without taking any notice, Poirot went on:

'But if so, *why did Gerard call attention to the possibility of foul play?* It is quite certain that, but for his statement to Colonel Carbury, Mrs Boynton's death would have been put down to natural causes. It was *Dr Gerard* who first pointed out the possibility of murder. That, my friends,' said Poirot, 'does not make common sense!'

'Doesn't seem to,' said Colonel Carbury gruffly.

'There is one more possibility,' said Poirot. 'Mrs Lennox Boynton just now negatived strongly the possibility of her young sister-in-law being guilty. The force of her objection lay in the fact that she knew her mother-in-law to be dead at the time. But remember this, Ginevra Boynton was at the camp all the afternoon. And there was a moment – a moment when Lady Westholme and Miss Pierce were walking away from the camp and before Dr Gerard had returned to it . . .'

Ginevra stirred. She leaned forward, staring into Poirot's face with a strange, innocent, puzzled stare.

'*I* did it? You think I did it?'

Then suddenly, with a movement of swift incomparable beauty, she was up from her chair and had flung herself across the room and down on her knees beside Dr Gerard, clinging to him, gazing up passionately into his face.

'No, no, don't let them say it! They're making the walls close round me again! It's not true! I never did anything! They are my enemies – they want to put me in prison – to shut me up. You *must* help me. *You* must help me!'

'There, there, my child.' Gently the doctor patted her head. Then he addressed Poirot.

'What you say is nonsense – absurd.'

'Delusions of persecution?' murmured Poirot.

'Yes; but she could never have done it that way. She would have done it, you must perceive, *dramatically* – a dagger – something flamboyant – spectacular – never this cool, calm logic! I tell you, my friends, it is *so*. This was a reasoned crime – a sane crime.'

Poirot smiled. Unexpectedly he bowed. '*Je suis entièrement de votre avis*,' he said smoothly.

CHAPTER 18

'Come,' said Hercule Poirot. 'We have still a little way to go! Dr Gerard has invoked the psychology. So let us now examine the psychological side of this case. We have taken the *facts*, we have established a *chronological sequence of events*, we have heard the *evidence*. There remains – the psychology. And the most important psychological evidence concerns the dead woman – it is the psychology of Mrs Boynton herself that is the most important thing in this case.

'Take from my list of specified facts points three and four. *Mrs Boynton took definite pleasure in keeping her family from enjoying themselves with other people. Mrs Boynton, on the afternoon in question, encouraged her family to go away and leave her.*

'These two facts, they contradict each other flatly! Why, on this particular afternoon, should Mrs Boynton suddenly display a complete reversal of her usual policy? Was it that she felt a sudden warmth of the heart – an instinct of benevolence? That, it seems to me from all I have heard, was extremely unlikely! Yet there must have been a *reason*. What was that reason?

'Let us examine closely the character of Mrs Boynton. There have been many different accounts of her. She was a tyrannical old martinet – she was a mental sadist – she was an incarnation of evil – she was crazy. Which of these views is the true one?

'I think myself that Sarah King came nearest to the truth when in a flash of inspiration in Jerusalem she saw the old lady as intensely pathetic. But not only pathetic – *futile*!

'Let us, if we can, think ourselves into the mental condition of Mrs Boynton. A human creature born with immense ambition, with a yearning to dominate and to impress her personality on other people. She neither sublimated that intense craving for power – nor did she seek to master it – no, *mesdames and messieurs* – *she fed it!* But in the end – listen well to this – in the *end* what did it amount to? She was not a great power! She was not feared and hated over a wide area! *She was the petty tyrant of one isolated family!* And as Dr Gerard said to me – she became bored like any other old lady with her hobby and she sought to extend her activities and to amuse herself by making her dominance more precarious! But that led to an entirely different aspect of the case! By coming abroad, she realized for the first time how extremely insignificant she was!

'And now we come directly to point number ten – the words spoken to Sarah King in Jerusalem. Sarah King, you see, had put her finger on the truth. She had revealed fully and uncompromisingly the pitiful futility of Mrs Boynton's scheme of existence! And now listen very carefully – all of you – to what her exact words to Miss King were. Miss King has said that Mrs Boynton spoke "*so malevolently – not even looking at me*". And this is what she actually said, "*I've never forgotten anything – not an action, not a name, not a face.*"

'Those words made a great impression on Miss King. Their extraordinary intensity and the loud hoarse tone in which they were uttered! So strong was the impression that they left on her mind that I think she quite failed to realize their extraordinary significance!

'Do you see that significance, any of you?' He waited a minute. 'It seems not . . . But, *mes amis*, does it escape you that those words *were not a reasonable answer at all* to what Miss King had just been saying? "*I've never forgotten anything – not an action, not a name, not a face.*" It does not make *sense*! If she had said, "I never forget impertinence" – something of that kind – but no – *a face* is what she said . . .

'Ah!' cried Poirot, beating his hands together. 'But it leaps to the eye! Those words, ostensibly spoken to Miss King, *were not meant for Miss King at all!* They were addressed to *someone else* standing *behind* Miss King.'

He paused, noting their expressions.

'Yes, it leaps to the eye! That was, I tell you, a psychological moment in Mrs Boynton's life! She had been *exposed to herself* by an intelligent young woman! She was full of baffled fury – and at that moment she *recognized* someone – a *face* from the past – a victim delivered into her hands!

'We are back, you see, at the *outsider*! And *now* the meaning of Mrs Boynton's unexpected amiability on the afternoon of her death is clear. *She wanted to get rid of her family because* – to use a vulgarity – *she had other fish to fry!* She wanted the field left clear for an interview with a new victim . . .

'Now, from that new standpoint, let us consider the events of the afternoon! The Boynton family go off. Mrs Boynton sits up by her cave. Now let us consider very carefully the evidence of Lady Westholme and Miss Pierce. The latter is an unreliable witness, she is unobservant and very suggestible. Lady Westholme, on the other hand, is perfectly clear as to her facts and meticulously observant. Both ladies agree on *one* fact! *An Arab, one of the servants, approaches Mrs Boynton, angers her in some way and retires hastily.* Lady Westholme stated definitely that the servant had first been into the tent occupied by Ginevra Boynton, but you may remember that *Dr Gerard's* tent was next door to Ginevra's. It is possible that it was *Dr Gerard's* tent the Arab entered . . .'

Colonel Carbury said: 'D'you mean to tell me that one of those Bedouin fellows of mine murdered an old lady by sticking her with a hypodermic? Fantastic!'

'Wait, Colonel Carbury, I have not yet finished. Let us agree that the Arab *might* have come from Dr Gerard's tent and not Ginevra Boynton's. What is the next thing? Both ladies agree that they could not see his face clearly enough to identify him and that they did not hear what was said. That is understandable. The distance between the marquee and the ledge was about two hundred yards. Lady Westholme gave a clear description of the man otherwise, describing in detail his ragged breeches and the untidiness with which his puttees were rolled.'

Poirot leaned forward.

'And that, my friends, *was very odd indeed!* Because if she could not see his face or hear what was said, *she could not possibly have noticed the state of his breeches and puttees!* Not at two hundred yards!

'It was an error, that, you see! It suggested a curious idea to me. *Why* insist so on the ragged breeches and untidy puttees? Could it be because the breeches were *not* torn and the *puttees were non-existent?* Lady Westholme and Miss Pierce both saw the man – but from where they were sitting *they could not see each other.* That is shown by the fact that Lady Westholme *came to see* if Miss Pierce was awake and found her sitting in the entrance of her tent.'

'Good lord,' said Colonel Carbury, suddenly sitting up very straight. 'Are you suggesting –?'

'I am suggesting that, having ascertained just what Miss Pierce (the only witness likely to be awake) was doing, Lady Westholme returned to her tent, put on her riding breeches, boots and khaki-coloured coat, made herself an Arab head-dress with her checked duster and a skein of knitting-wool and that, thus attired, she went boldly up to Dr Gerard's tent, looked in his medicine chest, selected a suitable drug, took the hypodermic, filled it and went boldly up to her victim.

'Mrs Boynton may have been dozing. Lady Westholme was quick. She caught her by the wrist and injected the stuff. Mrs Boynton half cried out – tried to rise – then sank back. The "Arab" hurried away with every evidence of being ashamed and abashed. Mrs Boynton shook her stick, tried to rise, then fell back into her chair.

'Five minutes later Lady Westholme rejoins Miss Pierce and comments on the scene she has just witnessed, *impressing her own version of it on the other*. Then they go for a walk, pausing below the ledge where Lady Westholme shouts up to the old lady. She receives no answer. Mrs Boynton is dead – but she remarks to Miss Pierce, "Very rude just to snort at us like that!" Miss Pierce accepts the suggestion – she has often heard Mrs Boynton receive a remark with a snort – she will swear quite sincerely if necessary that she actually *heard* it. Lady Westholme has sat on committees often enough with women of Miss Pierce's type to know exactly how her own eminence and masterful personality can influence them. The only point where her plan went astray was the replacing of the syringe. Dr Gerard returning so soon upset her scheme. She hoped he might not have noticed its absence, or might think he had overlooked it, and she put it back during the night.'

He stopped.

Sarah said: 'But *why*? Why should Lady Westholme want to kill old Mrs Boynton?'

'Did you not tell me that Lady Westholme had been quite near you in Jerusalem when you spoke to Mrs Boynton? It was to Lady Westholme that Mrs Boynton's words were addressed. "*I've never forgotten anything – not an action, not a name, not a face.*" Put that with the fact that Mrs Boynton *had been a wardress in a prison* and you can get a very shrewd idea of the truth. Lord Westholme met his wife on a voyage back from *America*. Lady Westholme before her marriage had been a criminal and had served a prison sentence.

'You see the terrible dilemma she was in? Her career, her ambitions, her social position – all at stake! What the crime was for which she served a sentence in prison we do not yet know (though we soon shall), but it must have been one that would effectually blast her political career if it was made public. And remember this, *Mrs Boynton was not an ordinary blackmailer*. She did not want money. She wanted the pleasure of torturing her victim for a while and then she would have enjoyed revealing the truth in the most spectacular fashion! No, while Mrs Boynton lived, Lady Westholme was not safe. She obeyed Mrs Boynton's instructions to meet her at Petra (I thought it strange all along that a woman with such a sense of her own importance as Lady Westholme should have preferred to travel as a mere tourist), but in her own mind she was doubtless revolving ways and means of murder. She saw her chance and carried it out boldly. She only made two slips. One was to say a little too much – the description of the torn breeches – which first drew my attention to her, and the other was when she mistook Dr Gerard's tent and looked first into the one where Ginevra was lying half asleep. Hence the girl's story – half make-believe, half true – of a sheikh in disguise. She put it the wrong way round, obeying her instinct to distort the truth by making it more dramatic, but the indication was quite significant enough for me.'

He paused.

'But we shall soon know. I obtained Lady Westholme's finger-prints today without her being aware of the fact. If these are sent to the prison where Mrs Boynton was once a wardress, we shall soon know the truth when they are compared with the files.'

He stopped.

In the momentary stillness a sharp sound was heard.

'What's that?' asked Dr Gerard.

'Sounded like a shot to me,' said Colonel Carbury, rising to his feet quickly. 'In the next room. Who's got that room, by the way?'

Poirot murmured: 'I have a little idea – it is the room of Lady Westholme . . .'

Extract from the *Evening Shout:*

> We regret to announce the death of Lady Westholme, M.P.,
> the result of a tragic accident. Lady Westholme, who was
> fond of travelling in out-of-the-way countries, always took a
> small revolver with her. She was cleaning this when it went
> off accidentally and killed her. Death was instantaneous. The
> deepest sympathy will be felt for Lord Westholme, etc., etc.

On a warm June evening five years later Sarah Boynton and
her husband sat in the stalls of a London theatre. The play
was *Hamlet.* Sarah gripped Raymond's arm as Ophelia's words
came floating over the footlights:

> How should I your true love know
> From another one?
> By his cockle hat and staff,
> And his sandal shoon.
>
> He is dead and gone, lady,
> He is dead and gone;
> At his head a grass-green turf;
> At his heels a stone.
> O, hó!

A lump rose in Sarah's throat. That exquisite witless beauty, that
lovely unearthly smile of one gone beyond trouble and grief to a
region where only a floating mirage was truth . . .

Sarah said to herself: 'She's lovely . . .'

That haunting, lilting voice, always beautiful in tone, but now
disciplined and modulated to be the perfect instrument.

Sarah said with decision as the curtain fell at the end of the
act: 'Jinny's a great actress – a great – great actress!'

Later they sat round a supper-table at the Savoy. Ginevra,
smiling, remote, turned to the bearded man by her side.

'I was good, wasn't I, Theodore?'

'You were wonderful, *chérie*.'

A happy smile floated on her lips.

She murmured: '*You* always believed in me – you always knew I could do great things – sway multitudes . . .'

At a table not far away the Hamlet of the evening was saying gloomily:

'Her mannerisms! Of course people like it just *at first* – but what I say is, it's not *Shakespeare*. Did you see how she ruined my exit?'

Nadine, sitting opposite Ginevra, said: 'How exciting it is to be here in London with Jinny acting Ophelia and being so famous!'

Ginevra said softly: 'It was nice of you to come over.'

'A regular family party,' said Nadine, smiling as she looked round. Then she said to Lennox: 'I think the children might go to the matinée, don't you? They're quite old enough, and they *do* so want to see Aunt Jinny on the stage!'

Lennox, a sane, happy-looking Lennox with humorous eyes, lifted his glass.

'To the newly-weds, Mr and Mrs Cope.'

Jefferson Cope and Carol acknowledged the toast.

'The unfaithful swain!' said Carol, laughing. 'Jeff, you'd better drink to your first love as she's sitting right opposite you.'

Raymond said gaily: 'Jeff's blushing. He doesn't like being reminded of the old days.'

His face clouded suddenly.

Sarah touched his hand with hers, and the cloud lifted. He looked at her and grinned.

'Seems just like a bad dream!'

A dapper figure stopped by their table. Hercule Poirot, faultlessly and beautifully apparelled, his moustaches proudly twisted, bowed regally.

'Mademoiselle,' he said to Ginevra, '*mes hommages*. You were superb!'

They greeted him affectionately, made a place for him beside Sarah.

He beamed round on them all and when they were all talking he leaned a little sideways and said softly to Sarah:

'*Eh bien*, it seems that all marches well now with *la famille Boynton*!'

'Thanks to *you*!' said Sarah.

'He becomes very eminent, your husband. I read today an excellent review of his last book.'

'It's really rather good – although I say it! Did you know that Carol and Jefferson Cope had made a match of it at last? And Lennox and Nadine have got two of the nicest children – cute, Raymond calls them. As for Jinny – well, I rather think Jinny's a genius.'

She looked across the table at the lovely face and the red-gold crown of hair, and then she gave a tiny start.

For a moment her face was grave. She raised her glass slowly to her lips.

'You drink a toast, madame?' asked Poirot.

Sarah said slowly:

'I thought – suddenly – of Her. Looking at Jinny, I saw – for the first time – the likeness. The same thing – only Jinny is in light – where She was in darkness . . .'

And from opposite, Ginevra said unexpectedly:

'Poor Mother . . . She was *queer* . . . Now – that we're all so happy – I feel kind of sorry for her. She didn't get what she wanted out of life. It must have been tough for her.'

Almost without a pause, her voice quivered softly into the lines from *Cymbeline* while the others listened spell-bound to the music of them:

'Fear no more the heat o' the sun,
Nor the furious winter's rages;
Thou the worldly task hast done,
Home art gone, and ta'en thy wages . . .'